IN THE BEGINNING

". . . Their eyes turned westward. They wanted to be the first to see the fabulous land of Virginia . . . They asked one another questions: Would the streets of the Indian towns be paved with gold? . . . Could they scoop pearls from the river, big pearls, the size of pease? . . . Would the pine-apple and plantain, such as they had tasted at Saint John's and Hispaniola, grow abundantly? . . . Would they find good shooting, grouse, pheasant and woodcock?

"The yellow light of the sky turned to crimson. It shone on the white bank of fog that clung to the shore, melting the fog into thin streamers and giving the shore color and form. Between the rifts the white crests of waves beat lazily against the sand. Far back the green spires of trees broke through the vapour. Here before their eyes was their new land!"

ROANOKE HUNDRED
by **Inglis Fletcher**

Read the other novels in Inglis Fletcher's great series of "Albemarle" historical romances published by Bantam Books: LUSTY WIND FOR CAROLINA, TOIL OF THE BRAVE, RALEIGH'S EDEN, MEN OF ALBEMARLE.

Roanoke Hundred
Inglis Fletcher

A NATIONAL GENERAL COMPANY

*This low-priced Bantam Book
has been completely reset in a type face
designed for easy reading, and was printed
from new plates. It contains the complete
text of the original hard-cover edition.*
NOT ONE WORD HAS BEEN OMITTED.

RLI: $\dfrac{\text{VLM 7 (VLR 6-9)}}{\text{IL 8-up}}$

ROANOKE HUNDRED

*A Bantam Book / published by arrangement with
The Bobbs-Merrill Company*

PRINTING HISTORY

*Bobbs-Merrill edition published October 1948
2nd printing............. October 1948
Doubleday Dollar Book Club edition published April 1949
2nd printing................. July 1949
Permabook edition published October 1951
2nd printing ....March 1952
Serialized in Philadelphia Inquirer 1949
Serialized in New York Post-Home News 1949
Serialized in Canada Wide Feature 1949
Bantam edition published March 1972*

*Bantam Books are published by Bantam Books, Inc., a National
General company. Its trade-mark, consisting of the words "Bantam
Books" and the portrayal of a bantam, is registered in the United
States Patent Office and in other countries. Marca Registrada.
Bantam Books, Inc., 666 Fifth Avenue, New York, N.Y. 10019.*

Dedicated to
DAVID LAURANCE CHAMBERS
A PRINCE AMONG EDITORS

"MY SWORD I LEAVE TO HIM WHO CAN GET IT.
MY MARKS AND SCARS I CARRY WITH ME
TO BE A WITNESS."

ACKNOWLEDGEMENT

I WISH to acknowledge my indebtedness for material used in this book: To Mariners Museum, Newport News, Virginia; The Library of Congress, Washington, D. C.; The British Museum, London; The National Portrait Gallery, London; The Bideford Library, Bideford, Devon; The Pine-Coffin Records, Exeter, Devon; Museum, Roanoke Island, Manteo, North Carolina.

To Sir Angus Fletcher, for advice and counsel in research; Mr. George Dunstan, of London, for assistance in obtaining prints; Mr. Sidney Harper, Bideford, Devon, for the use of his extraordinary library of Devon and Cornwall history; Commander John Stuart Fletcher, USN, for work on sailing ships of the Elizabethan period; Mr. A. L. Rowse, Fellow of All Souls College, Oxford, for use of material from his source book, *Sir Richard Grenville of the Revenge*.

And I am deeply grateful to Richard Hakluyt for *The Principal Navigations, Voyages, Traffiques and Discoveries of the English Nation*—that magnificent record of the great sea-captains of the Elizabethan period.

ACKNOWLEDGMENT

TABLE OF CONTENTS

BOOK I
WEST COUNTRY

CHAPTER 1
THE ROOKS FLY HOMEWARD

The day was dying. The rooks were circling, screeching their raucous sunset cries. As they whirled and planed, their strong wings beat black against the sky. The rooks were flying homeward, seeking a resting place in the great oaks of Stowe Wood. The herd-boy Colin, perched on a rock, laid aside a reed pipe on which he had been playing a plaintive tune. His blue eyes, wise beyond his years, looked out from his wind-browned face, following the rooks' restless circling flight over the low thatched cottages that clustered about the mill in the vale, then up into the grey sky, over the great house of Stowe, set high on its many terraces.

"Never the rooks rest on a poor man's land," he muttered as the birds flew upward toward King's Park field at the crest of the hill. Nurse Marjory had told them last night as they sat at the long table in the buttery, eating their supper, "Rooks always seek a rich man's abode."

He hunched his thin frame, clad in faded blue smock and slick leather breeches, behind a pile of rocks. Sunset brought the sea, and the sunset wind was chill even in midsummer. In the west, down the long vista of Coombe Vale, he could glimpse the sea, the wild, restless sea of the sinister coast of Cornwall. The Virginia Sea, as his master Sir Richard called it, lay beyond. It stretched forever westward to the shores of the New World. His mistress Lady Grenville always turned pale and became quieter than ever when her lord spoke of Virginia, as if she felt some menace in the word. Colin himself had heard her voice her fears as she walked with her husband one evening in the high-walled garden.

"I pray you, my dearest, do not say Virginia Sea. It is the Irish Sea, with only Ireland beyond, not that wild, savage land of Virginia."

"A great New World, my sweet Mary, a world that will give honour to our Queen and to our country, yes and to the men who conquer its wild beauty."

Lady Grenville laid her thin hand on her husband's arm.

3

"Richard, Richard, promise me you will not listen more to Walter Raleigh's wild dreams of conquering strange lands. Promise me."

"Nay. No promises, my sweet. A man's a fool who makes promises to a woman."

She said, "I think of the times you have left me to go abroad to fight the Queen's wars—to fight for Don Juan and battle the Turks."

His master laughed. "And Ireland—don't forget Ireland. Irish wars, more full of sound than hurt."

"I have cause enough to remember Ireland," she said. "How can I forget the savagery of Ireland when all our tenants had their throats cut, and Lady St. Leger and I barely escaped with our lives? No, I will not forget Ireland, nor Fitzmaurice of Desmond."

There was silence for a little. Then Sir Richard said, "I think we will ride to Bideford within the week. I must go to London, and 'twill do you good to stop awhile with your folk at Annerly. Would you not like that, my Mary?"

"Yes, Richard." But the life was gone from her voice.

"Then smile and raise your lips for a kiss. We will walk to the north garden. I have a mind to see how the gardener has done with my peaches. He was going to train them against the north wall."

Colin heard no more that evening. But there was talk enough in the kitchen and the stables, talk of the New World. It had been so ever since Master Drake had sailed his ships clean around the world and come safe back to Plymouth Haven.

He waited for the sun to go down into the sea and the deep heavy shadows fall on Stowe Wood. Coombe Vale would slide into darkness. Voices of home-going people would rise from the valley. He would whistle for his dog Hubba. A heathen name it was, but often he had passed the Bloody Corner where the great King Alfred had stopped the Danish King Hubba. That was long ago, but the traces of Danes still lingered in Cornwall and Devon. Sometimes he wondered about those old people. Then there was the long Roman wall in Stowe Wood. And he wondered about the Britons whose camps remained down near the cliffs, and the strange frightening folk who had made magic in great stone circles on the lonely moors. But it was foolish for him

4

to think of ancients. Enough that he lived now, in the days of Elizabeth—may Heaven bless Her Majesty!

He picked up his crook and whistled. Hubba came bounding down the hill, his tail wagging. Without words from his master he began to worry the bleating sheep, nipping at heels, uttering short barks, moving the flock down the hill to the fold.

The rooks set up a great new cry, scores on scores until the sky was black with them. He wished he could count as high as the rooks he saw. If only there were a few white rooks, he could count by difference. That was the way he counted the flock—one black and a hundred white.

Will Pooley, the head shepherd, counted on his fingers, but he, Colin, could count a hundred in his head. That was since Dame Philippa, his master's foster-sister, had told him he must sit with the young squires of a Wednesday when she taught them to count and write figures in a book. They worked in the counting-room, where clerks bent over their ledgers totalling up the gains from merchandise that came to Bideford from Portugal and the Azores, shipped in the name of Richard Grenville. For Grenville was a great man in Devon and Cornwall—aye, and in London too, where he sat in Parliament. Colin was proud to live at Stowe, and proud of the fame of his master.

The sheep were moving, bleating and baaing. Another day was passing. Colin paused in the narrow dusty path and dropped to his knees, his face turned toward the church at Kilkhampton. The square Norman tower stood solid against the sky, its stone walls faintly pink with the light from the dying sun.

He murmured a prayer, as many a Cornish man and dame prayed at that moment, in church pew or at wayside cross, a prayer for those on land with the lips, but the heart's prayer was for those at sea.

He dusted off his brier-scratched knees, examined a stone bruise on his foot with careful attention. The sheep paths carried stones—not rounded stones, such as he skipped along the beach where the waves pounded and rolled them from the green ocean's bed, but sharper slate stones that splintered.

He shouted, "Alert!" to his dog, turned a recalcitrant ram with his crook and started homeward.

The sun was behind the cliffs at the mouth of the vale.

Little pillars of grey smoke rose above the thatched roofs of the cottages clustered along the stream on the lower slope. The smoke columns, pierced by shafts of yellow light, held their vertical shapes until the wind from the higher valley caught the slender structures and spread the smoke into puffs and clouds across the crests of the low rolling hills.

Fat red cattle wound down paths pressed smooth by their hoofs as they grazed day after day along the roadside on their way to the deep green grass of the feeding meadows. Cow-bells tinkled, a quiet evening sound, as the herd stopped to reach the last sweet tuft of grass on their homeward journey. Heavy udders, rich with milk, would soon know the soothing hands of the milkmaids.

The long stone milking barns at Stowe would be filled with gay talk and laughter and the sound of milk splashing against the bright tin pails. The maids, gaily dressed in coloured calico skirts and white bodices, sat astride their three-legged milking stools, their smooth cheeks against the satin smoothness of the cow's flank, while they laughed or gave lively retort to the lusty banter of stablemen and feeders.

The evening quiet hung like a caress over the land. The voice of the restless sea sounded through the dusk. It beat like a strong pulse against the shore, pounding, tearing at the cliffs, hungry to make inroads, to wreck the tranquil land, to gain inch by inch, rod by rod. The high cliffs that guarded the moors and the gentle green vales stood firm, as they had stood before the age of man, back beyond man's knowledge. Yet the sea was always there at the foot of the cliffs, writhing, beating its green anger against the black slate, hurling ships and wreckage onto the narrow beach and the shingle.

> From Padstow Point to Lundy Light
> Is a sailor's grave, by day or night.

Colin waited at the gate to the home meadow for old Pooley, who moved slowly. Hubba waited too, for Colin's low whistle; then he bounded forward, nipping at heel and throwing his body against the fleecy sides of sheep, until he had moulded them into a fluid mass of wool moving through the narrow gate.

"Sharp through the gate!" called Will Pooley. "Watch sharp

that ye do not let them trample the young! The wee ones ban't strong as they belong to be."

Sheep in the fold, a long drink at the horse lot where the stream came clear over the stone trough, and Colin's thoughts were on supper and on a warm spot he knew above the bricked-in kitchen stove. But first food. He stopped at the court-yard. The great outer gate was open, under the strong Norman tower which rendered Stowe half-fortress, half-mansion. Carters and hay waggons driving in over the cobbles made noise and confusion. Men shouted and cursed at slow-moving oxen. Horses rearing and plunging were eager to reach mangers and crunch their evening meal. It was all familiar: the noise, the movement of animals, the ear-splitting shriek of turning wheels. It was the pulse of Stowe Barton, a strong pulse that had beat strongly down the centuries, from the time when the first Grenvilles came from France with the Conqueror, until now in the glorious days of Elizabeth.

As the shepherd boy disappeared down the long stone passageway that led to the kitchen, the restless, circling rooks flapped sombre wings across the grey sky and settled slowly into the protecting darkness of Stowe Wood, to take night sanctuary on rich man's land.

CHAPTER 2
THE TEMPLE

Richard Hakluyt, barrister, stopped at the shop of William Slater, fruiterer, at Temple Gate and bought two limes and a few oranges from the Canaries. He begrudged the money and would have refused to pay the high cost but for the illustrious company who were to meet in his chambers in the Middle Temple that night. He thought it becoming to have a good punch, for men grew more expansive, therefore more open to persuasion, after they had swallowed a few glasses.

Carrying his parcel under his arm, he went along the street of the Temple Bar and into the shop of Robert Monte, which leaned up against the tower. Monte's wife Joan, a swarthy woman of fifty with remnants of dark beauty in her lined face, made excuses for the absence of her husband. He had gone to Sussex to see an ailing uncle last week, then to Deptford to meet a fishing boat from Falmouth and purchase pilchards. Hakluyt knew Monte as an inveterate gambler and did not doubt that he was, at the moment, playing at dice in some dubious haunt of gamblers along the road that led to St. Paul's.

He was glad to see it was Joan who was keeping shop. She would help him select some choice bits of food to accompany the punch. She might, if her humour were good, make a saffron cake and bring it hot to his chambers that evening.

He waited until the shop was clear, leaning negligently against the counter. His sombre lawyer's dress was a contrast to the raiment of a group of young men of the city. They lounged beside the counter, buying to take to their lodging a meal which they would carry discreetly hidden beneath their long cloaks. Young men who lived Heaven knew how, but whose clothes were of the finest satin and whose ruffs were the fullest and stiff with lace from Honiton.

The tinkling bell sounded in the back of the shop; the last man had passed out. Hakluyt broached his plan with circumspection. He must be careful in his purchase. Quarter-day was close at hand and his rent was high since he had moved into larger chambers near the Round Church. Atkyns, who shared his chambers, never had hard cash on quarter-day. His stipend came in driblets at inconvenient times, and Hakluyt usually was his creditor to the tune of four or five pounds.

Richard listened to the usual amount of gossip from Joan. She always had gossip of the Middle and Inner Temple at her tongue's end.

"The poor-box has been broken into again by some lewd person," she told him. Mr. Popham, the Queen's attorney, had said in her presence that both the houses would be held responsible for repayment. After this the poor-box would be opened at the end of every term by a bencher of either house, and the money disposed of. In his opinion it was a direful deed, that of robbing the poor of a few pennies! Hakluyt agreed. Joan weighed the brown sugar and put it into a small stone crock. "Remember to return the crock," she admonished him with a toothless smile. "You usually do, but men seem to be more careless than ever."

Hakluyt promised. Seeing her in a good humour, he made his request for a saffron cake.

The woman's eyes lightened. "Ha! It's a Cornish gentleman you're having to your drinking bout, sir?"

"Cornish and Devon men," he answered. "But no drinking bout, I assure you."

"And who, may I ask? I be a Cornish lass myself, from Fowey."

"Mr. Philip Amadas, for one——"

The woman interrupted. "Ah, young Mr. Philip Amadas! You know he's bound to pay a fine for being out of commons in Lent. He and Mr. Anthony Skinner and James Harmon, him that built chambers at his own expense, lying on the north side between the mews and the garden of the Inner Temple. A pretty pass when a young gent thinks himself too good for chambers that once housed Sir Richard Grenville. I remember well how Sir Richard kept right on reading when the rest of the benchers fled and scattered about the city, afeared of the plague——"

Hakluyt interrupted. "Sir Richard will be one of our guests tonight."

The woman set the spices on the counter. A smile crossed

her thin lips. "Ah, there's the one that always has a word of praise for my pasties and saffron cake!"

"Pasties! Why didn't I think of pasties before! Of course, that is, if you will be so good as to make them." Hakluyt smiled, a pleasant smile that won him many friends at the Inns of Court.

The woman straightened her bright neck-scarf. "Well, it might be that I would, for a Cornish gentleman that is . . ."

He threw out more bait. "Sir Walter Raleigh and Mr. Hariot . . ."

She nodded briskly. "I know. Sir Walter's got himself up as a fine gentleman. I saw him no later than a fortnight ago, riding along behind the Queen herself; but I mind him when he was here reading at the Temple. Many a time he has stood me off for a half-crown."

Hakluyt took the small wicker basket containing his purchases Joan had set on the counter. "I can count on you for the cakes? Ten o'clock?"

"Aye. Not for the other gentleman, but for Sir Richard—he belongs knowin' the best of Cornish vittles and ne'er withholding praise."

"Excellent." Hakluyt laid the money on the counter.

As he opened the door, Joan called, "Before God, Mr. Hakluyt, I forgot to say my word of congratulations." Seeing the puzzlement on his face she grinned knowingly. " 'Tis said that you will be made an Associate the next term. And after, you'll be a Master. But no good without its cost—you'll be called to lend the treasurer three pounds for the building fund. That won't please you, Master Hakluyt, will it?"

Hakluyt murmured something and closed the door, the little bell jingling. How did the woman know so much? Damn it all! he thought. No one knew he was to be appointed one of the Masters of the Bench; a secret thing it was, and now the hucksterman's wife spoke of it as though it were common knowledge. He had told no one. Heigh-ho, that was the Temple! Everything ran from the barristers of the Middle to the Inner Temple, then to Gray's Inn and wound up at Lincoln's. There was nothing he could do about it. He made his way down the narrow lane, past the Round Church and up the narrow, worn, stone steps to his chambers. He had other things to think on before the meeting when

Walter Raleigh would come to talk to a select few about the new-found land of Virginia.

He opened the door. Walter Raleigh's friend Thomas Hariot was waiting for him, seated on the oak settle, looking out the leaded window. Hariot was a lean man with a thin neck and long face. His deep-set grey eyes were the dreamer's eyes. Hakluyt knew he was ambitious to become the greatest mathematician of Elizabeth's time but now he taught Latin and some English to divers noblemen's sons, a work he detested as unworthy of his abilities.

It was in character that he did not wait to greet Richard Hakluyt before he began asking questions about the origin of the Round Church and writing down Hakluyt's answers in his note-book.

"There are only three Rounds in all England. Isn't that true? What is the date?"

Hakluyt put his package of fruit on an oval walnut table and unwrapped the scarf from his throat. "I don't know the date. It is transition Norman, but I think it was consecrated in 1185."

"Yes, yes. So Master Hooker told me. The church, the buttery and the crypt are the only buildings that remain of the Knights Templars."

"So I've heard. But why are you so interested, Hariot, and why all these scribblings?"

"I've a mind to write a paper on Norman churches. I've been talking to a printer and he thinks the idea good. Dr. Richard Hooker approves." He leafed through the note-book. "Here are the items he gave me: 'First mention of the Temple as Inns of Court, 1449. The Agnus Dei symbol belongs to the Inner Temple; the Winged Horse, to the Middle. The symbol in the floor tile is old; that in the ceiling repainted in our time.'"

Hakluyt went to the window and looked down on the Round, as the church was affectionately called by the benchers. "It has some beauty," he said, "particularly the porch and the oblong chancel. I wish I knew who all the recumbent knights were. I suppose many a lawyer, waiting in the Round for his clients, has speculated on those stone knights and their stories."

"A good point." Hariot scribbled. "Lawyer waiting in Round for clients. Good point. Now I have only to get material on the library, the King's Bench Walk and the gardens of the

11

Middle Temple. By the way, was it not in these gardens that York plucked the white rose and Lancaster the red in the days of Henry VI?"

"Really, Hariot, I've never seen such a fellow for detail. I don't know."

"I'm a scientist, Hakluyt," the man said primly, without looking up from his notes. "Middle Temple Hall—I must mention that. The Queen is very proud of it, they say. But enough. Let's talk of other things. Who comes tonight?"

"The list is on the table. Read it while I prepare punch for my celebrated guests." Hakluyt took off his coat and hung it on a cane-backed chair. He pushed aside books and papers that littered the long table of dark oak, its carving black with age and smoke from the stone fire-place. With a thin knife, which he got from a drawer in the old commode, he began to cut lemons and squeeze the juice into a large pewter punch-bowl he had borrowed from a more convivial neighbor.

Hariot pored over the list, pulling his ear which had an extraordinarily long lobe. "Phil Amadas—I haven't seen him for long months. I used to tutor him, remember? Does he eschew London these days?"

"I think so. He pretends to read in the Temple, but I notice he's on the list of fines for being absent. No doubt he stays in Plymouth. There is much to interest him there. Drake is his idol, you know."

Hariot made a small gesture with his hand. "Master Drake is surely in the eye of the people these days. Since the Queen visited his ship at Deptford, he has been Saturn's golden man. 'Tis a gay blithe thing to sail tall ships, richly built and trimmed with brass, to put a girdle around the world."

"Aye, so it is, and pleasantly worded, Thomas Hariot."

Hariot raised his heavy brows. "You think so? Perhaps I should write it down before it escapes me."

Hakluyt laughed. "Let no idle word go by unnoticed. Hariot, you should be an historian, not a mathematician."

"Think so?" Hariot's voice showed his pleasure. " 'Tis what Walter Raleigh says. It may be that I——" He broke off quickly. Almost the secret had escaped on a traitorous, idle tongue. He did not know how much Hakluyt knew of his patron's plans for the Virginia voyage. "Yes," he said to cover, "Drake is of the world of Saturn, the Golden Age, when all men are equal."

12

"You speak like a nincompoop, Hariot. How can all men be equal? Some are born with brains and some not, and that's the end of it." Hakluyt spoke decisively. It was an old argument which came forth often of an evening in the common room of the Temple.

"You are old-fashioned, Hakluyt. That is the Welsh in you —to think a man must be born well to deserve honour."

"That is not what I said, Tom, and you know it. It's not a man's birth station that makes him great, but the brain that God has devised for him." He cut into an orange with such violence that the juice spattered the front of his puce waistcoat.

Hariot did not attend. He was perusing the list, murmuring the names aloud. "Is this to be a Temple venture? I find no name save those who read or have read in the Inner or Middle Temple. I thought to see some Bristol merchants, or some representatives of the merchants of London."

Hakluyt dumped the sugar into the juice and wiped his hands with a towel. "I know nothing, Hariot. Let's leave the matter until tonight, when Walter Raleigh speaks of his plan. What do you say to a stroll through the garden to the river? Perhaps we will see the Queen's barge as she travels to Greenwich."

"More like we'll see some poor devil on his way to the Tower by the Traitor's Gate. Mayhap, Richard, it is better to be born undistinguished and so escape the executioner's axe, that bloody axe which has severed heads from shoulders for some of our greatest men."

"Hist, Tom! Your tongue is as unruly as ever. Come, a walk and a draught of ale and a bit of cheese, before our guests come."

The nobility and the gentry dined at three, but it was dusk before Philip Amadas and his companion Arthur Barlow found their way to Hakluyt's chambers. They had wined and dined in Fleet Street near the Wool Inn, they announced as they came into the room.

"By heaven, Hakluyt, you save on candles as of old!" said Amadas, tossing his flat cap across the table. It fell on the settle beside the fire-place. "Two little flickers and not a light in the hallway. It's good that I remembered those two steps at the entrance, or Barlow and I would have landed in the court-yard with broken bones." Hakluyt laughed but Amadas didn't. "No thanks to you, Dick." He advanced into the

13

room, holding a candle high. "Is that Tom Hariot poring over maps? Upon my soul, I had not thought to see you outside the class-room." Amadas slapped Hariot's shoulder. "Have you heard of Arthur Barlow, the brave fellow who went with me to the New World of Virginia?"

Hariot pushed aside the maps and extended his hand. "Mr. Barlow, your servant, sir. I have heard Sir Walter Raleigh speak highly of your bravery and your accomplishments."

Barlow, not to be outdone, bowed low. "The name of Thomas Hariot is known to the world of scholars," he said, "a world to which, unfortunately, I do not belong. I'm but a rough sailor."

"Modestly spoken," Hariot said. "But I have read your Virginia report, sir. It does you honour and will, I am sure, place you among the scholars and geographers of our day."

"So many nosegays!" Amadas cried. He was young. He had a lively air, a twinkle in his brown eyes and a hearty laugh. He belonged to a South Devon family. They served the Queen as faithfully as they had served her father before her. They had once, during the latter's time, all but lost their property by espousing the cause of Norfolk. They had managed to keep out of the Tower by retreating to their estate near Plymouth and leading a quiet country-life.

There was the sound of laughter in the hall and men stumbling. A voice called, "Ye gods, what inky blackness! Open the door, Hakluyt, and give us a light. Our poor feet wander."

"Raleigh!" cried Hariot. He jumped from the bench and reached the door before Hakluyt could cross the room. "Enter! Enter, sirs!"

Two men stood in the doorway. They were elegantly dressed in silken hosen and brocade trunks and doublets. They wore dress swords, and on their smoothed locks were perched swagger puffed caps, laced with gold. Raleigh, Queen's favourite of the moment, and Sir Philip Sidney, courtier, poet and patron of men of letters.

Gallants of gallants, they brought the essence of the court into the scholar's sombre, low-ceilinged room. Well-being and good humour and all the amenities of splendid living attended the two friends.

"By Phoebus, 'tis many a year since I stumbled along the flags of the Temple, many a year!" Raleigh bowed to the group. "I bid you good evening, gentlemen, and good health to you, Richard Hakluyt. Here is Sir Philip, bound to come, though I told him 'twas only business we talked tonight, and secret at that."

Hakluyt bowed. "It is an honour to welcome Sir Philip Sidney to my humble chambers."

Sidney extended his hand, long-fingered and white as a lady's. "No apologies for Temple chambers, Mr. Hakluyt. I myself have occupied the same not so long since, but mine were on the other angle from the Round Church."

Hakluyt mentioned names. Hariot they both knew. Sidney spoke his pleasure when Amadas' name was mentioned. "Your brother I knew well, Philip, but you have grown up since my absence from Devon."

"Too long an absence, sir. Devon folk miss you. And this is my friend Arthur Barlow, who sailed to Virginia with me."

Sidney turned to Barlow. "Walsingham, the Queen's secretary, let me read your report on the new-found land of Virginia, Mr. Barlow. I swear, sir, it must be a Biblical land of milk and honey, if you tell the truth unvarnished."

"Sir, it is the fairest land under the cope of Heaven, a sweet perfumed land, abounding in all good things of the earth. An Eden, sir."

"Ah, yes. At court we call it Eden, Raleigh's Eden." His eyes twinkled. "Walt boasts so of its beauty and fruitfulness that I have sworn by my pedigree I would get the truth from Barlow himself."

The seaman blushed with pleasure, dark-skinned as he was. Praise from Sir Philip! He was indeed too flustered to reply, or say thank you for the praise. He could only stammer that Amadas was the one who deserved the honour. He was a noble companion, without fear. It was Amadas who had persuaded the savages Wanchese and Manteo to come home with them, when they returned from Roanoke Island this year of 1584.

"Do not be confused, gentlemen," Amadas said. "Barlow wrote the report, with only a suggestion now and then from me. . . . But where is Sir Richard Grenville? Is he not joining us tonight?"

Hakluyt turned away from the window where he had been observing the men who crossed the flags in front of the Round Church. "He assured me he would be here."

"And me also." Raleigh spoke quickly, his voice clear and incisive. "In truth I expected him to be here when I arrived."

15

Hariot went to the window. "Two gentlemen are coming, but one wears a gown."

"No gown for Richard Grenville. More like he will be accoutred in full armour, so fond he is of fighting." Sidney drawled his words, in sharp contrast to Raleigh's rapid speech.

Hakluyt impaled a candle on a tall brass stick, lighted it from a taper. He opened the heavy door, called to a servant in the passageway.

An old man, seemingly as ancient as the temple itself, moved softly in list slippers, changing chandles, removing a nub from the brass stick, then setting a new dip strongly on the spike. He lighted the new candles from the old, then with thumb and finger wet with spittle he dimmed the old flame.

"More light, John Pound, more light!" called Hakluyt, bent over a long oaken table where maps were spread.

" 'Tis all the candles you paid for, Master Hakluyt," answered the servant.

"Let us sit down," Raleigh said after the laughter subsided. "I see Hakluyt has a place for each of us."

Hariot moved over from the window. Amadas and Barlow stood together behind the bench on one side of the long table. Raleigh went to the head of the table, motioning Sidney to sit at his right hand.

"Pray be seated, gentlemen." Raleigh pulled the wooden chair from the table. "At least we can examine maps while we wait. It will take some time for them to cross the gardens and come up through the middle court." He unbuckled his sword, and laid it on the window-seat and sat down. The others followed, save Hariot who wore no sword.

"Or ask Barlow to tell us more about the island," Sidney suggested. He lounged back on his chair indolently, playing with a heavy gold chain that circled his neck and fell halfway down his chest.

"Why not wait until Grenville arrives, so all may hear?"

"Right, Walt," Sidney agreed. "Who else is coming? Our brave new admiral, Drake?"

A muffled laugh, quickly suppressed. Barlow glanced at Amadas and shook his head.

Raleigh explained: "No. Drake will not be here tonight. If we have a Grenville we do not have a Drake."

Sidney raised a perfectly arched eyebrow. "So lies the wind?"

"Yes, so lies the wind."

16

"I am amazed. Two illustrious Devon men at outs? Why is this?"

Amadas said, "There are Devon men who still look down their noses at Drake. An opportunist, one who plays his game and gives no credit to his men—the men who stood by him in the long voyage around the world."

There was a short silence, broken by Raleigh. "I suppose everyone here but Master Barlow and Captain Amadas knows that the idea of circumnavigating the globe was Richard Grenville's original plan, not Francis Drake's. Grenville put the plan in writing and laid it before the Queen. The Queen all but gave consent, then changed her mind. A woman may change her mind—even a queen. She said she couldn't spare Grenville from England."

"But she let Drake go with her blessing—and a competent subscription," Philip Sidney remarked.

Hakluyt, now hearing noises in the passageway, picked up a candle and left the room.

Raleigh answered Sidney. "Ah, the case was different! Francis Drake, a seaman of no importance, could be spared, but not Sir Richard Grenville, a Member of Parliament, a tested soldier in Continental wars, a representative of a great county family. So Drake went—and returned to glory."

"And Grenville stayed at home and voted on unimportant bills and endeavoured to submerge commotion in Devon and Cornwall." Sidney's usually lazy voice had an edge to it.

Raleigh showed no rancour. Grenville was his cousin. He knew his greatness and his weaknesses. "The Queen in times of war needs loyal men about her." He spoke soberly.

Amadas said, "The old Devon saying goes 'The Godolphins never lack wit, nor the Grenvilles loyalty.'"

The door opened. A tall thin man in clerical gown stood in the doorway. Behind him, a full head higher, was Grenville, a bearded man of noble proportions. Following them, Hakluyt's body was eclipsed; only his hand holding the lighted candle was visible.

The men in the room rose to their feet, bowed deeply to Dr. Hooker, the Master of the Temple. As he advanced into the room, Richard Grenville stood back, waiting for each man to speak to the famous cleric. Then quietly he found a seat beside Amadas, after Dr. Hooker had taken his place beside Raleigh.

Raleigh said, "This is a surprise and a very great honour,

Dr. Hooker. I have long wanted to talk with you, but, knowing how your time is engaged, I hesitated."

"Well, thanks to Richard Grenville, who has not the slightest hesitancy in infringing on my time, here I am—at a secret and very important meeting." The good doctor laughed. "In fact, Walter, your cousin made it very clear to me that I am the one who is honoured tonight, honoured to be allowed to be present at—shall we say?—the First Virginia Council." He put his hand, with the large ecclesiastical ring, on Grenville's shoulder. "This man, this Grenville, has a way of bending men to his purpose, and I am quite willing to be bent in this case."

Grenville's pleasant rich voice took up the banter. "I know, sir, you were on edge to meet these two venturesome young gentlemen. Allow me. Captain Philip Amadas, of Devon, and Master Arthur Barlow, sometime of Bristol, now London. They are, as you know, Walter Raleigh's first emissaries to the New World of Virginia."

"Yes, yes, I know. But how young! How very young to take such risks!" He sighed a little. "Well, perhaps it is always that way. Youth knows no fears. Fear, like caution, comes with advancing age." He leaned forward. "I am very short-sighted, but is this not Sidney across from me?"

"Himself, reverend sir, very much in your case tonight—eager to hear a report of Walter Raleigh's first venture to the shores of the new land."

Hakluyt set the bowl of punch at the head of the table and distributed cups. He then sat down between Sidney and Thomas Hariot, as Raleigh tapped the table lightly to command attention.

"We have a purpose in meeting here tonight in the Temple. It seems a fitting place to make plans for what we hope will be a great venture, one of the greatest ventures of our times. We all of us have read our law here, in the Inner or the Middle Temple. If we succeed in our endeavour, the world will know that we of the Temple have our horizons far afield, like those first men who met here, those Templars who came home from far journeying after they had fought in the greatest cause of all Christendom, the rescue of the Holy Land from infidels. Now in our time, in the twenty-sixth year of the reign of our Sovereign Queen, we have a new crusade. We must rescue the fair land of Virginia from

18

red savages, plant the cross of Christ and the standard of Elizabeth and bring peace and happiness on the country."

"Hear! Hear!" Sidney said loyally and tapped his glass.

"Excellent!" said Dr. Hooker. "I like that. We must carry the cross of Christ to all the world."

Grenville said, "And take new land for England."

Raleigh went on: "Each of you knows a little of the plan. I will proceed as though you know nothing." He took a roll from the pocket which hung from his leather sword-belt, put a candle close and spread the paper on the polished surface of the oak table.

"First, gentlemen, last year the Queen's Majesty saw fit to grant me a charter with permission to seat colonies in any or all of the new land: to govern, carry the law and to seat and plant. I will read you a paragraph or two of the Letters Patent, so that you may understand that the authority is vested in me.

" 'The Letters Patent, granted by the Queen's Majesty to Sir Walter Raleigh, now Knight, for the discovery and planting of new lands and countries, to continue for the space of six years, and no more.

" 'Elizabeth, by the Grace of God, of England, France and Ireland, Queen, Defender of the Faith, etc.

" 'To all people to whom these presents come, Greeting . . .' "

Richard Grenville settled back. If Walt intended to read the full of the Patent, he might as well ease himself with comfort. He moved a garter below his knee, where it bound, and settled his ruff by inserting two fingers at his throat and slowly moving his head. He had attended a levee at Whitehall. His dress was too rich with embroidery to give him ease. Walt was so prolix, so long-winded. Since he had gone to court, he had forgotten his soldiering, his ways of action and swift decision. Now everything was words, words, words. Grenville would not listen. Instead he sat quietly planning what he was going to do in the way of planting at Stowe Barton, if he decided to go on the Virginia voyage. He had not yet given his consent to undertake the venture. There was something about seating a colony in a new world that caught his imagination. But if he went, the command must be vested in him. It must be his way and say, on his terms, not

Raleigh's. Raleigh had no conception of such things. He had a smooth fine way of convincing people that black was white, but he would not have the ability to hold men together. Let him get the funds, the ships. He, Grenville, would choose the men. But let Walt squirm a little before he consented. This was the reason why he had brought Dr. Hooker, a shrewd man for all his godliness and his earnest Christianity. He knew men. He would back Grenville to choose his own followers.

The parchment crackled as Raleigh rolled it. The reading was over. Amadas' twinkling eyes met Grenville's. He gave no other sign, but Grenville knew Amadas was of his kind—*action,* not words.

Sir Philip Sidney broke the silence. "Now may we hear something from these two gentlemen who have been to Virginia and seen the country with their own eyes?"

"Certainly." Raleigh looked a little chagrined. He had intended making further talk, about how he would get ships and money; how he first happened to send men to scout the country.

But Sidney was questioning Barlow. "When did you sail, sir? How long did it take you? Where did you stop?"

Thus importuned, Barlow plunged into his tale. His voice was even, his thin sallow face without expression. He looked a sick man, which he was. "Sir, we had two barques. We sailed this year of our redemption 1584. On the twenty-seventh of April we departed from Bideford Haven, well furnished with men and victuals and having received our last letter and instruction, sir." He bowed to Raleigh. "We will not deal in detail with the voyage, for it would be tedious. By the tenth of May we arrived at the Canaries. By the tenth of June we were fallen with the islands of the West Indies——"

"Why did you sail so far south?" Grenville interrupted.

"Sir, you are observant. One need not go so far south. We expected that the current of the Bay of Mexico, between the Cape of Florida and Havana, had been of greater force than afterward we found it to have."

Grenville nodded.

"Did you stop at the islands?" Sidney asked.

"Only to take on sweet water and fresh victuals. We left on the twelfth day. On the second of July we found shoal water." Barlow paused, glancing at Philip Amadas, who nodded, remembering. "There we smelt so sweet a smell as if we had been in the midst of some delicate garden."

"Why, what was the smell?" Hakluyt asked.

"We know not. It was a land smell, though we saw no land. We kept a good watch, bearing slack sail. The fourth of the month we arrived on the coast, which we supposed to be a continent and firm land. We sailed one hundred and twenty English miles northward before we could find any entrance or river issuing into the sea."

He paused and poured a glass of punch. No one spoke. Grenville was following him on a map stretched on the table in front of him. Barlow went on: "The first opening that appeared to us we entered, though not without some difficulty."

Amadas leaned forward. "You remember my barque scraped bottom but that was Ferdinando's fault. I never trusted that insolent Portuguese navigator."

Barlow wiped his mouth with his kerchief. "We cast anchor three harquebus-shots within the harbour mouth, on the left hand. After giving thanks to God for our safe arrival, we went to view the land next adjoining." Barlow again looked at Amadas. Speaking was difficult for him. The effort raised a dry, hacking cough.

Amadas took up the tale. "We took possession of the land in the right of the Queen's most excellent Majesty, as rightful Queen and Princess of the same, according to your grant, Sir Walter, under Her Highness' Great Seal."

"What sort of land did you find?" Sir Philip and Dr. Hooker spoke simultaneously.

"Very sandy and low toward the water's side, but so full of grapes as the very beating and surge of the sea overflowed them—grapes, both on the sand and on the green soil on the hills and in the plains, as well as on every little shrub and climbing toward the tops of high cedars."

Barlow spoke slowly. "I hope you will pardon any immodesty when I say I have visited most of the lands of Europe, and many other countries in that latitude, and nowhere have I seen such plenty, such soft gentle breezes, so many animals. We journeyed inward till we found an island sixteen miles long. Roanoke it is called, inhabited by fat bucks, conies, hares, the best fish in the world. The red men have a stockade there, deserted now. We thought it a right healthy spot. Timber trees of great height—oaks, walnuts and those with mastic gum."

21

"Are the savages friendly?" Grenville asked. His keen blue eyes went from Amadas to Arthur Barlow.

"Gentle, kindly," Barlow replied.

"What about gold?" It was Sidney who brought up the question. A look of distress came over Dr. Hooker's intelligent countenance.

The men shook their heads. "The Indians wore brass ornaments, but the Indian queen had ropes of pearls the size of pease."

Sidney's eyes brightened. "Did you fetch some home?"

"Sir, no. The Indian king's brother offered us a box, but we refused them."

"Why, in God's name?"

Barlow's sallow face hardened. "We refused because we would not make it known that we esteemed pearls until they took us to the waters where the pearls grow."

Dr. Hooker nodded approval. "Excellent judgement, Master Barlow, excellent——"

Raleigh interrupted. "What think you of my new Eden, sirs? Is it a land fit to take in the name of our Queen? What do you say, Mr. Hariot? You have not ventured a word this evening. And Hakluyt?"

"I am in deep grief," Hakluyt answered, "because I cannot make the first journey to colonize."

Raleigh clapped him on the shoulder. "Never mind, Dick. You shall take down the stories of all the men who join the venture, and we will have the imprint of Chris Barker, the Queen's printer, on it in a fine volume. What a stir it will make!"

Grenville turned his head and watched them. His eyes were a cold blue and searching; his voice was caustic. " 'Twould be better to take our time making plans for the progress of the venture, rather than writing the story before it is enacted."

Raleigh raised his head. Anger clouded his handsome face. The eyes of the cousins met and held. The dark eyes fell before the unabashed scorn of the blue. The training of the courtier triumphed over the man.

Raleigh threw back his head and laughed. "Just as in the old days, Richard." He turned to Sidney, his eyes twinkling. "When we were boys my brother Humphrey Gilbert and I would sit with Richard by the seashore and dream dreams. Richard would want to know how many ships it would take, how many men, and where the money was coming from."

"Still a good idea," Philip Sidney said "Where *is* the money coming from?"

Raleigh's nervous fingers tapped against the table, "Some is promised, more must be raised."

He looked directly at Sidney, who said, "I reserved twenty-five shares in Frobisher's expedition, with my uncle the Earl of Warwick. I all but joined your brother Humphrey Gilbert when he sailed to his tragic end. I was in Plymouth ready to sail with Drake when he started on his glorious venture and sailed around the world, but the Queen learned of my intention and ordered my return to the court. I've worked on the Letters Patent for discovering new land in America. That is my small contribution."

Raleigh said, "All the more reason why you should become interested in this plan. At least it would be helpful if you used your influence with Sir Francis Walsingham."

Sidney straightened his full ruff: he had not yet had his cut to the new diminished size. "My father-in-law? I doubt my influence would avail you anything in that quarter or with Burghley either. The minister would turn away from anything I had a part in. Of that I am sure."

Dr. Hooker asked a question: "Will Her Majesty take shares as she did in Drake's venture?" There was a long silence. The men about the table looked at one another, then focussed their eyes on Raleigh.

"The Queen has granted the charter. She is deeply interested in acquiring territory."

Raleigh let his eyes fall on the table, as though he were studying the map. Hariot was loyal to him. He was eager to go. Barlow's feeble health would keep him in England. Amadas was primed for adventure. Hakluyt he did not consider. Grenville he must secure. One could never tell what lay behind his cousin's calm, searching eyes. If Sidney came in, even if he only bought shares, it would help to convince Grenville, for they were old friends. Dr. Hooker's influence with the Queen was very great, also with the secretary, Walsingham, and with Lord Burghley. He, Raleigh, approached his objective obliquely, as a courtier would. He began at once to talk about the duty of the Church to Christianise the savages, to counteract the influence of Spain and the Catholic Church.

Raleigh directed his eloquence, his native charm, toward the churchman.

Unwittingly Dr. Hooker played his game for him. "A noble undertaking," he said when Raleigh paused. "It has every chance of success if you have the right men behind it."

Raleigh reminded him that Walsingham had always been behind schemes to extend the influence of England, to build trade, to acquire new territory.

Hooker shook his head. "I don't mean the men who back a venture from safe harbour in England. I mean the men who take out the ships, who sail the uncharted seas, who govern new lands. What men have you in mind who will give the expedition life and power?"

Again there was silence. The men shifted in their seats. Through the open window came the sounds of loud talk, a snatch of song. A voice called, "Hakluyt, Hakluyt, are you there?"

Hakluyt went to the door and into the passage. The men inside heard him talking in guarded tones. His convivial friends went away.

Raleigh said, "I'm glad you spoke of that, Dr. Hooker. We think we know the very man, if he will lead the expedition to Virginia. He sits beside you—my illustrious cousin Richard Grenville."

Hooker nodded his grey head. "Ah, yes, certainly. No one could be better suited to undertake a bold project."

"Hear! Hear!" Sidney held up his glass to be filled by Hakluyt. "Let us drink to the new Admiral of the Virginia Voyages."

Grenville said nothing. He sat with his eyes on the map in front of him. It had been marked by Philip Amadas and Arthur Barlow in heavy lines, showing their route to the New World.

"Hear! Hear!" echoed the rest of the gentlemen present.

Dr. Hooker spoke. "This one thing is sufficient for me to vote an affirmation of the project, if a vote is necessary: that Grenville is chosen leader. He is a man I honour for his virtue, whose friendship I hold close to my heart, whose integrity is beyond question."

A faint flush showed on Grenville's cheek at Hooker's words.

"May I add my feeling, put into words?" Sidney spoke with emotion. "Since a boy I have been a close friend of the Grenvilles. I have never known men of more honest, forthright English hearts or more wisdom."

Raleigh took up: "Richard, my dear cousin, I think you *must* be our leader. In truth, I fear the plan will die in words, unless under your wise guidance you make our words flower into action. Give us your assent now, that we may proceed with full plans to seat a colony on the lovely island of Roanoke, that Eden which Amadas and Barlow have so well discovered to us."

Hakluyt, standing behind Sidney, said, "Raleigh's Eden. We must make it a reality now, within the year."

Still Grenville did not speak. He pushed back his chair, went to the window and looked out. For a little time he watched the riding lights of the barges in the river below Blackfriars Stairs, the black bulk of Bamande Castle. Barges moving slowly, to ease their way under the great bridge of London. Would one of these vessels carry an unwilling victim, to be disgorged at the Traitors' Gate of the Tower? A shiver passed over him. He moved impatiently. Why think of traitors or treason? He was a loyal man and held no converse with traitors to the Queen. Nor would he have any part in treasonable plots, though some West-Countrymen had spoken covertly to him—things that had better been left unsaid.

"Come now, Richard, declare yourself." Raleigh's voice broke into his meditation. When he turned he saw that all eyes were on him.

"Some things I must know before I give answer," he said, standing at ease, tall against the background of the open window.

"Ask what you will," Raleigh said quickly.

Grenville spoke directly to his cousin. "You are asking me to be subservient to you as commander, Walt?"

The swarthy face of Raleigh changed. His eyes looked anywhere but at Grenville.

"Well, why not answer, Raleigh?" Sir Philip Sidney questioned.

"You will be commander, Grenville," Raleigh said.

"You will take orders from me on the voyage?"

Raleigh again hesitated. "I am not going *this* voyage."

"What!" Chairs scraped as men moved closer, not believing they had heard aright.

"The Queen will not permit me to leave," Raleigh answered, gaining confidence with the words. Sensitive to opinion, he felt the astonishment, even hostility, in all the room. "There is work for me here, raising funds, victualing the ships and so forth."

"Ah," said Grenville, "I see you prefer the known land to the rigours and dangers of the unknown sea!"

Raleigh clapped his hand to his side. There was no sword.

Sidney, in his quiet even voice, said, "Raleigh would be of no help to you, Grenville. You need men of different calibre to stand beside you in such a dangerous undertaking."

The Queen's favourite slumped in his chair, his head bowed. Surely this was uncalled for, this belittling of his ability to stand hardships, danger.

Grenville spoke slowly. "I will go, but there are conditions to be met."

"Name them," Sidney said.

"First, complete command. Second, about the men: One hundred I believe you said would be necessary?"

Raleigh looked up. "There will be no trouble about the men, Richard. Why, half the young gentlemen of the court are eager——"

Grenville shook his head. "Ah, that is what I thought! Half the young gentlemen of the court I will not have. I want no muskcats of the court, no perfumed courtiers, their hands washed in civet. I said men—virtuous men, subject to no price but to soul and honour. I will not have men like kites that check at sparrows; falcons that forsake game to follow sparrows and reed-birds. I want men with strong livers; furious men, who will not pause except when victory is won."

Sidney's attitude of indifference fell from him as he asked the question that was on every man's tongue: "In God's name, what manner of men are these you seek, Richard Grenville?"

"West-Countrymen, sir. If I carry the standard of Elizabeth, let me have men of Devon and Cornwall beside me."

"Amen," said Hooker.

Philip Sidney rose to his feet. His eyes were bright; there was excitement in his voice. The nobleman who was called the most exquisite gentleman in Elizabeth's court had lost his indifferent, his casual manner. He raised his glass. "May I give a toast? To eight gentlemen of the Temple, here gathered! May the plans we have laid add a new empire to the realm of Elizabeth, our glorious Sovereign Queen!"

Not to be outdone, Raleigh's toast followed: "May history

be kind to us!" He glanced quickly around the board. "A Kentish man, a Welshman, a Londoner, and five gentlemen of Devon."

"Success!" cried Captain Amadas, as glasses clinked.

Dr. Hooker rose and clapped on his cape. "Let us go to the Round Church and ask God's blessing on this great venture, for no venture is great unless it has God's blessing on it."

Swords were buckled on, caps set jauntily; satin and velvet doublets and silken hosen went side by side with the sad color of scholars and the black robe of the Church.

Philip Amadas held the door open for Grenville, who walked with lofty brows as though clad in full armour. They went down the narrow stair, crossed the court-yard and waited under the portico for Dr. Hooker to precede them into the Temple church.

Courtiers unhooked their blades and hung them in the sword racks. Metal upon metal gave off a sharp ringing sound, amplified in the silence of the vaulted church. One by one the men dropped to their knees. Only the altar light cast a faint radiance in the heavy gloom of the sanctuary.

In silence each man made his prayer in the shadow of the cloistered marble pillars.

Grenville knelt by the floor tiles which carried the imprint of the winged horse and the lamb and flag. In his heart he felt peace and confidence.

After a time Dr. Hooker spoke. "Here in this Temple dedicated since the thirteenth century to the Knights Hospitallers of St. John, we ask Christ's blessing on a Christian venture as great as those of the Crusaders of ancient memory. A new crusade, to bring Christianity to the New World where savagery and paganism abide."

He rose, a dark shadow among the recumbent marble figures clad in armour. He lifted his hand and made the sign of the cross above the kneeling men. "Go with God, carrying Christ's banner before you!"

The men left silently, out of the church into the quiet night, east along King's Bench Walk, or by the Middle Temple lane through the gardens, where the perfume of red and white roses, late blooming, flooded the air. At the Temple-bar link-boys with flaming torches waited to guide them into the London night, with the vision of a New World shining before their eyes.

27

Thomas Hariot walked with Hakluyt to his chambers. As they passed through the hallway, Hakluyt glanced into the pantry. A single candle set on a table threw its light onto a basket covered with a white napkin. He made an exclamation that caused Hariot to pause at the door.

"The pasties! The Cornish pasties and saffron cake!" he exclaimed. "What will I do? After I importuned Joan to make them!"

Hariot laughed. "We'll have to eat them all, lest you fall into disfavor with that good cook, a thing not to be heard of. Come. I have a flat stomach. Let us begin."

CHAPTER 3
STOWE BARTON

Will Pooley, the old shepherd, paused in his climb up the long hill behind the garden. Colin also paused, pretending interest in the dogs, which had found a rabbit hole in the stone wall under the hedge.

The climb from the sheepfold to King's Park field was long, and Pooley's breath was short and his old heart beat painfully with the exertion. Colin made many such stops each morning, to give the old man a chance to rest without admitting that the hill was almost too steep for his rheumatic knees. The old shepherd was Cornish-proud. He often told the boy that a Devon man might be strong and sturdy, but a man of Cornwall had the strength of the sea in him, as well as the strength of the wild moors, and there was no giving out in him—unless he were dead.

After Pooley's breath came more easily, he pulled aside the branches of may-bushes that grew tall and rank in the old stone wall, and looked down the hill into the walled garden below. Colin, with the frank curiosity of youth, made an opening through the hedge.

Before him down the hill lay the great stone house of Stowe, which had for hundreds of years been the principal country residence of the Grenville family: a great rambling building, half-castle, half-dwelling house, with quaint terraces, decorated statues and hedges of yew and holly clipped in curious forms of animals, bow-knots and flowers. As far as the eye could reach across the rolling hills to the sea, and north to the borders of Devon, was Grenville land.

Fields and woods, upland meadows and lowland, all were lands of his master Sir Richard Grenville, High Sheriff of Cornwall and Member of the Queen's Parliament in London.

Their mistress Lady Grenville, she who was heiress of the St. Legers of Annerly in Devon, sat in her elbow chair on the lower brick terrace, her tapestry frame in front of her. About her were her children and the ladies of her household. The younger children played with the spaniels on the greensward

29

or the high terrace, while the older girls, young Mary and Catherine, with their guests the Dennys from Orleigh Court, were engaged in a spirited archery contest, their gay cotton gowns matching in brilliance the flower beds against the terrace's brick walls.

Dame Philippa, Sir Richard's foster-sister, born Tremayne, and the widow of Roger Tremayne, walked up and down the brick walk that connected the three terraces and wound in and out among the shrubbery massed below the walls. She was holding a book as she strolled, sometimes pausing to read aloud a line or two to Lady Grenville. A fine scholar Dame Philippa was, as learned as the men of her family.

She and her friend Mary Sidney, now the Countess of Pembroke, read Latin and Greek as readily as the students at Oxford and discussed law and politics as if they were members of one of the Inns of the Temple.

Colin wished he could contrive to see what book she held in her long fair hand. For more than a year she had given Colin instruction, along with the master's sons, young John and Bernard, and Master Richard Prideaux and John Arundell. The two young squires lived at Stowe as wards of the master. John Arundell was the son of Richard Grenville's half-brother Sir Alexander Arundell, of Trerice.

It was the custom in Devon and Cornwall for young gentlemen to come to Stowe to live under the guidance of Sir Richard, to learn the amenities and be guided in gentlemanly conduct. Horsemanship and hawking, training in arms and sword-play, became a game under the tutelage of the first gentleman of the West Country. Sir Richard was well versed in the conduct of seamen. His ships, built under his own eyes in the yards at Bideford East the Water, sailed the Irish Sea and the Virginia Sea and the Atlantic. They sailed as far as the Azores, trading and fishing, and sometimes helped sweep the English Channel of enemy vessels that preyed on Her Majesty's shipping.

It was Dame Philippa's idea that Colin, a poorly born boy of no pretensions, should take instruction in the presence of his betters, the young squires. It came about because she had observed him trying to count his flock by the aid of sticks and stones, taking away, then adding, as the sheep moved from one pasture to another. Then there was the incident when he saved her from falling over the cliff. Her mare, frightened by a broken bridle which flapped against its face, ran across the moor, out of her control. Dame Philippa sat well in the saddle, trying to halt the runaway by pulling on its mane. They were at the edge of the cliff when Colin caught the animal. He quieted it while he mended the broken headpiece. Dame Philippa was grateful. It was after this that she told him he could come once a week to the room in the counting-house where the young gentlemen took their instruction.

Doubtless she now read words from some book or manuscript which had been sent down from London . . . lovely words, strung together as beads are strung in a necklace.

Pooley tugged at Colin's smock. "Look, lad, look! By the good Lord, it is Sir Tristan the harper! I swear it is. Not since I was a lad like yourself have I set eyes on the great minstrel."

Colin pulled the branches of may farther apart. On tiptoe he raised his thin body until his eyes were on a level with the aperture. Taking care not to impale himself on the thorny hedge, he looked in the direction Will Pooley had indicated with his staff.

"Which one?" he asked. "The sandy-haired skeleton or the big fat man in monkish robe and with sandals on his bare feet?"

"Neither, fool. Look again. Cannot ye see the ancient one standing tall, with the harp in his hand, carrying himself proud? Cannot ye see the eyes that blaze darkly in a noble head? Cannot ye see the long white beard, like unto the Prophet Jeremiah?"

"Ah, I see. He wears the beard of Merlin."

A heavy hand descended on Colin's shoulder. He squirmed under the clutch of the strong fingers. "Hist, clod! Do not speak the name. Do you want to bring evil upon us and upon the house of Grenville?"

Colin laughed uneasily. "Ah, Will, do you think that Merlin will manifest himself to our eyes? 'Tis impossible. He is prisoned in his cave at Tintagel . . . imprisoned there by the wild Virginia Sea."

"Amen," said the shepherd. He crossed himself, then looked furtively over his shoulder. The new Law and the new Church did not hold with papish customs, but Will was old and new ways came hard.

Colin did not observe the gesture. He was absorbed in the garden scene. "Will he sing, think ye, Will? See, the footman brings stools for the guests. He has placed one for the harper near by our mistress."

"Aye, he will sing. And when you arrive at your oldest years, you will say to your children's children, 'I heard Sir Tristan, the great minstrel, sing.'"

Colin moved so that old Will could look through the opening. By so doing he lost his vision of the terrace. He saw only the old minstrel and Dame Philippa. She had seated herself on a stone bench, her rose silk skirt spread about her, her golden head supported by one slender hand.

The harper ran his fingers across the strings of his harp. Even at this distance Colin could notice how strong and supple his hands were, although his thin face was lined and old. Perhaps his heart was young as his hands.

"Fair stood the wind for France . . ."

The voice was golden. It grew in strength as the song advanced. A ballad of Agincourt and the great battle. Colin's heart leaped. Where had England shown her gallant spirit as she had done that day? Dame Philippa had told them of that battle.

"Upon St. Crispin's Day
Fought was this noble fray . . ."

The battle rose before his eyes. Brave Harry, England's King, fought as no king had fought before, or since. So intent was Colin on the story he did not notice when the golden voice was silent until he heard Dame Philippa's clear words: "Good harper, that ballad is unknown to me. But I think it has greatness in it."

The harper rose and bowed, a knight's bow, for Sir Tristan rated knighthood, though he scorned the honours. "Small wonder, madam. 'Tis written by a young man as yet without fame. He himself gave me the words and I have made the tune."

"The music does so complement the words that they are of one piece," she said.

"It is a most worthy song, most worthily sung." Lady Grenville spoke kindly.

Philippa rose and stood, her hand on the carved stone of the bench. Slim and tall, her long flowing robe girdled about her slender waist, she had the look of ancient Greece. She spoke slowly. " 'Fair stood the wind for France . . .' " She looked toward Lady Grenville. "Oh, I wish with all my heart I had made those lines out of my own imagining. Listen: I think I can repeat it all, for the words are written in my heart.

> "Though they to one be ten
> Be not amazèd . . .

"How heroically they ring, these words:

> "Armour on armour shone,
> Drum now to drum did groan . . .

> "Victor I will remain
> Or on this earth lie slain . . ."

The minstrel touched his harp. The children drew close; the young women left their archery. They sat, wide-eyed and eager, caught up by the power of the lines.

> "Upon St. Crispin's Day
> Fought was this noble fray . . .

> "O when shall English men
> With such acts fill a pen?
> Or England breed again
> Such a King as Harry?"

The children crowded about the harper. "Sing again, good sir. Give us a ballad of King Arthur's Round Table. Pray you, sing for us."

While they talked, young John Arundell, Sir Richard's kinsman, crossed the terrace and made his manners to Lady Grenville. "I heard it all as I was riding down the lane. It is a knightly ballad. It makes me sad that we do not live in the time of Agincourt and may venture all for our great King Harry. These are dull times, with no great venture before us to prove our love of country."

The minstrel turned his deep gaze to the tall youth with the serious eyes and strong though sensitive face. "Young sir, if we transpose a word or two we might sing a modern tune." He struck a chord. "Fair stood the wind for Spain . . ."

A sudden hush fell on the company in the quiet garden.

The rude and tumultuous world intruded. Lady Grenville's needle fell in her lap. The ball of wool rolled across the terrace.

"You have news of Spain, Sir Tristan? Has King Philip sent ships to ravage our coast? Pray tell me, is there evil news? . . . Or perhaps you saw my lord in London and he has sent you—?" Her voice betrayed her anxiety.

"Madam, I come from Plymouth way, not from the north. Spanish alarms are daily talk on the Hoe, at Fowey and Falmouth. They have sentries placed along the cliffs. 'Tis said the great Drake has asked the Queen for more ships to guard the Channel."

Dame Philippa put her hand on Lady Grenville's shoulder. "Cease your worrying, dear sister. Do not let fear turn inward. Richard will not go out to fight the Spanish unless the Spanish come to our shores, and that cannot be, with Lord Howard and the Queen's Navy to protect us."

The mistress of Stowe sank back in her chair. She said almost in a whisper, "Last night I heard the three clarions of Grenville sound clear in the night air. I saw young Richard Prideaux riding at the head of a long procession . . . and two others. I thought one was my John, but I could not see his face, for his visor was down. Young Colin rode beside them. He carried the banners of Prideaux and Arundell and our own. Another rode with him, carrying the banners of Courtenay and St. Leger. It was as though they rode on the waves and not the land of Elizabeth. A dozen banners fluttered in the air, and above all the long standard fluttered and it whipped about them as though it held the whole cavalcade in its encirclement."

Philippa took her hand, stroked the fragile fingers as if she would give strength and courage, but she did not speak.

Lady Grenville sat up rigid, her eyes on the distant hills, looking toward the west. "I do not see him. I hear his voice: 'Board ship, my brave lads! Board ship!' " She lay back, white and lifeless, her eyes closed. Philippa, alarmed, bent over her.

The harper approached. He put his fingers to her wrist. His voice was low. "Voices have spoken through Madam. Let her rest quiet. When she awakens she will not remember."

The smaller children drew near, frightened. Dame Philippa sent them away. "Run to Nurse, children. Tell her she can

34

take you for a walk up the hill where the sheep are grazing."
She kept chafing Mary Grenville's hands as she talked.

The children, at once recovered from their fright by
Philippa's calm matter-of-fact voice, ran off toward the
house, followed by their spaniels. The older girls and young
squires had already wandered toward the tennis courts, where
they played the French game.

The harper struck his harp once; it twanged softly,
piercingly sweet with the gentle sweetness of a flute.

Philippa's eyes searched the dark mystic eyes of Sir Tristan.
"What is it? What happened?" The words formed on her lips
were unspoken.

"She has the gift," he said slowly, "the gift of the pure in
heart. Sometimes she sees beyond the present. Stand away,
mistress. I think she awakens." Philippa went silently to the
stone bench and sat down.

Lady Grenville opened her pale-blue eyes. She looked
about her for a moment unaware. Then the blood mounted
slowly to her pale cheeks. "I am sorry," she said. "I must
have slept for a moment. Your pardon, good Sir Tristan,
that I closed my eyes while you played your harp. It was so
lovely, so tranquil."

Sir Tristan smiled. "You compliment me, madam. Music
was made for tranquillity, but often it is misused to arouse
passions in men."

Philippa thought, She has forgotten. How strange! 'Tis like
the classic mysteries when the oracle speaks.

But after the harper and his followers had gone to their
lodgings in the old house within the outer wall, Lady Grenville broke the silence that had hung like the far drone of
midsummer bees. "Sometimes I think it brings nothing but
unhappiness to love too deeply. In my heart there is always
the fear that he will go away to the Queen's wars—to
Ireland, to middle Europe or to Spain."

"Be at peace now, my dear Mary. Why bother yourself
about what may happen?"

"An uneasy peace, with Philip of Spain waiting, waiting."

"Be thankful Richard did not go around the whole globe
like Francis Drake."

"I am. O dear God, how grateful I am for that!"

Lady Grenville put her crewel needle into the canvas. For
three years she had been working on an arras that would
hang on the stone wall of the banquet hall behind the high

table. A design was in the making, brought from France by Mary Stuart, showing Diana, the fleet-footed, pursuing a stag through the forest. The chaste moon-goddess was afoot, in classic dress, but the ladies and courtiers who followed wore the gay costumes of King Francis' court.

"It will take a lifetime to finish," Philippa murmured. After waiting a moment she said, "God knows whether there will be war again or not, but if there is, on the sea or on the land, you must make up your mind that Richard Grenville will play his part. If the Queen calls, the Grenville clarions will blow."

"I know. I know. Sometimes I wonder, Philippa, why Richard chose me to wife—timid as I am."

"Because he loves you, my dear."

"The St. Legers are all timid." And weak as water, Philippa thought. "My brother is wild and extravagant. Richard is hard on John, my poor silly brother, handsome and vain, who would risk his patrimony on the cast of a die!"

. . . And leave Richard to manage Annerly and produce money to get him out of difficulties. Philippa did not say this aloud. She knew John St. Leger, his duels and silly frivolities and his pursuit after whores and women of no repute.

"I cannot think how Richard wanted me. He is so handsome, so bold and brave. He could have married——"

"Opposites attract," Philippa said lightly. She was tired of this talk. It led nowhere. To her mind Richard Grenville had done exactly as his ancestors and others of the Devon gentry—married into a county family of wealth and position, equal to his own. The Annerly acres might have had something to do with it. The Grenvilles loved their land, and Mary St. Leger brought thirty-six manors and many quarterings as her dowry—aye, and a royal line through the Boleyns. It was a Grenville habit to acquire land. Richard had inherited that, with his tall mighty frame, his heavy blond hair and his piercing sea-blue eyes.

Land-hungry, from the day the first Grenville came over with the Conqueror and became overlord of Bideford. The Grenvilles took by force, by preferment—nobles' land, and Church land granted by the late King Henry VIII. Not much had they got from Elizabeth, 'twas true, but she did not have the vast land to give to her nobles which her father had

36

seized from prelate, monastery and abbey and given to his favourites.

Of this Philippa did not speak. She was fond of Mary Grenville in her way. "Mary, you are sweet and patient. Perhaps one day you may tame that restless spirit and keep him safe at home, locked up in the walled garden of Stowe."

"It would be heaven."

Dame Philippa tossed a blond braid across her shoulder. She thought it would be dull to sit forever in the shelter of a garden wall, stitching tapestry, giving orders to lackeys, housewomen and dairy-maids. To be chatelaine of Stowe or Buckland or any other manor house in the West Country was not her ambition. Dull and unrewarding. Philippa was, in spirit, her foster-brother's kind. She lived in London. She went with the court when the Queen visited her nobles in the country. She spent much time at Penshurst in Kent with Mary Sidney. When she was with the Countess of Pembroke her eager mind found flame to light its imaginings; all the great minds—poets, playwrights and geographers—gathered in Mary Sidney's drawing-room—politicians, too, and men high at court and in national councils. Mary Sidney came less often to London now than had been her wont.

"You are one of the untamed, Philippa." Lady Grenville spoke suddenly, with one of those flashes of intuition that sometimes interrupted her serenity. "Even now you wish there would be war, that King Philip would send ships . . ."

"Bah! That coward send ships? Spain has not the courage. He talks and talks of his right to the English throne. How stupid he is to think that the English people want him for King of England, when we have our glorious Queen!" Her voice rose. "Yes, you are right, Mary. Sometimes I long to be a man, to fight battles, to defend the realm, or to go forth to conquer new lands in the name of our Sovereign Queen, Elizabeth."

"You would follow her anywhere," Mary Grenville remarked. "Anywhere, even to death. You know the old Cornish motto: 'The Grenvilles never lacked loyalty.'"

I know . . . I know . . . I do know, Philippa thought, adding to herself, And the St. Legers never lacked the quest for money. But she said nothing. She loved Mary. She thought she was the right wife for her turbulent, questing Richard Grenville. But sometimes she wondered. Mary could never satisfy the soul hunger of that haughty man or gratify his earthy passions.

She turned and began to walk along the terrace. At the far end she glanced up and saw Colin looking into the garden. She was about to call out to him, to reprimand him for eavesdropping, but she paused. The lad must have been attracted by the minstrel's song. She stood looking at the aperture in the yew hedge long after the face had disappeared. She liked the boy. He was quick, open to learning. He worked so hard, harder than Richard Prideaux or John Arundell. She tried to interest them in the poets, good books for reading, Latin. She taught to escape boredom. What was there for her in this wild Cornish country, or in Devon, save to hawk and ride and hunt, or divest herself of hampering garments and bathe deep in the wild ocean at the foot of the cliffs, at Hartland Point, or the shingle beach at Portledge? She sighed. London—she must go up to London as soon as Richard returned, not to savour the gaiety of the court, but to talk again with men who thought out beyond the present into the broad future.

She noticed the slim, tall figure of the shepherd boy climbing up the hill to King's Park field, his dogs at his heels. There was something in his back, the way he moved, the turn of his well-set blond head. A proud carriage for a shepherd, a proud carriage. It reminded her of someone. She stopped and looked intently at the retreating figure. A little thought caught in her mind. A quizzical smile touched the corners of her lips. She would ask her foster-brother. Richard had always been frank with her.

Colin reached the top of the hill. He paused and looked across toward the village of Kilkhampton. The square stone tower of the Norman church stood out against the sky, strong and bold, built for eternity. He wondered if the early Normans knew how well they builded their churches and watchtowers—those grey stone fortresses, the strength of the Church, placed so well to guide travellers across desolate moors, among the rolling hills. Down the centuries they had stood, monuments of faith. That is what Dame Philippa told the young squires: "Never forget what we owe to those Norman invaders. The early Britons left stones; they were sturdy men, cruel, without refinement. The Normans brought in another culture. The Normans left great buildings; crosses

for prayer at cross-roads; castles built by great families."
They were all recorded in one Domesday Book, as well as
the names of men who held the land. The Grenvilles, the
Arundells, Prideaux and Courtenays had come with William
the Conqueror in 1066.

That was long ago. Thirteen generations of Grenvilles had
held the same land in Cornwall and in Devon. "Be proud to
live under a Grenville," she had told them one day at
lessons. " 'Tis better to serve a great county family than to
serve the King or nobility in London. London men twist
their necks this way and that, to know whom to serve.
They are weak men who know not truth or courage. They
know only intrigue and money grabbing. They are given to
gossip and mean practises. The glory of England is in her
strong men, like the gentry of Cornwall and Devon and
Somerset."

Colin had never forgotten that. He was thinking of it at
this moment. He was proud to serve a great warrior and
sea captain. Perhaps one day when he filled out and could
throw a lance with a strong arm, Sir Richard would take him
abroad to the wars—or on the sea, the wild Atlantic that he
looked on from the cliffs. Some day . . .

He shaded his eyes with his hand, looking toward Kilkhampton. He thought he saw the sun glint on lance and
armour. His pulse bounded and he started toward a gateway
in the high wall, shouting to Will Pooley as he ran, "Sir
Richard! Sir Richard rides home to Stowe. God be
praised!"

Old Will called back, "Mind you the gate. It would fare
bad with you if your sheep go through and our master caught
ewe or ram in the lane." He hurried after Colin as fast as his
ancient legs would allow. He, too, would be at the gate, to
kneel and make his obeisance as the master and his fine
company of gentlemen rode down the lane on prancing
horses, with lances on toe and banners fluttering, as fine
a sight as old eyes could wish to see. Even the sheep-dogs
caught the excitement. They ran back and forth, barking and
cavorting. "Silence, brutes!" shouted the shepherd. "Want for
to get the flock astir? Down, Hubba! Stand quiet as the
master passes."

The little cavalcade rode along the walled lane. At the top
of the hill they drew rein—an old custom. From this point
Sir Richard got the first glimpse of Stowe, the low farm

buildings, the brick-yard, the broad-fronted house with its gleaming windows and sturdy Norman doorway, the high wall with its tower entrance. In the court-yard was life, men and women crossing and recrossing, going about their chores. Over the wall could be seen the outline of the garden.

There his lady sat waiting. He gave a signal. The trumpeter lifted the clarion, blew the home-coming notes. So eager was Sir Richard that he did not see the old shepherd and the lad by the gate. He turned to a young girl who rode beside him. With one sweep of his arm as though to encompass the hills and the Vale of Coombe, he said, "This is Stowe, Thomasine, Grenville land since the days of the Conqueror. Welcome to Stowe, my kinswoman!"

The girl, her wild-blowing black hair low over her eyes, did not answer. She was looking at the shepherd boy who knelt beside the hedge, making obeisance to his overlord. A smile crossed her full red lips; her stormy black eyes held scorn and a little contempt. To kneel, to bow the knee—that was contemptible. To be poor, of lowly birth, brought pity to her heart, but why should a young man bow to the earth because a great man passed?

The lad raised his head as though her brooding thoughts drew him. Blue eyes gazed steadily at her, frank, unafraid, measuring her; searching eyes that held no fear or subservience in them. He met her glance steadfastly until she dropped her eyes. Through her long black lashes she watched him rise to his feet. Tall and very slim, with broad shoulders, he stood beside the bent figure of the old shepherd, watching her.

Young John Grenville drew rein. "Heigh, Colin! I've brought a young falcon from London. We'll unhood her early in the morning. Will you carry the birds when we ride?"

The lad's voice came clearly as the little procession wound down the hill. "Aye, that I will. Stowe Woods at sunrise? Aye, soon as I set the flock to the lower vale."

"Excellent!" Young Grenville set spurs to his horse to catch up with the procession as it wound down the hill past King's Park field. The clarion sounded again, answered by the clarion at Stowe, a joyful welcoming call. The Lord of Stowe rode gaily into the court-yard, accompanied by his brave group of young men, and close-attended by his

40

steward, old Ching. Bridle chains rattled. Horses tossed their heads, neighing and champing their bits.

Sir Richard rode first to the derrick set up near the gateway. The farm smith was waiting to cast the chains, insert the iron hook into the stout leather belt at the back of the light armour which Sir Richard always wore when travelling, and swing him to the ground. Without waiting for his squires Grenville strode, armour clanking, across the stone-paved court-yard and greeted his curtsying people as he went. He was eager for the garden and the first glimpse of his wife. Only after he had kissed her on the lips did he allow his men to strip him of breast-plate and epaulets. Then he greeted his family one by one. Catherine he kissed on the cheek. Young Mary made a deep curtsy, kissing his hand. He laughed as he raised her, circling her slender waist with his arm. "Bravo, my girl! I doubt if there is a lady in waiting to the Queen who could do that more gracefully."

His daughter blushed prettily. "Thank you, sir."

"She's been practising," his wife said, smiling.

"And a good thing. The Queen wants her at court, to attend her."

"Oh, Father! When?" young Mary cried.

"In the spring. From May until October, I believe. Your mother will be notified."

"How gracious of the Queen!" Dame Philippa came forward to make a slight bow. "Welcome home, Dick." She put her hands on his shoulders and turned a cheek to be kissed. "Most gracious," she added, glancing from Mary to young Squire Arthur Tremayne who stood apart, a sandy-haired youth with a thin face and a long nose. He was watching young Mary's joy with visible misgiving.

"My young coz Arthur isn't happy," Dame Philippa said with a smile. "Are you afraid, Arthur, that Mary will lose her heart or her head to one of the gay London courtiers?"

The youth mumbled something and sunk his chin deeper into his starched ruff.

The girl walked over to him and thrust her hand through his arm. "Let's walk beneath the oaks," she said in a low tone.

He brightened instantly. "Yes, let us walk toward the wood," he said as they moved off.

Richard Grenville had a slight furrow between his eyes. "I am not so sure Arthur will bring happiness to our little

Mary," he said in a low tone to Dame Philippa. "I wish I could believe he could make her happy."

"What man can make a woman happy?" she returned lightly.

"You are cynical, Philippa. Cynicism belongs to London, not in the good West Country."

"Perhaps," she retorted. "But do you really believe, Richard, that cynicism is an attribute only of the court?"

He did not answer. He allowed his glance to wander to his wife. Lady Grenville had crossed the terrace and was instructing her tire-woman how to stick the plain blue background into her tapestry.

"I think I have made her happy," he said slowly. "I trust I have."

Dame Philippa gave him a swift look. He really believes he has, she thought. How stupid men are! She came near saying the words aloud.

"Your wife is an angel," she said instead.

"And I am a devil incarnate?" He smiled, his blue eyes atwinkle. "The latest thing I have heard about myself is that I drink my port at a gulp, then chew the glass tumbler and eat it."

"How disgusting!" Dame Philippa exclaimed. "How uniquely disgusting!" Then she laughed, a bright tinkling laugh. "What a monster they think you, my good Dick!"

"At least they make me a man of power. I'm sure no weak-livered nincompoop would eat and digest a glass tumbler."

"Without letting blood?"

"Without letting blood, they say."

"What else, Richard?"

He looked down at the slim, elegant figure of his foster-sister. A smile rippled his stern lips. He stroked his pointed beard with long thin fingers.

"Come, do not keep me in suspense," she teased.

"I am likened to Cesare Borgia by some."

"A poisoner?"

"No, no."

"Ah, let me see, wasn't he the fellow who wanted a fresh virgin every night?"

There was the shadow of a smile on Grenville's face. "Let us walk to the orangery. I wish to consult you in private."

"I hope you will tell me more of this gossip. It interests me."

"About my search for women?"

She shrugged her shoulders. "You are no different from any of the London men of my acquaintance. Scarce a day passes without a provocative tale of some young blade in some woman's bed. Your brother-in-law St. Leger has a pretty way with women, they say."

"Barmaids!" Richard scowled. "I've just paid twenty pounds to get the rascal out of a scrape."

They turned from the rose garden into the path that led to the orangery, a low brick building with glass windows, where the gardener kept his choice lime plants and miniature oranges.

Philippa said, "John St. Leger escorted me home one night after a festive party at St. James's. He insisted on coming in. I had my man bring the decanters. He drank three glasses of port, then tried to attack me. I thought for a few moments he would have his way." She smiled. "But a farthingale is as good a protector of virginity as an escort with a sword."

"The fool! The drunken fool!"

"Not too drunk, Dick. I saw him next day in the Queen's garden. I reminded him, 'You were drunk last night, sirrah.'

" 'So I was,' he answered, 'but not too drunk to regret what I almost attained.' Then he kissed my hand and said, 'One day fortune will smile on me.' "

"You shouldn't laugh, Philippa. I've a notion to cane the young devil. The impudence!"

"You'd be caning half the court, my dear brother. Don't think for an instant that I am more in demand than any other of the Queen's maids. Why, I've seen a favourite leave a private audience with the Queen, then go straightway down the halls in pursuit of some maid and carry her to one of the deep window embrasures." She sighed. "I wish they would at least have the grace to draw the curtains."

Grenville put his hand on her shoulder. "Is this the truth, or are you playing at being worldly?"

The young woman smiled with her lips only. "The truth, I assure you. Any lady in waiting can tell you tales. Ask Mary Sidney. She has seen so much that she stays at Penshurst more than half the time. I would not want a young daughter of mine at court before she married."

Grenville walked a step or two, then faced his foster-sister. "I think we will find an excuse to keep our daughter Mary at home."

Philippa nodded. "That is why I tell you these things, Dick. Little Mary is so lovely and unspoiled. I should loathe to have her disillusioned before her marriage. Let her serve her time at Whitehall after her marriage, not before."

"You are right, my dear, entirely right."

"Wickedness is rampant. You know Elizabeth and her ways. She minds not who is by if she wants comforting. The Queen is what Tom Seymour made her—Tom Seymour and her various stepmothers, who didn't get what they needed from the King, and secreted courtiers or stewards in their beds, like Catherine Howard. Too many good men have lost their heads for silly women. To lie with an ardent woman may be a pleasure. But to lie with a Queen—and then lie with your head on the block—is too great a price to pay for an hour's release."

"I never believed the tales about the admiral and young Elizabeth. She loved him no doubt. She was very young and he had a way with women."

"Like you, my dear Dick. Few women can resist you."

"You are indeed worldly. You know so much—as much as a man knows."

"Is that a crime? You are old-fashioned, Richard. You think all women are like your dear wife Mary. Mary is as innocent as a child, for all she has borne your children. We are not all Marys, my dearest brother."

He looked at her speculatively, his eyes narrowed. "We are not blood kin, Philippa," he said softly.

She met his eyes. "Questing, always questing." Her voice was brittle. She rose, her body taut and straight. Anger flamed in her blue eyes.

"Who is your lover, Philippa?" he asked, catching her hand. "Or shall I say lovers? We hear gossip in London."

"For shame, Richard! For shame!"

In an instant he was contrite. "Your pardon, my sweet Philippa. Your pardon. I do not know what made me speak such words."

She stepped away from him. "No matter. Other and more vicious tongues have wagged before now. I see Mary on her way to inspect the dairy. I think I will join her. There is something cool and refreshing about a dairy . . . after the fetid air of court gossip."

CHAPTER 4
THE BRAND

His wife lay sleeping. The moonshine flooded the room, the diamond-paned window making a pattern on the counterpane. Richard Grenville stood for a moment looking down on her quiet face, pale, almost waxen, in the argent light. His stern mouth relaxed. His blue eyes, which could be so hard and penetrating, held a gentle, protective look. How quietly she slept, worn out by the ardour of his loving!

Quietly he closed the door and made his way down the narrow steps, indifferently lighted by a lanthorn hung at the short landing. He could not sleep. His active mind raced with plans for the Virginia voyage. The very thought of Virginia adventure kept rising, pushing aside business of the farms. He had not told Mary. A dozen times he had been on the verge, and a dozen times backed away like a cowardly diver afraid to take the plunge. There had been opportunity, but he had hesitated. He told himself that he did not want to spoil his home-coming by talking of another absence before he had slept one night under his own roof-tree. Timidly she had questioned, "What was the news in London? Was there talk of more trouble with Spain . . . in the Low Countries . . . with France?"

He was glad to disabuse her of thoughts of war. She had not spoken of Virginia, poor child. She had little knowledge of the talk that pervaded the air, the very stones of London streets—talk of the New World. Glory for England lay across the Atlantic, to the north, to the west—glory for England. New Worlds in the name of Elizabeth the Queen. Glory and honour to the men who planted the first colony on the shores of the other world!

How he had risen to Philip Amadas' tale of the riches, the beauty, the untold adventure that lay across the water! He, Richard Grenville, would bring that glory to England. To seat a colony—that was far better than to sail around the world as Drake had sailed.

45

"Francis Drake." He spoke the name aloud. Drake, a man of inferior station, who had stolen his idea of circumnavigating the globe. He felt his anger rise as it always did at the name of Drake. He must put such thoughts aside. Drake had not seated a colony—just sailed straight home with gold from captured Spanish ships.

He paused, stopped by the murmur of voices in the hall. The young men had not retired. John Arundell and Richard's sons John and Bernard would be telling the stay-at-homes of London and its rich gaiety, its lusts and its vices. There would be no talk of Virginia. He had warned them on the way home to say nothing until plans were complete.

He opened the door silently and stood surveying the hall. A bright fire burned in the high stone fire-place. Half a dozen of his young squires lay before the blaze on the deerskins spread on the broad stone flags. Dame Philippa sat in the high-backed Italian chair. Beside her two of the staghounds lay at ease, their heads resting near her feet. Philippa had a way with horses and dogs. She hunted as a man hunted, riding hard from dawn to midday. His wife, since her children were born, rode no more. Sometimes she would go to the meeting-place in a farm cart and take her place on a hill-top where she could watch the stags being driven from the woods into the open fields.

Philippa glanced up. "Ah, Richard, welcome to the fire," she said, smiling. The youths sprang to their feet, John Arundell the first to attend him—a stool for his feet, a small tavern table for his elbow—while his son tapped a gong for a servant, ordered ale brought and a bit of cheese from their own dairy. Mugs were refilled with Devon cider or ale, as each man's taste ran. Dame Philippa sipped her white port from a delicate glass. She drank elegantly, with trained appreciation for fine drink, as for fine food. Grenville took his place near the fire on a high-back settle of dark oak which was worn to a smooth satin surface by the centuries. He sat quietly enjoying the amber ale, listening to the rising chatter of the young men, who sat at the game of hazard, near the diamond-paned window.

Youth had its advantage. Youth for adventure and change! With his robust health, his strong, well-knit frame, he seldom thought of the approaching middle age. He had never known illness. This he attributed to his ancestors who had left him a rugged constitution and a quick active brain, along with broad acres and manor-houses, flocks and herds. He glanced at the plaster coat of arms of the family above the fireplace.

The three clarions of the Grenvilles were known from the Netherlands to Hungary—aye, as far as the Holy Land. Now he would plant the Grenville banner in the New World, just below the standard of Elizabeth the Queen. He encountered Philippa's inquiring glance.

"You have something on your mind, Richard. Are we to have war with Spain? Has Philip the courage to bring his ships sailing to our shores?"

"Not for the moment. The Queen has outmanoeuvred Philip's ambassador once again. She has a miraculous way with her, our Queen."

"And a sagacious secretary in Walsingham." Dame Philippa spoke dryly.

"Burghley is not to be forgotten," Grenville said. "He is heart and soul in the Virginia venture." He stopped abruptly, having spoken without thought what was in his mind.

"Virginia adventure? Pray what is the Virginia adventure?" Her searching eyes sought his.

"Nothing. Nothing. I spoke carelessly, my dear."

She leaned forward; the soft mull of her gown revealed her firm white breasts. "I knew you pondered on some new idea, Richard. Do not try to cover your misspoken word. I know that look."

"What look, madam?" Grenville's face set in its stern lines.

Philippa paid no heed. "The look of authority that comes over you when you hold your courts as High Sheriff of Cornwall, or stride into the meeting of Parliament as Knight of the Shire, 'Overlord of Bideford am I, Richard Grenville.'"

Richard laughed.

"Your very bearing tells the story."

He looked remarkably youthful then, for he laughed with his eyes as well as his lips. "You make me feel a bit of an ass, Dame Philippa."

"Heaven forbid! Just a man of dignity and power, assuming the robes of office. But Virginia—we were speaking of Virginia. Wasn't it Walt Raleigh I heard talk of the wonderful New World across the Western Ocean?"

"No doubt it was Walt. He does little else——"

"But talk," she interrupted. "Such a fluent talker, using always the elegant word in its proper place! No wonder the

47

Queen prefers his talk to the feeble conversation of most of her courtiers. 'God's death! By me oath! 'Tis a monstrous fine day, ma'am,' " she mimicked.

"Now what would Walt say?" he asked, entering into her gay mood.

Dame Philippa pursed her lips. The tone of her voice grew higher, more precise. " 'Ma'am, forgive your humble subject if I say your presence brings radiance that pales the sun. You make the day for your loyal subjects, my Queen. Your smile is the sunshine, your frown the cold grey fog that swallows your city of London in drear November.' "

Grenville laughed aloud at her drollery. "Don't mistake Walt, my dear Philippa. Behind those la-di-da ways he has a shrewd mind."

"Shrewd for his own advancement. Oh, I like Raleigh. He amuses me. But he is always thinking of Walter Raleigh, whereas you, Richard, you think first of your country, then of the Grenvilles. That is as it should be."

He reached for her hand and raised it to his lips. "Thank you, my sweet sister and friend." Noticing the eyes of several young men on them, Grenville raised his voice. "A compliment from a fair lady is the occasion for a toast. Fill up, my lads, and drink to Dame Philippa, the most indefatigable, the most successful hawker in Stratton Hundred. Drink a long toast, my lads, till the bottom of the tankard is in sight."

As each man drank and set his pewter tankard on the long table, the old minstrel came into the room through the far doorway. He made his way across the flagged floor to do his obeisance to Sir Richard—a slight bow only, as became one who was at the top of his craft and knew it.

Sir Richard's greeting had warmth in it. He leaned forward to embrace the old man. "Colin lad, a mug for our honoured guest, my father's friend and my friend," he said affectionately. "It is indeed a rare welcome home to find you here under my roof. A good omen, I say. A good omen."

"Aye, Sir Richard, a good omen. I bring greetings to you from Arundell of Trerice. At Exeter I talked with Courtenay. They will be at Stowe before the week is out."

A smile lighted Richard Grenville's stern face. "Ah, good news indeed, ancient, good news indeed!"

The harper finished his drink. Excusing himself he left the hall.

"You are happy," Dame Philippa said to Richard after the

harper had gone, "extraordinarily happy. Why does the coming of Sir John Arundell and Rise Courtenay cause you so much pleasure? They come often enough to Stowe in their goings and comings from Cornwall to London."

Richard leaned toward her. "Sir John and Rise are but the earliest guests of many who will come to Stowe Barton within the fortnight. My squires ride through Devon and Cornwall to gather my friends together. There will be many of our cousins and friends to make feast, to ride down the fox, to unhood the falcon. The clans are gathering, Dame Philippa. The clans are gathering."

"For what purpose, my brother?" Philippa's fair face was grave, her voice quiet. "They come not for war?"

"No, no." Richard's voice was gay. He tilted his tankard, which Colin had filled. "They come to talk with me of a Virginia venture—Raleigh's venture, not the Bristol merchants' venture—the great venture across the Western Ocean that will bring honour and glory to our Queen."

He rose to his feet, the company with him. "To our courageous Sovereign Queen!" he cried. "Drink deep, lads, drink deep, to the most glorious Queen that subjects ever had! A Queen to die for!" He leaned forward and almost lost his balance. "Drink deep!"

Philippa steadied him with her hand on the sleeve of his velvet doublet. "Have done, Richard. You're drunk."

"Not I, my fair friend, not I—unless I'm drunk with the dream of the greatest venture a man ever had: a New World to lay at the feet of his sovereign."

"Hold your tongue. Do you want to spill secrets before these young squires? See how they watch you, their eyes filled with curiosity."

"You are right, Philippa. I remember how cautious you always were even as a child, cautious and bold too." He turned to the men at the far side of the fire. "Off to bed with you! At daylight we hawk at Coombe Vale." The men said their good-nights, bowed before Dame Philippa—all save John St. Leger, Grenville's young brother-in-law, who sat at the long table, his head resting on his arms.

"He has a weak head," Grenville said with contempt. "Night after night in London he is carried away to his bed. I think he will not stand up to the venture." He stopped Colin, who had picked up several mugs and was about to carry them away. "Heigh! You look a strong lad. Do you think you can make it up the stairs with the young gentleman over your shoulder?"

"Many a calf I have hoisted on my back, sir."

"Then hoist this calf and put him in his cot."

"Shall I undress him, sir?"

"That you shall not. Let him lie as he falls."

Colin stooped and lifted the limp form on his shoulder, lifted himself by the strength of his flexible knees and stood erect. He strode from the room, easily, as though he carried no burthen at all.

Grenville watched him. When the door was closed, he turned to Dame Philippa, a question in his eyes but none on his lips.

"You see the resemblance?" she asked softly.

"Resemblance to whom?" Grenville was obviously puzzled.

"No matter. I thought you watched the lad over-closely."

"Perhaps I saw in him good strength and a cool, confident air; a youth trained to fight and wear the Grenville colours."

"Blue and Silver and three clarions on his sleeve?"

"Yes. A badge to wear in all honour, my dear Philippa. Aye, in honour born out of dishonour." He pulled a leather-bound chair to the fire. "It pleases you to speak in riddles, evasively, as becomes a woman of subtlety. Must I now ask for an explanation?"

" 'Never explain,' " she quoted briefly. "But tell me more of this Virginia venture of Raleigh's."

He smiled at her, a quick easy smile that brought boyishness to his lean, stern face. "You must wait, dear Philippa. This day week there will be a meeting here. A hundred men of Cornwall and Devon will sleep at Stowe Barton. Perhaps we may ask you to be present and hear the talk."

"Ah, you will allow a woman to sit in the council of men?"

"Why not? You will manage to get the secret out of Philip Sidney or Walter Raleigh. You, with your little smile and your big, innocent eyes, so round, so full of candour—you will always drag secrets from men one way or another."

"You flatter me strangely."

"I flatter? Never! I speak truth as I see it."

"When it suits your convenience. You can be blind enough to truth when you wish."

"Have done with sparring, sweet sister. You know I have only admiration for you, though sometimes I deplore your methods. It is taking unfair advantage of a man, to sleep with him that you may have him whisper state secrets into your shell-pink ear."

"I have not slept with Walsingham!" Philippa's voice was indignant. "Never!"

Grenville teased her with a smile. "Ah, the strike went home!"

"I've never known you to listen to London gossip, Richard." Her tone was sharp. "If Walsingham chooses to sit often in my small cabinet, it is because he feels a tranquillity that he does not get at home. And if he sometimes talks of affairs that trouble and vex him, can I prevent?"

"No, no. Certainly not."

She did not heed his interrupting. "Those horrible women who are frozen in their veins sit in envy and speak venomously. I do assure you, Walsingham and I are friends only."

Grenville rose and stood by the stone fire-place, shifted his long legs to the fire's warmth. "I am glad it is Platonic solace of the mind, and not the lifting of the petticoats, that attracts the secretary. After all, I do not fancy Walsingham is much of a man on the bed. He has not the imagination to make dalliance a thing of beauty; leaves it merely convenience of the body."

Philippa laughed, her red lips parting over her white teeth. "You say the strangest things, Richard Grenville."

"Why strange? To me it is strange that a man can be so immersed in sedentary living that he has no joy or delight in——"

Philippa held up her slim hand. "No more of this, I pray."

Grenville allowed his eyes to travel the length of her lithe body, so elegantly and revealingly encased in rose-coloured silk. "Don't play the prude! By the living Jove, you are fashioned for a strong man's loving, if ever a woman was!"

"Perhaps I've never had a strong man's love, only weaklings who leaned on me, whom I mothered but did not meet on that high plane of equality." For some moments there was silence in the great room. The wood in the fire-place crackled and broke with sparkling flame.

"We are no blood kin," he said abruptly. She did not reply. Her face was hidden as she bent over the dog's head. "No blood kin," he repeated, his voice harsh.

There was a stir in the hallway. A door slammed. They heard the sound of running feet. The door burst open and the girl Thomasine ran into the room. Tears were streaming down her face. She stopped abruptly. Then seeing Grenville she ran to him, sank before him, thrust her arms about his knees.

"Take me home!" she cried hysterically. "Take me back to Tintagel! I loathe it here. I will not stay!"

Grenville unhooked the girl's hands. "Thomasine, this noise is unseemly. Quiet yourself and tell me what ails you."

She sent a swift glance over her shoulder. " 'Tis he. He pinched me and slapped at me and grabbed at my legs when I went down the hall." She pointed to Colin, who had just entered the room.

Philippa thought the lad's expression was one of amazement. Grenville thought differently. He unclasped the girl's clinging arms and told her to seat herself.

"Don't leave the room," he said to Colin. "Stand where you are till I give you leave to move."

He turned to the girl. Her hysterical cries had given way to sobbing. "Thomasine, stop that noise and say what you want to say without tears. Was this clod annoying you? Did he dare lay hands on you?"

"Sir, he did, he did." She laid her hand on her thigh. "Not once but twice he pinched. I was going down the dark hall. He was carrying a sotted man over his shoulder. He reached out at me as I passed him."

The boy Colin raised his hand as if to protest, but dropped it to his side. His usually alert eyes became devoid of any expression.

Thomasine leaned back in the chair and wiped the tears from her eyes with the back of her hand. The soft tangle of her hair fell across her face. Philippa looked from one to the other. They made a triangle, Grenville at the fire-place, Colin half-way across the room near the long table where the guests ate, a step below the family board.

Colin's head was erect. His shoulders were squared to meet the punishment he knew he must take. He stood almost as tall as Grenville, but his body was thin, with the rangy thinness of youth, while Grenville had begun to thicken in girth and about the neck. The man's eyes were cold as he looked across the girl in the chair to meet the calm blue gaze of the shepherd boy.

Philippa thought. This is cold anger I see. I would that it were flaming and sudden, like a flash of lightning, not this steady calculated anger. She knew Richard Grenville as she knew herself. She had seen him in all his moods throughout the years, and his moods were many and varied. A man of great generosity and unbelievable hardness. She had been frightened at the innate cruelty he sometimes displayed to a high-spirited animal. She was afraid now. Her fears for the lad made her stomach contract.

The boy must make some gesture of contrition, some excuse, kneel at Grenville's feet to ask pardon. Yet she knew he would not. He would stand thus, facing his master, until Richard's wrath came to the breaking point. She could not stand the tension. Suddenly she spoke. "What were you doing in the hall, Thomasine?" she asked. She hoped her voice sounded as calm as she wanted it to.

The girl's dark eyes turned slowly. She fixed her vengeful gaze on Dame Philippa. "I was going to the garden," she said sullenly.

"The garden at this hour?" Philippa lifted her hand and stroked the dog's head. "It is past midnight."

"I know not what the hour. I have no desire to sleep in a room with women who breathe heavily through their long noses."

Philippa laughed easily. She continued to stroke the dog's head. She hoped this interruption, this little device, would break Richard Grenville's anger.

"I often sleep out of doors, in my aunt's garden, or in the rocks near Merlin's cave, when I am home at Tintagel."

"Ah!" Philippa put a world of meaning into the exclamation. It was as though she had said to Richard, "See what a wild, wayward child! No doubt she provoked the lad Colin to pinch her buttocks and treat her the way the stablemen treat dairymaids." She raised her eyes. Grenville had not moved; he remained standing at the hearth, his eyes fixed on Colin. Eye for eye, glance for glance, there was no subservience in the one or lessening of anger in the other.

"Stand forth, shepherd!" Colin walked across the room. "Don't stand like a gawk. Make obeisance!" thundered Grenville, his voice even and hard.

The boy bent the knee and touched his forehead—a token of obeisance without humility.

"Not to me, fool! To the lady! Both knees to the earth and the forehead likewise!"

"Sir, that I will not. I make obeisance to you because you are my lord. But to no woman."

The girl leaned forward. Her eyes dark and vindictive turned from the tall blond youth to Richard Grenville. "Sir, I ask punishment for his touching my person."

"You will set the punishment. Make up your mind." He turned, took up the iron fire-stick, moved a log. The sparks hissed and the fire blazed up. It lighted the shadows of the long room, uncrowded now and silent.

Philippa's hand ceased to stroke the staghound's head that rested on her knees. She felt the silence, the almost tranquil silence, but she knew there was no tranquillity in the heart of the dark girl in the chair. The silence broke.

"He shall be lashed," Thomasine said decisively. "Twenty and one lashes."

Colin stiffened. Philippa could see him grow taut, but his face was expressionless as he stared over the girl's head to the darkened corner of the room.

"No," Richard said. "No. This is not a flogging matter. My men are never flogged for a thing like this. You must think of some other means. I believe it would be a Greek punishment if I made him your serving man, to wait upon you, to saddle your horse and ride as your groom . . . to stand outside your chamber, to guard you. I think it just—to remind him to pay respect to women under the Grenville roof-tree. Yes, a fair punishment." He turned his eyes toward Philippa. "A fair punishment. Do you not think so, Dame Philippa?"

In spite of her wish to be calm, her heart spoke through her reluctant lips. "An indignity unworthy of you, Richard Grenville, an indignity to his manhood."

Grenville did not listen. He was examining the point of the fire-iron. "Yes. I will give him a mark of honour. Hold out your hand!" His voice came clear and incisive.

Colin stepped to Grenville's side. Without hesitation he held out his hand, palm upward.

Before Philippa could intervene, Richard Grenville had set the iron on the lad's palm, a stroke down and one over. The arm muscle jerked in spasm. There was no weakness in the Spartan will. Colin thrust out his hand again. Again the iron seared—three quick strokes, two on diagonals, one across. Philippa thought she never would forget the pain in his eyes—where alone it showed.

Thomasine started up from the chair, her face livid. She gave one look at the iron as it seared the heavy pad below the thumb. She huddled back in her chair, then slumped down.

"I have marked fine letters T and A, to show you are a servitor of Mistress Thomasine Arundell," Grenville said.

Colin looked at Sir Richard once, then at a word of dismissal left the hall.

Philippa snatched up a half-filled tankard of ale from the table and sloshed it over the unconscious girl. "Call a serving woman," she said to Grenville. "Take her away. Lock her in her room is my advice. She's caused enough harm tonight, the silly wench."

Grenville stood looking down at Philippa, his calm unruffled. A slightly sardonic smile came to the corners of his firm mouth. "When you've seen as many men marked as I have, my dear Philippa, you will know that no harm has been done. It will grow out in half a dozen years and leave no sign."

"You fool!" she said. "It's not the mark on a man's hand that counts. . . ." She left the rest unsaid. She took up a candle and made her way across the long room to the door through which Colin had disappeared.

"Philippa, come back!" Grenville's voice was angry. She went on as though she had not heard. She must find the boy, do what she could to assuage the hurt, not to his hand—a little grease from the cook's stores would do that—but to the growing consciousness of manhood in a youth of great promise. Strange that Richard had not seen the Grenville in him as they stood face to face before the fire—or had she allowed her imagination to run away with her?

She took up the candle and groped her way through unfamiliar passages that led toward the kitchen. Never had she put foot in this part of the sprawling house, built by long-dead Grenvilles. Perhaps it might have been Sir Theobald Grenville himself who built Stowe Barton, the same Grenville who slept so quietly in the altar of the church in Bideford, his little dogs carved in stone at his feet. She stumbled over a rough stone in the flagging and stifled a scream as a rat scudded across the passage at her feet. Far down the stone-flagged passage she saw the light of a fire in an inner court-yard. She passed doors, some closed, some opening into blackness. The air was heavy with odours of cooked food. She must be passing the second court-yard beyond the kitchen.

55

A strong flow of wind came down the passage, a cross-current as she passed an open doorway. She heard heavy breathing, rattling snores. She dropped her silken skirts to shield the flickering candle from the wind. A moment later it went out, leaving her in complete darkness.

Philippa paused. Should she retrace her steps or go ahead, groping her way in the blackness? It did not occur to her to cry out for help. She moved slowly, feeling her way, her hand touching the damp stone wall, an unknown wall. She could not remember having passed by any entrances or doors for some time. Had she taken a wrong turn in the dark—back there where the cross-current of air had blown out her candle?

Turn back? It was always better to go forward. She moved cautiously, feeling her way in the blackness. She came to an uneven ridge in the wall. She paused and moved her foot, feeling her way. She found a rough stone step leading downward. This was the wrong direction, unless she had completely lost her bearings. She stopped, leaned against the wall to rest. It felt damp. She dropped the candle and could not recover it. No matter; it was of no use now, without a spark to light it. Her skirts had become a nuisance, impeding her movements. She stopped, caught up the trailing garments. She pulled them between her legs, fastened the train through her girdle, making a pair of pantaloons.

She moved now with more freedom. Testing each step with the toe of her satin shoe, she descended the narrow stone stairway. She counted up to twenty.

Her heart was thumping against her ribs. She told herself that it was absurd to be frightened. What in God's realm was there to fear at Stowe Barton? But she continued to breathe quickly.

Presently, after many uncounted steps, she felt the air change, grow cooler, with a tang of the sea in it. The blackness ahead gave way to a faint grey. Once she thought she saw the flicker of a light—or was it a star low on the horizon? She paused, then went on, step by step. She had no idea how long she had been walking in the dark narrow passage. Suddenly she heard the dull roar of the sea. She forced her aching legs to carry her on. There was a turn in the steps. They widened into a narrow path. The surge of the sea was loud. It reverberated. The warm air of the passage gave way to the bracing sea air. A few moments later she emerged.

She stood still, to get her breath. There was no moon. A myriad stars crowded for space in the dark heavens. The Milky Way sent a long streak across the sky, a path of pale gold for a giant to walk. Below her in the heavy blackness of the high cliffs was the sea. She could see the faint outline of the rolling hills, feel a trickle of water at her feet.

She must have come out the old Smugglers' Way. She had heard of the passage where of old times Grenvilles had had dealings with black-headed men from Lundy Island or the Irish coast, or perhaps a stray Spaniard who had brought his ship close enough to the cliffs to launch a small boat, bear his treasures ashore and traffic with those lusty Grenvilles who feared neither king nor man nor devil.

As she stood thinking, a shape rose from the darkness and moved up the path toward her. Her mouth was dry. Her heart beat violently. She spoke huskily. "Who goes?"

"The harper" was the guarded reply.

"Ah, Tristan!" she cried aloud in relief.

His voice showed his surprise. "Dame Philippa, what are you doing here?"

Her voice was controlled; it had a hint of laughter. "Such questions I have asked myself for the past hour. Or has it been a half-hour or two hours or only ten minutes that I have been walking?"

"You've walked farther than you think. It's a good hour from the hill-top to the cliff above the sea."

She sat down on a convenient rock and listened to the roar of the waves. "Where are we?" she asked.

He hesitated a moment. "An old path to the cove at the foot of the valley. A disused path."

"Ah, I was right. But how in the name of God did I get on it?"

"If you will tell me where you were going, Dame Philippa, perhaps I can answer your question."

For the first time since she found herself in the narrow passage, Philippa thought of the lad. "I came to search for the shepherd boy Colin." She hesitated a moment, reluctant to reveal Richard's cruelty. "The boy was hurt. He——" She paused. She could not see but she felt the harper's eyes on her.

"I know. The Grenville marked him as his own."

"I cannot think why." She spoke slowly.

"Many a man bears the mark of the Grenvilles, even though there is no brand to show it," he said evasively.

She said nothing. In the quiet the voice of the sea was heavy and menacing.

"It has always been so. The Grenvilles carry some strange power to bind men to them."

She did not reply. The harper was making a statement that required no answer.

"Always men follow them without question. In battle, on the land or on the sea, a Grenville speaks and men will follow to the death or to the ends of the earth, leaving all they value in life behind them—mother, wife, mistress, land or riches."

"Why?" she whispered, knowing he spoke the truth. "Why?"

"Why? I do not know." He waited a moment. "Perhaps it is their fortune, perhaps a doom."

A shiver ran down her back, though the night had the warmth of midsummer. She rose. "Show me the way to the sea," she said abruptly.

"Nay, Dame Philippa. It has danger, that path. By the light of day it is safe enough. Come, I will lead you the way over the hill to the house."

She thought of the lad Colin as she climbed the hill behind the harper. "I am afraid for the boy," she said.

"Do not concern yourself, madam. Long since I put grease on the wound. The lad himself must heal the wound to his heart. He has worshipped Richard Grenville and longed to follow him wherever he goes. Now . . ."

"The idol is shattered?"

"No, I think not. His hatred is toward the girl Thomasine, not to Sir Richard."

"Strange." She said the word slowly, not understanding why that should be. "Strange."

They climbed the long hill, Philippa stopping to rest from time to time. "You walk sturdily, harper," she said in one of the periods of rest.

"I walk much," he replied. "My old body is inured to the rough moors and the high cliffs of Cornwall; to the winds and the rains."

She was silent for a time, then she said, "You are free, harper?"

"Yes, madam, free to walk my own way. Few men can say that, this day."

Philippa thought of men she knew, lashed to their duties, to the service of the Queen, to their ambitions. " 'No man is free in all the world,' " she quoted, not knowing the harper would understand. . . .

> Chained to cities, chained
> To a thousand senseless things.

She wondered then about this man the country folk called Tristan. Was he really a man of their own quality who roamed the country singing his songs as a free man, or was he secretly in the employ of the Queen, to spy upon her subjects, or even upon the Queen's enemies? How easily he could grow to understand the temper of the people!

"I am rested. Let us go."

The harper led on, moving slowly along a narrow path upward until they came to the Wood of Coombe and the old Roman works. From there on they took the broad road to Stowe.

The dogs barked as they stood at the outer gates. A sleepy sentry challenged. The harper stepped forward to the light, spoke a few words. The sentry muttered something, pulled on the chains. The wide gates swung open and they passed into the outer court-yard.

A cock was crowing as the gates closed behind them, a shrill defiant challenge to the dawn.

CHAPTER 5
THOMASINE

The wind rose with the sun. The fresh clean smell of the sea drifted up Coombe Vale and spread over the rolling hill. The hills were yellow with ripened grain, set in rows of stooks along the hillsides.

At Stowe Barton the daily life began with the dawn. The cooks in the kitchens, dairymen and dairymaids, grooms and stablemen ate breakfast, each in his accustomed place according to rank in the household. The cowherds and shepherds were on their way to grazing ground before the sun touched the Norman tower of Kilkhampton Church. But Colin was not walking over the hills. He lay on a cot covered with straw in his stone hut behind the French tennis-courts, beyond the stables. His face was flushed, his blue eyes were shining with fever. Beside him sat the harper Sir Tristan, cross-legged, attempting to put a poultice on the swollen hand.

"Quiet, lad, quiet! Don't toss about so. Rest your hand now so I can tie this flax-seed on the wound. 'Twill ease the pain. Steady now, lad, steady!"

The boy muttered something unintelligible.

Marjory, the aged nurse of the Grenvilles, stood by, her face grave. "I do not like the look of it, mon. See the angry sunburst of red about the burn. I do not like the look of it, nor the glassy stare of fever in his eyes."

"Nor I, good woman." With a dextrous movement Sir Tristan secured the bandage in place.

"I'll go make strong tea to pour over it. Tea's very fine to ease a burn. Stop here, Sir Harper, till I come."

"That I will, for he's a good lad and I'd not like to see that strong arm made useless." Sir Tristan spread a canvas on the cot and gently rolled Colin over while he covered the straw.

In a short time the old woman came back, carrying a jug of strong tea. She put a finger in it and shook her head. "Too hot. We must rest a moment." She stood looking down at the long body, a troubled expression in her faded eyes.

"These Grenvilles," she murmured. "They're hard men. Hard. I've known them now for near to sixty year and they're all hard."

The harper got to his feet and pulled a three-cornered milking stool for Marjory. She seated herself near the cot.

"I don't understand this. I never knew Sir Richard to be unjust."

"The woman made him." She made a symbol of magic with her thumb and finger. " 'Twas the witch girl," she whispered, looking quickly about, "that witch girl from Tintagel. It is said she goes to the caves and holds conversation with the sorcerer Merlin."

"Nonsense, woman! There is no sorcerer living in the caves. 'Tis a myth—one that belongs to old days and ignorant people."

The woman's face set in hard stubborn lines. "It is no myth, Sir Harper. Many a man has gone to Merlin's cave to his undoing. No later than Whitsuntide a ship was drawn to the rocks and wrecked at the very foot of King Arthur's castle. Who but Merlin drew it there? A fair ship it was, sturdy, built at Bideford." She again made a circle against the evil eye. "Four Bideford boys sailed in her and they never came back, and their mothers stand on the quay and watch and wait, but never the lads return."

The harper saw it was useless to argue with the beldame; so strong was her belief in the sorcerer Merlin that no words of his could shake her. The lad was tossing about. Marjory laid her gnarled hand on his restless arm, quieting him with a word. After a time she turned to the harper, who had taken a seat on a bench at the head of the cot.

"You mind the trouble of Temperance Lloyd, who could cause prickly pains, as if hot awls were stuck into a body, when she was angered? Yes, and she could make herself into a grey cat or a magpie, and 'tis said she hunted with the Old Boy himself." She crossed herself, then looked slyly at the harper. " 'Tis not a papist sign," she muttered. " 'Tis for saving myself from the witches that I make a cross. They can't abide crosses. You know that." She drew the little triangular woollen shawl, which she wore pinned about her shoulders, across her thin lips. "You believe in crosses, don't you, Sir Harper?"

The harper nodded. He himself had in his travels knelt

61

beside many of the old stone crosses along the roadside and said his simple prayer.

"Yes, I believe in the Cross of Christ Jesus, our blessed Lord."

"Sir, you are a holy man. Say prayers now for this good lad, who rests under the evil spell of a witch girl."

The harper thought of the great unreadable eyes under a wild tangle of dark hair. "Why do you think the girl has powers?" he asked abruptly.

"Why should my master, my good master, burn the lad's hand, 'lessen she put a spell on him?" She leaned forward, watching intently. "See how long his body is, how strong his legs are, how broad his shoulders."

"A man to fight."

The woman did not hear the harper's words. "He is Grenville-tall." She had spoken aloud, words she intended to remain unsaid. It was then that she saw the shadow at the door. She rose awkwardly and made as much of a curtsy as her stiff old knees would allow.

"May the Lord bless you, Master Richard!" she said.

The harper turned. The great form of Richard Grenville, dressed for hunting, blocked out the morning sun and set the room in shadow. He nodded to the harper, laid his hand on Nurse Marjory's shoulder.

"They told me in the buttery that I would find you here, Marjory. Is the wound bad?"

"Sir, bad enough."

"What have you done for it?"

"Flax-seed, master; then cold tea."

"Nostrums, old woman's nostrums," Grenville said, but not unkindly. "Stay with him, good Nurse, and tend him well." He gazed at the shepherd, a puzzled line formed between his brows. "God's mercy! Why is this lad tending sheep when he might be carrying armour? I thought of that before, and must have forgotten it."

"Seen him often enough with your eyes, master, but not with your head."

Grenville moved his shoulders impatiently. "That's the trouble. Someone should remind me when these growing lads are ready to carry armour."

"Always armour and fighting, master. It was that way when you were *so* high. 'Give me a sword! Give me a sword!' you cried to your grandfather; and a little wooden sword he gave you. You didn't like it; you wanted one with a double-edge cutting blade."

Grenville laughed. "I remember, Nurse. I threw the wooden sword aside because it was small. I wanted one the size of my grandfather's."

"And ships," the old woman went on. "You must have little ships made exact. One day your mother, Dame Thomasine, cried on my bosom, 'He will walk in his father's footsteps on the deck of a ship.' Your father's death was fresh in her mind then—your hero father, who went down in the *Mary Rose* with five hundred brave officers and men."

A shaft of sunlight fell on Grenville's face. The harper saw a strange look come into his steely blue eyes—a fixed look, as though he saw beyond the narrow-walled room.

"Ships. Aye, ships. We Grenvilles have always loved a ship."

Colin moved restlessly. The nurse dipped a cloth into a small vessel of water and laid it on his forehead.

"I will send the tankard boy with some malmsey, with which to wet his gullet when he wakes up. Stay on, Nurse."

"Aye, master."

Grenville stopped for a word with the harper and then walked away. Nurse curtsied, watched him go, a tender smile on her wrinkled face. "Sir, see how gentle my master is when there is no witch girl."

The harper's eyes followed the figure of Grenville as he made his way toward the stables. A groom was walking a bay horse up and down. He led it to the upping block and Grenville mounted. Strong men sometimes did unaccountable things. He thought of the scene by the fireside the night before, which he had witnessed through the screen of the minstrel gallery. Sir Richard had put the stamp of the Grenvilles on the lad, without anger, as though it were a just punishment. He sighed. He had always thought of Grenville as a man who had some degree of gentleness behind the stern façade.

He left the cell and walked through the inner court-yard to the garden, where his little follower waited, guarding his harp and his few belongings. Today he would move on. He had a feeling he would like to bide a time at Tintagel. He always had welcome there with the lonely hermit who lived in the ruined castle on the cliff, high above the Atlantic. Something stirred within him, a restlessness he had not known

known since his youth when the sap in his veins ran thick and warm.

Lady Grenville stood in the great room, directing the hanging of a canvas between two mullioned windows that looked into the first court-yard. It had come that day from London, a portrait of her lord, Sir Richard, dressed in armour, his hand on his sword, his beard trimmed to a point, his heavy blond hair almost auburn and sleeked close to his well-shaped head. It was a good likeness; the blue eyes, clear and searching, followed one about the room. She was happy to have it. It gave life to the bare stone wall where she one day would hang the tapestry she was stitching. Two lackeys in blue livery stood by, while an old Devon man, a joiner, climbed a ladder to set the strong hook in the wall. At the far end of the room house servants were setting the long guest table. One never knew how many would dine any day, and it was a house custom to set places at table for the unexpected guests.

The morning had brought two young squires to join their household, young men who came to learn the ways of hawking, hunting and tricks of arms under the guidance of Sir Richard—Rise Courtenay, whose grandfather was the Earl of Devonshire and who resided near Exeter; and Robert Champernowne, a cousin of the Grenvilles, whose family seat was at Dartington. She saw them now, riding out the great gate with a dozen of the younger men. Sir Richard had left early to fly the new falcon on the moor, where the younger men would join him.

It seemed absurd to her that her husband was already training young men of the West Country. "Sorting the kites from the falcons," he called it. The talk at table and in the gardens of Stowe was always focussed on the manly arts of war—war on the land or on the sea. She sighed. If there could only be talk of other things than war! The lackeys had swung the portrait into place. The joiner had lifted his tools from the stone floor and gone away. The hushed talk of servants carrying the flagons and plates to the table did not intrude on her thoughts.

She sat down on a bench, which she had ordered placed in the center of the hall, and gazed at the painting. She did not like the new style of narrow ruff. But the high lights on his armour gave life to the richness of the metal. Spanish it was,

64

heavily embossed and enamelled. She remembered how pleased he was when it was sent to him from the Continent. She liked the effect of the helmet with the nodding mass of blue plumes, placed on the table beside him. Only twenty-nine when it was painted. How little he changed! The artist had caught the bold searching look in his eyes and the heavy brow that curved in upward sweep, framing his eyes, giving him a sort of Mephistophelean look. She must remember to have her woman look in his chest and air the gold brocade trunks. They looked so elegant with his long white silken hosen. If Mary decided to have her wedding this spring . . . She sighed. Richard was not too happy to have her marry Arthur Tremayne. He would have preferred a Courtenay or a Godolphin or a St. Albans. But Mary dissolved in tears until he withheld his approval. Richard could never withstand a woman's tears.

She heard a light footstep behind her and turned to see the girl Thomasine. Lady Grenville had not yet had the opportunity to question her husband at any length about the girl. That would come later. Now she watched her walking across the room, straight-backed, lithe with feline quietness. Thomasine made a little bow, awkward, almost crude. She must be taught how to curtsy, Lady Grenville thought. "Good morning, child. Did you sleep well?"

"No, madam. I slept not at all. The air is heavy indoors, and Nurse Marjory lets off such moans and belching of the ill-favoured stomach that no one could sleep near her."

Lady Grenville smothered a smile with her hand. "We will have to arrange more suitable quarters for you." She glanced at the poorly made frock of coarse red wool. "And some new clothes." Lady Grenville looked at the girl dreamily, with eyes half-closed. "Green, a soft grey-green, with a touch of tortoise. "Yes. It will be green. I must speak to the sempstress, to see if there is suitable material in the sewing-room."

The girl stiffened. An angry light shone in her eyes, but she spoke quietly. "Please, do not disturb yourself about a frock for me, madam. I sought you out to ask if you would not intercede with Sir Richard. I want to go back to Tintagel. I do not want to stay here longer." Her voice trembled. She moved her body restlessly, shifting her eyes, touching her full lips with her narrow, pointed tongue.

For all the world like a trapped animal, Lady Grenville

thought. Aloud she said, "Come sit beside me, Thomasine. Tell me how you like the painting of Sir Richard."

Thomasine turned quickly and saw the painting for the first time. She drew back startled, her eyes fixed. "He would have obedience," she said slowly. "One would be afraid to anger him too much."

"Is that all you see, child?"

"He looks as a king should look, wearing armour. He has a strong will but he could be cruel."

"Then do not cross his will, my girl. I think you have a will of your own. Or perhaps it is petulance and stubbornness that I see in your face. After a time you will accustom yourself to our ways, and the ways of Stowe are pleasant."

The girl started to speak; thought better of it and sat down on the bench. "I have had no one to tell me the difference between donkeyness and strength, madam. I am sixteen now. I do not even remember my mother. My old Aunt Matilda, you know, was cracked in the head."

"What is your name?" Lady Grenville spoke gently. "Sir Richard only called you Thomasine and said you were a kinswoman."

"I am an Arundell—not one of the great Arundells, a lesser branch than the Arundells of Trerice or Lanherne."

"Thomasine is such a pretty name! Did you know it was the name of Sir Richard's mother?"

"No, madam." She sat looking at the stone floor on which the rushes had been newly laid. "I know nothing but the sea and the little wild animals that live on the moor, and the birds that fly above me as I lie on the cliffs looking at the sky. Oh, madam, must I stay here, to have my middle held in a vise, and a skirt that gets in the way when I run, and a piece of muslin wound tight around my breasts so I cannot breathe?"

Lady Grenville glanced at the red kersey skirt, the leather half-jacket, the bare legs, feet encased in skins roughly sewn to resemble shoes. "You prefer what you are wearing to the costumes my daughters Mary and Catherine wear?"

"No, no, I do not prefer this." She made a contemptuous motion with her hands over her skirt. "I prefer what young John Arundell wears—long silken hosen of brown, with a green doublet and soft leather boots that reach the knees."

"But, my child, you are speaking of men's clothes."

"I know, I know. That is what I wear at Tintagel. Then

66

I am free to climb the cliffs, to look into the nests of birds; to take my bow and arrow and shoot a cony or a muskrat; to sail my little boat and help the men fish, with salt spray all over me, making my lips and cheeks sting with the salt of the sea. Ah, madam, let me go home!"

Lady Grenville patted the girl's hand. She noticed how shapely it was in spite of the roughness. Thomasine at once saw the contrast between Lady Grenville's slim white hand and her own. She drew away and hid her hands in the folds of her skirt.

"You are old enough now to learn the things a woman must know, to conduct a well-ordered household, to take good care of your person, to move easily and gracefully, to curtsy and to dance."

"No, no! Never will I do those things!" Thomasine cried.

Lady Grenville did not heed. "To converse with your elders and your betters; to learn to know people of your own years."

"I know people of my age. Jesse Tremoir, the fisher's son, is sixteen. I do not like him. Nor do I like the young gentlemen you have under your roof, who drink punch until they cannot stand on their own feet and must be lugged to bed by a lackey."

"It is not your place to criticise young gentlemen, Thomasine. Men have a world of their own, where women have no place. I see you have run wild like a hoyden. It is time for you to step into the women's world and learn your manners."

"But I don't want to learn manners. I want only to be free. I want my moors and my sea. I don't want manners. I loathe manners. Last night one of your fine gentlemen pinched my buttocks and tried to lift my skirts. . . . Is that the manners you want me to learn? To strip my body to the lust of men? To lie under the hedge and let men bestride me as a stallion bestrides a mare? Nay, I will not have fine gentlemen, drunken with much wine, try to creep into my bed and fondle my breasts. Why, no unmannerly rough Cornish fisherman dared lay hands on me, though I worked day after day with them hauling in the nets, the water deep against my thighs. They wouldn't dare even to think evil of me, let alone to touch my body amorously; no, nor a man overboard in his cups. He would find a wench of his own kind for horsing." Her voice rose. She stood, feet apart, looking down at Lady Grenville.

"Thomasine . . ." Lady Grenville did not raise her voice, but something in her tone caused the wild girl to pause. The two looked at each other, the one shocked and distressed, the other defiant. "Sit down again. Tell me quietly who caused you to make such charges. What man would defile a girl under the Grenville roof?"

The girl threw back her head and laughed. "The Grenville men have the name. I've heard it as far as Tintagel. 'The Grenville men take women as they take land—at their own choosing.'"

Lady Grenville turned white. She knew only too well the truth of the girl's words. She must curb her tongue. She must put other ideas into her head. But how to do it?

"Thomasine," she said gently, "you have wrong ideas. There are more fine men of good manners than evil men. Some are evil, I grant you, but they are few."

The girl sat down. She lowered her voice, for her sharp glance saw the lackeys were edging toward the end of the room where they sat, trying to hear what she said. "My lady, perhaps some gentlemen are good. I have not seen them. My father left me with John Piers's wife Margot at Tintagel and went away. When I was little we lived in the old castle at the cliff, King Arthur's castle. John Piers has the name of a pirate, and he is one. He watches for wrecks of ships and takes what he finds washed ashore. Perhaps he takes jewelled rings and golden chains from the dead. I do not know. I know only he was kind to me. And Margot they say is a witch. She can fly through the air on a broomstick, or change herself into a fox or a wolf and run the moors at night. I never saw her changed to an animal, but John Piers the pirate and Margot the witch both told me to hide in the furze and the heather if I saw young gentlemen come riding. And that I have done, for I saw two gentlemen take Jennie, a fisher-girl, and tear her clothes from her body and make her dance in the moonlight for their drunken pleasure."

"My poor child!" Lady Grenville murmured.

But the girl rushed on. Words tumbled out of her mouth like a torrent. "They would have had their will of her, those *gentle*men, save that I stopped them."

"Thomasine!"

"Yes. I stopped them with stones. First on one man's

head, then the other. Then I gathered up the poor frightened girl's clothes and ran with her to Merlin's cave and hid her. No one comes to Merlin's cave, my lady, for they are afraid of his magic. But I am not afraid."

Lady Grenville drew back. Even she had fear of the name of Merlin the sorcerer. "It is but a legend," she managed to say.

The girl looked at her keenly. "You are afraid, my lady. You are afraid of Merlin."

Mary Grenville said nothing. The girl terrified her by her frank outspoken talk. Why had Richard brought her to Stowe? Because his cousin Arundell of Trerice shirked his responsibilities? Should she have the care of this wild girl? She could not have her talking in this way to their Mary or the younger girls.

She ignored Thomasine's accusation, went back to the earlier question. "You must tell me the name of the man who spoke insult to you, Thomasine. Sir Richard will see that he is reproved."

A curious change came over the girl. Lady Grenville thought she saw fear—or was it regret?—in her black eyes. Her voice was low when she answered shortly, "He is punished." She turned then and went swiftly away.

Lady Grenville watched her go. Her eyes were troubled and fear lay in her heart. What was she to do with this untamed girl Richard had brought home to her, to gentle and weld into the counterpart of a lady?

It was evening when Lady Grenville spoke to Nurse Marjory about the girl Thomasine. The old woman's wrinkled face took on a look of fear.

"She is evil," she whispered, her fingers making a protecting sign. "She has already caused trouble enough with the shepherd Colin."

"With Colin?" Lady Grenville was surprised. "Not Colin, surely," she said, half to herself. Colin was a privileged child at Stowe; from a wee lad he had been allowed to play with the boys at their games. She had never had fear when they were hunting or hawking, if Colin was with them. He had always taken care of them and brought them safely home. He knew moors and the wood. He knew the tides and could tell by the look of the sea when storms were coming. Not Colin. She was so busy with her thoughts that she only half-heard Marjory's words, until she said, "It was this caused Sir Richard to set a brand on his hand."

"What are you saying, Nurse?"

Then the story came out: the branding, the fevered boy lying in the dark cell where the monks used to live when Stowe was a part of Hartland Abbey.

Lady Grenville rose. "Take me to Colin. I will see what unguents he needs for his hurts. Lead the way, Nurse." She followed Marjory's stooping figure. The *tap-tap* of the old woman's cane sounded hollowly down the long passage. They came out near the sheepfold, crossed a court-yard to the old cells. Marjory's garrulous tongue had not ceased.

"She says he pinched her buttocks. The girl lies. Why should a man pinch flesh hard and thin as a rangy colt? Men want softness. She has bewitched my master."

"Cease talking, Nurse!" The lady spoke with unwonted sharpness. When they reached the door of the cell, she saw Sir Richard standing in the doorway.

"I told you not to leave," he said sternly to Nurse Marjory.

She began to cry. "See, my lady? It is as I said. He speaks angry words to me, who suckled him when his mother's breasts were dry; angry words to me who comforted him, wee child that he was, when his father sank to his death in his watery grave, with all the brave men of the *Mary Rose*."

"Cease, Nurse. Cease." Richard's voice was not harsh but impatient. He turned to his wife. "Madam, this is not the place for you. Betake yourself to your women."

She did not answer. Instead she walked into the dark room. It faced east, away from the setting sun. A lanthorn placed on the ledge of the window gave feeble light. She moved across the mildewed straw that lay on the floor to the side of the cot. The boy's bright eyes met hers. They had no recognition in them. She bent over, lifted the bandaged hand. The arm above the bandage was swollen and fiery red.

"Remove the cloth, Nurse. Richard, call someone to bring a basin of water with a hot stone in it, and lint and towels; soft napery will do. We must get the swelling reduced."

"The wound is a burn," Richard said. "Will it be wise to put water on a burn?"

"No. The hot bandages are for the arm. I shall send for

unguents for the burned spot. Have my medicine case brought quickly now. There is no time to lose."

Nurse Marjory said, "Madam, it is the zern of dawn." Lady Grenville moved stiffly. The stool was hard. She opened her eyes. The first rays of light in the east cast a beam into the cell. The pale-yellow light fell on the lad's face. He was sleeping, breathing quietly. She leaned forward. The swelling had gone down. The unsightly red had faded.

"Thank the good Lord for His kindness!" she murmured.

"Amen," said Marjory softly. Lady Grenville glanced into the shadows where her husband was sleeping on a bench made of two planks. He stirred and with one lithe movement stood at her side. Mary looked up at him, smiling.

"All is well then. I see it by your face," he said softly.

"He sleeps naturally again. When you go in, send a man to sit with him. I will have gruel made. He will need nourishment when he wakes."

Richard bent down and kissed her cheek. "You are a good woman, Mary. I thank God, every time I am on my knees in church, that He has given you to me."

Tears came to her eyes, brushed quickly aside. "You are a good man. What other master would have slept on a board the whole long night beside a sick servant?"

"Nonsense! I've slept on the ground many a night in my campaigns. Come. Nurse Marjory will stay until we send her relief."

They stepped outside the door. The rim of the sun was touching the horizon, casting its light on the hills. All was dark in the court-yard. A figure crouched against the wall, moved, detached itself from the darker shadows.

"Let me sit beside him," the girl Thomasine whispered.

"Get to your bed!" Sir Richard said harshly. "You've caused enough of trouble."

"I did not lay a hot iron in his hand." Words came out of the darkness—accusing words that hung in the air.

Sir Richard took a step forward. The cobbles echoed to his firm footstep. The court-yard was empty. The girl had dissolved into the darkness.

Mary Grenville made no comment. In her heart she knew Richard had added another grudge to the girl's warped mind. She must find some way to reach her, to get past the hard, scornful shell. She sighed.

"You are tired," Richard said softly, "tired from good works." He put his arm around her trim waist. "You must sleep, my sweet. I'll ask Philippa to undertake the preparations for our guests."

"Guests? Oh, I had forgotten. Is it tomorrow or today that Walter Raleigh comes?"

"Tomorrow, and a score with him. Did I neglect to tell you, my sweet? Let Walter and Philip Sidney have the Red Room, the one where the Queen rested. Philippa will see that there is fair linen, and the new blankets woven from last year's wool."

"You did not tell me there were to be many. Do you think I will allow Philippa to see to my guests?" She quickened her pace. As she entered the long passage she rang the housekeeper's bell. "I must consult with Mrs. Brooks. Richard, you go to bed. You need the sleep. I don't."

He yawned, covering his mouth with the back of his hand. "Ching has the lists of our guests. I'm afraid you will think all Devon is descending on us. Can you manage?"

She looked up at her tall husband, smiling. "Have you forgotten the time two hundred men were lodged at Stowe for a fortnight? Has ever a man or woman gone hungry from Stowe?"

He let his hand follow her shoulder to her breasts. "My little housekeeper, I vow you bear the name with more reason than my ancestor Sir Roger."

Lady Mary laughed aloud. "You will spoil me with praise, sir. Begone to your bed before the household arises."

He lingered a moment, a curiously uneasy smile behind his close-trimmed beard. "You have no harsh words for me, Mary?"

"Harsh words?"

"Because of the boy? I will make amends. I will make him my armour-bearer on my next journey." He went away then. She stood looking after him until the tapestry curtain dropped behind him as he passed through the door.

"The next journey." She remembered then that he had not told her why Walter Raleigh was coming to Stowe. Walter never came now, as in the old days, to visit, to hunt, to hawk. He came to Devon only to intrigue, to get money for some scheme. A chill wind seemed to blow upon her. She moved slowly along the passageway, stirred by some unknown fear.

72

CHAPTER 6
"AND SHALL I DIE, AND THIS UNCONQUERED?"

Berries were ripening among the stones that walled the Cornish lanes. Thistle and wild tansy and yellow furze covered the moors. The furze grew rank, interlaced with bracken which had already turned to gold. Birds whirled above the stubble where the stooks of yellow grain stood in ranks, making a neat pattern in the hillside fields. Fat cattle grazed in the lush green meadow. Sheep were closed, ready for market at Stratton or Bude. The seasons do not change, nor does the yeoman who tills the soil.

Sir Richard Grenville stood in the tower above the gateway of Stowe and surveyed the landscape with his glass. "The land is eternal," he murmured when his wife remained silent. "It is eternal, and therein lies the strength and glory of England. Not in kings or princes, not in men who sit on benches and make the laws, but here in this good land that lies before our eyes. Here, the land, the men who till the land—these are our bulwarks against time, against our enemies within and our enemies without. My dear love, you are not listening. Why do you stand looking down the valley with fear written on your dear face?"

"And fear is in my heart, my sweet husband. I look at the sea and I am afraid."

Sir Richard's laugh rang out. Men working in the garden looked up, smiling as they mopped the sweat from their brows. It was good to have their master at home, even though they must work the harder. He brought them whips of apple and fig, or a new peach to plant; a new berry or a squash that they had not seen before. "Save the seeds," he would say. "We must keep abreast of the times in our garden and in our orchards."

It was the same in the stables—new stallions fine and strong, to put in the meadows with the brood mares. The best, always the best; even the wines that came in tuns from Portugal or the Azores. Stowe cider was termed better than their neighbors'; more care was taken to keep the presses

73

clean. No good trying to throw wormy apples into the press. He'd have a man disciplined for that. A harsh master, his tenants held him, but just and strong. They must keep the land sweet and well manured or set with marl, so that crops would improve. "Give something to the land for what you take away" was an adage often on his lips.

"Why should you fear the sea, my sweet wife? The sea is kind to the Cornish. Think of the pilchards; think of the herring and lobsters and sweet crabs."

"Aye, and think of the wrecks that lie along the shore from the mouth of the Tamar and the Torridge to Land's End."

"Well, think of them. Have we not pulled up many a stout timber from wrecks to strengthen our buildings at Stowe? Like the timber from the Spanish galleons, all carved and gilded, which holds the roof of our summer-house, and the king-beam of our farm-house."

"I do not like the sea," she repeated. "It puts fear in me."

"None in me, although my father lost his life in the sea. Come now, let us have a cheery face." He raised his spying glass toward Kilkhampton village. The church tower was black against the intense blue of the August sky. "Dust clouds rising? I think I see a banner fly. Yes, look, my dear one. In a moment you will see horsemen riding between the hedges. Presently they will be knocking at the gate below us. Let us go down. I will welcome my visitors with true Grenville hospitality at the gateway of my castle."

Lady Grenville followed her lord as he walked along the top of the high Norman wall to the stone stairs by the guardhouse. She left her husband there with his old steward Ching, who had served him well through the years, and made her way to the great hall. One look about to see that everything was in place. Not that men would notice. Plenty for his stomach, plenty to drink, a bed to sleep on, were all a man wanted.

She found Colin putting wine cups on a serving table. A bowl of late cherries to dip into the wine was placed beside the cups. She nodded approval. Colin made no sign of his hurt though there were lines of pain on his face, and the shadows under his eyes made them blue as the sea.

"Is there no one else to do this work?" she asked.

"The master said I was to be tankard-bearer tonight, and so I will be tankard-bearer."

She listened for resentment in his voice. There was none. "The guests will be tired tonight. Those who rode in today from Exeter have ridden from London two days before. They will want sleep."

"What of those who come from Newlyn and Padstow and Tavistock? They will not be weary. 'Tis Londoners who are soft, Your Ladyship. London does something, even to Cornishmen, if they stay too long."

Lady Grenville smiled. "I hope Sir Richard will never stay too long in London then."

"No, madam, not he. Even London cannot sap the great strength of him."

She looked up quickly, wondering. The lad set the silver tankards on a tray at the high table. He came back and stood before her, looking at her shyly. "Nurse Marjory told me my master stayed beside me the whole of the black night when my mind was out wandering on the moors. Did she say truth?"

"Yes, Colin. Yes."

He twisted a corner of the leather apron he wore as tankard boy. "Madam, do you think he would take it ill if I said a prayer for him and a thanksgiving that the kind God has given me such a good master?" He looked at her anxiously, afraid perhaps that he had overstepped.

"Do say a prayer for your master, Colin. I am sure the Lord will listen to you."

He touched his forehead with his fingers and made a stiff bow. "Thank you, madam."

"He bears no ill will to Richard."

Mary Grenville turned at Philippa's words. She had come in quietly. Now she stood beside the table. She wore a white coif and a petticoat of broidered Madras that floated out from a taffeta bodice of yellow. Very lovely she looked. Mary felt dull and drab beside her in her sober grey and white.

"No rancor," she said. "I am astonished. Yet I know Richard will always have the admiration and devotion of men . . . and charm women."

She spoke flippantly enough, but Mary knew Philippa meant what she said. She changed the subject abruptly.

"I am concerned about the girl Thomasine. She is so wild. It is difficult to understand her." She glanced up as she spoke. Colin was crossing the room. At mention of the girl's name

75

a look of anger came over his face. His body stiffened and the hand that held the punch-bowl trembled.

"There is one who hates the Cornish beauty," Philippa remarked as he walked out of hearing. She lifted a cherry from the silver bowl, dipped it into wine, holding the long stem daintily. "And with cause," she added. "I think that little wild one has made an enemy."

Mary shook her head slowly. "No, no. I think Colin could not hate anyone."

Philippa's sharp white teeth bit into the cherry. "I have in my mind that it was not Colin who pinched her buttocks, as she so elegantly put it. I have an idea it was someone else—a young gentleman who was in his cups and whom Colin carried to his room that night."

Mary stared at Philippa. Was that the reason why Richard had stayed the whole night with the herd-boy? Did he realize he had punished the wrong offender? One never knew with Richard. It was not his habit to admit himself in the wrong, no more than it was his habit to admit defeat. One never knew.

She bunched her housekeeping keys in her hand and thrust them into the woven bag at her long pointed bodice. "I must go to the nursery. The children must have their rest."

She found them playing a game of hide-and-seek in the hallway and sent them to the nursery. They protested against taking midday rest. They wanted to play under the great oaks. It put her in mind of her childhood at Annerly, when she begged one last circle of the great Hankford Oak. She little realized how deep wedged into her life that oak was to be.

It was under the great oak that she first saw Sir Richard Grenville, when he rode over from Bideford to call on her father. It was under the Hankford Oak he told her that her father had given his consent to their betrothal. She sighed. The children crowded about her, their childish protest rising; could they not go down to see the guests come riding along the lane? The servants had told them there was to be a great banquet—huge joints and legs of mutton; a hundred fowl had been killed; pheasants too, with lobsters sent up from Bideford Bay. Could they not look on from the minstrels' gallery?

Lady Grenville laughed. "No, no. Not a hundred fowl, my children, nor yet twenty." Tomorrow they could have jugged hare for dinner, if they were good, and perhaps a pheasant or a game-fowl. No, they were too young to go to the minstrels' gallery.

They capered about the room, while the young nurse and Nurse Marjory looked on.

"Did you take your rest, madam?" Marjory inquired.

Lady Grenville shook her head. "I forgot, really," she said apologetically. "There was so much to be done, there was not time to rest."

Nurse Marjory eyed her severely. "You will look washed-out at supper and weary, while Dame Philippa will be beautiful and sparkling and gratify the eyes of all the gentlemen guests." Mary smiled, and Nurse grumbled, "*She* slept all afternoon. Now she has had her woman sponge her with cool water from the spring, while you get hot stepping into the kitchen to see if the meat is properly turning on the spit. Why not leave cookery to the cook, madam?"

"I will rest now. Good-night, children." The children knew it was no use to tease. They came forward obediently for a kiss and went back to their luncheon.

Lady Grenville really meant to rest, but on the way to her room she stopped at her daughter Mary's door. She heard a muffled "Come in" and walked into the room. Young Mary was stretched full length on the bed, her face buried in the bolster. She sat up when she saw her mother, then burst into fresh tears.

Lady Grenville asked with concern, "What ails you, my child?" Mary buried her face deeper into the pillow, her shoulders shaking with the tempest of sobs. "What is wrong, my dearest child?" She pushed aside the rose-printed curtains and sat down on the bed.

After a time young Mary sat up. Her eyes were red, tears were running down her cheeks. "It's that girl! That terrible girl!"

"What girl?" Lady Grenville was truly puzzled.

"Thomasine. She has taken my puce taffeta gown. Look."

Lady Grenville looked in the direction little Mary pointed. A heap of clothes lay on the floor near the window. The black bodice, the red skirt Thomasine had discarded lay on the floor.

"If it had been any other gown I wouldn't have cared, Mother, but my puce! Arthur liked it so much."

Her mother withheld a smile. "It is really my fault, daughter. I told Thomasine I would find a proper costume for her out of your wardrobe."

"But she shouldn't have come and taken my puce without 'by your leave' or any polite words. And she stripped right in front of me—down to skin! She didn't even have on her modesty garment."

Lady Grenville thought a moment. It was difficult to appease Mary and keep from showing her annoyance at Thomasine. "Listen my child. Let me explain about Thomasine. Then you will understand why she does strange things." She repeated what her husband had told her: how his cousin Arundell of Lanherne had asked him to bring the girl to her for training. "She is wayward, with no manners, but she has good blood in her veins. She is an orphan, without training of cultivated folk; brought up by caretakers and a silly old aunt who died within the month. She has run wild like a moor pony, but she is courageous, without fear. There is the making of a fine woman in her, if we all help her and have patience."

Little Mary's tears ceased to flow. "An orphan?"

"She never knew her mother. Her father she barely remembers. He went away to Europe, to Maximilian's wars, and never returned."

Mary's sensitive face showed concern.

"Come, miss. A young female about to be married has no time for tears. As for the puce taffeta, I always thought the colour a little old for you. Tomorrow I will go to the sewing room and I will show you the new material your father brought home—bolts of cloth which my friend the Countess of Pembroke selected. You know there isn't a lady in England who has more beautiful clothes than Mary Sidney."

"Not even the Queen?"

"Perhaps, but she admires Mary's taste in clothes. Mary Sidney had a dress embroidered for the Queen as a present to give her at Christmas. A lovely thing: ivory brocade with pansies in colour, embroidered with seed-pearls. The Queen was delighted and wears it at her levees."

"Oh, Mother, am I to have a gown with a long pointed bodice, cut square, low to show my breasts, like the Queen?" Mary sat up straight, pushing up her little round firm breasts until they were like to burst out of her neckerchief.

Her mother smiled and patted her shoulder. "We will see, we will see. There is one piece of taffeta strewn with rosebuds which will become you. Your father has told me he wishes you to have suitable clothes, so that when Arthur takes you to London, you will not look like a country cousin."

"Oh, Mother, how wonderful!" Little Mary jumped from the bed as her mother walked toward the door. "Will you thank my father for me? And, Mother, about the puce taffeta—I think the taffeta with rosebuds would be nicer, much, much nicer." She tossed one long braid of dark hair over her shoulder and pressed her slender waist even smaller with her clasped hands, while she stood trying to look into the mirror. "I think I can wear a long bodice to advantage, Mother," she cried.

A tender smile came over Mary Grenville's lips. "Yes, my child, yes."

Little Mary threw her arms about her mother and kissed her cheek. "Don't scold poor Thomasine, Mother. Let her be happy in the puce taffeta."

Mary Grenville walked down the hall to her room. She was thinking that perhaps Thomasine had no capacity for happiness, poor restless tormented girl! She quickened her step; she must hurry below to the great hall to greet her husband's guests and make them welcome to Stowe. But she had a moment to think of little Mary—so quick to respond, so tender toward the unfortunate. What would life hold for her little daughter?

The housekeeper, Mrs. Brooks, was waiting outside Lady Grenville's chamber. "A number of the gentlemen have arrived. Sir Walter Raleigh and Sir Philip Sidney from London." She handed a paper to Lady Grenville. "Sir Richard sent this list, Your Ladyship. He says he can't remember how many more are to come."

Mary smiled. Was it not like her husband to invite the two counties and never question how they were to be fed or bedded? "How many have arrived altogether, Brooks?"

"Thirty or thereabouts, madam. Ching has placed Sir Walter and Sir Philip in the Red Chamber; Captain Amadas and Master Stafford in the Oak Room. They asked to save the extra bed space for Sir John Arundell, who will come by evening. The others are in the Long Room, with the screens all set so no one looks on the other. Each man has his privacy, just as we used to have it in the old days at Annerly, madam."

"You have done well, Brooks. That leaves the chambers in the West Wing free for late-comers."

"And rooms in the vacant cottages beyond the garden. Farmer Alsop says there are four chambers at the farm cottage, if necessary. A matter of housing ten men or more."

Lady Grenville checked the list carefully. "We can easily care for a hundred guests. Canvas tents can be erected if more should come. You have done very well indeed, Brooks."

"Thank you, madam. We want to make everyone comfortable."

Lady Grenville slipped a key from a bunch she carried in her side pocket. "Here is the key to the emergency linen room. It is fortunate that the new blankets were finished in early summer, since the nights are cool. Has Ching decided about the wines? You know how particular Sir Richard is about the wines he serves. Has the new shipment come?"

Brooks lifted her broad petticoat and abstracted her narrow housekeeping book. "I had this from your chamberlain Mr. Ching. The wine was brought in by postilion last week, well distributed so the horses were not overloaded: three tuns of white and two of claret, one tun of sack. There came also a hogshead of vinegar."

Lady Grenville was satisfied. "Please see if Sir Richard has given orders to his wine steward. If not, let Ching attend to it."

"Will you dine with the gentlemen tonight, madam?"

"Yes. Sir Richard has requested the ladies to dine with him. Dame Philippa will be at the high table."

"Miss Mary and the new young lady—will they dine at the table also?"

"They will be seated at the end. Miss Catherine has a sniffle from the weed blossoms and will not come down."

"Too bad, madam. Handsome young gentlemen are riding up every hour. Perhaps if I fill a pomander with ammonia salts she could manage. A pity to be deprived of seeing so many of the young Cornish and Devon squires." She had a knowing look, a match-making look.

"Stop by her chamber, Brooks, when you have settled about the wines. Perhaps you can persuade her. Let her hide her red nose behind a fan." The two smiled and nodded, fellow conspirators that they were. Only one of the Grenville daughters had married thus far—Bridget, to Christopher Harris, of Radford. Lady Grenville sighed. A pity that Richard had taken such a dislike to Christopher. Richard was angered because Christopher had persuaded him to sell Buckland Abbey to him, and then straightaway resold it to Sir Francis Drake. One other thing to add to his dislike of Drake. It irked him to think of the Drakes living in the abbey which had so long been the seat of the Grenvilles in South Devon. She was pleased enough, even though most of the money went into building new ships at the Chapman yards at Bideford. She had never liked living at Buckland Abbey. It was too conspicuously grand, and it still carried the monkish odour of old days. She liked Stowe best of all Sir Richard's manors. It was home to her.

Dinner was over next day. The ladies retired to walk in the garden or sit on the terrace, leaving the men to their toasts. The sun was hot but a little breeze stirred. The cattle that grazed on the hills along the edge of the wood were eating their way down toward the barns and the cow-sheds; fat and sleek, they made a handsome picture against the lush green of the meadow within the walled and hedged fields.

Lady Grenville soon left the group to consult with Brooks about the lodging of new arrivals. Dame Philippa took her ease in the arbour, while Catherine, sniffing her pomander, watched Mary and two young girls from Stratton vie for leadership in archery. The twang of the bow, as an arrow sped toward the target, cut the still air, and through the open windows of the hall men's voices rose and fell, some cultured, drawling, others more harsh with the strong un-diluted accent of the Cornish-bred.

Dame Philippa listened idly, her lithe slim body, elegantly attired, relaxed against the marble bench. She listened to the voices but her eyes followed the girl Thomasine as she strolled across the greensward, where she stopped under a tree to watch the archers.

Mary's puce gown had had a sobering effect on Thomasine. Throughout the meal she had sat quietly, not speaking, although Philippa noticed that the eyes of many a young man were turned her way. She is honey, thought Philippa. She will snare men; they will follow her, importune her—but not for marriage, my girl, not for marriage! A little wave of pity came over her.

She called to her, "Thomasine, Thomasine, I challenge you. Let us see who can hit the red heart of the target."

Thomasine came swiftly across the grass, her dark face

alight. Did I ever imagine she was awkward? Philippa asked herself.

Philippa was an archer of no mean skill. She fancied herself in the pose, her arm raised holding the bow, her slenderness outlined against the ivy-covered wall. Archery and playing the harp gave the two most delicious of attitudes to set men's hearts beating more swiftly. She practised both poses for their effect. In her heart she preferred galloping across the wild moors on a good mare, a hooded hawk on her wrist.

The girls moved aside. They were outclassed by Philippa. "Give me a heavy bow," she called to a lackey who was placing lanthorns on little iron tables on the terrace. The servant hurried away. "Perhaps you would like this bow, Thomasine," she said kindly. "I find it much too light."

"I will use whatever bow you use, madam. It would not be fair otherwise." The girl's voice was cool, low-pitched, but it had a velvet smoothness.

Philippa took the heavy bow from the servant, tested the pull, selected an arrow and took position.

"Well placed!" the girls called. "Within the circle!" A thin smile passed over Thomasine's lips. She glanced at Dame Philippa, who stood waiting, pleased with her shot. She hesitated a second, then placed the arrow, not in the heart of the target, but a little to the right, a shade farther from the center than Dame Philippa's. The girls clapped half-heartedly, Mary with her eyes on her puce taffeta gown, the others reserved, withdrawn, waiting.

"Ah, you could have beaten my shot!" Philippa said with a laugh. "You can't fool me, Thomasine. You placed your arrow too exactly."

Thomasine flushed. She was annoyed at being caught in an act of kindness. "The bow is heavy for me," she lied glibly. She would not tell them she could hit a cony running or an owl or a scavenger bird on the wind. These females, so elegant, so satisfied, so universal in their perfection—she would show them one day. She glanced at Mary, the silly girl exuding sweetness and condescension. She had better look to her betrothed, who was already casting sheep's eyes at Thomasine. Let Mary look to herself!

Some of the men straggled out of the hall. Two lackeys assisted a young squire of the county, whose head was not hard enough to drink with Grenville.

Walter Raleigh, seeing Dame Philippa on the terrace, strolled toward her. Thomasine could not take her eyes from him and his elegant dress, the clustered pearls that ornamented his satin doublet, his trunks stiff embroidered of gold and silver, his silken hosen, his elegant soft shoes. His hands, soft and white as a woman's, played with a brilliant locket hanging from his neck on a golden chain. The Queen had given him the locket, and it held her miniature on ivory. 'Twas said the likeness was identical with the lovely portrait, the one painted without shadows on her pale ivory face. Thomasine wanted to see that miniature. As Raleigh turned, she saw that he wore a great pendant pearl dangling from one ear. She giggled—and clapped her hand across her mouth.

"What amuses you, my lass?" Raleigh had seen her. "Tell me. Do not run away. I like young laughter." He caught her arm.

Thomasine stood trembling, her dark eyes looking out from the darker curls that fell over her forehead. "Sir, no, I cannot tell you."

"Indeed, yes. Speak out. You think me amusing. Now tell me why?"

"Oh, sir, no." She glanced at Dame Philippa, a pleading, almost frightened look. Philippa surveyed her coolly. Let her extract herself from difficulties of her own making was her thought.

"Come! A forfeit if you tell me."

Thomasine smiled suddenly. "A forfeit? May I truly demand a forfeit?"

"On my oath, fair damsel," Raleigh said with an exaggerated bow. "You were laughing at me. I must know why. My vanity demands it."

"Sir, I was not laughing at you. It was the ear-ring. I did not know that gentlemen wore ear-rings—only sea pirates."

There was silence for a moment, broken by laughter. Sidney had advanced behind them and overheard Thomasine's words. "I swear, Walt, the maid has paid you off in your own coin! What a story to tell the Queen!"

Raleigh joined the laughter. "Well spoken, maiden. Indeed, some of my friends have called me pirate more than once. But the forfeit. I promised you a boon. Ask it."

Thomasine advanced a step. Philippa started to reprimand

83

the girl for her audacity, but Philip Sidney raised his hand to silence her.

Raleigh waited, a little bored at the turn his momentary impulse had taken.

Thomasine said, "Sir, I would that I might glance within the locket you wear."

A change came over Raleigh's face, his body stiffened. Refusal was on his lips, but Sidney insisted: "Your promise, Walt. A boon for the maiden. Allow her to glimpse the royal countenance of her Sovereign Queen."

Raleigh snapped the locket and placed it in the girl's hand. Thomasine gazed for a moment, and as she returned it to him she lifted her skirts and made a low bow, not to Raleigh but the likeness of the Queen.

"By Apollo, a pretty gesture!" said Raleigh and turned to Dame Philippa. "Who is this charming maid?" he asked as they strolled toward the terrace. The girls who had watched the little play followed, leaving Thomasine confused, poised for flight.

Philip Sidney detained her. "You are a witch," he said, his eyes full of laughter. "You demand what is secret and most treasured."

"Oh, sir, was I so rude?" Her voice trembled. She had lost her eager assurance. She became at once a frightened child. "I did not mean to be rude."

Sidney lifted her chin with his long, elegant fingers. "Continue being rude and audacious, my little one. It will take you far along this weary world in which we live."

She broke away, catching up her flowing skirts, and ran swiftly along the brick path that followed the wall of the upper terrace. Dodging along the verge of a high yew maze, she ran full against Arthur Tremayne.

He closed his arms about her, half staggered at the impact of her body. "Why so hasty, fair one?"

Thomasine struggled to release herself from his arms. He held her close and after a struggle imprinted a kiss on her full red mouth.

She struck at his face, her nails leaving a trail of red across it.

"God's death! You vixen, you've scratched me!"

"I should kill you." Her face was distorted with rage. She flashed past him beyond the rose trellis into the path that led to the beechwood. He watched her whirling flight, his face like a thundercloud. Then he took out a fair linen kerchief from the pouch that hung on his sword-belt, and mopped the blood from his cheek.

"God's death!" he repeated. "Now I shall have to retire from the evening's entertainment or I shall be the butt of all their laughter."

In the great hall the tables had been cleared, the remains of the banquet set aside. The guests wandered to the gardens and terraces or walked in the orchards. Some flung themselves on the greensward and slept, as men do who have eaten to capacity. Others went to their chambers and divested themselves of their outer garments, arranging themselves to sleep until late afternoon, when they would assemble again for games—bowls, archery, wrestling, each young man eager to show his skill with arms, in feats of strength.

Sir Richard consulted his wife. "Tomorrow is the full of the moon. Do you think our guests would enjoy taking part in the harvest festival? Or shall I have the harper sing ballads, and later a dance in the hall?"

Lady Grenville thought for a moment. "The harvest festival by all means. The Londoners will be entertained. But I thought you had business to discuss."

"Tomorrow will be soon enough. I am expecting other gentlemen—Richard Hakluyt, Thomas Hariot and Ralph Lane, all from London; and perhaps William Cavendish; and from Exeter someone will come to represent the Earl of Devonshire."

She raised her evenly plucked brows. "You did not mention them before. Who is Mr. Lane?"

"An equerry of the Queen, a friend of Walt's. Perhaps you can bed him with Walt if you are short of bedchambers."

"I wasn't thinking of that. There are still some unoccupied rooms, Richard. I must have more food for supper."

Grenville threw his arms about her tapering waist. "Always thinking of a man's stomach."

Mary left him, still laughing, and went off to the buttery to talk with housekeeper and cook. She found them seated at the long oaken table in the buttery, each with a mug of ale and a plate of spicecakes. They stood up quickly when Lady Grenville came into the room, a large grey cat falling off cook's lap as he rose and made his bow to his mistress. He was a man past middle life with a face as lined as a map, a cross scar on one cheek-bone. He was as black-haired and

85

black-eyed as a Spaniard, and he boasted that he had gone round the world with Drake. "Though bain't see much as the galley was down below. I'd ha' died I would, the time we shot the Horn, weren't for Master Gorrell of Bideford who sewed up my wound with a sailcloth needle."

Lady Grenville told him now that other guests would arrive before nightfall, and asked what he would serve for supper.

"Pasties—pasties, ma'am, and some greens of dandelions mixed with young beet tops."

"Have you enough pasties, Cook?"

"Aye, enough. I always keep a roll of short-crust pastry by me; then 'tis nothing to cut up the raw beef and raw Irish potatoes, throw in some chopped onions and a sprinkling of fine herbs. Then I rolls out my crust thin, cuts it in triangles, fills it with the mixture, folds over and nips together, bakes for an hour. There you have the best pasties in Cornwall."

"That they are!" said Brooks, who had been silent until now.

"Sit down and finish your ale," Lady Grenville said kindly. "Don't forget to have two more rooms opened, Brooks." She walked out of the stone-floored buttery through the kitchen. Most ladies of the gentry never went near the kitchen, but she went often. It pleased the chef and the steward and kept the lesser servants on tiptoe to have the pots and kettles bright and shining. She paused in front of the great fire-place. She noticed the shallow tins of rich cream in the brick oven. She called out, "Cook, your cream is in rings."

Two young girls rushed out from behind the brick oven. With the corners of their aprons they lifted the cream pans off the fire and set them on the long table. They had just placed them in front of the window to cool when the cook came running in, his face red, his eyes darting sparks.

Lady Grenville left hastily, before he turned his terrible tongue upon the young girls. They stood close together, trembling with fear. Cook had the privilege of whipping if he liked, and not to watch his cream until it was properly clotted was a crime of first magnitude.

In the great hall she came upon Colin. He was standing over two lackeys. One was polishing the silver tankards for the high table, while the other worked on the pewter for the lesser table. Vinegar and salt for the pewter, fine silica for the silver. Bowls of hot water were on benches, ready for the final bath.

"Are you having ague again?" she asked, seeing how fatigued he looked. Nurse Marjory had told her that his fever rose every afternoon.

"Ma'am, thank you, Your Ladyship, not since Nurse Marjory went at midnight to the cross-road and buried a new-laid egg. The fever left me that very night and has not returned."

"I am glad, Colin."

"Thank you, madam, thank you." He was standing in front of her respectfully, with head bent. A slight noise behind her caused him to raise his head. Lady Grenville was again startled to see the dark look that crossed his face, and the hatred in his blue eyes.

She turned and saw Thomasine running across the terrace and into the house. She was clutching the voluminous taffeta skirts as though they hampered her free movement, and her face was stormy.

"You must not hold a grudge," she said to the boy.

"Ma'am?"

"You must learn to forgive, Colin. The one who is right can afford to be generous."

Colin's face had no expression. His blue eyes were without depth, were reflecting mirrors. She sighed. There were so many things that wanted righting here at Stowe! Sometimes she felt as though she were drained of all feeling, flattened between the heavy conflicting passions of the stormy people about her. It weakened her and left her tired and weary. She walked slowly across the stone floor, her soft leather shoes making a swishing sound against the rushes. A little rest, perhaps, before supper, a little rest.

Anxiety lay heavy in her heart; fears beset her, fears for some unknown torment that lay ahead of her. Richard had said nothing more of Walter's plans. Did they mean more days of anxiety in warring Ireland? A new fleet to engage Spain? She did not know. She dreaded the moment he would tell her he was leaving her again. Leaving her he surely would be. That afternoon she had heard him talking with Raleigh and Sidney. His full strong voice had floated up from the garden where the three men were strolling.

"'. . . and shall I die . . . and all this unconquered?'" Those were his words that lay heavy on her, a weight against her heart.

87

She met Philippa on the landing as they went up the stone stairs together. Philippa's room faced the sea, not far from the great Norman portal.

Philippa said, "You look weary, Mary. Can't you take your rest now? Surely your housekeeping chores are over for the day."

Mary smiled tiredly. "I thought they were until I saw Richard. He tells me other guests are arriving before night-fall. So beds must be sheeted and made ready."

Philippa leaned toward her and detached the bunch of keys from her belt. "Let me do that for you. I'll find Brooks and we will attend to it. How many more?"

"I'm not certain. Richard mentioned several of Walter's friends. Perhaps we should be ready for six at least." She stood at the door, waiting for Philippa to apply a bit of rouge. She wondered how much Philippa knew of Richard's plans. She hesitated to ask outright. It seemed in a way disloyal to her husband to pry into affairs that he had not confided to her. Yet if she could be sure it was not war . . . How beautiful Philippa was! Her body was slim yet rounded, almost like a girl's body, yet she was twenty-eight, not so many years younger than *she* was. Mary caught sight of herself in the reflecting glass, a white face, thin, pale, almost lifeless. She turned away.

Philippa's eyes met hers. "You must rest, Mary, or you will not be fit to greet the new guests tonight. That would disap-point Richard. He counts so much on this. What is worrying you, Mary? It must be something more than your house-keeping that pulls you down."

"I will go now," Mary said hastily. She must go. She would burst into tears if she lingered a moment. She went swiftly down the passageway, knowing that Philippa's blue eyes were following her, wondering.

Philippa had not left her chamber when she heard the clarion sound welcome. Her woman Mabsey, a sour-looking elderly female who had served her for years, bustled to the window and opened the diamond-paned casement. " 'Tis a cavalcade, madam. Look, madam, a dozen gentlemen and their attendants."

Philippa went to the window. Horsemen were riding through the gateway, their horses' hoofs making a great clatter. Banners were flying. She made out the swallows of Arundell; the black banner with silver crescents of Harris of

Radford; the sable chevron of the Devon Prideaux; the Courtenays, the Staffords, the Devonshires. There were others she did not recognize.

"Run for Brooks, Mabsey. Tell her I will join her in the linen room. Stir yourself or the gentlemen will have neither beds nor hot water for their bathing. Run, woman! Forget your dignity! Run!"

Mabsey hastened away, her skirts rustling, the black velvet ribbons of her mob-cap flying. Her mistress had no sense of decorum. How could Mabsey, at her age, run down a flagged corridor? She might slip and break her bones. She must be careful today, for last night she had dreamed of frogs and eels, a combination that could bring disaster. She slowed down as she turned the corner, and walked with stately measured tread. Suppose she should have had the bad fortune to meet Mr. Ching, Sir Richard's chamberlain, while she was moving in such haste. He would think she had no sense of propriety.

Brooks, in the linen room, was handing out sheets and bolster slips to four rosy-cheeked maids. "Hurry, Susie, the Grey Room! Elfrida, the room next to the Red Chamber! Mind, no wrinkles in the sheets. I'll be by presently to baste the bottom sheets at the corners to keep them smooth. These Londoners must find us as good housekeepers as city folk. Jeannette and Sara, to the North Wing with you! Scamper!"

Philippa came into the room. "I counted twelve gentlemen and their servants," she told Brooks.

"Yes, madam. Sir Richard sent word to me. Master Lane, the Queen's equerry, is here. He must have only the best, since he lives in the palace at Whitehall."

"Ah," Philippa said, "Master Lane! This meeting takes on official significance when Master Lane honors it with his presence." Her voice had a little tinge of sarcasm that was lost on the bustling housekeeper.

"Go with your maids, Brooks. I'll see that Mabsey counts out sheets for the other rooms."

The housekeeper paused at the door. "I had hoped to catch Miss Thomasine to help. Lady Grenville told me to find her, but she vanished at once after the meal was over."

"Where did she go?" Philippa asked, remembering that

89

the last she saw of her was when she was in swift flight across the upper terrace.

"The Lord only knows! Beg pardon, ma'am, but the girl gets me all atwitter. She's a queer one. It certainly upset me to see her running to the wood, wearing Miss Mary's puce taffeta. Wherever she is, she is up to no good." She sniffed audibly. "She is not the miss to wear any such fine clothes. A milkmaid's dress would suit her best."

She hurried away, leaving Philippa smiling. Why did the girl cast such a shadow of distrust wherever she went? She stood for a while watching Mabsey count the linen and check it against the list of rooms.

"Ma'am, there's no use of you standing here making yourself weary. Go take your little slumber, so you are in fettle tonight to meet the Queen's equerry."

A little secret smile played over Philippa's full red lips. Ralph Lane here in Cornwall! The last time she had seen him was at Kenilworth where the Queen had visited her good friend and faithful subject Robert Dudley. Lane had risen in the Queen's favour since then.

Lane and Raleigh friends? She wondered at that, when both were striving for the Queen's grace. Deep in thought, she did not see Thomasine until the girl turned into the passageway that led to the North Wing. The girl did not glimpse Philippa. She was walking swiftly, looking to neither right nor left. At the cross hall she stopped abruptly. Colin, carrying a silver tray with a pot of cider, was approaching.

The girl held out her hand, a conciliatory gesture, but he passed by without a glance. "It was not my fault," the girl said angrily, her voice rising, "not my fault. I did not brand you."

Colin could not have missed hearing her, but he walked steadily on to the Red Room as though unaware of her presence.

"May you be damned!" The girl's voice showed her anger. "May you be eternally damned!"

Philippa shuddered. She slipped into her room—unseen, she hoped. The girl was strange; a baleful light shone in her eyes when she spoke. What was it Nurse had said—that she lived in Merlin's cave? Philippa was sorry for Colin. It was not good fortune to have a curse set on one. It would have been better if he had listened to Thomasine's apology. He had ignored her, roused her anger. That was not good.

Suppose that she did know some of the secrets of the sorcerer, no telling what spell she might cast upon him.

Philippa entered her room and stepped to the window. The courtyard was crowded with guests who had come in from hawking, or cony chasing. She saw Grenville walk across the cobbles toward the Norman doorway almost directly under the window where she stood. He was talking to two men whom she did not recognise. As they were habited in dark sober clothes, she took them to be scholars, probably Richard Hakluyt and Thomas Hariot. She began stripping off her clothes. Naked she got into bed and lay between cool linen sheets. She would sleep until dark, then wake refreshed. Somehow she felt as though portentous things were about to happen at Stowe.

She heard the strumming of a lute, the harper's golden voice:

> "On a steep rock within a winding bay
> A castle stands surrounded by the sea,
> Whose frequent thunder shakes the trembling hill,
> Tintage of old 'twas called, Tintagel."

A little shiver went down her spine. The song was like an answer to her thoughts. The music went on:

> "Nor could the prince conceal the raging flame,
> But in false shapes to Tintagel he came,
> By Merlin's art transform'd from king to Duke. . . ."

She recognised the old song of Uther Pendragon, that Welsh prince who fell in love with the wife of Garlois, Prince of Cornwall. It was through Merlin's enchantment that he assumed the shape of her husband, and out of his adulterous ardour he begat King Arthur from the body of the Lady Igraine. . . . An old ballad known to everyone in Cornwall, yet now it had a sinister implication. What if that strange girl Thomasine knew the magic of Merlin? She remembered how the eyes of all the men followed her when she walked. Was evil born in her?

Philippa said aloud, "This is a foolish thought to which I give no credence." But before she slept she repeated the Lord's Prayer in Cornish, an earnest of her own pure thought. She drifted into sleep with the words on her lips: "Ny Taz ez Ny, neau, bonegas, yw tha hanaw."

91

CHAPTER 7
A GRENVILLE!

The hawkers were straggling into the court-yard in twos and threes. Grenville rode in, accompanied by his two sons John and Bernard, each with a hooded falcon perched on his wrist. Hostlers and grooms were standing about, waiting to lead the horses to the stables. Colin, dressed in bottle-green livery for the hunt, waited near the stone trough where the horses were watered, the hawk hoop hung from his shoulder. Bernard came over first; he transferred the falcon to his hand, placed it on the hoop.

John followed; he was in excellent humour. "We had luck this morning, Colin," he cried. "My bird brought down a grey heron and made him disgorge a six-ince fish from his gullet. It was like the morning last week when we were out. Say, where's Amos? Why are you carrying the hawk hoop?"

"I'm advanced from herd-boy," Colin said with a grin. "I now carry cider jugs and hawk hoops and stand behind gentlemen archers to hand them their arrows."

"I say! Do you like that better than shepherding?"

"Can't say I do, sir."

"Well, what would you like?" Bernard drew near in time to ask the question.

Colin hesitated a moment, gauging the distance between Sir Richard and himself, to be sure his master did not hear. "I'd like to bear armour for the master when he goes to the wars."

Bernard laughed, his merry eyes twinkling. "That is silly. You'd have to work all the while, right under my father's eyes. I thought you liked being off in the hills with the sheep, where no one could see you reading your books."

John, always more serious, said, "I thought you wanted to be a scholar, Colin. That is what Dame Philippa says. You should study hard; maybe my father would appoint you to a living. Wouldn't it be wonderful if you were curate at Kilkhampton or Morwenstow or even Bideford!"

"You are teasing," Colin said sullenly.

John hastened to reassure him. "Indeed I'm not. Dame Philippa says you are twice as studious as we are." He laid his hand for a moment on Colin's shoulder. "I know what you are thinking—that you are lowly born. Times are changing, Colin. There are men in London not of the gentry or of the nobility who have come to high estate—merchants and seamen. Sir Francis Drake, for one. Why, his father was a fisherman with only one small boat. Now he's a knight and the Queen's favourite navigator."

Colin shook his head and moved over to the gate to take a hawk from one of the guests who had just ridden into the court-yard.

"Why did you put such ideas in Colin's head?" Bernard asked as the brothers went into the house.

"Because I believe he can do what he pleases, once he makes up his mind. I don't see any reason for him to wander over the hills with the sheep every day. Sometimes I think we have other servants who could be advanced and serve us better."

Bernard stared. "What strange ideas you have, John! I believe you get them from reading Dr. Hooker's books."

"That is not true. I didn't get them out of books. I thought them by myself. Anyway, Colin is different. We've always been fond of Colin. Ever since we were children he has been our companion."

"More like a body servant."

"Bernard, how can you say that? Colin is too independent to be anyone's servant. Maybe he was born to a condition of servitude, but in his heart he is as independent as we are."

"Better not let our father hear your silly talk, John. He'd flog you—or maybe you'd ask for Colin for a whipping-boy." Bernard grinned impishly and ran up the steps two at a time.

John, always slower for all that he was two years younger than his brother, followed more leisurely. A solemn-faced boy, darker than most of the Grenvilles and quieter, he had more the disposition of his mother, but fortunately none of the wild blood of the St. Legers. In the old days John might have been a monk. He would likely choose the Church if it were not for the fact that the sea was in his blood. Bernard as heir of the Grenvilles had other work ahead of him. The management of Stowe and the twenty-odd other manors would be his.

When the brothers approached the long room in the west wing, it was to find Richard Prideaux and John Arundell in the little ante-room. They had stripped off the clothes they had worn hawking. A bath had been laid in a round tub made of wood, held in place by straps of copper. Arundell's man-servant was busy sponging the young men with cool water from the spring beyond the stables. Their clean linen lay spread on the bed.

John Grenville leaned out the window and shouted to his man to come bathe him. The lackey, a strong husky lad from Somerset, was seated on a stone bench conversing with a group of servants who belonged to the guests. The youth broke off in the midst of a tale of Cornish hawking and disappeared through the archway. A few moments later he knocked at the door, out of breath from running. He unlaced John's leather jerkin and dragged off his long boots.

Two young boys brought up water buckets, swinging from yokes across their brawny shoulders. There was much splashing and laughter and talk about peregrine falcons and tercels. John's young kestrel had behaved well, as well as some of the better-trained hawks. He flew easily, head in the wind, and checked at signal. Black John Arundell boasted that he had a hawk at Trerice that could outfly any he had seen at Stowe.

Prideaux also boasted. A peregrine falcon he had trained could outfly any in Cornwall. Wagers were laid, and plans made for a meet—each lad with his own bird, trained by himself.

A gong sounded. Bernard Grenville jumped from the tub. "Hurry! Hurry! Fifteen minutes till dinner. You know our father. He demands punctuality at meals."

Long hosen pulled on; trunks tied into place; doublets snatched from bed and chairs; wet locks coaxed into semblance of order. Chatter and laughter and boyish voices chaffing and teasing.

"I saw you making sheep's eyes at the new girl," Bernard Grenville whispered to John Arundell. "She's a wild piece to my thinking."

John Arundell's swarthy face reddened. "You never! I

94

didn't look at her. Besides, she's a cousin of sorts, one of the lesser Arundells. There's a pack of them in Cornwall."

"Do you acknowledge all your Arundell kin?" Bernard queried, stretching his handsome legs and pulling at his hosen.

"No, that I don't," Black John said, "particularly not the wild ones from Tintagel. They almost never come to Trerice —maybe once a year on a feast day."

Richard Prideaux's long Gallic face lighted with a slow smile. "If she were my cousin, I'd chain her—on feast days and other days. Did you mark how she walked, moving her hips sinuously, like some great cat or tiger?"

"She's got claws. Did you notice Tremayne's face last night?" Loud laughter followed John Arundell's queston.

"Did she so? Scratch our brother-in-law to be?" asked Bernard.

"It might have been trouble in a brier patch," Prideaux ventured. "But surely she spat at St. Leger a few nights ago. He pinched her when a lackey was carrying him to bed, the night he over-reached himself trying to drink as much as Sir Richard."

"No? What did she do?"

"Can't say; wasn't there. But he boasted."

"The beast!" John Arundell cried. "I've a mind to call him out for his insolence."

"Listen to the firebrand! Lad, your sword-arm hasn't skill enough to challenge St. Leger. He's famous for his sword in hand."

"I'll teach him not to bother the girl."

"Ah, Johnny, are you sweet on the wench?"

"Her name's the same as mine, even though I don't know the girl or ever spoke a word to her."

John Grenville said, "I don't think we should be flippant about any of my father's guests." The others were silent.

"Don't be a prig, John You sound like the curate. But let's be off. Get away from the glass, Prideaux. Your curls are in order. Give us a chance."

Prideaux ran his hands through the waves of dark hair, cut close to his well-shaped head. "I think I'll grow a beard when I go to Virginia."

"Virginia!" a chorus of voices shouted at him. "Are you going to Virginia?"

"Why not? They want young men, don't they?"

The others drew close to Prideaux. "What do you know about Virginia? Have you been asked to go? What is this Virginia talk?" John Grenville asked.

Richard Prideaux said airily, "I have ears. Why do you think all these great men are gathering at Stowe? Not to hawk or to harvest grain surely?"

John Arundell said, "I thought it might mean some plan to raid the Spaniards."

"No. It's a Virginia venture. I heard Sir Walter talking to Captain Amadas today while we were waiting for the falcons to take off. A great venture to the New World."

A second gong sounded. "The last bell. We'll be late to our places." Bernard led the way, Black John and Richard Prideaux close on his heels. They raced down the long hall to the stone stairs.

John Grenville, who was last out of the bath, found his hosen tied in knots. He struggled to untie them, but it made him late. He entered the dining-hall just as Sir Richard and his guests seated themselves at the high table. He stood at the door that gave on the serving pantry, his face red with embarrassment. How could he cross the room to the lower table without being in the line of his father's cold disapproving eyes? He felt a tug at his sleeve.

Colin whispered, "Quick, along the wall! There's a seat saved for you under the minstrels' gallery. Now, as the lackeys go in to serve the boar's head!"

Taking the hint, John slid along the wall, mingling with the lackeys who were serving the tables below the salt. Colin followed, carrying the wine jugs on a tray. John gained a seat on the long bench below the gallery and stood with head bowed as the new Rector of Kilkhampton, William Tooker, said a short prayer to bless the house, its guests and the food and drink that graced the board.

"Thank you," John whispered as Colin placed a pewter wine cup on the table before him. "Thanks." Colin moved on to serve the others at a near-by table. It was not the first time that Colin had stood between him and his father's displeasure. He looked about him. New faces were at the high table. He recognised Rise Courtenay—that handsome young son of the Earl of Devonshire—and Edward Stafford. Devon men were here to join the Cornish gentry. There was subdued excitement in the air. Broken sentences came to his ears: "Virginia"—the word was spoken quietly—"the

96

New World . . . how many ships? . . . The Spanish—may God damn them!—must be stopped, pulled from their high arrogance and . . . Florida in Spanish hands . . . the Plate Route to the Spanish Main . . . treasure, gold, silver and pearls . . . for the Queen and the Realm" . . . all words whispered among the young squires as they ate the hearty food set before them; words to capture a youth's imagination and stir hot blood.

John Arundell, sitting next to him, dropped his voice. "Lucky Grenvilles, you know what the plan is. You do not have to wait on tenter-hooks to find out what devices the great ones make for a voyage on the Virginia Sea."

"I know nothing," John whispered back. Better to acknowledge ignorance than to be caught in a lying boast of knowing more than he did. "Nothing."

The cheese board was passed; cider and wine and ale were poured into mugs and tankards. A shuffling of feet; the squeak of chairs on the stone-flagged floor; a rustling of taffeta skirts and subdued laughter, thinly sweet, as the women and girls slipped into the minstrels' gallery above them.

Arundell nudged John with a sharp elbow. "Look upward," he said softly. John glanced over his shoulder. Thomasine's profile was visible, clear-cut below a mop of unruly dark hair. Beyond her was little Mary's pale blondness.

A glance upward, no more. Sir Richard, splendid in blue doublet and fine hosen, rose. Raising the great silver-gilt bowl, he cried, "A toast to our Sovereign and Gracious Lady!" Every man was on his feet. The Grenville clarions sounded.

"The Queen! The Queen!" Half a hundred voices took up the toast. The great bowl passed from one man to the next along the table. "The Queen!" each man repeated as he drank. "The Queen!" . . . until it became, from repetition, like a chant, rising in volume as the lower tables lifted their mugs and tankards. "The Queen! The Queen! The Queen!"

John Grenville drank his cider with the rest, his heart pounding. How good it was to raise one's glass to toast their Gracious Elizabeth, the peer of all women!

Other toasts followed rapidly—to the Lady of Stowe; to Dame Philippa; to the young ladies of the household. It was grand. Sure in all England there could be no more distinguished company of gentlemen than these in the great banquet hall of Stowe. No, nor another so gallant as Sir Richard Grenville. John's heart throbbed with pride—proud that he was born a Cornish gentleman, knowing that he was born a Grenville, proud of the banners stacked against the wall behind the high table. All Devon, all Cornwall were here this day. Tears came to his eyes, prideful tears, to be brushed hastily away with the back of his hand. Out of the tail of his eye he saw Arundell's eyes were shining. Was he, too, proud to be Cornish-born, an Englishman, living under the greatest Princess the world had ever known? Was he proud to be born Arundell, as John was proud of his Grenville heritage? They stood equal, men of equestrian stature since the days of Norman William, they and the Courtenays and the Godolphins, the Trevelyans and the Staffords.

He lifted his cup to Sir Philip Sidney . . . to my Lord Burghley . . . to Sir Francis Walsingham. 'Twas cider of last year, and potent. The room grew hot and the figures of the men at the high table hazy. "To the Knights of the Shire!" . . . "To the Warden of the Stannaries, Sir Walter, Sir Walter!" Voices chanted the name. His cousin, the Queen's servant, rose to his feet.

How elegant he was, swarthy as Black John Arundell, in tight-fitting doublet of white with slashings of blue and silver! How striking the contrast! His pointed beard, thick and dark, fell over a white ruff. One long pearl dangled from his ear, a court fancy of court dandies. His words came swift, easy words, graceful words. His hands, fine and white, held tightly the hilt of a jewelled dagger. Sometimes he gesticulated, pointing to a great map pinned to the tapestry on the north wall.

"To Virginia, Captain Amadas, Virginia." He bowed to the sturdy captain with the merry dark eyes who sat beside him. "A call to brave men of Cornwall and Devon—perhaps one man from every hundred of our two counties! A summons for tall ships built at Bideford to sail down the Torridge and out to the open sea! Other ships lie even now in the Pool at Plymouth Haven. Three months only will take them to the long sandy banks of Virginia; then through a narrow entrance to the Island of Roanoke. Will any stout Cornishman or Devonian refuse so brilliant an opportunity to bring glory to his Queen, to shut Spain out of the New World?"

"Down with the Spaniards!" someone shouted.

"Hear! Hear!" came hearty voices raising the echo to the king-beam of the vaulted roof.

"Who will lead?" called Christopher Harris of Radford.

"Who but the greatest man of the West Country? Who but Grenville?" Raleigh answered, quick to take advantage.

"A Grenville! A Grenville!" The old battle cry of past ages. Men were on their feet shouting the name, while they banged pewter and silver drinking vessels on the smooth oaken boards of the long tables. "A Grenville will lead us to the New World!"

John Grenville tried to shout, but the words died in a sob that rose to his throat. Through the mist he saw his father's tall form, erect and noble. John swayed a little; the table felt steady under his hands. "A Grenville, strong as an English oak," Black John Arundell said, beating the table with the hilt of his dagger.

A mighty man, Grenville, thundering down the ages. It must have been like this when a Grenville banner waved beside William the Conqueror's; and in the Long Crusade; at Agincourt; at Crécy—at all the battles that made England great. "A Grenville!" Swords flashed aloft. The clarions resounded. The old rallying cry rang out again and again: "A Grenville!"

He caught a glimpse of Colin, his eyes alight, fixed on Sir Richard Grenville.

Black John caught up the banner of Arundell. Courtenay, Prideaux, Stafford, St. Leger, Champernowne were quick to lift theirs aloft. They crowded close. Tables were pushed back. . . .

Young John Grenville could stand no more. He turned and rushed out through the long window behind his bench, down through the garden. On and on he ran, across the bowling-green, across the upper terrace. Deep in the beechwood he stopped and threw himself on the ground, his heart bursting within him. He was not sixteen, far too young to plant the Grenville banner in the virgin soil of the New World.

CHAPTER 8
HARVEST HOME

The shouting died. Sir Richard Grenville, with one glance toward the minstrels' gallery and the white, stricken face of his wife, made a short speech of acceptance. From the tail of his eye he saw Philippa lead Lady Grenville along the upper gallery, young Mary supporting her. It must be a shock for her to hear the plans for sailing to Virginia, but perhaps it was as well to come this way. It would save him explanations and tears. Gad, how he hated women's tears! They took the strength from his veins and turned his liver weak.

He said what he had to say. One sentence came out clear and strong at the end: "Since Her Gracious Majesty the Queen has seen fit to make me admiral and general of this venture and place in my hands the full command of all ships and all men involved in this expedition to the new land of Virginia, I will assume the responsibility. The loyal support of the men of the West Country and the stout ships of Devon will carry us forward. With God's help we will succeed."

There was further talk and discussion. The shouting died. The guests went out of the banquet hall, scattered over the house, the adjacent gardens and terraces.

In a small antechamber off the great hall sat five men: Walter Raleigh, Philip Sidney, Captain Amadas, Ralph Lane and Richard Hakluyt. The western sun already low shone through the mullioned windows. Moving patterns of sunlight and shadow on the flagged floor were made by ivy that grew thick on the outer stone wall and hung in streamers across the window. Holland chairs covered in red leather, a leather-covered window bench and a long table of old oak formed the furnishing.

Raleigh was talking. In his face and eyes there was the remnant of that excitement which had blazed so short a time before. "You have seen for yourself what I mean, Lane.

In Grenville you have that rare thing called leadership. He has the quality to make men follow him to the death."

Lane sat stiffly while the other men lounged. It was said he wore a corselet of iron under his doublet to give his figure the prescribed flat stomach and straight back.

"We don't want men to follow to the death," he said, a slight edge to his voice.

"My mistake, Lane." Raleigh spoke good-humouredly. "I should have said, Men will follow Grenville to the ends of the earth."

Sidney lifted one silken-clad knee over the other and settled himself well in the high-backed chair. "It was mediæval, that demonstration. I kept thinking that the Crusades must have started in just such a way. That black-browed lad catching up the banner, the others following, the air heavy with their ancient battle cries."

"That is the West Country," Raleigh remarked proudly. "Our county families will always stand well together when it comes to an issue." He glanced at Hakluyt, whose long angular body was bent over the map. Amadas, from the window-seat, watched two wrestlers who were entertaining guests on the greensward, and said nothing. His time would come later.

"I agree with Richard. Some of my people come from the West Country. It is a society welded close, link on link. Its strength lies in its integrity and forthrightness. Did you ever see such a demonstration, Lane?" Sidney pressed the silent man for an expression.

The masklike features of the Queen's equerry did not change. "Often," he said in his flat, disinterested voice. "Often we have whipped up wild enthusiasm among the populace when the Queen is to make some public appearance."

Sidney glanced at him. "Ah, Lane the Londoner! Are your perceptions so blunted you cannot discern the difference between your staged demonstrations and one that comes from the heart?"

Lane flushed painfully. A new-comer, of doubtful ancestry, he was sensitive to any slight from a man of the position of Sir Philip Sidney. For a moment he was speechless. Without wit or quickness, he had not the grace to turn a phrase neatly. In a few moments he had command of himself. After all, was he not the friend of Sir Francis

Walsingham? And was not Sir Francis the Queen's principal secretary?

"I thought it well rehearsed," he replied, clinging to his original idea tenaciously. "I grant Grenville is a little king in this territory. I wonder if it is wise for a Knight of the Shire to have too much power." There was a veiled threat in his words.

Raleigh broke in quickly. This was not going the way he planned. There must be harmony, or the venture had little hope of success. "You misunderstand our people, Mr. Lane. We are a stiff-necked lot. We have a certain rugged independence, but we are loyal folk. From the lowest to the highest we are loyal to our Queen. You are mistaken if you think this display of enthusiasm you have witnessed was anything but spontaneous. Only a few of us present had ever heard anything of the plans before. Don't think this demonstration is any parallel to the whipped-up enthusiasm one sometimes sees in Westminster, which is engendered by proddings."

Lane disregarded Raleigh's explanation. "Who were those men?" he asked. "Whom do they represent? Are they Grenville's tenants and their sons? Fishermen? Yeomen? Folk who do Grenville's bidding?"

"I can see, Lane, that you have no conception of the West Country. Have you never heard of our county families who date back in unbroken line to the Conqueror—aye, and some of them beyond, to Saxon times?"

"I may have heard something at one time or another. It made no lasting impression."

Raleigh struggled to keep his composure. "Then there is no use to expound their virtues. Will you take my word that Her Majesty has no more loyal subjects than the men of the West Country who have fought her wars and upheld the dignity of the Crown?"

Sidney put an end to the discussion by joining Hakluyt at the table. Looking closely at the map, he called to Amadas, "Captain, will you show us the point where your ship made an entrance behind the long sand islands? Is there a bar? How deep is the water? How large is this Island of Roanoke?"

Amadas got up and followed Sidney to the table. Raleigh, tired of explanations, also went to the map. With the tip of his finger the young navigator traced the route

102

his ship had taken from the Azores and up the Florida coast to an inlet between the long islands to the haven near the Island of Roanoke.

"We knew nothing of the main," he said regretfully. "We explored only a little, but we know there is a great inland sea beyond the island."

"Why did you not investigate the main more thoroughly?" Hakluyt queried.

Amadas hesitated. "I wanted to," he said frankly, "but Barlow was against it. The Indians we had seen seemed friendly, but we were a small company, ill equipped with stores or small ships to go farther. Barlow contended that we had done what we had come for. I knew he was right, but certainly I wanted to see beyond the verge of the continent."

"You were not so cautious as Master Barlow," Sir Philip said with a smile at the young captain.

"Sir, no, I am not cautious. I wanted to sail on and on, but——" He shrugged his shoulders expressively. "Our Indian friends whom we brought home with us, Manteo and Wanchese, both advised against it. They said that the Indians up the great water were treacherous and at war with their people."

"Are you going on this journey with Grenville, Amadas?" Raleigh asked.

Surprise crossed the open countenance of Philip Amadas. "Why, of a certainty. You heard Sir Richard's quotation the other evening. It suited my mood perfectly. 'And shall I die, and this unconquered?' "

"Excellent. You shall have a ship of your own this time, Captain Amadas, and if you wish to explore the inland sea and the main beyond the Island of Roanoke, I am sure Sir Richard will voice no objection."

"Ah, that is what I want, gentlemen. I wish you could, with your own eyes, view that fair land—the gigantic pines; the monstrous cypress marching from shore far into the water; the myriad flowers and bushes unknown to us, and the vines thick as the compass of two hands with the luscious purple and amber grapes. A fertile land with lusty growth. Ah, again I say, 'And shall I die, and this unconquered.' " He paused, grinned a boyish, half-embarrassed grin. "I talk too much," he said and went back to the window.

"No, not too much. Not enough," Sidney said. "Come

with me, Amadas. Let's walk out and see the new mare Sir Richard has been boasting of. We can talk on the way. What you tell us catches my imagination, sir."

Lane got up from his chair, a look of puzzlement on his face. To Raleigh he said, "I hope Sir Richard Grenville has been informed that I, by the Queen's grace, will be the Governor of Roanoke for a year and a day."

Raleigh spoke shortly. "He will be informed."

Lane left the room. As he crossed the hall to go to his room, he saw Sir Richard walking up and down the garden path with the Rector of St. James-the-Greater, of Kilkhampton. The rector was talking earnestly, Sir Richard listening without interruption, but the heavy lines between his eyes were deepened almost to a scowl. Whatever Mr. Tooker was saying, it did not please the knight.

Lane smiled, a sly crooked smile. He did not like Sir Richard Grenville.

In the garden Mr. Tooker said earnestly, "I have done what I can by diplomatic means, Sir Richard. Mr. Paget has left but Mrs. Paget refuses to give up the rectory. I am at my wit's end what to do next. I have been here two months now, and she will not move out, nor will she allow me to have a room or go into the study, where there are many church books necessary to me if I am to go on with my work in the parish. I must have the lists, so that I may call on my new parishioners and become acquainted with them."

"The woman's a fool," Grenville said, "a silly, obstinate fool. I offered her a house in the village or one at Morwenstow, or even a dwelling in Bideford. She would not give way. I'll have to take steps."

"Dear, dear! I hope it will not come to the place where you have the law on her." The rector was plainly disturbed.

"My dear Mr. Tooker, *I* am the law in this parish, and I am likewise the Patron of St. James-the-Greater."

The rector hesitated. "Perhaps I should give way and resign. . . . Do you not think it ill advised to start off so badly? A quarrel with a woman, and that woman the wife of a former rector. . . . People will not take kindly to that, or to me."

"Give way, sir? How can you voice such a thought! Run from a woman? Mr. Tooker, if you haven't the humour or courage to take a stand, you are not the man to have the church. You would be the laughing-stock of all Cornwall if you retreated from a woman. Nonsense! We'll see that Mrs. Paget moves from the rectory before the week is up."

"Thank you, Sir Richard. You give me courage. I feared that you might think it unwise for a man of the cloth to descend to squabbling."

"I would think little of you if you retreated from a stand which you know is right. Cheer up, man. It's not a problem that can't be solved. Come. I see Dame Philippa and Lady Grenville. Shall we join them forthwith?"

Lady Grenville had been in the upper garden. The basket on her arm was filled with lilies. She smiled at her husband, but her face was as white as the lilies she carried, and her eyes had a hunted look.

Philippa, on the contrary, was still possessed of the excitement that had filled the great hall. She watched Grenville's approach. He is young, learned, virtuous and full-manned, she thought. Danger is in his blood. So is the sea in his blood; it draws him inordinately. What will come of this new venture? Will it win for him new laurels, everlasting fame, as Drake's voyage has done for him, or will it bring disaster?

Sidney had said to her, "He possesses that Promethean heat which kindles fire in other men." She recalled at that moment a look she had seen on Lane's face as she watched the procession of young men. He, in his narrow way, his unrestrained will and great ambition, could be a bitter and vengeful enemy. Richard, a spirit beyond the reach of fear, would not guard against little meanness. He might easily underestimate the Queen's equerry. Richard's reaches were simple and direct. An enemy he could slay. If he wanted a woman he would seize her. His was not a nature to combat slyness or intrigue of a mean cast. His was a splendid character for a prince. A couplet she had recently heard came to her mind because it fitted the man so closely:

> Who to himself is law, no law doth need,
> Offends no law, and is a king indeed.

That was Richard Grenville. Because he would not lower himself to intrigue or treachery, he would not recognise it in others. Should she warn him or let his self-confidence

105

carry him through? What a magnificent figure of a man he was! Physically and mentally of high stature, the sum of all bodily and mental excellence in man. She watched him as he spoke to his wife, now all solicitude. Before her gentle spirit he lost the calm remoteness that characterised his common attitude toward people. Mary had no conception of his fiery anger or his firm courage or his disdain of mediocrity in men or women. With her he was the eternal protector. I would be bored to death, if a man treated me so, Philippa thought. The Richard Grenville she knew was not boring. Mary Grenville went away and left them, intent on her household duties.

Grenville indicated a bench. "Please sit down, Philippa. I've been wanting to talk with you, but there has not been a moment."

Philippa spread her skirts and sat down. Each movement of her body was one of studied grace. "You are today's hero, Richard," she said, busy with the lace that ruffled about her sleeves.

He passed by the remark without comment, standing before her, stripping a short stick he had picked up in his walk through the grounds.

"What are you doing with that hazel stick? Do you intend to search for water?" she questioned, humour in her upward glance.

"No." He laughed and tossed the rod away. "No, I have a better use for it. I should, if I had my wish, lay it on the round bottom of Madam Paget."

"Richard!"

"Yes, and with some heat. The woman is causing Tooker trouble without end."

"How can anyone cause trouble for that pleasant little man?"

"She won't move out of the rectory. I told him to move right in with her. He was shocked. He began to shake as though he had a palsy."

Philippa smiled. "No one ever suspects you of humour, Richard."

"Am I so grim?"

"Not to my thinking. I fancy Lane imagines you to be as grim as a High Marshal."

"Lane!" There was contempt in his tone.

She ran her slim hand along the silk that covered her

106

knees. "Don't think too little of that gentleman, Richard. He has the ear of several important people."

"Let him. I will continue to think little of him. He might be good on horseback or at raping, but no more."

"I still say, have a care, my good brother."

He sat down beside her. "You are sweet when you worry about me, Philippa, sweet and lamentable. I like a woman who does not worry, who sends a man forth with a smile and with dry eyes. Let the prayer for his safety be in her heart, not on her lips."

"You are hard, my dear. . . . But we were talking of Lane. It is good sometimes to remember that an enemy at court is not a good thing. Nor is the Tower to be forgotten."

"You are morbid. That is not like you."

"Perhaps. But I saw Lane's face at dinner. It was not pleasant."

"Lane? Why think of him? An equerry to the Queen. A glorified groom."

Dame Philippa glanced over her shoulder and put her finger to her lips. "He rides beside the Queen," she said in a subdued voice. "There are many occasions to speak confidentially."

"Let him speak. A Grenville does not fear calumny when his conscience is clear. I will be a man who crosses the sea to win an empire for his Queen, not one who plods the earth to fetch fuel for a kitchen fire, nor one who cringes at the petty dictums of the court. No demi-Caesar am I, but a man to please his ancestors and himself, and perhaps—who knows?—the men who come after him. My own man am I, so let the Lanes vent their spleen or nip at my heels and yap to their own undoing."

Philippa's blue eyes widened as Grenville spoke. Her hand all unconsciously touched his that lay on his knee. "Your pardon, sweet Richard! My doubts and fears have taken swift flight. How could I be distressed or carry fear in my heart? You rise taller than any man within all England."

"Dear Philippa, thank you. I wish that my Mary would think as you think now." He stretched his legs and got up from the bench. "I am a coward when it comes to hurting her. Today I saw her white face as you led her from the minstrels' gallery. It was a dagger in my heart. For a moment I was all aflame to go to her and comfort her in my

107

arms. In truth, I took a step, but Walter caught my arm."

"You are going to her now?"

"Yes, I will put it off no longer."

"See that you do not wear her down. Tonight is the harvest moon, and all your guests will join your tenants to make merry."

"Aye, I know." He stood for a moment looking across the garden. His eyes fell on Thomasine as she ran across the upper terrace and disappeared into the yew maze. "That wild creature! I do not know how Mary will tame her."

"Why tame her?" Philippa answered. "Why clasp her in a mould? I think she is best left alone, with only small guidance."

Richard shook his head slowly. "Three days only, and half my young squires are running after her. She is a honey-pot. She draws men. If she is not careful, she will say farewell to her virginity before long."

Philippa said, "I think not. I saw her scratch Tremayne when he tried to snatch a kiss. I think she will take care of herself."

"I don't want my squires thinking of women. They must have minds free to think of nothing but the land of Virginia. Let Virginia be their mistress."

"A cold bed, if what I hear is true. Water and sand, a few tall trees, snakes and vipers . . ."

"A woman's thought, Philippa, not a man's. A man's mind will be set on glory—to be the first to seat vast new lands for the Queen's realm is honour enough for a man's lifetime."

Philippa lifted her arms behind her head. The wide lace-frilled sleeves of her gown fell to her shoulders, leaving her lovely arms bare. "When I marry again, I will not marry a man who seeks adventure on the sea or in far lands, but one who will take adventure between the sheets of my bed. Heigh-ho, here come Walter and Sidney, and behind them your Master Lane."

"I'll go now. I think Mary is waiting for me." He leaned far over, his eyes smiling. "You would be worth it, my dear," he said as he turned away. A lively blush spread over Philippa's fair face. She put her fan to her cheek to conceal the colour, as Walter Raleigh and Sidney approached her across the greensward.

A rim of red moon rose over the low-lying hill. From vale and woodland and field came the sound of laughter and hallooing back and forth. The tenantry was making ready for the harvest festival. There were pasties and seed-cakes and cakes of saffron, baskets of apples, jugs and barrels of good Devon cider, ale, cheese from home dairies, great bowls of clotted cream to eat on peaches or fruits preserved in spring for this occasion.

An old custom, the harvest festival. Old wives contended that it came to them from the Saxon times. Some anti-quaries insisted that it was planted on the island by the Romans. Ceres' Festival they called it. Whatever the origin, each year yeoman and tenant, herdsman and yokel and children looked forward to dancing and the harvest games.

The festivities at the great house began as the moon rose to full sight and dusk fell in the vale. Even the rooks caught the excitement, and long past their usual time they circled over vale and wood. Their heavy raucous cries seemed to penetrate the falling darkness as the roar of an angry sea might penetrate the fog over the rocky coast.

The guests were in the walled garden. Raleigh, Sidney and Lane were the center of a semicircle. The other guests and the members of the household sat behind them. The young squires lay sprawled on the grass. On the opposite side the servants were gathered, a hundred or more, dressed in the blue livery of the Grenvilles. Old Pooley had a seat of honour, while Ching the chamberlain moved quietly about to see that guests and servants sat in comfort. He kept his eye on the Norman gate in the outer wall where Colin, in his shepherd dress, waited to give the signal.

Tonight the tenantry, headed by the elder yeoman from each farm, would pay tribute to their overlord, each bringing with him the symbol of lease of Stowe land.

The ceremony would take place under the great oak, an oak so venerable that it was written into the Domesday Book, a ceremony as old as the Domesday Book itself. An earlier Sir Richard Grenville had had the Domesday record translated and carved into the stone above the fire-place in his hall. There it remained.

Sir Richard Grenville and his lady took their places under the Domesday Oak when the moon climbed as high as the Norman tower on the eastward wall. The knight was dressed in white, his doublet slashed in silver. He wore corslet and epaulets of silvery metal. Beside him on an iron garden table was placed his casque with blue plumes. The casque was cleverly arabesqued in damascene, with inserts of silver-gilt. His hosen were silk, his boots leather from Morocco as soft as a piece of Lyons velvet. His reddish gold hair was short-cropped: his beard, almost auburn, was trimmed to a nice point. Had he been going to a levee at the palace, he would not have been more elegantly dressed. He wore a Damascus blade which an early Grenville had fetched home from the Holy Land, where he had journeyed with Godefroy de Bouillon in the First Crusade.

Lady Grenville was all blue and silver, and her brocade gown swept about her in heavy folds. On her head she wore a heavy coif with a long lace veil that fell to the ground, giving her more height.

Grenville was attended by his sons Bernard and John, his lady by her daughters Mary and Catherine. They composed themselves in two great chairs with the Grenville crest carved at the top. By the side of each chair two Italian stone garden benches had been placed. The young people grouped themselves close to the chairs where their mother and father held court. Behind them and around the circle torches were being lighted before darkness descended.

"What is the meaning of this?" Lane inquired. "Why do Grenville and his lady seat themselves in throne chairs?"

"It is an ancient custom at Stowe. The tenants come once a year to pay tribute," Walter Raleigh replied. "I've seen the ceremony only once before, years ago when I was a lad. I remember how impressive it was."

Lane said nothing. Philippa watched him covertly. He likes nothing that concerns Grenville, she thought. Then she turned her attention to the west portal where the great double gates were swinging open. So heavy they were that they could not be negotiated by hand. A group of servitors turned a wooden crank that worked the machinery to open them. In ancient times a moat had surrounded the stout stone walls; now it was half-filled with rubbish and overgrown with brambles and ivy.

As the gates opened, Colin gave the signal and the clarions sounded. The procession, headed by the oldest yeoman, holder of the oldest land lease, stepped over the threshold and into the cobbled courtyard. Behind him a long line waited to move forward.

Beside each yeoman a young man walked carrying a lighted pine knot. The open gate gave a view of the long road that curved down the hill past Stowe Wood to the mill at the bottom of the vale. Flickering lights showed the procession winding slowly down the opposite hill, now heavy in shadow.

As the grey-haired yeoman advanced, dressed in his best leathern jerkin and short breeks, his buskin laced almost to the knees, the visitors saw that each man carried a red rose in his hand. Now the ancient one stood in front of his overlord, whom he saluted, not by the bent knee, but by touching his forehead with the fingers of his right hand. Then he laid his rose on the stone bench and, after a word or two of greeting from Sir Richard, passed on below the terrace where rows of benches had been placed. The torch-bearers stuck their torches in the ground, making a ring of light.

The harper, seated near a trellis covered with red roses, struck up a tune, a quick lilting tune which caused men to step more briskly.

For an hour the procession moved on; old tenant and young paid their tributes with red roses until the two stone benches were piled high. When the last man had touched his forehead in salute, the court-yard was crowded with women and children who came to watch and, when the ceremony was over, to join in the harvest festival.

Sir Richard rose to his feet. His clerk, grown old and bent leaning over ledgers, brought a scroll and quill pen. Grenville's full rich voice was heard above the lesser sounds and whisperings.

"Let all men that are present and to come know that I, Richard, son of Roger, son of Richard de Grenville, and of the Richards who preceded them, have granted such leases the liberties which have heretofore been theirs. Besides I have granted them fairs and markets throughout all my lands in Cornwall and Devon. Waters and pasturage, tolls and stallage shall be free to them.

"On Tuesday will I hold court, when each man may come for redress, or send a relative or friend if he be on pilgrimage or beyo 1 the seas.

"They may choose one burgess to be head officer. And

111

at the year's end ten shillings shall be paid to that officer from me and my heirs.

"On this I print my own seal before witnesses."

Colin stepped close and turned his back. The clerk used it as a desk. Then signed Sir Richard Coffyn of Portledge in Devon, Richard of Spekcat, John St. Leger and Sir John Arundell the Elder.

This ceremony over, the clarions rang out. The tenants crowded through the court-yard into the main yard, out through the lane to an open place by the stables where the harvest games would take place.

The guests rose from bench and grass. Philippa turned to Master Ralph Lane, waited for his comment. It came reluctantly.

"I must describe this to Her Majesty. She will be interested to know that such ancient customs and privileges still survive in the County of Cornwall."

Philip Sidney listened, his head tilted on one side. He held a red rose in his hand, which from time to time he lifted to his aristocratic nose. "I am sure Her Majesty will be interested. I was thinking I would describe the tribute of the rose to her. It will be interesting for the Queen to compare two versions of this most interesting ceremony."

Raleigh came up. "We are to go to the stables. Now that this formality is over, the fun begins, when we can watch the tenants take part in their harvest festival, a custom quite as old as the one we have just witnessed."

Philippa said, "Lady Grenville will lead a contra-dance with the chamberlain Ching, while Sir Richard will step off with Brooks the housekeeper. You gentlemen, if you are lively and arrive before the farm lads, may each choose a buxom milkmaid as your partner."

"Ah, how delightful!" Raleigh and Sidney exclaimed in one breath. "Let us make haste!"

Lane said, "A buxom lass is not to my liking. May I have the honor of stepping a measure with you, Dame Philippa?"

"Indeed yes, Master Lane—or should I say Captain Lane?"

"If it pleases you. But I should prefer simple Ralph—from you."

Philippa swept a curtsy. "It shall be as you request . . . Ralph." She pronounced the name prettily, with a little

112

hesitation. If Richard Grenville had been near by, he would have said it was time for Master Lane to beware.

When they reached the stable court-yard, a team of grooms and field men were drinking cider, each with a lighted candle set in his mug, while the crowd about them were singing:

> "Old Tom Tanner is come to town.
>   Heigh-ho, heigh-ho!
>   His nose is burned, his eyes are burned,
>   His lashes also."

And old yeoman named Jonas, with merry eyes and round red cheeks and a tuft of white hair standing straight up on his head, was selecting a bundle of grain out of a stook with great care. Only the best sheaf would do for "Crying the Neck."

Colin stood by. Philippa called to him, "What is the old man doing now?"

"Madam, they are about to Cry the Neck," he said, coming to her. "In a moment the game will begin. Pardon, Jonas is calling me. I am a contestant." He hurried away, to a crowd of reapers, men and girls, who had formed a circle about the stook. Colin stood in the center holding the sheaf, or neck, high above his head with both hands. The reapers stooped low to the ground. With a long wailing cry they began to sing:

> "The neck, the neck.
>   Wee—Yeu,
>   Wee—Yeu."

As they raised themselves slowly, Colin broke through the ring and ran swiftly toward the farm cottage a quarter of a mile away up the hill. There a dozen dairymaids stood guarding the doors and windows. They held water pails in their hands, ready to douse him as he came through. If he could get by the vigilant maids, the sheaf still held in his hand, and reach the sanctuary of the cottage, he might, as his forfeit, kiss the girl of his choice. Running along the hedge in the darkness, he avoided the doors which the maids were guarding. Swinging himself along the wall, he reached the roof and entered through an upper window.

The crowd followed. They rushed into the cottage and found Colin seated by the kitchen table, playing with a tabby.

Shrieking and crying, "Unfair! 'Tis witchcraft!" they circled around him. One maid after another came close, nudging his shoulder with elbow or hip, but he did not claim forfeit.

He raised his eyes and looked toward the door. Thomasine and young Mary stood outside peering into the room.

He leaped across the table and crossed the room. Mary hid behind a bush. Thomasine, with a frightened glance over her shoulder, picked up her skirts and fled down the path that led to the spring-house, well hidden from the cottage by a small copse of willows. Colin caught her there. He threw his arms about her and drew her to him. The girl resisted, struggling to break from his arms.

"Let me go, fool! Let me go or I'll call your master, Sir Richard."

"Call *your* master, the devil, for all I care." He was laughing as she fought in his arms. "You owe me something for a branding. I choose the forfeit of a kiss." He pronounced the customary words of the harvest game. "Give me your lips."

"I will not! It is my teeth you'll get." She bit at his arm but found no flesh, only the sleeve of his leather jerkin. "Unhand me! You smell evilly of sheep and cattle and manure."

"Health and fertility lie in manure, my fine lady."

She was breathing hard. "You hurt me," she said, making her voice pitiful. He laughed again a little wildly, for his blood was alive and racing at the nearness of her body. She kicked at his legs and scratched, managing to find his forearm.

"Come, 'tis lawful for me to kiss you. I won you fairly."

She still fought him, struggling in his arms. Voices sounded across the field calling to them. He picked her up and carried her along the hedge that walled the meadow.

"Where are you taking me?" she cried, her voice trembling.

"To a quiet spot I know where we can kiss without interruption."

"I'll scream——" She had no time to finish her words, for his hand closed on her mouth. On he walked up the sheep path, holding her slim waist with one arm.

"You are a wee light lass," he said. "I could carry you all night until the sun came up. Then we would be lying on the cliffs, listening to the pounding of the sea." He felt her lips nuzzling his palm, trying to fit her teeth. "Keep trying, pretty mistress. I like well to have you kiss the scar that you burned in my hand. . . . Don't you see what you have done? I wear your brand. I am your slave and, as your slave, I must be near you."

They came to the brow of the hill. In the rock was the shelter made of upright stones. Three sides of it were enclosed; the fourth, to the west, lay open. He released her but stood blocking the entrance. She tried to pass him. He held her arm.

"Have patience! I will make a light so I can see your beautiful anger." He struck a stone and a light flared up, which he held close to a tallow dip stuck on a stone bench. "Come sit beside me close, and I will keep the chill wind from you."

The feeble light flecked in the girl's eyes. She did not scream but held her body close against the wall, as far away as his encircling arm would let her go. "I will tell your master. I will complain in his court on Tuesday that——"

"That what?" His voice sounded cool. "Of what will you complain?"

She was silent.

"Of a kiss?" He bent over her. His lips brushed her cheek. "This is a lawful kiss. I so declare." He circled her waist, leaned to her, one arm about her shoulders, his hand caught in the hair at the back of her head. Slowly he drew her to him until her slim body lay against him. Then he put his mouth to hers, pressing against her until she opened her lips to cry out. Then he kissed her parted lips until she ceased to struggle and lay quiet in his arms.

He meant to kiss her only once, the lawful kiss, but fire swept him and set him trembling. He drew her to her feet, pressed her body hard against him. "The lawful kiss and then this unlawful one." He kissed her as though he would never have enough of kissing.

He released her then. She stood before him. Free of his arms, she darted to the doorway. The moon was well up now, and the path lay clear in the moonshine. Far below the lights and beacons of Stowe burned like fire-flies in the

115

night. He overtook her half-way down the hill, caught her arm. "Kiss me," he said harshly.

"I will kill you!"

"A happy death." He put his palm to her lips. "The burn will go away, and the hate."

Surprise forced her question: "Do you hate me?"

"Hate you? I loathe you. Are you so insensitive not to know it was you who caused me hurt beyond repair? To wear a brand like a criminal, burned into the palm of my hand for some silly play of St. Leger?"

"St. Leger? Was it he?"

"Who tried to pinch your buttocks? Yes, St. Leger, half drunk, hanging over my shoulder."

She spoke slowly. "I did not know. If that is true I am sorry."

"Keep your sorrow to yourself," he said angrily. "I'll have none of your pity, madam."

"St. Leger," she repeated. "St. Leger."

"Aye, St. Leger who laid his hands on you." He pulled her to him roughly, his hands heavy on her shoulders. He let them slide down her back slowly, across the curve of her waist, down her thighs. "St. Leger tried—but I succeed."

"Let me go! Let me go!" She was sobbing. "Oh, do not hold me so! It is beastly. It is lustful. Let me go!"

"Go!" he said thickly. "Go and complain to Sir Richard if you want. I shall claim harvest law for my kiss."

She put her fist against her lips to keep from crying out. Suddenly she turned and stumbled down the sheep path toward the house.

Colin let her go. He watched her over the first knoll until she was lost in the shadow of the hedge, behind the French tennis-courts. He threw himself on the ground and looked up at the sky.

I'm a fool, he called himself in disgust; a fool. I should have got her with child. . . . And swung from a gibbet, his better guide added. . . . Well, no woman is worth the gibbet. He began to laugh silently. She was terrified, he thought. That little wild one was as tame as a cony in my arms. . . .

It was not so difficult to tame them after all.

BOOK II
ELIZABETH'S
CAPTAINS

CHAPTER 9
EAST THE WATER

Grenville, accompanied by half a dozen men of the Stowe household, rode to Bideford in North Devon.

Here his guests Raleigh and Sidney were to take ship for Bristol after a conference with the merchants. Before they talked with Bristol men Grenville wanted to make sure what ships and supplies were available at Devon's own port. Merchant venturers of Bristol had for some years been instrumental in establishing trade with India and Cathay by the Cape of Good Hope route, following the example set by the Portuguese navigators. Sir Francis Drake had opened the possibility of the new route around Cape Horn, but that had not yet become a commercial reality.

The Spanish were taking more than their share of gold and silver from South America. The Plate Route from the Spanish Main to Europe yielded prizes in Spanish galleons, rich in treasure, to English ships.

The shrewd merchants of Bristol knew it was to their advantage to have a part in new ventures, and bought shares in freebooter enterprises. The Queen herself, secretly out of her private fortune, had taken shares in Drake's and had received a magnificent return in gold.

Raleigh wanted to get money from the Bristol men. Grenville had been against the idea. "Let us finance the whole venture in Devon. Let us take the risk and reap the gains," he had told his cousin. But Raleigh was already committed to at least one Bristol merchant, and Grenville had had to yield.

"I can provide at least three ships, perhaps a fourth, if the yard at Cleave House have it off the ways by April," Grenville told him. "I will hold my ships in the Appledore Pool as they come in from Lisbon and the coastal trade. If we sail in the spring, that will give the shipyard time for repairs, new sails and rigging. How many ships do you plan to send?"

Raleigh said, "I'd like to send seven, but I think five will be all we can outfit."

This conversation took place as they rode along between

the Devon hedges on their way to Portledge, Richard Coffyn's estate on Bideford Bay. Here they would stay the night and meet Dame Philippa, who had travelled down from Stowe two days before on her way to London.

The evening had turned chill and rain threatened all the way from Clovelly Cliffs. They had seen the dark mass of Lundy Isle rising from the sea. "A true sign of rain," Sir Richard had told them. "I've never known it to fail."

"Do you still own Lundy?" Walter asked.

"Yes, though I've thought to sell it. It gives me small revenue and much trouble. It is the haunt of piratical seamen, and I have not sufficient police to enforce the law. If I could sell it, I could build more ships," he said thoughtfully, his eyes on the island, and repeated, "build more ships. There is fortune in ships and in trade."

"You must own half of North Devon now," Sidney remarked. "Why do you seek more fortune?"

"The Fortescues, the Stukeleys, the Monks and the St. Legers have larger holdings than the Grenvilles now. Each generation of us has sold land unfortunately." He didn't say it aloud, but he had already made arrangements to sell another manor in order to finance more ships.

They had come to the gates that marked the entrance to Portledge.

"I don't seem to remember a Coffyn on your lists of available young men for our venture," Raleigh said as they rode among the woods in the vale that led to the house.

"No, there isn't a Coffyn who can go," Grenville told him. "His sons are too young. Richard himself is too lame from wounds in the wars."

They paused as the rambling stone house came into view. It was set deep in the vale between high rolling hills, which were partly wooded in oak and beech, partly lush green meadows where red cattle grazed. Portledge had been the seat of the Coffyns almost as long as the Grenvilles had been overlords of Bideford. It reached from Allwington to Bideford Bay, with many farms and tenants to bring wealth of the earth to the lord of the manor.

Grenville's young men galloped past the Norman portal and up the path toward the high-walled gardens. They dismounted at a gate in the old wall and hurried to their quarters in the monks' cells within the walled court-yard. Here the bachelor guests were always quartered. There were young

120

women staying at Portledge, and there was a pleasurable anticipation of a swim at the beach. Then they would return and array themselves in their best doublets and hosen and soft shoes before the supper hour. There was sure to be gaiety at Portledge, music and perhaps a ball in the picture gallery.

Raleigh and Sidney dismounted stiffly, unaccustomed to hard riding. Coffyn, limping, led them through the flagged entrance. Sidney paused to comment on the Spanish armour, mounted on pedestals on either side of the entrance. Someone had thrust a red rose through the gauntlet of one figure.

Coffyn, a thin man with a long nose and sand-coloured hair and beard, said, "My daughters take turns in ornamenting the Spaniard. They try to conjure up the handsome dark-haired *caballeros* who once wore the armour."

"Ah, youth! Youth!" Sidney exclaimed. "I wish I had not left that age behind me."

"Magnificent armour!" Raleigh commented.

"Yes, a trophy from a stiff fight—the Low Countries. I have another trophy here." He indicated the leg that dragged so when he walked.

"I hope no Spaniard finds that armour here," commented Grenville.

"What, Spaniards invade our Devon! Not while we can fight our good oak ships," Coffyn boasted.

"One never knows the strength of the Spaniard. He is a tough enemy and very resilient." Grenville spoke grimly. "One never knows. Each planning the Spanish make toward invasion brings them nearer success. When you think of how little strength is in our navy these days, I sometimes wonder. Now under King Harry we *had* a navy."

"The Queen is all for trade rather than fighting ships" was Sidney's comment.

"No trade comes without a fight, and a country must fight constantly to maintain it. Ship of war and ship of trade go sail to sail; the one complements the other," Coffyn maintained.

"Trade! Trade! You think only of trade, Coffyn, and ships." Raleigh laughed.

Coffyn stood aside at the door while his guests went inside. They walked into the great octagonal hall where a fire burned brightly in the stone fire-place. Other guests were assembled— James Stukeley, one of the Fortescues, other neighbors who had come to meet the distinguished guests. There was talk of the new venture that evening and arguments for and against it. While the elders talked, the young folk danced. In the morning they would ride on to Bideford four miles distant.

The company rode down the narrow Northam Road and paused to glimpse the beauty of the river and the curve of the bridge arches. The small white town nestled in the fold of the hills, with staunch stone houses along the quay.

They stopped at the chapel near the bridge-head. Grenville went inside to kneel for a moment at the tomb of his ancestor Sir Theobald, whose effigy in stone, with his little dog at his feet, was beside the altar.

Sidney lingered in the doorway, where once a Saxon portal stood. The Grenvilles are still feudal, he thought, still living in the long past. Shut off from the changing world of London, they are as mediæval as though the moats still surrounded their castles, and each morning and night the drawbridge rose and fell and shut out the world. The world Richard lives in is within the confines of his own acreage. There he is lord—at Stowe, at Kilkhampton and again at Bideford. . . .

"It is amazing!" he said to Raleigh, who had come out of the church to join him. "It is amazing that so splendid a life is still lived in our times. Indifferent to the world without are these little islands within our little island."

"These shires, these independent people of the shires, make England great," Raleigh answered. "Here you see our strength; in London you see our weakness. God grant the shires stay strong forever!"

"Amen," said Sidney fervently. "Amen."

Grenville's house stood close to the bridge-head, with the quay and the river and the shipyards in East the Water in plain view.

Dame Philippa stood near a window in an ante-room, watching the upper road. Grooms waited near the doorway to lead the horses down the quay to the stables. Footmen were there to carry saddle-bags to the rooms. The great gloomy town mansion was in gala array.

Her journey from Stowe to Bideford had been a succession of feasts of welcome by the country folk. But Bideford would top it all. As for her own feeling, there had been enough of feasting and long talks among the men-folk about Virginia. County life began to pall. She was ready for gay evenings of bright, brittle laughter, inconsequential conversation, a stolen kiss or two behind brocade curtains in a window embrasure. Things that she had painted as abhorrent when she talked about little Mary with Richard Grenville at Stowe resumed their lure.

Too serious, these men with a purpose. They gave no thought to women. They were moving in a man's world where feminine frivolities had no place. To be excluded was not to Philippa's liking. Soon she would be home in London. She was ready for new adventure. A little flirtation with Philip Sidney was not undesirable, even though he had lately been so devastatingly in love with Penelope Devereux Rich. She did not take too seriously his recent marriage to young Frances Walsingham, Sir Francis' daughter. She could think of her only as a little girl, and the marriage only as a family arrangement entered into on the rebound. She was glad he was riding up to London with her, and Raleigh well left behind at Bristol. A night at Bath would be pleasant, and no one would know whether she slept alone or had an ardent bedfellow. Philip was handsome as a god. She wondered why she had not thought of him as a lover before. The many times she had stayed with his sister at Penshurst, the thought had not come to her—or to him, for that matter.

But that didn't disturb Philippa. She knew well it was the woman who lighted the fire. Perhaps he would be slow to set aflame. What was it he had said last night—that all cats were grey in the night? The thought amused her. Perhaps his experience had been unfortunate, and the cats rather tame. She hugged her slender arms about her breasts and laughed. Let wild-fire whirl over him and give him a new world where all cats were not grey in the night. Let a thousand flames of joy spread over him, if he sought her bed, wild vicious flames that consumed and left no ashes of regret.

She saw the riders halt at the gates. She turned and walked swiftly down the long hall to the stairway. She must have time to dress carefully tonight. Tonight would be the beginning of a campaign. It must be quiet, subtle, with no gaucherie. He must pursue me, not I him, she thought. His dignity will not allow common dalliance. What mood will be mine—all innocence, boldly innocent; or wise in love, as wise as Lilith?

She hummed a song as she moved about her chamber, waiting for her woman to lay a perfumed bath: "My true love hath my heart, and I have his."

Richard Grenville, leaving his guests to their own devices and comfort, mounted his horse and rode across the Long Bridge on his way to the shipyards in East the Water. He rode at a sprightly pace, followed by Colin, his sole attendant. The Haven of Bideford had built ships since the time of Henry V, when the Admiralty ordered Bideford yards at Appledore Pool to build large vessels for the King's fleet.

The tide ran deep and strong at the quay near the street of the smiths, and ships up to one hundred tons' burthen, with prows and sterns greatly elevated above the water, were fashioned in these yards.

Many folk in the narrow crowded street touched their caps to Richard Grenville as he rode along, and greeted him with courtesy. Some he knew by name and with them he drew rein to speak a word.

Presently he came to the gates that led to the yards, where he found the small stone office of Edward Chapman, a cousin of Raleigh who lived at Buckland Brewer. Now superintendent of the yard, Chapman and his young son John, a lad of fourteen, walked with Grenville to the ways, where his ship the *Virgin God Save Her* was drawn up for caulking. A ship of two hundred tons, she had been launched two years earlier and had already made several trips to Portugal and the Azores. Near by was the bark *St. Leger*, one hundred sixty tons, owned by Grenville's brother-in-law, waiting its turn on the ways. The bark *Fleming*, two pinnaces and one snow were farther downstream.

Chapman, thin, with a high-bridged nose and light-blue eyes, stood taller than Sir Richard. He had deep lines from nose to lips, and the flat planes of his face showed the bony structure beneath. He coughed violently and confessed a cold that had kept him abed for some weeks.

He said, "Sir, we launched a ship yesterday. It now lies safely at the dock at Cleve House, where she will be ballasted —a hundred and four tons—and rigged to go over the bar at a moderate tide."

"Who owns her?" Grenville queried.

"Mr. Gorges, your relative, sir. He will load her with spirits, cordage, linen and cotton and some earthenware from Wales."

"To trade with Portugal?"

"Also woollen goods billed to Portugal, but the rest of the cargo goes to Turkey."

"I wager some gets to Spain instead of Portugal. Trade knows no enemies," Grenville remarked. He dismounted and tossed his reins to Colin. "Tie up the horses. I will go with Mr. Chapman to his office." He turned to young John. "Have you finished building your boat, lad?" he asked.

"Sir, it was finished last midsummer."

"Have you taken her outside the bar?"

"Sir, we have sailed her as far as Padstow, and she handled like a veteran."

"Good, lad. You'll be building ships as staunch as all your people have built these long years."

"Thank you, Sir Richard. That is my hope." He glanced at his father, smiling. The elder man smiled back. They were as alike as two pease.

"Not until you have spent a year or two at Cambridge," his father remarked.

The boy asked, "But, sir, how can Cambridge help me build ships?"

Sir Richard added a word: "Mathematics, my boy. Euclid."

"That's what my father says, and Cousin George."

"Ah, George Chapman, the poet who writes plays. I had forgotten he was your kin. If he would take you under his wing, you would be in good fortune indeed," Sir Richard said. "Now suppose you show Colin your boat. What kind is it, a sloop or a ketch?"

"A snow, sir, and very sturdy and seaworthy." The boys went off.

Sir Richard watched them striding away, headed for the quay. "How old is John?" he asked Chapman as they walked to the counting office.

"Going on fifteen," Chapman answered.

"I'm sorry. If he were older, he would be a fair one to navigate a ship for me when I go on my next voyage to Virginia."

Chapman raised his heavy eyebrows. "Virginia? Are you thinking of sailing to Virginia?"

"Yes, I'm making up an expedition to sail to the New World in the spring. That is why I have come to see you today. I want to know what ships may be had, and want you to look through the Sessions Book of Bideford to find out what shipwrights and quartermasters may be available for the voyage. I want sober men and diligent, those who will work

125

to the satisfaction of their officers," Grenville added as they entered the office.

Chapman pulled forward a chair. "Be seated, Sir Richard. I will have my lists brought up. In the meantime will you not tell me more about this Virginia expedition?"

On the way back Sir Richard stopped at the rope-walk where the long lines of hemp lay, fresh dipped in tar. Under a roof shed near by men were making ropes for rigging ships, combing hemp, spinning two or three strands into strong lengths. A shallow cistern filled with liquid tar had a windlass attached to the lip. Here a man fed the rope into the tar while a boy cranked a windlass which wound the well-tarred rope.

Colin, returned from viewing John Chapman's snow, stood watching while his master talked with the foreman. It was a new thing to him and new things he found of interest.

As he started across the long bridge on the way back to Grenville House, Sir Richard motioned Colin to ride closer. He had observed the lad's close attention to the rope making. He listened to the questions he asked young John Chapman about ships. An eager mind, was his unspoken thought. A good lad to have close beside me on the voyage to look after my interests.

He questioned him discreetly, learning something of the way Colin's mind worked, and he was pleased with what he discovered. It was quite apparent that Colin held no grudge against him for the branding. Sir Richard was deeply chagrined when he learned the truth of that little affair. Colin had not told him that John St. Leger was the culprit. He liked that; it showed good strength of character to accept the punishment. No tittle-tattle, but a lad who knew his place. He thought of Dame Philippa's remark that Colin learned faster than any of the young squires because he was eager for information. "A mind in which curiosity is lively" had been her comment. Another thing Philippa had said came to him: "Take a good look at his features and his carriage. Does he not have something in him that favours the Grenvilles?" Perhaps she was right. He glanced sideways at Colin. His Uncle William had been blond, with eyes as blue.

"Who was your mother, Colin?" he asked abruptly. A dark look crossed Colin's face. For a moment he hesitated. "Sir, my mother is dead."

126

"And your father?"

"He also is dead."

"And your name?"

"Colin." Nothing more. No explanation.

There was a fine dignity in the boy, Grenville thought. He would say no more. When he returned to Stowe, he would question Nurse Marjory or old Pooley about Colin. He thought of the numbers of young Grenvilles who had visited Stowe—their cousins the Champernownes, Gilberts, Arundells and St. Albans, who all had Grenville blood in them. Young blood sought young blood, and there were a dozen young milkmaids and farm girls to meet under hedgerows in the spring or the heat of summer. The lad was sixteen or thereabout. Sixteen years. . . . He must have been begot in the year 1569. He began to think back. Sixty-nine—that was about the time of the turning point in the relations between England and Spain, when Philip made his plan to send the Duke of Alva to the Netherlands to crush the Protestant resistance . . . the year when the northern earls were rising and when the Duke of Norfolk was flirting with the idea of marrying Mary of Scotland, a wild notion that cost him his head. Pope Pius excommunicated Queen Elizabeth about that time. Where was he, Grenville? Oh, yes, he remembered —part of the time in Ireland. But he came home when his Catholic cousin Sir John Arundell of Lanherne and Sir William Godolphin were at the head of a commission to muster Devon and Cornwall from Land's End to the Bristol Channel. A silly business, which died aborning.

He'd gone up to Parliament about that time as Knight of the Shire. There was trouble then over changes in the Book of Common Prayer, and his cousin Humphrey Gilbert became a defender of the Queen's prerogative in Parliament. Ah! He smiled a little under his close-trimmed moustache and beard. An incident came to him, one of those quick flurries of passion that sometimes overtake a man at the sight of a woman's bosom or of the curve of a thigh under a rainsoaked garment. Could it have been . . . He glanced covertly at the boy. One never knew in these cases whether one has planted a seed.

That midsummer night, when he rode in from a late visit in Kilkhampton . . . He had dismissed his groom, he remembered, and ridden alone. The moonlight was bright. Near the upper gate of King's Park he heard a woman cry out. He had reined his horse and dismounted, gone in through the gate. There he saw a farm lad making a poor attempt at covering a girl with his body. He sent the man packing with a lash of his riding whip about the yokel's shoulders. The girl, her hair falling over her face, her soft bosom showing under the torn kerchief, jumped to her feet, arranging her skirts with swift, frightened motions of her hands. The fragrance of new-mown hay was in his nostrils. The girl was young and soft and desirable. . . . Strange, he could remember so much detail after these years and could not remember whether he took the girl or not.

They had come to the gates of Grenville House. He dismounted at the block and left Colin to take the horses to the stable. His mind turned to the business at hand. He would let Raleigh convince the merchants of Bideford of the desirability of giving monetary aid to purchase ships.

Chapman had told him that the *Tyger* was available. The great door swung open and he entered the hall, walked swiftly to his room without encountering anyone except the lackey and footman wearing Grenville livery.

One thing was certain. At Raleigh's behest he had, by letter, engaged the attention of Dominic Chester, a merchant of Bristol. Bristol had been made ready to take shares in his earlier planned venture—to circle the globe—back in 1573, when certain gentlemen of the West Country were desirous to enlist themselves and their goods in the service of the Queen Majesty and the promotion of trade.

"May Francis Drake be damned eternally!" he said aloud in the silence of his own chamber. It was Drake who had snatched his idea and prevented Grenville from accomplishing that great adventure. Not only had he ruined Grenville's great plan, but he had, by subterfuge, got the Grenville manor of Buckland Abbey. "May he be eternally damned!" he repeated. He shouted for his man, who came hurriedly, alarmed by the volume of the summons. He stripped his master and followed him to the antechamber where the bath was ready. As his man scrubbed him energetically, Grenville's mind fell away from the thought of Francis Drake and turned again to the farm girl under the hedge on the midsummer moonlit night. Did he or did he not take the maid? Try as he would, he could not remember, and the question that had risen in his mind—could he have sired the blond Colin?—remained unanswered.

Sir Philip Sidney left the company of merchants and sought the company of Dame Philippa where she sat in the small room off the great hall. It was a pleasant room, with a deep seat in the window that looked out on the quay, a few chairs, and a table on which a footman, at Philippa's request, had left a flagon of wine and a few silver cups.

Sidney seated himself near Philippa at the window. "I could bear it no longer," he said. "The same talk, over and over. I know the words Walt will utter before they pass his lips."

"Are the Bideford men interested?"

"Yes, I think so. Walt is playing them off against the Bristol merchants. You know there is a fine competition in trade."

"Is Richard using his influence to persuade them to join the venture?"

"No. Wisely he sits back and listens. His part is to select the men who make up the colony, not to collect the funds. But I notice he has put his name down for a goodly sum."

"I know he is selling one of his manors to get money," Philippa said.

"I had no idea it was so important to him. Grenvilles don't like to sell land any more than the Sidneys. . . . But let's talk of something else, my dear Philippa. I imagine you are pleased with the idea of going back to London after so long an absence."

"Almost a year!" She sighed. "The country has advantages but one misses the stimulation of active, brilliant minds. Tell me what goes on. Has Mary Sidney found a new poet to write verse to her charms or a playwright to read to her?"

"No one new, I think." Sidney stretched his arms and rested his sleek dark head against the yellow brocade curtains. "Ah, yes, one—unknown quite until she found him. I can't recall his name, but he sits at her feet making calf's eyes. He has written a verse beginning "No spring till now . . ."

"I think it a lovely line," Philippa said slowly. "There was no spring in this world until I met you." She looked at him, her eyes lovely with innocence. "That is what he meant, wasn't it?"

"I suppose so," Sidney replied. "The sentiment must be pleasing to women. Mary has had it painted on her latest portrait, set in a wreath of leaves or flowers. I really don't understand the symbolism."

Philippa did not answer. She took up a lute and touched the strings softly with her long white fingers. "You are jealous of the unknown poet, Philip. You wish you had written those lines in a note to some fair one."

He laughed. "Perhaps. Who knows what lies underneath the mind of a man of thirty? Jealousy, passion, love, ambition —who knows?"

Philippa hummed a little, then murmured a few words of a ditty Sidney had written:

> "My true love hath my heart, and I have his,
> By just exchange one for the other given:
> I hold his dear, and mine he cannot miss . . ."

Her voice was pleasing. She looked at him as she played. Was there a question in her lovely blue eyes? He leaned toward her, seeking in the dim light to read her face.

> "There never was a better bargain driven."

He took up the tune.

> "My true love hath my heart . . ."

Her hand fell on the strings with a jangling sound. Her voice was very low; her eyes were veiled. "Have you no place in your life for a woman who can love? Do you think only of your early love?"

The room was silent; the moonlight lay on her face and her eyes looked, not blue, but black and mysterious.

"Only of Penelope?" he questioned. He was looking at her, not moving. He fell silent.

I have said too much, Philippa thought. She too, was silent, not moving. Her small plans had failed. Philip Sidney had no thoughts away from his beloved.

After a little he laid his hand over hers, but he refrained from speech. Philippa forgot the planned intrigue. She was stripped of old superficial thoughts. She yearned over him, as a mother yearns over a child, meeting defeat and loneliness. A tenderness she had not known she possessed rose in her heart, engulfing her. She wanted to soothe him, comfort him, share the lonely brooding thoughts that engulfed him. She could no longer stand the silence.

"Do not shut me from your thoughts," she breathed.

"My thoughts are dismal things. You would not want to share them."

She moved a little into the moonlight, knowing that moonlight became her, her white skin, the silvery glisten on her blond hair.

"Dismal and dark," he said half to himself. "I think of my own doom."

She shuddered at his tone. "What is it, Philip?" she whispered. "What is it that overwhelms you, that makes your eyes so tragic?"

"I do not know how the thoughts came."

She caught his hands, forgetting herself, thinking only to confort him. "Tell me! Tell me!"

"It is the way of the Sidneys to think of their doom. It is thought of my death . . . on a field of battle . . . far from England."

"What are you saying?" Philippa cried, caught up in his dark thoughts. "What are you saying?"

"I thought you knew of the prophecy, it is so old. I thought Mary must have told you."

"No. I do not want to know. I do not believe old wives' tales. You are young. You will live long, long, to the glory of England. Oh, Philip, you cannot, cannot die." She was trembling violently. He put his arm about her shoulder.

"There. You are shaking as though you had an ague. Listen, my sweet friend: I am going to London; from there I go out to the Netherlands under Leicester. I will not return. I shall die on a battlefield. All this is foretold, and in my heart I know it to be true."

Philippa put her hand to her face. Tears streamed down her cheeks.

His arm tightened about her shoulder. "Does that hurt you so much, my sweet?"

"I cannot bear it!" she whispered, her face against his.

"I did not know," he said wonderingly. "I did not know. Nor did I know before that you were so beautiful, so desirable."

" 'No spring till now,' " she whispered.

" 'No spring till now,' " he repeated. He got to his feet and pulled her to him. The lute which lay on her lap fell to the floor, giving out a faint discordant tone.

CHAPTER 10
SOME LETTERS

Richard Grenville let the words and arguments rumble about him. Talk of ships, of ways and means went on endlessly. He would have liked to escape from the room as Philip Sidney had escaped—by the simple expedient of walking out. He felt sorry for Walt, seized as he was in the vise of questions flung at him by the shrewd Devon men, who were first of all suspicious of Londoners. So often they had been betrayed by politicians and men intent only on moving themselves forward, ambitious men who had forgotten the soil that nurtured them. They were like yeomen who ploughed and planted and took from the soil without putting anything back to make it fertile.

They said the kingdom was depopulating from the increase of enclosures and from decay in tillage. They sorrowed over restraints put on the exportation of corn, while full liberty was allowed to export produce of pasture, hides, wool, leather and tallow. They complained bitterly about the high cost of everything. Prices were rising to a remarkable height, some indeed had doubled. That would make for stagnation. They wanted to tell of their grievances as merchants and landholders.

Because Raleigh was influential, they must tell him their woes. The extravagances of great men were spoken of. Raleigh protested he was not informed that the Earl of Derby had two hundred and forty servants; or that when the Earl of Leicester gave the Queen an entertainment at Kenilworth, three hundred and sixty-five hogsheads of beer were drunk. He disclaimed any knowledge of Burghley's plate, presumed to be no less than fifteen thousand pounds in weight. Was it true that the Queen never gave away habits she had worn, but put them away in wardrobes, until they now numbered three thousand garments?

Raleigh cast an anguished glance at Grenville, who came to his aid then by bringing the merchants back to talk of supplies for ships and the bright prospect for the port of

Bideford once trade was established with new and prosperous colonies in Virginia.

The evening ended finally, not without pleasure to Raleigh, when the company moved unanimously to undertake a great share of the venture. The worshipful mayor made the last talk. "Let it be the ships from Bideford Haven, lads. Have we not the stout oak, the stout men with stout hearts, to carry forward a great undertaking? Yea, and the Bideford black to paint the ships and the boys to sail them?"

A rousing cheer and lifted mugs greeted the mayor's words, and the evening came to an end. The merchants of Mill Street and of High Street, the Magnus Vicus of Roman days, took up their velvet caps and proceeded homeward, well satisfied. They were rich men, made rich by trade; so rich and important had they become that Queen Elizabeth had been led to grant them a new charter, which empowered the election of a mayor, aldermen and burgesses. Now they would be first to capture the Virginia trade, through their overlord and good friend Richard Grenville. So they walked home, that moonlight night of August in the year 1584 in good content.

Grenville sat down at a table in his cabinet and took up his quill to write to his wife:

Dearest:
Our guests have departed over the Long Bridge on their journey to Minehead, where they will take ship for Bristol and thence to London.
I think Walt was happy at the outcome. I was happy for him, and I liked him far better here than at Stowe. The longer he is away from London, the more he sloughs off the fictitious character that he has acquired as a courtier. A man may have courtesy and good breeding without losing kindness to all men, save only his true enemies.
Walt seemed to be franker, for he knew he was among folk who would not thrust a knife in his back or run to the Queen backbiting and talebearing. At first he seemed like a man living in the shadow of the Tower, but the longer he breathed free Devon air, the freer his mind became. It pleasured me to see him emerge a Devon man once more. He even talked of buying Hayes Barton in East Budleigh. This was, as you know, his birthplace. I was astonished when he told me that his father never owned that land, merely a tenancy. This may explain some of his actions: a man without land is a transient, and uneasy.
Philippa was very quiet when she departed with Sidney and

134

Walt. I think she wants the excitement of London, but Devon is bred in her. She told me she would come back to Stowe next spring when I sail on the Virginia journey. That pleases me, for she is good company for you, and she will really be a lady-governess to our children.

I will return soon to Stowe, but take ship from here to Padstow. Please send a letter in care of Richard Prideaux at New Place, for I will stay with him before travelling farther south. I must inspect defenses in South Devon and on St. Michael's Mount. When I am down there I think it will be very wise for me to interest some of the men of the Stannaries in our project. They are making many pounds out of tin mines these days.

Yrs. Faithfully,

RICHARD GRENVILLE

Bideford House.
To my best friend
Mary, Lady Grenville,
at Stowe in Cornwall.
By the hand of Ching.

Postscriptum. I am taking Colin with me and sending the lads home. John must tutor. I do not want him to fail his examinations when he goes down to Oxford.

My Dearest:
I am exceedingly glad to hear from you. I do desire you not to be passionate in my absence. I vow you cannot more desire to have me home than I am to be there; and as soon as I can dispatch my business, I will instantly come away.

News of the Virginia voyage travels in front of me. At the Prideaux' (they send best greeting) I saw Philip Blount, Captain Boniten and Cavendish. They will all sign papers to join us. They tell me young Francis Brooke is eager to go. Since he is a connection of the Dennys of Orleigh Court, perhaps that will influence some member of that family.

Make all haste you can to thresh out the corn for fear it may be spoiled, and observe how many bushels it is.

Let Charles the joiner make a board for the parlour as soon as you can; as plain and cheap as possibly he can make—only two or three deal boards joined together and trestles to stand on, and so long as to reach from the bay window to the little door, but not to hinder the going in and coming out.

We go to Plymouth next day. Colin deserves well of your praise. I think one day to give him the name of William Grenville, or would that displease Your Ladyship? He could remain Colin to the family. He is surely a natural son of some Grenville. One need only to look closely to know.

I will buy for you in Plymouth a broad tablecloth, twelve yards of damask, and narrow damask napkins. Dame Prideaux told me she had lighted on these in Plymouth, also Turkey work for stools and chairs. The damask cloth and diapers are pretty commodities, and I am told they are also cheap.

Your shoes and the children's are in making.

Have the gardeners make holes for trees. I am getting tops and roots from Tremayne.

I have bespoken four plumes of feathers for your bed. You must be careful to make ready the bedstead. I commend you and yours to God.

Resting Yrs. forever,

Richard Grenville

Francis Drake is not at Buckland Abbey, so I was spared calling on him.

Charge Postlett to keep pigs out of my new nursery and the other orchard. Let him use any means to keep them safe, for my trees will all be spoiled if the pigs come in, and I would not for a world.

Fowey, 6th Sept., 1584
To my best friend Mary Grenville,
at Stowe.

I found Dr. Hooker here, the guest of Dr. William Bradbridge, the Bishop of Exeter. He has made many friends for our venture and he will send his stepson Geffrey Churchman to go with us in the spring. I have heard that Dame Hooker is a lowly woman, once the good doctor's landlady. In his simple unworldliness she seemed to be doing things for him out of true kindness, so he married her, and her family as well. We will have the lad at Stowe for a time. D.V., he may be of good character.

Stafford's son Edward will go. All the great Protestant families of Devon seem bound to send a cadet. This pleases me, but I would have with us also some yeomen, well selected, who understand the land and the tilling thereof, for from the good fertile earth we must build our colony.

I have had no letter from you since Padstow. I trust all is well with you, my sweet friend. I will soon be at Stowe, there to rest for some weeks until it is time for Parliament.

I dread home-coming for one reason and one only. There is the matter of Mrs. Paget to be attended to, and I like it not. Contrary women cause even a strong man some anxiety.

Yr. affectionate

R. Grenville

From Exeter
to my best friend
Mary Grenville.
By hand. The messenger is paid, but give him one shilling more.

After he had written to his wife, Grenville penned a letter to Sir Francis Walsingham:

The pier and quay at Boteraux Castle in Cornwall are nearing completion of the repair work. They may well serve as a model for the defence of Dover or Folkestone. The Dover pier should be made of stone and chalk combined, and I enclose a drawing of the masonry.

I think, sir, that this will finish my work on harbor defences which I undertook at your behest.

I take occasion to deny the truth of the reports raised against me of having committed unlawful violence in the parsonage house of Kilkhampton, to the terror and danger of Mrs. Paget, who kept possession of the house after the arrival of the new rector, Mr. Tooker. If any terror was inspired, it was Mistress Paget who inspired terror in the breast of Mr. Tooker.

In the matter of the Cornwall Musters, and the collection of armour and munitions: I have a ship ready to carry cargo to the destinations along the coast, as soon as the officers of ordnance, Mr. Paynter and Mr. Bouland, send same.

I hope this plan will save the Cornish and Devon coast from piratical ravages. John Piers is in gaol at Padstow with several disreputable men. But so long as Sir John Killigrew's servants pass unpunished for smuggling, it is useless to gaol lesser men.
Your assured friend

R. Grenville

Private.
To the worshipful my loving friend
Sir Francis Walsingham,
at The Hatchet
behind St. Clement's Churchyard
in London.
My new man to carry this.

These letters safely on their way by messengers, Sir Richard spent the hour before midnight in his room at the bishop's palace, copying a poem given to him by Dr. Hooker. It was written by another Sir Richard Grenville, his grandfather. It interested him because he himself might have written the lines, so near were they to his own thoughts.

In Praise of Sea-Faring Men in Hopes of Good Fortune

Whoe seekes the waie to win Renowne,
Or flies with wynges of high desire;

137

Whoe seekes to wear the Lawrell Crowen,
　　Or hath the minde that would aspire:
Tell him his native soyle eschew,
Tell him go rainge and seek anewe.

To pass the seas some think a toille,
　　Some thinke it strange abrod to rome,
Some thinke it grefe to leave their soylle,
　　Their parents, kynfolke, and their whome;
Think so who list, I like it nott,
I must abrod to trie my lott.

He sat for a long time looking at the paper and the signature Richard Grenville. Ah, well, other Grenvilles, in earlier years, were questing gentlemen. Perhaps there would be others still to follow him.

Lady Grenville studied her husband's face as he sat by the fire, his dogs about him. They were alone in their chamber. She thought he looked tired, the lines heavy in his face. Ever since he had come back to Stowe a week or more ago, he had spent every day in the saddle riding from one field to another, from vale farm to the hillside acres, talking with tenants, planning for next year's planting. Many yeomen had been tenants at Stowe for three generations, one family for four. Good people all of them. He understood them, and they him. Life was good. The land gave bounteously. But now he must sell another manor, and there wasn't one with which he cared to part. The worst of selling was that the tenant, who held a ninety-year lease, might get a bad landlord, and he didn't like that. But he must have one more ship. He sighed heavily.

Mary looked up repeatedly from her knitting, her eyes on his face, but she said nothing. Long since she had learned not to break in on his abstraction. When the time came, he would tell her what troubled him. She was patient, content to wait, content to have him sitting beside her. These past days had been to her liking—their boys at home as well as their daughters, a family all together. That was as it should be. She could not conceive roaming from the roof-tree and the hearth.

"Mary, I've let the land at Eggafenne to Thomas Snellard. I doubt if he is a good tenant, but since he is married to one of our kin, I could not refuse him."

"He's Alice Grenville's husband, isn't he?"

"Yes, a far cousin, but still our kin. The rent runs from the Feast of St. Michael—one silver penny." He laughed at her expression of incredulity. "I knew you would laugh, but I can't have them wandering about without a home, now can I?"

"You are so generous, Richard. Why do you try to conceal your generosity?"

"It's the land out of Sir Theobald's holding, a good strip of field and two meadows, an indifferent manor but a roof over their heads."

He consulted a paper he took up from the table. "Symon Arthur is granted the right to carry and recarry with carts, waggons, horses and beasts over our lands for a year and a day. If he proves a good carter, I will renew the bill of indenture next year when I return from Virginia.

"I've let one messuage of ploughland with appurtenances in Cokemalone for twenty marks, the rents to be paid at Michaelmas. Then William Hale, bachelor, of Barnstaple, has taken the first close, called Beef Lears, and the soil of the pond in the same field; the west and south files, hedges and fences of Linhay; lease for twenty-one years from Lady day, for one broad piece of gold."

He folded the papers. "So you do not have to worry about these matters, sweet. I do not want you to have too much burthen when I am away. I'll go over the list of tenants with Bernard."

Mary looked up again from her knitting. "You are leaving Bernard behind?" she asked.

"And John also."

She asked, "Have you told them of your decision, Richard? They will be disappointed. I think they count on going."

Grenville took a turn or two about the room. Stopping near his wife, he put his hand on her shoulder. "Mary, it tears at my heart to leave you. Yet something stronger tells me I must go. But I will not take your sons from you. That will comfort you.

"I have made arrangements for John to go to Oxford. Bernard will be in my stead here at Stowe. He is a good lad and with Ching's help will manage. And by the way, when I was in Tavistock, I stopped the night with the Duke of Bedford. He gave me the name of a tutor whom he

139

recommends highly. I have written to the man to come here. He will coach the boys from now until next autumn."

"You think of everything, Richard. I had thought Mr. Tooker could read Greek and Latin with them, but they protested. They say they learned more from Philippa than they ever did from Mr. Paget."

A frown deepened on Grenville's forehead. "Paget! The very name annoys me. Tomorrow I must ride to Kilkhampton to see if his wife has removed herself from the rectory. Women cause all the trouble in the world, i' truth."

Mary smiled gently. "And all the happiness too, Richard."

He leaned down and put his lips to her smooth, cool cheek. "And all the happiness, too."

"If you are going to Kilkhampton will you take a package to Mr. Tooker? I made the singing cakes for the communion, and he should have them, so he won't worry about Sunday and no cakes."

He pulled her to her feet and held her in his arms, his lips to her throat. "You never tire of good works, do you, my Mary? Come, it is late and I must be up at sunrise. Let us repair to our bed."

Before they slept Mary said, "When you talk with the boys, explain to them why they are not to go with you. They will take it hard, particularly if John Arundell and Dick Prideaux are going."

"Very well. I'll talk with them tomorrow."

"Be patient with them, my dear. Boys need understanding and patience, and they are so proud of you, but they are a little afraid. If you take them into your confidence it will make them feel elated. Give them responsibility and they will accept it. They are old enough for the family councils, don't you think?"

"I suppose they are. I'm afraid I haven't given it much thought. How wise you are, my Mary, how wise and understanding!"

Grenville rode between the hedgerows toward Kilkhampton. A few paces behind him were his sons Bernard and John, and in the rear young Colin and Constable Smithers. He rode slowly, his mind heavy with the business before him. He did not relish making war with women,

Puritan women most of all. It had been annoying for Eusebius Paget to turn out so unworthily, getting himself into hot water continually by making accusations against the Rector of Philleigh, saying he was a dicer, and against the Vicar of Gulval because he was a drunkard. But when he accused the bishop of nepotism—and worse—there was nothing to be done for him. Paget was dismissed. This did not disturb Grenville, for Paget had proved more of a Puritan than a Churchman. He gave the living to his cousin William Tooker. Paget had gone peacefully, but his wife, who was an acknowledged Puritan, brought her kin to stay in the rectory and refused to leave.

If he put her out, which he must do, people would accuse him of hounding Puritans, as they had accused him of hounding Catholics. He still smarted from the case of Cuthbert Mayne, whom he had dragged out of a priest hole in Sir John Arundell's castle at Lanherne. Folk did not seem to realize that as Sheriff of Cornwall he had been obliged to carry out the orders of the Queen. She was determined to root out every vestige of Catholicism in Cornwall. The Arundells of Lanherne were known to harbour priests from Ireland. At any rate he had done his duty as sheriff and followed the law, even though it was obnoxious to him, going into the house of his dear friend and hauling a priest from his hiding place.

Well, that was over. Now the Puritans would take issue and put out untrue reports about his cruelty. Only one thing to do with this case: get it over quickly.

He left the young gentlemen at the London Arms near St. James the Lesser lich-gate. He proceeded to the rectory and dismounted, throwing the reins to Colin without words. "Wait here," he said to the constable. He gave a sharp rap on the lion knocker and opened the door.

He found Madam Paget seated in the hall, her new-born babe at her breast. She wore a grey dress with the white ruche neck-piece of the Puritans. She was surrounded by a company of six, who were drinking sweet cider and eating cake. Four of the six occupants of the room he knew; the others were a man and woman he had never before seen. They were laughing and talking animatedly.

When Mrs. Paget recognised Grenville, she snatched the child from her breast and put it in the arms of the woman at her right hand. Hastily pushing her protruding bosom within

141

confines, she began to button her bodice with clumsy fingers, even as she rose and made an awkward curtsy.

"I should be glad of a minute's speech with you, madam," Sir Richard said gravely.

The woman hesitated. She glanced at the unknown man, a dark, beetle-browed person. He stepped forward. "In a matter of business I represent my cousin Madam Paget."

Sir Richard looked at him, a cold, grave look; then he turned. "My business is with you, madam. If you prefer, I will state it before these persons. I give you two hours to leave the rectory. Carts will be here within the hour to move your possessions to a house I have secured for you in Clovelly, a house more spacious than the one you are now occupying illegally."

The woman started to speak. She turned her head from one side to the other, plucking at the mull at her throat. A dark spot began to show on her bodice. The babe began to whimper. It was evident that it had not dried up the milk in the woman's breast.

"I will not leave," she said sullenly. "Mr. Kempthorne, the justice, has told me I need not move from here."

"She need not move. That is the law," the man said belligerently.

Sir Richard did not pay the slightest attention. "Two hours I give you. If you are not ready to leave peacefully by then, you will be removed. If you prefer to be removed by the constable, I withdraw my offer of a house in Clovelly with a year's free rent. No use barricading yourself again, for I will have you brought before the Stannaries Court charged with trespass."

Without listening to the chorus of voices, the wails of the woman, the crying of the child, he turned and walked out of the room. At the door the constable waited for instructions.

"Go inside, Smithers. See that they do not pack any articles belonging to the rectory. Put a seal on the study before they get to it."

"Will she leave peacefully, sir?" the man asked. "She's been very cantankerous, very cantankerous, sir."

"I think she will leave," Sir Richard said grimly.

Colin held the stirrup. Grenville threw a long leg over the back of his horse. "I've given her two hours. If she hasn't gone by then, you'll find me at the London Arms."

He rode off down the street. The constable watched him

cross the circle to the inn. Smithers shrugged his shoulders and went inside the door with a certain amount of swaggering confidence. After all, this time he had Sir Richard to back him up, Sir Richard within stone's throw at the inn.

When Grenville went into the inn, he found his sons had been joined by Arthur and Diggory Tremayne and John Harris. While they ate, he regaled them with his experience.

"I gave the woman and her followers no time for words of protestation. I find success in giving orders, and no success in asking folk to do thus and so." He attacked a large portion of well-cooked joint with gusto and washed it down with a mug of ale. "Most folk want to be told," he added, eyeing the young men. "Remember that. There are always a hundred men to follow the one who leads."

They were eating the sweet, served by a pretty rosy-cheeked girl, when John, who sat by the window, exclaimed, "There go the carts!"

The others went to the narrow window. Madam Paget, her child and the two self-styled cousins were in one cart; the other two carts were piled high with household goods. They looked away from the London Arms as the carts rattled off down the road that led to Clovelly Village. Folk were peeping out of windows and doors, waving good-bye, but none went out to speak.

Sir Richard had not moved. He continued to eat his sweet and drink his ale. He was not ill-pleased. In a few moments he had settled a matter that had had the village on its ears for months. Now William Tooker could move in and begin his task of looking after the souls of the Parish of Kilkhampton.

He found his wife in the orangery, where she had been talking with the head gardener. They sat on a bench, while he told her the end of the Paget affair. "If it *is* the end," he said half-heartedly. "I don't want the whole of Cornwall talking and taking sides as they did in the Mayne business. I would not like to have a garbled report reach Walsingham —nor my friends among the Puritans either."

"Why not write to Sir Francis yourself? Let him have the truth before rumour gets to him."

"You are right, Mary. I'll do that this very day. I'll not have these people striking at my reputation. I can forgive an injustice aimed at me, but this horrid business is aimed at the Church."

"Your Puritans, Drake and Hawkins, won't agree with that," his wife said.

Grenville got up and paced restlessly, as he always did when disturbed. "Drake! How pleased he would be to do me an ill turn!"

"Nay, I think your own dislike outruns your reason, Richard. Sir Francis Drake is not likely to speak against you—you who are so just, so brave."

He plucked a small golden orange from a clipped tree and began peeling it. "Little you know the dispositions of men, my sweet. I've noticed that when a man has done another a grievous wrong, he speaks ill of him to cover his own conscience, seeking out his faults and magnifying them. His own guilty apprehensions make the other an enemy." He divided the fruit, laid an opened section in his wife's hand. He smiled down on her, a tender, loving smile.

"Yes, I'll write Walsingham this day. How is it that you have so much wisdom, madam? Do these inspirations come to you as you sit stitching on that great tapestry? I think perhaps you are Penelope. Mind you—no lovers while I am Ulysses and gone on my journey!"

Mary Grenville laughed. She loved her husband in this teasing mood; already he had banished the earlier worry. It was always so. Worry sat on him for a short time only, until he resolved on some action. Then worry fled.

Late that evening Grenville read the letter he had composed to Sir Francis Walsingham. He reviewed the circumstances; concluding with a paragraph which Mary heartily approved.

Whereas I being now prepared to commit myself to the pleasure of God on the seas, having a desire not to leave so great an infamy as this laid on my poor name unanswered before my departure next spring, I have thought it convenient even in plain sort to set down to Your Honour and other my honourable friends the whole and true course of all my dealings in this behalf.

CHAPTER 11
THE MOOR

Parliament met in November. By Christmas the Queen's pleasure and the sanction of Parliament were assured. Raleigh's charter was approved by a committee of eight men, with a large West-Country representation, including Sir Francis Drake. There remained only the financial organization. This was done through Raleigh and Sidney in London, and Grenville in Devon and Cornwall.

In spite of Grenville's distrust of him Ralph Lane was made Governor of Roanoke at the request of the Queen. Francis Brooke, of a strong Devon family, was to be treasurer, Edward Gorges high marshal, and Thomas Cavendish was given a ship. Twenty or twenty-five men were recruited in London by this group against the advice of Grenville.

"It's all wrong," he told Raleigh. "You take twenty-five city men and put them on a savage island for a year, and what happens? They cannot adjust to changed conditions. They are disgruntled, unhappy. They breed discontent. I tell you, the success of such an undertaking is in carefully choosing your men. You want adaptable men, not those who crave the feel of cobbles under their feet and the London street cries in their ears."

Raleigh agreed. "I can do no more," he admitted. "Lane has the Queen's ear. These are his men, and since he is to stay on the island the full year, I do not see how we can keep him from selecting some of his companions. After all, you have the selecting of seventy-five men, Dick. Isn't that enough?"

Grenville grumbled, though he had no alternative but to accept Lane's men.

Once again in Bideford, Grenville settled down to make plans in earnest. Four months was little enough time to secure the men and get ships in order. Five would sail out of Bideford to Plymouth, where a ship and two pinnaces would join the little fleet. The day of sailing was set for the ninth of April. This day was chosen because auguries were good, and the season the best to escape the winds of hurricane proportions which came on the equinox. God willing, it would prove auspicious to all concerned!

Sir Richard had at one time planned to have in his company one man for every hundred of Cornwall and Devon—a hundred was a sub-division of a county, having its own court—but he soon discovered that it was not feasible. He set Bernard and John making lists of the county families, segregating those who had cadets of an age to undertake such a venture. None under twenty, he told them when they started work. He gave them a room at Bideford House for an office. They were happy to have some part in the venture, if only a minor one. Richard Prideaux and John Arundell he put in Edward Chapman's shipyard under his brother-in-law John Stukeley. The more familiar they were with ships, the better was the chance of success. He was often absent from home, riding to Launceston, Padstow and Exeter to rouse interest in the forthcoming voyage. He was determined not to ask any man to go. Each man should come to him fired with desire, proud of the privilege to sail under the Grenville banner.

It was not long before a multitude of young squires and students besieged him and his associates. "To Virginia! On to Virginia!" became a rallying cry in the shires. So great was the enthusiasm that the Queen became alarmed. "Who will be left to guard our shores if the Spaniards come?" she cried to Raleigh. "That insatiable Grenville will absorb all my men and all my ships. Have done, Raleigh."

Raleigh calmed her. He wrote to his cousin Grenville:

I told her it meant only a hundred men and seven ships, very few out of the thousands left to defend her realm. "They go for your honour, fairest and most sagacious of all Queens, to add to your realm by annexation of territory and to your glory on the seas." She was then satisfied. But cease enlistment publicly, my good Dick. I need not tell you that I will sleep uneasily until your ships have sailed away westward. This terror called Spain hangs heavy over Her Majesty's head and disturbs her dreams. She is like a mother partridge who spreads her wings and calls her young to draw close to her for protection. So she would spread her arms and

146

draw in ships and men before the time when we must stand back to back and ship to ship against the Spaniards, who have gained friends and a haven in Ireland.

A man to represent each hundred in Devon and Cornwall is what you desire—a goodly idea, but too many men. What we want is bold young men to represent our Devon and Cornish families. Remember, it was but twenty-eight families of Devon who volunteered their services and swords to Her Majesty to rid her of her troubles in Ireland. Be content with a hundred men, my cousin, a hundred for Roanoke—or shall we say the Roanoke Hundred?

Grenville cursed, tore the letter into bits and let them fall to the stone floor, where the small white scraps buried themselves in the rushes. Tomorrow they would be swept out and burned. Grenville did not take orders readily. Let Walt write orders—he would follow his own course. But by the time he spoke to his wife about the letter his first flush of anger had subsided. What matter? What was to be was to be. There was something of the fatalist about Grenville—a belief that brought comfort to soldiers and sailors. A strong faith in God's divine will and protection had sustained him earlier in battles and would last him to his end. Often in the seclusion of his chamber he knelt in humility asking God's guidance to show him the rightful way. Harsh and stern disciplinarian as he was, he had a trust in his destiny too deep-rooted to be disturbed because he must at times give way.

With some impatience he sensed the situation of Raleigh, caught in the seething ambitions and jealousies, the subtle intrigue of Elizabeth's court. He must at times play his cousin's game, thanking God the while that he, in his own county, had a freedom of action unknown to the habitués of the court.

Let be the worries, he thought. He had tall ships in Appledore Pool, and some on the ways. Two more, *D.V.*, would sail in from Terceira within the month. He could do no more at present than scan the lists of volunteers that were coming in by messenger once or twice a week. Now he would spend the time getting his own affairs in order. A tutor was bargained for already. Bernard must be coached to attend the farm and tenants at Stowe and property near Bideford. Fortunately he was a friendly lad and got on well with the tenants, a necessary thing; friendly, yet not too

147

intimate. He must talk with John about his relations with women. Have a care to avoid unclean women, lest the French evil be the result, which would incapacitate him and make children improbable, or idiots. He would like to arrange a marriage for Bernard with Philip Bevil's daughter Elizabeth before he left, but the thing hung fire. Bernard had shown signs of being interested in sedentary and scholarly affairs. This Richard could not countenance, for Bernard must, as his heir, be prepared to assume the responsibilities of the farms and offices in Devon and Cornwall. John should go with him, not on this journey to Virginia, but the next. Grenville already planned to come home as soon as the colony was seated in order to recruit a second hundred, or perhaps two, yeomen and artisans in the most part, to carry on the work laid out by the explorers. So it would go on to development and trade, and to the devil with the Spanish supremacy in America!

It was dusk when he left Bodmin, but the December moon was full and the wild moor was swept clean of the snow that had fallen earlier in the week. Behind him rode Colin and a groom belonging to Arundell of Trerice, where he had been for a week. Ahead of him was a guide, a dark swarthy Cornishman who knew the moors. With good fortune they might reach Launceston by morning. His host, Alexander Arundell, had protested against night riding, and on Sunday at that, and particularly had he warned Grenville about the country after he left the River Camel and turned northward. " 'Tis an evil country," he had said as they drank the stirrup cup. "Evil, with unknown danger on the wild moors. Evil from the strange folk who cavort among the hills—those ancient folk who built with stones before the Romans came."

Grenville laughed and held his cup to the beaker. "Surely you don't hold with those old tales, Alexander?"

Alexander Arundell shrugged his shoulders. "One hears things," he said. "Those desolate downs hold many a secret. After the great Temple Downs there are other places of danger. Last week a wool train disappeared, and all the men who drove the packs. Next day six men were found near Brown Willy, all dead and laid in a circle, their feet pointing outward—dead, and not a sign on them to show how they went out of life."

Richard extended his cup for another refilling. "I'm not afraid," he said. "I'll keep my eyes and ears alert. 'Tis smugglers who are the danger, not the Ancient Ones."

Alexander looked gloomily at the floor. "I would say caution, if it were a word you knew, Richard. Caution when crossing Temple Moor; caution around the tower of Week St. Mary if you go to Bude by that path; caution around Brown Willy. 'Tis a wild country, and there are mighty cairns where evil folk may hide."

"I've no wish to be lost among the stones of Brown Willy, Alexander. Is not your man familiar with the track? If he is not, what good to send him? I will manage in front of me, Colin to guard my rear."

"My man is armed and he is strong in a tussle."

Richard Grenville had a twinkle in his blue eyes as he spoke. "But what if the Ancient Ones are playing bowls among the stones?"

"Hist! Do not speak so. You may bring evil upon yourself."

Grenville was thinking of the conversation as he rode along in the moonlight night. They had left Bodmin behind them and were now in the narrow track that crossed the wild Temple Moor. So deep were ruts in places that they could glimpse only the banks, not the moorland. No other riders could be seen, nor any human being on the moor, though there were hiding places aplenty behind rocks and cairns.

On a high spot where they could see for some distance, Sir Richard drew rein until the other riders came up. He whistled to the guide who was trotting along ahead on his sturdy moor pony.

There they held council. In the moonlight the guide seemed even more wicked than he had by daylight. He had a low over-hanging brow, his eyes were shifty, his mouth was sullen, and he seemed to have some impediment that made speech almost unintelligible. Grenville was obliged to question him several times before he seemed to understand. Finally he answered that there was a narrow sheep track across the upper moor which they could follow and thus escape going through Launceston. The man considered while his pony pawed the ground, impatient. They might turn off near Trewince Marsh. It would be bad if they lost the path and their horses floundered in the marsh. Men were known to have sunk so deep that the evil ground covered their heads. He seemed reluctant to go by the sheep track, but Richard was determined, and after a brief argument they turned off the road and made a line toward Tintagel, following the North Star.

The terrain changed and grew wilder. Rocks in strange irregular formation gave the impression of an upheaval, with stones pushed up from the bowels of the earth. The moon was rising higher; it spread a strange bluish light over the earth. The shadows cast by small hills and cairns were heavy and dark. The guide fell back until he was but a horse's length ahead of Grenville. Colin and Arundell's groom closed up, as if for company.

In the distance was a howl, which might have meant a wolf, and the sharp bark of a fox. Conies and other small animals scudded across the path in front of them. The guide turned aside and fell in with the two riders behind Sir Richard, murmuring he did not know the path. Since the master had chosen the sheep track, he would please to lead the way.

For a long time they rode onward. An owl hooted close by in a wind-swept tree. A frightened sound escaped the guide and he edged his pony in between Colin and the groom.

"It is no time to laugh," the guide muttered. " 'Twas hereabouts they took off with the wool train. Over there." He waved his hand in the direction of the sea. "They live in these round hills and make merry with travellers, using their heads for bowls."

"Nonsense!" muttered Colin. "Nonsense!"

" 'Tis true. My granddad was telling me this fortnight gone how he laid eyes on them when he be lad. They be quare, ver' quare folk, taller than most, with big eyes to see in the darkness, and their hands fall heavy on a man."

"Silence!" Sir Richard spoke harshly. "Silence, fool! Think to frighten good lads with your talk? Watch your horses now. We must cross a bit of marsh ahead."

Colin said, "Sir, do you wish me to ride ahead?"

"No, stay where you are. I'll lead. 'Tis not a long stretch. Best to cross before the cloud covers the moon."

Colin looked up. A long streamer of cloud lay in the sky, mottled like a mare's tail.

" 'Tis a way they have," the guide muttered. "They cover the moon so they can snatch."

150

Colin said, "Close your mouth, fool!" but there was a catch in his young voice.

"They cover the moon. Then they make their balls of fire in the hills."

"Ride behind, you fool!" Colin shouted. "Get behind, and quit your gibbering!"

They rode slowly, the horses' hoofs sucking up the earth in small cupping noises. "Easy!" Grenville called. "Turn left. The marsh deepens here." On they went, winding in and out, until at last they had all crossed the long thin finger that reached out from the main body of the marsh.

They came to a cross-path. Grenville called for the guide. "Which path?" he asked. The guide got down and ran around in small circles. It seemed as though he were sniffing the earth. Off his pony, he was short-legged and full-bodied, almost a dwarf, with heavy powerful shoulders and long arms. After a time he pointed to the right-hand path which forked from the one they had been following.

"This," he said.

Grenville said, "This seems wrong to me. It lies away from the sea."

"A short time and a turn to the left," the guide said. He mounted his pony and, waiting for the three to pass, fell in at the rear. They were among rocks now and the path narrowed. The clouds were crossing the moon, and the light grew dimmer.

The clouds darkened as they slid across the curve of the moon. A strange sheen seemed to cover the moor, a weird glimmer, not unlike the light that comes with an eclipse. Riding cautiously, they all watched the moon. Grenville thought, When it is all dark, perhaps we had better make a camp. He spoke over his shoulder to Colin and told him to ride forward. Side by side the horses stood while they talked. The horses were restless and uneasy. One whinnied, the moor pony. The moonshine faded, and the moor gradually grew black. The heavy rocks, the round hills were like ink against the grey shadows.

Suddenly the guide made a moaning sound. His voice cracked and creaked with fear. "Look! The moon lights! The moon lights!"

Grenville swung in his saddle. To the left some distance away three or four circular lights hung in the darkness. They

151

seemed to spin as an apple swings from a string. "Moon lights!" the fellow called out again, his voice filled with terror. There was a gurgling sound as though a hand clapped his mouth.

A moment later the groom fetched a frightened cry. "He's gone! He's gone! The guide's gone!"

Grenville rode back, cursing. "You fool, he can't be gone!"

"Sir, he is. He had caught hold of my arm when something wrenched him right off his pony's back. I smelled a sulphur smell! 'Tis the Old Nick himself." The fellow trembled and caught Colin's arm as he rode near.

Grenville circled, calling. There was no answer. The cloud was moving. A dim light pervaded, in which objects became visible again. He saw the moor pony, riderless. It was standing stiff-legged, its eyes wild, its body trembling. The other horses were shaking. Their eyes too were distended. Their hair was ruffled as in a strong north wind.

Grenville cried out in a mighty voice, "Guide! Guide!" An echo came back, "Guide! Guide!" and a sound like laughter.

"God's heaven!" cried Colin. "What's that?"

Grenville spoke angrily. "My voice against a rock. Have done with this nonsense!"

On a sudden the moor pony threw back its head and neighed, the horrible cry of an animal in fright. It reared and struck out with its hoofs. Whirling, it snapped the reins from the hand of the terrified groom and tore off, back toward the marsh. For half an hour they searched, calling, calling. No voice answered. Only Grenville's voice, reverberating.

"We may as well ride on," he said after a time. "The guide will follow us no doubt, now that it's light."

"Sir, he'll never follow." The groom got on his horse slowly. "The moor-folk have got him. Did ye not see their balls of fire and hear their wild laughter?"

"Folderol!" Colin said, but his voice carried no conviction.

Grenville tightened the gorget about his throat. His sword was slung in a boot at his knee. He had his pistols hanging in a leather case on the pommel of his saddle, and a strong knife at his waist. He wore light chain-armour under his doublet. He drew his cape about him; the wind was rising.

He was thinking, Why did the guide choose the right path

152

at the fork? The left was better marked and it pointed in the direction of the sea. What had he said? A short way, then the path would bear left? Instead, it was bearing farther right. His instinct told Grenville something was wrong. He had no belief that the moor-folk had snatched the guide from his pony and carried him off.

"Rein in!" he shouted to Colin. He turned and joined them, his horse brushing close to Colin's mount. "I think we have taken the wrong turn. We will ride back to the forks."

A moan escaped the groom. "Sir, sir," he pleaded, "not the forks! Before God, that is where they lurk! Let us ride on and put their faces behind us."

Colin said nothing. His face was an expressionless blur in the dim light.

"Turn your horse, fellow. We will ride to the forks and take the left turn."

With teeth chattering and hands trembling so they could scarce hold the bridle, the groom followed as they galloped back. "Don't leave me! Don't leave me behind!" he kept calling.

"Spur your horse then." Grenville's voice was harsh; he had no liking for a coward. If Colin was afraid, he did not cry out, but rode close to his master.

They found the forks without trouble and took the path to the left. It was poorly marked until they had gone a quarter of a mile. There it made a half-turn left behind what seemed to be barren rocks overgrown with scrub. Perhaps it was an old wall, or it might be the remains of a Roman camp or earthworks. It was impossible to make out. But the path was strong and well marked here. Grenville thought, There's a reason for this. Faint markings at first, many small paths spread among the stones. Now behind the barrier it becomes strong, as though the folk who travelled it thought they were far enough away for concealment to be no longer necessary.

They rode on and on through the night, sometimes in bright moonshine, sometimes in shadow. Presently they came to a second fork. Grenville continued left.

"A light, sir." Colin rode up close. "A light dead ahead."

The groom crowded them close. "Moor-folk," he muttered. "There will be more shining on the hills. 'Tis danger, sir. Let us ride back."

"I have no desire to back and fill across the moor. We will ride forward, but cautiously, my lads, until we see what is ahead."

"You will see—more lights will come, more lights to lure us to danger."

But no other light appeared. After a time they came to a low-lying pen in which kine were enclosed. The light was a ship's light, swung from a pillar, set before the dark mass of a building. They drew rein.

"Let us dismount and spy out the land," Colin said, standing by his master's knee. "Maybe it is a farm-house, but I hear no dogs."

"Nor I," Grenville answered. "More likely it is a moor inn of evil repute."

"So I fear, master. May I spy out?"

"Go ahead. We will stay by. Wait. Are you armed?"

"My dagger, sir." Colin handed his reins to the groom and disappeared into the shadows.

The groom drew close. "Sir, there is danger," he repeated. "I have smelt it."

"More like you smell the sty. Brace your back, fellow, and sit straight in your saddle. You will have more courage if your back is straight and your head erect."

The moon was under. Colin walked easily, as silently as an animal, until he came to the corner of a building. It felt cold under his extended hand. He drew back quickly, his stomach tight, the hair of his head stiffening. Then he chuckled. Slate. A building of slate that was chill against his palm. He walked slowly around, touching the walls from time to time. Once, twice, there was a break in the wall— a door, a window dark within.

Half-way to the front of the building—and it was a large one, long and low, all slate-covered on the windward side— he saw a chink of light. He applied his eye to the crack. He was looking into the kitchen. An old woman, bent, with a mob-cap over her scraggly locks, was at the fire-place. The window was an opening without panes. The woman's back was toward him, but she was speaking to someone.

"They be gone this some time. Bewse and Kendall go seaward. The wind will turn and mayhap a ship will come in against the rocks. Four men they have beside thyself. Tickle, he takes half a dozen brave boys and rides toward Launceston. There be a train of woolmen coming. Mayhap he will relieve them of the weight of gold they carry to pay the wool farmers."

There was a laugh. Colin edged closer, turning this way and that, until he got the second one in his vision. The laugh betrayed him. It was the guide, sitting at a long table, his elbows on the board, before him a meat pie.

" 'Twas about that I came to the inn this night. A mighty man rides the moor with a poor following, two only. He must have on him a sack of gold."

"Why didn't ye kill he and take the gold?" The woman stood before him, hands on hips.

"Why indeed? He had two with he, and he be dressed in a chain-mail that my blade would do naught but knick. Six men or more would do the trick."

The woman sat down on a stool and began to stir the contents of the pot with a gourd dipper. "Let be, Eyekut. Leave highwaying to they who know how. Best you stick to your smuggling and leading folk astray on the moors. Boys will soon be back and you can tell 'em about the fine gentleman with a bag of gold."

This was enough for Colin. He moved softly out from under the eaves and made his way back to the spot where Sir Richard waited.

"Ah," said Grenville when he had heard the tale. "I was right. Our guide intended us to fall into the clutches of the highwaymen. For that he must be punished."

Colin said quickly, "Sir, the others—the highwaymen—will soon be returned. Had we best not ride—?"

Grenville interrupted shortly. "Have done!" He gave his bridle to the groom. "Stay here until I deal with the villain. Stay you here, Colin."

He strode off toward the house. When he reached the wood rick near the entrance, he found that Colin was behind him. He grunted, but he did not send the boy back. Colin followed him around the house to the doorway where the lanthorn burned.

"Where is the kitchen?" Grenville asked in a low tone.

"Right," Colin answered. Grenville went inside quietly, threw open the kitchen door and banged on the door-frame with the hilt of his sword.

"Entrance in the name of the law," he shouted in a voice so terrible that Colin shrank back.

155

The old woman dropped the ladle. The guide tried to get up from the bench, but Grenville laid the flat of his sword across his shoulders.

"Truss him up, Colin." He threw a bridle part on the table. "Stuff his mouth. I'll deal with the crone."

The guide caught up a long knife, lunged viciously at Colin. Colin had no time to draw his dagger. He reached for the knife, fending off the thrust with his arm wrapped in his cloak. Twice the fellow thrust; twice his thrust was countered. Colin struggled to free the dagger caught in his belt. The guide, with foul words flowing from his evil mouth, pushed Colin back until he stood at the open door of a dark room that gave off the kitchen.

At last Colin got his dagger loose, but just as he did so the guide lunged again and this time pinked Colin in the shoulder. There was no pain, but blood began to drip from the right sleeve of his doublet. His dagger fell from his hand. The guide turned and rushed at Grenville whose back was turned while he dealt with the fighting, clawing woman. Colin cleared the bench in a flash and, before the guide had time to thrust the knife into Grenville's ribs, caught him on the jaw with clenched left fist. The blow jarred him and he swayed. Colin kicked him in the groin. He doubled up, screaming with pain. The long knife fell from his hand. Colin snatched it from the floor.

Before the guide could recover, Colin had his arms pinned behind him and a sleeve of his coat stuffed into his mouth. The woman fought on. She was stronger than one would think, but she too was soon tied up and gagged.

"Out with them!" said Grenville. "I will take them to Camelford and leave them with the mayor for a present." He picked up a candle and looked into a room that opened off the kitchen. "As I thought—bales of smuggled goods. Come. Out with you!" He slapped the woman with the flat of his sword. "Tie them to the horses' tails," he told Colin. For the first time he noticed the blood on Colin's sleeve. "Are you hurt?"

"Only a pin-prick."

"Well, if that's all——Secure now? Let them trot along. Ride ahead and keep a sharp look-out, Colin boy, lest we meet other smugglers coming in along Corbin's track."

"You know the lay of the land, sir?"

"Aye, well enough. In an hour's time we will be in Camelford, before dawn, and the sheriff shall have his men riding over the moor to catch the highwaymen before they waylay the wool train." He looked at the guide tied to the tail of Colin's horse, and the crone dragging along, well secured to the groom's horse.

He laughed. "I could have killed the fellow, but gaol is best. A little persuasion and he will tell the names of his fellows, and they will all lie in Launceston dungeon before another day."

They rode into Camelford as the first rim of light tinted the east. Grenville turned to Colin. "You did well, boy. I would not regret having you stand behind me in danger."

Colin was all but speechless at his master's words. "Sir, oh, sir, if I could always stand near you to do your bidding, I'd ask nothing more of God the Father!"

Grenville turned his searching blue eyes on the eager face lighted by the first rays of the rising sun. For a long moment their eyes met. Then Colin turned away. "Sir, I'm sorry. I spoke without your leave."

Above his beard a smile indented the corners of Grenville's firm mouth. "We shall see what the future brings, my lad." He spoke to his horse. The other horses pricked up their ears and broke into a swift trot. Into Camelford they went, the two frightened captives running behind.

Grenville rode to the square, stepped to the mayor's house and pounded on the door with the hilt of his sword. "Wake up! Wake up!" he cried.

A window was raised. A blond head appeared surmounted by a red night-cap. "Wake up, Mayor of Camelford! It is I, Richard Grenville, and I bring you two prisoners."

The mayor looked down and saw the prisoners. "Before God, what have you here?"

"Smugglers, and if you are quick and send your men by the Corbin trace, you'll catch a netful."

The voices raised the porter. A sentry cried out. A sergeant came running across the square, pulling on his coat.

Grenville said to him, "Take these rascals. A touch of the lash and they will spew out names."

The mayor, clad in robe but without night-cap, opened the door. "Step inside, Sir Richard. A bite of breakfast for you, sir. Your men will be taken care of at the barracks."

"Arundell's groom may go with your servant. This lad is

my squire. He's been pricked in the shoulder. See to his wound. Then he will breakfast with me, Mr. Mayor." He caught Colin's startled glance. A smile came over his lips. "My squire, after the old manner. He has won his spurs this night."

CHAPTER 12
SHIPS FROM BIDEFORD

The quay at Bideford was alive with the town's citizenry dressed in their best. April was at its pleasant prime. Gardens were abloom. A soft breeze blew in from the west up the Bristol Channel and the Torridge. The mayor, his aldermen and councilmen were aboard the *Tyger*, the ship that flew the Admiral's flag, dining with Sir Richard, drinking toasts, making speeches. Half North Devon, great landowners, yeomen, artisans, had come to call a farewell and wish a cheery voyage to the adventurers.

The men from the shipyard had laid off work. Shipwrights, caulkers, sail-makers, cord-spinners and sawyers were in holiday attire. Had they not built the ships, made the sail, tarred the decks and the ropes, and were they not entitled to an active part in the celebration? Merchants of Bideford had their pride. They had furnished the stores to feed the voyagers, selected the implements, the seeds, the cookery and the crockery. The housewives held themselves proud, too, for they had sent aboard the five ships preserves and dried fruits, breads and cake and other products of their kitchens.

The ships that lay in Appledore Pool, the *Roebuck*, the *Lyon*, the barque *Dorothy* and the *Virgin God Save Her*, were trimmed with garlands of flowers which the young girls had made. They festooned the decks and cabins. Unseamanlike, the sailors whispered, but let the maids have their way. Tears would be shed as the ships crossed the bar—tears for young lovers, for sons, for husbands, who sailed out into the unknown Western Ocean. Let them make merry now and dance on the decks and in the market-place with gay whirling skirts and flaunting petticoats, with curls and braids tumbling, lips that smiled tremulously, bright eyes with tears close. Children climbed on rope coils and hung perilously over the side of the quay, or clambered down the stone water-steps to jump into small boats that filled the Torridge from Bideford out toward the bar. How brightly the sun shone on the little white town nestled in the hills! How proud were the lads who

159

had been chosen to sail! How sad were the lads who must stop at home! How enviously they looked toward the ships dressed in gay flags! How jealous they were of those men who walked the quay with arms about maids' waists, unashamed!

Cavalcades clattered down the streets, banners flying. Those dressed in light armour, riding fine horses, were the fortunate young men who were taking ship at Bideford—North Devon men and Cornishmen—old names, Arundell, Gorges, Stukeley, Safford, Courtenay, Rowse and Prideaux. The people cheered and cheered, and the maids cast flowers, as the young cadets and their men rode by.

They would go aboard the ships after the mayor and the burghers came ashore. The rector from Kilkhampton and the vicars from Morwenstow and Hallam were already on the flagship. At sunrise that morning they had blessed each ship, to cast out all evil and leave only good.

When Sir Richard's ships made rendezvous at Plymouth with those of the governor, Ralph Lane, there would be a great ceremony at the cathedral. But here the men had gone to early morning service at the chapel near the bridge-head. They had knelt at the altar and partaken of the holy bread, each with his own prayer on his lips and in his heart.

Lady Mary Grenville had said farewell to her lord the night before. The couple had stayed at Portledge, and she would not go farther, in spite of his protestations.

"Tonight we are together for the last time," she said as they walked down the wood path to the beach. "Tomorrow you will belong to Bideford, to Devon, to the Cornish people, who have come to wish you God-speed. You will belong to them. Tonight you will belong to me."

He put his arm through hers and clasped her hand. "My Mary, I would like to think of you watching my ship sail down the river."

"No, my dear, no. But I will ride to Hartland Point. There on the cliffs I shall watch for your ships and see you out of sight as your sails carry you away."

He started to speak, but she silenced him with her words. "Let me finish, my husband. Do not importune me. I am jealous. I cannot share you, even with our dear Bideford folk or our friends. When you put foot upon your ship, you are the Queen's man, with a great task, a heroic task before you. Tonight . . ." Her voice broke. They had come to the high

160

cliff where the narrow path led down to the water of Bideford Bay.

He held her close, kissing her lips. She broke away from him. "Let us walk down the path to the water's edge," she said. "I have a desire to dip my hand in the water that will carry your ship to the far ocean."

They walked across the shingle to the water's edge. Mary stooped down, unmindful of her flowing skirts. She dipped both cupped hands into the water and lifted them. She stood quietly, her eyes fixed on the west. Lundy Isle stood out clear, and the dim purple line that marked the shore of Wales.

For a long time she stood with extended arms, the water dripping from her fingers. Richard watched her. She was like a Grecian priestess pouring libations to her gods. Perhaps she was. The thought came to him then that there were depths in Mary he had not fathomed. When he came home, they would be close, closer than they had been these years that had passed. They had been the children's years. Now the children had grown or were growing to their own estate. He and Mary would be together. . . . She made a quick movement with her arms and cast the water into the bay. When he saw her face he took her into his arms. "My dear," he said softly. "My very dear!"

The young folk rode down from Stowe. John was glum because he could not join the venture, even though his father had explained to him a week before that he must go to Oxford, and promised that he could go out on another voyage.

"This is only the beginning," he had told his son. "There will be another and another voyage. Ships and more ships will be sent until the Queen's colonies cover the whole of America. It will be only a matter of time until we force the Spaniards out of Florida and take over. So have patience."

"But the first one is the most important, Father," John persisted.

"No, my son, not the most important. The most important will be the one that survives. I have written to your principal at Oxford, telling him that I am committing you to his trust. That is a greater trust, John, than if I gave him my whole estate to administer. I want you to live as a gentleman should, and funds will be available for that purpose. But I warn you against prodigal living. Besides your studies you are to have

161

dancing and fencing for gracefulness and recreation, but do not let these devices interfere with your studies. Decent and genteel recreations are good for exercise and health. You must be a scholar. Bernard has the learning; now he must put his studies to practical use. I have already talked with him. He knows his responsibilities to the land. The Grenvilles have always taken their duties toward the land seriously. I will allow you eighty pounds a year, and ten a year for your servant."

John had asked him for Colin as his servant. "Colin will go with me on the Virginia voyage," Grenville said. "Recently he saved my life, giving no thought that he was weaponless when he came to my aid in peril. When we return, I intend that he shall have tutors. He will be your companion, not your servant."

John was pleased at his father's words. "Good old Colin!" he cried. "Does he know he will serve you?"

"I will tell him today. As to the eighty pounds, John, that amount will defray your diet, your chambers' rent, your clothes and your tutor. Do not write to your mother for money, for I have asked her not to send any. The amount is ample."

"Yes, sir."

"Now a last word of warning. Shun drunkenness. Drink your will, but be not drunken. Keep from drunken companions lest you share their ill repute and be utterly lost in my opinion. Again I warn you to keep within the compass of your allowance, for more you cannot have. Remember that your family has certain standards and patterns of conduct. Do not lower yourself by being less a Grenville than your forbears.

"One last word, my son. Present my service to your tutor." He rose and laid his hands on John's shoulders. "My dear son, I do beseech God to bless you and imbue you with wisdom."

Tears came to John's eyes. He brushed them away with the back of his hand. His father pressed his hands deeper against the lad's shoulders. "Be not ashamed of your tears. I find my own eyes clouding."

He had gone away. John, left alone, struggled to keep back the tears. Just then Thomasine came into the room. After one startled glance at him she backed away without speaking.

"Damnation!" said John softly. "Damnation! The girl is always about, eavesdropping. She will laugh and tell the fellows that she found me blubbering."

For all he knew his father's judgment was right, John could not help showing his disappointment now that the last day had come. The sisters, on the contrary, were in holiday mood, dancing on the deck of the *Dorothy* with John Arundell, Richard Prideaux, young Anthony Rowse of Bideford. Rise Courtenay joined them, and young Stukeley, with several of the Denny folk from Orleigh Court. The girls had brought packets, farewell gifts—knitted hosen, scarfs and new-made banners. Little Mary had stitched a standard bearing the Grenville clarions.

Thomasine moved on the outskirts, sometimes walking along the quay. She was searching for Colin to give him the hosen she had knit, but she could not find him. She had been aided on heel and toe by Nurse Marjory, who seemed to have forgotten her distaste for her. Nurse Marjory herself had sent a fine packet of herbs to Sir Richard, herbs that were health-giving and medicinal. In truth everyone in the north of Devon had brought some gift. The cabins and below-decks were piled high with gifts.

While the young folk were making merry, a solemn ceremony was taking place in the cabin. The worshipful mayor was in the midst of a speech as he presented to Sir Richard a great silver-gilt cup, richly chased, bearing the arms of Grenville.

Though the mayor was chubby and red-cheeked, his face was now set to solemn lines, for the occasion was one of great solemnity.

"In this year of 1585," he began, "a new era opens, one that Devon men will long remember. As you all know, the Grenvilles for many a generation have been overlords of Bideford. Now a worthy son of that ancient family sets his eyes toward a far land beyond the sea, so that he may bring honour and, later, trade to our city. A noble man, a gentleman of very good estimation both by his privilege and sundry virtues, is willing now to hazard himself on this voyage for the love he bears his kinsman Sir Walter Raleigh and for a disposition that he has to attempt actions worthy of honour.

"Sir Walter enjoins him not to tarry in the country of Virginia, but to leave some gentlemen of good worth and a competent number of soldiers there to begin an English colony.

"With him will go Sir John Arundell, Thomas Cavendish, Ralph Lane, Edward Gorges, John Stukeley, Edward Stafford, Philip Amadas, Thomas Hariot and divers other gentlemen and a sufficiency of soldiers.

"I propose, gentlemen, that you drink from this cup which we now present to him so that he may, once each day, drink to Bideford a lusty toast. To the good voyage of each and sundry, that by the grace and kindness of the ever-benevolent God they may come safely on those foreign shores and as safely return to us! But first, gentlemen, to our lady Sovereign Queen, God bless her!"

Toasts were drunk, as many as the names spoken, until the merchants of Bideford scarce knew when they left the ship or how they reached the quay.

Thomasine wandered from group to group searching for Colin, with the packet containing the hosen she had knit for him clasped under her arm.

A rude man tugged at her sleeve as she pushed through the crowd, whispering a lewd invitation. She snatched the arm away and went on. She did not even turn to heed him. She knew that only girls of the town walked alone, those strange creatures who lived in small huts near the river. She had looked inside a hut once and had seen, before the woman slammed the door, a half-dressed man lying on a bed.

The gongs were sounding. The boats that had brought the mayor and his aldermen were going back to shore. She was close to tears when she ran into young John Arundell. He was at the water steps, ready to embark in a skiff that would take him to the *Tyger*.

"John, John!" she called out and started to run to the steps. John saw her and turned back. "Ah, my little cousin!" he cried, clasping her hands. "Have you come to tell me farewell?" He threw his arms about her and held her close. Then he bent and kissed her firmly on the lips—a sweet boyish kiss that had in it affection and some of the sadness of farewell.

"Sweet Coz, be good and I will bring you a red Indian for a slave when I come home. Would you like that?"

Thomasine smiled up at him. She felt a sudden warmth, a loving-kindness for John. With swift decision she thrust the packet at him. "Take these. They are for you. Perhaps they will be welcome when the nights are cold in Virginia."

"Dear Thomasine! Something you made for me? This

164

touches me deeply." He kissed her again, this time with more ardour.

The crowds about them smiled kindly. These partings were sad. Someone from the boat called, "Break away! Break away!"

"I'll write to you if occasion offers," John promised, still holding her hands. "Write me and we will keep the letters till I return. And thank you, sweet Thomasine, for your gift. I shall treasure it because you thought of me while you were working."

She managed to smile at him, hating herself because she had not thought of him at all while she was knitting the hosen, but only of Colin—Colin who wore her brand in the palm of his hand; Colin who hated her. It was not until she was riding across the moor on the way to Stowe that she remembered the little message she had concealed in the toe of the hosen.

Later from the deck John Arundell tried to discover Thomasine in the crowd on the shore, but she had disappeared. The distance between shore and ship widened as the *Tyger* began a slow yawing with the tide. The dear girl, he thought, the dear girl! How beautiful she was, with her clouds of dark hair and her great dark eyes! Why had he not sought her out these weeks? What a fool he'd been! He tucked the hosen in a corner of his sea-chest. He would not wear them until he returned home so that Thomasine might see how he treasured her gift.

The ship bell sounded and the bells on shore. Sails were hoisted, and the ship made ready for the turn of the tide to fall down river. The others of the little fleet would be ready in Appledore Pool to fall into line.

A full complement of sailors lined the gunwales. The gentlemen adventurers were on deck, each with his man behind him holding his house banner. Each ship had its new broom to signify sailing. Crowds ashore sang and cried their God-speeds and farewells.

The banks were gay with moving figures in bright dress. Scarfs and banners flew.

Sir Richard, that man of equestrian stature, stood on the bridge beside the ship's master, dressed in armour, wearing his helmet with waving plumes, its visor turned back.

Ashore the young Grenvilles stood close one to the other, clasping hands, a small circle, away from the crowd: Bernard, tall and commanding, his father in younger years; John more emotional, waving his hand aloft; little Mary and the younger girls beside Madam Denny, in whose charge they were. They were strong in pride yet tearful. Mary turned away as the ship sailed past them.

"Where is Thomasine?" she whispered to John. "I haven't seen her all this afternoon."

John Grenville looked about him. "Nor I," he said. "Where has she disappeared to, the silly girl? Always running off by herself."

"Perhaps she thinks we don't want her. Mother says she is shy." Little Mary spoke anxiously.

John said, "Now don't begin worrying about Thomasine, Mary. She can fend for herself."

"But there are so many people, so many men in high spirits. They might——"

"No fear, sister. That girl is like a wild cat with her claws. Didn't you see Tremayne's face?" He paused suddenly. "I'm sorry, Mary. I forgot Arthur Tremayne is your betrothed. But he is a bit of an ass about women when he is in his cups."

Little Mary's gentle face crumpled as though she were going to cry. "I know," she said in a broken voice. "Ah, John, why is it? Is it because I am not dazzling enough to hold his love?"

John patted her hand and spoke with a man-of-the-world air. "Nonsense, little Mary! Men are like that. They like to stray a little. No harm in it. Arthur'll be as good a husband as the next one." But in his mind he wondered.

They caught up with the others as they came to the gate of Grenville House. They entered the great hall in silence, as if a sort of pall had fallen on them. Indeed the heart of the house had gone from it. The core and centre had sailed away into the unknown.

It was Bernard who broke the spell. He stepped into the place of the host. He was now the man of the house. He rang for a footman to take the guests from Orleigh Court to their rooms. "We will have refreshment in an hour," he said as the girls went up the stair, led by Madam Denny. He spoke to John. "Have Ching send men out in the town to search for Thomasine. God's truth, why must she cause trouble tonight, when we have sorrow in our hearts for *his* departure?"

"God knows, brother! Thomasine has little thought or care for anyone save Thomasine. No doubt she went home to Stowe with some of the yeomanry. So don't worry. Have pleasure, brother. Let us have music and dancing when sup-

166

per is over. Let us be gay, not sad. I am sure our father would wish it so."

"Perhaps you are right, John, but I worry about that girl."

"Don't worry. If she isn't found soon, we'll have the watch notified. But I'm bound to think she is on her way to Stowe, sitting on the knee of some yeoman or lying in the back of a cart."

"Don't be lewd, John. Don't forget she is well-born."

"But badly reared," John grumbled.

Thomasine was indeed riding in the back of a cart, but not bound for Stowe. Instead, she was on her way to Launceston with a kindly old wool merchant and his wife, with whom she had made friends at the quay. From Launceston she would find a way to get to Plymouth. She had time to spare to reach that haven before Sir Richard Grenville's ships made rendezvous with the ships of Sir Walter Raleigh at Sutton Pool. Hanging about at the edges, her eyes and ears alert, she had heard things.

The London men would be in Plymouth—Sir Walter, Sir Philip Sidney and the two scholars in the drab robes. London ladies and gentlemen would be in Plymouth, Dame Philippa among them, and perhaps the Countess of Pembroke. Wild thoughts ran through her head, wilder plans. She lay in the back of the cart on a bed of soft wool, the wool merchant's fat wife breathing heavily beside her. She hugged herself close, her thin arms across her breast.

She had escaped without anyone being wiser. She had two golden crowns in her belt, and the road to Plymouth lay open before her. She woke once. The stars were like great lanthorns in a dome of black velvet. Cassiopeia shone down on her. The old crone at Merlin's cave used to call Cassiopeia her star of good fortune. She lay quietly, warm and comfortable, secure in the belief in her star. After a time she fell into a dreamless sleep.

Ships built under Elizabeth were not beautiful, Grenville thought, as he stood on the bridge of the *Tyger*. He would like to build a ship after the Spanish style, all carved and gilded. Lundy Isle lay off, a purple blotch in the blue water of Bristol Channel—his own island, which he loved, although it gave him trouble enough. There was something in an island that always stirred his blood and caught his imagination. Lundy itself was a sort of haven, a protection for small craft, offering security for the little ships that navigated the Channel; a holding ground where a ship might lie peacefully when the wind was blowing; a pleasure to behold when a ship negotiated White Horse Race or had the ill fortune to be becalmed in that turbulent water.

Today there was no such problem in navigation. He had only to cross the bar. The tide served his ship well. The wind was just strong enough after they passed Appledore. There they had picked up the *Lyon* and the fly-boat *Roebuck*. The *Dorothy*, a small barque, sailed well and kept within easy distance. At the last Grenville had decided against taking the *Virgin God Save Her*. He would save her for the second voyage. The *Elizabeth* was at Plymouth with two small pinnaces, ready to rendezvous at Sutton Pool.

Cavendish would master the *Elizabeth* and carry the London contingent.

The bar was crossed. Clovelly lay snuggled against the cliff. Beyond lay the headlands and the long roll and power of the great ocean.

Richard turned his glass on Hartland Point, on that great barren cliff which the Romans called the Point of Hercules. When they rounded it, he called out that they were coming into a new sea. The mystery of stern dark cliffs, the high promontory led them into a new world.

But Richard Grenville had another thought: Hartland was a boundary between waters that were home and the unknown.

Before him were the West and the terrors of deep ocean. As long as Hartland was in his vision, England was there, strong and steady, to hold him.

The brisk wind filled the sails of the ships. Long rollers caught them. There was no storm, only another mystery of ocean. This would be their daily mead from now on.

He gazed eagerly through his spy-glass. Mary was there, somewhere on that savage rock against which the waves thundered. His last link with home!

The rendezvous at Plymouth meant nothing to him. His farewell to England had been said among his own people at the North Devon port of Bideford.

The swell of the ocean impelled them. The wind drove them south and west. The horizon dipped and rose again. On deck he watched the familiar coast. On the bridge he stayed until he thought he heard faintly the bells of Tintagel Chapel in faint farewell.

CHAPTER 13
SEVEN SEA-CAPTAINS

The seven captains sat in the Admiral's cabin in the *Tyger*. For an hour they had talked, trying to be prepared for every eventuality. "Accidents are a sign of incompetence," Sir Richard told them. Ralph Lane sat by, against a port-hole, spending his time looking out the window or paring his finger nails with his dirk.

Grenville paid no heed to his inattention, nor did Raleigh, who sat at the table by his cousin going over and checking the names of the men of the Roanoke Hundred.

Seated on deck outside the door were the two savages Manteo and Wanchese, who had been brought to England by Captain Philip Amadas and Captain Arthur Barlow. Wherever they had moved a crowd had followed, but the Indians walked with the high heads of princes, which indeed they were among their own people, and made not to hear the comments of the people. They had learned to understand English well enough under the tutelage of an Oxford scholar while they resided in England at the expense of Sir Walter Raleigh. Through his behest they had gone to court, so that they might see the Queen in all her magnificence and view the great concourse of people who rode and walked the streets of London. Their character was that of the Roman Stoics. They were expressionless when they saw troops march past Whitehall and when they visited the great abbey. Manteo became Christian, but Wanchese remained savage and was of moody disposition, speaking little, even to Captain Amadas.

Simon Ferdinando, the Portuguese pilot, knew the way of the ocean from the Azores to the Florida coast, having gone with Captain Amadas. He promised now to lead them safely to Virginia waters. A boastful man, low-browed, with eyes that looked away, he was not trusted too much by Sir Richard.

Thomas Cavendish, following Lane's example, took small interest. Sir Richard, in good temper though his blue eyes were cold, picked up a paper he had prepared and read it aloud.

"1. The admiral shall carry his flag by day and his light by night.

"2. Item. If the admiral shall shorten sail by night, then he shall show two lights until he be answered by every ship showing one light for a short time.

"3. Item. If the admiral, after shortening his sail as aforesaid, shall make more sail again, then he shall show three lights, one above the other.

"4. Item. If the admiral shall happen to halt in the night, then he shall show light over his other light, wavering the upper light from a pole. Then shall all ships gather round the admiral.

"5. Item. If the fleet should happen to be scattered by weather or other mishap, then so soon as one shall descry another, he shall hoist both topsails twice, if the weather shall serve, and strike them twice again; but if the weather serve not, then he shall hoist the main topsail twice and forthwith strike it twice again.

"6. Item. If it shall happen a great fog to fall, then presently every ship shall bear up to the admiral, if there be wind, but if it be calm, then every ship shall hull, so to lie at hull until it be clear, and if the fog do continue long, then the admiral shall shoot off two pieces every evening, and every ship shall answer by one shot, and every man bear to the ship that is to leeward, so near as he may.

"7. Item. Every ship shall hail the admiral every evening and then fall astern him while sailing through the ocean, and being on the coast shall hail him morning and evening.

"8. If any ship be in danger, any way by leak or otherwise, then she shall shoot off one piece and presently hang out one light, whereon every captain shall bear toward her, answering her with one light for a short time. Then he shall put it out again thus to give knowledge that he has seen her token.

"9. Item. Whensoever the admiral shall hang out his ensign in the main shrouds, then every captain shall come aboard his ship as a summons to council.

"10. Item. If there happen any storm or contrary wind to the fleet after the discovery of land whereby they are sep-

170

arated, then shall every ship repair to their last good port, there to meet again."

There was silence after the reading while Colin passed a copy to each captain present. As they studied his paper, Grenville said, "Our course, agreed on by Sir Walter Raleigh, Captains Amadas and Barlow and Pilot Ferdinando, is to steer directly on the Isles of Canaries for rendezvous at Fuerteventura. Our second rendezvous will be at Cotesa, a small island hard by the Island of St. John de Porto Rico, where sweet water is to be had. Another rendezvous will be Isabela on the north side of Hispaniola; and our final one, God willing, will be off Hatorask, into the harbour at Wococon; and so to the Island of Roanoke.

"If every captain present understands these instructions, he will please affix his name to this paper. But first—any questions?" Grenville turned to Cavendish. "Is all clear, Captain Cavendish?"

Cavendish glanced at the paper. "All is clear to a navigator, Admiral."

Captain Aubry asked, "Do our charts and maps coincide?"

Raleigh answered, "All maps and charts are identical. That has been checked and verified." He turned to Captain Boniten. "That is correct, Captain?"

"Correct."

"Any other question?"

Captain Clarke, who had been with Sir Humphrey Gilbert on his ill-fated voyage, asked, "Is the entrance near the Cape of Hatorask very narrow? Must each ship take pilot there?"

Grenville answered, "Yes, Ferdinando will see to the piloting."

Ferdinando spoke. "A dangerous passage that. It must be navigated by one who knows, else one's ship may go aground and block the way for others that follow. Captain Amadas will tell you it takes skill." He raised his brows and shrugged his shoulders suggestively. "Skill and a clear head. 'Tis not the work of ordinary navigation."

Amadas nodded. "We all but ran aground ourselves, Sir Richard." He rose then and put his name to paper. The others followed in order. Thomas Cavendish, John Clarke, Captain Aubry, Captain Boniten, James Browewich and Sailing Master John Gostigo of the flagship *Tyger*.

Lane got to his feet and looked at his round watch. "If you have no more need of me, Sir Richard, Thomas Cavendish and I will take boat to the *Elizabeth*. I am expecting a visit from Admiral Sir Francis Drake on my ship ere long. If you will pardon me?"

Grenville bowed. "We have finished with the business at hand, Mr. Lane. If the other gentlemen will remain, we will drink a toast to our safe voyage."

Cavendish said to Lane, "I will come to you shortly, sir. I would like to join this company of captains in a toast."

Grenville and Raleigh walked to the ladder, where a proper number of drums and side-boys waited, commensurate with the dignity of the Governor of Roanoke. As they crossed the deck, a sturdy red-haired man approached them, wearing a broad grin on his face.

Sir Richard stopped suddenly. "By the eternal God, it's Nugent!" Pleasure showed on his face.

Nugent saluted first Grenville, then Raleigh.

"Walt, you remember Nugent, my sergeant-major who was with me in Ireland?"

"Yes, indeed, I do remember," Walter Raleigh answered. "I remember every man who stood behind us those dark and bloody days."

"How come you here, Nugent?" Sir Richard asked.

"Sir, I was told in Belfast that you were sailing out on a great voyage of discovery. Sir, I came as fast as I could sail across the Irish Sea to Bideford. Sir, when I got there, they told me you had sailed. But I persisted, riding night and day. Sir, will you have me aboard your ship?"

"Will I have you, Nugent? Aye, as the sun dawns. Come to my cabin. You shall serve us the farewell toast we are about to drink with our seven captains."

The toast was drunk out of the great gilt and silver cup which the worshipful mayor and aldermen of Bideford had given to Sir Richard, an earnest of their affection and admiration for their distinguished lord.

"To the Queen! To the Queen!" the toast was drunk, and to Sir Walter Raleigh their patron, and to the seven great sea-captains, one after the other, and to England, blessed country. . . . Nugent served, Colin at his elbow.

It was sunset before the captains left in high good humour, some with bemused expressions and eyes glassy. Thomas

Cavendish had forgotten that Sir Francis Drake was supposed to be aboard his ship.

"What of it?" he said when he was reminded. Had he not been with noble friends, the seven captains? As for Drake, he, Cavendish, would accomplish a world voyage that would make Drake's appear no more than a sail from Deptford to the mouth of the Thames.

The pipes shrilled, water-boys brought up boats, and, clinging tightly to the ropes, the seven captains were rowed in all honours to their ships.

The last one, bearing Cavendish slumped down in the stern, passed a barge bearing Sir Philip Sidney and Dame Philippa, coming aboard the *Tyger* to give their farewells to Richard Grenville.

A slim youth, with clerk's quills and sand, passed across the deck. When he saw Sidney's barge, he moved quietly from sight behind the deck-house. Even as he hid himself from view, Colin stepped from the cabin. Wondering, he watched the lad move stealthily. A moment later the side-boys hurried to the companionway and piped the great lord, Sir Philip Sidney, representative of the Queen, over the side.

Still curious, Colin walked around the deck-house and came on the lad suddenly. With an exclamation the clerk dropped the ink-horn and quills; the ink ran out on the deck. With a muttered curse he bent over to pick up the empty horn, his face and neck scarlet.

"'Tis a strange habit that you wear, Mistress Thomasine," said Colin. "One not suited to a young woman. Are you waiting to see Sir Richard or do you follow some Bideford lad?"

Thomasine found her voice. "I do not follow a Bideford boy. I—I seek adventure, the same as others on this ship!"

"Oh!" His voice was harsh, his blue eyes were unfriendly. He started to leave.

Thomasine caught at his arm. "Don't go to Sir Richard, I beg of you. Promise me."

"Why should I promise? A ship's no place for a woman— or a girl. Surely Lady Grenville did not give her permission."

Thomasine looked down at the deck. "No," she said sullenly. "No."

Colin spoke passionately. "You think of no one but yourself. Get you ashore!" He walked away.

Thomasine leaned against the deck-house, dismay and discouragement on her face. Still, he had not said that he was going to Sir Richard.

A seaman came up and saw the ink run down the freshly holystoned deck. "God A'mighty!" he exclaimed. "You should wipe it up with your nose, Master Clerk."

But Thomasine had gone. Almost running she gained the clerks' cabin, where an old man sat at a slanting desk hinged to the wall.

"The ink, lad—where is the ink?" he exclaimed querulously.

"I couldn't find any ink-horn," Thomasine lied. "I'll look later. See, there's enough in the old horn, if we only water it a little."

The old man grumbled, while she fetched water from a vessel and dipped a small amount into the thickened ink. Stirring it with a quill, she exclaimed, "There! It is as good as new, sir." The clerk grumbled but began to write, his head within six inches of the book. Praise God, he's half blind! thought Thomasine, but that he might see too much was not her great worry. Colin had recognized her, Colin who hated her. He would notify Sir Richard and she would be sent ashore, after all the trouble she had had to convince the officer that she was a clerk, and to arrange her sleeping accommodation in the cubby off the old clerk's room. Misgivings crowded on her. How was she to keep away from the seamen? The privy was below decks, and there was no recourse but the bucket behind the press where the files were kept. Something else occurred to her. What kind of men were these? Were they like those lustful men she had seen on the moor? Suppose they would discover her and put her ashore at the Canaries? She began throwing her few belongings into the little case, preparing to go ashore. What a fool she was! Why had she come? Because of Colin? Colin who hated her . . .

She started for the gangway. She could go ashore with divers of the visitors and not be noticed. She hurried, pushing her way to the side, only to be stopped.

"Hey, lad! Wait your turn for a shore boat."

She stood behind a group, looking fearfully from time to time toward the Admiral's cabin in the high poop of the ship. Alas, it was not easy to masquerade! It might be readily done in a play on the stage, but how hard to accomplish in this world!

Presently she saw the door of the Admiral's cabin open. Colin stepped out. He stood looking down on the deck below. His eyes sought the spot where he had encountered her. For some time he stood searching, his eyes roaming across the deck. She made herself small behind a group waiting to go ashore. Then the time came for her to go down the ladder into a half-empty boat. The watermen were ready to cast off when an officer shouted for them to hold. Other passengers were descending. To her horror she saw Sir Philip Sidney and Dame Philippa. Dame Philippa stepped down with as much grace as a worldly woman could muster who had her wide skirts held around ankles by a scarf. She was laughing as she took Sidney's hand and stepped gingerly into the boat.

They took seats with their backs to Thomasine. She was drawing a deep even breath when Colin appeared at the loading opening in the ship's side almost even with the water. His eyes roamed across the boat. With a start he discovered her. She had pulled her cape over the lower part of her face. The action, on a warm April night, drew attention to her, rather than made for disguise.

He stood for a moment looking at her with level eyes. Then he called loudly, "Give my farewells to the folk at Stowe, Thomasine."

"May he be damned!" Thomasine muttered, for at his words Sidney turned. He, too, saw her poor attempts at disguise and said something to Dame Philippa.

The boat shoved off. The distance between her and the ship widened. Colin remained a dim shadow within the cavernous blackness of the hold behind him. The score was paid off, so he considered, for he smiled at her and made a gesture of farewell. Tears came to her eyes, which she whisked away quickly.

Sidney made his way precariously to the bow of the boat where Thomasine was, and sat down beside her. He appeared not to see the evidence of tears. "Dame Philippa has given me orders to bring you to her side as soon as we land." Then he smiled, a little twinkle in his eyes. "You must be swift and think up a good tale, my dear, a convincing one, for she will want to know why you are here, and not at Stowe, and why you are decked out in this outrageously becoming habit."

It was almost nine when Dame Philippa sent a servant to

Philip Sidney to ask him to come to her. The inn where they were staying was on Bideford Bar, with little privacy, but her sitting-room gave onto a private garden, which, in the moonshine, took on an illusion of beauty. They strolled down the brick path to the latticed arbour. The high walls were bright, planted with a hedge of may just breaking into tender bloom, for the season was early. They sat close on a stone bench and watched the ships' lights in the dark water.

"What did you say to the girl Thomasine?" he asked after they had sat a time in silence. "What did she have in mind to do in that disguise? Sail on the *Tyger?*"

"How did you guess?" she answered. "It was a pitiful story. It surprised me beyond words. It goes back some months." She told him of the night Richard Grenville had set a brand in Colin's hand at Thomasine's behest. "In spite of her hard shell she is soft as a little clam inside. It shocked her, that branding. She declares she wakes at night and smells burning flesh. She tried, in her queer way, to make some amend, but Colin hates her—rightly, she admits. She thought she hated him. But it seems that the night of the Harvest Festival he won the right to kiss her." Dame Philippa laughed softly. "He seems to have kissed her thoroughly. Then when she responded, he scorned her, she told me, and he said he loathed her. Instead of being prideful, she became the opposite—humble. She followed him, thinking to get aboard his ship. She succeeded."

"And he sent her back?" Sidney questioned.

Philippa laughed softly. "No, no. 'Tis absurd, but amazing. She got on without difficulty, engaged as a junior clerk to help a half-blind old man." Philippa began to laugh again. "It was the little cabinet. She hadn't thought of that complication before. How was she to go on a long voyage and not disclose her sex when it came to Nature's easement?"

Sidney joined her laughter. "What a sad death to romantic adventure! Where is she now?"

"I've put her in your sister Mary's room. I forgot to tell you that Mary and some Plymouth friends have ridden out to Buckland to visit Drake."

"And you didn't go?"

"No. I'm like Richard. Drake may have done great things for England, but I don't like him. Besides, at sunrise I pro-

176

pose to be standing on the Hoe watching Richard's ships sail out of the Haven."

"I will be beside you, my sweet friend."

For a long space no word was spoken. Then he said, "It is decided. I am to go to the Low Countries."

She drew close. "Sidney, tell me that you have forgotten those evil omens. Surely you, who have so much to give the world, must live until you have served your usefulness to the end. You are dedicated to great things, Philip. Forget those unhealthy portents."

"Dedicated? I wonder if anyone is dedicated. Life, well lived with all one's zest, may be full and overflowing before the years are advanced. We are young . . . and suddenly we are gone."

Philippa laid her hand over his, which rested on his silk-clad knee. "If you were three score and ten, you would still be young, for spring is in you."

"No spring till now, Philippa?" He spoke softly, his hand clasping hers. "Philippa, you believe my doom lies this year? I have convinced you?"

She shivered. He drew her to him. "I'm alive now, my sweet, and it is spring. Let us live valiantly while there is time."

Even as his lips pressed against hers, the image of Sidney vanished. She saw instead a strong man, one who stood on the bridge of a ship, courageous, alone, leaning on no one for strength. Then it was that she admitted to herself that she did not love Sidney. For him she felt affection and strong pity.

It was Richard Grenville she loved. She released herself gently. His arms dropped to his sides.

There was a sound of horses' hoofs on the cobbled street outside the walled garden. A coach was arriving. A woman's voice dismissing her coachman.

"Let us go in," Philippa said. "Your sister Mary has come from Buckland Abbey."

Richard Grenville sat by the table in his cabin, his writing-desk before him, and a candle placed beside him. A letter to write to Sir Francis Walsingham, and some final instructions to his steward Ching. Then a letter to Mary.

Dearest Dear:
Philippa will bring this letter to you, my last word before we

177

sail. Had I known that they would come down from London, I would have been tempted to insist that you come too. But perhaps your way is better. I like to think of you that night on the little beach, and the walk through the beechwood in the moonshine . . . of scarf waving as you stood on Hartland Point and watched our ships fade into the horizon. I can see you riding homeward. Our sons and daughters will watch over you diligently and well, tenderly too, and be close to you every day of my absence.

Today was very fine. The Plymouth men and women did us great honour. This was Raleigh's delight, this honour done to him, and he made a noble speech. I think there were tears in his eyes when he told them at the banqueting hall why he did not sail with us tomorrow. I felt his grief. He sorrows mightily. When he is in Devon, he loses the veneer London has put on him. He was among old friends who love him. Among all those who had come to dine us and bid us safe journey, no one in the room had a knife at hand ready to slip into his back. He was at ease and spoke his heart, and I liked him well, for he grows in stature when he is free.

Sidney is sad. He goes soon to the Netherlands under Leicester. If all goes well on that expedition, he will be made Governor of Flushing. He does not want to go. He told me he knows he will never return to England. Pray God his fears are groundless!

Mary Sidney is as wise and lovely as ever. But you will soon see her, as she plans to come by Stowe with Philippa on her way home. You will be pleased, I know. She is a woman of much wisdom and grace and deserves more of life.

Philippa, I think, is sad for Sidney. A look passed between them that enlightened me of some secret understanding between them . . . or perhaps the candle flickered and I read something in their faces that was not there.

I must have done. They will come to the ship after supper, to say farewell and take this my greeting to you.

My love and longing.

Your husband,

Richard Grenville

On board
the flagship Tyger
8th April, 1585
By the hand of Dame Philippa

I think the Plymouth people have not the gaiety our people have. They have more serious visages than we of the North. Every great man of this town, of South Cornwall, and the Stannaries was here today—St. Albans, Killigrew, Hawkins (talking of a new voyage to the West Indies)—everyone but Drake. He nurses a cold at Buckland, so they tell me. Devil take the fellow! I hope he has a *bad* cold.

Cavendish and the Londoners arrived too late to be banqueted. Lane came early yesterday but chose to spend the time with Drake at Buckland, I'm told. They expected Drake to sup with them tonight on the *Elizabeth,* but his cold prevented. Lane travels on Cavendish's ship, which suits me well enough.

Good night, dear wife.

In the small chamber of the Guild Hall a scribe sat late, writing by the light of a candle, setting a record in the Black Book of Plymouth. Fine beautiful writing it must be, as fine as ever the monks wrote in their missals.

On this day, the Ninth of Aprill, 1584/5. Sir R. Grenville, Knight, departed Plymouth with Seven Shippes and barkes, for Wingane DeLoy where he carries one hundred men or thereabouts.

The first day out the Admiral appeared on deck after the bos'n's pipe had sounded assembly. A prayer was read. Then the Admiral, as he was now addressed, made a speech to his men.

"We are now set on a hazard of prime importance. It is to the best interest of all to prepare ourselves for this task, so that we may be a credit to our Sovereign Queen and our country.

"I have noticed, in time of war and whenever companies of men are gathered together, that the Devil dwells in idleness. Therefore I propose that we in this ship avoid idleness and dissatisfaction by having daily tasks set, and that we live rigidly and according to rule, that our hands and our minds be occupied at all times, and that we prepare ourselves for the task of settling a colony.

"To that end, I have detailed certain plans.

"First, the ship's complement will be divided into a number of companies, each with a captain.

"These companies, or bands, will be in competition with other companies and bands—in drill, in fencing and in target practice.

"A group of musicians will be formed to play and sing.

179

"A company of players will be formed for the reading or acting of plays.

"Teams will be organized in deck games and such games as are suitable on shipboard.

"Books are available on soil and planting, on new methods of setting our orchards and fields, on minerals, botany, house-building, weir-building and the making of nets, for fishing will be a part of our industry.

"A man skilled in any craft will write his name in the book and tell what craft he is interested in.

"A number of young gentlemen have brought servants with them to attend to their personal wants. There will be one man assigned to each six gentlemen. The others will be put to more useful work when we go ashore. It is well, during this long voyage, for the young gentlemen to learn to do for themselves; so this plan will be inaugurated at once.

"All tasks will be performed by all men, so that each and every one of you will know how to sail a ship and keep her ship-shape; the tasks going in rotation, as assigned by the sailing master.

"We will have daily prayer, which all will attend. An evening reading of the Scriptures will be held after supper but will not be obligatory.

"That is all. At ease, gentlemen."

He handed the paper to Nugent, gave a nod to the bugler and walked to his quarters high on the poop deck, leaving consternation behind him.

180

BOOK III
THE OCEAN SEA

CHAPTER 14
FAR HORIZON

The young cadets of the county families soon found that the Admiral's orders were not empty words, nor was his drill-master Sergeant Nugent a man to trifle with. The second morning out drill began. A ragged drill it was. Orders were snapped out. Awkward lads responded as best they could. After two hours they were dismissed, a weary, bedraggled group. There was muttering and grumbling, but some stayed to watch the seamen go through their morning exercises and fire drill.

John Arundell exclaimed, "By the Eternal, lads, if those uneducated bully boys can do that well, so can we! I'm going to read the manual and see what this business means."

"What's the use of resisting discipline?" Richard Prideaux remarked, flexing his aching muscles. "We are in for it, and we may as well admit it. We knew the Admiral is a hellion for discipline. I agree with you, John. Let's get down to work." Half a dozen others fell in with them.

Philip Blount, who had joined the ship at Plymouth, and Anthony Rowse and four or five others fell into line and, headed by John Arundell, set themselves to learn drill. As an inducement to make their endeavour energetic, red-haired Nugent undertook to instruct them in sword-play. Since fencing was a sport, there was an enthusiastic response.

Grenville had in his equipment a goodly number of basket foils, and every morning after drill was over there was an hour with the swords in which teams competed. This sword-play made up in a measure for the rigours of drill and was in the form of reward for good conduct.

With swords Richard Prideaux and John Arundell were supreme, although Colin was a close competitor. With the cross-bow Colin led the ship, for not only was he the best marksman, but he could cut and feather the arrows.

Many of the younger men, led by James Lacie, a South Cornwall man whose brother had sailed round the world with Drake, thought the bow old-fashioned and not worth competitive exertion. They wanted musketry. This Nugent would not allow, for, by order of the Admiral, shot was not to be wasted. Life on board the *Tyger* was not spent in idleness as on some of the other ships.

The third day out the weather changed. The sky became overcast; the wind quickened. By night a great swell caught the ship, followed at regular intervals by another and another. Many of the young stalwarts sought the rail with a quickness they had not displayed in drill. These swells kept on with no sign of a storm. The sky was clear of clouds at sunset, and the stars were visible all through the night. A double watch was set to keep contact with the six other ships, which were held in sight.

The night passed without untoward incident and the morning of the fourth day dawned. The Admiral was on the bridge at daybreak. All the ships were in sight. He read morning prayer on the deck and thanked God for their preservation. But the great swells kept rolling, and the ships tossed over the swells' tops and into the troughs. Half the *Tyger's* company were sickened, and many lay inert on deck, too lackadaisical to move from a spot near the rail.

Colin and John Arundell swabbed decks side by side. They came upon a great dark spot that did not give way. Black John stood surveying it, his chin on the long handle of a mop, his two hands clasped around the stick. "If I did not know better, I would say it was a blot of ink," he remarked to Colin.

"It *is* a blot of ink," Colin replied. "Thomasine dropped the ink-horn."

John looked up quickly, an expression of surprise on his face. "Thomasine? You mean Thomasine Arundell? Whenever was she here on the *Tyger*? At Bideford?"

"No, at Plymouth."

"Plymouth?" John's expressive Gallic face showed his incredulity.

Colin told him how he had recognised Thomasine in spite of the boy's garments; how he had called to her as she was leaving ship in the same shore boat that carried Dame Philippa and Sir Philip Sidney.

"I wonder why she was here," John said. He thought of the fine hosen she had knitted for him. A pleasant thought came to him: Had she made the journey to see him?

184

"I wish I had seen her," he said. Observing Colin's expression, he hastened to add, "She's my cousin—far distant kin, but still my kin."

Colin had nothing to answer, so he said, "We had better sand off this ink before inspection."

John agreed. "I think someone will always be cleaning up after that young damsel. I fancy she will go through life leaving a burning trail behind her."

The disk of the sun hung in a horizon of crimson. The dirty-grey sea rose and fell, the waves tumbling wavering lines of fleck and spume. Dark descended, a heavy sullen dark, with no moon to show if clouds that banked the red horizon would float near to break into wind and storm.

Colin had watch at midnight. The air was heavy and the south came to meet them. He climbed the rigging to his station without thought of the rolling of the ship beneath. He moved swiftly and surely up the ratlines, holding by one hand. He knew he must be sure, for if he fell into that trackless sea, there would be no turning back to help him. That was the rule of the sea, a rule that would not bend or break. The bos'n had told it to them on the first day. It was the rule of the fishing boats of Cornwall, so it was no new thing to him; but he saw some of the lads turn white when it was read.

Aloft on the yard he felt his way to the nest, the dark sea below him, the heavens above him black, pierced by a few stars. Polaris was behind; he was sailing away from the Pole Star to meet the Southern Cross. As the night progressed, the sky grew starless: the solitude closed in upon him and he was alone between an unseen heaven and an ebony sea. His head turned at intervals to count the lights of the ships that followed. "One, two, three, four, five, six." All was well.

After a time the wind rose. The masts swayed and the topgallants cracked and whipped. He heard cries from below: "Let tack lines fly! . . . Let go! . . . Clew up! . . . Let go all! Now trice up and make fast! . . . Give us a haul! . . ."

"One, two, three, four, five, six," Colin called monotonously.

The cries that reached him were harsh and urgent. "Furl topsails! Bear a hand, men! Have you iron feet?"

Sailors were clambering, reaching for shrouds. Curses rose

like disembodied spirits, hurling imprecations upon slow and tardy men who, drunk with sleep, moved with the heaviness of beasts.

"One . . . two . . . three . . . four . . . five . . . six lights"

A man missed a ratline and cursed God. Up they came climbing, ten men or twelve. The bos'n yelled below, as the wind rose. The ship reeled. The mizzen brace slackened, and the great sail thundered and roared. Hands in the waist sprang to haul taut the murderous canvas.

The pressure of the blow put the *Tyger* on her side, careening. The yards buckled and bent. Colin clung to the shrouds. "One, two, three, four, five . . . five . . . five!" he shouted. His voice blew off to leeward and did not go below.

"One, two, three, four, five." One ship was out. The wind was roaring. A rag of canvas split from a sail slow-furled slapped across his back, binding him to the shrouds for a moment, then slapped back.

Again he shouted, "One, two, three, four, five." Someone on the yards heard his voice. His words were repeated.

In a lull in the wind came Grenville's mighty voice. "How many lights? How many lights?"

"One, two, three, four, five." Colin's dreary repetition beat against the wind.

Grenville shouted, "Make a wavering light above the light!"

The signal for the ships to gather round! But how could they in this dirty night, in this foulest of storm and wind? With chattering teeth and icy hand Colin clung to the lines, straining his eyes for six lights—but the sixth light was lost.

Black night and starless. Passionate men fighting a passionate sea. Where had he heard those words? Above the wind sounded the boom of a deck piece. Now only one light shone on the *Tyger*. And on each of five ships one light answered.

The wind beat them until the first streak of dawn cut through the heavy darkness. Grey was the sea and grey the sky, with only a streak of yellow lying along the eastern horizon. His eyes smarting with wind that brought salt to his eyes and lips, Colin peered into the sea. "One, two, three, four, five—" his cry was repeated on the deck below.

When full dawn came they knew it was the *Elizabeth*, Thomas Cavendish's ship, that was missing.

As light came and mountainous seas subsided, the Admiral had his ensign run up in the main shrouds to call the captains aboard the flagship.

A soft breeze wafted up that seemed to bring the southern lands to them. The sun was well above the horizon when relief came and Colin, stiff and weary, called his last report before he climbed down the ropes to the deck. "Sun up. Ships *Roebuck, Dorothy, Lyon* and the two pinnaces. *Elizabeth,* Thomas Cavendish captain, missing."

On deck Colin met Richard Prideaux, still a livid green from his late sea-sickness. "The Admiral wants you on the bridge," he told Colin. "He is in a wry mood because of Cavendish's ship."

"Thank you. Shall I go now as I am, or had I best wait to freshen up?"

"Best go now," Prideaux said. "He's been up all night like the rest of us. God, what a storm! I could have stood the weather if it hadn't been for Lacie making great tales about the storms his brother encountered when he sailed round the world with Drake. And John Payne laughed at the sea-sick lads. He thinks himself superior 'cause he sailed with Hawkins in '64. They laughed at us, said we were lubbers. I tell you, Colin, they sickened my stomach as much as the sea did with their boasting."

Colin said frankly, "I was scared. I thought the mainmast would touch the waves. I wondered what would happen if the rope that bound my middle gave way, and I fell into a huge wave. Were you scared?"

Richard Prideaux laughed. "I was too stomach-sick to think of anything but belching bile. I do remember wishing I hadn't drunk so much sack in Plymouth."

Colin found Grenville seated behind a table in his cabin, a pile of papers in front of him. He was talking to Sergeant Nugent when Colin knocked at the open door. He signalled for Colin to enter, and went on talking. "We'll know more about it when the captains come aboard. I can't think how Cavendish got so far away, unless he tried to sail out the storm."

Nugent said, "Admiral, he may overtake us when we reach the Canaries or at Dominica."

Grenville's lips were drawn to a thin line. "I won't wait one day at Fuerteventura, Nugent. There's something untoward in this. I would not put it past Lane to order him to

187

take another course so he might reach St. John's in Porto Rico before we do."

Nugent had a homely freckled face, usually smiling except when he drilled his men. Now he put on his drill face, severe and firm. "I na like Master Lane, sir. I'd put nothing past him. He's determined to show his authority as Governor, sir. As long as we are at sea, you as Admiral give the orders. When we get to Roanoke he will be the Governor and give orders."

Grenville said shortly, "When we arrive at Roanoke—and not before."

Nugent left then, and Grenville spoke to Colin. "What was your watch last night?"

"Sir, I was aloft twelve to sunrise." He did not say that it was well after dawn before he was relieved, that the mate had forgotten him in the excitement of the blow.

The Admiral looked at him, but Colin had the impression he did not see him. Grenville's face was stern—his habitual expression ever since he had come aboard the *Tyger*. It was no wonder he had acquired the name of disciplinarian. Colin waited. Looking through the door, he saw the sailors at work in the shrouds; he watched the water blinking and sparkling in the sunlight. It was warm and the water bluer now that they had passed the stormy Bay of Biscay. Strong-shouldered men were setting sails, singing, while the mate watched. There was a pleasant wind after last night's gale.

Grenville spoke abruptly. "Can you compose a letter and make a fair copy?"

"Sir, I think I can, if I know what I am to answer."

Grenville pushed the papers toward him. "Take these. There is a table in the next cabin. If you do the work to suit me, I will count you a scribe. That will clear you of deck work."

"Sir, I do not mind deck work."

"There are others to do such tasks. Few I can trust with this." He laid the mass of papers in Colin's hand. "I do not promise it unless your work be good."

Colin went out the door and into the adjoining cabin. As he passed along he looked at the deck below the poop, where a dozen men were putting things to rights after the storm. The mate's voice came clearly: "No, this won't do. See how you've let the water lie with edges showing dirt between clean strips. The deck must be as clean as a cook's deal table. Get stones, men. On your knees, and make it clean. This spot! It looks to me like ink—but who would be casting ink on a ship's deck?"

He passed into the cabin and closed the door. He seated himself at the table, arranged pen and sand and found an ink-horn.

Then he read the first letter. It was from Blount of Montjoy. Colin knew him, the father of the blue-eyed, bright-haired lad Philip, who had joined the ship at Plymouth.

My honoured friend:
This will be put in your hand by my first son Philip Blount. I pray you do listen to his pleas and allow him to go aboard your ship under your flag.

I had hoped ere now to have Philip at Stowe under your tute-lage, so that he might learn the amenities and such instruction as befits a lad coming into man's estate. For no one in all Cornwall or in all Devon can so instruct youth in the responsibilities of knighthood as you. I would have desired to have him with your own sons and with your wards Prideaux and Arundell. When I was about to ride to Stowe to make my request, I heard of your voyage. After Philip heard, there was nothing but talk of Virginia from his lips. So do, my old trusted friend, carry him with you in your ship.

Your sincere friend,

Blount

To my loving friend
Admiral Sir R. Grenville
on board Her Majesty's Ship Tyger,
lying in the Pool, Plymouth, Devon.
Third day of April, 1585

Colin looked at the back of the letter. The Admiral had scribbled a few notes: "Yes, will do what I can to instruct son along with other young gentlemen. Instruction in deportment, discipline, small-arms, swords, etc., as well as seamanship. Hard voyage, but England wants hard men to uphold her flag in the New World and on the seas."

Colin pulled up a three-legged bench and began to write. At first the groans and creaking of the ship's ribs cut into his consciousness, causing him to blunder, but he persisted, though at times he could scarce keep his eyelids from falling. Men came and went, shuffling along the deck, but no one opened the closed door. After a time it grew stuffy and he prized the cabin window open a few inches. The air was balmy and soft against his cheek. He heard the alarm for midday meal, but he did not dare to leave without permission. He worked on.

Next came a letter to Sir Francis Walsingham describing the sailing, the conduct of the crew, the storm, Cavendish's missing ship. . . . "We will have well-disciplined young men ready to occupy sundry rich and unknown lands. I shall have opportunity to send this by the captain of some English ship at the Canaries or Hispaniola."

Colin thought, There will be a home-coming ship or two in the Canaries. The post will be sent from there.

The sunset gun sounded. Sir Richard had long since sent his captains back to their vessels before he thought of Colin and the task he had set him. He walked to the cabin and opened the door. The boy sat at the table, his head pillowed on his crossed arms. He was sound asleep, but on the table beside him, weighted down by a bit of an iron bolt, was the pile of letters. The Admiral glanced through the fair copies, and a pleased smile softened his lips. There was a gleam of joy in his steady blue eyes as he looked at the tousled blond head resting on the rough brown cloth of the doublet.

He nodded his head in appreciation. He spoke. Coming quickly awake, Colin jumped to his feet and stood at attention.

Grenville said, "You have done the task to my satisfaction. Have your kit moved here as soon as you have had your supper. You will be my scribe and share these quarters with John Arundell." He left the cabin without hearing Colin's stammered words of thanks.

On the fourteenth day of April they fell with Lanzarote and Fuerteventura, Isles of the Canaries. The night before, the sea was filled with strange lights within the water, as though St. Elmo's fire lay all about them; the ship's wake streamed with fire; and dolphins broke water, leaped into the air and plunged back into the burning fire. The men crowded the rails. Some, frightened, protested it was Satan's fire following them. Old seamen such as Lacie and John Payne scoffed, said it was always so in these blue waters of the islands. But many turned their heads and hurried below to say their prayers, lest evil befall them.

The whole day they stayed on Fuerteventura playing at

games, talking to the inhabitants, loading fresh food and sweet water. At night they anchored off the shore, well prepared to make sail quickly if a Spaniard hove in sight. But no untoward incident occurred and at the sunrise gun they made sail and heaved anchor. By noon they were far off the islands, sailing westward toward San Domingo. With good winds and God's will they would reach it in four weeks.

There were nineteen or twenty men seated on the afterdeck where the cook had set up his cooking apparatus, made of a rectangular iron flooring with a gallery of iron six inches high for siding. Pots were suspended above the charcoal heat.

The men were finishing their meal when Colin came with his wooden platter and pewter mug to get his share. Cook Nicholas was a grim-faced German who had been picked up at Plymouth, where he had been in the stocks on a minor charge. He said, "Food's about gone." He grumbled as he scraped the stew from the bottom of one of the pots. "You should come on the hour, yes? Then you would have fish, fresh pulled in by me from my lines that drag behind."

"This will do," Colin said, accepting a chunk of bread on the point of a knife. He moved to the edge of the circle and sat down, his legs folded under him. Lacie was in the midst of an engrossing talk, so that no one bothered to glance up.

"Sir Francis Drake's men are tough and hearty, and Sir Francis Drake's as bold as a pirate. Why, my brother Edward said they'd kill and fire a village or a town, and pillage after, and the crew would get its rightful share. Once my brother went ashore with Captain Drake down at Port St. Julian, near Cape Horn, and there they found a gibbet already built. They hung some of the rude savages for an example, because they didn't bring baskets of corn. Aye, and the Indians then did come running with corn and other provender and laid it at Drake's feet. It don't pay to be mild-mannered with savages."

"I think that is a disgusting tale," Richard Prideaux said.

Lacie raised his heavy brows. "Yes?" His voice was insolent. "And what would our fine gentleman Prideaux have done in like case?"

"I'd have paid for the corn," Prideaux answered. "That would have been fair."

"In English shillings, I'll be bound."

"No, in trade goods—something the savages needed."

"Hm. I see. This isn't a venture, it's a christening mission we're on." Some of the listeners snickered. Prideaux's boyish features reddened. Lacie turned his back. "Aye, and that's not all. When they were down by Magellan's Straits, it was brought to Drake that one Thomas Doughty's actions were not what he looked for in a seaman, but tended rather to mutiny or disorder. In such case the success of the voyage would have been at hazard. So the captain called the company together and told the story of Doughty and brought out evidence. Now Drake was precious fond of Doughty, but a man's private affection can't stand in the way when a voyage is at hazard. So he took vote of the company and it was for death.

"But Drake did everything according to the law of England. He even requested our minister Mr. Fletcher to give the poor wretch Communion, and Drake himself took Communion with him on his knees and allowed him to take leave of all the company. And Doughty, with a prayer to the Queen's Majesty—he was a quiet sort—laid his head quietly on the block.

"Then, that being over, Drake made speeches to the company, praying for unity, courage, obedience, love and regard for the voyage. And in contentment every man went about his business."

Lacie waited a moment, then added, "So you see what a captain Drake is."

"We've a great captain ourselves." James Skinner, a stern-faced lad of twenty-two with a powerful body, broke in. "My father told me what a mighty man Sir Richard was in war, both in Ireland and when he went against the Sultan in Hungary. Devon men were all valiant on the plains of Hungary: Champernowne of Dartington, William Gorges, Thomas Cotton and Philip Budockshide. They all fought bravely, and they were young—younger than we are. They fought with fortitude like men born to arms and not to idleness. That is what my father said."

"No doubt your father spoke true," Lacie said. "I've no interest in land fighting. 'Tis the sea that shows a man's stomach and liver."

No one answered. Perhaps each youth bethought himself

of last night, and many of them wondered if they had stomach for the sea.

Colin listened but said nothing. He saw in Lacie a man to cause dissatisfaction if he wished.

Lacie got up and flexed the muscles of his powerful arms and shoulders. "Who's for the dice?" he said, looking about the group.

Half a dozen rose. "The dice and some sport? We can't spend all our hours seeking new worlds 'for gold, for praise, for glory,' as Drake says."

"The words were Sir Walter Raleigh's," Colin found himself saying.

Lacie turned quickly. "Who says I lie?"

"No one," Colin answered. "You are mistaken, that's all." He put his trencher on the deck and rose slowly as Lacie strode toward him.

"Who are you, and what name do you bear?"

Colin stood erect, eye to eye with Lacie. "My name is Colin," he said quietly.

"Colin what?"

"Colin."

"Ah, a king or a prince who bears but one name, or a——" He paused. He heard a low sound of protest from the company.

"Have done, Lacie," a voice called. "The lad's right. 'Twas Sir Walter who penned the words."

"Well, mayhap. I'm no such scholar. But 'tis Drake, not Raleigh, who seeks the new worlds." He strode away with his satellites behind him.

Prideaux edged closer to Colin. "He'd have bashed you in another second. What a forearm he has! He'd have put you on the deck in an instant."

Colin plunged his trencher and cup into the bucket the cook had set out for the purpose. "I've seen bullies among farm lads," he answered. He turned and walked down the deck, but not before he saw admiration reflected in the eyes of the remaining lads. It was a warming thought and not undeserved, for he had felt no fear as Lacie faced him.

Rise Courtenay overtook him at the foot of the companionway; a quiet fellow, Courtenay, and modest for all his great lineage; he was descended from the Earls of Devon, though the last earl of their name was dead, and the inheritance had passed into the hands of women.

193

"You are right, Colin. I know the fellow. He was always out to pick on smaller boys. He misjudged in the beginning. I saw him glance at your shoulders and appraise your strength. You are strong, aren't you?"

"Mayhap strong enough."

"Ah, that is good! But here come Sir Richard and his man bearing the great drinking cup. 'Tis sundown, and time for the company to toast the Queen."

Colin liked the ceremony. Each night as the sun hung on the western verge, the cook ladled out every seaman's portion of ale. All hands on deck waited, the Admiral, Sir Richard, standing among them. His man waited beside him, holding the Bideford cup filled with sack or ale or sometimes Portuguese wine. As the sun dipped, he spoke the words in a ringing voice that could be heard to the deck below, "The Queen and the Realm!" and the toast was drunk midst shouts and cheers. The cup passed around among the company and each man had his turn. Then the cup was taken away. Wrapped in its bag of white flannel, it was placed in Sir Richard's sea-chest which was pushed under his sleeping bed.

Tonight the sun was red, and the clouds that hung over the horizon took on its glory. The gentlemen quietly returned to their places abaft the mast. The seamen went forward. That was the rule. Colin thought, But for a trick of fate I would be forward. Yesterday he had been, and now he found himself in quarters next to the Admiral! He thought of Dame Philippa and blessed her, for was it not she who had taught him to draw words prettily as any monk?

He stood looking at the water in the brilliance of its evening colors—blue of indigo, pink, lavender and flame, like the clouds. They were deep into southern waters. He turned and made his way to his cabin on the poop.

There he found Black John Arundell spreading out his clothes on a berth. Richard Prideaux turned from the port to greet him.

"Sir Richard has sent us here," John said, "and Rise Courtenay's yet to come. Four of us share. But we must go our way on the deck when you start to scribble." They were laughing with merry eyes and lips.

"Gad, is it agreeable to leave that stinking place, where rats move about as men, and men as rats!"

Prideaux paced about uneasily, not speaking. Arundell

looked at him, a significant glance, as Colin set himself at the table. He noticed new books were piled there, vellum-bound, and one in red morocco.

Arundell said, "By the Admiral's orders we are to keep books together. I do the log and stand beside the helmsman, and with the navigator when he views his charts, and set all down. You are to keep a quire of the doings of the ship's company and the seamen, and write the weather and whatever befalls day or night, so that we have record."

Colin nodded, liking the idea well.

Prideaux began: "I spell John, and Rise Courtenay, who joins us here, will keep record of winners in sword-play and drills. In all, we will be the honourable company of scribblers." They all laughed, being young and in fine animal spirits.

"This for the first month, then there will be a change. A toast to the first month!" Richard Prideaux continued. "Let's set a record for the men who come after us. No blots. No blots. Clean paper and . . . What a record for fire-eating venturers!" They laughed again.

Arundell said, "Dick, you are to——" He paused.

Prideaux glanced at Colin, already at work with papers. He hesitated, but Arundell kept nodding to go ahead. "Colin, my lad, we want to have talk with you." Colin glanced up, surprised at his tone. "Yes, serious talk, but hang it, it's monstrous hard to say!"

"Go ahead," urged Arundell.

Prideaux looked one way and then the other in his embarrassment. Then he plunged ahead. "It's about your name. You know you've always been Colin, since long ago when we came first to Stowe and we used to play together with bow and arrow and wooden swords."

"And you taught us hawking," Arundell broke in, "and to ride a moor pony—remember?" They stopped and glanced at him questioningly. Colin said nothing. He looked first at one, then the other, a steady inquiry in his blue eyes.

"Oh, Phoebus!" said Richard. "It's this way. You can't go about being Colin, just Colin, now that we are out in the world. It was all right at Stowe, but here on the ship we are among strangers. You heard that tough Lacie. Damn him to hell anyway! He will make something of it, something to stand in your way. We won't have it. We've talked it over.

We have decided you must have a name, and a good one, for you are a good fellow."

They paused. Colin didn't help them. He sat very still, a withdrawn look on his face and in his eyes.

"Hang it, a good name with something behind it! So we've decided it must be either Arundell or Prideaux, whichever you choose."

Still Colin did not speak. He could not. His heart was in his throat.

"Won't you choose? Then we'll draw lots. We've already written our names on cards. Come, Colin, draw one, and whichever you draw is your name."

Colin found his voice. "You are good, but I can't do that. Whatever will your people say? A name can't be thrown about, one to another, like that."

"Why not?" Arundell spoke impatiently. "Why not? There's some law, I suppose. We can invoke it when we go home. Just now you want a name to write down in the ship's book. I hope you draw mine. I'd like that."

Prideaux, not to be outdone, cried out, "Prideaux is a good name added to Colin. Come now."

"It wouldn't be lawful," Colin protested.

"Come! Don't be a dunce. Draw, man, draw a name!"

Colin rose slowly to his feet, his eyes fixed on the door. The two boys turned and saw the Admiral standing in the doorway. How long he had been there, they did not know. His face was stern, but his eyes were twinkling.

"Young gentlemen," he said, advancing into the room, "your kind intentions do you honour. As you say, you both have names of high value, but you are too late. Look in the list of the company of adventurers and read aloud what you see written."

John Arundell, standing nearer the great volume, turned the pages until he found the place. "Colin Grenville," he read, "Colin Grenville."

The Admiral did not look at Colin when he spoke. "Colin is right. It must be all according to law. That was attended to at Plymouth. The papers were taken to Stowe by Dame Philippa for Lady Grenville to sign. By this time it is entirely legal." He placed his hand on Colin's shoulder for a second and left the room before the boy had found tongue.

"Jesus!" John Arundell exclaimed. Richard caught Colin's hand and pressed it. Colin did not move. He stood white and

196

shaken, looking at the page before him. The first thought that came to him was that Dame Philippa would be pleased. A second later he saw the mocking face, the impudent dark eyes of Thomasine. She would laugh, laugh, laugh. Well, let her laugh, damn her! He would prove himself as strong, as stalwart a Grenville as any of them.

When he looked up he was alone.

CHAPTER 15
TROPIC ISLE

The small Spanish horses were restive and giving trouble to the men who were endeavoring to load them onto the *Tyger*. After an hour's struggle two more horses broke halter and got away. This angered Grenville who was watching the loading from the bridge. He sent his cabin boy for Colin.

"Go ashore and show those men how to handle animals," he said. "I want the mares handled gently, else we shall have wild, untamable animals on our hands. See that the kine, bulls, goats, swine and sheep are kept in pens until the tide turns and we move closer in shore. It is unfortunate that we did not bring sheep-dogs from Stowe to do the work."

"Sir, I brought my dog Hubba. Do you want me to work him?"

Grenville nodded without taking his glass from his eye. "Damnation! They will ruin those horses." He lifted his voice and shouted to the mate, "Have done. I'm sending a man ashore to look to the animals." To Colin he said, "Tell the bos'n to have a sling made, strong enough to swing them from the small boat to the deck."

"Perhaps the Spaniards have a float we could borrow."

Grenville turned on Colin, his eyes blazing. "Christ! Do you think I'd ask a favor of a Spaniard?" He glared at Colin. "Get them on board without help. I want them loaded before I send a boat around the island for salt. Bring me your quire before you leave. I want to see what you have recorded."

Colin left quickly. He encountered John Arundell outside the door of their cabin. "The Admiral wants you at once," he said with a grin.

"What's his humour? Is he chewing glass or beating up furniture?"

"No, but he's wrathful. I think it's because our men are stampeding the animals and making a display of their ignorance before the Spaniards."

"No doubt. I don't like it myself." Black John looked shoreward. "There must be a hundred of them sitting around watching. I can't see the grins on their faces, but I know their silly mouths are smirking. Judas Iscariot! I could put the lash on those bungling yokels." He turned. "What does he want of me? Will he skin the hide off me with his tongue?"

"He wants the stockade made strong enough for defence in case they should attack in force. For all they pretend friendship, he does not trust them."

"Christ! I know nothing of building a stockade. Tell me how, Colin. There's a good fellow. I'm too liverish today to stand a tongue lashing. I've had Nugent on my neck since early morning. The drill manual won't stay in my head."

"Remember how we drove strong saplings or stakes into the ground and laid others across the top, lashed together with vines or thongs?"

"Yes, yes." John's dark eyes brightened. "Yes, of course. Heavy uprights at the corners where sentries can stand. Right? Thanks. Shall I give out as though the idea were my own?" And not waiting for Colin's answer, he walked quickly toward the Admiral's quarters.

Colin went into the hold and got Hubba, who was tied to a stanchion. The dog barked when he saw Colin, short, happy barks, nuzzling his cheek against his master's hands and licking at his face with red tongue. "Easy, Hubba." Colin rubbed the great white ruff gently. "Easy. We've work to do."

He found the bos'n on the after-deck and inquired about a sling.

"We've got such already, quite strong. I told the mate, but he would have none of it. He thinks he can lighter the animals over on a pontoon. A stubborn mon is the mate and will take no telling from me." He spat copiously over the rail, a gesture of silent contempt.

Colin said, "The Admiral has ordered me to get the animals aboard. He says they are to be slung."

A slow smile curved the boatswain's thin-lipped mouth. He relished Colin's words mightily. He had an old feud with the mate—not only a personal feud but the inherited feud of centuries between mates and boatswains.

"Aye, sling them we will." He winked a bleary eye at Colin. "I'll be ready with the derrick windlass and sling by the time you get them alongside. You'll be wanting a net for the small animals—sheep, kine and swine? They work easy in a net."

"You're right, Bos'n; a net also."

"Aye, aye, sir. Just be giving me the signal when you want to hist they."

"Right, Bos'n."

Colin got into a boat, carrying Hubba. The dog struggled at first, but he soon was quieted by gentle words from his master.

On shore he found everything in confusion. Half a dozen men chased squealing swine, some escaping to the woods, others running down the beach.

"May God damn all Spaniards!" shouted a sweating lad who stood looking after a lean black pig that had got away. "They've greased the beasts." He looked at his hands.

"Fall on them!" Colin cried as he made his way toward the glowering mate who was cursing and swearing at men and animals indiscriminately. Sweat ran in rivulets down his dusty cheeks. He had stripped off his jerkin and was naked from the waist up. Sweat beaded his face and his hairy chest and back.

"God damn all swine!" he muttered, mopping his face with the back of his dirty hand.

Colin said, "The Admiral says for me to take over."

The mate glared at him. "Take over and welcome. How can I move animals with a lot of greenhorns like these?"

"I've brought my dog. He's trained," Colin said, repressing a smile. The mate grunted and walked off. Colin called three men who were standing knee-deep in water, looking after swine that ran down the narrow beach. Sheep were huddled against a rock. Mares and stallions were galloping up a narrow path that led to the high land. A rough pen had been set up, made of driftwood and stubs stuck into the sand.

"Stand between the pen and the water," Colin said to the three men. "My dog will run the animals in. Then you can throw a gate across the entrance."

Whistling to Hubba, he made his way up a path and came down to the beach beyond the stampeding animals. Hubba was barking, his great plumed tail wagging from side to side. He kept looking at his master, waiting for a signal. When it came, he began to work the excited kine toward the pen. With sharp barks and quick short plunges at the

200

heels of the recalcitrant animals he headed them along the beach.

Colin turned his attention to the horses. Some had run toward the marsh, pursued by a dozen men. He must reach them before they entered the bog. The smaller animals were moving along now; soon they would be housed in the pen. He waited until they were all in. Then he whistled to Hubba and walked along the beach. Ankle-deep in sand, he made slow progress.

The marsh lay three or four miles from the stockade that Sir Richard had had built when they reached the Bay of Moskito in the Island of St. John de Porto Rico a week before. The Admiral had no intention of being at the mercy of the Spanish there on the island. He was taking no chance of treachery. They had seemed friendly enough. Upon the arrival of the ships they had come down carrying white flags to show their peaceful disposition. They had made signs of parley.

Sir Richard had sent out two men to parley, Edward Stafford and Philip Blount. The Spaniards were pleased when they found they spoke their language, and brought greeting and inquiry from the governor of the island. But they made protest against the company for occupying their land and fortifying on it.

The two Englishmen sent word to the governor that they wanted nothing but water and victuals. They would stay only long enough to build a pinnace. The messengers told them that their governor was a man of proud humour, and they did not know whether or not he would permit trespass on their land.

Stafford had replied that their Admiral also was a man of proud humor and that he had falcons of power and he proposed to stay on the land as long as he pleased and would sail at his own convenience.

The two men had come back, and the *Tyger's* men and those of the other ships built a makeshift stockade, where they stayed at night, keeping a strong sentry. In the morning they felled trees and set about building the pinnace.

A river ran at one side and the whole compound was surrounded by forest, excepting on the sea side.

Three days later eight or more horsemen had come out of the woods half a mile away. They sat on their fine caracoling horses, their splendid armour glistening in the hot sun. Sir Richard sent ten armed men marching along the beach. The Spanish horsemen watched them approach, then turned and rode away.

Three days after that a great excitement had come to the company. The look-out discerned a sail and sang out, "Sail ho! Sail ho!" Bare feet pattered on deck as men and officers ran to look. A Spaniard? A Frenchman? What ship lay in the offing? Signals were called among the ships, and the Admiral wakened from his siesta (as the Spaniards put it). Spaniard or Frenchman or war? In either case an enemy. Sir Richard studied with his glass, waiting. An order went from ship to ship: "Make ready to hoist anchor." For it was ever the humour of the Admiral to be first to attack—a sturdy attack was the best defence, he had frequently told his captains. "Let the enemy do the guessing while you do the manoeuvring." Larger and larger grew the sail until at last he discovered that it was Master Cavendish's ship that sailed toward them—lost since the great storm three days out of Plymouth.

Seamen and the companies of each ship had shouted for joy, thrown caps into the air and danced on the deck. A gunner fired off the ordnance—a welcome shot that sent some onlooking Spaniards fleeing for safety into the wood. There had been toasts and gaiety far into the night, so glad were Cavendish's men to be at the rendezvous in time, and so glad were Sir Richard's men over the reunion.

Sir Richard and Master Cavendish had foregathered with the captains in the Admiral's cabin to plan and give thanks, but Master Lane did not come, offering as an excuse that he suffered from ague.

Of the men, those more moderate in habit had contented themselves with talk and the swapping of yarns. But now as Colin ran along the beach he saw evidence of wilder jollity. Many of the company had drunk too much and were stretched out on the sand. He noted with satisfaction that none of these were from the *Tyger*. The *Tyger's* men were too well disciplined for that. They knew that sottishness would mean the hold and leg irons.

At length Colin came close to the horses. In order to get beyond them he must clamber up the low cliffs and go through a forest. The marsh lay ahead. He planned to get behind the mares before they reached the quagmire. Two of the company joined him, young Allyn, whom he had known at Stowe where his father was one of the Grenville tenants, and James Skinner. He was glad of their company, first because he did not know whether Spaniards were hiding in the woods, and then three were better than one to fan out and turn the horses. It was a full hour before the mares were stopped. One of them was gentle enough for Colin to vault to her back and drive the others before him. Hubba skirted the woods along with the men and kept the horses running toward the rough pen.

The loading progressed in a more orderly fashion now. The horses were driven onto a pontoon. Plunging to their knees in the water, splashing and snorting, they fought every inch of the way. Strangely enough, once the slings were secured about their bodies and the blindfolds on, they made no protest even while they were swung out over the water and into the loading down in the hold of the ship.

The kine and swine squealed endlessly and the sheep gave frightened bleats as they were cast into the nets and made the trip above the water. It was sundown before the task was completed.

" 'Tis enough to drive a man wild," Lacie remarked. He was waiting to go aboard, standing in the water while a servant scrubbed out the boat. The frightened animals had left many tracks behind them, and the smell of urine was strong and nauseating. "They'll make the ship stink like a prison ship," Lacie continued. "Why do we have to take a shipload of these damned animals? I thought this was a ship for a company of gentlemen adventurers, not one filled with farm-yard stenches and manure."

Colin looked at him in surprise. Didn't the man realize they must live on the Island of Roanoke for a year? How could they do that without fowl and cows, milk and butter and beef? He said nothing. Lacie had neither looked in his direction nor addressed him since the fracas aboard ship. That suited Colin; he had enough on his hands. But there was smouldering hatred in Lacie's breast, and more than one man had warned Colin that he bore a grudge, and that he would wait his own time to satisfy it.

Darby Glande, who had sailed to the Indies for the Bristol merchant Thomas Aldworth, had stood sentry one night with Colin. He had been outspoken. "Watch yourself lest he take you unawares, my lad. Lacie has boasted he will lay you by the heels."

Colin thanked Glande whom he liked, a stalwart man with mild blue eyes that met one full and steady. He had a thin face. The bones of his cheeks stood out under tight-stretched skin, thickened by the winds of the sea. In spite of a sabre scar that crossed his cheek, and his golden ear-rings, he was a quiet man, but Colin thought he could be harsh enough and quick to fight when aroused to anger. He was kin to William Saltern of Bideford. He had come to the *Tyger* when Cavendish's ship reached St. John de Porto Rico, giving as an excuse that he wanted to be with North Devon men.

A good navigator, Glande had sailed to Muscovia. He was watchful, as he had been taught to be in dealings with the Easterlings and in traffic into Turkey.

Tonight they walked the beach at sunset. Sir Richard's seven ships riding at anchor were a goodly sight. Glande talked of trade and the wealth that trade had brought to the merchants of Bristol.

He held the company on the *Elizabeth* in scorn. "They talk of gold and silver and pearls," he told Colin. "They should be thinking of pitch and tar, hemp for cordage, and masts. Hides and rich furs and the like will bring more wealth to England than gold and silver."

This was a new idea to Colin. "You think there is no gold in Virginia?" he asked.

Glande shrugged his shoulders. "I do not seek gold, Colin. I seek a place to abide, where trade goods are easy and cheap. Mayhap I will set up a station and make my contacts with merchant companies in England and Europe. That is my hope. Another voyage, perhaps two, and I will settle myself in a new country and gain my wealth through trade."

John Arundell joined them then, throwing himself on the sand beside them. "God's visor, I ache in every bone! My feet are burning, my back aches, and look at these blisters." He held his long white hands before Colin. At the base of each finger was a huge puffed blister.

Glande said, "It is best to draw off the water."

"Best how?" John asked helplessly. "How? Never before have I seen such things."

"Ask the bos'n for a needle and a shank of thread. Sew directly through the skin and let the water drain off through the thread."

204

John shook his head. "I don't know what you mean. I'm sure I can never sew my skin."

Glande laughed. "I'll fix them when we get aboard ship tonight."

"I'll never go aboard ship. I'll lie right here in the sand until the tide bears me away."

"And let the mosquitoes feast on your skin?"

"God, no! They liked to have eaten me last night. They stung me until the blood streamed down my face."

Glande said, "That is not good, Master Arundell. Sometimes, after the mosquitoes bite, a fever comes with chills and one wants to die of aches and pains."

John laughed wryly. "No one tells of these plagues when they talk of Virginia and the New World. They speak only of grapes and fruits. Trees and flowers of incredible beauty. Fish in the streams. Game in the woods. Pearls in the rivers. A veritable Paradise, to listen to Amadas."

"And so it is." Glande got to his feet and took up his harquebus. "These little nicks and pricks of Nature come to remind us that perfection is the attribute of Allah alone." He went off to walk his rounds.

John said, watching him move off to the stockade, "Why does he speak of Allah? Is he a barbarian?"

"No, not so. I think he was prisoner to the Barbary men. Note the scar he wears across his face. 'Twas made by a scimitar stroke."

John said enviously, "Some men walk in danger and excitement while we fight only gnats and mosquitoes and break our backs making arbours, so that high dignitaries may dine in state even on a savage island."

Colin glanced at him. Was the heavy work beginning to break Black John's spirit? Then he knew he was only making fun of his own ineptitude. "How goes the stockade?" he asked.

"Well enough. It fell down twice, until we set the poles deep in the sand. I can't see why we must keep strengthening the stockade. The Spanish are fearful of us. They stay watching us from among the trees, not daring to come close. They sit there all day on their horses. By Jupiter, but they have fine mares! I'd give something to own the one the captain of that troop rode."

"Perhaps it is because of the ships' guns that they stay at a distance," Glande remarked shrewdly as he returned from his rounds. "They bear watching, those fellows. You can't trust them."

Arundell lay on his back, his arms over his head, gazing at the great cumulus clouds that drifted slowly across the blue intensity of the sky. They moved slowly, compelled by some lazy wind drifting in from the south. It was all lazy—the sky, the clouds, the little stream—and all a place to love.

A picture of Thomasine crossed his mind. It would be good if she were here, a part of the slow easy life of a tropic isle. His eyes closed. His thoughts drifted into dreams. He dreamed he saw her riding down the beach on the back of the beautiful mare he coveted. Her hair was floating behind her, caught by the wind. She rode without saddle, her fine white thighs firm against the satin flanks of the bay mare. They were one, the horse and the girl. A depression came over him. He could not move—only watch her riding away from him, never turning to look back. He groaned and wakened. Colin was laughing at him.

Glande was saying, "The Admiral has a stomach for Hispaniola. He must sail to that island. Once when I was there I saw a bull-fight. A gory one it was."

John made a face. "Barbarians! I can't abide the thought of a man chopping at a bull with his blade, trying to disembowel the brute, leaving gory entrails to drag in the earth. Now give me a good bear-baiting. There is a sport!"

"I see no choice," Colin said rising. "I'm going to bathe. I am thick with dust, and a thousand little flies are at me biting like hot needles."

Glande said, "They say sharks abound in the water. One man had a leg nipped off. The Spaniards won't go in."

Colin smiled. "I'm so thick with dirt and sweat that even a shark would veer off."

John sat up languidly. "Well, I suppose I'll have to follow you. Can't have you saying that Arundell of Trerice is a coward."

They stripped and ran toward the water, Hubba bounding along beside them. Their example was followed by others. Soon half the company were cavorting in the water. From the hills the Spaniards watched. One, a low-browed fellow with evil eyes, took up his cross-bow. A companion knocked it upward before he could speed the arrow, for the governor's orders were absolute: no Englishman was to be touched while the ships' guns were trained on the shore.

206

The pinnace was finished and launched. The time had come to test the promises so readily given concerning food stuffs. Grenville's men waited by the marsh, waited long hours in vain. When they went back and reported to the Admiral, he flew into a fit of rage such as John and Colin had never seen before. He cursed with a serpent's tongue dipped in venom, in a voice so loud that the seamen on deck paused in their tasks to listen, proud to have a leader whose wrath was mighty.

Colin saw Lacie on the deck standing stock-still at the sound of Grenville's voice. He appeared, for a moment, to hesitate; then making up his mind, he ran up the companion-way and approached the Admiral. He stood deferentially, cap in hand, his sharp eyes fixed on the man of wrath.

After a time Grenville's anger abated. "What do you want, sir?" he shouted. Lacie stepped closer and spoke for a moment. From his position in the door of his cabin Colin caught Drake's name, then the word "fire," an arresting word which seized Grenville's attention and held it. A smile crossed his lips, a thin, cruel smile. He smashed his closed fist against the rail like a man who has seen his vengeance gratified.

"Go!" he said sharply to Lacie. "Go, and may the devil's fire be put in your hand!"

John Lacie was grinning broadly. "Aye, sir." He turned and clattered down the steps. A moment later he was calling loudly for a boat to row him ashore.

Eight ships stood out to sea when the tropic night closed down on them in velvet darkness. The ships' company saw sparks from the burning stockade, small fires along the edge of the woods. Brighter and brighter they grew until it seemed that the whole island was ablaze. Devil's fire licked up the trees, a beacon fire of vengeance.

On the burning isle the Spanish governor wrote diligently on a letter to Diego Hernandez de Quiñones, Governor of Havana, reporting the visit of the English ships who came upon his isle without permission and set about building a pinnace and an entrenched fort. He had sent a lieutenant with forty men to view the position they had usurped, and later despatched thirty-five harquebusiers to harass the men when they left the fort to take wood or water. The pirates, he wrote, raised a flag of truce and told his lieutenants they were

Englishmen of good intent, who wanted only to build them a ship, bargain for animals and provisions and then sail on to settle. He had let them have a few cattle for a goodly price. With them were two Indians dressed in splendour.

He pleaded with the governor to write at once to King Philip and beseech His Majesty to send ships of war to protect his trading ships and his island people.

And so the darkness fell on the dismal island and a frightened people—and eight ships, the *Tyger* in the lead, sailed on through the blue seas of the tropics, leaving fear and destruction behind. Late that night they took a Spanish frigate near St. Germans' Bay. In fear the crew fled and left the ship waiting for them. More fear and more destruction were to come. Before they made another landfall they had taken a second Spanish ship, with good rich freight and some Spaniards of high rank and circumstance. It fell to Colin and John to give over their cabin to the highest dignitary, and to Richard Prideaux to wait on him as a young knight should wait on a grandee.

Don Fernando de Altamirano was a man of wealth and must be treated with all respect, Grenville instructed the young lads, but it was Glande who told them that the Spaniard would be ransomed for a pretty penny once they reached Hispaniola or Cuba. Captains kill, burn, ravage, prey on commerce and hold for ransom—that was the way of the sea and the wealth of the victor.

Glande's lined, scarred face wrinkled in mirth when he saw John Arundell's look of dismay. "You'll have many a new thought before your eyes behold Padstow Light again, my lad. 'Tis the hardening that comes to a man of the sea, and it will come to you."

"Never!" said Black John with vehemence. "Never will I kill, burn or hold for ransom. Never, so long as I live."

Glande was unimpressed. "Then you'll rape—mayhap a Spanish girl of Hispaniola. They be fair fine girls at Isabela Port—practised too, in the arts." He winked broadly. John's lips closed in a fine line. Glande sensed his embarrassment and his stubborn will. "Or mayhap it will be an Indian savage. I've never tried one myself, but mates have told me they do the measure right merrily."

John stamped off down the deck. Glande watched him go, a smile on his rugged face. "A fair fine lad, when he's strengthened himself a bit. And you too, Master Colin. You'll find out that the best way to learn the language of a strange country is to lie with a woman of it."

Colin said nothing. He'd seen enough of hedgerow frollicking not to take Glande's words amiss. He knew what Glande was trying to tell them was that they must slough off boyish ways and habits. They were in a man's world, a harsh, hard world, where a man had to have a strong stomach and unbroken will if he wished to survive.

Don Fernando de Altamirano sat at table in Grenville's cabin. He was a dark thin man, tall, with keen, intelligent face. He listened impassively to Grenville as he talked. Course after course was set before them—the ship's fare, supplemented by fruit and green stuffs that had been brought to them from the island. Grenville ate heartily and pressed Altamirano to eat more bread made of wheat flour, for he knew the Spaniards' bread was poor stuff made from cassava. The service was all of silver, the finest Grenville had brought with him, and the wine goblets of silver-gilt to match the great cup that had been presented to him by the mayor and council of Bideford. Altamirano's quick, shrewd eyes appraised the table service, the fine carved oaken chairs, the French tapestries that hung on the panelled walls. Sir Richard's habit was of the best cloth and he wore about his neck a fine chain of golden links set with precious stones. The don weighed shrewdly his captor's bearing, the deference accorded to him by his young squires, who were no doubt gentlemen of quality.

They spoke in Spanish, in which Sir Richard was not too proficient, so he had beside him his pilot Simon Ferdinando to translate in case of difficulty in understanding. The pilot was a man of poor station, a Lutheran, Altamirano discovered by questioning. There was a second Portuguese, of higher degree, one John Gostigo, whom Sir Richard had sent to wait on him when his man had been put ashore on Porto Rico. Gostigo spoke Castilian, which set him apart in Altamirano's eyes as a person of standing.

The don had learned things from Gostigo: that a great English fleet lay off St. Anthony. Perhaps they were going to take over Spanish possessions, Trinidad or Dominica. Gostigo had told him also of the great Sir Walter Raleigh, favourite of the Queen, who was sending out ship after ship to settle in the

New World. They were not to kill Spaniards but to be friendly, so the New World would belong to both England and Spain.

This Altamirano did not believe. The English feared Spain. The Queen—God put a curse upon her!—sat on the throne that belonged by every right to Philip of Spain. They were waiting only to gain courage to fight. Well, they'd best seek courage in haste, before Philip sent ships and took their country and put the usurping Queen's head on the block.

He crumbled the bread on the silver plate that bore the Grenville arms, and planned ways to get this information to the governor. Grenville leaned forward. Don Fernando could not read his eyes; they were cold, though his bearded lips smiled. His bearing was that of a host. Grenville spoke of indifferent matters. He was versed in the arts. He had visited in Madrid. He knew surpassing well such Spanish poets as De Hita and Garcilaso, and the ballads of the Cid.

He spoke, not too unkindly, of Philip's claims to the throne of England, but on the subject of religion he was courteously silent. Truly he must be a great man in his own country of England, thought Don Fernando de Altamirano, a very great man, surrounded by persons of distinction.

The don's eyes roamed as they sat listening to the sweet music the Admiral had commanded to play as they dined. On another ship he caught a glimpse of two Indians surpassing tall, most elaborately garbed.

The music ceased. Grenville said, "It is sunset. Will you do me the honor of accompanying me to the bridge for the evening ceremony?"

Don Fernando rose from the table after he had dipped his fingers in the silver bowl filled with water which John Arundell held. His hands he wiped delicately on a serviette which Richard Prideaux presented. He plunged his jewelled dagger, greasy with fat from the roast, into the water and cleansed it thoroughly. Sir Richard did the same, remarking that Don Fernando's dagger was one of great beauty.

"From Toledo," the Spaniard said. "It would give me pleasure if you would accept it as a slight token of my appreciation of your hospitality."

Grenville bowed and smilingly accepted the gift. "Your courtesy and thoughtfulness make it almost impossible for me to hang you, Don Fernando—providing of course that the Governor of Hispaniola refuses to ransom you."

Don Fernando smiled, showing his narrow white teeth. "I cannot imagine such a contingency. The governor will be only too happy to pay the needed gold in order to have me at his side."

Grenville said, "It is not gold that we shall ask. Horses, kine, calves and mares shall be the ransom price." He waved Don Fernando through the door. "Precede me, sir," he said with a bow.

They stood at the rail. The young gentlemen of the ship's company were drawn up, twenty on either side. On the deck below, the trumpeters waited, while the seamen and servants stood at attention in double ranks. It made a brave show. The Spaniard took in the placement of the heavy guns, twenty-pounders.

Before Sir Richard gave the signal for the clarions, the don answered his captor, "The horses and mares shall be from my own stock. It will give me pleasure to know that the breed which has been in my family for many generations will be in your colony—" he looked into Grenville's eyes—"wherever the colony shall be," he added.

"Thank you, Don Fernando. Believe me, the mares will have the best possible care."

He turned quickly and gave the signal. The clarions sounded. John Arundell and Colin stepped forward, Arundell carrying the great cup, Colin a tall silver ewer with wine for refilling. Arundell presented the cup to the Admiral. He raised it. For a moment he hesitated, then he said, "To a lusty wind!" drank and passed it to Don Fernando. When the Spaniard had answered the toast, Grenville took the cup from his hands and gave a second toast: "To the Queen, may God keep her!" The cup passed from hand to hand until it reached the deck. Stewards there were to fill it with ale, for ale is a seaman's drink until he reaches the Golden Islands, where rum takes its place.

The Spaniard leaned against the rail watching. Nothing of his thoughts showed in his face. After a time he raised his eyes. Over a sea of glass the sun lay on the rim of the horizon. Directly in the path was the purple shadow of Porto Rico, no more than four leagues across the strait. To his left he saw his frigate, so lately loaded with wealth in merchandise destined for Spain. A bitter smile crossed his lips and his hands tightened on the rail. Ah well, he had blood of the Moors in him, and that made for patience, for who can wait

211

longer without complaint than a Moor, or who can remember longer or strike more swiftly when the time comes?

His thoughts went swiftly to the seaports of his country. He could see ships riding in the roadsteads or building in yards. Soon they would sail—sail northward—but now he must smile and bow, and hide his hatred for an arrogant man who spoke of hanging.

John Arundell polished the silver cup, rubbing it gently, while Richard Prideaux put the wine bottles in a chest after carefully corking them. Colin sat at a table, ready to begin on his writings.

John said, "Did you glimpse the look on our Spaniard's face when he walked to his cabin? If he had had a dagger in his hand, I think he would have struck our Admiral as he walked through the door."

Prideaux turned the lock and put the key in a crevice between the panels by the door. "He has no dagger. Didn't you see him present his dagger to Sir Richard? I think it was noble of him. It is an elegant Toledo." He stood off, to see that the key was well hidden.

Arundell gave the cup an extra flourish before he put it into the flannel bag. "Silly fellow! A gift offered in that way means nothing. By the time Don Fernandez gets to his cabin, the dagger will be lying on the table."

"Why? He gave it, didn't he?" Richard's face showed his incredulity. "A free gift it was."

Arundell answered, " 'Tis a custom in Spain to make such offers. 'Everything in my house is yours, *amigo*. . . . This is your house, *amigo*.' One accepts graciously and returns the gift."

Colin joined in: "John Gostigo told me that at some of the great houses in Spain and Portugal a guest finds a pile of gold coins on a table in his bedchamber. He is supposed to use what he needs while he is under the roof."

"A fine custom," Arundell said quickly. "Perhaps we should have aimed to take Spanish islands, instead of sailing for Vir——"

Prideaux clapped his hand over John's mouth. "Hist!" he whispered. "The Admiral has given orders not to mention the word." He got up, glanced down the passage, closed the door. "It's like this," he told them, his Gallic features carrying something of the importance of the disclosure. "John Gostigo

212

told me in great secrecy last night. The Admiral attached Gostigo to Altamirano as his interpreter. When Simon Ferdinando went back to the *Roebuck* Sir Richard told Gostigo just what to say when the Spaniard questioned him. He was sure to question him. Gostigo is a Portugal, born in Lisbon, and the Spaniard would consider that as they are neighbors they are friends. Especially would they join hands against the English."

"What fun!" Arundell broke in. He sat down on the long bench near Prideaux. "Do you think we can trust Gostigo, Dick?"

Prideaux hesitated, thinking about Gostigo's expression when he told about months in a Spanish cell and his treatment by the Inquisition. "I think so. If you can trust a man who bears a grudge, yes."

"Tell us more," Arundell said eagerly. "I'd like to know just what he has told Altamirano. Does he think the Spaniard believes these tales?"

"That we are sailing for Trinidad and the Spice Isles? He thinks so. He tried to make it sound truthful. He says it is a good thing Sir Richard has sent Ferdinando to the *Roebuck* now. He doesn't trust him."

Colin looked up from his writing. "But Gostigo and Ferdinando are both of the same country."

"I know that, but John Gostigo thinks Ferdinando has been dealing with the Spanish. Like as not, he'll take us the wrong course or do some other treachery."

"How can he, Dick?" Colin questioned. "He isn't to do any navigation until we come to the Virginia shores. Captain Amadas would know whether or not he were sailing correctly."

"That's so, he would. I had forgotten about Amadas," Arundell said. "He is to transfer again to the *Tyger* when we make the Hispaniola landfall—he and a Devon man named John White, who makes wonderful drawings of fish and fruits and colors them."

"I'd like to see the drawings," Colin said. "Wouldn't it be nice to send some to Lady Grenville at Stowe?"

"Excellent idea." Dick turned his purse inside out. Five shillings and a twopence clinked on the bare table. Arundell added three shillings and an odd penny.

Colin shook his head. "Nary a penny have I. But I might do some lettering for Master White in exchange." The lads agreed that would be the thing, but the mention of Lady Grenville and Stowe set their thoughts backward.

"Strange," said John, "strange how far away Stowe seems. It seems endless days since we were hawking at Hartland Point."

"Two months, excusing eight days," Colin said.

Dick laughed. "He counts the days like a lovelorn swain. Who is she, Colin? Come, give us your confidence. Have I not told you about pretty Nell Slater, and Barbara of the Barbican, and some other wenches who made merry with me?"

Colin got red in the face. "There's no one," he said shortly.

Dick turned to John. "And you, Arundell of Trerice, don't you have a thought of a woman to give you sons to bear the name?"

"There are enough John Arundells as it is—five or six to a generation. I declare when I have a son I shall give him another name. Alexander is good—my father's name."

Dick was roaming about the room, walking nervously, flicking his lower lip with his finger, a way he had. He stopped behind Arundell and slid his hand on his shoulder. "If you marry the fair Thomasine, John, may I step to the altar with you? Or are you thinking of the altar?"

Arundell jumped to his feet. "By Gad, you've said enough, Dick! I thank you to leave her name out of your talk."

"Don't be an ass, John. The whole ship knows she came aboard the *Tyger* dressed in men's clothes. She was set to go to Virginia just to be near you." Richard's voice was teasing, his eyes were merry. He winked at Colin, who bent his head over the paper.

John said nothing. He stood with back against the wall, his feet spread to catch the sway of the ship. His eyes, his whole dark face were flashing. "Hold your tongue! 'Tis not the truth. I said good-bye to her at Bideford Quay."

"You are angry. Therefore my words are true. You dream of a fair—or shall I say dark?—Thomasine."

"Hold your tongue! It's a lie when you say she was on the *Tyger*."

"Colin knows." Dick laughed, untouched by John's anger. "You saw her, didn't you, Colin?"

Colin looked at John. Had he forgotten the great spot of ink on the deck, which they had sanded away with some effort? Of course he remembered. He did not want Richard

Prideaux to know he was aware that Thomasine had followed the ship to Plymouth.

John muttered, "Anyway, she didn't come to see me."

"Whom else?" teased Richard. "Didn't she knit fine silken hosen for you?"

John turned away without answering. Colin thought, He loves her. He loves Thomasine. A strange feeling spread over him, a depression which seemed to clutch at his stomach.

Richard crossed the room and threw his arm over John's shoulder. "Sorry, John. I did not mean for my teasing to hurt you."

"She's my cousin." John spoke slowly, trying not to betray the tremor in his voice.

"A far cousin, you told me yourself, and why not? You're a quiet fellow, who thinks deeply and doesn't speak. She doesn't think—she acts. A violent person. But maybe you can calm the devil in her. Who knows?"

John picked up his cap and went toward the door. "Perhaps that's what I like in her—the devil. . . ." He walked out, slamming the heavy door behind him.

Dick looked at Colin. "Whew! I didn't realize or I wouldn't have teased."

Colin turned his steel-blue eyes. "Realize what?"

"That he is sunk in love with that wild Thomasine." He, too, took up his cap and went out, leaving Colin to think over his parting words in gloomy solitude. Why should he feel as he did at the knowledge that John loved her? He hated her. Unconsciously he opened his hand and gazed at the two letters T A, a brand that Thomasine Arundell had put on his hand. He hated her, he who had never hated anyone before in his whole life.

In the Admiral's quarters a conference was going on. His captains, Edward Stafford, Philip Amadas, John Clarke and the others, were with him. They were discussing the terms of Altamirano's ransom. Clarke and Stafford wanted gold. The others were willing to agree to what Grenville decided, whether in horses and cattle or gold and silver. Clarke was empowered to speak for Lane, who lay ill of a fever on the *Elizabeth*.

"Gold was Governor Lane's verdict," Clarke said, "and in plenty, so every man has his share."

Grenville sat quietly, but a deep frown gathered on his

broad forehead. His blue eyes were hard as Cornish slate and dark with anger.

"I prefer to talk to Governor Lane himself, but since he is ill, that cannot be. Need I explain to you, Captain Clarke, that the success of any colony lies in its ability to plant and grow food. In order to survive you must have cattle and herds—horses also, not only to plough the fields but for the use of horse soldiers. Horsemen are often most effective against an enemy, particularly when the men are equipped with hand cannon. Foot soldiers with harquebuses are excellent, but backed by horsemen they are well-nigh invincible."

Clarke, who was a short, rugged man, with heavy features and over-hanging brows, shrugged his shoulders. "I'm a seaman myself, Admiral. I know only the sea and my ship's ordnance. Will not Governor Lane be responsible for the conduct of the men, once our ships land the company on Roanoke?"

"That is correct, sir." Sir Richard rose, a signal that the conference was over.

Amadas, seeing his anger, intervened. "The Admiral is quite correct, Captain Clarke. Knowing the country from having been on the island and the mainland for three months, I would say that horses and cattle are a necessity. The Indians are gentle, seemingly, but if you talk with Manteo—I do not trust the sullen Wanchese—he will tell you that they are constantly at war with other tribes. How do we know that they will not turn on us?"

Clarke answered shortly, "Our guns will take care of any disaffected Indians."

Stafford, who was a quick-moving, energetic man with a broad smile and white, handsome teeth, had remained silent during the discussion. "I think, Captain," he said to Clarke, "we should consider seriously what Admiral Grenville has said, and again consult with Governor Lane. Perhaps he has not given so much thought to settlement as he has to occupation."

"As you wish, Captain Stafford," Clarke answered. But the men present knew he would not be in favor of Grenville's plans for settlement, nor would Master Ralph Lane.

Grenville sat silent and immovable at his table long after the captains had departed, looking straight ahead. His eyes were not on the glassy sea or the slack sails or the men sprawled half naked on the deck waiting for a breath of air to strike the ship.

His mind was on Clarke's words, which he knew were Lane's. It was the first rift. Lane was beginning to assert his authority as Governor of the new land of Virginia.

CHAPTER 16
LANDFALL

Colin wrote industriously, following Sir Richard's words. The Admiral walked back and forth, turning abruptly as he reached the walls of the cabin. He had stripped off his doublet and wore a thin linen shirt; the linen had been spun and the cloth woven in the weaving rooms of Stowe and the shirt stitched by Lady Grenville against the hot weather in Virginia.

Colin thought how ill suited his master was to the narrow confines of the panelled cabin. His tall body, his broad shoulders shut out Colin's view of the deck as he neared the door. He must stoop to leave or enter the room.

Today Sir Richard had been silent as he ate his morning meal. For a long time he had read from the ship's Bible, as though to draw strength from its wisdom. Colin sat quiet and withdrawn, making little of his presence in the room. He had learned that this quietness was pleasing to Sir Richard. More and more he studied his master's ways, trying to penetrate his thoughts, but without success. One thing pleased him greatly: Sir Richard had come to lean on him, not to give him his confidence, but to send him on small errands; to transmit his orders or to stand between him and the numerous petty annoyances that come to a man in command of a company. Sometimes he spoke of Stowe—for the most part of the farming or the improvements he would make. Again he would talk of Roanoke, of the things that should be done to assure a successful colony.

"We must not be like the Spanish," he would say. "They colonize poorly. They take from the land and oppress the people. It is a way of greed. Short-sighted. Take—take—take will not build an empire. Take and give, live and let live—that is the way of success. Make it a land where a man and his family may live well, where tenants are happy and feel secure." Colin listened and learned.

Today there was no talk of conquest or of Stowe, no words were spoken whereby a young man might glean wisdom that

218

would make for maturity. Grenville sat drumming on the table with his fingers or pulling at his golden beard. Was he thinking of what he had left behind, home-sick for his family, for Stowe? Or was he seeing a long vision of the future?

For half an hour Colin watched the full sails as the ships moved swiftly under a strong wind. They were sailing northward now in the great stream. Frigate-birds and sea-robins flew across their path or followed the great triangular wake left by the ship. Then with screams and fluttering and shrill sound they dived into the blue waters or the white crests of the waves to snatch at the scraps from the cook's galley that the pantry-boy bucketed overboard. He could see two or three sailors fishing, throwing lines from the afterdeck. The wind was warm, the land not too far distant, though held from view by the haze that lay along the littoral.

Colin turned to thinking of the bull-fight which the Spanish Governor of Hispaniola had upon their coming arranged for the entertainment of the great English gentleman; of three white bulls, strong with life and mountain living, which lay dying or dead in the arena, their gory entrails stretched between fighting dogs; or prancing horses, their coats shining: of matadors wiping blood-soaked swords on velvet hosen—a scene to remember in its wild savage beauty.

One memory troubled Colin. Lane and his aide, Comptroller Francis Brooke, had pushed ahead to be the first seated at the bull-fight, the first to greet the Governor of Hispaniola. How black had grown Sir Richard's face, how his eyes had blazed until a thought came to him! He lingered till all the company entered the arena of the bulls before him. Let the governor wait a few minutes. Then with clarions trumpeting, banners flying, he entered, followed by his company in full armour, grandly, as a king would enter a field.

The Spanish governor had not been slow to gather the significance. Here, vested in Richarte de Verde Campo, as the Spanish spoke Grenville's name, was the might and glory of England. Lane was the courtier, with the courtier's ineptitude. The Governor of Hispaniola was a soldier, and to Grenville he gave deference, whereas he had given to Ralph Lane simply the courtesy of a host to a guest. He approached Sir Richard on foot, waited until he dismounted, then led him to the seat of honour. Lane scowled and made to rise from his seat. At a word from Francis Brooke he sat down again.

What a sight this entertainment had been! Colin, country-born, had not dreamed that in an island so far from the homeland men would surround themselves with the accoutrements of grandeur evidenced in the armour and court dress, the vari-coloured rugs spread on the earth, the high-backed chairs covered with red leather for the distinguished guests.

Surely the good Lord had been kind to him, that he was allowed to behold such splendour.

He thought, too, of the banquet, under a pavilion covered with leafy green boughs, which Sir Richard had given for the Spanish governor and his richly attired men that evening in the glory of the dying sun.

The English were magnificently dressed. Sir Richard was in full armour. His gold-encrusted helmet he had won from a Saracen when he was in battle with the Turks. Lane was in pale-blue satin and silver, with a velvet cape slung across his shoulder in spite of the heat.

The English were not to be outdone by any Spanish show. Their plate was heavy, their wine goblets of chased gilt and silver were handsome. As the banqueting progressed, their heads proved stronger and steadier while the goblets passed and repassed, filled over and over again with wine the Admiral had purchased from the Portuguese merchants when they anchored in the harbour of the Canaries. Many a Spaniard sank back on the Turkey carpets and slept, while others staggered into the woods to relieve their stomachs' fullness, or were carried off by their servants and were seen no more.

Don Fernando de Altamirano, yet unransomed, had sat beside Grenville. He spoke not at all, drank deeply, showing no change from the wine except a flush on his olive skin and a smouldering fire in his intense dark eyes. Colin, who with John Arundell stood behind Grenville, had noticed that the governor from time to time was surreptitiously pouring his wine on the ground. Grenville also must have seen, for he had his wine-bearer fill the governor's cup whenever it was empty.

Lane had leaned across the governor and spoken to Grenville in English. "Sir Richard, will you make terms of the ransom or shall I? Let it be gold." He belched and put his fingers to his lips. He was far gone with wine. "Gold," he said, raising his voice. "Gold."

Sir Richard had glanced at Lane without expression. Lane

lifted his goblet to his lips, a swallow too many. When Sir Richard spoke, he addressed his words to Francis Brooke. "Will you escort Master Lane to his ship, sir? I am sure the governor will understand and excuse him from the company."

Brooke spoke to Lane in a low voice. Lane, after a momentary refusal, rose unsteadily. " 'Tis gold, gold," he muttered. "Let him ask ransom in gold." He stood swaying. One of his men stepped forward quickly and caught him before he fell across the governor.

Grenville had smiled. An answering smile was on Menendez' dark-bearded lips. "Your Excellency will pardon?" Grenville said. " 'Tis a light head. Do not censure his acts."

The governor had nodded. He glanced about. Others showed that they, too, were light-headed. Sir Richard, as host, rose and gave the sign that the company was dismissed. Some men walked away to the beach on their own legs. Others had had to be helped to the boats.

The music of guitars was heard then, and Spanish men singing:

> "Three dark maids—I loved them when
> In Jaen——
> Axa, Fatima, Marien.

> "Three dark maids who went together
> Picking olives in clear weather. . . ."

Grenville, standing, had watched the exodus. He turned to the governor and Don Fernando, who remained seated. He quoted a bit of poetry, the legend by a hero of Spain:

> " 'What tower is fallen? what star is set; what chief come
>   these bewailing?'
> " 'A tower is fallen! a star is set!—Alas! alas for Celin!' "

His Excellency was pleased. He said, "You have read our poets. Surely you have understanding of the proud Spanish heart." He looked meaningly toward Don Fernando.

Grenville sat down. He beckoned John Gostigo, who stood back of them, to come near. "Perhaps it will be well if Don Fernando goes back to the *Tyger* while we discuss the terms of his ransom." The urbane manner of the host had gone now. The negotiator was a different man, cold and wary.

221

The governor had nodded, and after a ceremonious bow to him Don Fernando had followed Gostigo. Two of the young gentlemen of the company joined Don Fernando to accompany the prisoner to the ship. Gostigo had returned.

Grenville said, "My knowledge of your language is too slender to trust in such an important task as negotiating a man's ransom. Gostigo will act as interpreter, if that is agreeable to you."

The governor had signalled one of his own men. "Perhaps two interpreters would be more agreeable, señor."

"As you wish, sir. As you wish."

Colin had been dismissed then and wandered away. He had not learned the outcome of the discussion until the following morning when horses and cattle were loaded on the *Tyger*.

The Admiral's voice broke in on Colin's reflection. He took up his dictation in the day book:

"On the seventh of June we departed with great good will from the Island of Hispaniola; but the wiser sort do impute this great show of friendship and courtesy toward us by the Spanish rather to our force and vigilance and the watchfulness that was amongst us than to any hearty good will. The merchants sold us, at a price, sugar, tobacco, bull-hides, ginger and such, as well as some animals.

"Doubtless if they had been as strong as we, we might have looked for no better courtesy at their hands than Master John Hawkins received at Saint John de Ullua, or John Oxnam near the Straits of Darien, and divers others of our countrymen in other places.

"On the eighth day I had certain adventures when the pinnace I was in was all but cast away. We had been hunting for seals.

"On the ninth day we came on the Isle of Caycos. We searched for the salt ponds which the Portuguese Simon Ferdinando, the pilot, promised us. We found no salt. The Portuguese deserves a halter.

The Admiral stopped. "If it had not been for Amadas, who begged me to spare him, I would have hanged the fellow," he remarked to Colin. "Amadas persuaded me that no one excepting the Portuguese knew how to bring the ships safely through the narrow straits at the entrance of our harbor behind the sand-banks."

He took up the tale again.

"Had it not been for the *Roebuck's* men under Master Lane who had got salt at Roxo Bay on the southwest side of St. John's, we would of necessity have turned back. I will be ever watchful of the treacherous fellow.

"I believe, after a talk with my navigator, that we should lie off the Island of Roanoke by the end of this month of June. We give our fullest thanks to God for bringing us across the treacherous sea to the shores of Virginia.

"In good health and likewise in spirits."

Grenville yawned, and rubbed his eyes. "That is all. You have found it easy, Colin, to keep up with my words today. My thoughts go slowly, sluggishly. My mind keeps turning back to Stowe. . . ." He got up, went to the open port-hole and stood looking out on the water. The wind sent the whitecaps scurrying. A great white bird dashed itself against the port window. Its wings flapped and beat against the side of the ship. Too big to pass through, it clogged the opening. One claw caught on the Admiral's thin white shirt and tore a great rent, leaving an angry bloody scratch across his shoulder and down his breast.

Colin leaped forward. Papers and quill scattered to the floor. He caught the bird by the legs, forced it backward. Then he released it, but not before its heavy beak had caught his hand, crushing the bones of his little finger. He drew back quickly and stood against the table, his face pale, his hands shaking.

Grenville was solicitous. "You are hurt!" he exclaimed.

"No, no," Colin stammered. "It is not that. It is the sign, master."

Grenville spoke sharply, "If you call me master again, I'll have you flogged. What sign?"

"The bird, m—— sir. Death follows a white bird."

"Nonsense! Have done with such nonsense!"

"A white bird brings death," Colin said stubbornly.

"Then we must die together, you and I, for the bird has set his seal on both of us."

That night the wind rose to gale proportions. The ship rolled, dipping from side to side, until it seemed as though the masts would touch the turbulent waves.

A seaman mounting to his watch in the look-out missed his footing. With a scream he slid, struck the rigging and plunged into the water.

223

The deck watch shouted, "Man overboard! Man overboard!" and flung a line into the dark shadows, but no hand clutched at the hemp to draw it taut.

Colin and John Arundell heard the cry and rushed out to the deck.

"Why don't they slacken sail?" John cried, his voice high against the wind.

The Admiral joined them. "There will be no turning back. We will sail on. You must not question the rules of the sea." To Colin he said, "You are thinking of the white bird?"

"Aye, sir," Colin replied. He was not easy in his mind. What had a white bird that flew to Grenville's window and marked them with its evil talons to do with that seaman's death?

For three days they sailed—"within smell of land," the old seamen quoted. The young men, Colin and John and Richard, smelled no land smell, though they stayed on deck sniffing vigorously, facing the west. Nor could their straining eyes catch more than a low dark cloud bank that grew deeper and darker as they neared the latitude of the dreaded Cape Hatorask.

Captain Amadas explained to them and drew a chart showing the jutting headland that extended far out into the Virginia Sea. "A dread cape, where hurricanes and gales are caught and snagged and blow outward to the ocean, or wreak their violence on the long reach of sandbanks that follow the shore water to the islands and the main beyond." They had had many violent storms, crashing thunder and lightning bolts, the summer he and Captain Barlow had spent on the island.

Richard Prideaux said, "Biting flies, bugs, worms that burrow into your flesh and between your toes, lightning bolts that could readily kill a man, winds up, gales that blow in the twinkling of an eye—what is this country? Eden, the fairest land under the cope of heaven? God's death! It seems the end of the world to me." He fixed his black eyes on Amadas. "Why did you not tell us these things before we sailed from Bideford?"

"Why, indeed?" echoed Philip Blount, who came up from behind them. His face was beaded with sweat, his hands were black with tar. "There must be gold and silver and precious stones, aye frankincense and myrrh to make us forget the

224

seven plagues of Egypt that we encountered on the Island of Hispaniola. I scratch in my sleep and wake to find myself bleeding where my finger nails have gashed my legs."

Amadas smiled. "No Eden without its serpent, you know."

Lacie, who was near by sewing canvas for a new sail, had his word. "These la-di-da gentlemen have tender skin. Me the biting flies leave alone. You will harden, my masters, before you are quit of Virginia."

"Who spoke to you?" Prideaux stepped across the deck, his hand at his belt. He had forgotten he was swordless.

Lacie got to his feet, dropping the canvas from his lap. "The gentleman makes to draw a sword—a brave fellow behind a steel blade. Lift up your fists like a proper Cornish lad, and we'll make a ring and test our muscles."

Captain Amadas spoke. "Keep your mind on your mending, Lacie, or the bos'n will take over. We'll have no fighting aboard the *Tyger*."

Lacie walked away, muttering that Amadas had best look to his own ship where there was plenty of fighting between-decks.

Amadas did not hear him. He turned to the three lads. "The Admiral wants no quarrelling. We are all set off on a noble adventure. We must put our strength to our work."

"Lacie stirs up trouble wherever he goes," Prideaux began.

"The mate will look to Lacie. Come, my brave lads, the Admiral wants a fencing competition."

Blount cried, "Who can fence with his sword when the deck rolls under him and his opponent dips and rises before his eyes?"

"You dip and rise before the eyes of your opponent, so honours are easy. Come now, lads, the company is only as strong as its weakest man. Let us build for strength."

John asked, "Do you think we must fight the savage Indians, sir?"

Amadas shrugged his shoulders, "Who knows? But let us be ready. A lionlike instinct becomes a strong male. It aids him in gaining height and full proportion. Let it be a game if you will, but quicken your eye and strengthen your wrist, and make your body move as a cat moves. One day you may need all your valour and all your skill."

"He speaks like a parson," Prideaux muttered as Amadas walked out of earshot. "I'm weary of preachments. Before

225

the dawn rises, Nugent has us by the ears, marching and manoeuvres. Salt pork and slops that turn your stomach, stench of dirty bodies forever in your nostrils—and we are at it again. Then the fencing master and the bowman. Down we go into the hold to lift cannon-balls with all speed, with the ordnance sergeant standing by to count aloud the minutes it takes one to carry a ball, load and light. I'd give twenty thousand crowns to be free again to ride across the moors, following the flight of my falcon."

"Please, Richard—" Black John Arundell spoke up—"do not lose your head. We sit close to the Admiral. Do you want lesser lads, seamen, to hear your disaffection?"

"My every muscle screams out. My legs are filled with water instead of bones," grumbled Richard, but he lowered his voice and managed a grin.

From aloft voices rose from seamen climbing the rigging, furling sail:

> "In Amsterdam there lived a maid—
>   *Mark well what I do say!*
> In Amsterdam there lived a maid,
> And she was mistress of her trade—
>   *And I'll go no more a-roving*
>   *With you, fair maid!*
> *A-roving—a-roving—since roving's been my ru-u-in,*
>   *I'll go no more a-roving*
>   *With you, fair maid! . . .*
>
> "But when I'd blowed my twelve months' pay—
>   *Mark well what I do say!*
> But when I'd blowed my twelve months' pay
> That girl she vanished clean away—
>   *And I'll go no more a-roving*
>   *With you, fair maid!*
> *A-roving—a-roving—since roving's been my ru-u-in,*
>   *I'll go no more a-roving*
>   *With you, fair maid!*"

"God eternally damn all ships," Prideaux mumbled, "and all men who sing about roving!"

He walked away, the laughter of his fellows following him to his cabin door.

"Does he really hate the sea?" John asked Colin.

"I don't think so, but a man on shipboard must complain

226

just so much. Let him grumble. It does no harm, and perhaps it does him some good."

"He'd better not let the Admiral hear him," Philip Blount broke in. "He'd cast him below or put some stripes on his back. The Admiral doesn't hold with such talk. Why, it's mutinous!"

"Nonsense! Dick doesn't mean a word. I'll wager my little dagger against your silver doublet buttons that he's forgotten by now."

"Mayhap he has, provided he's asleep."

"Come on, let's go down and pick up some foils. I've a notion to match my skill against Colin's." Blount started toward the companionway.

Colin hesitated. "I've writing I should be doing."

"Golden Phoebus! Haven't you written yourself out by now? What is it you write about? You keep me awake nights listening to your scratching quill."

John cried, "A lie! You snore the moment your head hits the bed. Come on, Colin. Write your stint after supper. Let's get to the foils before night comes. I don't like to fight by ship's lanthorns."

In his room Richard Grenville took up his quill and wrote a page or two on the report he would send later to Sir Francis Walsingham.

We had brought a Bible translated into Spanish. I do not think Altamirano was too pleased when I suggested that he take it to Porto Rico, so that the people there would understand what their preachers were saying, and how they were deceiving them. I made inquiry about what the Inquisition was doing. But he evaded my question. I think misgovernment extends to the Spanish isles as well as the home country.

When we left Hispaniola, we sailed southeast a little way, so they would have no knowledge of where we were going.

I have got no word of Drake, although we came upon an English merchantman at the Island of St. John's, whereby I sent reports to you and letters to my good wife at Stowe. I sent also pictures limned by John White of the people and the fruits and fishes of these tropic islands, and a great sea turtle. White, who is a Devon man, has a pretty skill in such matters. He will make pictures of the new country when we

227

arrive in Virginia, so that you may present them to Her Majesty the Queen. Then she will have in her mind the nature of her new subjects and how they live and dwell, for I shall take over the land with all ceremony in Her Majesty's name as benign ruler, and in the name of my cousin Raleigh as owner of the Charter.

This I will do, before I give over to Master Ralph Lane as the island's governor.

The morning of the twenty-sixth of June the *Tyger* came to anchor at Wococon, one of a long chain of sandy banks that protected the main.

Colin and John were up before daybreak, pulling on hosen, jumping into shoes and doublet. They tried to waken Dick Prideaux, but he muttered and swore and buried his head deeper in the pillow, his dark hair falling about his face.

Philip Blount was already out, on watch. Shivering in the early morning air they made their way up to the bridge.

The navigator shouted at them and drove them down, but they stayed on the companionway, their eyes turned westward. They wanted to be the first to see the fabulous land of Virginia.

The first streaks of light, the false dawn, showed behind them on the eastern horizon; long shafts of light, faintly yellow, pointed to where the globe of the sun would show beyond the ocean's curve.

During the first moments they were silent. Then the inner excitement burst out. Boyish and eager, they asked one another questions: Would the streets of the Indian towns be paved with gold? . . . Could they scoop pearls from the river, big pearls, the size of pease? . . . Would the pine-apple and plantain, such as they had tasted at Saint John's and Hispaniola, grow abundantly? . . . Would they find good shooting, grouse, pheasant and woodcock? Fishing they knew to be beyond any they had dreamed of. Two days before, when they had anchored in a small harbour for the night, the nets had brought up in one tide enough to have sold for twenty pounds in London. Nugent had told them that. They had no way of calculating costs, for they had neither bought nor sold fish. At Stowe and at Bideford all that was done to get table fish was to send two or three lackeys or kitchen boys to the river or to the sea down at

Coombe Vale, and they'd take what was needed. It was the same with crab.

"We don't want for fish," John said, hanging over the rail, looking landward. "I wish the fog would lift. It lies like a long streamer or veil. If it would rend, we could see the shore, supposing the navigator is correct."

Captain Amadas came up and joined them at the rail. "Have patience, my lads. Have patience. Presently the sun will drink up the fog and you will see the long sand-spits that lie like a reef along the coast." Amadas' eyes in the half-light were sparkling and eager. His hand trembled a little, and his voice betrayed his excitement.

"What does the Admiral plan? Do we anchor and wait until the other ships come up, or do we sail into the entrance when the sun rises?" John asked the question.

Amadas said, "The ships answered the signals last midnight and hove to. All but one. Cavendish's ship lingered behind." He glanced over his shoulder, for they were not far from the Admiral's quarters. "I think we will make entrance soon after sunrise, if the tide be right. The Admiral is impatient to claim the land of Virginia in the name of our Sovereign Lady."

Colin asked, "Will we take land before the governor comes?"

Amadas smiled, a smile that quickly vanished from his firm, bearded lips. "You remember the play that says: 'The sea-faring man has prayed on his knees night after night for a westerly wind to carry his ship forth. Sometimes he shakes like a leaf lest his ship be wrecked'—as we nearly were on the treacherous shoals at the Cape of Fear—'He is ever at odds with the weather. The clouds are too barren of wind, or the heavens forget themselves and let down wind too strong for his liking. He is like a farmer, sometimes the harvests do not answer his hopes, or the season is too fruitful, so the corn has no price.' I think our Admiral's ideas follow the play's. Now that land is at hand, he will brook no interference with claiming it in the name of England."

A black bird with a red bill flew in front of them, followed by another and another.

"Terns," Amadas said, pointing. "Terns. Land is very close. See—the first rim of the sun! Perhaps we should make our salutations to it like the heathen of old."

"Look!" said Colin, pulling at Captain Amadas' arm. On

229

the highest deck was the tall, strong figure of the Admiral. He stood apart, motionless as a statue. His armour—for he was completely accoutred—caught the shafts of sunlight. His head was bare, proudly held. In the sunlight his hair looked as though it were a golden cap.

What thoughts were passing through his mind? What dreams, what lofty dreams of empire? Or was he giving his silent thanks to the Blessed Lord who had brought him and his company safely to the New World?

The three men watched their commander in silence. The sunlight brightened behind him until his armour, like his hair, became pure gold.

"He looks a pagan god," Amadas murmured. At the moment the sun came into its full circle. The yellow light turned to crimson. It shone on the white bank of fog that clung to the shore, melting the fog into thin streamers and giving the shore color and form. Between the rifts the white crests of waves beat lazily against the sand.

Far back the green spires of trees broke through the vapour. Here before their eyes was their new land.

"Thank God!" Captain Amadas spoke reverently the seaman's prayer. "Thank God for a safe voyage and a safe haven!"

A shout came from the look-out, Philip Blount's voice roaring down the wind. "Land ho! Land ho!" From the deck the seamen and the company took up the cry, "Land ho! Land ho!" Voices charged with excitement rose and fell: "Land ho! Land ho, Virginia!"

CHAPTER 17
THE FALCON AND THE TUDOR ROSE

Grenville paced back and forth inside his cabin, while the Portuguese pilot and Captain Amadas sat in the high-backed oak chairs.

"How long until the tide turns?" Captain Amadas glanced at the dark-browed Ferdinando.

"With the half-hour."

Grenville banged his clenched fist against the table. "We will delay no longer for Cavendish's ship!" his voice rasped. "Look you below. My men, all impatience to set foot on land, cannot be denied. By sunset all ceremonies must be over, so that the sunset gun will mark their end."

Simon Ferdinando rose. "Sir, I am well suited by your decision. I must pilot in nine ships through that narrow way. Sir, which ship sails first?"

Grenville stared incredulously. "Which ship sails first? The *Tyger* certainly."

Ferdinando lifted his cap from his knee, bowed to the Admiral, left the cabin. Captain Amadas followed a moment later, after Grenville had given the order in which the ships were to sail. The *Tyger,* the *Roebuck,* the *Lyon,* one of the ships taken from the Spanish at Porto Rico, then the *Dorothy* and the three pinnaces. Cavendish's *Elizabeth,* with Governor Ralph Lane and the London gentlemen, would enter last since she was not even in sight.

Colin, John, Dick and Philip waited outside for the Admiral. Every seaman and ship's officer, every member of the company was attired for the ceremonial. Ships' flags flew. Every ship was dressed.

Banners of each family were staffed, ready to be carried ashore. On the cabin table lay the great flag of England, furled in its casing of canvas. Beside it was the banner of Elizabeth, which the Queen had presented to Walter Raleigh, denoting her interest in the planting of England's first colony in the New World.

Twenty men, led by Captain Aubry of the *Roebuck* and

Captain Boniten of the *Lyon,* had gone ashore on Wococon to select the spot where the ceremony would take place. As soon as the ships had anchored at a small harbour five days before, an invitation had been sent to Wingina, the Indian King on Roanoke Island, to attend. This had been arranged by Prince Manteo. Wanchese sullenly refused to have any part in the plan.

The Admiral called Colin. "You will go ashore with Master Blount and ten men whom you will select. I charge you with seeing that nothing untoward transpires when we step ashore. I suggest you take Master Anthony Rowse for one."

"Sir, may I select Master Darby Glande and Master Joseph Gorges?"

"Glande, yes. I hesitate over Gorges. Perhaps it would be better to have him among my gentlemen-at-arms since he is one of my kinfolk. I shall take among my guard John Harris and Master Stukeley. I would choose Master Hariot, but he is aboard Captain Cavendish's ship. Go now. Get your men and inform those already ashore to meet us on the beach when we land.

"It is well that the two Indians went aboard the *Lyon.* If they had stayed on Master Cavendish's ship, we would have been sore put to it for an interpreter."

The work on shore had been completed when Grenville's young aides reached the strand. The boatmen pulled the long-boat up on the beach well out of the water. They made their way to the hillock of sand and consulted with Captain Aubry, who told them all was in readiness for the arrival of the Admiral.

Indian canoes to the number of twenty or more lay in protected water inshore, and a large company stood close together not far from the point where the canoes were idling.

Colin's curiosity was whetted by their number and the strength of their almost naked bodies. They were a warm copper colour. Their skin was oiled, so that it seemed to shimmer and reflect the light of the sun. Some wore small aprons of fringed, dressed deerskin to cover their nakedness. Tied, braided tails hung down over their buttocks, for all the world like cows' tails. Some of the Indians were tall, but not so tall as Prince Manteo, nor as fair-favoured in features and eyes. The greater among them had a sort of scarification in a series of circles that began at their shoulders and made a design ending at their lean bellies.

Their stiff black hair was braided—some had feathers thrust through the braids—and they wore divers strings of beads about their necks, which hung as far down as their umbilicus depression. Some had copper about their arms and legs, of such a colour that at first it looked to be pure gold.

Colin noticed one man deeply wrinkled, with hair touched with grey, who carried in his hand a mighty bow. On one wrist he wore a chain of beads: on the other, the bow arm, was a strip of deer leather, wrapped tightly for strength. He had a clever device across the fingers of his hand, a sort of guard, also to give strength when he shot the arrow.

This Indian was surrounded by others, younger men, of tall stature and muscular. Colin took him to be a king, or at least a high chief, for in his ears he wore large pearls, very orient, and the beads he wore were likewise pearls, though dark.

As Colin watched, two young savages brought forward a bench of sorts. They put it down beside a green bush which was the height of a tall man and had small glossy leaves like a tea plant. This bench they covered with a deerskin. They drove stakes into the sand behind it and cast another deerskin, most beautiful in hair, before it. The old man sat down, resting his back against the stakes and his bare feet on the skin.

Near by other savages arranged small pieces of driftwood, all pointing toward the center, to make a fire. The blaze rose and sent off black smoke in a cloud—perhaps a signal to other savages on sand-banks or the main, or perhaps only for warmth as a number of them made a circle about it.

John Arundell leaned over and spoke into Colin's ear. "There are no women, only men. A good thing, no doubt."

"Indeed yes," Philip Blount broke in, "with our seamen and laborers continent for so many months."

"The Indians have wisdom in these matters," Darby Glande informed them. "They demand chastity in a young maiden or any unmarried woman."

"What about wives? Do they have the same strict rules for them?" Philip asked.

"I think not. Only the maidens."

The conversation was interrupted by the arrival of other boats. Colin turned and saw the *Tyger* moving slowly through the narrow entrance between the sand islands. She looked a great ship then, even with her large sails furled.

The Indians turned to watch her progress with blank, stolid faces. The Englishmen, drawn up in a group, also watched her, and pride glowed in their eyes. A proud ship she was, with her high prow and gilded figure-head pointed directly toward them, and the company in shining armour drawn up at the rails.

They saw Sir Richard Grenville standing motionless on the bridge, as they had seen him earlier, but now he was not alone. Behind him were his gentlemen-at-arms and his trumpeters and players of the kettledrums.

John said, "The Admiral is annoyed. He told me that he planned to fetch the organ for this ceremony, for the Indians love music, but alas, both organs are on Captain Cavendish's ship!"

There was no time for further comments, as the *Tyger* put to anchor in the deep hole. The seamen began to lower the small boats in order to bring the first members of the company ashore. Sir Richard stayed as he was. He would come when the other ships had anchored and set ashore their complement.

After a time Manteo and Wanchese came ashore in a long-boat. The eight men of its crew tossed their long oars and held them upright as the two princes stepped from the boat to the sand. The Indians had discarded their elegant English habits. They were dressed as the chief was dressed, in white deerskin heavily fringed, and they wore golden bracelets and chains set with precious stones.

They went at once to the old chieftain. Kneeling on the sand, they touched their foreheads to his feet in obeisance.

"He must be King Wingina," Colin said to his companions. "See, he is motioning them to sit beside him, but on the ground."

"That shows they are inferior," John answered. Philip did not take his eyes from the Indians.

"They have strong bows, but I don't see any falcons or pistols. At that, they could be a danger to us." Anthony Rowse made the comment. "I've been told that they lie in ambush on dark nights or even on moonlight nights. They carry long knives and small hatchets, see, like those standing well behind the king. The Indians that are carrying spears

234

have knives in their girdles. They are warriors who protect the king's person."

"As our gentlemen-at-arms protect our Admiral and governor."

"They look cruel to me," Philip Blount remarked. "I'm glad we have our heavy ordnance aboard our ships."

Glande nodded toward the hillock where Captain Aubry and Captain Boniten and their men waited. "We have a cannon ashore, to fire a salute no doubt, but it will give the savages knowledge that we have protection."

Arundell slapped his cheek. "The same devilish gnats biting like hot needles. It is good that we have the cover of our armour and boots."

"Aye, and they come out heavily at night, buzzing and hovering over, so that a man is hard put to get proper sleep." Glande caught at a winged pest with his cupped hand. He crushed the gnat. Holding out his palm he said, "See, it's barely of a size to be visible, yet what agony it can inflict!"

"If Dick were here he would counter by saying, 'Show me the golden streets.' "

The men laughed. They were light-hearted, filled with anticipation. The new country was achieved. They had set their eyes on the savages. Even Manteo and Wanchese were different. Stripped of their English clothes they took on a new aspect. They became one with the ever-increasing company of savages which were landing from the canoes.

"I wish I were a king," grumbled John. "Then I could sit me down and rest my weary body. This armour which my father wore like a feather is too big for my bones. How heavily it weighs on my shoulders!"

Darby grinned. "Your father was a mighty man. I remember him well. He rode like the wind, and his sword had strength behind it."

Black John was solemn for a moment, then a smile made his face radiant. "Perhaps Virginia will bring me to man's estate and raise my stature."

Glande nodded. "These ventures make men—or destroy them."

He was interrupted by Colin, who cried, "The ships are through—all of them—excepting one."

"Which one lingers?" Philip asked.

"I can't be sure. But one appears in danger of grounding."

The high shrill whistle sounded, followed by the roll of kettledrums.

"That means the Admiral is being piped over the side. Let us hurry and take our positions."

There was a stir among the Indians. Without moving their bodies, they moved their heads, looking with their obsidian eyes toward the *Tyger*. The sand dunes, covered with low scrub, obscured the landing.

The clarions and the drums broke the stillness that had settled over the Indians and the company.

Presently Grenville appeared in full armour, with plumed casque on his head, visor open. The flag of the Grenvilles with three clarions whipped in the wind. Three musicians blowing clarions came next, then the drummers. A company of a hundred men followed the Admiral across the sands, with seamen making an aisle through which they passed. Ten gentlemen-at-arms were each accompanied by a tall West-Country man who carried the house banner of his particular county family. The standards would be unfurled when the time came for Grenville to take the land in the name of the Queen.

The Admiral went at once to the gaily striped tent which had been set up on a dune in view of all the savages, the ships and the Englishmen. Captains, masters, gentlemen and soldiers gathered about him, Colin and his companions among them.

They faced the Indian king, who stood with Manteo and Wanchese on either side and his warriors behind him.

Captain Amadas handed the Admiral a scroll of parchment, sealed with the Great Seal. The clarions sounded "Attention," followed by a long roll of the drums.

The Admiral began to read the Charter given by Elizabeth the Queen to her most loyal and devoted subject Sir Walter Raleigh. He read openly and solemnly in a clear voice. He took possession of the land by right of the Crown of England.

A soldier, brightly dressed, presented on his knees a silver tray. On the tray was a bit of turf, out of which sprang a few small reeds, this year's growth. A second soldier presented a wand of hazel, stripped to whiteness, betokening sovereignty. These were delivered to the Admiral after the law and custom of England.

When this act was accomplished, a young Indian boy, tall, erect, stepped forward. From under his cloak he produced a second block of turf. Through the turf was thrust an arrow, feathered in white, with the plume of an egret bound to the shaft. This betokened submission by the Indian tribe, for the arrow was without a point.

The soldiers fired a volley. Every man drew his sword and held it aloft. The flag of England was unfurled and set up on a staff on the hill of sand. A second long roll of drums, and the Falcon and Tudor Rose, the standard of Elizabeth, caught the breeze. The Falcon and Rose were the symbols of the Queen's Grace; the banner was without the sceptre which denoted her presence.

The sun's afterglow was over the rim of the main when the heavy cannon was set off. The savages, startled, jumped. Some turned and fled to the canoes. Paddles dipped. The king, though startled by the intensity of the cannon's shot, spoke to Manteo, who raised his voice and in his own tongue assured the frightened people that all was well.

Sir Richard stepped across the intervening space, accompanied by Captain Amadas. The latter carried a handsomely carved casket of silver. Sir Richard opened the lid, took out a long chain made of large golden links, from which hung a medal bearing the likeness of the Queen. This he threw over the head of the Indian king.

He spoke through Manteo, saying that they, the king's subjects and the Queen's men, would dwell in peace, living under the laws of England and the Crown.

A gentleman stepped forward from the company. Master Rowse it was, and he read a paragraph from the Bible, which Dr. Hooker, clergyman and Master of the Temple, had sent with the ship. This was to show that the law and Christian dominion went hand in hand—the majesty of the law as temporal power, and the law of the spirit, symbolised by the Church.

Then Sir Richard Grenville grasped the banner of the Queen's Majesty and set the staff beside the flag of England, driving it firmly into the sand.

Every man fell to his knees, and the great prayer was said by all Englishmen present. This was followed by a hymn, Sir Philip Sidney's rendering of the One Hundred and Thirteenth Psalm, sung valiantly and with great purpose.

> "O you that serve the Lord,
> To praise his name accord;

Jehovah now and ever
Commending, ending never,
Whom all this earth resounds
From east to western bounds.

"He monarch reigns on high:
His glory treads the sky.
Like him who can be counted,
That dwells so highly mounted?
Yet stooping low beholds
What heav'n and earth enfolds."

The Indians were silent and watchful, awed by this display of banners, flags, arms and solemnity.

The long salute—and the fair land of Virginia was now a part of the domain of Elizabeth of England.

Colin breathed deeply. Men all about him were stirred. Eyes were wet. The long journey was over. They had fought the ocean and won. But ahead of them was a land to be conquered.

As the last cannon was fired, the sunset gun, a shout rose from the water. The Spanish barque was in trouble. Man after man was leaping into the water, swimming and wading to the beach, as the ship, piloted by the Portuguese Ferdinando, struck against the shore. It listed sharply, seemed to shudder from stem to keel as it settled into the water, blocking the entrance.

Outside on the blue ocean the white sails of a ship were visible—Master Cavendish's ship the *Elizabeth,* carrying a company of London men and Master Ralph Lane, Governor of the Island of Roanoke by virtue of Her Majesty the Queen.

And on shore a group of West-Countrymen lifted their voices in fine unison and sang the "Gate Song of Stowe."

"Like a fruitful vine
On the house's side
So doth thy wife spring
And thy children stand
Like olive plants
Thy table round."

In his cabin on the *Tyger* the Admiral heard and smiled. His men shared his triumph that he, Richard Grenville, a

West-Countryman, had planted the standard of Elizabeth in the New World.

Fires burned brightly on the main and on the island, blazing in the velvet of the night; Indian fires, beside which warriors sat, speaking their thoughts in their strange and savage tongue. Indian drums sounded, vibrating warning.

Colin, on the deck, looked shoreward. He thought of the wild moors of Cornwall, of strange pagan rites practised in the stone circles. Those had been savage days in a young land. What was transpiring now beside the fires in the soft Virginia night, in another young and unconquered land? Some wild dance, some strange ritual, a human sacrifice to a pagan god?

He went slowly toward his cabin. The ship was silent as a tomb. The feasting and the drinking had left men dead for sleep. As he crossed his threshold, he saw a candle was burning in the cabin beyond. His master, Richard Grenville, kept vigil in the night.

239

CHAPTER 18
LORD WARDEN OF THE STANNARIES

Walter Raleigh, Lord Warden of the Stannaries, made his triumphal way across South Devon. From St. Austell in Cornwall, where the great tin mines were located, to Exeter, where he was to be the guest of the bishop, he was entertained by the mayors of cities and the gentry and cheered by yeomen, farm lads and artisans. The women-folk were not behind in their admiration. A great ball was held at Buckland Abbey, although the master of the house, Sir Francis Drake, had already departed from Plymouth with a fleet of twenty sail. Drake's destination was unknown, but many guessed he would attack the Spanish islands.

Between Raleigh and Drake there was no great love lost, although the one had no occasion to dislike or distrust the other. Raleigh agreed with the opinion that had been general among the gentry in South Devon. To be sure, the Earl of Bedford, whose seat was at Tavistock near Drake's birthplace, had stood godfather to him and remained his adviser and friend. But they still remembered that he was a son of mean parents and recalled the talk that as a youth he had served a poor mariner, who owned a small boat that sailed to Zealand and France, trading in a meager way.

However, when Drake returned from the journey around the globe, a great legend sprang up about him, which persisted. The gentry forgot to look down their noses at the man of inferior birth and sought him out. They would share the acclaim that had come to the circumnavigator. They recognised that he had a head to contrive and a hand to execute whatever promised glory to himself and good to his country.

Drake's bride, the heiress of Sir George Sydenham, did the honours at the ball with grace and distinction. She was a tall, handsome woman, composed and distinguished. Raleigh tried, in his subtle way, to glean from her some inkling of Drake's destination, but she turned the question by asking him to step into the gallery to see the portrait of her husband, done at the request of the Queen.

Raleigh must perforce follow her and make comment on the painting, which was indeed a good likeness, giving a fair presentation of Drake's very round head, his brown hair, his comely beard and sweeping moustaches. It showed his large strong eyes to advantage, and the artist had caught his cheerful, engaging expression. Being a bust painting, it did not show his short stature.

Lady Drake said, "It grieves me that my husband and Sir Richard Grenville are not friends. Here are two of England's great captains, and they must remain cool and stand afar from each other. I cannot imagine why, nor will my husband answer when I question him."

Raleigh allowed his eyes to wander about the beautiful room. They rested on chest and desk, chairs and finely carved table. The ancient Grenville arms above the fireplace had not yet been erased and replaced by the newly granted arms of Drake.

"I know, I know," she said, biting her lip. "We occupy the house where the Grenvilles have lived for many generations. We dine on their table, sit in their chairs. But he sold it to us willingly."

"Not to Drake, madam," Raleigh said gently. "Richard Grenville sold Buckland to his son-in-law Harris."

The lady dropped her eyes. For a moment she was silent. Her voice was low. "It was a trick, Sir Walter, a trick that I am sure my husband sometimes regrets. You are his true friend, I think. You know he does not love to admit a wrong, any more than he will brook a defeat."

Raleigh turned the pages of the Bible which lay on the table, the Holy Book that had journeyed around the globe. After a moment he said, "The qualities one might not like in a weak man become part of the strength of a strong man. Francis would not be defeated in purchasing a house any more than he would accept defeat in battle. Do not let this annoy you. Between two strong men, both ambitious to achieve the same thing, there will be animosity. What matter? There is glory enough to go around when Englishmen may sail the seas, find new lands and seat them with their fellow countrymen."

Lady Drake watched the expression change on Raleigh's face, a look of longing replace his usual calm. Impulsively she spoke, laying her hand for a moment on his arm. "You wished to sail to Virginia?"

The sound of music came from the ball-room, laughter and gay voices from the terrace.

"Someone must remain behind," he answered. "It is not given to every man to fill his eyes with the restless sea or a far horizon. Someone must stay behind to look on narrow streets and know the sting of voices that carry envy and venom."

Lady Drake pressed his hand. "Come, let us return to the ballroom. I have kept you too long from your admirers."

At the door she turned. Her fine eyes held an expression of deep kindness. "You are on your way to Stowe. Would it be presumptuous for me to send a message to Lady Grenville? Will you say to her that I, too, know what it means to wait . . . to wait in loneliness?"

Raleigh thought of this conversation as his little cavalcade approached Exeter where he was to pass the night, a break in the journey to Stowe. Because of his attempts to colonise the New World, he was in high favour at court. When the captains Philip Amadas and Arthur Barlow returned from the first journey with such glowing reports, Elizabeth had knighted him. Soon she made him Lord Warden of the Stannaries and later bestowed on him the title of Vice-Admiral of the Counties of Cornwall and Devon. The royal privilege of vending wine throughout the kingdom was most lucrative, and from the great tin mines he drew a goodly revenue. Revenue was welcomed now because his funds, drained by Sir Humphrey Gilbert's disastrous voyage, must stand the strain of still another expedition when Richard Grenville returned. He must produce more ships, more men —this time yeomen, artisans and husbandmen. He had promised Grenville before he left Plymouth in April.

He lifted his mind from his deep thoughts. His young squires were singing as they rode along. Their hearts were light. Had he not promised that they should go on a journey to Virginia or to the Golden Isles?

Promises he made them, over and over, with scarcely a thought, court promises spoken lightly and as lightly broken. He thought of other things, of his boyhood, of his mother's understanding when he and Humphrey Gilbert would return home late to Hayes Barton, their eyes shining, their tongues eager with tales of the Ocean Sea told to them by the old seaman as they sat on the cliffs.

Humphrey had gone out first on that Ocean Sea and had died with words on his lips that were indelibly stamped on the minds of Englishmen: "We are as near to heaven by sea as by land." Humphrey had been very near to God in his fine, gentle spirit. He was without ambition for himself; he wanted only the nation's good. Raleigh sighed. Perhaps one day he could be as gentle in spirit as Humphrey. They had had the same mother; surely her goodness fell evenly on both her wandering sons.

Humphrey had not sought the court as he had. Glory had come to him by his deeds.

Raleigh thought then of the line he had once written on a windowpane. He had known the Queen would pass that way. He had hoped in his young heart that she would pause to read what he had written:

Fain would I climb, yet fear I to fall.

How his heart had beaten! How he had trembled when she stopped! How beautiful had been her smile as she finished the couplet, scrawling the letters on the pane with the diamond in her ring:

If thy heart fails thee, climb not at all.

Oh, divine Elizabeth! That had been long ago, when he was so young, so audacious. Now he would be afraid lest some courtier, someone envious of his closeness to the Queen, would make light.

The Queen's herald had found his lineage and given him a crest and coat-of-arms, but Raleigh knew that some had disputed his right to them. What matter, as long as he held the Queen's favour?

But how long would that favour last? In his time he had seen favourites rise, only to lay their heads on the block for some so-called treason. How far had Leicester slipped from the Queen's affection? Was this handsome young Essex a hazard to Raleigh's rising fortune?

The dull pomp, the heavy routine of life at court stifled him at times. His was a restive spirit. He knew well that one must strive eternally to keep in favour. He had no great estate where he could entertain the Queen and her court for days on end, even for a month, as some great lords, such as Leicester, had done.

This new thing, this searching for new lands and planting colonies had caught the Queen's fancy, and the people's also. See how Drake had risen from nothing to a high place.

Drake was too wise to linger in England. Sail and search; sail and sail again. New lands, Spanish cities sacked, made to pay ransom. Gold for Elizabeth. That was the thing! Even in his secret heart Raleigh did not dare to call her greedy, but she gave away little of her own wealth. Honours and property she took from some traitor, or some Catholic family or the Church, and gave them to some favourite—he had had his share—even as her father had done before her. That was her way. Perhaps it was always the way of princes.

He tried to convince himself that he would have sailed for the New World as Drake and Gilbert and Grenville had done, or brought shiploads of slaves from Africa like Hawkins. But would he? He had found excuses for not going on dangerous voyages even before the Queen forbade him to leave England.

He must send out ships, and more ships.

Hakluyt, his friend and Hariot, his tutor, already beholden to him for past favours aplenty—they would help him keep alive the Queen's interest in Virginia, and the people's. Grenville was already a man of distinction. He needed nothing more to add to his stature. But he was ambitious. He wanted to be one of the sea-captains who were enriching England in land and in wealth. He was a man who strode forward toward danger as others fled from it.

Raleigh's mind turned to Hariot. He had instructed him to draw up a topographical account of Virginia. Was that a mistake? Hariot was a most ingenious fellow, a mathematician who thought away from the mathematicians at Cambridge and Oxford. He thought away from some of the clergy. Secretly Hariot doubted the authenticity of the Mosaic account of the creation, but he was no deist. Raleigh had given him instructions to instil religion into the Indians. That was part of his office in the new colony.

Sir Walter turned schemes in his head whereby he might acquire more ships without giving over control of the ventures. Gold—if only they would come back and report that they had found gold and other precious metals, how easy his path would be!

244

He pushed the dark thoughts aside. That was a way he had—thrusting off unpleasantness. Humour had come to his aid in more than one tight spot. He remembered a wager he had made with the Queen about the weight of smoke from a given quantity of tobacco. Elizabeth enjoyed the "Queen's herb" as much as he did, and she likewise enjoyed a wager. He wagered he could tell the amount. She challenged him. He weighed the tobacco, then the ashes, and computed the smoke by the difference. The Queen had been delighted by his ingenuity and paid the debt in gold.

Said she, in front of all the company gathered to witness his discomfiture, "I have heard of those who turn their gold into smoke, but never before have I seen a man who turned smoke into gold."

To make the Queen smile was an accomplishment. To make the Queen laugh was a triumph. . . . Aye well, pleasant thoughts.

He looked up. His eyes fell on the tower and walls of Exeter, suspended like an enchanted city above the blue haze that masked the earth. He had come to Radford Place, down Halloway, to the South Gate with its great round towers. He passed under the archway. Across the square was the bishop's palace. Here he would find welcome and rest, and good company after the evening meal.

He reined his horse and waited for his men. Recognising the great Sir Walter Raleigh, the guard passed him unchallenged.

At the gate to the palace Raleigh dismissed his men with full purses and a day's leave. They rode off to the marketplace. It was a fair day, passing noon, and this gave the men more than the allotted twenty-four hours, which ran from sunrise to sunrise.

Coming to Exeter was not without plan, for Exeter was the center of the wool trade and not too far from the potteries. Wool merchants, weavers and fullers held their meetings at Tucker's Hall. No doubt the bishop could advise him which of the rich merchants had ships.

The wool merchants traded with Germany and France, Portugal and Holland. Raleigh knew the Queen had chartered the Merchant Adventurers more than twenty years before, and a governor and four consuls had been appointed. If

245

they had gold and ships, why not gold and ships for his Virginia venture?

The bishop, he was informed by a curate, was absent on a visit to Tavistock and Hartland. But the knight was more than welcome; a room would be ready instantly. As soon as his servant had put his horses away in the stables, Sir Walter's luggage boxes would be taken up. In the meantime there was refreshment ready, or perhaps he would prefer something in his room. The great bell of St. Peter's rang the hour, making it impossible to speak. When five had struck, and the vibration died away, Raleigh said he would go to his room.

The curate, a frail, delicate man whose skin had an earthy whiteness, led the way through the stone-floored passageway up the stairs to a cell-like room, part of the old palace built heaven knew how many centuries before.

The curate extracted a large iron key from a bunch he took from the pocket of his rusty black wool cassock. As he bent over to fit it to the lock he said, "I have put you next door to Dr. Hooker, but he will not disturb you. He reads his devotions in a low voice, and the walls are very thick, four feet of stone or more."

A smile lighted Raleigh's face. "Dr. Hooker? Is he here? Will you tell him I would be pleased to see him."

The curate turned the key and opened the door before he answered, "Dr. Hooker is in the Lady Chapel. It is a fast day and he will pass the whole day alone, locked in. At midnight perhaps or maybe it will be morning before he comes out. Until then no one may speak to him, nor will a mouthful of food pass his lips."

"Surely this is not Ember-day?" Raleigh asked, showing that he knew the good doctor's habits.

"Sir, no, but he now goes within the chapel in solitude on other fast days. His mind and heart are set on spiritual things, sir."

Raleigh nodded. "Very well. I will converse with him in the morning. In the meantime, if I may have hot water and food, I will take my rest."

"The order has been given, sir." The curate put the keys into his pocket. He bowed and went toward the door.

Raleigh stopped him. "Do you know if there is a meeting of wool merchants at Tucker's Hall tonight?"

"I think not, sir. The wool governor and his consul have

departed for Totnes and Hartland. Early this morning they rode away."

A servant came with a pewter ewer filled with steaming water. Another boy carried a tray covered with a white cloth. Raleigh's man arrived a few seconds later with his boxes and travelling case. Bathed, dressed and fed, Raleigh sat down to write. An idea had come into his head. If Hakluyt was to publish the reports of the various navigators, a compendium of all great English voyages, why should not he, with his greater knowledge, write a history of the world?

The sun, streaming in through the lancet-shaped window, fell on Raleigh's face. He waked to full knowledge of the world about him. He rose, dressed, walked across the close, went into the Lady Chapel and made his devotions. He found himself dwelling not on his sins of ambition but on the welfare of the Virginia colony, a most earnest prayer for those men that they should fare well in the far land among savages and strange circumstances.

As he entered the room where he was to breakfast, he found Dr. Hooker already half through, the bones of a pheasant breast, with remnants of a slice of cold joint on his plate, a rasher of bacon and two eggs. He had a cup of ale to wash them down.

His prominent eyes lighted when he saw Raleigh. He greeted him quietly in his usual slow manner, but there were warmth and affection in his voice when he inquired after Sir Walter's health and Lady Raleigh's. Having wiped the egg from his lips, he began his inquiry about the colony.

Raleigh could tell him little. He had seen only one communication from Grenville, by way of a home-coming merchant ship which the colonists had met at Hispaniola. He had with him other letters for Lady Grenville, but supposed them of a personal character.

The colonists were in good health and spirits. Cavendish, fallen behind in a storm, had rejoined them. Grenville had sent Dr. Hooker a message. He had delivered the Bible translated into Spanish which Dr. Hooker had sent with the expedition. The Governor of Hispaniola received it graciously enough, but the lusty friar who was always at his side had cast black looks. However, the Bible had been delivered in a great company of people, so that many inhabitants knew about it.

247

Dr. Hooker smiled with pleasure. "I shall say prayers for Richard Grenville. He is a man of sensitive, spiritual feeling. I like him well. I shall ask the good God to watch over him and his people. May they live always in grace!"

Sir Walter cast a surreptitious look at his companion's coarse gown, his worn canonical coat, the heat pimples on his face which came from his sedentary life of inaction. He leaned close to the table, shortsighted and stooped. With all these deficiencies there was something there, something of the spirit that shone through, which gave him dignity and a grave honesty that compelled men's respect. He did not ask about his stepson Geffrey Churchman or any other individual except Sir Richard Grenville. He spoke of the colony as a unit. Raleigh thought that it should be so, a common cause, undertaken in common enthusiasm.

He was a little piqued because Dr. Hooker had nothing to say about Raleigh's own share in the venture. He spoke of it always as Grenville's expedition. This disturbed Raleigh somewhat, but he quickly dismissed his ill humour. After all, what did Dr. Hooker know of worldly things? He was a man of God. He was filled with the Holy Ghost. Only twice in four years had he been absent from chapel prayers when he was in his diocese. He was regarded as a holy man. Persons of quality and note would turn out of their journeying route just to gaze at him, and the country-folk would kneel for his blessing.

Raleigh tried to draw some information from him concerning the rich wool merchants, but Dr. Hooker soon let him know that as a cleric he wanted the wool merchants to continue to pour gold into what the people called the "wool churches," rather than donate to uneasy ventures. These ventures, he told Raleigh with rare discernment, were often turned into voyages of destruction, with attacks on richly laden ships belonging to foreign countries, or slave-trading expeditions, both of which he held to be against Christian principles. Converting savages to Christianity he upheld, but not the wrong-doing of slaving or licensed piracy.

He did not mention names when he spoke of adventurers, but Raleigh knew well whom he meant. Raleigh dropped the subject.

Early next morning he continued his journey across the moors to Stowe. He would tarry one or two days there in order to read to Lady Grenville a communication that had

248

been sent by Sir Richard from the Island of Hispaniola and deliver other letters from him to her.

That night after supper, before the sun had set, Raleigh sat in the garden terrace at Stowe. On one side of him was Lady Grenville, on the other Dame Philippa. At his feet, on small three-legged stools, were the younger women, Mary Grenville and Thomasine Arundell. The smaller Arundell children, Sir Richard's wards, sat on the grass. Behind the little group were the young squires of the family, John and Bernard Grenville, St. Leger, Denny and the youngest Stukeley. They waited eagerly for Sir Walter to begin reading the letter from the voyagers half-way across the world.

Sir Walter, who had the knack of making all his speech and action seem of first importance, took his time. First he had his smoke, in which Dame Philippa joined him. Earlier in the day he had instructed the younger men in the art of smoking the Virginia weed—or the Queen's herb as he called it. He had, he told them, introduced the habit to the court, after Captain Amadas had fetched the tobacco from the Island of Roanoke. The French and Portuguese had brought tobacco back to their countries earlier, but Sir Walter had introduced it in England.

He told them how, when he first sat smoking and blowing clouds about, a lackey, thinking he was afire, had thrown a bucket of cold water over him, leaving him like a drowned rat. The girls giggled at the story. The young men guffawed. Philippa smiled. She had heard the tale often. Lady Grenville was slightly disapproving when Raleigh passed his long-stemmed pipe to Thomasine, who took a great puff. She spoke sharply to the girl.

Philippa interposed: "Why scold her, Mary? If she goes to court, she will smoke. How much better to have her learn to smoke with grace! Little Mary, too, should learn to smoke a small pipe, now that she is betrothed to Arthur and will surely go to court."

Lady Grenville set her jaw and drew her lips thin. For a gentle person she had a strong will. "No, they are not to smoke. It is an unclean habit, and it occupies time that could be spent advantageously. Don't tease them, Philippa. Please don't stick ideas into their heads. I'm sure my girls do not want to form a filthy habit."

"Indeed no, Mother," Mary said quickly. Thomasine

said nothing. A look passed between Philippa and Walter Raleigh. They knew Thomasine would not follow Lady Grenville's request. The sparkle in her dark eyes gave her thoughts away.

The pipes were finished and removed by liveried servants, to be washed and scalded and all brown trace removed. Raleigh took up his letter case and began to read.

"My honoured and sweet cousin:

"Today a trader's ship put into the harbour of Isabela on the north side of the Island of Hispaniola where we have been anchored since the first of the month.

"After our arrival at the Island of St. John's de Porto Rico on the twelfth day of May we lingered to build a pinnace. The Spaniards did not like our coming, but they found it too hard to remove these resolute Englishmen by violence. They came to parley, notwithstanding their multitude.

"Master Cavendish arrived at St. John's with his ship and Master Lane, who begins to feel that the importance of being appointed by the Queen Governor of Roanoke outweighs my importance as Captain General and Admiral of the Fleet adventuring to Virginia.

"I allow him rope and proceed to make my plans.

"The Spanish Governor of Hispaniola, having much discernment for a Spaniard, treats with me and ignores Lane as a man of lesser rank. Lane sulks and most of the time remains on the Elizabeth, surrounded by his gentlemen.

"Since we estimated more than two weeks' stay on St. John's in order to build our boat, I had Master John White, a Devon man as you well know, draw plans for a proper fort for this island, plans that might be used on a larger scale on Roanoke when we arrive at that place. It is in the form of a square, with a narrow opening to seaward: On the land sides three points, like great arrow-heads, give storage room for salt and provide watch-towers for sentries. When we had completed the wooden stockade, we threw up earthwork bastions to make it impregnable.

"Our young men behave well. I keep them busy with drill and navigation, fencing and sports. Idleness is something I will not countenance.

"I have written Sir Francis Walsingham by the same hand that I send this letter. Of Sir Francis Drake, who was rumoured to leave Plymouth shortly after we sailed, we have heard nothing. The Spanish, however, have news that he will come with twenty-three ships. It is said that the Spanish ambassador who resides in London has means to know whatever transpires at court. He sends the news to King Philip at Madrid, and then it moves as quickly

250

as sail can bring it to the Governor of Hispaniola and from there to the Spanish islands hereabouts.

"They want very much to know to which port we will sail. But I shall circumvent them. From Hispaniola I will sail a little way on a southeasterly course, so that they will not suspect a Virginia voyage. Therefore they will have not time to send a company up from their stations in Florida to raid the Virginia coast. This latter, I understand, is a country they raid every so often, and they talk of planting a colony there, a little farther north.

"It is God's blessing that I am arriving in Virginia in order to put an end to any idea of Spanish dominion from Virginia to Newfoundland.

"I am enclosing letters for Lady Grenville. Will you please send them to her forthwith, at my house at Stowe.

> "Your assured loving friend,
>
> "R. Grenville

"Address to Walter Raleigh, Knight,
in Care of Master Richard Hakluyt,
The Temple, Strand, London,
From Isabela, on Hispaniola,
the fifth day of June, 1585."

John was ready with questions; so were Bernard and young St. Leger. But Dame Philippa spoke first. "Has Lane any great authority in London, Walter?"

Raleigh nodded. "I believe so. He has the ear of the Queen, and of Walsingham as well."

Then came questions from the squires, in the most part about the next expedition.

When the young folk had wandered off for a trial at archery before it grew too dark, and Lady Grenville had gone to the nursery with the children, Philippa continued her inquiry. "It would be the part of wisdom for Richard to endeavour to keep in agreement with Lane?"

"Yes, but you know our Richard. He can be as arrogant as a Spaniard if he sees fit."

"I know," sighed Philippa. "He detests mediocrity, and it is my opinion that Lane is mediocre. Richard is like all of us: we make out well with our own class, and with the lower, but we find trouble adjusting ourselves to mediocrity."

"As you say, Philippa, it would be the part of wisdom to allow Lane some of the prerogatives of rank even before he is the governor of the island. But there is nothing to be done about it from here. Richard will not be in Virginia much longer."

Philippa raised her thin arched brows. "I thought the colony was to be on trial for a year."

"The colony, yes, but not Richard. Three months only and then he is to return to take out the second colony." He looked troubled. "I haven't secured the ships nor have I enough money. That is my worry now. I must have ships, men and equipment to sail next spring, and not a ship have I, and only a few shares sold!"

Philippa said, "Raising the funds is not the easiest task, Walter. It bears a great responsibility."

"Thank you for your understanding, my dear."

She looked across the greensward. The group about the archery target held her attention. After a time she spoke. Something in the tone of her voice caused Raleigh to turn his searching eyes on her face. She was so tuned to guarding her thoughts, he could at first read nothing by her expression, nor by what she said.

"A year has gone by since you were all here at Stowe. The harvest time comes again. How slow, how prolonged the days have been!"

"Strange words from you, Philippa."

"Why? Do you think me incapable of weighing the passage of time? Dear God, sometimes I count the hours as they drag by! Endless hours, filled with despair."

He leaned toward her. "Philip?" he asked, his voice low. "Do you wait for Philip Sidney's return?"

She did not meet his eyes. Everything about her was still. Her slim beautiful body, her long tapering fingers, her very thought were still, as though she were suspended in some timeless world. "Not Philip. That was a fleeting moment, sweet but not lasting. Oh, Walter, it is sad to know what love means when it comes too late." She turned slowly. There was a tragic hopelessness in her blue eyes as she watched Mary Grenville walking through the garden.

Raleigh put his hand over hers. There was warm sympathy in the gesture. "You and Richard. You and Richard and Mary."

"I must not hurt her, ever," Philippa whispered.

Lady Grenville joined them, and Raleigh spoke no more to Philippa. In the morning he rode on. The young gentlemen of Stowe accompanied him as far as Bideford, where he took ship.

Late that night Thomasine crept into Philippa's room. She

252

seated herself on the floor by Philippa's bedside. "I could not sleep. It is the moon. At home, at the full of the moon, I used to run out on the moor. I would throw myself on the earth and dream, dream, dream: I was happy then. Now Lady Grenville tells me I cannot run on the moor. I must behave like a lady. Ah, Philippa, good, understanding Philippa, why must women love? Love without hope?"

Philippa's heart contracted suddenly. Who was this girl that she asked aloud the question that was eating at her own heart?

Thomasine, not wanting an answer, went on talking. The moonlight playing on her face gave it a pale, unearthly look. Her dark eyes seemed to burn red, as a cat's burn in the night. "Lady Grenville let me read parts of her letters. Did you know that Colin wrote them for Sir Richard? The letters said so. You taught him to write. Now he writes for Sir Richard. Are you not proud?"

Dame Philippa did not speak. It came to her suddenly that it was Colin about whom this wild girl dreamed. Mary thought it was John Arundell. She listened now to the low voice.

"He wrote the letters. He inquired about everyone at Stowe. Everyone, even nurse Marjory. Not one word about Thomasine. Oh, Philippa!" She put her head down on the white counterpane. Her thick dark hair hid her face completely and tumbled over her shoulders.

Philippa reached out her hand and laid it on Thomasine's head. Why indeed did women love so blindly? Thomasine had come to womanhood with an ancient cry on her red lips. Why should a woman eat her heart out for the love of a man?

Again Philippa sighed. Why indeed?

BOOK IV
VIRGINIA

CHAPTER 19
NEW FORT IN VIRGINIA

The ships were anchored, lying off the northeast shore of Roanoke Island. The Spanish barque had righted herself with the high tide. A line from the *Elizabeth* was used to drag her off the sand and set her in channel. A steady stream of Portuguese vituperation came from the lips of Ferdinando the pilot, which ceased only when he had dropped anchor.

Vituperation, the English variety, came from the bearded lips of Governor Ralph Lane, although not publicly. His intimates, gathered around him in the cabin of the *Elizabeth*, heard and sympathised.

"It's what I would have expected of Grenville. He tricked me—taking possession of the land while I was trapped, virtually a prisoner, on the *Elizabeth*."

Francis Brooke, thin, sardonic, with raised black brows and oval black eyes, sat on the edge of a table swinging his long legs. He had thrown his lot with Lane, since Raleigh had named him comptroller, but he did not follow Lane blindly, as some of the others did.

Now he spoke, in his lazy, well-bred voice. "It seems to me, if my memory serves me, that we were remiss. The *Elizabeth* lagged behind." He glanced at Captain Cavendish who, stripped to the belt, sat near the port to catch the east wind. "Why was that, Captain? Is the *Elizabeth* the slowest of the ships, or is your navigation inferior to eight other navigators?"

Cavendish glared at Brooke. He was a hot-tempered man and Brooke's easy careless ways annoyed him. "Our navigation is as good as any. Grinding over the shoals at the Cape of Fear held us back. Bad luck."

Brooke played at cat's-cradle with a bit of string. "I noticed none of the other ships grounded over the shoals. No offence, sir. I just wondered."

"Gentlemen, I beg of you to quit quarrelling," Lane broke

257

out irritably. "It's enough to have a division in the company without this eternal bickering among ourselves."

Brooke raised his brows, shrugged his shoulders—gestures quite common among the elegant courtiers who visited at Wycroft, his father's seat in Axminster. His assumption of blasé indifference irritated Lane still further. Lane could, by using the weapon of sarcasm, get under the defences of his men, but not under Brooke's. Brooke smiled, making Lane conscious that only on the Island of Roanoke was he in a superior position. Sometimes he suspected that young Brooke admired Grenville.

Lane turned his eyes landward. What he saw did not please him. His men who were ashore were playing at bowls or lying in shaded places on the beach. Grenville's men were working industriously. They had already set about making bricks, laying out foundations for their houses. One house was well advanced, with a strong foundation. They had cut out a section of trees—pines, cedars, oaks and bays—and had begun work on their side of a fort similar to the one they had built at St. John's according to Master John White's drawings. Darby Glande took charge. The work had progressed well. Now after a month on the island there was a goodly showing of house foundations and walls. Down by the shore where the reeds grew thickest, thatch was being woven.

The first day he set his foot ashore on Roanoke, Lane had proclaimed himself governor with a suitable ceremony, which the entire company witnessed—all save Grenville, who had taken a few men and crossed the water to the Indian village on the main. It was a thoughtful act on the Admiral's part, for it left Ralph Lane the ranking man on the island.

A goodly number of the governor's men at once took up their abode on shore, cutting out a clearing at the top of the long hill. Here in a grove of beautiful trees some set about building permanent houses.

Sir Richard lived on his ship and moved about the waters at will, examining and exploring. Every day Indians came to the island, bringing fish and game or wild birds, to exchange for small trade goods. They were Wingina's men, and they came in long canoes, each of which was burned out of a single long log and would hold twenty men comfortably. On the main the village had good cornfields, which would be ripe in another month or more.

Lane decided it was too late to plant this year. But some of Grenville's men, under Colin's direction, planted a field they found near the site of a deserted Indian village on the island. It was a well-cleared plot enclosed within the village palisade, which they repaired. This enclosure made the field safe from the ravages of bear or deer or even small animals.

Brooke picked up Lane's glass and inspected the group of workers. "They are industrious folk. Their maize patch has put out good growth, and they have done well with their houses. They know how to provide for themselves certainly. I wish we might say as much for the men on our side."

Thomas Hariot, who was busy writing in his quire, looked up. "We have on our side many men of nice bringing up, but they come from cities or towns and have never seen the world before. They have known only dainty food and soft beds of down and feathers. The country is miserable to them."

Lane answered quickly, "When Grenville leaves in a month's time, we shall see which side fares better and labors better."

"I loathe to see it working out thus—first one side, then the other side. The company should be in unity at all times. I myself do not intend to take sides." Hariot spoke quietly, scratching at his cheek with his feathered quill, his fine large eyes on Lane. "I shall go with the Admiral on some of his journeys to the main and the islands, in order to make maps and to write reports. That is my duty to Sir Walter Raleigh, by whose orders I am here." He gathered up his papers and made off for his cabin.

Cavendish said, "It is difficult to deal with all the people, some thinking one way and some another, but I agree with Hariot—unity is essential."

Lane spoke sharply. "How can there be unity with divided command? When Grenville sails, you will see—we will be one company."

"Let us hope that it will be set to Admiral Grenville's standard of work." Brooke lounged out of the cabin after he had made this last remark.

Spurred by the knowledge that his own men were criticising his inaction, Lane made plans to send his men out on discoveries. Fifteen men, with their luggage and victuals for seven days, he sent southward beyond Sir Richard's discoveries, all within the inner water. They were to journey into waters too full of shoals for a pinnace to sail.

Early next morning Lane boarded a pinnace, taking with him Captain Cavendish, Hariot and twenty others. Captain Amadas, Captain Clarke and ten men went in a ship's boat. Francis Brooke and John White, with ten more, passed over the water to the mainland with victuals for eight days.

With so many of the company out on voyage of discovery —each man in his heart hoping to discover gold or pearls— the work of building the palisades to surround the fort inevitably suffered.

Darby Glande and Colin were progressing well with the task assigned to them—brickmaking, felling trees for the rough planks. There was sand in plenty on the island. Mixed with oyster shells obtained on the banks, it could be manufactured into a good fabric. It was set into brick moulds, and it dried hard and firm. Such fabric they had seen used in the Spanish towns for walls and the foundation of houses. Even for houses themselves it had proved warm in winter and cool in the hot season.

Darby sat on a log smoking his Indian pipe, watching his men work. Colin stood near by. He had just come up the long hill from the beach, where he had half a dozen North Devon men cutting reeds for thatching the houses. They had begun a general house, with an upper and a nether floor, and the walls were well up, with openings left for windows.

Not far off two men were sawing a great cedar, and two others were busy with long saws to rip out rough planking for the outside of the building where the fabric was not used. They had a little plan of the building to guide them, which Master White had made. When it was finished it would be not unlike the inn at Kilkhampton across from the church. Men liked to be surrounded by familiar things.

" 'Tis black and white houses we want in the New World, not earth huts or barns. We must show the savages how Englishmen live." These had been the Admiral's words, and they would carry them out to the letter. A little forge had been set up for making nails, and the carpenters and joiners were hard at it, working merrily in spite of the derisive calls of the men who lazed on the beach or in the dense shade under bay trees.

Darby smoked his tobacco and puffed smoke with great enjoyment. "Let them waste their lungs," he told Colin.

"There'll be another cry come winter. We will be fast and snug, and they will be crying for our fireside."

Colin said, "It is worrying that some laze so long. They do not even wet a line to cast for fish, but lie on the sand in their nudity day after day. Why, even the savages plant and fish and hunt. When we went across to the village on the main, I saw hundreds of fish hung on a long line, drying. And they had deer flesh, drawn in strips. It also was drying over a fire. Our Indian guide told us a man could travel for days with only chunks of dried deer's meat to sustain him."

Glande said, "Good! We'll dry some venison over a fire, to put away. Did they salt it?"

"I think so, but I'm not certain. It would be sure to keep if it were smoked and salted. Come with me, Darby. I'm going to look at the horses and cattle. I have some men making shelters, for we know not how cold the winter will be. No one has stayed the seasons through. I want a warm place for the sheep. They may lamb early."

Darby rose. "You're a smart lad. How does it come you know so much about animals?"

It was on the tip of Colin's tongue to say that he had herded sheep for many seasons, but he remembered Sir Richard's warning not to talk. Instead, he said, "Sir Richard has great flocks and many fine horses and herds of cattle at Stowe."

They walked through the woods to a point on the shore. A meadow had been fenced in by intertwining small saplings. Here the livestock wandered, feeding on native grass, down the slope to the water to drink. Three cows stood knee-deep in the water on the shallows, slapping their tails lazily to ward off flies.

In an enclosure to themselves were the horses.

Glande said, "Look, the mare has dropped a colt."

"Yesterday morning. The feeder ran for me, but everything went normally. They're beautiful horses, aren't they?"

Glande nodded. "So it seems to me, but a Spaniard told me that their governor had driven away the choicest mares, so Sir Richard would not set eyes on them and demand them for Don Fernando de Altamirano's ransom."

"They have tricks, those Spaniards. But I'd have done the same in like case."

When they returned to the beach the sun was low. The same men were still lying on the beach. To keep off the insects some had covered themselves with sand, and only their arms and heads were visible. Three were dicing, using shells for money.

"You'll get the fever," Glande said. "After sundown the gnats and stinging flies come out in force."

The men laughed. They did not stir, but went on with their dicing. Glande went back to send his workers for a quick bath. To rid themselves of sweat came first, then a run down the beach, and the row in the boats to the ship for supper.

"They'll sleep well tonight," he remarked to Colin. "A tired body and a sound sleep put a man in good trim, with no time for complaints. A good leader looks after his men's needs. Feed the body and occupy the hands and mind— that's the way to keep trouble out of a camp. Look at Lane's men. Already they're picking quarrels with our men and with one another. Lane has ordered stocks built. Better if he saw that his men were busy every day. Then they'd have no time to get into trouble or reason to stand in the stocks."

The Admiral, with Master Stukeley, John Arundell and Philip Blount, came aboard the *Tyger* shortly after Colin got back. They had been to Aquascogok, an Indian village near the great lake the Indians called Paquipe. Philip and Black John came into the cabin when Colin was washing his hands. They began to tell him about the journey and the Indian village they had visited.

It was only just now at sundown that John discovered the Admiral's silver cup was missing. They had dined at the village. The Admiral had taken his own service with him. As a matter of courtesy he had offered to the chief his silver-gilt cup filled with wine. The chief drank the wine at a gulp in a savage manner, John told Colin. Other Indians had crowded about to touch the cup. When they got back to the ship, it was missing.

"It's my fault," John said. "I should have made sure. I thought the Admiral's servant had packed it with the dishes. But he swears he never saw it after the Indian chief drank from it. Now I must tell Sir Richard. I'd rather be shot."

"He'll be furious. I'm glad I don't have to tell him," Philip Blount remarked.

"Is it the great cup? The cup from Bideford?"

"Yes, the great cup. How could they have concealed it?" John put the question to Philip.

Philip shook his head. "I can't conceive—unless it was when they all gathered around the chief to examine it."

"No, I saw it after that. They must have taken it when our men were packing the plate. Well, I'll have to tell him. I may as well go now." Black John got up and went toward the door. "Pray for me," he said as he left the cabin.

Philip and Colin exchanged sober glances. Philip said, "He'll take the hide off John. I wouldn't be in his shoes for a hundred crowns. You know the Admiral dotes on that cup. And who wouldn't?"

"Will he put him in the stocks?" Colin asked.

Philip shook his head. "I don't know. You can never tell what that man will do when he's in wrath. I'm afraid of him, Colin. I've never been afraid of anyone before—that is, since I've been a man."

Colin did not envy John, but somehow he no longer feared Sir Richard, not since he had written letters for him to Lady Grenville, so full of tenderness. He understood how deeply the Admiral cared for his men, particularly for the young men of his command. He wanted to strengthen them— "harden" was the word he used—so that they could step into life prepared. "To play the part of English gentlemen means a long and severe training," he had once told Colin when he was planning a program of daily work with Nugent. "A man must think honestly, as well as act honestly. Integrity of mind and spirit will bring comfort when things are dark about one." A stern sense of justice was inherent in Grenville.

Colin said, "I think he will be just."

Philip did not hear. He was standing close to the partition. A rumble of voices could be heard, but no words. After a long time, inordinately long it seemed to the two lads waiting, John came back into the room.

He went directly to his chest and took out his sword and two pistols. He strapped his sword-belt about his waist and looked to the pistols.

"For the love of God, what did he say?" Philip demanded.

"I'm to take twenty men, two boats—ten men to a boat —and visit the Indian town."

"What? Now? At night?" Blunt words rushed out.

"At once. Without delay."

"Who captains the second boat?" Philip asked.

"James Lacie."

"Lacie? Why not Nugent? Glande? Some older man?"

" 'Tis time we accept responsibility without leaning on older men. Sir Richard was eighteen when he fought the Turks."

Philip didn't comment. He took up his sword and buckled it around his middle. Colin followed. He carried a sword and dagger, but no pistol.

John stopped them. "You weren't on the list to go, either of you."

Neither Colin nor Philip answered. They followed John out of the cabin, clattered after him down the companionway to the main deck.

John spoke to the boatswain. Boats were swung. As they were being lowered, Sir Richard Grenville stepped out of his room. He watched the three lads getting into the boat. A half-smile came over his lips. "They stand together, those three," he remarked to Nugent.

"Four of them," the sergeant replied. "Four of them. If Prideaux were here they would be four."

"Where is Prideaux? I haven't seen him for a day or two."

"Governor Lane sent him to the banks in charge of a boat crew . . . fishing . . . looking for oysters and clams."

Grenville said, "I'm not sure whether it is good policy to weaken our company, sending out so many men at a time, at least until the fortification and palisades are completed."

"The Indians seem gentle enough. Manteo returned today. He says all the Indians near the coast are favorable to us. He cannot vouch for the Chowanooks, a mighty tribe that live far up a broad river."

"Ah, we must discover these rivers, Nugent. We must add to our maps before we sail for home. New discoveries will be welcome to Sir Walter."

"So Master Lane thinks," Nugent said shrewdly. "He is sore afraid that you will discover more than he does. That's why he is sending out men here, there and everywhere."

Grenville nodded. The boats had been lowered. The oarsmen were in place.

The sun had set, but a fiery afterglow lay on the western rim. Spires of tall trees on the main broke the horizon. There was no far horizon, as there was on the sea. The forests cut the venturers off from the unknown land, a hidden land of deep mystery.

Nugent watched the boats shoot out from the shadow of the ship. "Sir, there are no canoes about tonight," he remarked.

Grenville paused, looked back over his shoulder. "I wonder," he said absently.

The sergeant searched the main with a glass. "Not a canoe, or a cooking fire."

Grenville stood in the doorway. "I did not give any orders to Arundell. I want him to handle the situation."

"Sir, you think the cup is gone?"

"Yes." His face changed. He seemed tired and dispirited. "The Bideford cup is gone. I am not sure but that I am responsible." He turned and entered his cabin.

A feeling of uneasiness came over Nugent. "I wish to God he had allowed me to go," he muttered to himself. "That frightened boy will never get the cup from those wily savages."

By the time they had reached the mainland, dark had set in. Arundell was first to leap ashore, closely followed by Colin and Philip.

" 'Twill be dark as two black cats by the time we reach the Indian town," Philip grumbled. "And vipers are out. I saw one flathead lying in the water up the creek this morning."

Arundell gave orders to light the pine-knots which the boatswain had put into the boats for torches.

Lacie demurred. "Sir, let us sneak up on them, see them gloating over their treasure cup, leap upon them with sword and pistol and take what is ours without ado."

"No, we will not. We will march into the town in good order and make our request for the return of the great cup."

"Ah! Shall you say, 'Your Lordship, our Admiral begs of you to return his property'? Have done with fooling, sir. These savages do not worship your gold lace. They will not stand bare and bend their hams. They are thieves. Treat them as such. Put them in the stocks after they have felt the flat of your sword against their buttocks."

Philip Blount stepped close to Lacie. "The Admiral has set Arundell in command, not you, my good fellow."

Lacie laughed. "Arundell in command! Well, let it stand. He can make obeisance to the savage king and tell him from what stock the Arundells descend, how many knights there are in the family and what coats they quarter. I seem to have heard such talk on a London stage. It is not the battles that our forbears fought that count today among this savage horde. 'Tis a Drake or a Hawkins we need, if we keep order here."

Arundell had walked off. His men had begun the march in line behind him. Two men carrying torches of pitch-pine lighted the way.

Lacie, grumbling, called his boat to follow and fell in.

Philip moved swiftly ahead. Colin lingered to give orders to the men who held the boats. They were to light lanthorns, so that the detail could be easily discovered when it returned, and to have harquebuses ready set on tripods for use in case the savages should be up to some beastliness.

The forest was silent and full of night mystery. Birds made soft cooing noises. An owl's hoot—from man or bird Colin could not be sure. He did not know Indian signals, only the signals made by moor-folk or poachers who roamed at night. These savages moved furtively, with no effort. He had watched them as they came and went on the island; at their fishing wiers; bending over their paddles. All muscles rippled with one impulse in co-ordination. So silently, so stealthily, they glided in and out among the trees and thickets, alert, moving like swift swords, as when they cast spears at fish jumping in the water. These were their woods. The Indians were at home. They knew the forest and streams, even as he knew the moors and woods in Coombe Vale.

He walked last, shifting his glance from side to side. The moon was rising, a small silver crescent, glimpsed between the tall pines. How far upward the trees spread their crowns! The thick carpet of pine-needles made for silent movement. He thought he saw a shadow flit from tree to tree at his left hand. He paused beside the trunk of a noble tree and waited motionless, but there was no sound. The men ahead were silent, too, as though the forest silence had fallen on them. Sometimes as the path turned he caught the glimmer of the torches. How far was this village, and where were the canoes? Where indeed?

Colin stopped. He heard a twig snap. Between him and

the light of the torch a shadow passed. He held his breath. Had the Indians surrounded them, cut off their retreat?

He waited, peering through the gloom, but no shadow moved. After a time he moved on. The path was well worn now, an earth path without the pine-needles that caused a man to slip and lose balance. The voices and shouts of his companions fell on his ears as he left the path and came into a clearing. The Indian town was empty. Arundell's men were running from hut to hut, finding each one empty. Fires were still burning; there was food in a cooking pot. The Indians had fled at their coming—fled as guilty men flee from the law.

Arundell stood in the center of the king's mat to watch that every hut was well searched. Philip Blount poked into corners and mounds with his sword, but found no cup concealed. It was Lacie who picked up the woollen bag that belonged to the cup. The Indians had the cup, and with it they had fled.

Forest paths circled the village and broke off like the spokes of a wheel, leading on one side to the deep forest and to a swamp dark with heavy rotting undergrowth. Beyond the corn-fields that surrounded the village was more water.

After a time the men wandered back, grumbling, voicing their disappointment.

Blount said, "We were an hour too late. The beasts!"

Arundell gave orders: "Fall in. Single file. To the boats. March."

Lacie drew near. "Do you want me and my men to go into the woods?"

"No. There is no use tonight. It would only risk losing our men. We must wait for daylight."

"Daylight? They will be miles away by daylight!"

John said, "I had no orders to enter the forest—only to search the village." He turned and moved off. Lacie gave an order to his men, who were in the rear of the others. Colin waited a moment, then followed Arundell, leaving Lacie behind.

Arundell's boat was out in the water when someone shouted, "Fire! Fire! The woods are afire."

Everyone turned, almost swamping the boat. "May God damn Lacie!" Colin said in his throat. He understood, too late, why Lacie had lingered behind. He remembered his words when they were sailing from the Canaries: "Fire and ravage

267

and kill—that was Drake's way. That is the way of all great sea-captains. Fire and ravage, ransom and kill."

The boat moved silently through the night. Lacie's boat put out from the shore, a dark moving shadow on the water.

Men lined the ship's side. Arundell was the first aboard the *Tyger*. He had not spoken since the alarm of fire. Philip Blount followed him. Black John went straight to Grenville's cabin. Seamen and men of the company were asking, "The cup—the cup—did you find the great cup?"

"God blast the savages to hell!" a sailor cried out. " 'Tis our last link with home. Every night when the toast was drunk, I could see the Cornish headlands. Now . . ."

"Who fired the village?" a dozen asked. "Not Arundell. He would not have the liver."

"Lacie fired the corn-field and the woods. Lacie himself fired the chief's house," answered men of the detail. Below decks Lacie was the hero of the venture.

In the cabin John made his report. "Sir, the king and all his people were gone when we came to the village. We searched but found only this." He laid the woollen bag embroidered with the Grenville Arms on the table. "It was too dark to pursue. We saw no sign of Indians or Indian canoes."

He faced the Admiral across the oaken table. The Admiral sat in his high-backed chair. Arundell was standing. "The village is burning," John said after a long silence, "and the corn-fields, I fear."

Grenville banged the table. "You fear? Didn't you set fire to the place?"

"No, sir, I did not. I do not fire villages or burn food."

Grenville's eyes were cold. "But your men did. A captain is responsible for his men."

John said nothing. Grenville continued to look at him with his hard, unwavering, cold eyes. At last John said, "I did not know until we were crossing the water that the village had been put to the torch."

"What do you mean? Did you, the captain, leave before all your men were in the boats? Don't you know that a captain never leaves his ship until the last man is off? Don't you know that a captain on land has the same responsibility as a captain on a ship? God damme, sir, you are a disgrace to your family! Before you go, think of this: Suppose the

268

chief acted in good faith. Suppose he thought the cup was a gift. How would a savage know the value, or judge between a cup of tin and one of silver?" His voice rasped. After a pause he said, "Leave me. I must think."

White-faced, John came into the boys' cabin. His fingers trembled so violently that he could not unlatch the buckle of his sword-belt. Colin leaped to help him. Colin and Philip got his heavy collar unhooked and drew off his boots. No one spoke. John sat on the bench by the table, his head in his hands. Philip and Colin looked at each other with frightened eyes. After a long time Philip asked, "Didn't you tell him that Lacie fired the village?"

John said, "A captain is responsible for the actions of his men. A captain is last to leave his ship, last to leave the land." His lips were stiff. He lifted his head and stared straight ahead of him. " 'Think of this: Suppose the chief acted in good faith. Suppose he thought the cup was a gift.' "

"Good God!" Philip leaned forward and put his arm about John's shoulder. "Did the Admiral say that?"

"Suppose a village starves because we burned the corn?" John looked from one to the other.

Try as he would, Colin could not think of anything to say that would give comfort.

"I have brought disgrace on my name."

Philip jumped to his feet. "So help me, that's a lie. You didn't fire the woods or steal the cup. I'm going to the Admiral. I'll tell him what I think."

John caught his arm and held him back. "It isn't what the Admiral thinks of me that counts, Phil. It's what I think of myself."

CHAPTER 20
THE CHALLENGE

The week after the burning of the Indian town
Aquascogok, Governor Lane and his men returned
from their journey to the main that lay to the south.
Because of the long islands on the sea-coast, entry with the
large one-hundred-thirty-ton ships was very difficult, so some
of the greater ships lay off Trinity Harbour, the entrance
nearest to Roanoke Island. Wococon, where the first entrance
had been made, was held as base for discovery to the south.
Roanoke Island was a base from which to sail west in the
great Inland Sea and up all the rivers that fed it. So many
rivers of great depth, so many inland seas, no man amongst
them had ever seen before.

Nor had they seen such tall pines. They noted a new kind
of cedar with great spreading roots that grew in the black
water of the swamps and along the shores of the sound.
Every day brought discoveries in trees and birds and fish.
Great flights of white cranes rose at a gunshot. They flew up
the broad water behind the island, their cries echoing along
the streams. Great grey herons rose from their feeding
grounds in the rushes, and other waterfowl, which made
loud squawks as they flew off.

Talk about the firing of the Indian town, which had died
out, rose again with Governor Lane's return. A dozen of his
men ran at once to tell him of the circumstance which led to
burning the village.

Lane's anger rose. Here was something tangible. He sent
Francis Brooke to arrange a meeting with Grenville. First, he
requested Grenville to come to his camp. Grenville refused.
If Master Lane wanted words with him, the meeting would
take place on the *Tyger.*

When Brooke reported, Lane's face flamed to a dull scarlet.
He swore he would not go.

Brooke said, "The Admiral will not leave his ship. I am
convinced by the tone of his answer. If you want talk with
him, it will have to be on his terms. 'I lose time to talk to

Lane' are the words he used. He is making preparation to sail up the broad water before sunset."

Lane grumbled, but yielded to the advice of Captain Clarke and Brooke.

"I'll tell him what I think," Lane remarked. "He is bound to know that I, Ralph Lane, am the Governor of Roanoke."

Brooke said, "You are acquainted with Sir Richard? Do you know him in his rough moods? By heaven, I think his wrath is as mighty as Jove's! He makes me tremble just to look at him. If he is in the humour, he flings words as a husbandman flings dirt. He can abuse. Sometimes I think the moon maddens him. Take heed, sir, lest he lash out. Beware lest he tie you up with words. Beware also lest he draw quickly. He has might behind his sword-arm, and a long reach."

Lane did not see Brooke's grinning face. He was busy buckling on his sword. The day was hot, but he was attired in a suit of heavy corded silk, and his ruff was starched and stiff. He stamped out of the cabin and called for his oarsmen. He went unattended. If Grenville got the better of him in words, he wanted no one to witness his defeat.

The Admiral sat in his cabin. He wore no doublet. His thin linen shirt was belted over his trunks like a tunic. The neck was ruffed with a fine Honiton, and at his wrists were doubled ruffles of the same. He sat at his table but rose when Colin announced the governor—rose and bowed courteously, and asked the governor to be seated.

To Colin he said, "Bring a cup of cool spring water. Governor Lane is flushed with heat, and perspiration beads his forehead."

Lane's flush deepened at Grenville's words. He was uncomfortable and therefore at a disadvantage. Grenville continued to speak of the weather. "I know from my experience in the Mediterranean countries that it is well to consider climate. One dresses accordingly and moves with caution—never in the heat of the day. Consider the savages. They lie under trees during the sun's meridian. They fish and hunt in the cool of the morning or the evening."

Lane was wordless, his anger increasing. "I am perfectly comfortable," he managed to say. "I do not feel the heat."

Grenville raised his brows. "No? You are fortunate indeed. Looking at you, at the colour of your face, one would think you were about to have a stroke."

271

Colin put a ewer of cool spring water and a cup in front of Lane. He waved it aside, sitting stiffly erect.

"I will call you if I need you," Grenville said to Colin, who left at once.

Lane said, "My visit concerns your act in arbitrarily burning an Indian village while I was at Wococon. Sir, I believe you have done a great wrong. My men tell me that not only the village was burned, but the maize fields were destroyed, leaving these good people homeless and hungry. Men, women and children are homeless, with no grain and no place to lay their heads—all for the loss of a cup, a valueless cup."

Grenville's smile broke. "Is that what you'll write Walsingham? Or perhaps my cousin Raleigh? Or perhaps Sir Philip Sidney? Or even all three? You can send them when John Arundell goes home in August."

Lane said nothing. He was prepared for a storm of protest and was taken unawares by Grenville's control.

"Don't bother," Sir Richard continued. "I will inform them when I return to England. I am not in the habit of explaining my actions, Lane. But since you have got yourself into a fever over the poor savages, I assure you that it was not their village, only a temporary fishing camp, a seasonal camp. The maize field was small and mean. It had already been raided by deer. It was of poor consequence, since the Indians had not troubled to make a watchman's platform in the middle, as they do in their main fields, to drive off birds and animals. And as for the cup, it was by no means valueless. In truth, it was of great value. By God, man, can't you understand that you must not let the savages think they can take from you without punishment? What kind of government will you have if laws of property are not established and swift punishment meted out to any who break them?"

"It is well enough for you to talk about laws. You don't have to enforce them. You, through your rash act of burning a village, leave me and my men to reap the consequences." Lane spoke slowly, impressively, as though to a company.

"Nonsense, Lane! I've been an officer for the enforcement of laws all my mature life. My father was one before me, and his father and his father's father, back ten generations. Don't you think I know whereof I talk? Indians and whites

272

both must bear punishment for evil-doing. The group must be protected. If the evil-doer is protected, your whole system of justice breaks down. Now, sir, if that is all that troubles you, think no more about it."

He looked at Lane, hot, sweating, uncomfortable in those London clothes. The little smile still lingered in the corner of his mouth. "You are new at governing men, Lane. It is well to learn values. Do not let the unimportant incidents concern you. Save your mind and strength for governing a colony and protecting your men."

He rose. The interview was over. Lane left without further speech. He had no retort ready to meet Sir Richard's words. His planned interview had been quite different. He had, in his mind, humbled Sir Richard Grenville for an act of wanton cruelty and destruction, which jeopardised the safety of the colony. Sir Richard would be meek, would sue for pardon, beg the governor not to report to Sir Francis Walsingham or to Raleigh. Lane would put Grenville in his place with excellent skill. Suavely he would humiliate a county gentleman with his fine, rapierlike tongue. . . .

And what had happened? He had had no tongue, nor could he even now think of what he might have said to hold ascendancy over Grenville.

His gentlemen had no need to question Lane on the outcome of the interview. The truth was written in his face. Any zany would know that Grenville had worsted him.

Brooke laughed when the door banged, and started to speak.

"Go to, Brooke!" Captain Clarke said sharply. "Let's have none of your prating. His Honour is in a direful mood, which can spread to us if there is too much talk."

"Right, Captain! Let him learn of himself. A man must make his own mistakes—that is, a stubborn man, who will not listen to the advice of his betters."

Lane had not gone over the side of the *Tyger* before Grenville called Colin to his cabin. "Sit down, lad. I have writing for you to do. Put a cloth close by. I do not wish moisture from your hand to draw too near the paper, for I write to Sir Francis Walsingham."

Grenville paced the cabin for a time, a way he had when troubled in his mind. Colin counted. Three strides and a half brought him to the partition; a quick turn and three

273

and a half strides to the opposite wall. A dozen times he paced back and forth before he began to speak. His words came slowly at first, then with increasing swiftness, until he noticed that Colin was hard pressed to keep up with him. Then he slowed down. Grenville was telling of the loss of the Bideford cup, and on through to the end, where the village was burned.

Colin wrote steadily. He had no feeling about the circumstance. In truth, neither John nor Philip had spoken of it once since the night a full week past when Sir Richard had called John a disgrace to the Arundells. Colin knew that each of them resented the accusation. That their hero, Sir Richard Grenville, would use such heavy words to John was unbelievable. Each knew the inner feeling of the other, but no word was said.

Sir Richard knew how they felt. There was a remoteness, a distance, established between the three lads and himself. They remained well-mannered, cheerful to do his bidding, but their eyes, which met his so steadily, were clouded, unreadable. The close bond of youth shut him out. This he regretted. The point of discord was tenuous and withdrawn. There was nothing he could do. Colin, who was with the Admiral for longer periods on account of his clerkship, could read his mind. Once or twice he had been on the verge of speaking but turned aside, the words of explanation unsaid. The white flame of passion burned readily in Richard Grenville, but the flame died quickly, except with Drake. He was not harsh with such men of little mind as Lane. He was more like to disregard them.

Meticulously set down was the story of the Indian village. Each man who played a part was named in order. He lingered long over the closing of the letter.

"How vainly I try to place blame, when the blame, if blame there be, rests on my own head! As I spoke harshly to young John Arundell, the thought came to me that I spoke of myself. I have not trained my captains as I should, or they would not dare to fire a village without orders. I spoke harshly to John because he is close to me, and seated by my side he must to others be my representative.

"But in him I liked one thing, a thing that shows the compass of a man. For all my harshness, he did not speak the name of Lacie, who had done the firing. He took the burden on himself, nor would he betray another. You, my friend, know what that means in a man so young—a stout heart, to take punishment as it comes and never give away a friend or a subordinate. I like it well in John. It gives me faith that he will stand firmly on his own feet. If, perhaps, I was overly harsh, the lesson will sink in. He and his companions will not forget.

"I smile a little. They have closed me from their fraternity of friendship. I am outside. I see this in their cold young eyes, which look at me with disapproval, where once they were warm and friendly. Ah, well, the role of teacher is always difficult! In time it will be as it was before.

"I am confident now that John has the stomach to be made a captain. I will put him in charge of the first home-going ship next month, and he shall bear this letter to you."

Colin copied down the words. His heart was light. He did not want to lose John as a companion, but . . . He looked up quickly. Grenville's eyes were upon him steadily. A little twinkle seemed to shine through their clear blue depths.

"A clerk's work is secret work," he said. "But there are times when speaking is not amiss." He left abruptly, before Colin could thank him.

Colin went to their cabin only after he had copied part of the letter. He was afraid to trust his memory. John must know every word exactly as Sir Richard had said it. This would prove a better cure than any physician could bring. It would restore life to his listless spirit and the old sparkle to his eyes; lift the heavy load from his heart. Good John! How happy Colin was for his friend!

He found Richard Prideaux and Philip Blount sitting on the bench in front of the long table, which was littered with papers.

Dick was sketching a little map. "Here is a broad inland water as great perhaps as the sound behind Roanoke, with many streams coming in." He looked up as Colin slipped into a seat on the opposite side of the table.

"Please continue," Colin said.

Dick took up the story. "Heavily wooded shores, and the water teeming with fish. Indians came to Wococon, watching us from their canoes. Master Lane ordered me to take a pinnace and ten men and sail to Hatorask. We were to watch for shipping, live on fish, oysters and mussels, and look for pearls."

"Did you find any?" Philip asked quickly.

"None that would bring crowns. A few pied or black, but none orient. We had a man with us versed in such things. He is very hopeful because of the strings of pearls that some of the savage women wore about their necks. He traded some cloth for several pearls of the size of pease. The savages told him they came from the northward in a great water." Dick turned to Colin. "Want to go back with us tomorrow? Stafford is taking twenty men to Croatoan. They are breaking ground for a second planting of corn. The wild-fowl are plenty and the savages very kind and good."

Colin shook his head. "My work is here."

"Still clerking? I feel sorry for you, Colin. What a life! You sit inside four walls when the sea and the woods are at your service. I sleep on the ground every night, rise with the dawn, take my fowling-piece or my net and go abroad. My men snare rabbits, and we have shot two bear and half a dozen deer on the main. What more could a man want, I ask?"

"A woman perhaps," Philip said with a sly look.

Prideaux reddened. "Their women are not uncomely. I look the other way when some of the seamen lure them into the bushes. The governor has given strict orders to leave the Indian women be . . . but . . ." He laughed. "The seamen are old hands at finding women in every port. So why should I preach morality to them? Let them have their pleasures. If they should fall on the sands in the moonlight, who am I to investigate whether or not they have a woman under them? At least that's what Darby Glande, my second, tells me—and he's a wise one."

"Your men had better have a care. I've heard that the chiefs demand chastity in their women. Isn't that so, Colin?" Philip asked.

"Darby told us that it is only the maidens who are chaste. The tribes kill them if they find out."

Dick got up, stretched his long arms over his head, yawned. "I can't be bothered, nor charge my men with orders I can't enforce. 'Tis wisdom to look away and let the men frolic if they will."

"Where are you going now?" Philip asked as Dick took up his cap.

"To the Master of Victuals. I must get supplies for

twenty days. Provost Marshal Gorges is going with us. Better change your mind and come, Colin."

"No, I can't, though I'd like being by the ocean."

"Yes, the ocean. Sometimes I sit on the strand and look eastward. Across the water are the Cornish coast and my home in Padstow. Sometimes I dream I can see New Place rising out of the water."

Philip Blount laughed. "You are sick for home, Dick."

"Not I," Dick said with a grin. "I'm all for adventure, and gathering up gold and pearls, and going home as rich as Croesus."

"So you can marry and settle down at New Place?" teased Philip.

"Who said so? I'm not thinking of marriage just yet. 'Let me go, warm and merry still.' Isn't that the Spaniards' song we heard on San Domingo? Farewell, you landlubbers!" He went out whistling the gay little song.

Philip watched him. "I think I'd like to go to the shore. I'm not an island man—that is, a small-island man."

Colin said, "Sir Richard is going to talk with you about organising a troop of light horse. He wants you to go to him in the morning."

Philip let out a roar and threw his cap in the air. He whacked Colin a mighty thump on the back and jumped over the bench on his way to the door. "I'm off to look at the horses," he said over his shoulder.

Colin heard him clattering down the companionway, shouting for a boat to take him ashore. Very mercurial was Philip—spirits in his boots one moment, touching the sky the next.

Colin felt old. Not that his years were greater, but his way of living had aged him. Hard work he'd known since he was a little lad, helping the feeders with the cattle, helping the farrier shoe horses, being herd-boy for sheep, fetching and carrying in dairy and kitchen, driving oxen to the plough, gleaning in the harvest fields. There had been play too, hawking and hunting with the young masters, setting snares for wild hares and conies, fishing off the coast in a small boat. Yes, pleasures had been many. But he had grown hard and tough, with no aptitude for play. Dame Philippa had often told him he was too serious. "Smile! Laugh aloud! There is no harm in laughter."

277

The thought brought Stowe before his eyes, the great stone house, the high, enclosing outer walls, the terraces, the walled gardens and orchards. The rolling hills green now with waving grain. Men singing in the fields, cattle grazing in the meadows. Giggling girls in dairy and kitchen. Grooms hanging about, waiting to steal kisses from dairymaids, who could not resist because their arms were weighted with crocks of cream and butter. Savoury odours from the kitchen. Ripe strawberries with heavy clotted cream.

A heavy feeling lay on him. In his mind he saw the women's garden terrace, the archery. Figures moved about. The soft flowing skirts of the women. Thomasine, standing slim and straight, bending a great bow that only men used. How strong were her slim arms, how sinuous was her body! She moved with animal grace. Only her stormy eyes and her full, petulant lips were ugly in his sight.

He stared out of the port. In the water were Indian canoes, twenty men to a dugout. They rowed slowly as they neared the fishing weirs.

He thought of the harvest festival. A year had passed, but he still felt the fragrance of her lips. Sometimes he dreamed. . . . He straightened his shoulders and moved his head impatiently. He must stifle such thoughts. He glanced at his hand, which lay, palm upward, on the table. Her brand stood out red on his flesh—T A. A mark of shame, even as a felon is marked, a thief. He hated the girl.

John came into the room. He stood in the door looking at Colin, amazed at the expression on his face. "A tuppence for your thoughts," he said.

Colin glanced up. The look of anger faded. "Not worth a ha'penny," he replied. "Come sit down, John. I have something to show you." Colin gave him the copy of Sir Richard's letter, the lines that concerned him.

The cabin was quiet. Noises from the outside entered the room: the dip of Indian paddles, water lapping against the ship's side, the exultant cry of a fisherman as he landed a big one, the low murmur of voices from the shore, the sharp tapping of a hammer within the fort.

Colin waited with patience. After a long silence John heaved a great sigh. "It is well," he said slowly. "It is well. I have suffered in my heart, Colin. I cannot tell you how deeply."

Colin said, "I know, John."

"It is a devilish feeling, to wear a goose cap for ineptness, to think you have been false to your family, have denied your station by cowardice. Sir Richard has a way of driving a dagger deep."

"You need worry no more, John. The wind must now blow eastward."

"Ah, yes, it is time for a lucky wind. These days I have been as a beast taking soil; like a hunted beast, a stag or a boar that has sought refuge in a swamp or stream and knows not which way to turn." He got up and laid his hand on Colin's shoulder. "Thank you, my comrade. I will not forget."

"It was Sir Richard's suggestion, so do not thank *me*."

"That gives me a stronger feeling in my liver, but I thank *you* for other things. I have not spoken, but I felt your comforting sympathy—yours and Philip's. Does he know?"

"Not from me," Colin answered. "I have spoken to no one but you."

"Then I shall tell him. It is good, is it not, to feel that one has friends near, good friends who share sorrow without spoken words?"

"This is the first time I've ever had friends of my own age, except Bernard and John," Colin said simply. "I find it a warming thought."

John took up his cap. "Come, let us search for Phil. I want him to share my happiness. I must have been a devilish poor room-mate these days, casting my gloomy thoughts on you both like a pall. St. George on horseback! I feel good. I tell you, good! A ship of my own. Did you mark his words? Captain of a ship!"

"Your west wind is blowing strong." Colin laughed with him. Arm locked in arm, they left the room, making themselves narrow to get through the doorway. John's laughter was good to hear, Colin thought happily. No angry shadow hung over him. His face was young again, and his heart light.

The days were long now. The sun was still well up when the evening meal was eaten on the deck of the *Tyger*. The men were restless, walking about after supper. Nugent, who watched the seamen closely, sensed the restlessness. Immediately he set about organising games, first swords, then archery. Someone called for fisticuffs, good Cornish fights with bare fists.

It was Lacie who stepped forward then and cast his hat onto the deck. "I challenge Master Colin No Name to meet me in the ring," he shouted. "No bare fisties but a wrestling match, Devon against Cornwall. I stand for Devon."

Philip Blount, who had just won the sword-play, stepped close to Lacie. "Master Colin Grenville, my fellow. See that you remember. The name is not unknown in Devon, nor is it without honour."

Lacie tossed his head. "Name or no name, the challenge stands."

Colin, who was across the deck from the crowd, had not heard the challenge. Lacie repeated it louder. His voice boomed out. Colin turned about from watching a sailor exhibit parrots he had snared. He realized that the eyes of the company were on him. He looked at Philip Blount who was standing near Lacie, and asked, "What's up? Did I hear my name shouted?"

Lacie said, "That you did, unless you are deaf. I challenge you. I've thrown my cap into the ring. A Cornish lads' bout, a wrestling match, fought fairly till one or the other falls to the boards and a man counts out."

Colin detested bouts. They were brutal, bloody affairs, which settled nothing. He realized Lacie had been planning this encounter for some time, hoping he would refuse.

"Accepted," he said without hesitation.

"Make a ring, lads!" Lacie shouted. "Make a ring and lay your wagers. I bet five to one I'll put him on the plank in five minutes."

"Done!" said Philip Blount. "Though I loathe making a wager with a braggart."

Lacie grinned. "We'll see who's a braggart."

There was movement, the shuffling of bare feet on the boards. Nugent came on deck. "What's this?" he called, eyeing the ring.

"A wrestlin' match," someone told him. "Cornwall against Devonshire."

"We'll have no wrestling on the deck of a ship, as dark as it is at this moment, my mates. Tomorrow we'll go ashore after work, make a proper ring and fight it out."

There was a low-voiced rumble of disapproval. The men wanted to see a fight now, any fight.

280

"No grumbling!" Nugent called out. "There'll be no fight tonight." He turned and went below.

Lacie raised his voice. "Sergeant Nugent's right for once. 'Tis too dark, and ground is best for falling. I don't wish to break a Cornish back, or even a rib."

There was a laugh. Colin sensed that the crowd was for Lacie. They liked his blustering ways, his swagger. Colin would have preferred to go at it now and get it done.

Philip tugged at his arm. "Come on. Let's go for a swim." To Lacie he said, "Better watch yourself, or it will be your back on the floor, and you'll be gathering sticks on the moon tomorrow."

The company laughed. 'Twas an old tale, back before the days of King Hal, that the man in the moon bore faggots on his back as a punishment.

The crowd broke up, seeing there would be no fight.

Philip said to Colin as they ran down the beach, "Frightened of Lacie, fellow?"

"Frightened? No. He's strong, but he's got a soft belly. He drinks too much. He eats too much and he takes too much ease."

"Don't be over-confident. He's got a powerful pair of shoulders, and his arms are long. A bear's hug is what he'll have. So save yourself. I wish I knew something about this business. I don't, but I'm right behind you."

"Thanks, Phil." Colin could have told Philip that he'd wrestled since he was a small lad, but never in anger. There would be anger behind this match—anger and confidence.

Well, he, Colin, had confidence and no anger. Let tomorrow come.

Colin went to bed and slept like a child. In the morning half a dozen Cornish lads came to offer assistance. They'd stand behind, watch for foul play, carry the sponge. Colin was touched. He had been so busy with clerk work that he'd seen very little of the men of the company. It was evident that they did not hold grudge because he was near to Sir Richard. He felt heartened.

All morning he worked with the horses. Sir Richard had told him that he need not work. He said nothing about the fight, but Nugent was sure to have told him. Colin was philosophical about the match. He would do his best. Lacie was a full stone heavier, broader through the shoulders, with

281

a heavier chest. His legs were heavier too. Colin hoped he could move faster.

John and Phil were as nervous as old women. They followed Colin around, insisted that he rest and do no hard work, save his strength and in no circumstances eat any food until after the bout.

Darby Glande came over from the main late in the afternoon and went at once to talk with the Admiral. The Indians of the village directly across were coming over to the island to a man. Even the king, whose legs were impotent, was coming. They wanted to observe a contest between white men.

"How did they know about it?" Sir Richard asked.

"God knows! Excuse me, sir, for speaking roughly. But they do know, and there's great excitement. As near as I can learn, the women are annoyed because they are excluded."

Sir Richard laughed. "Well, if we are to have an audience, let us arrange a good show." He called his man. "Find Sergeant Nugent and bring him here. Then ask Master Arundell to tell Captain Amadas that I would like to speak with him as soon as he can come to my cabin." He walked about, rubbing his hands, smiling as though his thoughts were pleasurable.

When the men came, Sir Richard told them what Darby Glande had said. "Now we must make plans. If the Indian King Wingina comes, he must be received with all honour. Let me think. Suppose before the bout we have preliminary games: small swords, marksmanship. How shall we arrange it so that the Indians may see how skilled our men are?"

Sergeant Nugent said, "Sir, why not let the contest be Devon versus Cornwall all through. Let the Cornishmen, the onlookers, sit all together, and the Devon lads likewise, with banners, bugles and kettledrums to announce each event, and umpires to read the rules of each contest."

"Good! Excellently good!" Grenville said. "Captain Amadas, the details of the tournament will be in your hands to plan."

Amadas said, "Would you like tilting, old-fashion? We have some excellent horses. I saw Master Arundell tilting with a long reed at a wasp's nest hanging on a tree. He made a swift retreat, followed by a cloud of insects."

Everyone laughed. Grenville said, "Yes, yes. Tilting first.

Then swords. Perhaps we had best give up the idea of marksmanship, because we would have to move the company to a range somewhat distant."

"We could have archery," suggested Nugent.

"Yes, I suppose we could . . . but do the Indians excel our men shooting?"

"Sir, we do not know, but we have men who are fine archers with the heavy long-bow—Master Allyne and Glande here. I doubt if there is an Indian who can equal them in shooting." Grenville nodded approval.

Amadas wrote the names on a paper.

"About the wrestlin' match?" Nugent asked.

"Ah, the wrestling match. Let it be the last event. Make it important. After that, a feast for our guests. Do you approve of the plans, gentlemen?"

Everyone approved.

Grenville said, "Let's hear what you have written. Who are to be the contestants? We must keep it to Cornwall against Devonshire."

Amadas took up his paper. "We open with the tilt: Master Anthony Rowse for Devon, Master John Arundell for Cornwall. The bow: Master Allyne and Thomas Harvie for Devon. For Cornwall——" He looked up from his paper. "Here, this won't do. Glande is an Irishman."

"That I am, sir."

"That rules you out. We must have Cornish bowmen."

Glande said, "Master Prideaux is a fair fine man with the long-bow."

"Prideaux has gone to Hatorask," the Admiral said smiling. "We have Cornishmen who are expert. Name one or two."

"Randall Mayne, Rowland Griffin, Bennett Harris, George Eseven . . ."

"Good! Let them contest among themselves this morning. There should be two on a side."

"Sir, we haven't selected swordsmen." Glande spoke.

The Admiral turned to Nugent. "The best swordsmen?"

"For Cornwall, Master Philip Blount. For Devon, Master Francis Brooke."

"Good! Captain Amadas, I charge you with carrying my invitation to the governor. Ask him to select one of his company to act with you in planning the tournament. Come, gentlemen, the time is short. We must act quickly. Nugent, call as many men from the ship as you need. Lay out an arena with logs as seats, or pine boughs. For the king and the governor provide something special—chairs, perhaps, with elbows and high backs. All matters of the ring are in your hands. Glande, I want you to remain."

Captain Amadas and Sergeant Nugent left. The Admiral walked about the room. Glande stood waiting, his cap in his hand.

"You must have wrestled in your days, Glande."

"Sir, I did, and had no mean reputation, either."

"I am sure. Now this is what I want you to do. Go to Colin Grenville, talk with him, see what he knows about the art. There are fine points which we must presume Lacie practises. Do you think you can show our man how to defend himself? I do not think he can win, but I want him to make a fair showing."

Glande cocked an eyebrow. It gave him a curious, rather Pan-like look, an old, raddled Pan, who knew all things and who laughed. "Your Worship, I'm not so sure that Lacie will outclass young Colin. He swills a lot of ale and eats more than two men. There's not too much time, sir, but I'll do what I can."

"Excellent, Glande. We can't all win, but we can put up a good fight while we last." He spoke slowly. His eyes had a far-off look. "A good fight while we last," he repeated. "That's the best a man can do."

The Admiral stood looking out of the window, seeing nothing, thinking. Glande waited a moment, then went quietly away. He would teach Colin a trick or two, that he would. He was grinning when he left the ship. A seaman said, "The old man's up to mischief, I'll be bound."

"Mayhap he'll fight Lacie hisself," another said, looking up from the rope he was plaiting.

"Lacie will surely win the bout. There's other Cornish lads could fight stronger 'n the young'un."

"So? Well, perhaps, but give the youth his chance. He's a rare good lad, he is, and bound to hang on. Have ye noticed he with the horses, trainin' they? He's a stubborn fella, he is, and in prime strength. No fat around his entrails like Lacie. I give ye two shillin' he wins."

"Taken. And mind ye pay up forthwith."

The first sailor said, "Master Lacie is fair undone. He made his plans for a big play and hisself for a big hero.

But now there's to be other bouts, some on the back of a horse, and the young masters with French swords. Yes, he's fair undone. He wants the middle of the field, does Lacie."

" 'Tain't that so much, Willie, as he wants to bring young Master Colin to his shoulders in the ring. He has ne'er forgiven him since that day he faced him down on the ship."

"He is a man to carry a grudge, but he's a bold fellow, too, afearing nothing on God's green earth and always talking of Sir Francis Drake. He's a fair man, is Drake, but so's Sir Richard. Say, I'd like to see him mad and chewing glass goblets till the blood runs down his fine beard."

"And I." The other seaman laughed. "I doubt if it's true, though his man do say he can lift the hair right off a man's head when he gets in a cursing mood. He's as good a sailor as any Frankie Drake e'er dare be, and he's a gentleman born, kind as kind. To me he says, 'I watched you make sail in the storm last night. 'Twas excellent work. Excellent.' That was the storm off the Canaries, when Master Cavendish and his ship got lost. He misses nothing with those sharp blue eyes."

The sun was over the meridian. The day was hot and humid. Colin lay on a bed of pine-needles on the ground and watched the men who were acting as grooms work the horses. The animals appeared languid and sweated in great layers of foam. They, too, felt the heat. By night, when the sea wind blew in, they would frisk and caper and show their mettle.

John Arundell and Philip Blount searched in their chests for bright velvet cloaks to use as horse blankets, while two of the best carpenters were fashioning tilting lances of wood. There was activity on the northern side of the island, where the arena was being cleared among the trees. Chairs had been set up on a platform like thrones. A gay striped canvas which had served as shelter on the after-deck of the *Tyger* in the tropics had been stretched on four poles as a canopy for the chairs. Here the governor and the Indian king would sit to view the games, surrounded by their men.

Sir Richard had given the order and supervised the arrangements, for the games were to take place on the part of the island allotted to him and the men of the *Tyger*.

Glande found Colin after a search of the ship. He sat down beside him and at once began to question him about

285

wrestling. He had not talked for long before he was convinced that Colin knew more of the art than he or Sir Richard had supposed.

"I watched at fairs, and when I was fourteen, I entered myself in a match at Kilkhampton. I was sadly beaten, but I learned. Next, I made a match at Bideford Fair, and one at Barnstaple. I was soundly trounced. But each time I learned a trick. The fourth match I won, and the next, and from then on."

Glande nodded. "I suppose your opponents were younger and smaller?"

Colin grinned. "No, they were older and weighed more. Some had more skill, but I managed."

"Sir Richard should know this," Darby said. "He's sitting in his cabin, no doubt, lost in worry. He wants that you shall be winning."

Colin's eyes shone. "Don't tell him. Perhaps I may have misfortune, and the Admiral be disappointed." He pulled something from his girdle and showed it to Darby. "Look, I'll wear this. It's the foot of a hare that I snared in Kilkhampton Churchyard. It brings good fortune."

"Merciful Mary!" Darby exclaimed. "If it's the hind foot of a hare you're depending on, you may as well give your bow to Lacie as the victor."

Colin grinned boyishly, "The hare's foot—and my own footwork. So don't be adding to your worries, Master Glande."

Glande got to his feet. "I won't, but I'll have my two eyes open to look for fouls and any other evil work. Do your best, lad. There's a might of shillin' that will change hands tonight."

Colin's bright blue eyes clouded. "I don't like to think of that," he said seriously. "It makes a weight come on my shoulders."

"Well, keep Lacie's weight off your shoulders is my advice. Watch him that he don't knee your middle. That's an old trick—a foul one, but who can see when it happens? You are sinewy and you have a frame built for strength, but these games are won by skill, not bull strength. Watch him close. Shift position often. Don't let him get your head under his arm. I doubt if you have the strength to throw him by that hold, but try, lad, try if the chance comes."

He stood looking down at Colin sprawled on the pine-needles. "No use telling you all this and warning you. When you're in the ring, your brain will tell you what to do. I'm counting on that. Have you got your skillibegs handy?"

"Yes. Two Cornish lads made some fair fine ones. 'Let him kick with his Devon boots, and pay no attention' is what they told me. I know they made my skillibegs thick and tough out of wild hay and laced them firmly about my legs."

"Good! Very good! I'll be right there, where your water bucket stands tonight, and good fortune to you!"

"Thank you, sir. Thank you."

Colin watched the Irishman walk away until his stocky form disappeared among the trees. How kind everyone was! It was a comfort to think that Glande would be there with the sponge. His mind was made up to win. He would be careful, watching for tricks. It would be Devon kicks against the hugs of the land of "Tre, Pal and Pen," as they called the Cornish.

It wasn't Cornwall he wanted to win, but Stowe. The honour of Stowe. He wondered idly if Lacie had qualms, whether he was baking his heavy Devon boots in bullocks' blood until they were as hard as flint. But no, he thought, sleepily, there were no bullocks on Roanoke. Lacie would have to use deer's blood on his boots. Would deer's blood burn as hard as flint? His eyes closed and he slept quietly, his young body relaxed, drawing fresh vigour from the earth and the pines and the soft sea air.

CHAPTER 21
THE TOURNAMENT

King Wingina with fifty of his men arrived about
four of the clock, a proper time, for the wind had
changed, bringing the sea, making the air cool and
delightful. A delegation from the ship met him and escorted him from the beach, whither his warriors had carried
him on their backs, so his feet might not be made wet by
wading. He was tall and imposing for a savage, but his face
was set to hard lines, more like Wanchese' than Manteo's.
Glande told the Admiral that Wingina's people were enemies of Manteo's people, so he had heard. Neither Manteo
nor Wanchese had been on the island for some days now.
They came and went as they pleased. Manteo came more
often than the other, always in the same friendly spirit.
Since the death of a brother whom Amadas and Barlow
had befriended the year before, Wingina had begun calling
himself Pemisapan, the Serpent.

When the Indian king had stepped on the shore, and his
men had arranged his long mantle and taken their places
near him, a bugle sounded from the high bank and sailors
came down the beach and waited, a guard of honour to
escort him up the long hill to the high ground.

There Governor Lane waited, well apparelled in his fine
silk of blue and silver. On his head he wore a small puffed
cap laced with silver. A blue plum waved valiantly in the
gentle breeze. Very elegant he looked, with his gentlemen
standing about. They also were apparelled in vari-coloured
silk, with short swords and jewelled daggers.

The salutations over, the king was led to his seat in an
elbow-chair under the canopy. Governor Lane sat down on
his right hand. Sir Richard was nowhere to be seen.

Colin lay on the ground under the pines that rimmed the
arena. All about the semicircle the men of the company
sprawled or sat, their backs against the logs. When the bugle
sounded for the first event, they got to their feet and stood
until the flags were brought in. Men marched in, separated

and, having planted their flags in the sandy soil, took positions on either side of the platform, all in good military order, thanks to Sergeant Nugent's training.

Then the bugle sounded for the first event. Out of the woods from behind a thicket of bay trees the horsemen galloped, a dozen in full armour, visors down. They circled, manoeuvred, as clarions played and drums rolled. They wheeled smartly and formed a semicircle opposite the platform. A single horseman, in armour with visor open, followed.

"Sir Richard Grenville!" the herald cried. "A hall! A hall for Sir Richard Grenville, Master of the Tourney!"

Grenville rode to the center, advanced until he was close to the governor and the Indian king. Pemisapan shrank back, then straightened. Grenville reined his mount, saluted the Indian with lowered lance, then the governor, and wheeled to the center of the ring.

The herald announced, "Riding for Devon, Master Anthony Rowse. For Cornwall, Master John Arundell."

Visors open, the two contestants galloped in from opposite sides, rode up to the Master of the Tourney, saluted. Then they saluted the governor and his visitor. Each closed his visor, took position. Grenville moved out of the circle to his post in front of the horsemen. The wide velvet capes, blue and red, and the bridles decked with colour made a gay spectacle.

A fair blow on the breast-plate would constitute unhorsing, the herald announced. The horses, keyed to excitement, pranced and pawed the white sand. The riders advanced, circled with lances poised, made another circle.

Colin rolled over so that he might watch the faces of the Indian visitors. Stoical, unmoved, they sat, but their black roving eyes expressed surprise, excitement. Truly they could never have seen such pageantry before.

The riders were evenly matched. "A Devon!" shouted the crowd, when a lance touched armour. "A Cornwall!" came close after. This was as it should be, first one, then the other. Horses dancing, rushing forth, checked to sit on haunches; lances thrust and withdrawn. It was a matter of ten minutes before Devon with a true sure thrust hit Cornwall directly on the breast-plate. His lance broke. With a quick turn Cornwall knocked the broken lance from his foe's hand.

A shout went up, "Unfair! Unfair! The joust is Devon's."

The Master of the Tourney judged it so, and Devon had one point.

The horseman circled the field. Victorious Rowse dismounted. Black John removed his helmet. Rowse advanced to the governor, who placed a wreath made of bay leaves on his head, while Devon men, on their feet, shouted until the victor and all the horsemen rode away.

Pemisapan spoke to the governor through his interpreter. "Why do you lay leaves on his head? Does he ache in his head? We lay wet leaves on the forehead of one who is ill of the trembling disease."

Lane explained the ancient Greek custom of the laurel, but the Indian king was not satisfied. Sitting on the back of an animal had made the man ill. That was evident. He would send for his medicine man, who knew the ways to make a man well. "Wet leaves on head. Hot stones at feet. Wrap close in skin coat. Build fires all around until drops of water run out of him."

Lane tried again to explain, but gave up. The young Indian who stood near the king said he was a cousin of Prince Manteo. Manteo had taught him the English language. He asked permission to explain to the chief what the laurel wreath signified. He was still explaining when the fencers took their places.

A large arena had been used for the tilting. Now the crowd closed in to make a smaller crescent, so that all might witness the sword-play. Again Devon and Cornwall were so evenly matched that it seemed impossible one could get advantage over his opponent.

King Pemisapan lost his stoicism. He leaned forward, watching intently the parry and thrust, the graceful postures, the flash of blade on blade.

He turned to the governor. "Why does he not throw the knife deep into the heart of his foe?"

Lane looked hopelessly at the young Indian interpreter, then at his gentlemen. His eye fell on Philip Amadas. "You explain, Captain. You understand these savages." He turned away to watch the fencing. The chief drew back, affronted.

Amadas, sensing trouble, spoke quickly, explaining that it was sword-play, not a duel where men fought to draw blood. The king listened without expression, then turned his shoulder to the governor. Amadas was troubled. He said to Lane, "You must not ignore the chief. He will take offence."

"Let him take offence. Why am I seated here? Why should I sit on the level of an Indian?" He rose and walked away.

The king spoke; the young lad interpreted. "The king says this man is not a chieftain. He is of inferior rank, who does not know the habits of kings. The chief lord of the English is he who rides on a horse."

Amadas said, "Master Lane is the governor. He rules the land. Sir Richard Grenville is the Admiral. He rules the ships and the sea."

"Ah, yes. The sea is greater than the land. It eats the land, nibbling a little each day."

By chance—or was it prearrangement?—Grenville came up at the moment. He greeted the king courteously, with dignity, and sat down in the chair vacated by Lane. The shadow of a smile came over the copper face. The black eyes had expression in them. Pemisapan said to the young Indian, "Two kings sit side by side."

Amadas had picked up enough of the tongue to understand. He smiled. The savage had more comprehension than he had imagined.

The match was over a moment later, and though it was so close as to be almost a draw, Philip Blount appeared the loser.

The two contestants came forward. Grenville laid the wreath on Francis Brooke's dark head.

The king leaned forward and said, "I would tear the leaves apart and lay half on one head and half on the other."

Grenville was startled at the Indian's perception. "You are quite right. Nugent, another wreath." When the sergeant handed him the second wreath, he put it into the hands of the Indian.

The king leaned forward and placed the wreath on the blond head of Philip Blount. He sat back, smiling with satisfaction. The company cheered, which pleased the king even more. The look of worry in Philip Amadas' eyes vanished. He, of all the Englishmen present, understood the Indian character. He alone knew how close to fierce anger the king had been at Lane's affront. This little honour, graciously given by Grenville, had cleared the air. Amadas wondered then what kind of governor Lane would be, and how long they would keep the friendship of Pemisapan.

Archery was next. Four men contested. When the arrows

had all been placed in the target, made of skin and stuffed with grass, no one had struck the bull's-eye. Devon won, with Thomas Harvie and Master Allyne closest to the mark.

The chief turned and spoke to the young Indian boy, whom he called Okisko. The boy hesitated, looked down at the ground, then off in the distance. "The chief says, May I show my skill with the bow, sir?"

Sir Richard replied instantly. He called for a bow and arrows. Okisko stepped forward, tested the bow that James Skinner handed him. Without seeming to take aim, he put an arrow in the very center of the target. Then deliberately he put six arrows, one after the other, side by side with the shafts already in the target.

The applause was hearty and instantaneous. Men got to their feet shouting. Others ran to the target to see how close the arrows had sped.

Grenville gave an order. The clarions sounded, and he himself set the wreath of victory on the Indian boy's head, while the four archers stood by, clapping their hands vigorously.

The chief sat very erect and silent, obviously pleased. Okisko stood beside him with folded arms. He tried to remove all expression from his face, but he was young and proud and very happy to show these Englishmen that Indians too had skill.

Grenville said to him, "I have never before seen such marksmanship."

The crowd, having given their approval and applause, became restless. It was time for the wrestling.

Colin stood up, took off his leather jerkin and kicked off his shoes. Darby Glande fastened the straw skillibegs around his legs and bound them in place with leather thongs. John and Philip helped, "for all the world like horse trainers!" John exclaimed.

"Now remember what Darby said," Philip cautioned. His blue eyes were earnest. "Don't let him get your head under his arm, and watch for knee fouling. A kick in the groin will settle you. So have a care."

After the archery a dozen or more men had tramped the spot where the wrestling would take place. Darby straightened up and walked away to the ring. He stood watching two seamen mark it off. Okisko joined him, looking at the white sand that covered the spot. He walked slowly over the circle after the men had moved away. He paused and glanced up at

Glande, who was observing him. The Indian set his moccasined feet on a little ridge which ran across from Colin's corner toward the center of the ring. Then he knelt, dug his fingers into the sand, pulled hard. The crowd was watching him closely, wondering what he could be doing.

In a moment they knew. Okisko jumped up. In his hand he held a bush covered with long spines. He spoke slowly but quite clearly. "Devil's-club. Very bad for gentleman with bare feet."

Eyes turned from Colin, who was barefooted, to Lacie with his heavy boots. There was silence, an ominous silence. No accusation was made, but from the Cornish side mutterings could be heard. Lacie started to speak, but thought better of it. Glande called attention, explained the rules. Kicking was allowed, and head holds. A fall was to be acknowledged when the umpire ruled that both shoulders were on the mat. The match was for a true backfall. The men were to catch what holds they could. Two sticklers had been selected, one from each county.

When Lacie stripped off his jacket, a murmur ran through the onlookers. What had appeared to be a fat stomach was muscle, not fat. His shoulders were heavy, and his arms muscular. As they faced each other, Colin looked slimmer and lighter, but his flesh was hard and he moved easily.

Each side eyed its champion. The Devon men chortled with glee. "Look at the strength of Lacie. The other's but a wee lad."

Cornishmen grew truculent. Muscle alone did not win bouts. Wait till their man got his Cornish hug around Lacie's body. They would see. Bets were called, and holders came forward. Cheers and catcalls rent the air when they saw the great boots Lacie wore.

"Devon men must have boots to win battles," someone shouted. "For shame!"

"Take the little lad home, before our man near kills him."

Then silence came. Colin cleared his mind of anger at the jeers. It was not an accident that the nettles lay in the sand, directly in his path. A first wrath gave way to an exultant thought. Lacie had fear of him or he wouldn't stoop to trickery.

The odds were all with Lacie at the outset, but as the fight progressed, some small honours went to Colin for the agility with which he escaped Lacie's attacks. He was always moving,

293

weaving this way and that, watchful, remembering Darby's instructions, keeping well out of the way of the heavy Devon boots. "If he kicks, let them be glancing blows," Darby had warned. Blows had come, but his skillibegs withstood and held.

There came a time when Lacie crouched toward him as though to grab him around the waist. But Colin knew better. Lacie's attack would be a heavy kick, then up with his knee to catch his groin. Instead of jumping aside where he would have met Lacie's knee, Colin leaped straight up in the air. Lacie's foot encountered nothing. His knee twisted and met only air. He fell to the ground on one hand and knee.

Colin could have grabbed him for a head hold then. He did not move, though the crowd on the Cornish side yelled for him to close in. Instead, he stepped back and waited for Lacie to rise. A long groan came from the audience. But one of the sticklers shouted, "Good lad! A fair play, a fair play!"

Lacie's face was twisted with rage. He went at Colin like a mad bull, arms and legs flying in ferocious attack.

The violence of his movements kept Colin leaping. "Close in, Cornwall! Close in!" the crowd shouted. "He's winded. Close in!"

Lacie saw his wild attack was doing no harm to anyone but himself, so he played cautious.

"Two cocks! This is a cockpit! Have done with playing! Get to work!" The crowd edged closer. The Indians, too, drew in.

Colin remained cool in spite of taunts from his own side. Evasive he must be until he caught Lacie off guard. Lacie had not the patience for such tactics. He must kick his fury against some obstacle. The toe of his boot caught Colin on the shin, a true kick that set him limping for a moment. He watched the fire in Lacie's eyes. They shifted in the direction he meant to kick. Suddenly Lacie plunged, head down, reaching out his arm to grasp Colin about the middle. Colin shifted quickly, let him pass. Then with a rapid turn he had Lacie's head under his right arm.

"The Cornish hug! By Gad, he's got him with the Cornish hug! Hang on, boy! Hang on! Squeeze his windpipe and lay him on the mat!"

Colin squeezed hard. He felt Lacie going limp. He shifted his legs to get better balance. A fast twist, a good heave, and in a flash the big man was over Colin's shoulder. He hit the earth and lay flat on his back, quite still.

Turmoil rose. The green bough of the cedars overhead had never felt such wind except from a hurricane. Men clapped one another on the back, danced and shouted, "A Cornwall! A Cornwall!" until someone changed the shout to "A Grenville! A Grenville!"

Colin stood still, his chest rising and falling. Blood pounded in his ears, oozed from his nose. Sweat dripped from his forehead over his eyes and blinded him. He panted in short, heavy breaths that racked his lungs. He heard Darby's voice: "Well done, lad, well done!" He felt the slosh of cool water over his face and shoulders.

"Come, lad, pull yourself up and get your crown. God's breath, but you've earned it!" Phil and John were by his side. He heard their voices but he could not see them. The roar of the crowd was dull in his ears.

Someone was splashing water over Lacie, pail after pail, until he groaned and cursed and made to sit up. The effort was too much. He fell back again. Half a dozen Devon men lifted him and carried him down the hill to the seaside.

Colin's eyes cleared. He stood in front of the Admiral. Grenville was smiling. He laid the victor's wreath on Colin's dripping yellow hair, plastered against his skull like a golden casque. "Well done, Cornwall!" he said.

The feasting came then. White men and Indians gorged on pork and wild-fowl, washed down with ale. The two little organs had been brought off the ship, and sweet music was played as they ate. The governor came back in time for the supper and took his place on one side of the Indian king while Grenville sat on the other. Pemisapan paid slight attention to Lane. Only when the governor spoke directly to him did he respond, and then in as few words as possible.

Lane said to Philip Amadas, who sat next to him, "You know these people, Amadas, from your visit last year. Tell me why this Indian holds no malice toward Grenville, who ordered his village burned, yet he attempts to ignore me."

Amadas shrugged. "That I cannot tell you."

Okisko, who stood behind the king, answered, "The burning of a village was an act of punishment for wrong-doing. It is a matter of law. The insult to the dignity of a king is another matter."

Lane looked confused. There was a little fear lurking in his eyes.

Amadas said non-committally, "You have your answer, sir."

At sunset, when the feasting was over and the king was making ready to go to his long canoe, he turned to Grenville. "It is the wish of the boy Okisko that he stay for a time near the lad with the hair of wheat and eyes of the sea. He wishes to learn what the boy knows. Perhaps, if he proves eager to learn, he may go to that great land of yours, as Manteo has done."

Grenville looked at the tall Indian boy for a moment. Then he said, "It shall be as you wish, O Chief. It is well for some of your people to learn the ways and to think the thoughts of the white man. It will serve us well, both Indian and Englishman, to read each other's open hearts."

The chief bowed his head in approval. Escorted by the seamen, he made his way to his canoe where his oarsmen awaited him. As he slipped into the canoe, the clarions sounded a farewell. The king touched his hand to his heart and was rowed away.

Amadas said to the Admiral, "I think this has been a good day for friendship."

Grenville looked pleased. "I hope so. One must move cautiously with these people. It would indeed be well if we could learn to think as they think. Our lives if they ran parallel would move along pleasant lines."

Lane, who had heard him, said nothing. He seemed confused and ill at ease. Presently he excused himself and went away.

Philip Amadas watched him go. In spite of his merry eyes, his genial smile and air of simple good will, Amadas was a shrewd man. He was thinking that Lane had much to learn before he could make himself master of Roanoke Colony.

The lads in the cabin next to the Admiral's tried to keep their voices down. John was regretting that he hadn't outridden Rowse; Philip, that he hadn't gained a clear victory over Brooke. Only Colin had achieved, given Cornwall a full score.

"But what good did it do?" he asked glumly. "Wrestling's a trick. No keenness of mind, no real skill, just brute force or a lucky twist."

His companions paid no heed. Black John looked across to blond Philip. "What shall we do with him? He never told us he was Cornwall's hope. Shall we douse him in the bay? Make him walk the plank? What shall be his punishment?"

Colin began to pull off his hosen, groaned. The stocking stuck to his leg. The drying blood from half a dozen cuts held the wool fast.

"What a sight!" exclaimed Phil. "Quick, John, get witch hazel from the bos'n! Hey, man, don't drag at your hosen. You'll start the bleeding all over."

" 'Tis nothing," Colin grumbled, annoyed to show scars of battle. "The ache in my shoulder is worse."

Philip pressed the shoulder with both hands. There was a snapping sound, as though the bone had moved back into place. "By Phoebus, I believe it was out of joint! How does it feel now?"

"Better. It no longer pains. You must have put it in place. You should be a surgeon, Phil."

"Yes, that's what I'd really like to be, but you know I can't. My family wouldn't allow it. I must learn to manage estates and check stewards to see they don't cheat, and a thousand other uninteresting things . . . maybe go soldiering in Europe or fight in a ship against Spain."

"Probably the last. The Admiral thinks it won't be long before the Spanish will attack our coast—a year or two. We've very few ships."

"I suppose he wants to seat this colony firmly before the Spanish move north and sink what ships we have," Philip observed.

"Yes, so I think. Another time he will bring more artisans." Colin laughed. "The Admiral says we're overloaded with gentlemen now."

John came back with a beaker of white fluid. "Wait," he said to Colin. "Let me pour this on the hosen and soften the blood. That's what the bos'n said to do."

The cooling liquid eased the hurt. After a time the stockings gave way.

Philip whistled. "By the great Jove, that Lacie surely kicked! Hey, this wound looks like a horseshoe. Suppose the rascal had iron in his shoe?"

Colin shook his head. "No, I don't think so. Hard leather makes a cut, you know."

Darby Glande came in with a basin of hot water and some

white cloths torn in strips. "On the bed, sir! Stretch yourself out, while I bandage your honourable scars of battle." He leaned over and examined one on the shin-bone carefully.

John and Philip watched him. He looked up and caught their eyes. "Iron?" Philip asked.

Darby nodded, looked at Colin, whose eyes were closed. He was breathing evenly. "Sound asleep," Darby remarked. He wound the cloth about Colin's brown legs from knee to ankle. "Poor lad, he's beat. He put strength into his arms and he never lost his head, not once. It's a proper fighter he would make."

"Aye, but he doesn't like fighting. He won't fight again."

Darby grinned, a curious lop-sided grin. "I'd be pleased to see what he'd do if he liked it."

He finished tying the cloth and got up. He stood for a moment gazing down at the sleeper. "He has a bitter enemy, an enemy who plays him dirty, what with nettles for his bare feet and iron for his shins. The Lord looked after him this day."

He said good-night and left the two youths looking at each other. Darby had uttered what they had been thinking. Colin had an enemy who didn't fight fair.

"There's no good warning him against Lacie," Phil said. "He won't believe a man can have so much evil in him. We must watch over him, John. He'll never watch for himself."

John shook his head gloomily. "How can I, when I am sailing for home next month?"

"That's right. I'll have to find someone else to help me. I can't be looking out for him day and night."

John grinned. "Colin would surely clout us if he heard such talk. He's able to take care of himself. So let it go at that."

"Maybe you're right," Phil said as he got out of his clothes and threw them in a heap on the floor.

John stretched out on his cot. "I'm as weary as though I'd fought the Battle of Agincourt. That mare I rode had the gait of a camel and . . ." He didn't finish the sentence. By the heavy breathing he knew Philip was already asleep.

In the next cabin Sir Richard Grenville was writing in his daybook a lively description of the events of the afternoon. He ended with "Lane is a nincompoop. He has managed to antagonise the one chief we must keep as our friend."

He closed the book. He put it into his chest, which he

298

locked, and hung the key around his neck. He walked out on the warm deck and looked across the water to the main. Fires were lighted where the village had stood that Lacie put to the torch. Perhaps Pemisapan slept there, or some other tribe had come down to the sea to fish or to view the strange white men.

It was quiet, the night very dark. The stars were close, shining in great brilliance. It came to him that they should not be here in this far-off land. Why should they leave their home shores for this unknown world to conquer, to kill or be killed, to impose their civilization on the savages, to take their land from them, push them deeper into the untracked forest?

The English would conquer. Perhaps not his men, but others. They would come, and keep coming, until the New World yielded to them. What would happen to the Indians? They had evils of their own. Would they take on the white man's evils as well?

He felt old and very tired. He wondered whether he was doing right to bring these young men out to fight battles against unknown enemies—the Indians, the climate, the loneliness, the utter loneliness of the deep forest.

He returned to his room, blew out the candle and undressed in the dark. No use to allow himself regrets. He remembered some words about the grace of perfect knowledge. If he had that, if he could see beyond to the grand works of eternity, would he hold to a rational course and know tranquillity? By the grace of God, no! He would despise himself if he did not take the chance to move forward.

He, too, slept, and in his sleep he cried mercy for the things he had done.

A week later Okisko came to the ship and presented himself to the Admiral. Colin was in the room at the time, writing, setting down Sir Richard's accounts, making lists of the farm implements he would bring on the return voyage. Okisko looked at Colin in astonishment. Why should a man who could fight sit like an old woman in a chair, use his hands holding a goose-quill, his strong legs idle?

Sir Richard smiled. "In England a man must do many things. He does not hunt or use the bow every day. Did not Manteo tell you how we live?"

The Indian said, "Yes, but I do not understand why he

299

idles so. There are birds on Lake Paquipe and on Wococon, and fish in the stream."

The Admiral was tired of this. "Do you still want to go to England with me?"

The Indian hesitated a moment. "Sir, I will go. There are things to be learned. Manteo tells me it is best that I go and learn. Englishmen have come to our land and they will stay, he says."

Grenville said, "That is true. Colin, will you take Okisko to his quarters? The cabin beyond you. Then send John Arundell to me. I wish to speak to him."

John came into Sir Richard's presence with some hesitation. He did not know what his guardian wanted. In truth, since they had been on the island he had all but forgotten that he was the Admiral's ward until he was twenty-one. One year more was all. Now his mind was running on a thought that had come to him some months back. He had for a long time struggled to arouse his courage and consult Sir Richard. Perhaps today was the time. But first he must listen to what the Admiral wanted.

"It is the matter of your ship, John. I have been thinking of the Spanish barque we took at St. John's. She proved herself a good sailor, swift and steady at the same time. You will be alone, without convoy. I want you to have a ship that will outrun any pursuers."

John said, "Do you think I can captain a ship, sir?"

"Why not? You've sailed ships since you were a lad. I see no difference. I'll put a good navigator and helmsman on board. You'll sail on the fifth day of August, twenty days before I set sail with the *Tyger*. That will give you time to see Sir Walter, go to Stowe and begin getting supplies ready for our return at Easter of next year."

John was silent for a moment. "Sir, am I to come back next spring?"

"Why not? Are you not satisfied? Does it not pleasure you to be a part of this great undertaking? God's blood, man, what do you want?" The Admiral spoke sharply.

John looked away and did not meet his steely blue eyes. "I've been thinking, sir. I believe I would like to study for holy orders."

Grenville did not answer. He stroked his red-gold beard. "Sit down, John. Let us talk about this idea. When did you get it into your head?"

"Sir, I've thought of it for a long time. It seems to me that is all I am suited for. I do not like to fight. It turns my stomach to see blood. . . ."

"That is not a reason to turn to the Church. The Church needs leaders. It is not an easy sheltered life, where you can shut yourself off from the world. You must have strength to hold up the faltering and the weak, spiritual strength, unless you are thinking of something more sheltered—" his eyes bored into John—"unless you are, like your uncle Sir John, a Catholic, and you yearn to fly to a monastery and evade your duties."

John was shocked. "Oh, no, sir! Indeed, I'm no Catholic. I like our Church. When I step inside, I feel peace and quietude."

"You're not alone in that, my good sir. I have been a soldier and fought bitter wars. I am a sea-captain. I have seen bloodshed in plenty. But I, too, find peace in my religion, when I read the Holy Word or when I kneel on the stone floor in our chapel in Kilkhampton, where my fathers have knelt. I find peace and solace from the world's ills and my own infirmities. But I do not want to take orders, John, and I do not want you to. I do not think you are a godly man. You are too young to know the world. I doubt whether you have ever lain with a woman. How can you lead people out of sin, if you know nothing of it?"

John couldn't speak, nor did Sir Richard expect him to. He went on: "Consider other things, John. Your forbears have left you a goodly tradition. The Arundells are gentlemen born. They have always met their responsibility to their Queen and country, to families their equals and to men of lesser station. You have tenants on your land who have cultivated your acres for you for three or four generations. Some leases have run to the fifth or sixth generation in the same family. Your people have been loyal and faithful to you. They have planted and harvested. They have followed the Arundell banner into wars since the days of the Conqueror. Are you going to betray them now?"

John, his face solemn, answered, "Sir, do you think I will betray my people if I go into the Church?"

Grenville said, "You are the heir to your father, John. Not the second son or the third, but the heir."

The room was silent. The sound of laughter, the rubbing of bare feet on the deck, the song of birds on the shore, the splash of a paddle seemed only to make the quiet room more silent.

"What must I do?" John asked in a low voice. "Tell me what you expect of me, sir. You are my guardian. Do you know my dead father's wishes?"

"Your father would have had but one wish for you, John: To live worthily, do your duty to God, to your country, and to the land that is yours. You must remember that you have two sisters. Do you want Arundell land to go to their husbands, to another name than Arundell?"

"No, no. I would not have it go like Gorges'. I have always resented that family inheriting Dartington and all the lands of the Champernownes. Surely there were some cousins who would carry on the family name without turning to the distaff side." John spoke quickly, energetically.

Sir Richard smiled behind the hand that stroked his beard. "You have not thought far enough. The Gorges have power in court."

"You are right, sir. I thought only a little way. . . ." He leaned across the table. "What is it you want of me, sir?"

Sir Richard's long fingers drummed lightly on the table. "From you, John? The same that I want from Bernard and John Grenville, for in my thought you are a son. Learning enough to meet all men equally. Science to keep up with the movement of the vast new world we are living in. Husbandry, for you must know what to expect from tenants, yeomen and tillers of the soil. A wife and sons, strong sons to make your name live."

John looked at his guardian. "I want to marry Thomasine, sir. I ask your permission to marry Thomasine Arundell the day I am twenty-one."

It was a full hour later when John left the Admiral's room and returned to his cabin. Colin and Philip were waiting for him to go ashore. Their eyes asked questions, but their lips were silent. An hour and more with the Admiral—what could that mean? Not bad news surely, for John was smiling. He was in excellent spirits, but he kept his own counsel.

Late that night, when they were walking up the beach after a swim in the moonlight, John said, "Sir Richard has given his approval of my marriage with Thomasine if Lady Grenville also will approve."

"Good! Who is Thomasine?" Philip clapped John on the back.

John waited a moment. "Aren't you going to congratulate me, Colin?"

"Yes, yes, of course. I hope you will be very happy . . . both of you."

John was too happy to notice Colin's hesitancy or how flat his voice was. He laughed. "Sir Richard warned me that she would need some taming, but I like her wild ways. He discouraged me about taking holy orders. He said I'd best not make Thomasine a curate's wife. She would have the parish by the ears."

"Curate!" Philip was aghast. "You can't be in your right mind, John. I don't know Thomasine, but I hope she goes on keeping the parish by the ears. You're not a man for the Church, John. You go home and attend to your land, just as I must do, marry, have a brood of children. She has a nice name. Who is this Thomasine of yours? You've never told me, you ape."

"She's an Arundell," John answered, "a far-away cousin."

"Well, marry her, and let her burn her hair on the altar for your safe return from voyages, like the Roman matrons. 'Berenice's ever-burning hair,' " he quoted.

"I won't go voyaging when I marry. I've promised Sir Richard to wait until I'm twenty-one next year. An old married man! Colin, why are you so quiet?"

"How can he talk when your mouth is so busy with questions? Eh, Colin?"

"He knows Thomasine. She lives at Stowe. She's a ward just as I am."

"Excellent! You won't have to ride any distance to court your lady. I take it she is beautiful and demure, sits with downcast eyes at her broidery frame."

John laughed. "She's pretty, but nowise demure. She's as wild as a moor pony. Didn't you listen when I told you Sir Richard said she would take some taming?"

"I'd forgotten. Maybe she won't be tamed, eh, Colin? I say, come back from wherever you are."

"Your pardon, Phil. I was looking at Ariadne's Crown. How brightly it shines tonight in the heavens!"

"You're moonstruck. I hope you're not in love. I couldn't make out, living with two love-lorn fellows. Are you in love, too, Colin?"

"Not I, Phil. No I."

Colin couldn't go to sleep that night. He turned and tossed on his narrow bed. He felt heavy, and there was an ache in his vitals. He must have eaten something. He lay with his face pillowed in his hand—the hand that bore Thomasine's brand.

CHAPTER 22
RIVER CHOWAN

July was a hot month. Day after day small showers
fell, with heat following. Some days the wind blew
from morning until night, a land wind with heat in it.

The houses progressed rapidly. Two main houses were complete in the quarter given over to Grenville's men. Now he
was on land every day by sun-up, urging the men to speed.
He wanted to report to Sir Walter Raleigh, perhaps to Her
Majesty, what progress had been made, that houses were
built, crops ready to harvest. His presence livened the men.
Each day they looked to him for words of praise.

Governor Lane stayed at Wococon most of the time or
pushed his way up the creeks and rivers and along Lake
Paquipe. With him went Hariot, John White and two men
who knew about minerals and gold, Edward Chipping and
Sylvester Beching. He kept other men stationed on the long
islands that guarded the mainland. Prideaux, Stafford and
Rise Courtenay, with twenty men, remained at Hatorask.

This puzzled Grenville. He thought it poor generalship to
scatter forces. He spoke of it several times to Colin. One
day Colin said, "Perhaps the governor looks for Sir Francis
Drake to come this way."

"There is no gold to be had here. You'll never find Drake
if there are no plate ships to be taken."

"Does Sir Francis know there is no gold to be found in
Virginia?"

Grenville paused in his stride. "By God, I believe you're
right! You've put a thought into my head, my boy."

He said no more about Drake. Colin thought he had forgotten. Sir Richard was like that. He troubled about things
for which he had no answer. Once he found an answer to his
liking, he put the affair out of his mind.

Now he was interested in the great sound that lay back of
Roanoke. He made ready a pinnace to journey up as far as
the point where two great rivers met, one coming from the
north, one from the far west. Okisko had told him about the

305

Chowan, a broad river from the north that divided the territory of his grandfather Okisko from that of the Chowanook Indians, who gave it their name. Here was a good country where crops were heavier, forests deeper and trees taller. In the spring the herring and greater fish also swam up in schools to spawn. There were small creeks of sweet black water, which drained the heavy swamps of cypress and hardwoods. Grenville knew by the Indian's description what trees and fish and other things he meant, though he did not often have the English names for them. One thing interested Sir Richard more than any other: the mention of freshwater creeks of great depth, where he could take his ships. The *Tyger* was foul and needed cleaning, and there were no ways where the bottom could be scraped and made ready for the voyage home.

He would go up first in the pinnace to test the depth of the channel. Okisko insisted it was very, very deep, but how could an Indian know when they had only shallow canoes?

These things the Admiral talked over with his young men. They were eager to go. They would take the Portuguese sailing master Juan Gostigo with them.

Master Hariot came in from Hatorask and asked permission to accompany Sir Richard. "I have listed the beasts, birds, flowers and trees of the islands. I want to go inland. I am sure there is more to be seen."

Grenville agreed. He was a trifle annoyed that Lane had kept certain men away from him. He saw through Lane. He was trying to win over the scientists, White the limner, Hariot the historian. He was wooing the young men of great families to his party, the all-powerful Courtenay, Gorges, Brooke, Stafford and others of like station. He was trying to build a strong bulwark against criticism if the colony should fail when he was governor in full charge of its destiny.

Hariot was Raleigh's man. He owed too much to that knight not to tell him the truth on his return. Grenville would send the most disaffected men home on John Arundell's ship or take them on the *Tyger*. He would do that much toward Lane's success.

John White followed Hariot to ask if he might go on the voyage.

A sunny morning came when the Admiral considered the wind was favourable. His personal clothes, his second armour were packed. Necessary instruments were on the pinnace, spy-glass, small ordnance, harquebuses, together with such trade goods as pots, pans, cloth and beads. He ordered his silver-gilt tableware carried aboard; also one small organ and some musicians, for the Indians liked music. Twenty in all made up the party, including rowers, in case the wind failed on their return. Okisko went with them to interpret and assure the Indians they came in peace, not for war.

Colin, John and Philip lay on deck watching the shore. The inland sea, or sound, was wide, the channel in the middle of the stream was deep, the forest heavy on either side. When they had sailed westward for an hour or more, they saw Indian canoes coming out from shore. The Indians rowed along within hailing distance but made no effort to come closer.

Captain Amadas came out of the little cabin where he had been talking with the Admiral and sat down beside them. He told them of his first journey. "We thought for a time that the island was the mainland. But when we sailed into the sound, we found that the main lay beyond—a great land with deep spacious waters. We found the people gentle and loving. When we landed at their town, they brought us broth, very sweet and savoury. Their meat was cooked in earthen pots, good and wholesome, and they served it on platters of sweet wood."

"Did you go ashore?" Philip asked, rolling over on his side so that he might see both the speaker and the shore.

"Yes. When we had eaten, they invited us. We saw the place where they lodged. They gave us a drink in which they had boiled ginger, black cinnamon and sassafras. We saw their town, and the women, very comely and unafraid, brought us wine crushed from their grapes, which grow wild in immense quantity."

"Is the wine fermented," John questioned, "or is it the sweet of the fresh grape, like our Devon cider?"

"Both," Amadas said. "Some was set away in large earthen pots until it had fermented." He sat with his arms about his knees while he watched the shore. "I remember while we were at meat several men with bows and arrows came in. They had been hunting." He laughed a little. "Barlow reached for his weapon. When the woman who served us saw our mistrust, she was very much moved. She sent some of her people out to take away the bows and arrows and break them, and beat those poor Indians out of the gate again."

"Do you think they will be as kind to us when we visit their towns?"

Amadas said he didn't know. "When I was on St. John's Island, I understood a Spaniard to say that his people had been raiding up the coast, looking for pearls. If the Spaniards have been here, the Indians will not be so guileless. They will be watchful and afraid, and it may be that they will attack us."

But there was no attack that journey. They visited several Indian towns. The last was on a little bay, a few miles below the meeting of the waters of the Chowan and the red river of the falls.

It was at the little place Weapemeoc that they surprised the Indians. Indians had met the pinnace at the other villages, sending out men in canoes to greet it. Sometimes the chief or the chief's son came aboard, and Sir Richard would give him small presents and have food served him. Musicians played as he ate. The Indians liked it well.

At Weapemeoc a great feast was in progress, which could be observed from the shore. Colin took the tiller. Sir Richard ordered sails lowered, so that they might run in close to the shore of the small bay.

The Indians were so engrossed that those on the pinnace had time to observe a circle of upright logs about which they danced. On the top of the logs, facing inward, heads had been carved.

The masks looked like the heads of veiled nuns. Sir Richard called attention to the resemblance. "Have the Spanish been here before us?" he asked Amadas.

"Perhaps some Indian has been a prisoner in Florida or on one of the Spanish isles, and he carved the nuns' heads."

In the center of the circle three men stood locked in an embrace. In the dancing circle the men carried rattles made of gourds, and twigs with green foliage. A priest, with his hair cut in a crest that resembled a Roman helmet, beat on a drum. He wore a short cloak made of rabbit skins, and at his feet was a pile of wild-fowl, ducks, swan and geese.

At this point the sentry discovered the pinnace. There was a great outcry, and the women who were onlookers ran to the forest, dragging children with them and all uttering piercing screams.

Sir Richard asked Okisko to step out on the deck and call to the people of Weapemeoc to say to their king that the English were there with all good intentions, and request that he send a deputation on board the ship, so that the English leaders might show their friendship by giving him presents.

From the ship Sir Richard watched the consultation which took place on shore, Okisko standing on one side of him, Captain Amadas on the other. Thomas Hariot came out of the cabin which he shared with John White. The latter sat on a stool, his drawing board propped up on a bench, and made a brief sketch of the dancing arena. Few words were spoken. Now and then the Admiral questioned Amadas or Okisko.

"The priest makes prayers," Okisko said. "He gives an offering to the sun and asks for guidance. If the sun goes down in full glory, the portents are good. If a cloud bank covers the sun, then the portents are bad."

"And what happens if the portents are bad?" the Admiral asked. "Will they send out boats to attack?"

Okisko hesitated a moment. "I do not think so. Perhaps if I say to them that their friend Captain Amadas is here among us, it will ease their suspicions."

The Admiral agreed at once. "Step forward. Cry out again that we come as friends. Then you, Amadas, remove your cap, stand out where they may see you and say a word to them."

"If I can remember their tongue." Amadas smiled ruefully.

Okisko stood at the rail. Cupping his hands, he cried out in a full, strong voice. He talked a few minutes. Several Indians walked down to the shore. One stepped forward and replied. After he had finished, Okisko turned to Captain Amadas. "Sir, the chief remembers you well, you and your brothers. He remembers you by your great generosity. You came and brought gifts. 'Let the captain speak!'"

Amadas greeted them with a few words in their language. Then, through the interpreter, he said, "Why is there fear among you, O Chief of a great tribe? When my brother Captain Barlow and I were here with you a few moons ago, you and your people made no show of fear or doubt. We

309

brought you, of your own accord, to our ship, and you liked our meat and our wine. You left our ship and fell afishing, and you divided the fish into two parts—one for our larger ship and one for our smaller. Neither you nor your people were afraid. You stood as a king stands, and you listened not to a man speaking over your shoulder. Are you no longer a man to come and go as you choose, O King? Do you pay tribute to Wingina, who calls himself Pemisapan?"

The king shouted and beat his hands on his breast. He was his own man, he said, a king in his own right. He paid tribute to none. As for Wingina, who now called himself by another name, he had a grudge against him. He carried a wound in his thigh from Wingina's bow. But he did not fear him, nor the English.

"Then either come aboard our ship to make trade, or we will come ashore."

The king's warriors had gathered around him, listening to Captain Amadas. Now they made a great hullabaloo, shouting, gesticulating. Foremost among them was the man Okisko said was the priest. He was expostulating, waving his arms, shaking his rattles.

Okisko said, "If the Admiral would now speak?"

Grenville stepped forward. He stood head and shoulders above the others. The sun shone on his armour. "We will come ashore. We bring gifts from the great Queen of the English. We come in peace. But we must have a chief's word that we will be received in peace. Send two young warriors aboard our ship, that they may see the gifts with their own eyes."

Grenville turned and went into his cabin. The men left the ship's sides. Some went below. Others sat on the deck and made sweet music with their small instruments.

An hour passed. Okisko, who had been watching from a secluded place, spoke to Captain Amadas. "They will come now. The priest has gone away to sit in his temple. He will pray to his gods. He sees that the king is determined to send someone to the boats, so you may depend on it the god will give a favourable sign. It may be a few hours, it may not be before morning, but they will come."

Captain Amadas went to speak to the Admiral.

"I have no intention of waiting until tomorrow to deal

with an Indian chief," Sir Richard said. "Give the order for the navigator to make sail."

This was done. At once there was activity on deck. Seamen manned the ropes, hauled up the sails. Men walked round and round the creaking windlass, hauling up the anchor.

Colin gave over to the helmsman. A breeze was blowing from the east. The sails caught the wind as the ship swung. It was a small wind, but enough to tack across the bay into open water.

On the shore the villagers ran to the water's edge, shouting and throwing their arms about. They were ready to deal with the captain. By now the pinnace was out of the curving bay. The mainsail was hoisted. A stiffer breeze caught the canvas. The ship took a northward course.

Okisko was silent. When they were well out in midstream, he allowed a brief smile to come to his lips. "My grandfather is a great leader, a very great leader. He does not allow a small king of an insignificant tribe to play fast and loose. You will see. The chief will send out canoes to beg the English leader to return. Is it not so, Captain?"

Amadas nodded. He, too, was well pleased. Grenville had grasped the situation. He knew when a firm hand was necessary.

John Arundell and Philip Blount joined them. "Look, they are sending out canoes—two—three—big canoes. Are they going to attack us?"

Okisko said, "Sirs, no. They will now request respectfully that you make a visit to the village of Weapemeoc."

"How does it happen that you know so much about what these people will do, Okisko?" Philip asked.

A broad smile came to the face of the Indian. It was so unusual that both lads stood looking at him in amazement. "This town and Pasquenoke the women's town are under the jurisdiction of King Okisko of Weapemeoc," the Indian boy said.

"Your father?" cried John.

"My father's father. Therefore I know these people as far up as the Chowanook country where the river becomes sweet water, broad and still."

Captain Amadas said, "Yes, I know we sailed up the Chowanook to where the river grows no wider than the Thames between Westminster and Lambeth. The land be-

311

yond the left bank is fairly high, and on the high bank is a town which the savages called Ohanoak. I remember it had fine grain fields and is subject to Chowanook."

"Yes, yes." Okisko spoke quickly, with black eyes alive and sparkling. "Chowanook is a great town, and its people are a fighting tribe. The king, Menatonon, suffers from a lameness, but he is a very prudent king, and he knows well his neighbours and the country to the far north."

The canoes of the Indians set out, but, having only ten rowers each, they could not get out of the bay fast enough. They turned and paddled back.

"It is well," said Okisko. "Let the king speak for himself and not for the priest."

Amadas made his way to the Admiral's quarters. It was near sunset. Grenville was sitting at the port, watching the Indian town through his glass. He smiled and stroked his beard. "Sit down, Amadas. Your Indians look disappointed."

"So they are, sir. Okisko says it serves them well, or something to that effect. It seems these towns are ruled over by a chief named Okisko."

Grenville looked up quickly. "So? So?"

"Our boy's grandfather."

"What has he to say about our manoeuvre?"

"He says it is excellent; that a king should know a king's mind and not lean on a priest."

Grenville nodded. "We went to them. Now let them come to us. Tell me, is there good anchorage for the night beyond?"

"Sir, yes. Set for the long point at the meeting of the waters. Beyond is a deep creek, where a ship can anchor. I remember it was there that we saw deer in great herds coming down to drink and fish leaping from the water. It is a quiet spot and safe harbour."

"Good! We will steer for the point. Will you give directions to the helmsman?"

They anchored in the mouth of the creek. Heavy forest lay all about them. Great cypress trees set deep in the water guarded the banks. The creek was large enough for a big ship to enter. The shadows of the great trees were reflected in the water. Fish leaped, breaking the dark stream. A gunshot frightened the water-fowl. At sunset a doe and three fawns walked out of the forest and stood knee-deep in the creek.

312

Startled by the noise from the ship, they lifted their heads and crashed into the forest, showing nothing but white tails and rumps. Birds sang. Little parakeets studded the forest like variegated jewels. The air was soft and sweet from the scent of flowers on the bank, honeysuckle and shrubs. Vines grew heavy and rank, a tangle of green, while blossoms of the bay hung over the water, little accents of pure white in deep green.

Colin remembered what Amadas had told him: "The sweetest land under the cope of heaven." Standing alone, he looked up the wide creek and thought of the Cornish coast, rocky, forbidding. This was a gentle land, rich in lush, overflowing with fecundity. If it were cleared, what crops would spring from that virgin soil! He thought of Stowe: long generations taking from the soil and giving little in return, a thin spread of manure and another planting. Here, away from the coast, the land was dark and abounding. If he could only plant crops, graze sheep in the plenteous vegetation of these meadows!

Suddenly he saw himself clearing a forest, building a house . . . sheep and kine . . . a noble outlook of river and trees . . . standing in the door of the new house, a woman . . . fecundity, promise. . . . He closed his eyes, but he could not close the eyes of his mind. It was Thomasine Arundell he saw in the wilderness dream. This could not be. She was a girl that he loathed. She was the girl John Arundell would marry. That was as it should be. They were of a kind, Thomasine and John, of one name. They were born to their place in life, gentle-born.

He felt a whack on his back. Phil and John were beside him. "The Admiral wants you," they said in a breath. "We are all going to eat a supper—fish, fresh caught—and afterward Captain Amadas will tell us about the upper rivers, and Okisko will tell us about the people. John White is making a little map, so we may visualize the country and not be ignorant."

After supper the Admiral's chair was brought out, and the others grouped themselves about him. Some of the older men, Hariot, John White and Captain Amadas, sat in chairs, while the younger sprawled on deck. The seamen made a circle about them.

Colin would long remember that evening: the dark

mystery of the forest behind them; the black water of the creek; the low, mournful call of doves; an owl's deep hoot; the sudden bark of a fox; the snapping of limbs and twigs in the woods, as some large animal crashed through the tangle of grape and wire vines.

The sun went down behind them. The land across the river was still bright with sunshine, but the shadow of the great cypress trees lay almost their full length in the water. After a time the sun faded and the bright afterglow hung in the sky. The soft shadows slowly darkened. Stars came out. A quarter moon rose and cast its light on the rippling water. For a time they listened to the forest noises. A fish broke on the water. An eagle planed and swooped. White cranes flew by, their great long legs dangling behind.

Most of the men smoked the new weed, which they had brought with them from Roanoke, liking its soothing quality. Across the water lights began to twinkle. On the side where they were anchored was another town which belonged to the Chowanooks. "We are anchored in their river now," he said, "a day's journey perhaps from their great town of Chowanook."

Amadas, who sat next the Admiral, said, "Chief Menatonon's town is on the high land on the left. Chowanook is the greatest province and seigniory on the river. I recall that this one town can put seven hundred fighting men in the field."

"Sir, that is true," Okisko answered. "But the King Menatonon is of good discourse. He keeps peace with his neighbours."

Amadas called to a servant for coals and bent forward to light his long pipe. The light reflected on his face, showing the eagerness of his searching eyes. "Okisko," he said, "I remember well my visit to Menatonon. We went, Captain Barlow and I, to his village. We sat on a mat and fell to trading—chamois, buffalo and deerskins in exchange for tin dishes." He laughed. "I remember the king wanted a bright tin dish to hang in front of him like a breast-plate. For it we got twenty skins worth twenty crowns, and for a copper kettle, fifty skins. They wanted our swords and hatchets and axes, because they feared a war from the people of the north farther up the river."

Okisko said, "Yes, from the people who fish for pearls." There was a long silence after these words. "The queen of the Chowanooks wears pearls in her ears and wrapped about her neck, hanging down to her middle." Amadas said nothing, nor Grenville. "The women wear white coral about their heads, and around their arms and legs metal that shines like the sun."

Grenville asked a question or two about the Indian town. Then as an afterthought he said, "You say they fish for pearls?"

"Sir, no. Not the Chowanooks, but the people farther north, a wild, warlike people, who live on an island in a great body of water called Chesepiooc. There are two other kings at the great town of Chowanook."

Grenville said no more about pearls. That was enough for the present. Like Amadas, he did not want the Indians to know that they sought pearls or gold.

"Tell us about your great gods, Okisko. We will then tell you the story of our God Almighty, and His Son the Lord Jesus and the Holy Ghost."

Okisko sat cross-legged. He had not moved since they all gathered on the deck. The English lads squirmed. They found the boards hard to their thin bodies. John Gostigo took out his little stringed instrument and began to play a sad tune, picking the strings, humming softly. A bird flew over the ship, flapping great black wings.

"What's that?" one seaman cried. "A devil! I felt the sweep of his wings across my face, and the smell of sulphur is all about."

" 'Tis true. . . . I smell an evil smell." Half a dozen joined in.

Their awe-struck voices reached the Admiral. " 'Tis but a bird," he said in a loud tone so it might be heard across the deck.

"Sir, no bird could be so big. Its wings shadowed the whole deck. I saw it with my eyes as I lay looking at the stars. It shut off the very moon. It had a great evil head, and it carried something dangling. . . ."

John Gostigo struck a soft chord on his instrument. "An alcatras it was, a bird with a long beak and a pouch that hangs, which it fills with fish."

"What did you call it?" one seaman asked timorously.

"An alcatras. It's a big black bird with a wide spread of wings. You will see more such on the river and at the shore, when the fish run."

315

The men muttered, some of them unconvinced. "But it was big, big, black . . ."

"All things unknown are big at night," said Gostigos, "and the night gives black shadows to grey and brown and even white. Have no fear. The alcatras wants nothing but the fish that jump in the water at the ship's side."

Grenville thought this talk about the black bird had gone far enough, the explanation sufficient. He called for his men to remove the tankards and he put a question or two to the Indian.

"When we go to war," Okisko told him, "we carry clubs into which have been set the short sharp horns of a stag. These are for hand-to-hand fighting. We have bows, strong, made of hazel-wood. The arrows are headed with shells or teeth of fish sharp enough to kill a man without armour. Sometimes our warriors wear armour made of reeds, held together with thongs of leather. Our swords are of hardened wood, and we sometimes have breast-plates of wood.

"The image of our god of war we carry with us that our priests may ask counsel of him. Do you, sir, ask counsel of your priests before going to war?"

Grenville hesitated a moment. "We ask our churchmen to say prayers in church for our safety and our victory."

"It is the same," Okisko commented. "Do you sing as you march into battle? But no, you have the horns to blow instead."

Amadas said, "Tell us about your gods, Okisko."

Okisko, nothing loath, began his story. The Indians were natural orators, and his voice was round and full. Manteo had taught him his English well, and while at times it carried the sentence structure of the Indian language, it was understandable to all the listeners.

"We have many gods, whom we call Mantoac. Of the gods some are more important than others. There is one only chief and great god, who has existed for all eternity. When he purposed to make the world, he made other gods to help him. The sun, the moon and the stars are lesser gods. Before the land the waters were made, out of which were formed many creatures. A woman was made first, who by the working of one god conceived and brought forth a child. That was long ago.

"The gods are of human shape, and therefore we make images of them in the likeness of men. In houses and tem-

316

ples they sit and think. We worship and pray and bring sacrifices. The soul lives beyond the body. If its work is done, it goes into a heaven of bliss everlasting, which is in the farthest part of the earth where the sun sets."

Okisko's audience sat quietly. Perhaps each man was thinking what Grenville thought, that these savages had a religion not so far removed from their own. It would not be difficult to Christianise them and lead them to salvation.

Okisko told them the story of a wicked man who had died and been buried. The next day the earth of his grave began to move, and he came up to say that his soul had been near entering Popogusso, which the English call Hell. But the *good* gods saved him. Now he must walk the earth again and teach his people, so they would not go to that terrible place of torment.

Okisko had just finished the story when a watch called out that canoes with lights were approaching from up the river. Men scrambled to their feet and sought weapons. Gunners jumped to their guns.

The Admiral called, "Each man to his place, but don't fire a shot unless I give the signal!"

Out of the darkness the canoes came floating, twenty or more. At the bow and stern of each was a burning pine-knot. They moved silently; even the sweep of paddles was muffled.

"They come in peace," Okisko said to Amadas, who stood beside him.

"Are you sure of that?"

"Sir, if they came in war, they would come without lights, in the blackness of night, from the land and from the water. They would attack swiftly, from behind trees or in dark canoes, and only later perhaps would use fire-burning arrows. At war Indians come in the dark, or at day dawning, but never carrying lights."

Grenville joined them and spoke to Okisko. "Address them. Ask who they are, and why they come at this hour."

Okisko spoke. His voice carried out over the water where the canoes had made a great semicircle in front of the vessel. Presently he turned to the Admiral. "They say they are a delegation from the three kings of the Chow-anooks. They have heard through the waters and by land that a great king in a great ship is within their seigniory. Their rulers wish to make him welcome. And in the morning they would lead the great king to their town, where he and his people would be received with all honour."

Grenville had two lighted lanthorns brought and held on either side of him. He stood fair and tall in the light, so that all might see him. He thanked the three kings for their welcome, and said that tomorrow he would sail up the river to their village. In the meantime the canoes might return home with the assurance that the English gentlemen had come with peace in their hearts.

For a time the canoes circled about, now in the bright moon path, now in the darkness. An owl hooted, answered by another.

Amadas said to Okisko, "That was a man with an owl's voice. Indians are in the woods on the shore."

"Sir, yes. They watch all night. But rest secure, great captain: they are here in friendship, without treason."

"They had best be without treason, or we will unlimber our great guns on their villages."

"Sir, no need for war, when peace is so easy."

That night Grenville wrote in his journal: "We must hold peace very dear and preserve it. We must think only of friendship. We can then trade with them for furs, gold and pearls, and show them the ways of Christ according to Dr. Hooker's plan."

The morning was clear and warm. After a breakfast of fresh fish they raised anchor and tacked across the river to catch the wind. The breeze was gentle, and they lazed with slack sail. An hour out they saw the Indian canoes rowing to meet them. The Indians greeted them with cries and gestures of pleasure, holding up strings of fish and water-fowl in a net. These they flung on deck with every evidence of good-will.

There was so little wind that two days had passed before they lay opposite Chowanook. The town was thirty or more feet above the water. It was in a great clearing of the forest, which stretched around three sides of it, dark, green, menacing.

The ship lay out in the channel in midstream. Only the near side of the town was visible, above a great circle of palisades. Moored in rude floats built of logs were many canoes, great canoes that would carry twenty or thirty men.

These canoes began to fill with copper-coloured savages, clothed only in deerskin clouts. They all carried bows

318

and arrows, so Grenville ordered the ordnance unhoused. This was merely a showing, but he wanted nothing untoward to happen. Grenville had made up his mind that he would leave behind him only thoughts of peace between Indian and white man. If war came later, it would not be his responsibility but Lane's.

The first canoe brought messages. Would the Great Chief come ashore? The Great Chief would not. He was preparing a feast for the king of the Chowanooks. He would receive the king on the deck of the ship within sight of his warriors and his town. The king would sit under a canopy to shield him from the sun.

The messenger returned to shore. After a time a boat larger than any they had seen swung up to a float. A man was carried down the bank and carefully placed in the stern.

"Menatonon himself," Okisko announced, "he who is impotent in his limbs and must be carried."

The Admiral called to the boatswain, "Rig a chair and let it be dropped overside so that a canoe may pull under it. We will make it easy for the king to come aboard."

Already chairs had been placed under the canopy, and a table with food and drink cooled in buckets of water.

The king hesitated. The chair seemed formidable to him.

"Get into the chair, Okisko," Grenville said. "Show him how simple a device it is." Okisko rode up and down a couple of times. The king was satisfied and allowed himself to be hoisted to the deck of the pinnace.

Once aboard, the king showed his delight at his reception. He examined everything in the way of arms and ordnance, ate heartily and drank wine with a certain gusto, saying that he himself had wine made from black grapes and amber, which grew near the sea-shore.

He had a ship, too, put together with wooden nails. Some time ago a white man's ship had been wrecked off Hatorask. The Chowanooks had been out on the point at the time, fishing. They had found boards and planking, held together with nails. These wood pieces they saved, drew out the nails and manufactured a boat.

Amadas looked at Grenville. "The Spanish," Amadas said.

All afternoon the king was fed and entertained. He was well wined, but he was in nowise drunken. He carried with him many presents when he left, and went with great protestations of friendship.

All night the canoes patrolled about the ship, to the uneasiness of some of the crew and the younger men.

John White made drawings of Indian canoes, the great alcatras and some of the Indians, showing caste scarifications.

Thomas Hariot scribbled, day and night, questioning Okisko on matters he did not understand about the Indian tribes.

John and Colin had watch. They sat on deck, their eyes following the movement of the canoes, dark shadows on the darker river. At their post gunners slept an uneasy sleep as they lay on the deck, fingers twitching to pull a string that would release a blast on the quiet river. But no blast was necessary. After a time the moon hid its light under a mass of clouds. A few raindrops fell. A chilly wind blew up-river.

One by one the canoes disappeared into the darkness. They heard them bang against the floating docks, for sound carries far over quiet water.

Always alert for danger or attack, they moved about the ship. The rain came, softly at first, then a steady downpour which lasted until morning.

Before sunrise a canoe put out from the shore. Six oarsmen rowed one man who sat in the stern. A tall figure stood on the prow and worked the long sweep.

The passenger came aboard and delivered a small box, wrapped and twisted with narrow rushes that were formed into a mat. "For the great English King from King Menatonon of Chowanook," he said and at once returned to his canoe.

Colin, only half awake, carried the box to the Admiral's cabin. The earliness of the hour did not disturb him, for he knew Sir Richard was awake by daybreak.

In answer to "Come in," Colin entered. Grenville was sitting up in bed, dressed in his white brocaded night-robe. He had his Bible spread open on his knees and he was reading aloud.

He looked up and waited for Colin to speak. "The king sent this package to you—a farewell gift, his messenger said."

"Open it. Let us see if our entertainment has borne fruit."

Colin removed the reed mat and revealed a small casket of wood, painted in various colors. It resembled Spanish work.

"Raise the lid," Grenville said.

Colin lifted the simple lock and opened the casket. His blue eyes grew round with astonishment.

Grenville took the box from his hand. "Pearls!" he exclaimed. Pearls by the hundred dripped through his long fingers. He held some in his hand, scrutinzing them carefully. Some were pied, some black—but some very orient and large. What a present for Her Majesty! A pleased smile came over his stern face. "I think, Colin, our entertainment has borne glorious fruit."

CHAPTER 23
JOHN ARUNDELL SAILS FOR ENGLAND

The whole camp was engaged in writing letters—on Roanoke, on Wococon, at Hatorask. The quills were scratching over paper. Those who knew the art wrote their own letters. Those who did not dictated to a scribe. Colin wrote a dozen letters for seamen and men of the company. A letter home from a man in the wilderness was a revealing thing. Into it were poured hope or hopelessness, longings, nostalgia for family and homeland.

A few were buoyant, filled with tales of hunting, of fish in such quantity that "you'd never think again of fishing for pilchards," as a Cornish seaman named Amos Treloar wrote to the "Old Woman." He told her great tales of Indians and war canoes on the river. When he had finished he said with a twinkle, "Better let Old Woman think it is danger I live in, else she will be putting another man to her bed."

So it went on all one day and the next, up to the very night before the sailing on the fifth day of August.

The followers of Lane wrote most furiously, to offset any tales that John Arundell might take home. They did not know that Grenville had given John orders not to criticise anyone. The opportunity was too good for Lane and his closest friends to miss. They dispatched packets to Sir Francis Walsingham, Sir Philip Sidney, Sir Walter Raleigh, Lord Burghley and others high in government.

Thomas Hariot wrote a long letter to Richard Hakluyt marked "Secret."

Of our company that return, some for their misdemeanours and ill dealing in the country have been worthily punished. They by their bad natures will not only speak malice of their governors but slander of the country itself.

Some, ignorant of the state of the country, will tell more than they ever saw, daring this because they think no one will be about to disprove them. Others will make difficulties of simple things

322

because they do not understand them. The cause of their igno-rance is mainly that they never left the island where we have our settlement. After gold and silver were not found, they had little care for anything but to pamper their bellies.

And there are others who have little understanding, less discre-tion and more tongue than is needful or requisite. Some of them have had nice bringing up, but they lived in cities or towns and (as I may say) had never seen the earth before. Because there were not to be found here any English cities, any fair houses, any of their old accustomed dainty food nor any soft beds of down or feathers, the country has been to them miserable, and they report accordingly.

My purpose is to give the reason for the malicious opinions of these men. Envious, even slanderous, reports will be made. I do not mean to trouble you, but just to let you know. These trifles are not worthy of mention.

Many of the men in our company are worthy to be remem-bered, as the first discoverers of the country—Sir Richard Gren-ville, our general, Ralph Lane, our governor, and divers others who worked under the government of the captains, mates and masters of the voyages.

Thus referring my relation to your favourable construction, expecting good success of the action from Him who is to be acknowledged the Author and Governor of all things,

I take my leave of you

Thomas Hariot

*To Richard Hakluyt,
The Middle Temple, Strand,
London.*

Governor Lane sat in his room late into the night. By the light of several candles he, too, wrote letters marked "Secret." One was addressed to Walsingham.

I think it is good to advertise you concerning Sir R. Grenville's complaints against M. Cavendish, the High Marshal Edward Gorges, Francis Brooke the Treasurer, and Captain Clarke. They have been faithful to me and industrious. To this I certify.

The conduct of Sir Richard from first to last has been tyran-nical. It is through his default that action has been made most painful and perilous.

I refer you to an ample discourse of the whole voyage in the hands of the bearer, our Treasurer Francis Brooke, directed to Sir Walter Raleigh. Sir Richard's intolerable pride, insatiable ambition and proceeding toward us all, and to me in particular, are beyond telling.

I have had as much experience as Grenville. I desire to be freed from this place if he is to carry any authority in chief.

Your humble well-wisher,

Ralph Lane

August.
Port Ferdinando, Virginia.
To Sir Francis Walsingham.

Other letters were going into pouches. Phil Blount was struggling over a letter to Mistress Courtenay, Rise's sister, not a love letter but trembling on the verge. He called in Colin to make a fair copy. His thin face was slightly flushed, for he had never admitted to his comrades that his affections lay in this direction, though they suspected it.

Colin thought of no one to write to until the Admiral suggested that he write to Dame Philippa. This he did, telling her about the company, about the new houses, the fine horses Sir Richard had taken from the Spanish.

As for foxes, they are here by the hundreds, and grey wolves and deer, bear too; good sport both for bear and deer. The Indians beat the woods, making great noises, or set fire to the brush to drive the animals out through a narrow tunnel. They shoot with bows and arrows. Sometimes they dig a great pit, set stakes in it, cover it with brush, and then drive the bears toward it. The animals crash through the brush and are impaled on the sharp stakes. A cruel hunting you will say, Dame Philippa.

We attended a deer drive where the method was to drive the animals toward a stream. Indians wearing deerskins and heads with antlers waited on the opposite side. When the driven deer came to midstream, the Indians shot them with bows and arrows in great number. This may seem slaughter to you, but the Indians dry the meat, hanging it in strips over a fire, and it is their food for the winter or when they go on their journeys from the principal towns on the mainland to the seashore during their season to catch fish. These fish also they dry.

I think they are a wise people, because they know how to sustain themselves in a wild land. Everything they do for themselves, from providing food by planting corn, melons and the like, to tanning skins for their clothes, making their earthen cooking pots, weaving their baskets to store corn and grain and weaving mats for their sleeping huts. I find them a very fine and gentle people. Although the Spanish on Hispaniola told us terrible tales of their cruelty and tortures, we have seen none of this.

Perhaps the cruel savages who drink human blood and roast human flesh all live in Florida and the Spanish possessions. I think we must be kind and fair to our Indians, else they too may become savage.

Grenville read the letter Colin had written with a great deal of interest. "I am pleased with you, Colin. You show keen observation and sensitive perception. I shall not trouble about you when I am gone."

Colin looked down at the floor. He was disappointed. He had hoped he would sail with Sir Richard and return with him on the next journey to the colony.

Sir Richard saw his disappointment. He ignored it and went on talking. "I want someone here to look after my interest. You will have complete charge of my horses and all the animals. There are only a few here who understand husbandry. I'll leave my men Smolkin and Robert. They will live with the animals at the stabling place. I will leave Tom Skeuelabs and John Fever too. They will cruise the woods and endeavour to estimate what naval stores are to be had—tar, pitch, turpentine and resin. Mast poles will be cut and laid out to dry, so we may carry some back to England later. Since gold and silver do not lie in this part of the land, we must turn our thoughts to such objects of trade as are at hand. Captain Amadas will take this in charge, with Rise Courtenay and Master Allyne. They have asked me to let them do these things, which, coming under the head of naval stores, fall in my jurisdiction as Admiral.

"Philip Blount will be with you, for he too is interested in horses. I suggest you breed the mares. They will drop foals in the spring. Do you think you will be happy in this work?"

Colin's blue eyes met the Admiral's steady gaze. "Sir, you are my master. What pleases you pleases me."

"I don't like the word 'master' between you and me, Colin. You are as a son to me, like John Arundell and Richard Prideaux. I am your guardian, standing as your father. Please remember."

325

Colin's heart was near bursting. He struggled to keep back the tears. "Sir," he said, "sir," but no other words came.

Grenville put his arm about the lad's shoulders. "You are to forget past sorrows, Colin. When you go home, you will live at Stowe as my ward. Or perhaps you may wish to stay here. Perhaps you will find a place for yourself in Virginia. Marry, bear sons, prosper in power and well-doing and build a great new world. The old world is lost in its age. It is weary with wars and hatreds. The new world will be vigorous. Let it grow in grace and forget the evils of the old. Praise God, it will grow strong and, in its strength, be kind!"

Grenville took up his cap and left the room. Then at the door he said, "All the letters are completed, but one that I will write this evening before bedtime. Go now and help John. He is overwhelmed by his new responsibilities. I've sent my servant to help him pack. In the morning we will sail him down to Wococon, where his ship is waiting, already loaded with skins and enough poles for ballast. He will have an excellent navigator, George Eseven, and for a mate Erasmus Clefs, who is one of our best seamen. So he will fare well."

Colin found John standing in the center of the room, which looked as if a strong hurricane had struck. Sir Richard's servant was lifting clothes from the floor, where John had tossed them when he took them out of the carved oak cupboards.

"Ah, Colin! Just the one I wanted. Over in the corner are clothes I'm leaving behind. You and Phil can fight for them. Sir Richard said to leave everything behind except what I would need for the voyage. By Phoebus, what does a man need for a voyage? Armour, one fine suit, leather jerkins, a few pairs of hosen and velvet doublets? I've left my second-best satin doublet for you—the blue one—and six pairs of hosen with velvet tops, four Holland shirts, one suit of light armour, three pairs of shoes and one pair of long boots for winter. Heaven knows what your winter will be!"

"Some say the winters are mild here, but with much rain and wind. Some say they're cold; others that they're warmer than in England, not so warm as on Porto Rico. Who knows?"

"It can't be very cold or the savages would not go about

in their nakedness all the year, as I've been told they do," John observed. "Stop!" he called to the servant. "Cease, and find us some ale and a bit of bread and cheese. St. George on horseback, this work is wearing! I feel my strength oozing away." Black John flung himself on the bench full-length. He lay on his back, his knees up tentlike.

"In three months I'll be at home in wild Cornwall." There was a gayness in John's voice and his eyes sparkled. "Lovely Cornwall, lovely Stowe, lovely Thomasine!"

Philip stood in the doorway. "You do your lady no honour to put her last in your exultations."

"Well, I'll exchange and cry 'Lovely Thomasine!' first."

Philip moved aside. "Here are ale and cheese, my young Cornish worthy. Get up and drink to tomorrow's sailing, and to the company of sorry men you leave behind." Philip raised his glass. He held the tankard in mid air, looking at Colin. "You're not going, are you?"

"No, I'm staying."

"Good! We'll have Rise Courtenay to sleep in John's bed."

John beat the table with his empty tankard. "Ah, so you can talk of Mistress Courtenay!"

Philip reached a long arm and gave John a shove. He rolled from the bench to the floor. He sprang up and dusted himself off. "Have done! You do wrong to put a worthy captain on his hunkers," he cried in mock solemnity. "Ah well, 'tis the last scuffle. Tomorrow, beginning at sunrise, I will be Master Arundell—I mean Captain Arundell —of the good ship *Coombe Vale*."

"Is that the new name they have given the Spanish barque?"

" 'Tis the name I have given her. Heavens knows what will be painted on her stern when we see her tomorrow. Come on, let's get out of here. We're in the way." He grinned at the servant. "You finish. I'm worn down."

The servant suppressed a grin. "Very good, sir."

The three lads went on deck. "I've a mind to look at the horses before I go. Come on, my boys." John cried out loudly for a boat, and when one came alongside the three went ashore.

After they had seen the horses, which were kept just beyond the stockade in stables built of stakes and covered with boughs, Philip suggested that he and Colin find themselves a house to live in, a small house for five or six. Prideaux would be back from Hatorask soon. They'd take in Rise Courtenay and one or two others. They went in and out of the half-finished buildings, looking for one that met Philip's approval.

Colin asked, "Won't we have to apply to Governor Lane after Sir Richard sails on the twenty-fifth?"

Phil said, "No. We'll ask the Admiral to assign us to shore quarters. Part of this place is for the men of the *Tyger*. I'll ask for this one, right against the palisade, not far from the common-room. I suppose we'll eat in the common-room, won't we?" He turned to John. "How now, Captain, is that the plan?"

John grinned, said he didn't know. No one had asked his opinion.

"I'll ask Sir Richard tonight. Better be early than late, say I. . . . I say, there's your old friend Lacie, Colin. He's looking into the houses too. Shall we invite him in with us?" Philip gave Colin a poke in the ribs. "Old Sobersides!" he taunted.

Lacie did not come their way. They did not know whether he saw them or not, or whether he avoided them. He disappeared in the opposite direction, toward the west gate.

John said to Colin as they plodded back through the sand, "Have your eyes open for Lacie, fellow. He's bound to make trouble for you in one way or another."

Colin grunted. He was tired of Lacie and tired of warnings. He was able to look after himself, but he didn't say so. John meant well . . . and John was sailing tomorrow.

Candles burned in the Admiral's cabin that night when all the rest of the ship slept.

He had written a long letter to his wife Mary, setting down the words of love that were in his heart for her. At the last he wrote:

John had asked for Thomasine's hand. I have told him that I have no serious objection, but that I must talk with you before I give a final answer. John is a fine lad. I want him to make a marriage that is suitable. Thomasine has a sufficient dower, but I am not sure that she is ready for marriage. You must think it over, my sweet wife. You see how I lean on you in all things? Soon I will be at Stowe. Then I will tell you with my lips and my arms how necessary you are to me.

328

My sweet and loving friend, good night.
Your husband

R. Grenville

On board the Tyger
Roanoke Island in Virginia.
August 4, 1585

The Spanish barque sailed on the tide. It was near sunset, with a spanking breeze from the west to lift her sails,
from mains to topgallants. The light fell on her and
coloured the canvas, golden sails on a golden sea. John
Arundell stood on the bridge. Very fine and noble he looked,
his comrades thought. His new command had given him
stature in their eyes. He was no longer their companion to
tease and taunt with rough boy's play, but a man who
captained a ship on the great Ocean Sea.

Great Englishmen had sailed the waters of the Ocean
Sea—Drake and Hawkins and Frobisher—great captains all,
men who had raised the glory of Elizabeth high—Grenville
also—and now young men to follow them, each dreaming
his dreams of conquest.

It was a quiet and subdued crew who sailed back to the
island in the pinnace. Their good companion had left
them. He sailed toward Land's End and the Cornish coast.
They must stay behind, to wrest what glory they could
from the forests of a new world—grave thought for young
souls, a little sad perhaps, an ache for a softer life in an old
land. But youth is resilient. By the time the sun rose on
another day they were deep in new plans. Sir Richard would
take them on one more journey before he, too, hauled
up anchor and set sail for England.

Secotan was four days' journey away to the south and
west. Grenville wanted to visit this town, because it was
near here that a ship had been wrecked. He had heard the
story from Captain Amadas. He thought it might be possible
to find some trace of the ship or the people, who had had
white skins and worn clothes like the English.

The tilt-boat was launched. The Admiral took with
him Master Stukeley, Hariot, Stafford and Cavendish. At the
last he invited Governor Lane and John White, and
much to his surprise Lane accepted.

The passage was through a sound within the mainland,
yet so wide a water that no land was in sight. Full of flats
and shoals, it was too shallow for boats of deep draft.

Colin sat near Master Hariot on the journey and held much conversation with the scholar, who was writing the history of the colony.

"Sir Richard tells me that you write a fair fine hand, Master Grenville. What would you say to making a copy for me, when the Admiral sails for Bideford?"

Colin thanked him. "Perhaps, Master Hariot, it would be well for you to ask the Admiral. He has laid out some work for me, but I am sure there would be time enough."

"I will speak with Sir Richard today. I find much writing puts a cramp in my hand, and sometimes my neck is as stiff as a stork's from sitting and bending over a table. If you could find time, it would be a great help."

And so it was arranged, for Sir Richard had no objection, in truth was well pleased. It would be one more phase in the education of this eager youth.

Secotan was an open town, with large gardens planted in straight rows—tobacco, which the Indians called *uppówoc*, maize and large-kernelled corn. Colin walked among the houses, which were far apart. The whole town was set in a goodly clearing in the forest. The houses had round roofs. The walls were of reed mats. Some of the walls were rolled up. The women had been sent away, perhaps to a women's town, for the season was well advanced, and there was no work for them in the gardens until harvest time.

The chief entertained them at a meal of cooked beans, corn and venison. Mats were placed in the wide street, and food served in earthen plates.

Near by were the dancing ground and the temple hut, inside which a fire burned. The same wooden stakes with carved nunlike heads that they had observed before surrounded the fire and the dancing circle.

Colin, walking about, came upon the end of the gardens, behind which the river curved. Here a hut had been erected on poles set on a platform, higher than the tallest maize stalks. A watchman was sitting in the hut, beating on a drum, singing and making a disturbance to frighten away crows and other birds and beasts that might feed and destroy the crops before the harvest time.

As they sat at the feast, the king told the Admiral about the great ship which had been wrecked. According to the Indians, who reckoned time by the moon's advent, it

330

must have been twenty years or more ago. He repeated what Sir Richard had already heard, that the men of white skins had spent ten days or so on one of the long islands where no one then lived, Wococon. His men had found them and helped them fasten two canoes together to make one boat. They made masts for them out of young trees and aided them to get the boat into the water.

"What did they do for sails?" Sir Richard asked after dinner had been removed. They were all puffing at long pipes, smoking the lowest of all the leaves on the tobacco plant.

Colin saw how interested Lane and Hariot were, and Captain Stafford also. John White was sitting farther down the street, making a little drawing of the village, while half a dozen copper-skinned natives sat around him, watching him carefully, their faces solemn and unsmiling.

"They used their shirts for sails."

"Then they got away," Lane said.

"No, they did not. We gave them food. Three weeks they were here."

"And then?" Grenville waited while the interpreter listened to a long conversation.

"He says his people found the boat on another uninhabited island not far away. They admired the white skins of the men. Never since had they seen any people like these until now."

Captain Stafford said, "Could it have been some of Sir John Hawkins' men? He was in this part of the world about that time."

Grenville said he thought not, although Hawkins had told him that he visited the French Huguenot colony in Florida, where he had put in, searching for fresh water. The French were near to starvation. He went ashore and visited the commander René de Laudonnière. Hawkins left them beans and salt, wax to make candles, and fifty pairs of shoes, for they were almost barefoot. The French were suspicious. They did not know whether France and England were at war or not. They were afraid to trust the English.

The king watched Grenville's lips as he talked, as though to read what he said. When the interpreter translated the conversation, he lost interest. It was nothing that his people knew about. He knew the English—that was all. These other tribes were as nothing to him.

Grenville's party left shortly after, but not before they had given the people presents of cooking pots and lengths of cotton.

On the way back Stafford brought up the subject of the wreck again. "I seem to remember vaguely about that French colony in Florida, but my memory is short. Do you, Master Hariot, know anything more?"

"The Huguenots were sent over by Admiral Coligny. They were seeking refuge because of the difference between their religion and that of the state—or Catherine de' Medici's. Then Spain had a rival in Florida. Philip the king could not endure that, so the eternal struggle for power began."

Grenville added, "It was said that Coligny had sent an earlier colony farther north. But I know nothing of the details."

Lane said, "Why does it matter? All this is ancient." His voice displayed his lack of interest, his weariness of the discussion.

Grenville gave him a brief glance. "If the Spanish were here once, they may come again. Whatever one has to say of Philip of Spain, he has determination."

"It takes a determined man to have four wives, and all of royal blood," Lane answered.

A laugh arose. " 'Tis his third mother-in-law—Catherine de' Medici—that would take all of a man's guile and determination to outmanoeuvre." It was Hariot who spoke.

All this was above Colin's head. He determined to ask Dame Philippa about these things.

They returned home without incident. Grenville sailed west again on the way back, into the mouth of a broad river the Indians called Cipo, where they went for mussels.

Lane's eyes glistened when he heard the word mussels. Mussels might mean pearls. Since there was no sign of gold or silver, pearls must be found. He would find a fortune in pearls. But he would let it go until Grenville left and he was *really* the governor. Then the search would begin.

Late in the month, the twenty-fifth of August, the *Tyger* stood out to sea from Wococon. Some disaffected persons sailed with Grenville, and some others who would return at Easter with him. The Indian Okisko went as the guest of the Admiral and Sir Walter Raleigh. Easter was not far off. Winter would pass quickly, and another spring begin. Greater hope comes in the spring, new life. No, it would not be long.

No sooner was the *Tyger* in the Ocean Sea than a change swept over the island. The first night there was a great feast given by the governor. Lane sat in an elbow-chair on a raised platform and watched the feasting, a secret smile on his small mouth. His hand caressed his moustache and his beard as his eyes roamed over the company. It was as though he were counting his men and those who were loyal to Grenville. Colin felt Lane's eyes rest on him, although his own were on his plate. He would get short shrift from the governor. The best thing to do was to stay out of his sight.

That night as they got ready to go to bed, Phil Blount said, "Life will be different now. I could read it in the governor's eyes as he glanced our way."

"He is going up the Chowan day after tomorrow. He will be too busy to think of us."

"Umm. I don't know. I wonder how long we will be allowed to keep our comfortable quarters here." Phil looked about. "Crude but comfortable," he said. "Smells nicely of wood, fresh cut. When Rise Courtenay comes next week, and one other——"

He was interrupted by a knock at the door, loud and demanding. A voice called, "Open up!"

"What braying! Do you bring unhappiness?" Phil called.

"Open up! 'Tis I, Dick Prideaux. Open, I say."

Phil leaped from his bench, unlatched the heavy lock, threw the door open, while Colin lighted the candle lanthorn.

Prideaux stood blinking on the threshold, staggering under bundles of clothes thrown over his shoulders. A pair of long boots hung from one hand, a canvas case with a pillow from the other. His face was red, his glistening nose was peeling. He wore on his head a black cap, which dangled over his shoulder. Behind him were two sailors carrying his heavy sea-chest, and behind them came his armour-bearer, a red-haired youth with a wide grin. He held the breast-plate and collar tied by a thong and carried the metal helmet on the back of his head.

"Where shall these boys put my chest and my armour?

333

Step in, my good fellows. Throw the armour in the corner or on top of the armoire, if there's no room inside."

"The bed on the far side has no occupant," Phil said, slapping Dick on the shoulder. The bundle of clothes dropped to the floor—white camelot, leather jerkins, velvet mantles and fine Holland shirts.

"Hey, you! Wait, fellows! Put my chest there, against the wall. You may go now. Do not drink so much ale that you'll have no stomach for work tomorrow." The seamen laughed, pulled at their caps and went away.

Dick sat down on the bench at the long table, stretching his legs. "Jesu, it's good to feel a floor under my feet, even if it is earth and rushes! I've stridden the deck so long that I spread my legs when I walk to straddle an ocean swell."

Colin, whose tasks had prevented him from going to Wococon, asked, "Did the *Tyger* sail?"

"Aye, and a grand sight she was. Her decks were as white as my Holland there, and her sails billowed out, from topgallant to mainsail. Rows of shields hung along her rails with newly painted devices, and her forked banners flew from taffrail and yard-arm. You'd have thought she was the *Great Harry* herself, she looked so gallant."

Phil said, "The crest of St. George makes a brave show, and the Tudor Rose."

Colin gave an involuntary sigh.

"Why so gloomy, Colin? You're stuck here for a twelvemonth, and you, Phil, and a hundred more of us. So what matter?" Dick inquired.

Colin set a tankard in front of him. Dick caught it up and drank deep. "A month I've had at Wococon, with naught to do but stand on the shore watching for a sail, or cast for fish or make bets on which crab can back most swiftly to its hole. It's good to see your silly faces again." He grinned and looked from one to the other. "We'll miss old John, will we not?"

Phil said, "Rise Courtenay will come in with us."

Dick looked around the room, counting the beds which took up one side of it, six roughly made, bough-covered narrow beds. "Who else will join our house?" he asked.

"It has not been decided. I believe they cast lots."

Phil unlimbered his long legs and got up. He took a candle from off the mantel-board. He lighted it, snuffed the old one which had burned to the bottom of the lanthorn and set the new one in its place. He said, "If we don't like the others, we can freeze them out—give them the blank wall."

He had no sooner spoken the words than a knock sounded. Prideaux, who was closest to the door, got up and lifted the latch.

Captain Amadas and Stafford came in. They greeted Prideaux. The others got quickly to their feet. Amadas said, "Stafford and I have decided to move in with you. We like this house—" he smiled a little—"and the company seems desirable. Have you extra beds?"

Philip Blount waved his hand toward the shadowy corner. "Two, sirs. We are honoured."

The men unbuckled swords, unbuttoned jerkins and pulled off their long boots. Colin brought tankards and got out a round Devon cheese he had in his chest.

Phil made a small fire on the hearth and put a rag in the flame. "It will smell evilly," he remarked, "but Glande says the biting flies don't like smoke."

"Sometimes I think the smell worse than the bite," Amadas said. "My men will bring over our chests in the morning and a tick full of husks to sleep on. Tonight I could sleep on a stone floor. If you will pardon me, I'll rest my body this instant."

The others stripped to small clouts, rubbed their skin with grease to keep off insects and climbed in on the pine boughs, after putting their muskets within reach and their knives under their pillows. A sentry walked along the stockade, his boots making a scuffing sound on the planking. The night was warm, the moon almost at the full. Colin couldn't sleep. He kept thinking of the white men shipwrecked on the lonely coast so many years ago. On the other side of the stockade the feast was still going on. Men were drinking, singing. High sharp words cut into laughter. Grenville would not have had this. Lane was relaxing the discipline the Admiral had maintained, to show what a good fellow he was. It was a bid for good will.

In the silence of the forest dark shadows moved from tree to tree, listening, watching, keeping always out of sight of the sentinels. The sentinels walked along the high platform or sat in the blockhouses, looking out over the low treetops, seeing nothing that moved in the thickets

335

of bay trees and small pines, nor the canoes hidden in the reeds along the shore.

Colin thought, The *Tyger* is gone, and with it the heavy ordnance, the trained fighters. What have we left? A few cannon, a few men practised to war, and the rest an untrained crew. . . . Tomorrow, after Lane sailed up-river, he would talk with Captain Amadas. He would feel more at ease if Glande and Nugent were domiciled near them, and Master Allyne and a few other men he knew had cool heads. It would be well to have a little company of trained men. The drunken voices were a long way off . . . tomorrow . . . his eyes closed.

Early in the morning he sought out Sergeant Nugent and urged him to take the hut next to them. It was not quite finished. Colin offered to assemble a crew from Cornwall, whose work he knew to be good. "They will have it plastered and thatched before the week's end," he told Nugent.

"I am sorry, for I would like to live with Glande and Allyne and near you, but the governor has put me on his staff—a sort of valet-servant-handy-man," he added bitterly. "Though I should not say so, it will not be like the good days under Sir Richard. . . . I am fearful of what may happen."

"You mean you think the Indians may grow unfriendly?"

Nugent showed surprise. "No, they are afraid of us. They will fetch and carry as we bid them. It's here in the island that trouble will come, among our own people." He stepped close and lowered his voice. "Lane's not the man to keep order or command respect. Your men of Devon and Cornwall won't relish taking orders from a London courtier. That they won't. There's where trouble lies, right in our own camp. Don't give the red savages a thought, sir."

Colin did not agree, but he kept his own counsel. He walked over to the north entrance to watch the men loading Lane's ship. Tomorrow they would go up-river to visit Chowanook and make discoveries farther on.

Quantities of trade goods were being piled on the beach to be loaded. "Food and clothing for a ten-day cruise," one of the seamen told him.

As he watched, Master John White joined him. He was carrying his colours in a box and had an easel under his

336

arm. He said to Colin, "Am I too late? Has the ship sailed?" Perspiration dripped from his wide brow.

"The ship hasn't come in from Wococon yet, Master White. It sails up-river tomorrow, not today, sir."

White dropped down near Colin and set his boxes on the pineneedles that covered the ground. "Thank the good Lord! I will have time to finish a sketch I was working on, of a rare land crab that a seaman brought me this morning. I want to record it before it dies." He opened one of his boxes. A large-clawed crab, pink in color, moved lazily out.

"How beautiful it is! See that delicate color, almost violet, with pink edges, blue and red and white," he muttered as he began mixing his paints. "Look: one large claw, one small. Hold it still, Colin. Don't let it nip you. I saw one like it when we were on San Domingo."

Colin made a little fence of pine-cones stuck into the sand. The crab moved slowly, trying to find a way out.

"Good! Good! I'll have it sketched in a minute. Eight legs and the pinchers."

Colin watched Master White as he worked. He had always seemed a quiet, reserved man who talked little. He was different now, his face alive, his eyes alert, his long sensitive hands so sure.

"There is so little time and so much to set down. Sometimes I lie awake at night, restless, waiting for the day to come, so I may paint new things, flowers and plants, birds and animals—and the savages. How magnificent their bodies are, all bronze and muscles! I can scarcely contain myself until I get to Chowanook. That is the warrior town. There I will draw them as they move with bows and arrows or with shield and spear, strong and lithe. I will draw them as they dance, grotesquely beautiful."

He looked up, saw the surprised look on Colin's face. "Ah, it is like this to be an artist, with no thought but to make representation of people and animals, to catch them, imprison living things on canvas! It is good, is it not?"

"It is wonderful, Master White. I do not understand how you do it. It is the most remarkable thing I have ever seen."

A pleased smile came over the artist's face. "Thank you. Thank you. If Sir Richard hadn't taken it with him, I'd show you the little picture I did at Secotan of the

337

sorcerer dancing by the fire—his ugliness, his venom, his evil face under the black raven-wing cap. He has evil in his heart, and I saw it shining through his eyes." White dropped his voice. "I made a little cross on the drawing so the evil did not enter the picture."

Colin said, "That was wise, Master White. One does not know how devils get into one, or when. At Stowe, where we live, there is a woman who is possessed. At night she turns into an animal and roams the moors, committing evil, bringing ill luck to people she does not like. I know, for her grandson told me he had seen her turn into a cat and jump out the window and run away right under his very eyes."

White nodded. He was only half listening. "A little cross will dispel evil," he repeated.

After a time Colin got up and went away. The artist was too engrossed to notice when he left. Colin thought, Today I have seen another man—not the Master White I talked with on the voyage. He felt good. Somehow he had glimpsed a rare sensitive soul under quiet exterior.

That afternoon Thomas Hariot moved into the next hut. With him came Cavendish the navigator. Hariot said, "Hello" as Colin came up from the stables with his dog Hubba at his heels. Hariot patted Hubba's shaggy head. "I didn't know there was a sheep-dog on the island," he said.

"Sir, I keep him with the animals. He likes the horses and holds a good watch over them."

"I've moved my work here. There is too much noise where I am living at present." Master Hariot looked at the house. His dark eyes twinkled. "I'd like it better if there was a thatch over it, instead of a bay tree for a roof."

"Sir, I will undertake to have it thatched in two days' time."

"Excellent! In the meantime I will store my work in my chest. I have sent home a goodly report by the Admiral. He was well pleased." He looked more closely at Colin. "Ah, you are the lad Sir Richard recommended to be my amanuensis, are you not?"

"Sir, yes, I am the one."

"And you live here? That is excellent. I can call on you at any time."

"Yes, Master Hariot." Colin hesitated a moment, then said,

"Sir, I've been told that you are a great man for mathematics."

"Ah, you are interested in algebra or the calculus?"

Colin flushed to his brow. "I know nothing but the most simple figures, but I could learn, could I not, with you to teach me?"

Hariot was pleased. "Indeed you can learn, if you are not a dullard. I have taught many. My most promising student is Sir Walter Raleigh himself." He said this proudly.

Colin answered, "You may find me a dullard, but, sir, I want to learn."

"Half the battle, my boy, half the battle! Now if you will see that this cottage is thatched, I'll move in as soon as you you tell me it is ready. The sooner it is finished the sooner lessons begin, eh?"

"Yes, sir. We will make the greatest haste."

The camp was in a great stir all that day and half the night. The morning after, the *Elizabeth* set sail up the west water toward the meeting of the rivers. The governor took with him his closest companions, London men for the most part, with Captain Clarke in command. Master Cavendish went with him, and young Stukeley, twenty in all beside the seamen. Lane waited until all were aboard. Then he left his house dressed in armour, with a guard beside him and trumpets and standard-bearers preceding him. Sergeant Nugent was with him, Glande and James Lacie and other men who were good seamen and soldiers.

Deck guns were in view, and a gunner on shore set off a salute as the ship's sails were lifted.

Dozens of canoes carrying Indians turned and scurried this way and that at the sound of the cannon. A great flock of white cranes, disturbed by the noise, rose screeching from the reedy banks and flew swiftly toward the main.

Philip Blount, who with Colin was standing on the sentry platform, commented, "Our governor departs in splendour, with pomp. I trust he returns in like manner."

CHAPTER 24
BLACK PEARLS

It was the week following Lane's departure for Chowanook when Colin had the first proof that Indians were landing on the island secretly at night.

He was walking along the bank on the side of the island opposite his quarters. Hubba was bounding along, first in front of him, then behind, when he noticed a small path hidden by the bushes and vines that grew rank in a copse of pine and cedar. He entered the path. Suddenly Hubba barked, one short bark of warning, followed by a deep-throated growl. Colin froze in his tracks, looking from side to side. His glance travelled along the path. A short distance from him, half obscured, he saw a snake, a dark stub-tailed, evil, venomous reptile. Its flat head was raised, swaying gently from side to side. Almost at the same instant he saw a brown quail, quite motionless, perched on a low bush.

He looked about quickly, wishing for a stone or a sharp scythe such as a husbandman used in Devon. There was not a branch, a stick or a stone at hand. Slowly he drew his long knife from its sheath and inch by inch raised his arm to a position where he could take aim. An instant later the knife flashed through the air and pinned the snake down, directly through its head. A lucky shot! He knew it wouldn't hold long in the sand, with the snake thrashing. He leaped to a tree to break a branch, and saw an old log lying on the ground. He dragged it from the encircling vines and brought it down with all force on the snake's back, breaking it. Hubba barked ferociously and sprang forward, but Colin caught his collar, holding him back.

"Steady, steady! Good boy! There's a lot of venom left in that beast yet."

The bird fluttered off a short distance, one wing dragging. Colin thought, The snake has broken its wing. Then he laughed. How often had he seen a mother grouse feign a broken wing to draw an intruder away from her nest! The nest was near. The snake was after the nest, not the bird. He

340

walked up and gave the snake a finishing blow with the length of wood and drew out his knife. He drove it deep in the sand once or twice to cleanse it of any poison, and wiped it on a dock leaf.

Hubba barked and jumped at the dead snake, which still moved. Colin lifted it on a long stick, walked down the path to the edge of the bank and flung it over.

A wild shout broke the stillness, then another. An Indian, who had evidently been crouching below the bank, sprang into the open beach. The snake had fallen directly on him and still hung over one arm. A second Indian followed. They ran along the narrow strip of sand and disappeared into the reeds that grew along the water's brink. Soon Colin saw them paddling away in a canoe. He counted six Indians in the dug-out.

He stood on the bank and watched them until they were out of sight. He slipped his knife from its sheath, gave Hubba the signal of silence and made his way over the bank. A ladder, cleverly woven of grape-vines, gave easy footing. Below, he found a shallow cave, well out of the reach of the water. There was evidence of occupancy—the remains of an old fire, a pile of mussel-shells, and two arrows stuck in the wall which evidently had been overlooked as the Indians fled.

Colin walked along the beach. There were a number of other vine ladders reaching down from the top of the bank. They were so cleverly made that one would have had to look closely to discover that they were not natural vines. He took off his boots and obliterated his track. He walked back, carefully stepping on the balls of his feet, toeing in, as the Indians walked, and climbed a ladder to the high ground.

Hubba was waiting, his tail wagging. He fell in behind his master.

Half-way back, where he had killed the snake, Colin put on his boots. He was disturbed by what he had discovered. Why should Indians be hiding under the bank? From what he had seen he was certain that they had been there before. Perhaps it was an old haunt, even before the English came to the island. . . . He would speak to Captain Amadas, but to no one else.

He stopped at the stable and left Hubba with Robert. "Watch the horses closely," he warned the man. "If you ever see anything disturbing at night, call the sentry." Robert looked at him with startled eyes. There was no need to alarm him. Colin said casually, "There are still bears on the island, and perhaps wild cats. Keep all the animals well housed."

"Never fear, sir. Hubba won't let anyone get near here at night. Strange thing, now that I think of it: he was quite restless a few nights ago. I heard him prowling about the stalls, but he didn't bark. I knew everything was all right, sir."

"I pray you be watchful, Robert. You know Sir Richard sets great store by these mares. We must have them well conditioned when he comes to Roanoke next spring."

"Sir, we will, if rubbing and polishing and lush green grass will keep them. We are all proud of the horses."

"Plenty of corn. We will harvest our little garden soon and put the corn high, near the roof, so it will be dry and safe. Good night, Robert."

"Good-night, sir."

Colin stooped to rub Hubba's long muzzle and went his way. He did not feel so uneasy, now that he had reassured himself that Robert was watching the animals with such care.

That night, when the others had gone over to the common-room for games of dice or draughts, he stayed behind to speak to Captain Amadas.

Amadas listened to Colin's story without comment. He rose, took tobacco from a box made of cedar wood, lifted his long pipe from its place on the wall, filled and tamped it.

Colin wondered if he had spoken foolishly, jumped at the wrong conclusion. How often Sir Richard had warned him to withhold speech until he had thought the matter over carefully.

"Have you spoken to anyone?" Amadas asked.

"Sir, no. I——"

"It is fortunate. I will speak to the governor myself. I am in charge of the island until he returns, so I will warn the sentries to listen for crackling brush. Let me see. I shall say that a great brown bear has been reported."

Colin asked, "Want me to send half a dozen hunters out?"

"Good! It will make the Indians more cautious. And we will organise some night hunting with flares."

Colin said, "I was afraid you would think me foolish."

"To tell me what you have seen? On the contrary. Lately I have been wondering. The Hatorask Indians have not been near us. It has been days since Manteo visited the island."

"I think Manteo told Sir Richard that he was going far up the river on a journey."

Amadas tapped the ashes from his pipe and hung it on the wall. "Come, let us go to the common-room. I feel lucky. I think I can beat you at a game of draughts."

They walked through the pines. The night was quiet. Stars were bright, but there was no moon. A soft wind soughed in the trees. The smell of pine was strong in the air.

Amadas said, "Such beauty! It is sad that there must be a serpent in this Eden. Remember: this is between us."

"I will not speak to anyone, sir."

Two weeks went by swiftly. Every day Colin was writing for Master Hariot. Every day he had a lesson from him in mathematics. Then there was the small grain to harvest, corn to be stowed. The training of the horses continued, although Philip, now that he had become interested, took on most of that work. The light horse, ten riders, had to be whipped into shape. Aside from the men who volunteered for it, most of the company lay about under the trees, swam or fished. The huts Sir Richard had laid out were almost completed, and no others had been started.

One morning in early September the *Elizabeth* came into sight, speeding along under a strong west wind. The company sprang to life. Camps were cleaned, rubbish was burned. By the time the ship had anchored and the governor come ashore, the stockade was redded up and the men were on the beach to welcome the voyagers.

The Governor of Roanoke gave out a proclamation through Master Gorges, his high marshal, that he would that afternoon at four by the clock, following dinner, meet the company in the central compound near the common-room. At that time the full details of the journey up the Chowan River would be revealed. It would not be necessary for those who stayed behind to question the men who made the journey. They would hear everything from the lips of Governor Lane himself.

The sun was still high when the company assembled under the pine trees near the central building. No benches were available, so they sat in circles on the ground.

A young boy dressed as a herald sounded a bugle. The governor came out and mounted a small platform which had

343

been erected for the purpose. He sat down in a high-backed chair.

The high marshal, suitably accoutred, made a speech. He was nervous. His voice broke once or twice, which caused a titter to ripple through the audience. He limited his talk to a few words. The company, he said, had been called together to listen to a message from the governor, Master Ralph Lane, one of immense importance. They were shortly to hear something that would probably influence the course of their country's history, perhaps the history of the whole world of living people. When these discoveries were known, the governor would be one of the great men in the English nation.

There was scattered applause, a craning of necks, a shifting of position and considerable scratching of nether extremities and exposed skin. The chiggers were at work, as anyone who sat on logs soon found out.

The governor bowed to Gorges, thanked him for his words. "Since the facts I am going to tell you are in the nature of a report, I will remain seated, for it will be of some length. If anyone is without the range of my voice, let him move closer in."

Since Master Lane's voice was light and of high pitch, a number of men moved in. Among them were Dick Prideaux, Philip Blount and Rise Courtenay, who seated themselves directly in front of Lane. Colin stayed where he was, at the edge of the circle, his back against a young pine tree. He could both see and hear, and he did not want to make himself conspicuous in the governor's sight.

Lane waited until the confusion had died down, and began:

"Thanks be to God our Heavenly Father, we of the *Elizabeth* have returned from a voyage of one hundred and thirty miles up the Great Sound and the Chowan River. We went far to the north, to where the river becomes as narrow as the Thames at the Isle of Dogs. That journey, by itself, will be one that Mr. Hakluyt will publish in the book he is preparing on great English voyages and discoveries.

"The Chowan River, after we sailed past the meeting with the tawny river at the head of the Great Sound, we found deep and calm, and all these waters to be fresh, with no tide but a wind-tide.

"We sailed by a number of Indian towns and stopped at

none, although we fired a salute at each as we passed. Not knowing the kindness in our hearts toward them, many took great fright, ran from their villages and hid themselves in the forests.

"We saw many canoes on the river, fishing or ferrying across from one town to another to trade; for there was no war among the tribes on either side of the river at the moment."

He paused, glanced at the papers he had for reference and handed two or three to Master Gorges, who stood close to him.

"Sir Richard Grenville went as far as the seat of Menatonon, the King of the Chowanooks, but he did not leave his ship. The king came, instead, to meet him. I, your governor, had different ideas. I went ashore, accompanied by my guard. Before the Indians knew we were there, I had taken Menatonon prisoner."

He paused here, waiting for some sign of approval. The crowd was silent. One man looked at another. Some eyebrows were lifted. Rise Courtenay opened his mouth to speak. Prideaux shook his head.

Lane looked down at them. "Have you young gentlemen anything to say?"

No one spoke.

The governor took up his story, but he was flustered. After he spoke he had recognised Courtenay. He wanted no argument with Courtenay, whose antecedents had been Earls of Devon, and whose family, even now, had powerful connections.

The governor looked down, after a moment found his place and proceeded: "The king is crippled, but he is very grave and wise. He talked of matters of state, not only of his own country but the others around him. He gave me understanding and light on the country while I held him prisoner."

There was a faint rustle of men stirring. One man cleared his throat, as though he would speak.

Lane hurried on. "And now we come to the pearls."

The men leaned forward then. All gazed intently at him. Their eyes were greedy. Some mouths were slightly open. One man had a film on his tongue and over his lips. Not a soul moved. Avid for wealth, Colin thought as he looked about the circle.

"The king told me that, by going far up his River of Chowan by canoe and then descending to the land, you are within four days' pass overland northeast to a certain king's country, whose province lies in the sea. The place of his greatest strength is an island in a bay, and the water around the island is very deep."

Lane paused here, called to Nugent to fetch him a cup of water. His audience moved and twisted, speaking to one another in low tones. The man next to Colin said, "May he be damned for keeping us hanging by our heels this way!"

"Hush!" said another. "Hush! Let us hear about the pearls."

Lane drank deeply, handed the cup back to Nugent. The Irishman's face was unreadable. Colin knew he raged within himself. Sir Richard never required menial service of Nugent.

"There is so great a number of pearls in this country that not only the king decorates his tunic and mantle with them, but his warriors also. The beds in the king's house are set with pearls, and he has such a quantity that it is a wonder to see."

One man, greedier or more impatient than the rest, shouted, "Show us the pearls! Let us go to this place."

Lane's face grew black as a thunder-cloud, but he held his peace. "In good time, my man. Do not interrupt until I tell the story. The King of the Chowanooks had pearls from this king, which he had bought or traded for copper."

"Let us see the pearls!" . . . "The pearls! Show us the pearls!" The cry came from one side of the company, then the other.

Lane did not heed. He went on: "He gave me a rope of the pearls from this country. They are black and very great in size." He looked up and said, "Nugent, bring out the case with the string of pearls."

Nugent left and went toward the governor's house. He did not go swiftly, but with dignified tread he crossed the space between the two houses.

Lane went on: "I had with me a man who understands these things. He says there are many very great white pearls at this king's place, white, great and round. Black pearls they take from shallow water; white pearls from deep."

Sergeant Nugent came back then. He carried a leather case, such as a woman has on her table to hold her jewels. He handed the box to the governor. Lane opened the lid and took out a long string of black pearls, some indeed of considerable size. The men exclaimed in admiration. They were accustomed to white pearls. They knew nothing of black. They were caught by the beauty of them, shimmering softly in the light.

Lacie cried out, "Your Worship, has a black pearl any value?"

Lane spoke frankly. "I do not know. They imprison the light softly."

Someone said, "You are sure there are more pearls? How can we get them?"

Questions came quickly: "Where is this place? . . . Can we go? . . . If there are black pearls, can we know there be white also?"

Sergeant Nugent passed among the company. Men reached for the pearls, ran them through their fingers. Colin seemed to see them hanging about Thomasine Arundell's neck. Pearls, he had heard, take light when they are against a woman's skin.

Philip Blount took the string from Nugent's hand and held it up. "Sir, may I ask who will receive this wonderful gift?"

Lane smiled and shook his head. "Who but Her Majesty the Queen?"

A murmur of approval went through the crowd. The Queen! Lane would take them to the Queen as a gift.

He was talking again. "I caught the idea from what the King of the Chowanooks, Menatonon, said—that white men have traffic for pearls with that country, men who have clothes as we have and who come for white pearls."

"When are we going?" someone called out boldly.

"I must plan carefully. Menatonon, when he paid his ransom and was dismissed, promised that he would give me guides to go overland into the king's country whenever I wished. He advised me to take many men with me, and goodly store of victuals. He said the king was loath to suffer strangers to enter his country, and especially to have them meddle with the fishing for any pearls. He was able to put a great many men in the field, and they could fight well."

"Let us go for pearls! Pearls are better than gold!" It was Lacie who cried out. Men were on their feet now, crowding forward, their eyes ravenous, their lips slobbering.

Lane banged on the table. Gorges shouted, "Sit down, men! Let the governor finish." The men obediently seated themselves again, but the circle crowded the platform.

Lane held up his paper. "This is what I will send to Sir Walter Raleigh. You, as my people, shall hear it first." He read slowly so everyone could hear distinctly.

"Hereupon I resolve with myself that if your suppliers come before the end of April, and you send a store of boats and men, with sufficient amount of victuals to last us until the new corn is in, we will go, for that is the time of fishing."

"Sir, April is six months away," Rise Courtenay broke in eagerly. "Can we not go now? Must we go up this river and cross land to the east? Why can't we sail north on the sea and reach this bay?" How shrewd Rise Courtenay was! He had thought of things that had not come into Colin's mind.

Lane held up his hand, for others were repeating the questions. He resumed reading his message to Raleigh:

"I am resolved to send a small barque with two pinnaces about by sea to find the bay and to sound the bar, if there be any, while I, with all the small boats I can make and two hundred men, go up to the head waters of the River of the Chowanooks, accompanied by Menatonon's guides. They will be his best men, for I have prisoner even now his best-beloved son. But Menatonon himself and the savages of Moratoc report strange things of the head of the river. Some say it is thirty days', some forty days' journey. The river springs out of a main rock and makes the most violent stream. This huge rock is near the sea. Storms come outwardly from the sea so strongly that waves are beaten into the fresh stream. Other strange and fearful things they say transpire at the head of the river. These things might deter a more resolute man than I."

"The pearls!" someone cried.

Lane flushed, but he did not answer. "Remember: I brought Menatonon's son in the boat as an earnest of the Chowanooks' good behaviour."

Lane folded the papers and handed them to High Marshal Gorges, who laid them carefully in leather-covered boards, which he tied with a leather string.

"Now you, as my company, see what confidence I have in you. I have read you a report before it goes to Sir Walter. You know just what I know. I am resolved that as soon as winter passes, we shall sail up the river from the sea, and from the river make rendezvous at the Island of Pearls."

Men shouted, throwing their caps in the air. "The Island of

Pearls! The Island of Pearls!" they chanted.

Lane lifted his voice. "Remember what Menatonon said, 'They have so many pearls that their houses and furniture are adorned with them.'

"Now my fellows, there is ale for everyone, and I want from you a promise to build a fleet of small pinnaces so we may navigate to the head waters of the river as soon as spring comes."

A great shout went up: "Your Worship, we will build ships and more ships! Hurray for the Governor of Roanoke and a toast to our great Queen Elizabeth!"

Lacie, whose voice was louder than most, made himself heard above the clamour. "If the Queen would once wear a string of black pearls, the whole world would wear black pearls. Let us get black pearls and white! Let us fill our hosen with pearls to take back to England!"

They trooped off to get their ale. Lane and Gorges, Clarke and Stafford went to Lane's house.

Amadas walked back with Colin. Their friends followed. It was almost dusk. The last rose colour of the afterglow touched the clouds that floated along the eastern horizon. Suddenly Amadas said, "Let us walk down the path you told me of. I want to see for myself."

"I am not sure that we can get down and back before dark."

"No matter. We'll take a candle."

"Where are you going?" Dick Prideaux called as they passed the house.

"To the stables," Amadas answered. Prideaux went on inside. "It is well. We do not want others with us. Let us walk swiftly before the light fails."

When they came to the spot where Colin had killed the snake, they heard the soft flutter of wings, and the swift scurrying mother quail and her brood ran across the path into the brush. Amadas and Colin came to the bank quietly, shielding themselves with branches of bay held in front of them.

When they flung themselves on their stomachs to peer over, they saw no sign of Indians on the narrow strip of sand. Colin started to rise, but Amadas held his arm. A movement in the reeds had attracted his attention. Soon a canoe moved out from among the osiers and paddled to open water. When it was clear of the reeds, the boat made a silhouette against

349

the light. It was a small canoe, with only six men. They paddled away out of sight. Again Colin started to rise, and again his companion held him. Two more canoes moved silently out of the reeds, following the first.

Colin felt a sickening chill of fear clutch at his vitals. With Amadas he lay a long while, silently watching, until dark fell. Cautiously they rose then and found their way into the path that led to the deep woods. At first they stumbled against roots or were caught by thorny vines. After a time their eyes became accustomed to the dark and they could discern a variation in shadows, the heavy shadows of trees or bushes that blocked the way.

When they opened the door of the house, they found Phil and Rise dicing vigorously. Dick Prideaux sat strumming on a little stringed instrument. He was singing a song.

> "Charming sweet maids in your smocks,
> Set open your locks.
> *Down, down, down.*
> Let chimney-sweeper in.
> He'll sweep chimneys clean.
> *Hey, derry, derry, down,*"

Phil looked over his shoulder. "That's a silly song. I wish you'd sing something else, something more lively, a love song maybe, a song about spring and true love."

The others laughed. "Man, to the point! Sing a song of pearls and gold!"

Rise Courtenay spilled the dice from one hand to the other. "Lane is more shrewd than I thought," he said.

"Shrewd? What do you mean?" demanded Phil Blount. "I thought him a great fool, going to such lengths to explain why he didn't go after pearls when he was up there." He mimicked Lane's voice perfectly. "If I had had more men . . . if I had had boats . . . if there wasn't a great rock at the head waters of the Chowan . . . A thousand *ifs*. That was what he was really saying. It looks to me as though he knows he is doomed to failure and is already showing why he'll fail."

"I hadn't thought of that," Prideaux said slowly. "What worried me was that he took the King of the Chowanooks prisoner and made him pay ransom."

"In pearls," one said.

Dick went on soberly: "It is all so unwise. He breaks down, where Sir Richard builds up. The Indian king gave pearls to Sir Richard as a present. He left Menatonon in good humour with the English. Now Lane takes the king prisoner, a great indignity to a proud ruler, and gets a string of black pearls as ransom."

"You are quite right, Dick," Amadas joined in. "And as an added insult, Lane takes his favourite son and brings him here captive."

Courtenay leaned his back against the long table. He, too, spoke seriously. "Strange, all that didn't occur to me. To me it seemed that he was giving the company something to think of, something to do during the long winter days ahead—build boats, get ready for an expedition when spring comes—and dangling a string of black pearls before their eyes to make up for not finding gold. He erases disaffection, and believe me, gentlemen, there was plenty of disaffection among the men on Hatorask."

"You are both right," Amadas said. "I am gratified that you observed so keenly. Here we are, five men among one hundred and eight and some seamen. Perhaps, beside Lane's intimates, we are the only ones not blinded by a string of pearls. We cannot say as much when Stafford is here. I am not sure whether or not he is fooled by Lane. Let us make ourselves into a little band who keep eyes and ears open. We all want this colony to succeed—perhaps I more than the rest of you, for this is the second time I have come. I believe in Virginia. I believe in its great future. I believe that it will one day be a jewel in the crown of our Queen. Let us pledge ourselves to do everything in our power to make the colony successful."

Blount jumped to his feet. Dick Prideaux put away his lute. They circled around Amadas, their hands clasping his hand, one above the other.

"We're your men, Captain," Courtenay said. "You are our captain and our commander. Tell us what you want."

Amadas' face showed his pleasure. The brown merry eyes were clouded for a moment. "Thank you, my companion. We are a band to follow the lead of our Admiral. Be friendly with the Indians. Work and do not idle. Most of all, be watchful."

He turned to Colin. "I think it is time for you to tell your story. This is among us."

Colin told them succinctly about finding the Indians.

351

With a strong stocky body Courtenay had a stubborn tenacity. He felt contempt for men who turned each opportunity to their own advantage. He had also an inquiring mind, with some discernment. He looked questioningly at Amadas. "Do you think we are in danger, Captain?"

Amadas was busy lighting his pipe. It was a moment before he answered. "No, I don't—that is, not immediately. But I think we should be vigilant and watchful." He took a few puffs. "I spoke to Lane about increasing the guard. He laughed at me, called me an old woman full of fears." Amadas' teeth closed over his pipe.

"Lane's a silly fool," Courtenay said. "Suppose each of us takes turns doing sentry. From midnight to dawn is the time Indians attack, I'm told. Come, I'll cast dice with you to see who goes out tonight."

He threw. "Gad, I did it! Threw myself."

"What Indians are our foes?" Philip Blount asked Amadas. He considered a few moments. "Our new foes would be Menatonon's people; our old foes Pemisapan's."

"Why Pemisapan's? Because Lacie burned their village?"

"No. Didn't you hear Okisko say that was lawful retribution, because they had not delivered the thief to be punished?"

"That is queer."

"It's the way they reason. There's another cause. Remember that Lane turned his back on Pemisapan when he was our guest. Lane showed his boredom plainly. Pemisapan was insulted. His dignity was hurt. That was a deeper crime than firing a village."

They all looked at Amadas, puzzled. Here was something they had not fully thought of, that an Indian had pride and dignity.

Amadas saw what they were thinking, and sounded a note of warning. "Think of an Indian king as a man supreme in his own country, who lives by a set of rules which are as vital to him as our laws are to us. Try to put yourself into his place, think as he thinks. Unless we Englishmen do that, we will never be able to govern. The Spanish drain their colonies of all wealth and give nothing in return. If we follow them, we fail. We must exchange gift for gift. We have a saying in Devon, 'For each field harvested, give a prayer of thanks—but give a load of manure as well.' "

They laughed, but they had something to think of. Amadas was well pleased at the eager questions that followed, questions that showed him he had set them thinking. Finally Courtenay got up. He put a fresh candle in a lanthorn, threw a warm mantle over his shoulder.

Colin also got up. "I'll go with you. I'm not sleepy tonight."

Amadas said, "The path to the river, I think. Tomorrow we will investigate further. Good luck, Courtenay!"

Rise laughed. "And no Indians!"

The candles burned late in the governor's house. Ralph Lane was merry with wine and knew he spoke more freely than was wise. But what matter? He was surrounded by loyal men of his own choosing. His ruff thrown off, he sat back in his chair, stripped to the waist, for wine made a man's blood flow hotly.

He boasted, as a man in wine boasts, of his own grandeur and his accomplishments. "I gave them something to think about tonight," he said to Captain Clarke. "Pearls, pearls, instead of gold . . . build boats to get pearls . . . keep men busy building boats, all winter . . . that damned Grenville . . . he keeps men busy . . . Lane will keep men busy . . . no idle men on Roanoke."

He laughed, throwing his head back against the chair and looking around him for the approval of his fellows. "Stafford, Gorges, speak up! Hariot, what think you? You are a scholar."

Hariot, who had been moderate, said, "Men are happy when they are occupied and——"

"That's what I say," Lane interrupted. "Amadas, that killjoy, asked me today to put on more sentries at night. I told him he was a fool. The Indians are afraid of me. Did I not take their great king prisoner? Have I not his son as hostage?" He pounded the table. "My meaning is to go on the expedition in April. We'll go into bays and sounds and up notable rivers, the Moratoc, the Chowan. We'll fish and sail. At the head waters I'll raise a sconce with a small trench and palisado to guard my boats, and I'll leave twenty or thirty men there. I'll march with the rest of the men and so much victual as every man can carry, and their furniture, mattocks, spades and axes. And every two days' march I'll build another sconce, and so on and so on, till we get to that bay where the pearls are. And I'll build a big fort there. And as for Pemisapan, I'll . . ." His head fell on his chest and he slept, like a man overcome by his own boasting.

Edward Stafford left first. Only Nugent was left. He lifted Lane and slung him across the couch. He snuffed the candles, went out and closed the door. He stood on the stoop and spat contemptuously against the house. He said aloud, "The smell of pines is sweet in a man's nostrils and cleansing to his soul." He made his way under the trees to the tent where he slept in the deep shadow of the pines.

That night men moved restlessly on their cots or beds of boughs. They dreamed of wealth, immeasurable wealth, to carry home with them . . . black pearls, beautiful against some loved woman's white breasts.

Philip Amadas was awake reading when Stafford came in. Stafford glanced at the cots. Prideaux and Phil Blount were fast asleep.

He raised an enquiring eyebrow. Amadas said, "Courtenay and Colin are out doing sentry."

Stafford made no comment and began to remove his clothes. Presently, stripped to drawers, he sat down across from Amadas and folded his arms on the table, looking at nothing.

Amadas glanced at him from time to time, but Stafford remained motionless.

Amadas had known Stafford's family for many years, but he had never met Edward until this voyage. He knew that there was some connection between the Marquis of Stafford and the Grenville family, but it dated a good while back. He was not sure enough to speak of the thing that was troubling him now. Stafford had been much of his time on Wococon, but he might be close to Lane, so it was best to say nothing. It made things difficult, because he was the only one in the house left out of their confidence.

After a long silence Stafford said, "Is everyone here for gain, to make wealth to carry home to England? In the name of God, isn't there one person on this island who is here to build a colony for the glory of our country?"

Philip Amadas laid down his book and extended his hand across the table. "Thank God!" he said.

It was near morning when the two men stopped talking. Much had been said and much promised. Rise and Colin came in as false dawn broke in the east. No one who lived under the roof thought differently from the others. There was agreement. Amadas' last thought before he turned in was, Stafford is a strong oak. It is good to have a united house, for the strength of the house is unity.

BOOK V
THE LONG PENNANT

CHAPTER 25
THE HOMEWARD BOUNDER

The *Tyger*, with Admiral Sir Richard Grenville aboard, made her way southward into blue waters.

She was out but a few days when the look-out shouted, "Ship off port bow!" Sailors ran up the rigging, the guns were manned, for any ship they encountered might be Spanish.

Word was brought in to Sir Richard's cabin, where he sat by the gilded Gothic window smoking his pipe. He was meditating on how he was to help his cousin Raleigh get more ships and enough money to buy supplies for the colony he had left behind.

"A tall ship of four hundred tons or thereabouts," the mate told him.

"What says Simon Ferdinando? Is she Spanish or Portuguese or English?"

"The pilot thinks she is Spanish. He believes, from her rig, that she is the *Santa Maria* of St. Vincent. If so, she is part of the merchant convoy that should be sailing the Plate Route from the Spanish Main to Spain."

"Does she lie deep in the water, mate?"

"Sir, very deep. No doubt she is heavy laden. She is travelling briskly under full sail."

"What course does she take?"

"East by southeast. No doubt she plans to make rendezvous at the Azores."

Grenville got up from his chair and took his spying-glass from his cabinet. "A merchant ship, you say. She must indeed be one of a convoy, either ahead of the other ships or behind them. In any case we are going to attack with utmost dispatch. Give orders to man the guns. Have shot and powder issued every seaman. I will have a boarding party ready."

The mate spoke hesitatingly. "Sir, are we at war with Spain?"

Grenville's anger rose. His blue eyes flashed fire. "God's death! What do we care whether we are at war with Spain?

359

Does Francis Drake ask such questions? No! He boards and takes—and the Queen gives him honours because he brings in gold. Off with you! Take my orders to the sailing master. Ask Pilot Simon Ferdinando to step here."

The mate fled the cabin. Grenville went to the window and opened the casement. On his port side he saw the ship, a tall galleon of perhaps four or five hundred tons. A slow sailor, he thought, exulting. His little *Tyger* could sail around her in circles. He recalled that he had no proper boarding boat. He went to the door, shouted for the ship's carpenter, the second mate, the boatswain. His urgent voice carried to the deck below, where seamen were already running back and forth, carrying shot, preparing the guns.

The ship's carpenter came first, an old Bideford man from Chapman's shipyard.

"Get your men, Mallet. Knock a boarding raft together as quick as you can."

"Aye, sir. How large a raft does Your Worship require?"

Grenville thought a moment, pulling at his beard. "I will take a boarding party of thirty-five or forty. I won't try to grapple, as the stranger stands too high in her decks. We will launch the raft and board from the water. Have we timbers?"

The wrinkled old face broke into a grin. "We've some sea-chests. The boys can stow their gear in bags. And there's the planks we ripped off when we repaired her at the island."

Grenville smiled and put his hand on the old man's shoulder, a gesture of confidence, for the carpenter had sailed in more than one of Grenville's ships. He knew that Mallet was capable of tearing every sea-chest apart to get lumber, if the need were great.

"Just get us afloat, carpenter, and we'll manage the rest."

"Your Worship can have confidence in me. Don't have the raft on your mind. He'll be ready by the time we overhaul yon ship."

"Good, Mallet! I knew I could count on you. I wish I were as sure of all my men."

The mate's raucous voice sounded, giving orders to the helmsmen, the seamen and the gunners. "One to the top, to watch ship! . . . Outer-set the ship! . . . Flat about! Handle your sail, men! . . . Step lively, my boys!"

Simon Ferdinando came up the companionway and waited for Grenville to take his glass off the ship and give him permission to speak. There was an expression of almost wolfish satisfaction on his face. He was like an animal closing for the kill.

Grenville had not had full confidence in the pilot since he had all but wrecked a ship at the Wococon entrance. However, the Portuguese knew ships, and he was obliged to take his judgement now. In answer to Grenville's question, Ferdinando said, "Sir, she is certainly of the merchant fleet plying the Plate Route. She is heavy loaded; therefore she has visited either the Golden Island or the Main."

"Do you think she is a good prize, worth overtaking?"

The pilot's tongue licked his lips, a slow movement of sensuous anticipation. "Sir, I believe her to be a treasure ship, perhaps as rich as the *Cacafuego,* which enriched Sir Francis Drake."

A coldly calculating look came into Grenville's eyes. He, too, was anticipating as great a treasure as Drake's *Cacafuego.* If that could only be, he would come to Plymouth, not as a man who had engaged in planting a colony in the new land of Virginia, but as a great sea-captain sailing into haven, homecoming pennon streaming behind his gallant ship! . . .

As great a treasure as Drake's—the words burned in his mind. Envy of Drake? No, he was not envious. But bringing in treasure would set him high with the Queen. Then he could ask for ships and men for the westward adventure.

Simon Ferdinando watched the Admiral with his shifting black eyes. He is greedy, Simon thought, as greedy for gold as any seaman. But Simon said nothing. He waited, bareheaded, long cap under his arm.

Grenville spoke again. "Do you think the *Tyger* can outsail the stranger?"

"Sir, she can sail a ring around her, if you wish."

"Excellent! That is all. Stand on the bridge and watch. Perhaps you may be of use to Captain Kendall. When will we overtake her?"

"Before nightfall, if we keep this breeze."

"What is our position?"

"Not far above the islands. She has turned. She is now heading directly east under full sail, as you can see."

"I see. Topgallants, mainsails and lateen. Get to, Ferdinando, and see that we come up on her port side."

"You will board her? Will you sink her after you have stripped her?"

A gleam of satisfaction shone in Grenville's eyes. He stroked his blond moustache. "I don't want her damaged. I intend to sail her into Plymouth Haven, with the Standard of St. George flying." He noticed that Ferdinando lingered. "Well?"

"Sir, there will be prize money for the crew?"

Grenville's expression changed. His eyes were cold, his face was expressionless. "The Rules of the Sea will be in effect," he said shortly.

The wind died toward sunset. Grenville realized that they would not overtake the Spanish ship before dark. He gave orders to follow the course, hoping that a fresh breeze would come with the rising sun. He did not go to sleep until after midnight. Then he threw himself, dressed, on his bed.

There was little sleep on the *Tyger* that night. A double watch was set. Seamen prowled about the decks, looking anxiously into the blackness. Gunners slept by their deck guns, powder boys beside them. The men prayed for a strong wind and a good fight, with treasure to carry home to Moll or Becky or Jane.

Ferdinando had given out the news that the Admiral promised the Rules of the Sea would be in force. That meant piracy rules, under which every man had his just share of the booty. Each risked his life against the chance for treasure, sometimes winning, sometimes losing. There was a buoyancy about the ship that spoke confidence in the outcome. No matter what the individual thought of the Admiral's terrible temper, there was no doubt of his bravery or of his sagacity in a fight on land or on sea.

Those who were awake speculated on the cargo. Older men told tales of Drake and Frobisher and Hawkins. The younger ones listened and wondered how they would act under first gun-fire, at the sight of men's blood drained out of them in battle. They prayed, perhaps that they would find courage somewhere and lose the awful emptiness that obsessed them. Worries drive fastest at night. Perhaps morning light would bring bravery.

A servant brought Grenville hot chocolate before sun-up. He was already awake, peering out the window into the darkness.

The breeze freshened as the dawn came. The look-out caught sight of the galleon. "Ship in sight!" he called, and

362

repeated his cry at intervals. Men stood at every gun in the two tiers.

By ten in the morning the *Tyger* was near enough to make out the Spanish standard. Ferdinando's surmise had been correct. He now definitely identified her as the *Santa Maria* of St. Vincent.

The Admiral stood on the bridge. Beside him were the sailing master and Simon Ferdinando.

"Jesu! What do they do now?" Ferdinando muttered. "They are trimming sail. The fools! Do they not know that we will overtake them?"

Grenville watched the manoeuvre. "They must think we are one of their convoy. This is our chance." He gave orders to the mate.

"Gunners stand by! Company seamen ready to launch raft! Boarding party ready with small-arms! Lay the ship by!" shouted the mate. "Three to the top!" They manoeuvred to windward.

Through the glass the Admiral saw a white puff of smoke hang over the port side of the Spaniard. A moment later a shot crossed the *Tyger's* bow.

The mate shouted the order to open fire. When the noise ceased and the smoke cleared, they saw that the Spaniard's shrouds were riddled.

The *Santa Maria* shivered under the cannon fire. She set all sail and tried to escape, but the *Tyger* could outsail her. The *Tyger* fired several rounds, but there were no answering shots.

"They have no cannon," the gunners shouted, jumping about. "Shall we sink her?"

"Hold fire!" The Admiral's voice rose above the uproar of the deck. "Give her two near the water-line. Then hold."

These last shots settled the Spanish. They began hauling down sail. "Lay to!" the mate shouted across to them. "Lay to for the boarding party!"

The Spanish captain did as he was bidden. As the *Tyger* drew near, her men saw the *Santa Maria* had only one cannon, that for firing a salute. The Spanish seamen were armed and had evidently been prepared to fire, but the shots on the water-line had frightened them. They ran about like ants. Some of them jumped into the water, thinking the ship about to sink.

Sir Richard Grenville boarded the *Santa Maria* with thirty-five men. His raft fell asunder just as the last man jumped aboard the prize. The Spaniards made no resistance. How could they, with the guns of the *Tyger* trained on them?

Something happened to Richard Grenville when he entered the captain's cabin and saw the richness of the furnishings. It was a foretaste of an even richer cargo.

Don Antonio Osorio received him with dignity. He had lately come from San Domingo. While there he had heard of Don Richarte de Campo Verde; heard of his stay on St. John's de Porto Rico, his visit to Hispaniola; heard also how the Admiral had taken a Spanish barque under the very eyes of the governor. He had been informed of the greatness of the English Admiral—that he dined off gold plate and his servants wore fine livery, and music was played by many musicians while he ate at table. Evidently a very great captain was this English Admiral, with a mighty temper when roused. It would be best to appease him, give him what he asked, without cavil. The commander of the *Santa Maria* had no desire to come under the Englishman's wrath.

So, over a glass of excellent Madeira, he told Sir Richard that the *Santa Maria* was one of a convoy of thirty-three merchant ships. She carried a heavy cargo of spices, sugar and hides. The ship was the vice-admiral of the San Domingo contingent which at Havana had joined the fleet of New Spain and the mainland.

Sir Richard asked for the inventory and set a man looking through the lists. Two others were sent to check the stores.

He sat in the captain's room, ate excellent food, enjoyed the wine. When he had finished to his stomach's satisfaction, he said in Spanish, "Now let us list the gold and silver."

Don Antonio's face darkened. He had hoped that two thousand hides, great quantities of sugar and spices, would satisfy the English pirate. He put the demand aside, telling Grenville in great detail how he had had bad fortune. Two days out from Havana they had run into foul weather and were forced to lay to overnight. By morning only six of the thirty-three ships were in sight. During the day these drew away.

"The *Santa Maria* is a poor sailer," he told Grenville. "It is a hurt to the heart to captain such a ship and see others forging ahead, larger and richer ships." He looked at Sir Richard out of the corner of his dark oval eyes.

Grenville did not raise his glance from his wine-glass. He

knew the mind of the Spaniard. It was as open to him as though it were a printed page in a folio. Don Antonio wanted him to leave the *Santa Maria*, convinced that greater prizes sailed ahead of him. The Spaniard trusted that he was greedy for gold, would be content to take the cargo of hides, sugar and spices and go after the other ships.

The Portuguese, Simon Ferdinando, came to the door. At his signal Sir Richard stepped out to speak privately with him. Ferdinando said, "Sir, I have talked with a merchant from Lisbon who is on board. He has told me that there are gold bars and bars of silver and a great quantity of pearls on this ship in the captain's care."

Grenville said, "Excellent! I suppose he gave you this information so that I would not trouble to search the passengers."

Simon grinned. "That is what he thought, but I knew different. I told him they would do well if you spared their lives. Let them know fright."

Grenville asked, "How many passengers are there?"

"Sir, twenty or more; some very wealthy."

"Go to them, each in turn, and get the keys to their strong-boxes. Bring them to me." Simon turned to leave. "See that you deliver *all* the keys. There will be no private looting on this ship. Let that be an order to all my men. No rape. The women will not be violated."

The Portuguese pilot's face grew red, but he did not utter a word. How did the English devil know what he had planned? "Deliver all the keys." The man was capable of hanging anyone to a yard-arm if he discovered him concealing even a pearl ring snatched from a woman's finger. . . . There was a woman, luscious and inviting, the maid of the captain's wife. She had looked at him over her bull-fighter fan with provocative eyes. An hour or a night spent with her would not be considered rape, surely. His tongue ran over his lips. No, not rape.

Sir Richard went back to the captain's room. The Spaniard was stitting at table, nervously tapping his fingers on the board. A servant was clearing away the dishes. He looked at the English leader with frightened eyes.

When the servant left the room, Grenville said, "And now, Don Antonio, suppose you have your private inventory fetched up. I have a desire to see how much gold and silver you have secreted. I have an idea you have more hides, sugar

and spices on your own list than on the one you handed me."
Grenville smiled, but his eyes were hard. They seemed to have
changed from the calm of a blue sea to the grey of angry
waters before a real storm.

Don Antonio went to his cabinet and took out a strong-
box. This he opened with a key that hung to his wrist on a
golden bracelet. The bracelet matched the golden rings, set
with precious stones, which he wore in his ears. Grenville
noticed there were several rapiers in the cabinet with silver
basket hilts, heavily encrusted with stones. A rack of jewelled
daggers hung in the back, a goodly collection which would
look well in his armory at Stowe.

He ran his eyes over the parchment. "Ah!" he said. "Seven
thousand calf-skins instead of two thousand. Two hundred
boxes of sugar, about forty arrobas each—that is well over
three hundred pounds. A thousand quintals of ginger. Other
items . . . Let me see. You have totalled it at one hundred
and twenty thousand ducats. . . . Now we will look to the
passengers."

The Spaniard started to protest, then dropped back in his
chair. Why should he sacrifice himself to save passengers'
gold?

Ferdinando came to the door again. He handed the keys to
Grenville, who laid them on the table. "I've changed my
mind. Bring the passengers here, five at a time. Tell them to
bring their strong-boxes with them."

The people were herded into the small room. Guards stood
at the door. One or two men protested. A woman wept when
she gave over her jewels to Grenville. He opened her box.
There was little of importance, old-fashioned jewels of the
last century. *Mia madre!* The old woman wept.

Grenville shut the box and put it in her hand. "Keep
your mother's jewels," he said.

The woman clasped the box to her bosom. *"Gracias, gracias,* señor!" she cried.

Grenville leaned forward in the chair. "But I will take the
pearl string. It is not quite covered with your hair, señora."

The woman wailed loudly, but took the string of pearls
from their concealment. A heavy braid of blue-black hair
tumbled over her shoulder. Several rings set in diamonds and
large emeralds fell into her lap.

"And the rings," Grenville said unsmiling.

The woman wailed the louder, but her husband grabbed

them from her and laid them on the table. "I did not know," he said sullenly.

So it went for an hour until there was a pile of jewels which Sir Richard thought must come to the value of forty thousand ducats. Not too bad! Some, indeed, were good enough for the Queen herself. There was one beautiful globular pearl that belonged to the captain's wife. She had fought, holding the jewel in her fist, but he opened the fingers one at a time, took the pearl, then kissed her hand. "Señora, one so beautiful does not need jewels. Leave jewels to ugly women who need adornment."

"Your ugly Queen, perhaps," she had spat out. "Well, let her wear it, and may it bring a curse upon her!"

Grenville was tired of this. He gave over to one of his young men. He went out on deck and ordered the prize goods made ready to take aboard the *Tyger,* using two of the *Santa Maria's* boats to load the treasure. The choicest jewels he kept himself, close-locked in Don Antonio's strong-box, the key to which he now wore about his neck.

A great shout rang out from the *Tyger* when they spied the riches. There would be plenty for all.

Grenville ordered the Spaniards taken to the *Tyger,* leaving only twenty of them aboard the prize, including the merchants. He remained on the *Santa Maria* with his thirty-five Englishmen. After the goods were safe in the *Tyger's* hold, he ordered the two ships to set sail. If by any chance they were separated, the *Tyger,* under Master Kendall, was to sail direct to England. Being the faster ship, she must be free to go on. She could outsail any enemy ship.

When they neared Bermuda, they ran into a storm. The *Santa Maria* lost sight of the *Tyger* and did not see her again during the long voyage home.

The *Santa Maria* had ill luck. She was hard to handle. Ferdinando said, "I am a Terceira man. We have difficult ships to sail, but this devil is the most difficult I've ever encountered."

Grenville's men were made sick by the pitch and toss. The ship was so slow that food grew scarce and had to be rationed. They came to the point where a day's ration was no more than a little rye, cooked in water to make a thin soup. Men grumbled and forgot that they had treasure to be divided. They thought they might never see Land's End, that this was an ill-omened ship and might wreck, or they might starve. They lost count of the days in their discouragement.

367

Finally, in the second week of October according to the Spanish calendar they had to rely on, they beheld the Island of Flores.

Grenville did not know the strength of the garrison or what boats anchored there. He sent the English below, with orders to keep out of sight. He placed the passengers and the few Spanish sailors in plain sight. When some small boats put out, he forced the captain to request food to be sent out to the ship.

A boat of five men came to the *Santa Maria* and clambered aboard. Grenville's men came out of concealment then, and the Admiral himself threatened, saying he would not let them go unless they promised to bring supplies. At first they refused. Grenville cursed. He would throw them and all the passengers into the sea, but first his men would slay them.

When the islanders learned who it was that had captured the *Santa Maria*, they were in great terror. Richard Grenville's name brought fear, even as Drake's brought fear.

"He will sack the town," Ferdinando told them. "He sacks and burns and kills, aye, even tortures men who refuse to do his bidding. It will be best to bring supplies to the ship. He will pay you in gold, for he is an honourable enemy."

The islanders huddled in a group to talk it over. Urged by the captain and the passengers, they decided to go ashore, get supplies and return to the ship. This they did. Grenville paid them as he had promised—"out of *my* gold!" the Portuguese merchant wailed. Not only did he pay, but he sent the passengers ashore, though at the last he had the men stripped and found a few hidden jewels of value.

The women he allowed to go without bothering them. All the rest were in the boats when he kissed the hand of the captain's wife and told her it would be always wise to trust to the gallantry and courtesy of English gentlemen. "If you had done so, you would have pearls on your pretty neck at this moment."

Shining black eyes blazed at him. "Spawn of the devil!" she cried.

He laughed. He caught her arm, pulled her to him and draped about her throat the string of pearls he had taken from the old woman.

She stood stock-still, looking at him. The fire died in her eyes and tears came suddenly. She moved toward him and threw her arms about his neck. She clung to him. "Thank you, thank you, thank you," she whispered.

Grenville lifted her chin with his fingers and looked into her tearful eyes. "You are a sweet morsel," he said very low. "Kiss me for what we have missed, my little spitfire. Kiss me hard. Let me see what passion I have missed."

She glanced over her shoulder. No one could see into the room. She fastened her arms about his neck and curved her body against his. Raising her half-open mouth to him, she whispered, "You kiss—a kiss to remember what we have lost."

Grenville said, "If I had been a ruthless captain, as you Spanish say I am, we could have had pleasure. But I am not ruthless. I treat my prisoners honourably—do you bear witness, señora?"

She gave herself into his embrace again. With her lips against his she whispered, "Why were you not ruthless, Richarte de Campo Verde?"

He walked with the señora to the companionway. "One day we will meet again. Then you will have no cause to complain." He bent over her hand. "I follow the pearls down to your fair breasts," he said softly. She looked away then and let the seaman lead her down to the deck.

Grenville watched her enter the small boat and row away. He sighed regretfully. The woman had been sweet and soft in his arms. Perhaps honour toward a prisoner was a poor thing, if the prisoner were a lovely woman and willing.

He went to the bridge. The last boat had put off and was well away from the ship. His spirits rose. There was a merry breeze. He heard the whip of canvas as the sails were hauled aloft.

He turned to Ferdinando, the man from Terceira. "North by northeast!" he said sharply.

"Nor' by nor'east," the pilot repeated. Ahead of them were blue water and racing whitecaps, and the light of the sun upon the sea.

"Nor' by nor'east," the man in the top called out. "Nor' by nor'east and a merry gale."

Below, voices rose. "Home-bound for England!"

The wind caught the long blue pennon that streamed out behind. "Home-bound for England and the West Countree . . ."

Richard went to his cabin. The thought of the woman

was in his mind. Ah well, he still had the great pear-shaped pearl he had taken from her. He would not give it to the Queen. He had the casket of Indian pearls for her. The pear pearl he would have mounted in a brooch and wear it in his cap, as Walter Raleigh wore a pearl of inferior lustre. An earnest of what might have been—the idea made him smile. His men looked at him as they passed. "The Admiral must have a treasure for us to divide. Praise God for His mercies!"

All Plymouth was out on the Hoe, or walking the Barbican. The worshipful mayor had proclaimed a holiday, so that the people might see Sir Richard Grenville sail into Plymouth Haven in the great Spanish galleon *Santa Maria,* which he had captured on his way home from Virginia.

It was late in October. There was a taste of winter in the air. The people of Plymouth were wrapped in warm mantles, and the women covered their locks with bewitching hoods or scarfs.

Grenville had been expected twelve days earlier. His *Tyger* had fallen with Land's End then, and the same day come to anchor at Falmouth.

The Corporation and the Council had been set to receive Sir Richard with fitting honour, but they discovered that he had transferred his flag from the *Tyger* to the Spanish prize. Now she was in sight, so the mayor, Sir Walter Raleigh and many persons of quality waited to welcome Sir Richard and get from him news of relatives and friends who had been left behind on Roanoke Island.

They had received letters when John Arundell's ship came in some three weeks earlier. There had been letters and little packages on the *Tyger,* too. Now they could talk to Grenville himself and find out the whole truth. So many rumours were afloat concerning the colony that there was uneasiness about the fate of those gallant young men.

The tall ship of Spain was beautiful as she lay off the entrance. To those who stood waiting on the Barbican, she was as fine a ship as they had ever seen, perhaps as fine as the *Great Harry,* with her golden sails, which now lay at the bottom of the Channel. How graceful the long homecoming pennon! How happy the faces that lined the rail and looked out of the gilt-rimmed windows!

Distinguished men and women of Devon and Cornwall

watched. Lesser folk, fishermen, men of the wharfs and women who walked the Barbican, all had common thought that day: Another great captain of England was coming home! The news was in every mouth. Coming home in a great Spanish ship, filled with Spanish gold for the Queen's use to fight her wars with Spain!

A beautiful tall ship with red and yellow sails. Those were the colours of Spain, but above them floated the standard of England, the Dragon of St. George and the three clarions of Grenville.

What a day for England! What a day for the West Country, with her boys coming home!

In his cabin on board the ship Grenville marked off the last day of the journey on the calendar—October eighteen in the year 1585. In an hour he would be on shore.

He went on deck dressed in his first armour. The headpiece with blue plumes stood on the table in his room. His first sword was about his waist, and a Spanish dagger with jewelled hilt was thrust into his sword-belt. He saw all Plymouth spread out on the beach and the press of people standing on the Hoe to receive him, for this was his day, his home-coming.

Who would be there to meet him? Mary, Bernard, John, Philippa? Raleigh, he was sure, for word must have reached him from the *Tyger* that there was a great Spanish galleon as a prize. Yes, Walt would be there.

Drake? He wondered if Drake could possibly be still in Plymouth. He hoped so. He wanted Drake to see his triumph. Simon Ferdinando had said the *Santa Maria* was as great a prize as Drake's *Cacafuego*.

He had a little time left. He turned and went to his cabin and took his quill to write a short report to Sir Francis Walsingham.

Honoured Sir and Friend:

I am taking the moment, as the prize ship which I captured is entering the Haven of Plymouth, to acquaint you with the success of the voyage. I have performed the action directed to me. We have made discoveries in the new country named Virginia, have taken possession of it for the Queen's Majesty, and have peopled it. We have stored it with cattle, fruits and plants from the Indies.

The commodities of the country are such as my cousin Raleigh advertised you of.

I have left your people in good health under the government of

Master Ralph Lane. They are all eager to continue living in the land.

I plan to return by Easter next with men and supplies to make permanent our establishment.

I will at the earliest time repair to London to kiss the hand of Her Majesty and apprise her of the details concerning the Spanish galleon Santa Maria *and the value of the cargo.*

Until such time,

Your true friend and faithful,

Richard Grenville

Plymouth, in Devon.
Eighteenth of October.
By the hand of
Walter Raleigh, Knight.

A knock at the door interrupted Grenville as he was affixing his seal to the letter. A seaman stood at the door, saluted and said, "Sir, a boat with lords and ladies is approaching. They ask to be allowed to come on board. Sir Walter Raleigh sends his greetings and asks if you will receive them now."

"Request them to come on board," Grenville said. He finished applying heated wax to the paper and sealing it with his crest.

He met the visitors on the deck where his quarters were located. Mary, his wife, came up the companionway first. She had changed not a whit. Her smile, the tranquil light in her eyes were the very same. Dear, dear Mary! He put his arms about her and kissed her sweet lips. Then there were Bernard and John—they seemed to have filled out to great hulking lads, men really—and Philippa, poised and graceful.

They came into his cabin. Walter Raleigh followed a few moments later. The cousins' greeting was warm and affectionate.

"Richard, you have achieved greatly. Our venture in Virginia is on everyone's lips." Raleigh looked about the richly furnished room. "And you have won us fame and wealth."

Richard smiled. He sat on the long velvet-cushioned bench beside his wife, relishing her nearness. "There was Grenville luck in it, Walt. Thrice the Spaniards did not fight. Three barques I have captured now—or rather a frigate, a barque and this galleon."

"Was the cargo rich?" Raleigh asked, all curiosity.

"Rich enough. I am sending the inventory to Sir Francis Walsingham. There are sugar and spice and hides."

Bernard cried, "No gold, Father?"

"Gold enough, my son, as well as commodities I have mentioned. But where is John Arundell?"

"John is waiting at Trerice to welcome you. He was here last week when the *Tyger* came in, but he had to go home."

"And little Thomasine?" He glanced at his wife.

She looked about, startled. "Where is Thomasine? She came out in the boat. Go find her, John."

John got up reluctantly. He wanted to hear about the capture of this beautiful ship, but he went. He came on Thomasine standing by the rail, watching the ship pull in her anchorage.

"My father wants you," John said. "What are you looking at?"

"This ship," she said breathlessly, her eyes shining. "Look how gaily she is dressed, her standards and banners flying and rippling in the wind! How proud and elegant is she, like a beautiful woman! Do you think she knows that every eye in Plymouth is looking at her, that all the people are waiting, eager to welcome her home?"

John looked at her radiant face. There was a twinkle in his eye, but he spoke soberly. "You've forgotten she isn't coming home. She's coming into a strange port. I think she must be sad, for I'm sure she doesn't speak English."

The light went out of Thomasine's face. "John, you think of such cruel things." She followed him into the Admiral's room.

Thomasine walked across the floor and swept a curtsy, holding her wide green skirts daintily.

Richard pulled her to him and kissed her brow. "Thomasine is a grown woman," he remarked, looking at her.

"Sir, I am only six months older, but I swear it seems five years since you sailed away to Virginia."

"Ha! She is even composed and able to let a graceful phrase slip off her tongue as readily as Philippa here."

Mary smiled and made a place for Thomasine beside her. "Philippa is responsible. She has taken a hand in Thomasine's training. Now she vows she is going to take her up to London."

"There is time enough for that. Tell me, where are my daughters?"

"Waiting at Stowe, Richard. We are so many as it is."

Thomasine looked about. "Where is Colin?" she asked suddenly.

"Colin? Why, he is on Roanoke Island, I hope," Grenville answered.

Thomasine looked away. No one but Philippa noticed the pain in her eyes.

Raleigh, who had gone out for a moment, came back. "The worshipful mayors of Plymouth and Falmouth and the Councils are waiting to be received."

Grenville got up. "I will receive them in the banqueting room. Come, Bernard. Come, John. It is pleasant to have my two fine sons at my side when I meet these august gentlemen." They left the room, preceded by Walter Raleigh.

Mary said, "He is thin. He has a worried look, and there is a deep frown between his eyes. I know he needs good food and plenty of cream. When we return to Stowe, I will put weight on his bones. Men without women to care for them never eat the right food."

Philippa laughed indulgently. "Dear Mary, what a sweet little housewife you are!"

The following day the Grenville family departed for Stowe by way of Padstow. They zigzagged across Cornwall. Many friends and relatives who had come to Plymouth accompanied Sir Richard until it was like a troop of horse riding out to the wars. This cavalcade was peaceful and included women and children. They rode by day, stopped for dinner and at night stayed at the home of some friend or as guests of some municipality.

Following the example set by Plymouth, other towns and villages sought to entertain the hero. Then too there was Sir Walter Raleigh, Lord of the Stannaries. So the Stannary towns vied among themselves to entertain the party. St. Austell, Truro, St. Ives, Launceston, Bude and Stratton wanted them.

Philippa maintained they were the Canterbury Pilgrims come to life once more. She chose to be the Wife of Bath and tried to induce others to take names, but they refused. The young men fought for turns to ride between

374

Sir Walter and Grenville, so that they might hear Sir Richard's tales of the new world.

Grenville himself fell often into silence. Once Mary said, "Richard, come back. You have been away from me long enough. What are you thinking, that puts you into such deep abstraction?"

"I was looking at our walled lanes and our hedges and our trim, neat fields. It is as though I were seeing our West Country for the first time."

"You missed it so much?"

"Yes, I missed my own. But, oh, Mary, there is a magnificence about a primeval forest that you will never know unless you see it!"

The old fear rose in her breast. Already he was thinking of going back to that savage country.

Grenville looked away over the rolling country. Presently he raised his eyes and focussed them on Thomasine, who was riding ahead. She was riding by herself, hunched low in the saddle. Richard said, "Did John Arundell talk with you, Mary?"

"Yes. He seems determined. I see no reason to object, Richard. Only Thomasine . . ." She paused. She too looked at the girl riding ahead on her moor pony. "She is still rather wild. . . . I feel that John will have a weary time taming her. Yet she has softened somewhat. She may change more. . . ."

Richard shrugged his shoulders. "I doubt if John can really tame her. She needs to live in a wild country like Virginia. The country will tame her or break her—I don't know which."

"Don't think of it, Richard. Don't think of letting John take her out there. John must be here on his own land, with his own people. Promise me, Richard."

"No promises, sweet. Here is Philippa. Does she know of John's hopes?" Grenville pulled up and waited.

"Yes, John told her."

"What do you say, Philippa? Shall John marry Thomasine? Shall we go ahead and arrange a marriage?"

Philippa said, "I don't know. She will not talk to me. She is very sweet to John, but I don't think she loves him."

"Why not? The girl is a child. She does not know her mind. She will marry whom I say, and when." Richard's voice showed his impatience. "Why should we talk of love between children? They must marry suitably, let love come later. You know that, Philippa. You are ridiculously sentimental, and you too, Mary. I say the girl knows nothing of love. Marry her to the right man before she has time to think such nonsense."

"If you think that, you are already too late. Whether she knows it or not, she is in love with Colin."

Mary's "No, no!" was almost automatic.

Richard turned his head toward Philippa, a look of incredulity on his face. "By the Eternal, I won't have it!"

Philippa bridled. "Colin is a good lad, with more brains than any of the young ones at Stowe. And he's got blood in him, good blood." She stared straight at Richard. "Good blood. You should know."

Mary cried, "Just what do you mean, Philippa?"

Philippa's face was white. Her eyes were very dark. "I'm sorry, Mary. I lost my temper. Richard knows what I mean."

Richard said, "Yes, I know what you mean." He put his hand on his wife's arm. "I'm sorry, Mary. Our uncle, our young and very amorous uncle, was not always careful where he took his pleasure."

"Oh, I remember what you wrote me from Fowey. That is the reason you gave him the name of Grenville," Mary said. There was a lilt in her voice. She turned to Philippa, who sat very stiff and straight in her saddle showing nothing of her face.

Richard said, "I find him a good lad. I do not know that even if John had not come to me first, I would allow Thomasine to think of Colin. Besides Colin loathes her."

Philippa said, "I wonder."

Richard Grenville slept well that night. The past few days had been great days for him. He felt that he had reached a high point in his life. All men were giving him honour. The Queen had sent loving messages to him by a member of her own household.

Only one man was missing. If Sir Francis Drake had been there to witness his home-coming . . .

But Drake was out, sailing the Plate Route and gathering riches for the Queen.

CHAPTER 26
INTERVAL

Geffrey Churchman paddled into the little cove on the north side of Roanoke Island after three months on the mainland. He had followed the broad waters, the rivers and the creeks day after day, visiting Indian towns and hunting and fishing camps. He was lean as a deer-hound, brown as an Indian and wore as few clothes as one. He carried with him a poke made of deerskin, filled with maize kernels, dried fish and smoked deer-meat; a fishing-rod and a bow and arrows; a mantle made of tanned deerskin; and his Bible. He had followed Dr. Hooker's instructions faithfully and likewise the teachings of the Saviour to preach the Gospel to all people.

A great change had taken place in Geffrey. He had left Wococon a boy, with a boy's round childish face. He returned a man. His face was narrow. Lines from mouth to chin and the look of selflessness in his eyes bespoke a man with a mission to fulfil.

He carried also a long staff in the form of a cross, the cross-arm held secure with a lashing of rawhide.

The night after his return he told the company what he had seen and heard during his stay among the Indians. The men who listened to his quiet words, as he stood by the fire talking, wondered how they had overlooked him on the voyage out. Surely here was a man with the burning fire of an apostle to convert the savages to Christianity. He had, he told them, studied the savage all the way over. He was on the same ship with Manteo, who had taught him the Indian tongue, informed him of the tribal laws and beliefs and their way of living and instructed him in their taboos, lest he unknowingly should offend them by breaking some rule.

Colin could not take his eyes from Churchman's face as he talked. He thought of him as a young John the Baptist while he stood in the glowing light of the fire, his crude cross stuck in the sand at his side. This was his staff and his comfort. He had been well received in each town he visited, he said. Each night he planted his cross, his symbol of Christianity, by the night fire. The Indians sat on the ground, listening to his story of Christ the Redeemer. First he would read a chapter from the New Testament, explaining in simple language as he went.

He had not baptised, since he was a layman. He had not yet taken holy orders, but he thought he had not offended God, because in his heart he wanted to do good to these Indians. In every village where he stopped, he had taught the people the Lord's Prayer and the Apostles' Creed and to sing a hymn or two.

He brushed a long lock out of his eyes. He showed his strong white teeth in a wide smile. "I think the Indians liked the hymns more than the prayers, but I would not sing until they had repeated a prayer with me."

A few had not liked to have him come to the towns, incited by the sorcerers no doubt. The Indian priests were very jealous of their power. They seemed to sense in the cross something that would oppose them.

Every man listened without moving. When he had finished, the governor took his hand and thanked him. "You have done us a great service, Master Churchman. I do not know why none other of us has thought that the Church must go first. No one but you."

"My father Doctor Hooker told me what I must do. I must not accept praise."

"You are modest. All good men are modest. Come to my house tomorrow. I want to talk with you."

The governor, Master Gorges and Captain Cavendish went away.

Philip Amadas dismissed the company and carried Churchman to his house to rest. Colin was pleased. Geffrey would surely talk more freely to a small group, tell them more about the Indians and about his own adventures. It could not have been so simple as he had made it seem.

Colin went down to the stables, as he did every night. John Fever was seated on the stump of a tree near the barn lot, waiting for him. Fever said, "Sir, you told me to speak to you about anything that happened which seemed unusual to me. Last night the dog barked loudly. I wakened and went out to see what disturbed Hubba. I found him walking in and out among the mares, very restless and alert.

I went to every stall. I could not find any reason. There was no sign of prowling animals to make the dog bark. I looked around again when it was light. About fifty yards from the stables, I saw the print of a moccasin in the sand. I tried to follow, but the pineneedles are thick, and there was no trace."

Colin said, "Do you think it might be Indians, or one of our men wearing moccasins?"

"I don't know. But why should one of our men be prowling?"

"That's so. Why should he?" Colin thought a moment. "Perhaps it would be wise if you and your partner took turns watching. You could build a little fire near the lot, a sign that there is an outlook."

"Yes, sir. I wouldn't want that anything should happen to Sir Richard's horses."

"Nor I. When I go back I'll speak to Captain Amadas. He knows the way of Indians."

Fever walked a short way with him. "I'm no scatter-brain or easy-to-scare man. I thought you should know."

"Quite right, Fever. Thank you. Don't shoot me if I come down during the night." Colin laughed.

Fever opened his toothless mouth in a grin. "Hubba won't bark for you, sir."

The men were drinking ale and listening to Churchman when Colin went to the house. Only their own men were in the room—Amadas seated, the lads sprawled about, Stafford standing by the fire, for the November night was cold. Churchman also was standing, or rather walking up and down the room as he talked.

"Something is happening. I sensed it in several of the towns. Perhaps it is just restlessness. Winter is coming on. The harvest was not so good as usual; there is less grain. The hunting parties have not been so successful as usual this autumn. One Indian told me that the acorns were few, a sign of a hard winter. Fortunately fish were plentiful. They have smoked and stored quantities."

There was a moment's silence. Stafford said, "I wonder if we have any smoked fish against the winter."

No one knew. Blount, who was on the floor near the fire, said, "I doubt it. Lane has been so busy running from one town to another trading for pearls that he hasn't given much attention to what winter will bring."

Churchman was aghast. "This is unthinkable. The Indians tell me the winter sometimes lasts for four straight months. Cold, rain, sometimes snow, certainly storms. Neither fishing nor hunting can be so good as in the autumn. Surely the governor must have given thought to the comfort of his people."

Prideaux said, "He counts on trading with the Indians. From what I have seen, he is leaning on a broken reed. The granaries are not even half full."

Amadas, who had been silent during the discussion, said, "Perhaps we should appoint a few to go to the governor and find out. We have nothing to do with the administration of the colony, but we have the right to know if there is plenty of food for the winter."

The others agreed. Stafford and Amadas should be the ones.

Rise Courtenay said, "He won't listen to us. He thinks we are callow youths. I can hear him: 'Leave the government of the colony to your betters.' He said as much to me when I protested against his taking Indian princes prisoners and demanding ransom."

"He does that?" Churchman's increasing dismay was obvious. He was about to say something more when there was a loud knocking on the door.

Prideaux called, "Come in."

The door opened. Lacie stood outside. "The governor wants Grenville to come to his house at once." Lacie walked off as soon as he had delivered the message.

The men looked at Colin. "What's up?" Amadas said to him.

"I don't know. Nothing pleasant, I'm sure. Lacie wouldn't be the bearer of good tidings."

He went at once to the governor's house. There he found six or eight men. The room was heavy with smoke. Two clerks were seated at a long table. They seemed to be checking lists. Lane was at the end of the table, a tankard in front of him.

Colin stood in the door for a moment. No one looked up or spoke. He advanced a step and waited.

Lane turned. He looked at Colin from head to foot, a long, calculating gaze. Colin made no move; he stood quietly at ease.

"It has been brought to my attention that you have

been spreading the word we will soon be attacked by the Indians. Is that true, Grenville?" He lingered over the name, making a sharp emphasis, pronouncing it *Greenvile*.

Colin answered, "Sir, it is not true."

"I have been told by people in whom I have complete confidence."

Colin said nothing. He met the governor's eyes steadily.

"No matter. I have decided to send you to Wococon. From there you will take journeys along the rivers and to the great lake. I want a report on the activities of Indians in all the towns thereabout."

Colin bowed.

"Can't you speak?" Lane said sharply.

"Is it necessary? The governor has given an order."

Lane flushed. "You will go tonight at moonrise. You will take a canoe. I want you to go alone."

Colin waited silently.

"I said *alone!*" The governor's voice rose. The men in the room stopped talking.

Colin thought, He wants me to make objection. He wants to prove that I am afraid. Well, he will never prove that. He turned to leave.

"I don't want you to take anyone from Wococon, either. Do you understand?"

"Sir, I understand. I am to take a canoe at moonrise tonight, to go to Wococon, from there to visit Indian towns on the islands, rivers and the great lake."

"Yes, by God! And I want a complete report. If I find you have disobeyed and taken men with you, I'll have you in the stocks."

Colin smiled slightly. "Sir, I will leave at moonrise. Have you further orders?"

"No, by God, no, nor do I want insolence from you, Master Greenvile!"

Colin met his angry glance steadily, gave him back a long level glance. He turned and left the room without bowing, his tall erect body moving easily, without betraying any outward sign of emotion—or was there contempt in his blue eyes?

There was silence in the room as he walked out and closed the door quietly.

Cavendish said, "God, Lane, you put a burden on that boy! Do you want him to be killed?"

"Churchman went alone among the Indians. He was not killed."

Gorges stirred uneasily. He remembered that his family were kin to the Grenvilles. "Churchman went as an evangelist, a man of God. You are sending this lad out to spy. Won't the Indians know the difference?"

Lane hit the table with his fist. "The Indians? They are little above beasts. Do you think they reason as a white man reasons?"

No one spoke. Lane turned to Gorges. "I intend to break up that house, that little nest of malcontents. I'll have no little cabinet run by Amadas and Stafford, or those so-called cadets of noble houses. By heaven, I'll show them that there is only one Governor of Roanoke Island and his name is Ralph Lane!"

No one answered. Lane turned to the clerks. One at a time the others left. The governor did not appear to notice. The last to go was Provost-Marshal Gorges. He said, "There is time for me to catch Grenville before he leaves, if you decide to change your order. It is an hour before moonrise."

"I won't change my order, Gorges." Lane's voice rose again. "I'll take the responsibility."

Gorges shrugged. "As you wish, sir. But if anything happens, there'll be a row from here to the Throne." He walked out. The door slammed.

Lane lifted the tankard. The clerks picked up their papers and slipped out noiselessly. The governor sat alone.

Colin went back to the house. Everyone looked up when he opened the door. They had been waiting expectantly.

"Well?" Amadas was first to speak.

"I'm to go to Wococon tonight at moonshine." He went to his bed and began taking clothes out of his chest and putting them in a bag.

"Say that again!" Stafford cried. "What do you mean? Who is going to Wococon tonight?"

"I am—and from there along the rivers and Lake Paquipe."

"Alone? Why, God's death, Lane must be out of his mind!" Phil Blount was on his feet, strapping on his sword-belt. He ran out of the room before anyone could stop him.

Amadas called after him, "Prideaux, Courtenay, don't let him do anything foolish!"

382

The two snatched up their swords and followed. Colin went on stuffing clothes into a bag.

Amadas said, "Wait until I see the governor. He must be drunk."

"No. He was drinking but he was not drunk. He hates me because . . ." He did not say because he bore the name Grenville. They all knew it as well as he.

Colin stood, his feet apart, his canvas bag in one hand, a bundle of hosen in the other. "Don't try to stop me, Captain. I am going. I said I would go. Don't you see, he wants me to stay so he can declare me a coward?"

Stafford agreed. "You are right. After all it's not a bad journey to Wococon. I've made it half a dozen times."

Amadas paced the floor. "It isn't the Wococon trip that worries me; it's his having to go up the rivers and streams among savages of the mainland, Indians we don't know, and who don't know us."

Colin said, "Tell Phil to watch the stables." He repeated briefly the conversation he had had with John Fever.

"I'll tell Blount. I suppose you will have to go to the island. Wait there a week before you start up the rivers. He may change his orders."

Stafford said shrewdly, "I don't think so. I think this is the beginning. He is afraid of us in this house. He thinks we are all against him."

Amadas raised his heavy black brows. "Well?"

Stafford grinned. "It is better not to start a mutiny. We all want this colony to survive. We must use some diplomacy."

Amadas turned. "Where's Churchman?" he asked.

"I think he went out with the others. Perhaps, Amadas, we'd better see what they're doing. Hot blood won't help Colin."

"I don't need help. If Churchman can follow the rivers, so can I. Good-bye." Colin slung his canvas bag over his shoulder, took his bow and arrows. Stafford thrust a musket at him. Colin shook his head. "No. I think I'll get on with the Indians better if I carry only their weapons."

Stafford set the harquebus down against the mantel. "You are quite right. Well, here's luck! I may be in Wococon myself before long. I like that place. The air has a good sea smell at Wococon."

The governor was still sitting at the end of the table when Philip Blount burst into the room without either knocking or asking leave. Lane was startled. He looked at the young man standing before him, feet spread, anger blazing in his eyes.

"You can't send Colin off by himself! It's criminal!" Philip said, trying to keep his voice calm.

Lane half rose, then sank back. "You will leave the room and enter properly!" he shouted. Recognising Blount, he dropped his voice. "Who has given you the privilege of entering my house in this peremptory manner, Master Blount?"

"Ah, you know my name? I'll tell you quickly enough. We do not intend to have you take out your spleen on Colin Grenville."

"Have a care, Master Blount. Your voice is loud, your manner insolent. Will you leave?"

"No, I will not. Not until you change your orders."

"I have no intention of changing my orders. I will send my subordinates when and where I will. I am the governor. I have a good notion to put you in the stocks."

Philip laughed.

Lane banged on a bell. No one came. He shouted, "Nugent! Nugent! Come here, you sluggard!"

Nugent put his head in the door.

"Remove this insolent fellow."

Nugent looked from one to the other, but he didn't advance into the room. With a straight face he said, "I dare not, Your Worship. The man has a strong sword-arm. I am afraid."

"You fool! You silly fool! Come here, I'll take the hide off your back. Throw him out!"

"Oh, sir, I dare not. Besides, what has he done, sir?"

"Done? He entered this room without my permission. He demands that I rescind an order."

Blount did not turn his head. "Nugent, I warn you not to touch me. This fool is sending Grenville out to Wococon in a canoe tonight, alone, and then up the rivers alone. That's what I'm here for. He can't do it."

"Take him away, Nugent."

"Sir, I have fear in my heart. Master Blount can outdo me with a sword."

"Coward! Call the guard!"

Nugent advanced into the room. "Sir, consider what you are asking of me. I am afraid of Master Blount. I am afraid of Master Blount's family. What will happen to me when I go back to England, if I lay hands on him?" He turned his head toward Philip and slowly closed one eye. "Why not send me out to Wococon with Master Grenville, sir?"

"God's death! Tomorrow you will get forty stripes." Lane turned to Philip. "Why do you come here begging for Grenville. He didn't object. Why should you?"

Philip took a step nearer. His thumbs were in his belt. "He's no coward. Why are you sending him to the Indian towns alone? That's the question I ask you. Do you want him killed because his name is Grenville?" He moved closer, glaring angrily.

Lane drew back in his chair. "Blount, you're in love with the fellow. That's it, you're——"

Philip raised his hand and slapped the governor across the mouth.

Nugent caught at his arm. "Easy, Master Blount, easy!"

Philip threw him off. "The foul-mouthed devil!" he shouted, drawing his sword. "Stand up! I'll have your blood for that."

"Easy! Easy! Can't you see he's in drink?" Nugent urged. "He don't know what he speaks."

Philip said, "Move aside, Nugent."

Lane cried, "Guard! Guard! I'm being murdered."

"Stand up and draw. What kind of a man are you? Draw, you fool!"

Lane got to his feet and fumbled for his sword. He could not loose it from the scabbard.

The door burst open. Lane cried, "Guard, guard, arrest this fellow!"

Richard Prideaux, followed by Rise Courtenay, entered. They were winded from running.

"Phil, have done! Are you mad?" They took places quickly, one on either side of Blount. They saw Lane's face. His lip was bleeding.

"Take him away before I do him harm," Lane said.

"You must go, sir," Nugent urged. "I'll get the governor to bed."

"I won't leave until he apologizes."

Lane didn't want to fight a Prideaux or a Courtenay. "I apologize," he said thickly. "What d' I say?" He dropped

385

back into the chair and laid his head on the table. With a sort of defensive cunning he pretended to sleep.

Nugent lured the angry lads out. "Leave it to me. I'll see what can be done. Tell Master Grenville to linger at Wococon."

The three were satisfied. "Good fellow, Nugent!" Prideaux said. He thrust his arm through Philip's. "Come on. Captain Amadas wants us. There's going to be a council of war, and he wants you."

Blount didn't speak, but he slid his sword into the scabbard. Together they walked off to the house.

Colin went down to the water. Two men were guarding the boats and canoes. One of them stepped forward with a sharp challenge. Colin gave his name. The second man, a shadow in the darkness, said, "Here is your canoe, sir. It's stocked with victuals." He bent over the boat to push it off, gave a groan and clapped his hand to his back.

"What's wrong?" Colin asked, for the man seemed in pain.

"Nothing, sir. Just a spice of sciatica. All the Morgans have it. It runs in the blood."

"I'm sorry. Why don't you go home and put a hot flannel on it?"

"Sir! And leave my sentry go? The old fellow would have me in the stocks in no time. No, sir, I'll stay right here."

The second sentry came up. "I'll hold the canoe, sir, while you step in. Right in the middle. She's a tricky lass, this canoe, but she's fast. I've put in two paddles. When I heard you was going, sir, I knew you'd want the best."

"Thank you. That's kind of you." Colin's heart warmed at the unexpected kindness.

"Yes, sir. We fixed it all good for you, on account of the Admiral."

The second man, the one with sciatica, had straightened his back by now. He said, "His Altitude the Governor is fair set on getting pearls and gold, but the Admiral, he's more of a mind to plant and make the land provide. Me and Jim here, we're West-Countrymen. We know the land will feed and provide. This soil is virgin, sir."

Colin stepped in, balancing himself carefully. He sat down and took up the paddle before he answered. "The Admiral will be back in the spring with men and seeds and farm implements."

"God be praised! His Altitude, here, he don't know one grain from another. That he don't. He's got what grain we have thrown in on the earth without ventilation under it. It's bound to go bad on him."

Colin dipped his paddle. "Good-night, and thanks, boys."

"Good fortune, sir," they said in one voice. "Good fortune to you!"

The moon was visible above the island as he paddled away. Soon he forgot the twisted feeling he had in his vitals. The air was cool, but the blood soon ran warm with the sweep of the paddle. Small strokes, even and rhythmic, sent the canoe ahead swiftly.

She was a good boat. For that he was thankful. If it was to be his home for weeks to come, they must get on together, he and this boat, form a unity. He smiled a little.

The shadows were dark along the shore, where bushes grew and vines heavy with grapes interlaced. Most of the vines on the island had been stripped. The men were busy making wine against the long winter months, when there would be nothing to do. The ale was getting low, and no wonder, the way some of the men swilled it.

The moon cast a light on the water. Colin avoided the moon path and kept to the shadows along the bank. He was thinking of the Indians who crept up to the farside of the island, watching ... waiting ... for what?

His mind lingered on the idea for a while, then went to other things. Strange how the water and the woods cut him off! He wondered about the house, what they were doing. He hoped they did not get into trouble because of him. Phil was so impulsive, almost violent. Then his thoughts passed to other things—the island, the colony. He had not given them great thought these last days. There had been plenty to do at the stables to occupy him.

He thought how disorganised the company had been since Sir Richard went away. The men would not put their minds or their energies to the gardens or the fields. Even hunting palled, the ducks and geese winged through the sky in such immense numbers. Once, for two days they had not seen the sky for the flying pigeons. He wondered where the ducks and geese flew to winter. If the men had only shot enough of them to dry or smoke for winter food!

But no, they were soon surfeited with water-fowl. Perhaps it was just as well that they had not used more shot. They might be short of ammunition before Sir Richard came at Easter.

No one seemed to worry about food. The talk among the groups around the night fire was of the inexhaustible mines of the Spanish conquests, of the glorious wealth Pizarro's men had tapped. The Spaniards were a lucky people. They had discovered untold riches. He smiled grimly—"for Drake and Hawkins and Grenville to take from them."

Still and all, it would be better to be the discoverers, rather than to take from the discoverers.

He had his paddle poised. In the silence the screech of the waterfowl sounded very loud. A strange, weird cry followed. His liver was against his throat. He was tense, waiting. Then he relaxed. A laughing loon. He had heard one before, but it sounded different at night. He drew his canoe in under some overhanging bushes. He thought he heard another sound, the quiet dip of a paddle, not far behind him. But when he stopped, there was no sound. After a time he went on. He wanted to get to an open place before the moon set. He knew the entrance from the time they stayed on the island when they first landed on Wococon, before they went on to Roanoke.

His mind turned to the continuous mass of forest that clothed the mainland. He began to wonder. Perhaps the devil lived in the boiling water the Indians talked about at the head of the river, or perhaps beyond the forest lay Cathay and the South Seas. If he could crash through the forests, perhaps he might be the discoverer of the short road to Cathay, to the islands where spice trees grew, to the rare silks that rivalled the looms of France. Often he had heard Dame Philippa talk of porcelains without peer and wondrous silks and brocades.

Again he drew his paddle from the water and let the little eddy pull him near the shore. When he paused, the sound of the paddle behind him stopped also. Perhaps it was an echo. A little chill of fear crept over him. An evil spirit might dwell in these woods, waiting to attack one who travelled alone. He had heard such tales at the fires. He tried to think of other things, but fear kept creeping in on him.

Silence of the water. Not a fish broke. Not a night-bird

called. Even the silly loon was still. A cloud drifted over the moon, a thin cloud that let a strange livid light seep through, making an eerie shadow on the water. He took up his paddle with hands that trembled.

This would not do. Tomorrow, when he came to the outer island, he would make a cross to carry. Evil spirits fled before the cross.

He paddled on and on, making headway. His back was bent with fatigue. His arms cried out in weariness. Once his eyes closed and he almost lost his paddle. Evil spirits or no, he must sleep. He turned toward the bank and beached his canoe in the shadow. It would not do to let the moonshine fall on him as he slept, for then the evil ones would creep in and occupy his body, driving out his soul.

He made a sign with his closed fingers against evil, trusting they wouldn't fall apart as he slept. He must sleep.

He was still sleeping at sunrise, when Geffrey Churchman came upon him, asleep with his fingers firm in the symbol against evil. Churchman smiled and drew his canoe up beside Colin's. He, too, slept, for he had followed all night.

Colin awoke. The sun was shining, the birds were singing, the fish were jumping in the water. He sat up. His eyes grew big and round with surprise. Side by side with his canoe another was drawn up on the sand. Geffrey Churchman slept in it flat on his back, his mouth open a little. His staff, the sign of the cross, was planted in the ground between the two canoes. Colin stretched his cramped limbs. He got out of the boat quietly, knelt before the cross and said a prayer deep from his soul. God had been merciful.

They breakfasted on fish, which Colin had caught and cooked while Geffrey slept.

Geffrey said, "It is fortunate that I will be going up and down the rivers. We can travel together."

Colin shook his head. "No, I must go alone. Those were the governor's orders. Geffrey, there is another reason. I am going to spy out. . . . If the Indians found out that you were connected with me, all the good you have done in the name of the unselfish Christ would be undone. You can see that."

Churchman agreed reluctantly. He said, "At least I can give you a map of the rivers and towns, explain which tribes are friendly and those who are not. I will be a week at Wococon. While we are there, I will give you information about these people and make up a little vocabulary for you. You must allow me to help you that much."

They found only ten men at the camp at Wococon. Several had gone to the mainland, hoping to trade for pearls. Four were at Hatorask, keeping look out for ships. The others under Anthony Rowse had gone ten days before to the lake to shoot water-fowl.

The following day it began to rain. The cold dampness penetrated the body. The men huddled by day in one hut, used as a common-room for cooking and dining as well. At night they slept in the sand-dunes. Each had hollowed out a little tunnel, lined with pine-needles. There they were not uncomfortable, but the wind whipped the sand in on them. If the wind were high, they were obliged to tie handkerchiefs over their heads and eyes. Even their mouths and nostrils would be filled with the stinging white sand.

There had been no leader on Wococon since Master Cavendish went back to Roanoke. The shooting party had the ship *Lyon*. When it was anchored in the deep water inside the entrance, the men stayed aboard. This was more comfortable, especially when it rained.

The storm lasted five days. The wind blew bleakly off the Atlantic, splashing rain and sand into the shelters. On the sixth day the sun came out for a short time, but the east wind was cold. By nightfall the fog-bank settled down. On the morning of the seventh they heard shouts. The fog still lay so heavy on them that the low pine trees appeared to be a slowly marching army.

The men ran to the place where the ship usually anchored, thinking the hunting party was returning. It was the pinnace from Roanoke. Captain Stafford had come to take charge of the little outpost.

Colin was pleased. Stafford was a wise man, with sea experience. Colin felt as though he had a solid wall behind him.

Stafford greeted him cheerily. "I hoped to get here before you went to the mainland," he said as they walked to the hut. "The governor has softened a little, but not entirely. You may come back in two months' time instead of three."

Colin said, "That means into February. It may not be

390

too bad, if I don't freeze to death." He pulled his sheep-lined mantle closer. "This air turns the marrow to liquid."

"It won't be so cold after you leave the coast. These flat sandbanks protect the inland waters and the mainland."

Are you going to stay here, Captain Stafford?"

"Yes, thank God! The air on Roanoke is not to my liking." He lowered his voice and told Colin about Philip Blount and his encounter with the governor, the part Nugent had played, and how Dick and Rise had come in just in time to prevent Philip from forcing the governor to fight him. "Now Philip is under house arrest—'confinement' is the word Lane uses—for three weeks. His story is that Philip was drunk and attacked him."

"No one would believe that," Colin said indignantly.

"I'm not so sure. Lane has his toadies. He dared not give a severe sentence. Nugent tells me that he was frightened. Phil fairly lifted his wits off their hinges." Stafford laughed. "At that, I don't like to see disagreement cropping up." He added soberly, "It is not good to have a divided company.

"Lane is off again with twenty men to the mainland, going up beyond the meeting of the waters. He says he is looking for a passage to the South Seas. I hope he doesn't take any more prisoners, or the Indians will unite against the English. It's safer for us if some of the tribes are warring against one another."

Some men came up then, and there was no more talk.

In the morning Rowse's shooting party returned from Lake Paquipe. They brought quantities of game-fowl, four deer and one bear. They immediately set about smoking the meat for winter's food. "We won't have to have Lenten food every day," Rowse said, referring to the fish and mussels which had been their main diet. They had traded with the Indians near the lake and had several bags of corn, which could be ground into meal. And best of all, the Indians had shown them a bush called yeopon, the leaves of which, when steeped, had the savour of tea. Everyone was in good humour. There were laughter and high spirits. Colin thought this was a good camp, this Wococon.

He talked with Churchman before he went to his shelter to bed. He had his vocabulary of Indian words, small, but enough to get along. The map he put in a little leather pouch strapped about his waist under his leather jerkin, where he carried an extra knife.

Churchman looked through the clothes Colin had brought with him, selecting and discarding. He would travel light, but he must have a few presents to give to Indian kings. Geffrey insisted on extra shoes and four pairs of heavy woollen hosen. Colin had brought two pairs that John Arundell had left him. He shoved these into the toe of his canvas bag, which was now a quarter the size it had been.

"You will be coming back to Wococon every fortnight or so," Churchman said sensibly. "You'll have no time to feel lonely or put upon, if you do that. And remember, I will be handy on the same route, some days ahead of you, some behind. Perhaps we may meet at an Indian town, Secotan or Aquasocogok."

Geffrey set out the next morning, Colin the following day. The men had moved back to the *Lyon,* where the quarters were drier.

It was raining when Colin started in his canoe. Captain Stafford urged him to wait until the weather broke, but Colin said no. He would be wet many times no doubt. He might as well learn to fend for himself in alll manner of weather. He did not say he had fended since he was ten, in moor storms and in foul weather on the rolling hills and among the giant rocks along the coast at Hartland. That was another story, one he kept to himself.

The whole company came down to see him off. His canoe was laden with gifts for trading and with small presents that would make travel comfortable.

"Bring home the pearls!" Stafford called as Colin dipped his paddle into the water. "Bring home the pearls!" the men shouted in unison.

He pointed his canoe west by south. At the long point he would come to the mouth of a great inlet almost as wide as the sound behind Roanoke. Into this inlet flowed many streams. Here on the banks he would find Indian towns. That is what Churchman had told him. He knew, for he had visited each one in turn. Churchman had found the Indians gentle and friendly. Colin hoped he would be as fortunate.

Richard Grenville returned to Stowe from London. "A furious man," Dame Philippa called him, "driven by witches with flags."

For once her badinage did not amuse him, the hurt was too deep, a wound given by the Queen herself. She had no intention, she had told him at a private audience at Whitehall, of allowing her gentlemen and captains to drain her Navy by taking ships out on the Virginia venture.

He was to be content to stay in Cornwall. If he must have adventure, why not join Leicester in Holland? No, for the present she would not allow a ship to leave England except for the purpose of war.

Grenville was not tactful when he muttered that Francis Drake was out with a goodly number of ships.

The Queen's temper flared. "Drake will stay in England in the future. We need our captains here." At the end she melted, thanked him for the casket of pearls and for the Crown share of his prizes. She also bestowed a manor on him. She said, "Grenville, do not be downcast. I have issued a stay for all shipping—believe me, not your ships only, but all ships of Devon and Cornwall. I am afraid, Grenville, afraid for our Navy. Spain waits her chance." She gave him a rarely beautiful smile which lent life and inner light to her mask-white face.

He said nothing more about the colony he had left behind. He knew they had corn; they could fish and hunt. How was he to know that the corn would mould and the men grow too weak to hunt or fish?

The Queen sent a note to him at St. Leger House a day or two later:

Perhaps we will allow you one small ship, if it is your own. You may take over some men and implements, if you wish, but no convoy of five or seven ships. This We forbid. We have informed Raleigh what We have already told you. He begs for three small ships. We may relent for him, but for you, one ship only, and you may not leave the West Country before February of next year.

"I will not get there by Easter," he told his wife glumly. "I gave my man's oath—and now it must be broken."

"There is nothing you can do, Richard. Why can't you accept what comes? You told me of the belief of the Spanish Moors, who accept the will of Allah and do not fight against stone walls."

Grenville remained silent. For long moments he brooded, trying to find a way out.

"At any rate I'll have my ship made strong and tight, my supplies ready. I will talk to yeomen and find out who wants to go."

"You'll have no trouble. Half the young lads in the country are ready now, your sons included."

Grenville shook his head. "This time we must have artisans and husbandmen. We must succeed. Walt has thrown everything into this venture, nearly forty thousand pounds sterling."

He got up and drew his fur-lined mantle over his shoulder. "I am going to walk in Stowe Woods. Perhaps I may think of a way out of my difficulties."

Philippa met him in the hall. "Where are you going, furious man? From your face I think you are prepared to fight the world."

"No, not the world, Coz. Just one stubborn woman." He left the house and walked through the great gate. Down the road toward the woods he tramped, his head down. The bright leaves had fallen from the trees. Only a few, sere and yellow, clung to the branches. The pines made him think of the island.

Half-way down to the wood he paused. He looked across the rolling hills and into Coombe Vale. Near the mill he saw riders. John Arundell and Richard's sons Bernard and John had gone hawking in the early morning. The Grenville boys rode ahead. Arundell was some distance behind. Beside him rode Thomasine, gay in her Lincoln green habit. He hoped John would tame her.

He smiled a little. They were all so young; they had no reasponsibility but to hunt and hawk and shoot and dance. It was a good life for a county gentleman. But beyond the sea that beat the ramparts of their county lay a wild new land that needed strong, gallant men to subdue her and bring her to full fruition.

He moved slowly. He felt dispirited and very tired.

CHAPTER 27
THE WINTER OF DISCONTENT

The governor with ten of his light horse and twenty others embarked on the *Elizabeth* and sailed west up the great sound. Manteo went with him, to guide and interpret. He left Provost-Marshal Gorges in charge of the camp on the island. Captain Amadas was not asked to accompany Lane, nor was Philip Blount, although Lane took Prideaux, Courtenay and Captain Cavendish. He made a great mystery of his destination. It leaked out through some of his men that he was going to the country of the Mangoaks, but if they went overland it would be for not more than from one sunrise to another. He announced that he was looking for copper for assay, but Amadas knew Lane was seeking the pearl country.

The ships made excellent time up the sound, for the wind was favourable. It was not so strong when they moved into the Chowan River. The helmsman was obliged to tack from side to side to catch a favouring breeze. They saw dozens of Indian canoes, but none approached closely enough to hail and so find out who they were.

The governor had been lured into this journey by the story of his prisoner, the Chowanook chief's son. He told of a red metal which was taken from a river under a great falls. The Indians there would take a bowl the size of a target, he said, wrap it in skin over the hollow part, leaving an opening. They would drop this bowl into the shallows and drag up as much ore as it would hold. The ore they cast into a fire, where it melted. It yielded five parts metal and one of clay. The Mangoaks had such a store of metal that they decorated their houses with plates of it.

Lane was eager to discover wealth of any kind to take back to England. He coveted gold. Perhaps this metal was gold.

He had no interest in the beauty of the river or the great forests, of the cypress trees that grew deep in the black waters of the swamp. He did not see wealth in timber or prospect of trade in turpentine pines, in tar, in pitch. Only on gold or pearls was his heart set.

When they had come to a place of portage, he went ashore and made a camp, taking with him some of his men. The rest he left on the *Elizabeth*.

They had not seen any Indians all day. They were in a strange country above the land of the Chowanooks.

Manteo was uneasy. Rise Courtenay joined him at the rail. They were to go over in the next shore boat. Rise said, "Do you know this country or the people, Manteo?"

The Indian shook his head. "Sir, I do not know them, but I have heard that they like war and fighting."

"Did you tell the governor?"

"Sir, I told him, but he gave no heed. He said we are a goodly company. We have cannon on our ship and our men have arms and powder."

Rise looked shoreward. It was a lovely sight at twilight, the great pines, the little cove made by a bend of the river. There was a flat sandy beach, pine-covered. The bank rose to a height of thirty or forty feet. White cranes stood in the quiet water. Two eagles planed overhead. Birds sang little night songs. A partridge called from the bushes on the bank, answered a moment later by its mate.

Manteo pointed to a spot behind some vines. Two does stood drinking. The buck was on guard on the ground above.

"It is so peaceful," Courtenay said.

Manteo made no answer. His black beady eyes followed the bank. He was alert.

Courtenay joined Dick Prideaux, who was whetting his hunting dagger on a piece of stone. "I'm sure Manteo thinks there is some danger here."

"Nonsense!" Dick answered. "You imagine things. He didn't tell me to expect trouble."

"Look at him," Rise said. The Indian had gone to the stern of the ship. His eyes were focussed on a point of land down-stream where the cypresses were growing far into the water. "He sees something moving. A canoe?"

"I can't see anything at all. Come, here is the boat. Let's go ashore. We can examine the bank. If I listened to you, I'd see an Indian behind every tree. You're dreaming, man. Wake up! Tomorrow we'll find gold. I feel it in my marrow."

Dick was so exuberant, so eager to examine this new place, that Rise shook off his uneasiness. After all it wasn't his own thought, it was Manteo's actions that had caused him a sense of alarm.

They went ashore. A small fire had been made, a cooking-pot set up. Two men came in with a dozen grey squirrels, enough to cook for supper. They sat down to skin them. Dick wandered along the beach. He came to a little spring in the bank. The water was clear and cool. Lying flat on his stomach, he drank. The beach curved sharply here. He had no wish to go out of the sight of his fellows, so he returned to camp. He found the horses being unloaded.

Suddenly they heard somewhere in the forest above them a strange, wild song, accompanied by drums.

The governor sat on a log and listened, beating time with his finger. He had a smile on his face. "The Indians are singing a song of welcome," he remarked, well pleased.

Manteo leaped to his feet at the first drumbeat. "A warsong!" he cried. "A war-song! They mean to fight."

The governor, alarmed, shouted to take the horses back to the ship. "Everyone on board!"

A volley of arrows descended upon the company, and another was aimed at the *Elizabeth*.

No one had his weapons at hand. There was a rush for the shore boats, where the hand weapons lay. The men took up the harquebuses, set them on tripods and fired upon the bank. The Indians fled into the woods. It was now sunset. The governor consulted Manteo. There was no time to pursue the Indians before nightfall.

The men chose a good spot for a camp, set up a strong guard and several sentries.

Lane strode up and down the beach, dressed in full armour. "Before the rising of the sun I will lead you into the forests and deal destruction upon these Indians."

By morning the company decided to move on. They were anxious to arrive at the place, supposed to be one day away, where copper was to be found. They left a guard with the ship and marched up the bank into the forest, following a well-cut animal trail. They carried with them food, supposedly enough for a two days' march. It was gone in one day. The second day they walked—but not far—without anything to eat. They still had not come to the place where the great falls were. On the third day they started back, tramping through the woods wearily.

There was grumbling and complaining as they made their way through bush and bramble and heavy vines. They found the camp late one afternoon. They had seen nothing of Indians save a few dead fires in the woods.

The governor did not want to give up. With Manteo, Courtenay and two others he rowed farther up the river. It took them four days to reach the source. They came on no rapids or great falls.

They let the boat drift down-stream. They were stranded for a while on an island. They had nothing to eat but leaves from the sassafras tree and grew tired and dispirited.

When they returned, they found that those who had stayed behind at the camp had fared as poorly. They had eaten little in five days, with the exception of a dog they had killed and made into a stew.

All the company got on the *Elizabeth* in silence and sailed downstream.

Prideaux lay on the deck, sick and heaving. He had thought the stew was squirrel.

Courtenay said, "The Indians misled Lane. Falls in the river! Why, it's quiet and calm."

Prideaux gagged, managed to say he didn't care for anything but to leave this foul place. Others lay on deck, trying to sleep, resting their weary bodies, their brier-scratched legs, their blistered feet.

Lane sat in the cabin writing in his day-book.

If I had found a good mine by the mercy of God, or had discovered a passage to the South Sea, we would have all profited. Unless we find one or the other, nothing can bring this country to be inhabited by our nation. If only either had been discovered! Then this would be the most sweet and healthful climate and the most fertile soil, so well manured, and its gums and sassafras and other roots would make good merchandise. But we must find a better harbour to take ships of great draft.

He wrote no more. The *Elizabeth* had left the river and entered the sound. The wind was blowing great billows. The ship rolled. Men rushed to the rail or lay sprawled on the deck too weak to move.

The horses stamped and neighed and were tossed from one side to the other of the pitching, rolling ship. The governor lay on his bed unable to move. The few whose stomachs were stout tried to minister to the sick, but finally gave up and left them where they lay.

Then the wind died down and the ship reached an Indian town in a little bay. But all the inhabitants had fled, so there was no corn to be had. Two seamen raided the weirs and got a few fish, but not enough to satisfy the hunger of the men.

The next morning the *Elizabeth* arrived at Roanoke. All on the island were at the beach to greet them, calling out, asking questions before the ship anchored. They soon saw by the wretched appearance of the voyagers that the news they brought was not good. So they too grew quiet and pulled long faces.

Provost-Marshal Gorges rowed out to the *Elizabeth*. He went into the governor's cabin and closed the door.

The news he brought was melancholy. The Indians of the mainland had refused to sell corn or trade for any foodstuffs. It was almost Christmas season and the food supply had dwindled. The rats and vermin had been at the stores. And, even more alarming, the grain was damaged by mildew, because it had been improperly stored. Even fish were scarce and would not bite.

The men on Wococon had come in for supplies. Gorges had been obliged to refuse them corn until the governor returned. They were tired of clams and mussels. They wanted ammunition, so some could hunt. He refused this too, not knowing what disposition the governor would make of their shrinking residue.

Lane sat snapping his fingers against the table. He was hollow-eyed and pale from sea-sickness, and his temper was short. "Don't tell me any more. One misfortune follows another. We have had ill luck put upon us."

Gorges spoke quickly. "Ah, you knew? I did not intend to tell you."

"Knew what, fool? Speak out."

Gorges hesitated. "Your man has found clay images, stuck full of thorns, hidden under your pillow three mornings in a row. 'Tis sorcery, sir."

"Fools! Fools! Do you think I believe old wives' tales of sorcery? I pass that by. The state of our granary is more urgent. In God's name, why wasn't the maize stored properly?"

"No one knows, sir. At least no one will take the blame. You will find the men in low spirits, sir. They think a doom is hanging over us, a black doom, the work of some Indian devil. Sir, will you speak to the men when you go ashore? You can raise them from their lethargy. I had hoped you would bring hope of discovery to them."

"There was nothing, nothing but disaster. Only the Lord's mercy delivered us from pain and peril." Lane got up wearily. "I will go ashore and speak to the men. I would to God I had something to say that would give them encouragement!"

Gorges had one more blow to deliver. He held it until the last. "Word has come through Colin Grenville, who touched at Wococon after one of his journeys, that Ensenore, the father of Pemisapan, is dead. He was, as you know, our friend like his other son. They had influence over Pemisapan. Both are gone. Grenville thinks the savages up the rivers are now becoming unfriendly."

Lane blazed out, "Damn Grenville and his evil tidings! I don't believe what he says. I don't believe Pemisapan is unfriendly. Don't you remember how pleased he was to be banqueted here? How much he enjoyed the sports and games?"

Gorges remembered, but he was wise enough not to refer to the time Lane had offended the chief. "Perhaps Grenville is wrong," he said, agreeing with the governor. "It's difficult to understand Indians and their ways."

Lane cursed. "Why should we try to understand the savages? We will march on them and blow their towns to bits. That's what Drake would do—" his voice rose defiantly—"blow them to bits."

Gorges opened the door. There was nothing he could say when the governor was in such a mood. He wondered if it were fear. The provost-marshal was not sure.

The days that followed brought increasing gloom. It rained steadily through Christmas and the New Year. The Christmas pudding did not taste like home pudding, for the cooks had been forced to use bear's suet and the men complained of the flavour. The cooks were angered. They had struggled to make a tasty meal. They had bears' meat, deer meat.

They killed one of the little pigs and served it whole, with a pine-cone in its mouth instead of an apple. But the bread had a poor taste, for the grain was ill-flavoured, and they had come to the end of the ale. The wine made from wild grapes was still green and made the men ill. Almost the whole company grumbled and cursed and moped about through the holiday-time. They talked more of home than they had since they left England.

One day Captain Amadas and Master White were playing at draughts. Several visitors had come to the house to cast dice with Prideaux, Blount and Courtenay. Philip had the luck. They were talking about the horses. One had been shot. Its leg was broken when they were coming down in the ship.

Suddenly Prideaux said, "I haven't seen Colin's dog Hubba for days. What has become of him?"

Philip said, "I heard they made a stew of him on the trip up-river."

Prideaux turned green. "Christ!" He rushed to the door, his hand over his mouth.

The men looked at one another. Blount said, "Whose hellish idea was that? Surely they weren't that near starvation." He glanced at the open door. "Poor devil! Fancy eating Hubba! It's beastly. Couldn't anyone have killed a deer?"

"They were afraid to go shooting," Courtenay said. "It's not pleasant to hear war-drums and horrible war-cries. Nor is it pleasant to have to duck poisoned arrows."

No one commented. After a moment's silence he went on: "I'm glad I wasn't hungry that night. I think that dog stew will weigh on Dick's stomach this long time. Here he comes. Let's cast."

Prideaux came in, still looking sick. Courtenay moved over to make room for him. "Your turn. Good fortune to you, my lad!"

February was cold and wet. The food grew steadily shorter. A few men went out to shoot. One or two wild turkeys, a deer, made the bag that month. They were forced to live mostly on fish. One morning they found the weirs were broken up. The Indians had come in the night and destroyed them. No one knew how to set the stakes to repair them.

The friendly Indians who camped at the upper end of

Roanoke Island had gone without anyone knowing. Lane sent a deputation across to the mainland to visit the Indian town. The savages told them that the king had gone away, and they had no corn to sell, nor any dried fish or deer meat. The Englishmen offered tin pans, even bits of armour. The natives refused, although their eyes glistened. They wanted armour, they wanted knives, but they would neither sell nor trade. So the men went back to Roanoke Island empty-handed. Only White and Hariot carried on their work.

Early in March Colin came back to Roanoke Island. He had been away for three months. He was as brown as an Indian, but in excellent health. He was shocked by the appearance of the men of the company whom he passed on his way up from the beach to the governor's house. He went at once to give his report to Lane.

Lane lay flat on a bed in the room where he received his guest. He was very thin. His eyes were hollow. His lips turned down at the corners. Dejected, without hope, he seemed to have forgotten his anger. He greeted Colin with a small degree of enthusiasm, as a man bored beyond endurance welcomes a diversion in the drabness of his days.

"Nugent, bring a chair for Master Grenville."

Colin saw that Nugent, too, was thin, sallow and hollow-eyed. What had happened to them all?

"Tell me what you have seen. Were you able to get corn . . . to trade? Did you find the pearling grounds?" The governor spoke languidly, as though the effort of speech were too much for him. He focussed his eyes on Colin. He seemed, for the first time, to realise the youth's vitality, his exuberant health. He pulled himself up by his elbows until he sat with his back against the pillows. "You are not starving. What have you done? How have you kept alive, while my men are starving?"

"I had no trouble, sir. I had my line. There are fish in the rivers. I had my bow and arrows. There are hares and squirrels and many deer. I've cooked frogs' legs and turtle stew and made meal cakes."

"Don't! My stomach touches my ribs. Wait. I want Gorges and Captain Clarke here while you tell me about the Indians."

Nugent brought the two men. They also showed signs of

short rations. They stared at Colin but made no comment on his appearance. Colin stood, leaning against a long table, while he talked.

"Sir, I will tell you at once that I saw no pearls except those worn by the Indians. They all tell the same story. The pearl beds lie to the north. I found no indication that there is a passage by river to the South Seas. The rivers grow narrower and narrower as one ascends. I went some distance to the west following two different rivers, which come into the lower sound."

"What about the Indians on these rivers? Are they willing to sell grain?"

Colin shook his head. "Sir, the Indians are unfriendly. Something has happened during the three months I have been out. At first they welcomed me. Then I came to a town where I was chased away. An arrow struck my arm as I rowed off. I was able to cut it out with my hunting knife. It was not poisoned. My canoe is a swift one, so I escaped. I got to a village where I had been well received before, but here again the people were hostile. They did not send me away, but they fed me very little. One young Indian who has been to Roanoke and been well treated here came to me in the night and told me to go away. He said the Indians had fear of us. Everywhere the English had visited a strange malady had appeared within a few days and people had died. Their sorcerers had made sacrifices and danced before their idols, but they could not conquer the magic the English put upon them."

Lane said, "What could this disease be?"

"I do not know. I thought perhaps Master Hariot would understand and be able to cure it. I asked the young Indian what the symptoms were. He told me that the werowance—their name for chief or king—was grievously sick. He lay languishing, and his priest could not help him.

"Their corn began to wither by reason of a drought. He said their gods were displeased. The Indian boy begged me to pray to our God of England to cure them." Colin smiled ruefully. "I prayed, but I do not think my prayers were answered."

Captain Clarke said to the governor, "Do you suppose that this belief that we have practised evil against them is the reason why they will not sell corn to us?"

Lane said, "It may be. Continue, Grenville. Tell us everything the young Indian told you."

"Sir, I think I have already done so. A few days after our departure from an Indian town, the people began to die very fast—in some villages twenty, in some forty, and in one town six score. The Indians said the disease was so strange they knew neither what it was nor how to cure it. According to the oldest men it had never happened before, time out of mind."

Joseph Gorges, who was a shrewd man, asked a question. "Do you think some of our active enemies have used this plague, this mysterious sickness, to put the more friendly Indians against us?"

Colin replied, "I thought of that and said as much to Geffrey Churchman when I met him at the lake. He thinks not. He is a godly man. He cannot see evil in anyone."

Captain Clarke said in sharp tones, "There is nothing godly about an Indian. I say, let us march on them and destroy their villages from here to Chowanook."

There was a slight stirring outside the door. A twig snapped. Colin was at the door in an instant. Dark had descended as they talked, but he saw a shadow, deeper than the tree shadows, move stealthily toward the beach. There was no use to follow. He came back into the room. The three men looked at him questioningly.

"An Indian," he said briefly. "No one but an Indian can move so noiselessly."

The governor said querulously, "I don't want eavesdroppers. Where is Nugent? Where is my guard?"

Colin asked, "Are there any Indians in the camp?"

"No one but the interpreters and my prisoners. The Chowanook prince has full freedom of the camp——"

Clarke interrupted: "I've always opposed such soft methods. A prisoner is a prisoner. Let him be put in irons."

"Does the Chowanook prince speak English?" Colin asked. "You were speaking of destroying the Chowanook villages."

"So I was, and what matter?" The captain was truculent.

"Let's not quarrel," Lane said. "I am trying to think about what this man has told us. Where is Churchman?"

"Sir, I do not know. I have not seen him since we met at Lake Paquipe. He expected to be here by now. It is coming toward Easter when we expect the Admiral."

404

"If he doesn't come with food and men, he will find us all skeletons from starvation."

Colin looked closely to see whether the governor spoke in jest. He decided he was in earnest. "Why should anyone die for want of food? There is fish in the streams and game in the forest."

"Not one of my men has strength to hunt," the governor replied.

"You mean they are afraid of the Indians," Clarke said contemptuously.

"Let them set traps for conies and squirrels and dig pitfalls for larger game. Have they given up hope?" Colin questioned.

Clarke said, "You have spoken the truth." He looked at Lane who leaned back against the pillows, his fingers twitching at the bedcovers.

Colin stood still. He expected the governor to scorch him with a tongue of flame for his boldness. But no word came. Gorges and Clarke were silent, each busy with his thoughts. After a long silence Colin said, "Sir, may I be dismissed?"

Lane opened his eyes. "You are dismissed. You are the bearer of evil tidings, one more evil to add to our fast-approaching doom." He closed his eyes.

Colin looked in surprise at Gorges, then at Clarke. Gorges was looking out the window. Clarke followed him to the door and walked with Colin a short way down the path.

"The governor has lost hope," Clarke said. "I think he has some disease that causes him to be indifferent to all his responsibility. His apathy has passed on to the company. I think you will find a sad change in our men."

He began to laugh silently. "Lane sent you into the forest so that you might disappear. Then he would no longer be reminded of his enemy Richard Grenville. Now you return, the only hearty man amongst us, and Lane—well, Lane has forgotten his anger with you. Did you notice?"

"I expected nothing less than the stocks," Colin acknowledged. "I was amazed, but more shocked at his appearance."

"He is an ill man—aye, ill in body and indolent in mind. That is not good in a leader of men." Clarke turned and tramped off.

Colin made his way to the house. He found everyone

seated at the long table casting dice. The men leaped to their feet and rushed to him.

"Colin!" Phil shouted. Courtenay was wringing his hand. Amadas clapped him on the shoulder. Prideaux threw an arm around him.

Amadas was first to question. "How does it come that you arrive home looking as strong and buoyant as a Marathon runner, after three months in the forest? And look at us—flabby muscles, shrivelled flesh and eyes burned out."

Colin was embarrassed. He felt ashamed of his strength and good health. He replied, "It is always good to live out of doors and sleep under the stars."

Prideaux groaned. "It's a poet we have with us."

They all laughed, then looked at one another astonished.

Phil said, "That's the first laugh we've had for three months. Come, sit down. Tell us what adventures you've had." Blount poured some dark liquid into a mug. "Don't turn up your nose because it doesn't sniff pleasantly. It's wine made from the pokeberry. By God, it's not too bad when one has nothing else to drink!"

"Why not drink milk?" Colin teased.

"Milk? Gad, he doesn't know the cows were killed long ago! It makes my mouth drool to remember that last joint."

Colin's heart skipped a beat. "What about the horses?"

Phil Blount answered that question, his finger on his lips. "Hist! They were lost, or the Indians got them in a raid."

Colin's face flushed. "Do you mean to tell me that you let those horses get away? I say——"

Blount caught his shoulder. "Boys must not get excited." He dropped his voice. "The governor gave orders to kill the horses. We got word of it privately. We put them on a pontoon, dropped down to one of the uninhabited outer islands and turned them loose."

"But they will starve!"

"Not so, my hearty. We've visited them once or twice. They are fat and sleek. They eat scrub. I don't know what the bush is, but they thrive. They burrow into the sand for shelter. Why, one of the mares has dropped a foal. Even the little creature flourishes."

"Doesn't anyone suspect?"

"No, I'm sure no one knows, except John Fever. He went with us. The other grooms we got drunken with the last of our choice Madeira. So now we drink the juice of the pokeberry—but in a good cause."

With one accord they all lifted their mugs. "To the mares and stallions—may they often meet!" Dick Prideaux gave the toast.

Captain Amadas laughed heartily. "Colin, bless you for returning. You have brought us back our humour. A man cannot live without laughter. Now sit here and tell us what happened to you, slowly, with no omissions. And tell us about Churchman. Where did he overtake you?"

Colin, weary as he was from the long days of paddling the canoe, found it good to be back, with these companions waiting. The months of silence slipped away and became a scene in the play-house, with the forest for back curtains, the river the stage. He began his tale.

While he talked, Master Hariot slipped in and sat down near the fire. When Colin paused and appeared about at an end, he asked, "After the Indians showed hostility, did you have any serious trouble?"

A strange look came over Colin's face. The bronzed skin reddened. He waited a few moments as though deliberating. He said, "The Indians have a strange belief. They think we are not born of women, but are men from an old generation, who have risen again to immortality; we remain dead only for a time and then return. There is a prophecy that many of our kind will come to kill them and take their places. They foretell that we will be in the air, yet invisible, without bodies, and will shoot invisible bullets to kill them."

Amadas exclaimed, "Before God, it is a good thing they don't know how few bullets we have left! . . . Pardon. Pray continue."

Hariot pressed for more. His eyes were glistening. His fingers itched to set all this on paper.

Colin grew restive, he had talked so long. "One thing about the bullets: the medicine men suck strings of blood out of sick bodies and say these are the strings to which were fastened the invisible bullets that we have already been using. One Indian told that he had seen us shoot ourselves out of our pieces of ordnance. We can destroy, from any distance, any town that offends us."

Hariot said, "This is important to me. You must come to my place, so that I may record it for posterity. But, Colin,

407

you haven't told us yet whether you were in any danger while you were on this notable journey."

Colin had not wanted to speak of that night on the lake when he had given up all hope, that strange experience when he had prayed to the good Lord to come to him—his capture by two evil Indians as he leaned over his small cooking fire; the journey through the dismal swamp at the dead of night; the council by the fire in the depths of the marsh; the twelve men wearing horrible masks, who danced and capered and tortured a live animal by tearing out its entrails and eating them. The terror of it lived again. But why not tell them?

The little company sat silent as he brought before them the stark horror of that night and told of the boy who had tried to save him.

"They tortured him, stripping the skin from his face inch by inch, slitting the skin of his belly and limbs to make little pockets. They stuck splinters of lightwood into the slits. It was then I knew they would burn him alive before my eyes."

No one moved. They scarcely breathed as they watched Colin's face, listened to his flat impersonal voice. They could see he was strongly stirred.

"It took a long time," he said after a pause, "before they lighted the splinters of pitch pine. They rendered him impotent with sharp hacking knives, so that he would not arrive in their heaven in the guise of a man."

"Great God!" someone breathed. Every man present could see it all, the heavy blackness of the forest, the soughing pines, the smell of pitch. . . .

"The stench of burning flesh is horrible." Colin's voice was low. "I think I prayed . . . perhaps I fainted. I had no sense of time. The Indian boy never spoke or cried out. Only his eyes . . . there was an agony in his eyes too dreadful to endure. I think I must have fainted against the stake where they had bound me."

He was silent, remembering something of which he would never speak. At that awful moment in the swamp his mind had been cloudy, hovering between the conscious and the unconscious. Despair and terror weighted him like loadstone. He told how he had worked his hands loose from the binding thongs. He had heard a voice crying out to him, Thomasine's voice. At first the words she uttered were not clear.

They seemed to come to him like a rushing wind: "Raise your arms to the sky . . . the sky . . . the sky." The voice had died away. There was only the soughing in the pines overhead. Almost without thought he had raised his hand, pointing. The Indians turned. They saw it then. . . .

"What saved you?" Amadas' voice was rough. "Tell us. In the Name, tell us!"

"It was the comet. It blazed in the sky, a great fiery beacon. It reflected in the black waters of the lake." To Hariot he said, "Sir, you told me it would come."

"Surely you are loved by our Lord the Christ," Hariot said reverently.

"Somehow I loosened the bonds. It was too late to help my Indian friend, far too late."

Colin slept that night without moving, but his were the only eyes that closed. Terror and savagery had entered the quiet room and would not go away.

The days dragged on. The spring was late coming. One morning after a week of foul weather Colin walked to the east end of the island to look after his trap line. Almost overnight the forest had become a fair land. Trees had burst into white bloom, as white as the foam on a green sea wave, and as delicate. It was as though the deep green of the forest were the sky, and the satin-white petals of the flowers were stars in heaven. He had never seen such beauty. He paused and sat down on a log to gaze into this world of transcendent loveliness. These must be the stars that bloomed for the gods, invisible to man's eyes. Only in this New World paradise could there be the like. He sat very still, filling his soul with beauty.

A noise startled him, the faint cry of an animal, a small sound but it caused Colin to spring to his feet. He made his way cautiously to a tree near by, under which he had a trap. It was as he thought. A man was bending over in the act of wringing the neck of a cony. Colin shouted. Lacie sprang to his feet, the rabbit hanging from his hand.

"So you are the poacher," Colin said.

Lacie's sullen face flushed. "I'm no poacher. These woods are public domain. I'm as free to catch a cony as you are."

"Not in my trap." Colin's eyes fell on the knapsack under

Lacie's arm. It was stuffed with small animals. "You've sprung all the traps, I see. Hand over those skins."

Lacie stepped back. "Go to hell, you Grenville, with your airs of God walking on earth!"

Colin stepped forward. His eyes blazed. His jaw was clamped tight.

Lacie threw the knapsack on the ground. "Take it, you devil! A starving man doesn't ask who owns traps."

A rush of pity swept over Colin. The poor fellow! He stooped to take up the knapsack, intending to divide the animals. As he bent over, Lacie's knife flashed. The blow caught Colin in the ribs making only a flesh wound, but it unbalanced him so that he fell to the ground. Lacie snatched the sack and ran down the path. After a time Colin rolled over and got to his feet. The breath had been knocked out of him, not by the blow, but by a root that he fell upon.

He made his way with difficulty to reset each trap before he went home. By the time he got back, his tunic was wet with blood.

No one was in the house but Captain Amadas. He helped Colin remove his tunic and washed the wound, staunching the flow of blood with lint, tying it into place with a cloth.

"It wasn't an Indian," said Colin, grinning in answer to Amadas' question.

Amadas nodded. "Least said—Phil and Dick are edgy these days."

Colin nodded. "I'm sorry about the traps. I'll go back at twilight. We may have a stew after all."

"Don't trouble. I shot a squirrel with my bow." Amadas sighed. "I missed two. I'm not improving much with my bow."

One evening Colin and Amadas walked the trap lines. They found two conies. As they turned to walk back, they heard Indian drums. The sound seemed to come from a distance. They listened without speaking. A long silence followed. Then the drums sounded again.

"I don't like that, Captain," Colin said. "Listen. Count the intervals. It may mean something serious. It sounds to me like a call to council."

Captain Amadas answered, "Lane has done wrong in taking chiefs' sons prisoners and holding them hostage. Did you know he now has several prisoners? He thinks it makes for security. I have a contrary belief."

The drums were silent. They waited a full half-hour but heard nothing.

"They may be assembled for a deer drive by night," Colin said.

On their way home they saw a fat, slow-moving opossum in the path. Colin killed it with a club. They had stew that night, opossum cooked with sassafras leaves to give flavour. Washed down with tea made of yeopon leaves, it was not unpalatable.

Amadas and Colin talked late that night while the others slept, worn out with the day's tramping through marshes on the mainland, stalking deer. They had had nothing to report, only that they had seen remains of Indian fires where the old village had been.

Amadas said, "Here are some of Lane's blunders that happened while you were gone. Pemisapan came to the island. Whether he came in friendship or to spy out our strength, I do not know. The governor was in one of his moods. He seated the king below him. That was ill advised. Then they had argument over the king selling corn. The Indian swore he had had no corn; there had been a drought. Lane took the tack that Pemisapan didn't want to sell. He accused him of listening to Wanchese, who has become our open enemy. He told Pemisapan that he and his allies hoped to starve us out. He ordered that one of our enemy kings be removed from the neighbourhood, else we would march on Pemisapan and destroy him.

"I was there, close by. I saw the beady eyes of the crafty Indian wander over to the stockade, look at the listless men who were lounging about. Even the guards held their arms in a slovenly way. He refused, got up and marched away before he had eaten."

"What do you think will happen, Captain? You know the Indians."

Amadas filled a pipe. When he had put a burning stick to the bowl, he said, "I do not know. What I fear is that they will all unite—all the tribes, even those who have been friendly—and come upon us. A common cause will pull them together against a common enemy. What chance have we then, a handful of men against thousands?"

"None, God knows, none."

411

The door opened. They looked up to see Geffrey Churchman. His clothes were in rags, his bare legs bruised and scratched. He sank into a chair without words. Colin brought him a mug of water. He did not pause until the last drop was gone.

"I've just come from the governor. I've told him that hundreds on hundreds of Indians are gathering on the mainland. They are coming in great canoes from the west. Lane laughed. He said the Indians were always gathering. He was tired of false alarms. Perhaps they were coming for spring fishing." Churchman grunted. "What month, what day is this? Has Easter passed. Where is Admiral Grenville?"

They answered that Easter was long past; it was near the end of May. No sign yet of the Admiral. They feared something had happened.

"Where is Captain Stafford?" Churchman asked.

"He is at Hatorask watching for a ship. Prideaux is going out tomorrow in the pinnace. He will take twenty men."

"Why twenty more? It takes only a few men to sight a ship."

Amadas explained: "The governor sends out twenty at a time to fill their stomachs with mussels and crabs and turtles. We are on short rations here."

Churchman did not appear to listen. He was counting the number in the camp. He asked questions about ammunition. The others caught his urgency.

"If Lane won't take precautions, by God, I will!" Captain Amadas stood up. "You think the attack will be tonight, Churchman?"

"Tonight or tomorrow night. It's that devil Pemisapan."

Colin said nothing. He was marvelling at the change in Geffrey. When he last saw him, he'd said that Indians were gentle creatures, and childlike! Now he evidently thought them about as childlike as rattlesnakes.

Amadas said, "Wake the boys. Tell them to dress and go out on sentry. I'll talk with Hariot and John White. God knows, a scholar and an artist are not soldiers, but they have common sense. No use to talk with anyone else—for the present." He left the room.

Churchman finished the last of the stew, while Colin wakened the lads.

The attack came shortly after midnight. A blazing arrow struck the empty stables and caught the dry thatch. A second fell inside the palisade. It blazed. The alarm sounded. The drums across the island were beating at fever heat. The sentry shot in the direction from which the arrow had come. He made a hit, for an Indian screamed and jumped out from a thicket. In the firelight his oiled body glistened. He held a hatchet in one hand. He lifted it to hurl at the sentry on the high wall of the palisade, but the Indian dropped to the earth and lay still. The sentry's shot had gone home.

The whole company was out, with cries of "Fire! Indians! Fire!"

A burning brand fell on the governor's house, but Nugent and the guard ran with buckets of water and had put it out even before the governor came to the door. He was in his night-shirt. When he saw the roof had been fired, he ran back and came out bearing his dispatch case and a bundle of clothes over his arm. The night was windy. The night-shirt whipped about his legs.

His inertia had disappeared. He began calling out orders. Somehow he rose to the necessity for prompt action.

The cannon were set off. The gunners shot into the thickets. From the yells that followed, the shot had not been wasted.

There were no more arrows fired that night. The thatch on the governor's house was saved except for a small section. A few men had been wounded slightly by arrows. One Indian had scaled the stockade but had been cut down by Philip Blount as he dropped over.

If it had not been for Churchman and for Captain Amadas' prompt action in setting extra sentries, the stockade would have been taken, the houses burned, perhaps the ships set on fire.

One good came out of the night's excitement. The officers and the company were alive to danger. Before, an Indian attack had been talked about as a possibility, but the quiet of the winter had lulled them into false security. The lethargy that had held them vanished. Now they were alerted.

In the morning two companies marched around and across the island. No Indians were discovered beyond the dozen or so that had been slain.

The governor acted promptly, with something of his old decision. King Menatonon's son was caught trying to run away. Lane straight-away ordered him into the bilboes and

413

threatened to cut off his head, which frightened the youth into confessing that Pemisapan had been the instigator of the attack.

The governor then called a council of war. He said that the mischief having happened, he must instantly move in retaliation. In the meantime he had sent an Indian interpreter to Pemisapan, telling him that the governor would visit him as soon as he had gone to Croatoan to receive his fleet, which had arrived from England.

"Gentlemen, I do not expect the arrival of the fleet and I have given up hope that it will ever arrive. Easter is long gone. Tomorrow will be the first of June, and we have done no planting because we had no seed. Sir Richard Grenville has not fulfilled his promise, and we must act promptly. We must move on the Indians' village, drive them inland and take their corn."

Gorges rose to speak. "Why can't we sail to St. John's? We have ships."

Captain Clarke jumped up. "Not a ship is seaworthy. They have lain in the water almost a year without having once been careened. They are all foul."

"Why haven't they been careened?" someone shouted from the back of the room.

The governor paid no heed. Knowing nothing about ships, he had refused Clarke's request to be allowed to build ways. He went back to the subject in hand. "Pemisapan will think we are going to Croatoan. We will cross to the mainland and fall upon his village."

But the governor did not fool the wily Pemisapan. Some of the English went out at sunset in canoes to look over the scene and seize as many of the Indians' dug-outs as they could find. They were surprised by an Indian sentry. A fight ensued in which the Englishmen cut off the heads of two Indians, but not before the others had raised a great cry. The alarm was given. Lane's men were hard put to escape with their lives.

The next morning he and a great company were to set forth in canoes for the mainland and the village of Pemisapan.

CHAPTER 28
PEMISAPAN'S HEAD

The men who were left to guard the camp, when the governor went to the mainland, rushed for safety to small boats and climbed aboard the ships that were left behind.

Blount and Courtenay at the last moment were ordered to Hatorask with Prideaux in the pinnace. Colin and Geffrey Churchman were to stay in the stockade to keep sentry. Amadas was to go with the governor. He was very dubious about the proceeding, but Lane was in no mood to listen to reason. His anger mounted with each passing hour. He was in a new rage because Osacan, one of Pemisapan's braves who hated the English bitterly, had tried to carry off Manteo.

The Camp was sleepless the whole might, waiting only for false dawn to move.

Lane came forth onto the beach dressed in full armour. He made a prayer for success and gave the English their battle-cry, "Christ Our Victory." Then he told them his plan of attack.

He said, "I must move first, so as to protect our scattered men by any device that I can imagine. I sent word to Pemisapan demanding that he punish Osacan. I have been pretending that Manteo is my enemy instead of my friend, so that he might get for me news of the Indian villages. Our men in the first boats will wait in hiding along the shore and come forward at the signal. I with twenty-five men will land first. Forward now! Man the boats! Christ Our Victory!"

He entered a boat with ten light horsemen. Nugent and an Irish boy named Edward Kelley were with him as guards to his person. The group of small ships and canoes set out in a southerly direction so the Indians would still think they were bound for Croatoan, but the party landed on the mainland, their armour shining in the sun, their harquebuses ready, pistols and swords at their belts. They moved slowly because of the undergrowth tangle of thorn vines and scrub.

They came upon an open space. There they found several werowances who professed friendship. But Lane's followers, Clarke in particular, urged him not to trust them, for it was a trick. So a guard surrounded them lest they escape.

Clarke, as colonel of the advance party, started ahead. At the same time the cry "Christ Our Victory" came from the rear-guard.

The Indian drums began to beat. The sound seemed to emanate from all the dense forest about them. Clarke, in the lead, came suddenly upon King Pemisapan surrounded by his best warriors, all with hatchets. Behind them were the archers with drawn bows. At the same moment the werowances broke from their guard uttering great war-cries. The unseen savages in the forest joined them in creating an uproar.

Clarke, now cut off from the other Englishmen by the advancing braves, drew his pistol and shot the king. Pemisapan fell to the ground and lay as one dead.

The war-cries increased in violence. The arrows fell like rain on Lane's troops. The governor gave the order to fire. The harquebuses on their tripods blazed and boomed. The Indian bowmen, having spent their first arrows, made for the woods or for the swamp, where canoes had been hidden.

Suddenly Pemisapan leaped to his feet and dashed for the forest. Kelley, who had the governor's petronel, shot him in the buttocks as he fled. But the king ran on like a deer. In spite of the press of Indians about them and the invisible presence of unnumbered enemy in the forest, Nugent and Kelley dauntlessly pursued him, Nugent lumbering in his heavy armour, sword in hand, Kelley running free and shouting, "Christ Our Victory!"

The governor yelled and waved his pistol. He cried angrily to Clarke, "You're a fool! Why didn't you kill him? Now I've lost the king and my serving-men. Surely the Indians will kill them now."

Clarke said nothing. He was ashamed of his marksmanship. He and his men beat the woods, fanning out in a circle, but only one Indian did they see.

Lane ordered the trumpets sounded. The colonists straggled in from the woods. Some brought back hatchets, and others Indian bows, but only one had a scalp-lock. They marched to the boats singing. Just as they were climbing into the canoes, they were halted by a shout. Nugent appeared, followed by Kelley. Nugent was holding high in his hands the head of Pemisapan! Then the victorious cry of the company rose to the heavens.

It went even louder and higher when they marched up the hill to the stockade on Roanoke. Nugent went first carrying Pemisapan's head. The face had taken on the grimace of a horrible mask. Blood dripped from the neck, where Nugent's sword had severed it from the body—a ghastly sight, but a goodly sight in the eyes of the company.

The governor ordered the trumpets to sound assembly. All gathered around the flag-pole.

Lane, his face shining with triumph, told the island guard how victory had come through the goodness of God. At the last he said, "One less enemy! Let us thank God for His mercy." They dropped to their knees.

The gory head of the chieftain was impaled on a pointed stake by the north gate.

Far distant on the mainland the Indians beat the slow drum as defeated warriors danced a funeral dance around the headless body of their king.

Colin watched Geffrey Churchman and Captain Amadas, who stood beside him. Neither face showed flush of triumph. Colin remembered then that other threats still hung over them. They had killed an Indian king, but they had no corn to eat.

That night the men drank the last of their pokeberry wine to celebrate a victory. They were rejoicing, carefree, with no thought of the morrow.

Churchman went alone to walk in the woods and pray for understanding. Amadas talked to Colin far into the night. He planned to make weirs to catch sturgeon and other fish; to send Colin far up the rivers to get seed corn; to fortify and to set men to drilling. "Who knows what may come out of the north?" he said. "The Chowanooks may now join in war upon us to avenge the death of Pemisapan." He went out to speak to the son of the Chowanook king in his prison. When he entered the hut, he found it empty.

In the morning Colin had word to join Captain Stafford who had moved to Hatorask to watch the entrance from the ocean. He was alone in the house when Nugent arrived with the message. The sergeant was heavy-eyed and his face was pale. There was no air of victory about him.

"I spent the night washing and scrubbing the Indian's blood from my hands and my body. I scrubbed with water and then with sand, but I can still smell blood."

Colin did not know what to say. He went on packing his small bag.

Nugent went on: "I did wrong. We should have taken the man prisoner. He would have been a hostage to keep off attack. But I lost my head. So did he." Nugent laughed grimly. "It does seem my head has not been right since Sir Richard sailed away. If his ship would come, things would be different."

"What can have happened?"

"I don't know, unless the Spanish have descended on the coast of England." Then he grinned. "Or maybe the Irish have got out of hand again. You know the Queen is one to call on Sir Richard when trouble shows in Ireland."

"It must be something dire. He would never break his word."

"Your boat will be ready in an hour." Nugent left.

Colin stood looking out the door. Pemisapan's head was still aloft. Flies and insects buzzed about it. Sometimes a crow swooped. Bustards wheeled in the sky. The day was sunny, but a chill wind was blowing. He would dress warmly. He emptied the bag he had carried on his long journey. At the bottom he found what he was seeking—a pair of hosen, green, of good weight. They were new, unworn, part of the parcel John Arundell had given him when he left. Colin remembered stuffing them into the toe of his canvas bag when he set out on his long journey up the rivers.

Now, as he held them, the faint odour of lavender seemed to rise. He turned the packet in his hand, then untied the string that bound it. His fingers encountered a fold of paper. The hosen must have been a gift, which John had never worn. He read inside the name Thomasine, written in her uncertain childish hand. A strange heavy sensation assailed the pit of his stomach. He turned the packet with fingers that trembled. A sort of anger came over him—why he could not fathom. Well, he would wear the hosen even though they were fashioned for John Arundell. John had thrown them aside, or perhaps he had forgotten them in the excitement of leaving the island.

He unwound the cord and shook them out. The scent of lavender was stronger now. He felt something in the toe of one and supposed it a sprig of lavender that had dried. But when he drew it out, it was another small folded piece of paper. He hesitated a moment to open a message that was meant for John. But a second thought came: Why not? John had cast them away. He would read what she had written, that wild girl.

A picture of her rose before him—tempestuous eyes, red lips parted, vivid face framed in a cloud of unruly dark hair. He remembered the fragrance of her lips against his that night of the harvest festival. How alive her slim body had been! How his heart had pounded when he held her in his arms! How he loathed her! But he had subdued her with his kisses.

A sense of triumph rose in him. By God, she was something to master, that girl! Then he remembered. By now she might be wedded to John Arundell. John was his good and true friend. . . .

He opened the paper. One line only: *I grieve because I have set a brand on your hand.*

Something seemed to burst within him. It was a freshet in spring, an exultation far beyond anything he had known. It was triumph such as a ewe might feel when it lambed. It was the white blossoms he had seen in the forest. It was the nightingale's song. Thomasine! Even her name had beauty. Why had he never felt it before?

He ran from the house to the beach, stripped himself and plunged into the water, splashed out again shivering. He scrubbed himself with white sand until the blood tingled and his skin shone. His blue eyes glowed in his tanned face. His even, white teeth glistened. He ran back to the house and thrust his long firm legs into the green hosen. He put on his best tunic, the pale one with silver buttons. He strapped on his sword and thrust the jewelled Spanish dagger, which Sir Richard had given him, into his sword-belt.

He strutted around the empty room, struck out a long leg to admire. "Green," he said, stroking the hosen; "green for spring, for eternal spring."

He was interrupted by a hearty laugh. Captain Amadas

had come in on him, all unaware. "Well, my young cock o' the walk, what ails you?"

"N-nothing," stammered Colin, red-faced. "Nothing. It's spring. They say men go mad in spring," he finished lamely.

"You misquote, sir. Lovers go mad in spring. Not men."

Colin's heart went against his breast. He had buttoned the note inside his tunic. He felt for a moment as though the captain's eyes had pierced the cloth and the words on the paper were bare to his eyes. "Lovers," Colin repeated, "lovers on Roanoke?"

"There may be, one day," said Amadas soberly. "But I thought you were off for Hatorask."

"So I am." Colin grasped his bag and flung it over his shoulder. "So I am, and now. Good fortune, sir!" he said as he stood in the doorway. "Good fortune!"

"Thank you. We will need it," Amadas replied.

When Colin with five men reached Hatorask he found Captain Stafford, who greeted him with enthusiasm. "It is dull to the point of distraction here. Nothing to look at but the sand and the sea and the gulls. Not even a storm in a month." He left Colin to settle himself in one of the sand burrows while he saw the men off who were taking the boat back to Roanoke.

Colin stripped off his fine raiment and dressed himself more soberly. He buried his armour in the sand to keep it from rusting. When it came to putting away his green hosen, he was at a loss where to lay them. Finally he thought of his helmet. He put them inside the head-piece and wrapped the whole in a sad-coloured mantle. He could hear the laughter and teasing of his companions if they found him dressed like a fop.

Phil, Dick and Rise came in at sundown. They brought crabs and one fish for the evening meal. When they saw Colin, they set up a great shout and dashed along the beach.

They wrung his hand, slapped his back, poked his ribs. He flinched, for he still felt Lacie's knife thrust.

They all gathered in the common-room while the cook prepared their supper. The others plied Colin with questions. When they were told about Pemisapan's conspiracy, they were loud in their regrets that they had missed a fight. "Our only fight is with crabs, when we wade out into the sea for a bath," they complained.

Stafford smiled at them and smoked his pipe. In answer

420

to Colin's question, he said they hadn't seen an Indian for weeks. "They must be planting on the mainland," he said "They'll be here later to eat mussels."

Colin said, "It's already June. They must have finished planting by now." No one commented. They really weren't interested.

Phil Blount was busy with his shells. He had collected a great variety. He must take them back to Devon when he went home.

Stafford said, "The Admiral is overdue by two months."

Prideaux spoke up. "What will we do if he doesn't come? I don't want to eat sea-food all my life."

"Nor I," agreed Courtenay. "But I don't worry too much because the Admiral doesn't come. Sir Walter will send someone else."

They dismissed the subject and began to talk about a whale they had seen spouting in the sea. If they could kill a whale, there would be a change of diet for themselves and the company on Roanoke.

Colin slept well that night. He had put Thomasine's little message in the amulet bag he wore about his neck. Nurse Marjory had given it to him. "It will keep off evil, Colin," she had said. "Promise me you will wear it night and day." He had done that. Now it was a hiding place for the words Thomasine had written to him.

The sea sang a pleasant rhythm. The taste of salt stung his lips and nostrils. Toward morning he woke. An unhappy thought filled his mind. How had John Arundell come into possession of the hosen which Thomasine had intended for him? He tried to puzzle it out, but he found no answer. He felt annoyance with John at first. Then the annoyance grew into something deeper.

It was not yet day. He got up, dressed and went down to walk on the beach, just as the first streamers of light spread like an open fan in the east.

He stood looking across the grey water, shielding his eyes with his hand to make sure. There, against the rising sun, were the dark outlines of ships—one—two—three—plainly visible!

He let out a great cry, "Stafford! Captain Stafford!" He cupped his hands and cried, "Ship ahoy! Ship ahoy! Ship ahoy."

The men ran tumbling down to the beach. Roused from

deep sleep, they came as they were—some naked as the day they drew first breath, others in night-clothes which their women-folk had made as farewell gifts before they left the West Country.

By the time the sun was full above the horizon, they counted seven ships. They were sailing from the southeast.

The lads jumped and capered around, up and down the sand. Stafford steadily watched with his perception glass. After a time he said, "Phil, you and Dick take a canoe and two men and go to the governor. He must be prepared, put his men on alert."

Blount spoke quickly. "It's the Admiral . . . isn't it? Surely it can't be anyone but Grenville."

Stafford handed the glass to Courtenay. "At first I saw three ships coming out of the haze. Now there are eleven. I don't believe that Grenville would have more than three or four at the most. These might be Spanish ships."

Blount was off like a flash, his thin legs flying along the beach. Prideaux followed. The sun shone on his naked body as he ran splashing down the wet sand.

There was nothing for the others to do but wait. They sat down on the beach. The cook brought fried fish for their breakfast. He saw the ships. He waited for his turn, then looked through the glass.

"I count nineteen," he muttered. "They look proper big ships. One's a six-hundred-ton vessel, or I was whelped by a stableman out of a trull."

No one smiled. Everyone watched intently. By bright daylight the vision was not so clear, for the sun danced on the waves and tired the eyes.

After a time Stafford gave the glass to the cook. "You're an old sailor. What do you see now?"

"I see twenty-three ships, or abouts, somewhat blurred. I think they be Spanish ships."

"Are you sure?"

"Been't sure about anything, sir, since my stomach's so flat for lack of food. Mayhap they be Spanish captured by some bold English captain, like our Admiral took a barque at St. John's."

His words did not give much comfort to Stafford. He and the cook tried to estimate the time it would take them to sail close enough to make out what banners the ships flew at the yard-arm.

They waited until nightfall. When the moon rose, twenty-three vessels stood in the roadstead off Hatorask, but no boats had been sent ashore, and they were still unable to discern the nature of the banners.

That night was one of anxiety. The men lay on the sand waiting. They had their harquebuses beside them, and all their side-arms. Everyone had resolved to sell his life dearly if Spaniards set their feet on this soil, which was now the soil of England.

When the sun came up, they watched with tired eyes for a sign of life from the ships. Presently they saw a boat launched from the greatest of the fleet. It was pointed directly toward them. From its direction it would beach not far below the spot where they lay.

Colin's eyes were keen. He had been accustomed from childhood to search the desolate moors for lost lambs. He was the first to see that the boat flew St. George's Banner.

"It's an English flag!" he said excitedly.

Some of the men were on their feet ready to run to the water's edge. "Hold!" Captain Stafford called. "They may be Spanish. Let us wait."

"You are right, Captain." A new voice spoke. Colin and Stafford turned. Behind them, Captain Cavendish, Anthony Rowse and Darby Glande were approaching their position, crawling on their stomachs. "It would be like the Spanish to play a trick and fly our banner."

Captain Stafford asked, "Have you come up from Wococon?"

"Yes. We brought the *Roebuck*. She's anchored yonder in deep water behind the sand island, out of sight. We saw the ships. We counted sixteen. Surely Admiral Grenville would not be sailing in with such a fleet. They must be Spanish."

Stafford said, "If they are, we'll fire a volley to make them welcome. That's all the ammunition we have," he added grinning.

He handed the glass to Cavendish, who took a long look and whistled. "I count twenty-three ships lying off. I am sure of the number now. That's a fleet of great size." He passed the glass to the others. Darby Glande had it last.

The ship's boat had run into the beach. Barelegged men waded ashore holding onto the gunwales to set the boat well up.

423

Glande let out a shout. " 'Tis England! 'Tis West-Country lads!"

"Quiet, fool!" cried Stafford. "You may be mistaken."

"Nay, sir, I am not, for I know them as well as I know my own finger. There's Master Abraham Kendall, and Master Herne seated in the stern. Aye, 'tis West Country."

Stafford's voice showed his excitement. "Plant the staff, boys, here in the sand. Plant her hard and fast. Let them see Old England flying in the New World."

Two men lifted the staff and let the banner ripple out in the strong breeze.

Men were tumbling down the beach shouting and crying out their welcome.

Cavendish and Stafford were the last to get to the boat, just as the two captains were stepping ashore. Stafford saluted, "Sirs, we make you welcome to Virginia. Stafford, commanding the outpost."

The salute was quickly returned. "Kendall and Herne. We bring the compliments of our admiral and captain general, Sir Francis Drake."

"Drake!" the ragged, half-starved men shouted, and pounded one another on the back. Drake, the greatest of them all, had come to rescue them. There would be food and clothes. Drake!

Stafford conferred with the two captains. They had come, they said, to bring to Governor Lane the compliments of Sir Francis and to inquire if he could do anything for the governor and the colony.

Drake's captains looked at the colonists. They were indeed a sorry lot. Some were laughing, some had tears in their eyes.

"We are well supplied with food," Kendall added.

Stafford said, "We have lived on fish and crabs and mussels for a month."

Kendall called to his men, "Bring the supplies ashore. If someone will cook, you can have a meal of good beef we got from the Spaniards."

Darby Glande stepped forward. "Captain, you know my cooking of old. Will you trust me?"

Kendall nodded. "Ah, Darby Glande. 'Tis a fine thing to see you again. We thought you had gone to the Spanish Main with Hawkins."

"No, sir. I'm here, and I'm that hongry that my ribs are sticking one to the other."

424

Kendall said to Stafford, "Sir Francis' compliments. He asks that the commander and five or six of his men come aboard the *Elizabeth Bonaventure* to dine with him. Herne, you will stay ashore and see that these men have a proper dinner?"

"Aye, that I will. They look drawn-out and thin to me."

Stafford called Courtenay and Colin Grenville. "Will you come with Captain Cavendish and me? We are going on board the flagship, the guests of Sir Francis Drake."

The young men came quickly.

Cavendish said, "I would like to include Anthony Rowse, if you please, Captain."

Kendall said heartily, "Bring your young lads. We have food aplenty—aye, sir, food and riches, for God has furthered our hopes. In His great goodness He has given our admiral the cities of Santiago, San Domingo and Cartagena. What a ransom they have paid in gold and jewels and Spanish coin!" He spoke boastfully. "And we have harried the Florida coast giving the Spanish the scare of their lives."

"Drake's star shines as bright as ever," Cavendish said. "He is fortune's man."

"Aye, he is, and a good bold man to sail under. We never lost a ship and gained several Spaniards, and he divided the prizes equally among his men."

Captain Stafford entered Drake's cabin alone. The others waited without until he had spoken with the admiral and learned his wishes.

Stafford had glimpsed the great Drake only once, at Deptford when the Queen gave her sanction to the sea-captain by dining on board his ship. He had stood on the bank with a vast press of people while Queen Elizabeth conferred the honour of knighthood on the successful circumnavigator of the globe. That was five years earlier.

The great man sat in a chair in the splendidly furnished cabin. He did not rise or extend his hand. He sat silent. His keen dark eyes, set deep in a broad swarthy face, were unwavering. His hair and beard were black, and he had a bold look, composed, as becomes a man who has been successful in large undertakings.

Stafford remembered words he had heard concerning Drake: "He has a head to contrive and a hand to execute whatever promises glory to himself and good to his country."

Surely there was never a man who was a greater architect of his own future and fame.

Yet with all he had carried an air of truculence, as one who is ready to fight. So he had fought from his early years, without proper education, for he knew only the sea. He had given himself to the sea with all his heart, and the sea had given to him in return.

Stafford waited. When Drake spoke his voice was higher and thinner than one would expect from so eminent a man. He said, "Captain Stafford, will you please give me an account of the colony? I have come hither to ascertain whether the governor is in want of any service, and whether supplies are needed."

"Sir, we are in dire need. In fact so great is the need of food that we have been forced to stew a broth of roots and herbs, to live on small animals like conies and squirrels. Our clothes are worn to tatters. We have very little ammunition left."

Drake tapped the table with the hilt of a jewelled dagger. He was elegantly dressed and wore about his neck a golden medal with a great pearl dangling from it. "I take from that Admiral Grenville has not arrived."

"Sir, he has not come. When he sailed for England, his plan was to return by Easter."

Drake said, "Perhaps the war with Flanders has prevented his sailing."

"War with Flanders? Are we at war with the Dutch?"

"Of course you did not know, having had no ship to visit you. We are helping the Dutch against the Spanish. The Earl of Leicester commands an army in Flanders. His kinsman, Sir Philip Sidney, had been made Governor of Flushing." This news they had had from an English merchant ship which they had met in the Spanish islands.

Drake spoke then of ways to strengthen Governor Lane's position. "Perhaps if he will come to me here on my ship, we can discuss this matter."

"Sir, Roanoke Island is a day and night's journey away. I will start at once to give him news of your arrival. The whole company will kneel at your feet in thanksgiving, sir."

Drake looked pleased, but he said, "I don't want any English to kneel to me. If anyone kneels, let it be Spaniards." He shouted for a servant.

When he came, Drake sent for his captains who were

426

aboard his flag-ship, Martin Frobisher, Christopher Carliell, Francis Knollys. They looked curiously at Stafford and his wretched garments. Stafford stared back. He knew Carliell was Sir Francis Walsingham's stepson. Young men of rank all of them, eager to serve with a great sea-captain. When Drake mentioned his name, they changed their attitude. Stafford was a great name in England, and even a cadet of the house was important.

"We will dine now," Drake said.

Stafford spoke of the young men he had with him— "Rise Courtenay and Colin Grenville, Anthony Rowse and a young navigator, Thomas Cavendish, who has great ambitions to follow your example and sail around the world."

Drake hesitated only a fraction of a second when Grenville's name was mentioned. With a wave of his hand he invited them all to dine with him. To Carliell he said, "Captain, will you escort our guests to the dining-hall? I will join you later."

They had finished dinner before the admiral came in. The wine was brought, and toasts were drunk—to the Queen, to Drake, to the Governor of Roanoke. Sir Francis himself proposed one to the success of Sir Richard Grenville's colony in Virginia.

Colin thought there was a curious smile on his dark-bearded lips as he raised his golden cup. Colin only tasted the wine. They had been so long without proper wine that it made his head giddy.

Drake turned to him. "My Madeira does not please you, Master Grenville?"

"Sir, I have not tasted wine for months. My stomach is collapsed for want of food. I fear to drink lest I might lose my balance."

He spoke so frankly and looked at Drake with such friendly eyes that the admiral's frown disappeared. He laughed heartily. Pointing to Knollys he said, "Some of my captains have weak heads, but they don't know it." Knollys had a sickly grin on his lips. There were bright red spots on his cheeks and his eyes were beginning to glaze.

Drake turned back to Colin. "I thought all Grenvilles had iron stomachs and hard heads."

"Sir, perhaps I am not a good Grenville."

The admiral showed curiosity. "Do you live in Devon or in Cornwall?"

"Sir, in Cornwall, at Stowe." Colin smiled. He would give no satisfaction to Admiral Drake. "I am one of Sir Richard's wards," he said.

Drake nodded and turned to Rise Courtenay. A Tavistock boy, Drake knew the Courtenays of Exeter and all their great kin.

He sat back, fingering his wine-cup. He was content. Among these young gentlemen of the West Country he was a hero, a noble figure. Now that he had come to their rescue, they and all their families would be in his debt. After a little time he rose and with a few cordial words returned to his quarters.

Stafford and his men went ashore. He left that night at moonrise. Drake wanted Governor Lane to wait on him on his ship in three days' time. Stafford himself would carry the message of hope to the starving colony.

That night Sir Francis Drake paced the deck of his ship. He looked toward the long barren islands of sand. His active mind was busy with new plans.

Three days later Governor Lane sat across the table from Admiral Drake. The door was closed so that no one could overhear.

Drake said, "I am shocked by your appearance, Lane. You are not the same man I saw a year ago at Buckland Abbey."

"I am not the same man. By the living God, it's all the fault of Grenville! He burned an Indian town, then he sailed away and left me to face the hostile savages. It's only because of God's goodness that we are alive today." He began to tell the story of ill luck which had befallen them.

Admiral Drake appeared to listen. After a time the governor's voice faltered. He wondered what Stafford had told Drake. He had always thought well of Stafford. He had been a man to obey orders and never deviate. . . . He wondered. . . . He lifted a cup of wine to his lips.

The admiral rose and rang for a scribe. "I will put in writing what I am offering to you. It is better so. Then no trouble will come of it. After you have signed your request, I will consult my captains." He waved his hand toward the door, which now stood open.

Lane waited, wondering at the turn. He did not want to put his request for help in writing. He had spoken of Francis Drake as a bountiful and good man. What could he do now

428

but sign the paper the scribe set before him, asking for victuals, ammunition, clothing, barques, pinnaces and small boats? The boats were to be victualed, manned and furnished.

Presently, after all had been written down, the captains came in. After some wrangling it was decided and all signed.

There would be enough victuals to last until August, and barques to carry the company to England if no ship came.

Lane stayed until Drake had promised to leave good masters, skilful navigators, who would sail them home to England after helping them seek a better harbour farther to the north; also a supply of calivers, hand weapons, match and lead, tools, apparel.

"Leave me something in my ships, Lane," Drake said with a laugh, and the council broke up.

Lane was riding in the sky with happiness. Food was being unloaded on the beach and carried to shelter. The barque *Francis*, with Masters Abraham Kendall and Griffith Herne, was anchored close to shore. Lane had put Masters Cavendish and Rowse aboard to represent his company before he went aboard himself.

He sent Nugent and five rowers back to the Island of Roanoke to bring suitable clothes. He intended to live on the *Francis* until the admiral should sail a week or ten days hence after he had filled the casks of all his ships with sweet water.

The governor ordered Master Stafford to return again to the island as his emissary and bearer of good tidings. All the colonists who wished could come to view the great fleet, provided they left a sufficient number behind. As Stafford set off, the governor told him that the admiral wished to speak particularly with Master Hariot and Master John White. Sir Francis had heard of Master White's fine pictures and wanted to see samples of his work. He desired to renew his acquaintance with the learned Master Hariot.

Governor Lane received his principal men on the *Francis*, a good ship of seventy tons. The pinnaces were anchored at hand, and there were several smaller boats which Drake set aside for the colonists.

The men of the company began to arrive in two days' time. Many brought their goods, for they were determined to ask passage home with Sir Francis' fleet. At least fifty were assembled near the entrance.

When they saw the great fleet in all its majesty, they fell on their knees in the sand and thanked God.

The governor, too, was greatly moved when he came to greet them.

He told them of Sir Francis' noble offer. They could see with their own eyes the boxes of supplies that were being put ashore. There was a dinner prepared for them in the common-room at Master Stafford's house. Lane's voice broke. "The Lord has held His holy hand over us. Let us rejoice and pray for the eternal success of our colony, the first colony of Englishmen in the New World, for this is our honour. The praise of our Queen and our nation will be upon us."

The men walked soberly to the shelter where food was spread. They did not bolt their food as ones condemned who had their last meal set before them. They ate quietly, with propriety, for their days of starvation were over. Had they not seen the supplies being carried ashore? Boat after boat was being rowed in from the fleet, loaded to the gunwales.

Sir Francis Drake's name was on every tongue—the greatest sea-captain in all England, the greatest benefactor. Had he not, in the abundant generosity of his heart, sailed for long days off his course to visit their colony, to see that it did well, and that the people wanted for nothing?

Surely it was as the governor said, the very hand of God was stretched out to them.

Colin walked along the beach. Everywhere he saw little groups of men. Some had their possessions at their feet. They were talking and laughing and making merry. Much of the talk was of home. They questioned Drake's seamen as they unloaded the stores.

Every day now some of the men ate aboard the vessels, Drake himself graciously entertaining Marshal Gorges, Masters Hariot and White. Captain Amadas, even Dick Prideaux and Philip Blount came back singing praises of Admiral Drake. Colin thought, Everyone is impressed by him. Can I be wrong? Perhaps it is only my imagination, but I have the feeling that he does not want Sir Richard Grenville's colony to succeed.

His thoughts were interrupted. He heard voices. A pleading voice cried, "Sir, do not take them from me. I mean them

430

for Sir Richard to present to the Queen." There was a gruff, sharp answer and the sound of a scuffle.

Colin sprang forward, for he had recognised Lacie, who was saying, "The Queen will get the string of pearls, but it won't be Grenville who presents them to her."

Colin came upon them behind a thicket of yeopon. Lacie's back was toward him. He had his hands about the man's throat, shaking him violently. Colin recognised the man's face but did not know the name. He was an old fellow who knew about metals and jewels. Colin had heard that he had managed to collect a great quantity of pearls by trading with the Indians when they came to the fishing grounds. He was clutching his breast with both hands, as though he had the pearls concealed on his person. His face was purple, his eyes bulged out. He cast a despairing look at Colin. He could not speak, for Lacie's great hands were tightened about his windpipe.

Colin shouted, "Lacie!" Lacie whirled about. The old man dropped on the ground and began to crawl away on his hands and knees.

Not a word was said. Lacie faced Colin. His face was distorted with rage.

Colin drew his sword. "Draw, fellow! You will get your punishment for this outrage."

"It won't be you, a Grenville, that administers it." Lacie drew and lunged, not waiting for the amenities.

Colin called out, "On guard, Lacie!" His voice carried, as he meant it should. Men came dashing up from the beach. Some ran for Captain Amadas. Others made a circle.

The old man sat upright. His hands clutched a long string of pearls. They glowed softly in the light. He kept crying, "He tried to steal them from me. My pearls, my beautiful pearls! Thief! Thief! Thief!" He pointed a trembling finger at Lacie's back. "He is a thief. I brand him a thief."

Someone helped him to his feet. His friends surrounded him, giving dark looks at Lacie.

Lacie did not see them or hear the old man's hysterical cries. He was watching, watching with sharp eyes. Thrust and parry, thrust and retreat. Sand was poor foothold.

Presently Captain Amadas joined them, out of breath. He pushed his way through the ring and stood in the front line. He would see fair play.

Lacie was the taller, the heavier. That carried more advantage in wrestling. But Colin moved swiftly. His body was hard and muscular, his step light as an Indian's. The long days' travelling silently through the forests had taught him co-ordination of body and mind.

Lacie's skill with the sword might be greater, but Colin was ever wary. His blue eyes scanned, not the sword, but the eyes of his opponent. No tricks! It must be straight sword-play. He could tire the man.

Once Lacie slipped and went to his knees. A sound came from the silent watchers like a long breath.

Colin dropped his sword to his side and waited for Lacie to get to his feet.

"On guard!" he cried, when his opponent had recovered his balance. "On guard!"

The circle deepened. Seamen quit their work and gathered round. Both men showed beads of sweat. Colin was dressed in leather jerkin, but no armour. Lacie wore neck-piece of iron over his leather tunic. Both men were bare-headed, their faces exposed.

Once or twice Captain Amadas stopped the fight to give the men breathing space. Lacie was weakening. The long days without proper food told on him.

Colin defended, letting Lacie attack. At last Lacie had his guard down for a second, only a second, but long enough for the point of Colin's sword to catch him on the wrist. Lacie's sword dropped to the ground. He grabbed for it and thrust wildly. Colin stabbed at the sword-arm. A moment later Lacie's blade described an arc in the air. A dozen men ducked to get out of the way, and fell in a tangled heap on the sand.

Captain Amadas raised his hand. The bout was ended.

Lacie protested. He would finish. No bout was over until blood was drawn.

Amadas said, "Look at your arm, Lacie!"

Blood dripped slowly from under his tunic sleeve where Colin had cut the leather and pierced the upper arm. Lacie forced his way through the crowd and walked off, nursing his injured arm with one hand.

The men watched him go without expression. Then they went back to their places.

Colin walked up the beach with Amadas and Stafford. "The old man had a great string of pearls, some very large, all beautiful. He told me there were five thousand in all. He

432

is determined to take them back to England to give to Sir Richard Grenville. And Sir Richard is to take them to the Queen, so he said. He told me also that he had not had a good night's sleep for this long time. More than once men had tried to rob him. The governor tried to buy them, but he refused."

That night Captain Stafford set a guard in front of the old fellow's burrow. The wind blew heavily. Lightning flashed on the horizon, but the oldster slept peacefully, his pearls secure.

The morning of the thirteenth of June dawned. The sky and the sea were leaden. The wind had blown steadily for twelve hours and rose to a stronger gale as the daylight came and the morning advanced.

There was a long swell on the Ocean Sea that rocked the ships. The captains went each to his bridge. The sails were close-reefed. By noon the sky had the strange yellow light that betokened a heavy storm.

Drake signalled to his captains and hung storm warnings from the mast-head of the *Elizabeth Bonaventure*. Governor Lane came ashore to consult with his leaders. The storm rose with such fury that the small pines on the shore lay with their crowns in the sand under each gust of wind. Men bored deeper into their burrows or lay flat in the sand clinging to small bushes behind the dunes for protection. Boxes of stores were broken up or covered by the driving waves and scattered along the beach.

Each day of the storm more of the company struggled in from Roanoke Island. They reported boats wrecked, roofs carried away, trees lying on the earth. They were frightened. Again doom had descended on them. They swore that the head of Pemisapan opened its mouth and spoke, sometimes shrieked with laughter, as trees fell and roofs whirled away in the air.

"The doom! The doom!" they repeated endlessly.

The fourth day of the great storm Sir Francis Drake's ships put out to sea. The men on the beach watched them sail with sinking hearts.

The *Francis*, with many of the company, started to weigh anchor. Panic struck the others left on shore. They rushed to the beach as though pursued by a great army. They crowded into boats, overloading them, capsizing some.

433

Men struggled in the angry waves, while those in the boats beat them off with oars.

The governor and Captain Amadas shouted, trying to raise their voices above the roar of the wind, "Come back! Come back to shore!"

Stafford ran up and down, making his endeavour to calm the people. "The ships will return," he cried. "They are standing off so that they will not be dashed on the beach."

No one listened.

Colin and Dick, running to help a man who had been washed in on a wave, saw Lacie and the old fellow struggling in the water. Lacie was dragging at his breast, trying to get the pearls. Colin shouted to Dick, "He's a devil incarnate."

A great wave came. Dick and Colin ran back, dripping, eyes burning with salt. When Colin had cleared the spray from his lids, the sea was empty.

The next morning they found the body of the old silversmith on the beach, a few pearls clutched in his hand.

The *Francis* was gone. Whether she had sailed away or lay on the bottom of the ocean, they did not know. Once more they were alone, without a ship that would carry them home.

On the fifth day the wind died down. The men who were left behind wandered aimlessly up and down the beach, gathering up the few boxes of provisions that remained. No one spoke, from the governor down. The doom was heavy on every man.

In the morning the sun rose, the wind was subdued to a brisk breeze. A man who was salvaging some wreckage let out a mighty shout. Drake's fleet was standing off the coast! Drake had returned to rescue them!

After that there was no holding the company. The governor pleaded. Amadas harangued. White and Hariot added their voices. Stafford went from man to man. He told them that summer was coming on; there would be corn growing, schools of fish; they had a few stores; they were in much better case than they had been for six months past. Churchman prayed. No one listened.

One man with a wild light in his eyes said the doom had come on the colony as a punishment for Lane's cruelty, for his outrages upon the poor savages.

Drake came ashore. He offered more provisions and ships,

434

smiling his secret smile as he looked about at the havoc the storm had made.

The company voted. Only seven voted to stay—Colin, Dick, Phil, Rise, Amadas, Hariot and Stafford. John White was engaged in looking through his books, saving what might be saved.

Drake turned to Lane, "What say you, Governor?"

"The hand of God beckons us. We must go. We must obey the will of the majority. That is the law of the Charter and the Company. The minority must accept the decision."

Amadas' face was red with anger. "And leave no one here to protect this land where we have planted the Queen's banner? Surely we must stay."

Edward Stafford agreed. "We must protect what we have won, sir."

Drake watched them, his bright dark eyes first on one face, then another. "I have room for you all. A safe journey is what I offer. Three months and you will see Land's End rise out of the mist."

There was no holding them back. No one returned to the island.

By nightfall Drake's ships were sailing south-east for the Azores.

Colin stood at the rail watching the long strip of sand until it vanished from sight. Here he had been happy, a man among men. What would happen when he returned to Stowe? Would his newfound manhood stand for something?

Drake's ships had scarce time to reach St. John's in Porto Rico, a fortnight's sail, when Grenville's ship lay off Port Ferdinando. With his ship came three others sent by Sir Walter Raleigh, well victualled, with settlers to till the soil, to build houses, to make the Virginia colony firm and sound.

Sir Richard's ship sailed through the entrance and came to anchor at the north end of Roanoke Island.

A scene of desolation met their eyes. The hurricane had made havoc, but that was not all. Men's belongings lay scattered about. Houses were deserted.

Alone, Grenville climbed the hill to the fort. No one knew what his thoughts were as he stood looking at Pemisapan's head stuck on a post over the gate.

After a long time he came back to his ship, entered his cabin and closed the door.

In the morning he ordered the ship to proceed up the sound, but he could not find a trace of his hundred men, nor were there any Indians in the towns on the lower waters.

He spent some days searching. In the end he gave up. Something dreadful had happened—an Indian attack or a Spanish raid. Whatever it was, some terror had overtaken the colony and wiped it from the earth.

He was unwilling to lose possession of a country which Englishmen had held so long. But what was he to do?

One night a group of men, fifteen in all, came to him. They had held deliberation, they told him. They wanted his permission to stay on the island and hold the land for the Queen.

Grenville could not speak for emotion. One by one he clasped their hands and looked into their eyes, his own filmed with tears.

The next day he sailed, Raleigh's ships with him, leaving behind provisions for two years and ammunition in great plenty.

"We will return next year," he told them at the last. "Be of good faith. Deal fairly with the Indians. And may God have you in His keeping!"

The men went up the hill to the stockade after the ships had sailed. They noticed then that the Indian's head was gone. Grenville had buried it decently, with his own hands.

It did not enter Grenville's mind that the men he mourned were safely lodged in ships of Francis Drake's victorious fleet homeward bound for England.

CHAPTER 29
WITHOUT BANNERS

Sir Francis Drake's fleet was about to sail into Plymouth Harbour. Church bells were ringing. A great press of people had waited from the time his ships were spoken in the early morning.

What a thrilling story he would have to tell! What triumphs! Santiago on the Cape Verde Islands he had seized and burned. He had taken San Domingo on Hispaniola by assault and been paid a ransom of twenty-five thousand ducats to spare the ancient city. He had sacked Cartagena on the Spanish Main of its merchandise, and that key to the treasure-house of Peru had paid him a hundred thousand ducats more after a furious night attack. Everywhere he had humbled the pride of Spain and taken his fill of gold and jewels.

Drake's ships, trailing his long home-bounder pennon, ghosted up the Channel in a light following breeze leaving scarcely a ripple in their wake. His honours would be almost as great as when he sailed around the world. Drake, the greatest of all sea-captains and the glory of Devon, was coming home again.

The miserable men whom he had brought back from Roanoke would have no share in the welcome accorded Drake and his captains. One by one or in little groups of two and three the wretched planters of the first colony in Virginia prepared when they disembarked to travel quietly to their homes.

Every day of their long voyage home they had been aware of failure. There would be no prize money for them to divide. For them there would be no banqueting and feasting. No women would follow them offering their favours to heroes.

Grenville's men had nothing to show. It was a year and three months since they had sailed from Plymouth. Why did they not bring home a cargo to the Queen's taste and tall tales of full flavour about lusty fights, of ships and barques

437

captured and treasure won at the point of the sword? Again that dark little man would swagger across the stage, another Caesar returning with the spoils of victory.

Colin talked with Captain Amadas. They stood side by side on the deck of the *Bonner* and saw the purple mist divide and show the coast of Cornwall. Happiness set Colin's pulses tingling when the first shout went up "Land ahead!" A fine glow was in his breast. His eyes feasted on the home shores.

But the exultation died down quickly in his heart and the hearts of his fellows. All they could think of was that Raleigh's colony had failed. They were coming home without their Admiral. They were poor wretched men who had been rescued by a great leader. Drake again came first, Drake and his men. Tomorrow they would all be gone on their way, each to his home, each to tell his story of failure that might have been success, if——

In his cabin Lane was writing furiously. Every paragraph of his long report was laden with explanations. If—Lane's everlasting if. The word failure is bitter on the lips and it makes poor display on a written page. Men are judged not by the effort but by the result. . . . So it would be with these weary men.

"No fanfare for failure." Amadas spoke the words aloud.

Colin said, "If we had only stayed, our Admiral would have come to us. I am certain he would have come if we had waited."

"But we didn't wait. We ran like rats from a sinking ship. I am ashamed."

"And I," Colin said. "I am ashamed to look into the eyes of our comrades. We are all ashamed, I think."

Amadas nodded. "I will go again to Virginia, Colin. I think it necessary. We must try and try, until we are strong in that New World. I believe it will be like that. We will go again and again until we conquer the land."

Colin watched the coast rise higher out of the water.

Amadas spoke reflectively. "We were not strong enough. We were timorous. We were beset by fears, fears of the loneliness, of the vast forest, of the great Ocean Sea that divided us from our known world. We were afraid of the unknown. We were small souls, Colin, or we would have defied Lane's order and stayed on."

Colin's voice was very low. "We failed our Admiral. We

438

had neither loyalty nor courage. We deserve what we get. We slink into England with fallen crests. By the Eternal, when I go again no words spoken by any man will make me turn back!"

His voice had risen. Two or three seamen, Drake's men, turned. They looked at one another and smiled.

"God's truth, we deserve smiles and sneers!" Amadas said.

They were silent. Finally Amadas spoke, repeating himself. "We will go back to Virginia, Colin, you and I and some of our brave boys. We will wipe out the ignominy of defeat by determination to succeed. We cannot fail now. We cannot allow Spain to rule the New World." He held out his hand. Colin grasped it firmly. "We will make a bond, take oath together. In the name of Elizabeth and with the help of God we will go back to Virginia!"

"God with us!" Colin said. "Perhaps that is the destiny of the land—to make men struggle to win her."

Amadas nodded. His arms were on the rail. He was watching the coast line with eager eyes. "It is beautiful, this land of ours, but it is an old, mature beauty. There is an excitement about a new land——" He held his tongue. Others were walking along the decks. In a short time they would go ashore.

After a while Colin said, "I trust I can find a moor pony in Plymouth strong and willing and cheap. If it isn't cheap, I'll walk across Cornwall to Stowe."

"I will not stay in Plymouth a day," Amadas said. "Let Drake and his men ride along the streets in full view of the populace, with banners flying and drums beating."

"We will hasten to our homes, Captain Amadas—all of us, for I think every man among us feels as we feel."

There was no tinge of the old merry look in Amadas' dark eyes. They were reflective, sad. "It is not good for a man to feel defeat rise in his heart. It is not good."

Colin said nothing. What would he find at Stowe? Would Sir Richard be there, or on the sea? What of Thomasine? Of John, Black John Arundell? Of the household of Stowe? His mind refused to move farther. Tomorrow and another day, and he would know. . . .

Another thought came to Colin. At the island he had had the companionship of men. He had been one of a goodly company. What did the days ahead hold for him?

439

He could never make a new life in this ancient world, never.

Philip Blount came up and joined them. He was yawning. "I suppose it will be studies again for me. Oxford will be tame after the wild life we have lived." He addressed Captain Amadas: "Sir, did you ever think that our living here is overlaid by traditions made by other men, years on years built up of custom? In Virginia we are at a beginning. We make our own customs. We are the ones to found traditions." He laughed shortly, slightly embarrassed. "I say! What am I talking about? Silly business, trying to figure out why one does things. Better to live right along, not questioning deeply." His lips widened in a boyish grin. "It can't be that Master Hariot's logic is taking effect on me, and I'm beginning to use reason!"

Captain Amadas laughed. "If you go back to Virginia, you won't need to reason. You can be all action."

Blount sobered. "If I go back to Virginia," he said slowly.

Dick Prideaux came up from behind and stood gazing at the coast. "We'll soon see St. Michael's Mount. I wonder if any of my people will be in Plymouth."

Blount said, "How could they know that we are coming home in Drake's ships?"

"They can't. But they might be there to greet Drake. I've an idea that most of Devon and Cornwall will be near at hand, all those who have been within reach of messengers sent out from Land's End." Dick said to Amadas, "Captain, it's a sorry way we come back to England, limping on a crutch handed to us by the great conqueror. I don't like it. I wish we had stayed on and taken our chance with fortune. Somehow I feel this should have been our course. This slinking in like dogs with tails between their legs doesn't suit me. We are Drake's captives, as it were, starving castaways that he picked up on an island. It catches in my craw, sir. What do you think, Captain?"

"We've just been discussing the matter," Amadas said. "No one likes it, Dick. But there we are. We may as well swallow the fact that we are slinking in—and get away as swiftly as we can. I'm like to vomit with the idea of being commiserated by a lot of stay-at-homes who are beating drums for Drake. I am eternally damned if I can stomach it!"

"Never mind. No one will even cast a look at us. They

will be too busy making laurel wreaths for Admiral Drake. We will take up our few belongings and depart." Phil chuckled. "One thing sure, I'll have welcome enough when I get to Exeter and my family."

Colin wondered if anyone would welcome him. Without Sir Richard what would be his position in the household at Stowe?

Dick said, "Colin, I want you to go home with me. I've some kinfolk at Plymouth who will furnish horses for us. We will ride to Padstow. You'll find a warm welcome from my cousin at New Place."

"I want him to go home with me!" Phil Blount exclaimed. "It's not too far to Bideford, if he goes by way of Exeter. He can come to you at any time, Dick. You Cornish are always traipsing around, visiting one another."

Colin was warmed by this friendly squabbling over him.

Captain Amadas said, "I'm going to throw my clothes into a bag. I'm going to get off the ship and go home as quickly as possible."

"I won't need a very big box to carry my belongings. Only Colin here looks as though he belonged to Drake's men—a fine jerkin, elegant green hosen. Why, I believe he expects to meet a woman. Dick Prideaux poked him in the ribs.

Colin's fair skin flushed.

"Ah, I was right! Look at his face. On second thought I believe I'll go to Stowe with him. I have matters to discuss with my guardian Sir Richard. I wonder whether John Arundell has been successful in his suit for the fair Thomasine. I don't envy him. She'd keep a man worrying."

Colin turned away. He did not want to discuss Thomasine with Dick. John Arundell would marry her. He might as well keep that in his mind.

"I will talk to the boys," Captain Amadas said. "There's no use for us to linger in Plymouth. If there is any spare praise to slop over the cup, Governor Lane can have it."

So it was agreed, and so it happened. Plymouth was alive only to her hero, Sir Francis Drake. Words on the lips of the conquerors were strange ones. They mouthed Santiago, San Domingo, Cartagena, St. Anthony. No one mentioned Virginia or Roanoke save only those who had lived on the island for a twelvemonth, those downcast men who had ventured so much in the name of the Queen and England.

Dick and Colin rode down the hill to Stowe at sunset. They paused at King's Park, where Sir Richard always stopped to catch the first glimpse of Stowe, the walls that encircled the house and the farm cottages, the court-yards, the stables and the folds.

The great gate was open to welcome travellers. Little figures, small and indistinguishable, moved about. The stooks of grain stood in serried rows on the hilltops. Cattle grazed in the meadows. Sheep were nibbling slowly down the vale. Old Pooley with his dogs moved behind the flock. Colin recognised him by his slow steps, the way he bent his back as he walked, leaning hard on his crook.

The milkmaids ran along familiar paths. Some were intercepted by stable-boys or feeders who snatched kisses in the shadow of the wall or a high bush.

Pale grey smoke rose from the chimneys. Colin could almost smell the delicious odour of a joint roasting.

Stowe in its beauty hugging the hilltops . . . the apple trees . . . how peaceful, how finished, how very rare it all was in its quiet splendour! Stowe was as eternal as the great cliffs of Hartland.

Colin's eyes glazed over. He turned his head sharply lest Dick Prideaux might witness his weakness and laugh.

But Dick's mood was near his own. "We always last, we county folk," he murmured.

Colin said nothing. He was disturbed. Which should he do —go directly to the stable court-yard or ride in through the great gate as one who is an equal of the master's family? This was the question that had been troubling him ever since he left New Place, where they had spent the night with Dick's kin.

Dick said, "They've seen us. Look on the terrace. See, people are moving about, waving their hands."

A few moments later the blast of a clarion rang out. Men ran to the great gate. Colin and Dick saw horses being brought up. Three figures galloped out the gate and up the long hill toward them.

"We should have had our herald sound our trumpets," Dick said. "Alas, we come quietly, stealing in like the harper. Let's ride to meet them." Half-way down the hill he cried, "I know now who they are—Bernard, John and Thomasine."

When they met, all the boys leaped from their horses. Bernard and John pounded Dick on the back. They wrung

442

Colin's hand. There was no lack of warmth in the welcome given these two poor colonists. Thomasine did not dismount, but there was a glad light in her smile and in her dark eyes as she extended her hand to them.

After the boys' hearty greeting was over, Dick asked, "But where's John Arundell? How does it happen he's not here?"

"John is in London. He went up with the family a fortnight ago." Bernard laughed slyly, glancing at Thomasine over his shoulder. "He went to visit his tailor. We think he must be ordering his wedding garments."

Colin's heart sank. Now that he saw Thomasine again, he wondered how he could ever have thought he hated her.

She sat quietly on her horse, her eyes downcast. She was controlled. Even her hair in its black net was orderly and in place. Now and then she laid a slim hand on her restive horse to pat its satin neck, murmuring soothing words.

The others rode off. Thomasine and Colin were left to follow. After a silence Thomasine said, "You are quiet, Colin. You have said nothing at all. You are different." She turned the full splendour of her eyes on him. "You are so manly. Do you know you are the image of Sir Richard?"

Colin flushed, hesitated, then said, "Sir Richard has discovered that I am a Grenville, a distant cousin." He found he could say the words steadily, without a tremor in his voice.

"Ah, Colin, I'm glad! I admire all the Grenvilles. There is something magnificent about them, something strong and ancient. Dame Philippa says the Grenvilles 'walk with the gods.' Of course she is joking. There aren't any gods."

Colin smiled now. He was pleased at this childish moment. She was not so grown-up as she looked. Colin rode beside her down the hill. When they came to the gate to the park, Thomasine had to dismount and walk to the opening in the high hedge.

"It's my favourite view of Stowe," she said as they stood looking over the rolling hills down the vale toward Stowe Woods. "It is beautiful now in midsummer greenery, but I think it loveliest in the autumn with the woods in patchwork color, the fields harvested."

Colin looked down at her standing so close beside him. Their horses cropped the grass. The other riders were far down the hill. They were quite alone in the wide, beautiful summer.

"Do you remember another harvest?" he spoke abruptly, hoarsely.

She did not look at him, but turned her eyes to the little stone house on the hill above them.

Colin laid his hand on her arm. "Do you remember?" He caught her in his arms, pressed her body close to him. He kissed her, his lips hard against hers. "I have hungered for you, Thomasine."

She released herself gently. "Ah, Colin, Colin, didn't you know? I am to marry John when Sir Richard returns."

The next day Colin found John and Thomasine at the tennis court, playing the French game, batting a small ball against the high stone wall. He stood watching them. A strong feeling of loneliness came over him. Something set him thinking of quiet hilltops where he used to sit watching his sheep, playing mournful tunes on his little shepherd's pipe. He remembered how he had watched the young folk of Stowe playing at games on the terraces, dancing on the green grass, laughing and singing. They were so gay and happy. He wondered then if he would ever know laughter with gay comrades. Those days seemed so long ago, yet little more than a year had passed.

In that year he had known the warmth of friendship. John had been his friend.

He walked up the path through the wood to King's Field. He heard a terrified feeble bleating. He left the path. A little lamb had strayed from the flock. It had wandered into the heavy hawthorne hedge and imprisoned itself. Colin bent down to release it from the thorns and circling branches.

He tucked it under the crook of his arm, a natural familiar movement. He smiled crookedly as he looked down at the fine-fashioned sleeve of his jerkin, velvet slashed with leather. The lamb snuggled close against his body, as hundreds of lambs had snuggled to him. He walked quickly, led by the bleatings of a hundred sheep, to the open hilltop that overlooked Kilkhampton and the whole of Coombe Vale to the sea.

So familiar this land, so loved! The church tower square and strong, the great mound of the ancient Britons, the heavy crowned oaks. The hurt in his heart faded.

There in the shade of an old oak sat Will Pooley. A young lad was on the ground near him, listening with upturned face and eager eyes to some yarn the old man was telling.

Colin saw himself in the young boy. He stood without moving, watching. There was something eternal in the picture before him: age to youth; the wisdom of age passed on; the lore of the countryside, of field, of wood, of animals, transmitted from the lips of the old to the ears of the young.

It was the story of a people, the story of the fields themselves, the recurring seasons. For forty generations, aye and more, he thought, this scene had been re-enacted. Age to youth . . .

Will Pooley looked up and saw Colin standing with a stray lamb under his arm. A slow smile came over his lined face. " 'Tis the wee one that strayed away last night. I thought we had lost he for fair. He's welcome, he is, for his ma has been a-fretting."

Below, on the courts, the little ball flew back and forth against the stone wall. Colin did not hear the laughter of Thomasine and John Arundell. The voice of old Will filled his ears and his mind again. He threw himself on the grass at Will's feet, his hands clasped under his head, his eyes on the white clouds floating across the blue sky.

Colin's feet led him up the sheep path to the top of the hill. He walked the familiar way without thought of where he was going. He was thinking of Thomasine, of every encounter with her from that first time he had seen her riding down the hill from Kilkhampton in Sir Richard's company—the wild mop of her black hair, her great dark eyes, her contemptuous smile as she looked down on the shepherd lad.

What was it that held him? What was her power that set his pulses thundering, his heart beating. "She brings more joy than any god—she brings more woe"—Dame Phillipa had read the line. He remembered now the end: "Oh, may it be an hour of mercy when she looks on me!"

He paused abruptly. His feet had brought him to the old stone hut on the hilltop. Here it was that he had held her, his lips pressed against her fragrant mouth. How she had trembled in his arms, like a wild thing! That was what she was, a wild thing. The moors were her roaming. The smell of bracken and furze had been about her, clean and fragrant, the smell of gorse and the autumn woods. He faced about, looking down Coombe Vale in the glory of sunset.

A small figure was moving along the path from the upper

terrace. He watched the slow progress, his heart beating swiftly. It could not be, but it was. He knew every lithe movement of her young body, the turn of her head. His heart was pounding like the beat of the sea against the high cliffs, but he did not move.

At last she came to him swiftly, like the darting of a swallow. Her eyes were wide and glowing, her lips parted. "Colin, Colin, why do you run from me?"

"I do not run," he said, stoutly he hoped, but his voice trembled.

"Were ever lovers so crossed as we?" she went on, not stirring.

Lovers! His heart leaped.

"Unhappy, ill-starred lovers, who can't speak of love because of honour. What is honour?" she stormed. "A word, nothing more!"

Colin spoke then. "It is more than a word, Thomasine, much, much more."

"I do not care for a man's world where friendship counts more than love. I am a moor girl, Colin. I want life and love and the sky and the evening star, and a love to match all beauty, Colin."

He caught her in his arms, forgetting all he should have remembered. "You are a witch girl," he whispered against her lips, "a witch to draw a man in the passion of love."

Dusk came and the first bright star shone. A young crescent moon rose above the trees, a lovers' moon. As Colin watched her running down the hill toward Stowe, he murmured, "A witch girl to drive a man to madness."

Philippa stopped at Bideford on her way to Stowe. She had been to London for a few weeks. Lady Grenville had been there, too, staying at the St. Leger house. For some reason London bored Philippa. Many of her friends were in the north shooting or at their country places.

Lady Grenville had promised her daughters that they could go to Penshurst for a week. Philippa refused to go. Something pulled her toward Stowe.

Mary had said, "I'd like very much to go home, but the girls would be so disappointed. They have counted on seeing Penshurst."

"You must take them to Mary Sidney's. It will mean only a week longer. I will wait at Grenville House for you and the girls to make your visit to Penshurst. I've had Bideford in my bones all day yesterday and today. So I'll go down in the morning."

Philippa looked out the window. A cavalcade of riders was coming across the Long Bridge from East the Water. She watched idly. The wind was still. Banners hung limply on their staves. A few stragglers stood at the bridge-head. Some knight and his train were riding through Bideford.

The house was quiet, staffed by a few servants in the kitchen and scullery, a footman who acted as butler, the housekeeper, a parlour-maid, her own woman; that was all.

She was glad she had come on ahead. For three or four days she had been restless and uneasy. Every amusement palled. Perhaps Walter Raleigh's heavy gloom had had its effect on her, his depression as he considered the effort it had cost him and Richard to get ships, the greater effort to gain the Queen's permission to send those few ships out.

She sat in the embrasure watching the horsemen, without seeing them until they were half-way across. She got up and knelt on the padded window-seat. Her long yellow wool skirts lay in folds about her, sweeping the floor. She pressed her face against the small pane, wishing the glass were clear and did not distort so heavily.

Surely it was Richard Grenville. She recognised the way he carried his head, his broad shoulders, the bold fashion he sat his horse. She waited breathlessly, not stirring. Only her fingers moved restlessly crumpling her handkerchief into a ball in the hollow of her hand.

The riders came to the bridge-head, paused for a moment. Some rode off to the left. A group of four rode swiftly to the outer gate and entered the court-yard of Grenville House.

She ran quickly down the passage to her room, straightened her blond curls, dusted her face with rice powder and slipped a long furred robe over her yellow gown. She stood for a moment scanning herself in the mirror. What she saw satisfied her.

She walked slowly down the hall and waited. A moment later she heard Richard's voice. He was in the entrance hall speaking to the footman. "Lady Grenville here?" she heard him inquire.

"Sir, no. Dame Philippa came from London yesterday.

Her Ladyship is to arrive Saturday next. She and the young ladies are visiting in London and at Penshurst."

"I have just come from London. Strange I did not meet them there. They must have gone to Penshurst."

Dame Philippa leaned over the rail and looked into the hall below. Grenville's man was relieving him of his armour piece by piece, unlacing clasps and buckles, removing gorgets and shoulder-pieces.

"Welcome home, voyager!" she said.

Grenville looked up. "Philippa!" He ascended the steps two at a time. "I was disappointed not to find Mary here. It's good to see you, my dear."

He stood a step below her, looking up. "The voyage was a failure," he said abruptly. "I suppose you've heard."

"Yes. Drake brought your men home."

"Damn Drake! If Lane had waited a fortnight, our ships would have been in sight. Is he always to stand between me and accomplishment?"

Philippa put her hand on his shoulder. "Your destiny is far greater than Drake's. Why do you bother?"

He turned and went down the steps without answering.

They sat long at supper. The great banquet room was lighted only at the far end. They sat side by side before the many-paned window that opened on the river and the Long Bridge.

Richard Grenville spoke little. Wine-glass in hand, he looked absently on the river. Many boats were lined up on the opposite shore. They were being repaired and made ready.

" 'If the Spaniards come' . . . 'When the Spaniards come' . . . It seems to me I have heard nothing but the Spaniards since I came back. In London little else was spoken of—except Drake's exploits and the treasure he brought home to pour into the Queen's lap. What did Grenville bring home? Nothing but the disappointed men I carried out to enlarge our colony. I can see the sly smile on Drake's face.

"Lane is a fool, Philippa. I saw his report in London; also Master Thomas Hariot's record. Richard Hakluyt showed them to me."

Philippa started to speak, but she withheld comment. She realised that Richard was scarcely aware of her presence. The bitterness, the bile of his disappointment boiled at the surface. Better to let him talk without interruption. She was

448

alarmed at his thinness, his lined face, the look of tragedy in his eyes. She saw fully how deeply he had been hurt by the sorry fate of this first effort to seat a colony in Virginia.

"I had only ambitious dreams for the Virginia venture. Like Raleigh I saw a way to fame and glory: discovery, development of new land that would make England richer than before, visions of the extension of England. I saw, too, the pleasure of the Queen when we should out-distance Philip of Spain, beat him in his game of discovery. But I have failed in this as in other things. I would have been proud to add land and riches to England—to have pleased the Queen, to have laid a great colony at her feet, to have heard her words of praise."

Philippa said, "A Boleyn can bestow nothing on a Grenville, my dear. Anne's daughter has no power to add grace or prestige to one of your name."

Richard did not smile or show appreciation. He drank the glass of wine and reached for the decanter to pour another. The footman had been sent away with the admonition to leave a dozen candles in the cabinet, for he had writing to do.

"Lane is indeed a fool," Philippa said. "His talk in London is certainly a fool's talk. He has nothing to tell but what he might have done, *if——*"

"I know. A weak man soothes himself by excuses. A strong man takes the blame."

Philippa moved slightly. A candle sputtered and went out. She lighted it again from another. The light fell on her face. For the first time Grenville looked at her as though he saw her.

And in his blue eyes she thought she saw shining a curious flame, a blue flame. She had seen the color of burning driftwood that has floated in salt sea-water. She might be mistaken. It might have been the flame of the candle.

Her own feeling for him was changing. She tried to turn her mind to other things. But he was too near. She raised her eyes toward the window. It had grown dark outside. The window was a black mirror reflecting them. They were indeed equal, she and Richard Grenville, in colour, in stature. The yellow-green gown she wore blended against the great Aubusson tapestry that hung on the stone wall of the banqueting room opposite the window. The two of them fitted in with the knights and ladies of the hunting scene depicted in wool.

Richard sat looking at her. She saw him turn his head to watch her. Once he reached out his hand to touch her arm, but he drew it back again and shook his head slightly. He did not know she saw him reflected in the window.

A great moon began to rise. Richard stood. "Let us walk in the garden. My man tells me that the orangery is at its best."

"Will it not be too dark to see the display?"

"I don't think so. We will have candles brought."

Philippa followed Grenville down the long hall out into the high-walled garden.

Grenville did not speak. He held a candle protected by circular glass set in iron. It gave a feeble light. She moved beside him without effort, although he did not shorten his stride. She had caught up a dark cloak from a chair as they passed down the hall. She drew the cloak closely about her. The wind from the river was cold.

The footman was bolting the heavy oak gate set in the high stone wall. Grenville called to him to fetch candles—and a decanter of wine, he added as an afterthought. The lackey hurried away.

They walked up and down the garden path. The moon cast a pale light on the garden, making it unreal, filled with mystery of night. The pleasant odour of spices seemed to hang in the air. The shuffling of horses' feet on the cobbled road was far away.

Richard looked at the moon. It was at the full. It brought to his mind memories of a moon shining on the water behind the island. He had thought even the moon was untamed then, amid the towering spires of pine trees, while the air pulsed with the low strange screeches of water-fowl, the eerie hooting of an owl, the shrill cry of a bird before the jaws of a savage animal closed.

The moon he saw tonight was an orderly moon in a cloudless sky. The garden, too, was orderly, with its paths neatly bordered in yew and its hedges that hid the stone wall. Even the stone benches at the end of the path fitted into the well-ordered pattern. This was Mary's garden. Only the orangery was his. He had had it built ten years before after a visit to Italy.

His thoughts were interrupted by Philippa's voice. "You are sad, Richard, too sad. This one voyage is neither the begin-

450

ning nor the end. There are other ships and other men and other voyages."

"You speak as a woman trying to bring comfort. I cannot sleep at night for remembering that deserted island. I cannot sleep seeing in my mind Drake carrying away my people and sitting in his cabin laughing, laughing. I think I can never smile while Drake lives in my house, destroying the enterprise I built. Drake! May God blast him! I will find a way to level the score."

Philippa was alarmed at the violence of Richard's tone and words. She must break this mood, this black destructive rage. But she would have to be cautious. He would brook no interference. She saw him now as others had seen him, arrogant, prideful, a man to walk his way without regard.

In his very arrogance he was dear to her. Once when they were very young, he had come to tell of some childish trouble. She had forgotten the reason, but she remembered through the years the weight of his head on her knees while her hand stroked the blond hair.

Now she longed to take him in her arms and hold him close. She yearned to take away the hurt, the bitterness of defeat. But she dare not move or speak, for fear he would retreat from her. He would never talk to Mary. His feeling for her was too protective, too gentle. Philippa must be watchful lest in her eagerness to serve him she close himself away from her. He was like that—so strong, so unwilling to show weakness or accept help. That was his character; it was also his knightly code. Every word she uttered must be guarded. O merciful Lord, guide her and give her wisdom!

Without words they moved down the long path. The candle gave a thin light. The small panes of the orangery windows were overlaid with a leaden design. The light reflected in the bull's-eye panes was caught and imprisoned in diminishing circles.

She shivered and drew her mantle close. "Do you feel cool, Philippa? Let us go into the orangery. It will be warm." He opened the door. The heavy fragrance of blossoming oranges came to them, a fragrance sweet, almost overpowering. They walked among the little trees and came to the small cabinet, to which Grenville retired when he worked with his papers or studied his books on orcharding and the making of gardens.

A table was there, three or four chairs, a great seat of oak

451

covered with soft leather from Cordova. Two candle-stands were on a long table. A little fire of peat burned in the fireplace. Over the mantel-board was a plaster-work crest of the Grenvilles. The moonlight came into the room from windows high above the mantel-board. The footman brought the candles and wine and withdrew.

It was a small room, but it bore the stamp of Richard Grenville. Folios and quartos, models of ships, a book opened to a piece on grafting garden trees—all as he had left them when he went away to Virginia.

Philippa sat in the great chair near the hearth. The silence grew unbearable. She said, "Richard, what are you going to do about John Arundell and Thomasine?"

He stopped his pacing. It took a moment before he brought his thoughts upon her question. "John is only a little beyond twenty. When he is twenty-one he shall marry Thomasine. It will be a suitable match. Thomasine has a goodly dower, with several manors. John will need her dower, for he does not come into any great inheritance until he is twenty-five."

"And what will you do with Colin?" she questioned.

Grenville's face clouded. "Philippa, I don't know. I thought Colin's destiny would lie in the New World. Now I'm not so sure."

"He will have strength and character," Philippa said thoughtfully. "The Grenville blood runs strong in him."

"I know. He has more than proved himself. But many other young lads proved themselves."

"Thomasine is in love with Colin." She hesitated; perhaps this was not the part of wisdom.

Grenville scowled. The old black look was in his face. "Thomasine doesn't know her mind. She will love John Arundell as readily as she will love Colin. Thomasine is my ward. She will marry whomever I desire. I will select the man who will be her husband, as though she were my daughter. She and John are of the same noble house. It is a suitable marriage, I say." He leaned toward her. "What has come over you, Philippa? All this talk about love! A year ago you would have scoffed at love as a plaything for a worldly woman."

Philippa said nothing.

"Can it be that you love, my dear Philippa?"

"Why do you ask?" Her voice was low.

"If you love Philip Sidney, it is useless. Sidney will never love anyone but Penelope; not his young wife or the women who kneel at his feet. Perhaps I should not talk to you in this way, but I don't want you to be hurt. I am not blind. I saw you together here in this house. I think he came to your bed that night."

Philippa flashed a look at him. "And if he did?"

He said, "I have no control over you, my dear, nor do I wish to interfere." He moved about the room, closing the door to a small cabinet, turning over the leaves of a book. "Perhaps I envied Sidney."

The scent of orange blossoms was heavy on the air. Philippa's eyes were cast down. She had allowed the dark mantle to fall from her. Her bare shoulders were very white and well modelled.

He touched her shoulder gently. "Perhaps I envied him," he repeated.

Philippa was trembling. Something in the sadness of his voice hurt her, roused in her a passion of tenderness. "You need not envy any man, my dear."

He moved over to her side. "Do you mean that, Philippa?"

She did not raise her eyes. There was a swift urgency in his voice. She rose and walked across the room and stood beside the rows of orange trees. She stripped blossoms from the rounded bush and held the white beauty against her cheek. What had she said . . . what was she doing . . . after all the long months of telling herself that she must never let him know how passionately she loved him?

Grenville leaned over the table and blew out the candles. Then he came to her swiftly and took her in his arms.

The scent of oranges rose strong, a heavy fragrance drowning her senses, blotting out reality.

"My dear, my dear, my need of you is very great."

She stirred in his arms, pressing against his strong lithe body. She wanted to tell him how long she had waited, but his lips were hard on hers. She could not speak. She could only give herself to the violence of his passion.

The herald of Elizabeth the Queen came next morning while they were at breakfast. Grenville opened the parchment, glanced at it and passed it to Philippa.

The Queen
  to Sir Richard Grenville:
Whereas We have some occasion offered to us by reason of

453

certain ships of Spain that came about Scotland and the West of Ireland . . . we mean to rendezvous in the River Severn and send ships to Waterford or Cork in Ireland. We have made choice of you for this service following:

We require you to make all shipping on the north coasts of Devon and Cornwall meet for transport of soldiers to Ireland . . . to give charge that it be made ready with masters, mariners and maritime provisions. . . .

So on the next warning from Us or Our Council be prepared to sail. Sir Walter Raleigh, Knight, will inform you when for Our service to pass into Ireland.

Philippa pushed back her fruit. Her corn-flower blue eyes were filled with fear. "What does it mean?" she whispered. She knew well enough. He got up and led her to the window-seat. She sat, her back against the window, he beside her. The orange blossoms she had thrust into her bodice moved slightly with her breathing.

"You know, Philippa. By tomorrow I will be gone."

"Alone?"

"I and my young gentlemen-at-arms, John Arundell, Colin and Dick Prideaux. This is the beginning of something portentous for England. We may lose to superior ships and vast armies, but whatever happens, we will lose greatly." He lifted her hand to his lips. "You will not forget, Philippa?"

She pressed her hand over his. "Between us, Richard, there will be no forgetting. Oh, my dear, my dear!"

He lifted her face in his cupped hand. "No tears, my sweet. You must help me gird my armour and buckle on my sword, a smile on your sweet lips." He bent and kissed her mouth.

When Grenville was ready to leave, Philippa helped him with his sword. He drew the blade from the scabbard and held it aloft. "I leave my sword to him who can get it." He smiled but there was no gay lilt in his voice.

A feeling of desolation came over her. She would never know which came first with him—love of a fight on the sea or of a battle on the land. Whichever it was, love of woman came after. She must wait, for that was the part of women who loved the Grenville men. She, Philippa, would be one of the company who waited . . . with a smile on her lips and black despair in the heart.

He turned to her then. "Your scarf as a gage of battle, after the old fashion?"

454

She unwrapped the green scarf from her throat and tied it around his arm, weaving it in and out of the leather band.

He sent his man out ahead to bring his stallion around to the door. He circled her waist with his two hands. He looked deep into her eyes, a long look, to keep her in his memory. "I have looked on you a thousand times, Philippa, but never as I look at you now. In all my life there has never been any woman like you. If there is nothing more in life for us, you will remember."

She put her hands in his. "I will always remember." She spoke the words solemnly, like a vow.

She watched him ride away from her over the Long Bridge, as she had seen him ride toward her such a short time before. The sun shone on his armour and the bright casque with its nodding plumes. She would see him no more. He would gather his men about him and set sail, as he had ridden away this morning, without a backward glance.

In the street she heard childish voices. Children were playing a game, dancing blithely and singing a little song:

"O western wind, when wilt thou blow?"

Philippa waited at the bowed window until the little company reached the far end of the Long Bridge, until she could no longer distinguish his brave figure, only the blue plume of his casque, floating.

She pressed the white blossoms to her lips. Whatever came, she would have no regrets.

CHAPTER 30
THE ARMADA

Grenville lingered in Ireland, together with Sir War-
ham St. Leger, his wife's cousin. They undertook to
secure for the Queen the country of Kerrywherry
and Kerrycurrihy and seven plough-lands in Ballingarry in
the County of Cork. He had a dwelling in the castle of
Carigroghan and, together with Alexander Arundell, John's
uncle, an estate of twenty-four hundred acres.

Here he fortified against Spanish invasion. The work being
finished to his satisfaction he departed for the court in London. He had been away from home for over six months and
he longed for his family and for Cornwall.

The household of Stowe longed for him. Mary his wife
had carried on the labour of the master with the help of
Ching. Their son Bernard was taking more and more of the
responsibility. John was in Bideford, where he spent his time
at the shipyards, with his young cousins at Annerly or with
the Dennys at Orleigh Court. He had given up the idea of
taking orders for the Church. The sea was calling. His father
had written from Ireland that the barque *Virgin God Save
Her* was to be his. It was his ambition to sail her to Virginia.

John sat in the Grenville pew near the altar in the Bideford church. It was the day when the Indian Okisko, whom
his father had fetched from Roanoke, was to be baptised, a
proper ceremony with the clergy present from near-by
parishes, Kilkhampton, Clovelly, Hartland and Buckland
Brewer.

Raleigh was the name to be given to the Indian, and the
great Sir Walter had sent a complete habit, made of elegant
material, braided and slashed in London fashion. The Queen
sent a golden chain, a duplicate of.those she had presented to
Manteo and Wanchese.

John watched the ceremony until he grew weary. Resting
his eyes on the tomb of his ancestor Sir Theobald, he fell to
thinking about the little dogs, carved in fair stone, that lay at

456

his feet. It was the little dogs that made Theobald come alive to him; not the recumbent figure of the knight, but the dogs he had loved. He thought, Will I be buried here at Bideford or at Kilkhampton? Will there be any puppies with me? He smiled. Remembering where he was, he covered his lips with his hand.

At last the ceremony was almost over. Bernard sat in his father's place, with Mary and her husband Arthur, and Lady Grenville dressed all in russet brown, her sable cape across her shoulders, looking straight ahead. She was very sad these days, John thought. He wished his father would come home from Ireland; failing that, he wished Dame Philippa would come down from London. She could always enliven the family with her wit, her tales of the court. Her lively letters were an event.

John let his glance roam about the church. There were some lovely women seated in the ancient pews. He supposed he would marry one of them, a Stukeley, a Denny or a Fortescue. He thought he would rather marry in Devon than in Cornwall. Perhaps his father would make a match for him with one of the Courtenays of Exeter.

His eyes fell on Thomasine, that little witch, sitting so demurely with cast-down eyes. He scarce recognized her of late. Dame Philippa had made her into a young gentlewoman. He liked her better as a hoyden, hawking or riding to the hounds. Bernard was glancing her way too. Good old Bernard! He had grown quite an old man since his father went to Ireland and he had taken on the responsibilities of Stowe. Bernard could be counted on to tread, in a kind of magnanimity, the honoured steps of his ancestors.

The rector droned on, and now the Vicar of Morwenstow mounted the pulpit. Thanks be to Heaven, he was a canny man; he knew that sermons must be short! Okisko must be tired waiting. John was. He would like to sail down to the Pool to look at his ship. . . .

Feeling a draft on his neck, he turned his head slightly. The Grenville door, by which the family entered the church, was being slowly opened. His father's powerful figure blocked the doorway. He entered. John Arundell and Colin followed.

Thomasine saw them at the same time John did. The expression on her face changed from surprise to swift pleasure. She did not look at John Arundell. Her eyes were all for Colin. What did that mean? Was she seeking excitement, shifting from one man to another like the women at court? John didn't think much of that. Thomasine could be fun, but she could scratch like a cat.

He could not see his mother. Bernard blocked his vision. His father had now seated himself beside Lady Mary. Quietly as he had moved into the pew, half the congregation of Bideford folk had seen him. They focussed their eyes on him instead of on the vicar. It was always this way. People turned to him. Merchant and squire, seamen on the quays, yeoman and husbandman touched their caps as he walked the streets of Bideford or rode along the country lanes.

John took pride in his father. He had heard men talk at Stowe. Once he had heard Sir Walter say that a new and dominant force had sprung up in England since the discovery of the New World: the "royal hearts," fearless men and true who fought the seas and conquered new lands.

His father was one of these. The sailor as well as the statesman had the ear of the Queen. His father was both. In Parliament his wise words had weight, and on the sea he was one of the great captains. Drake, John and William Hawkins, Frobisher were others.

What was it my Lord Bacon had said about Captain Drake? "He climbed a tree in Panama and saw both oceans. Again he had climbed a cliff at Terra del Fuego and leaned his head out over the southermost angle of the world."

John sighed. Another year to wait before he was old enough to chance the sea. He would have liked to sail to Virginia with Master John White, when he carried out a new colony.

He and Thomasine had talked it over. She, too, wanted to go to the New World. Master White, who was a Devon man, was taking women and children with him, as well as artisans and implements for farming and seeds for planting.

This was to be a permanent colony, Sir Walter had told him when he visited Stowe a week past. "You'll have your chance, John. I promise you that I'll take you with me when I go on a voyage." John had thrilled at the great man's words.

The sermon was over. It had not been too tiresome. Now Okisko stood up. His sponsors rose to stand beside him, Sir John Stukeley and a man John did not know. His father also rose and walked across in front of the altar.

The Indian saw him. A quick smile crossed his lips. John

thought, Even that stoical being has love for my father. He has a true and princely mind, has my father, even as great loyalty as Sir Theobald, the ancestor who lies there at the altar.

He thought of the words of an old ballad about an earlier Grenville. The Grenvilles never would be free of Mars. The name would go on in the service of Mars, the god of war.

He sighed. A burden was upon him, and upon Bernard, to carry on the Grenville name. Here near him lay another Richard, who had had the overlordship of Bideford far back in the year 1200, holding three and a half knight's fees. Suddenly John felt oppressed by all the men of his name who were buried here.

The rector was sprinkling the holy water on Okisko's head. It splashed his hair black as channel coal and trickled down his red-bronze cheek.

The prayers were said. The Indian knelt. When he rose, his name was no longer heathen Okisko, but Christian, a name as great as any in England, Raleigh.

The Rector of Clovelly said the last prayer, and the congregation moved slowly out of the church. They lingered at the door in little groups and knots to greet Sir Richard, gone these long months in wild Ireland amongst the rebels.

Lady Grenville clung to his arm. Catherine was on one side with her betrothed, Justinian Abbott of Hartland Abbey, standing near by.

His father would miss little Mary. Arthur Tremayne had carried her away to Collacombe. It was well. Arthur had always yearned after Thomasine.

John Grenville walked with the others to the Norman door. When he stepped outside, he saw horsemen galloping across the bridge. A press of people followed, running along shouting and yelling, "The Spanish are here! The Spanish are here!"

The messenger jumped from his horse and ran up the stone steps that led from the street to the chapel. Several boys followed him, shouting shrilly, "There's Sir Richard! There's Sir Richard! He will save us from the Spanish dogs."

The herald doffed his cap and handed the scroll to Sir Richard.

Grenville unrolled the parchment and read its brief contents. He descended to the ground and walked to the retaining wall that surrounded the churchyard. He stood on the wall to speak to the press of people in the street below. The congregation had followed him. They grouped around him. The people waited in breathless silence for him to speak.

He raised his voice so all might hear. His voice carried to the citizens who stood at the bridge-head.

"An alarm is sounded for all England to rise and defend her shores. I have here a summons from Sir Francis Drake, Admiral of England. He calls all true Devon folk to the defence of the Realm.

"The Spanish galleons have been sighted in the Channel, a mighty force of ships which they call the Invincible Armada."

He rolled the paper and handed it to John. "Gather together on the quay, you men of Bideford! Call out, you who will volunteer to man our Bideford ships!"

A mighty shout rose from the street, from all the length of the bridge. Men were running across from East the Water and along the quay. The crowd was growing more dense each moment.

Sir Richard said to his wife, "I must meet with the Corporation, Mary, to tell them the plans for the defence of the North Devon coast. I talked them over with Walter and Francis Drake in London. I did not have time to meet with the Corporation here. Now this news arrives." He smiled a little. "But it is not unexpected."

The church bell began to ring—three short peals and a pause, then three short peals again.

Urgency was in the sound of alarm. He turned to the herald. "You must be weary from your long ride, sir. Come to Grenville House. Food and sleep will set you aright." He looked at the lad with more attention. "I seem to remember your face. Do I know you?"

"Sir, my name is Amadas. It is my brother Philip's face that lingers in your mind."

Grenville smiled, "Yes, yes, my dear and loving friend Philip Amadas." He put his hand on the lad's shoulder. "Walk in your brother's footsteps, my lad, for he has greatness in him."

"Sir, Philip has already joined Sir Frances at Plymouth. Every ship, every hulk, every fishing boat in South Devon and the coast of Cornwall is in the water, ready to sail."

"North Devon will follow. In Cornwall ships are waiting for the signal from Lundy Light to Padstow."

They walked toward Grenville House. Thomasine held her skirts daintily. John Arundell was on one side of her, Colin on the other. John, ignoring Colin's presence, said, "Thomasine, I thought we would have the banns said at once."

Thomasine glanced up from under her long dark lashes in a manner she had observed when she visited London last year. "Sir Richard says there will be no talk of marriage until we are rid of the Spanish."

Colin drew a long breath.

Sir Richard kissed his wife when they stepped into the hall. "My dear, when we have beaten the Spanish back from our coast, I will be home—this time to stay."

Mary's lips quivered. "Oh, my husband, will it always be like this—you going away to some unknown danger while I wait and wait, full of fears?"

"No, no, my dear wife. When I return, we will go to Stowe. But alas, I have now only this moment for you, my dear!" His hands about her waist, he lifted her off the floor and kissed her lips.

"John, you are to take out the *Virgin God Save Her*. Bernard, watch over your dear mother and the children. Colin and John Arundell, be at dock side in half an hour. You left your gear on the ship?"

They both spoke at once. "Yes, Sir Richard."

"Where's Prideaux?"

"On the *Tyger*, sir, waiting."

"Good! You sail with the tide so we may go over the bar readily. Young Amadas, will you join our ship?"

The boy's face was wreathed in smiles. "To sail on the great Grenville's ship! Oh, sir! Sir!"

"Thomasine, we'll talk of weddings when I return."

He was gone, the door slamming after him. Colin slipped away, leaving John Arundell and Thomasine together.

Lady Grenville walked quickly to the window. She had a view of the river and the bridge. She did not see her husband. He must have gone down the street. She turned and went upstairs, taking no notice of Thomasine and Black John who sat in the window-seat on the far side of the door. She walked slowly, her russet skirts trailing behind her.

Grenville stalked quickly in the garden, looking neither to right nor left. He opened the door of the orangery and went in. He stood for a moment looking at the rows of neatly

461

trimmed trees, some white with bloom, others with golden fruit. For a brief instant only, his eyes travelled to the room where he and Philippa had known such rapture.

He let himself out the gate cut in the high wall, where his men and his horses waited, and rode down the quay.

Colin finished packing his small kit in a few minutes. From his room he heard the sound of excited voices raised in the streets, the surging back and forth of the press. He went to the window. Men carrying sea-chests on their shoulders were walking swiftly, while women hung on their arms and children clutched their coats.

All the movement was toward the quay. Several small ships were ready there to take the men to Appledore Pool, where the great ships lay.

Colin ran down the stairs. A painful depression came over him. John Arundell had his arms about Thomasine. His dark head was bent over hers. She broke from his embrace when she saw Colin.

John shouldered his bag. "Where the devil is my man?" he grumbled.

"Waiting outside," Colin said. His eyes met Thomasine's and for a moment they held. Then she looked away.

She made a curtsy, deep, with all her new grace emphasised. "I wish you good fortune, Colin," she said gently, "very good fortune."

Colin bowed stiffly and moved toward the door. John went out first. Colin turned as he closed the door. Thomasine was standing in the center of the hall, her hands clasped above her breasts. "Colin," she whispered. "Colin."

The blood rushed to his face. "Good-bye, good-bye. God keep you, Thomasine!"

"Call me 'little witch,' " she whispered; "little witch, as you did that night at the stone house on the hill."

"You are a witch," he said huskily. "You lure men to you. You are bound to John, my friend who trusts me. Oh, my dear, let me go before I lose all sense of honour, of manhood. Let me go, Thomasine."

She stood close, looking up at him. Her dark eyes seemed to Colin to burn red. "I will not let you go. Remember, you wear my brand—on your hand and in your heart."

He turned and walked quickly away. His face was white. His hands were clenched.

462

Thomasine watched him go. A little smile played on her full lips. "He loves me," she said aloud.

The quay was bursting with excitement. Every lip was repeating Drake's "Burn the Spanish king's beard!" . . . "Down with the devils!"

Colin and John found a boat waiting at the water-steps.

Every small boat, every fishing boat, every available ship was being manned as quickly as names could be called and entered into the ledgers. Clerks sat at tables checking. Food wagons drove up. The river was crawling with small craft. From Bideford Bay to Hartland Point it was the same. If the Spanish descended on the West Country, men were ready.

They found young Amadas on the deck of the *Tyger*. About him were a dozen Bideford boys. He was telling a tale about Drake.

"He was playing at bowls on the Hoe when a pirate landed on the Barbican. The pirate had been cruising off the Lizard when he caught sight of the Spanish fleet in the Channel. He sailed for Plymouth to warn the people. The mayor ran to the Hoe crying, 'The Spaniards are coming! The Spaniards are coming!'

"My brother Philip was playing with Sir Francis. My brother told me that the admiral never turned a hair. 'Let us go on with the game, gentlemen,' were his words, and they did. He finished the game of bowls, right there on the Hoe."

The lad paused and looked quickly over his shoulder. "Then a strange thing happened. There's magic in it, sirs. The admiral threw the balls over into the Haven." The lad's eyes grew round, his voice shook. "When they looked again, they saw ships lying in the water—a ship for every ball he threw."

Breathless silence followed. "He is a sorcerer!" . . . "A Merlin!" . . . "No Spaniard can touch him." But the voices that uttered the words trembled, and faces were grave and troubled.

The little fleet from Bideford sailed on the tide, down the river, over the bar, out into the bay and onto the wild sea: the galleon *Dudley*, Captain James Grifey, which had been the *Santa Maria*, the ship Grenville took in the Indies; the *Virgin God Save Her*, with John Grenville commanding; the *Tyger*, which was the admiral; the barque *St. Leger*, captained by John St. Leger of Annerly; the barque *Fleming*, sometime called the *Golden Hind*, with Fleming captain.

Following the major ships came pinnaces and small barques and the fishing fleet. The sky was crimson, with angry clouds across the horizon. They crossed the bar. They came into the stormy Atlantic to meet King Philip's Invincible Armada.

The storm grew in the night and high winds beat the Channel. The Spaniards mistook a promontory for Land's End and all but grounded the first ship.

Grenville saw his fleet sail. His horse was waiting. He mounted and rode straight for London to take up his duties as one of the nine councillors to the Queen.

Then, back to the West Country, he rode from one weak spot to another, strengthening defences. He had raised three hundred men at his own cost in the army of seven thousand five hundred. And so it was that Grenville defended the land while Francis Drake sailed out in his staunch ship the *Revenge*. Lord Thomas Howard, Admiral Drake and the God of Storms defeated the Spaniards. Some say the God of Storms made the greatest fight.

The winds drove Spanish ships around through the North Sea to be shattered on the rocky islands of Scotland and the coast of Ireland, and so it came that no Spaniard put foot on the West Country shores. But Spanish ships were wrecked on the wild Cornish coast. Spanish corpses drifted in onto the strands, and galleons were ground to pieces on shelving cliffs. The tides brought beams and bones of ships and gilded planks into Bideford Bay for the country folk to salvage and build into their homes. And the name of Drake rose to the sky.

Philippa wrote to Lady Grenville to tell her how the people of London rejoiced at the death of Spain's great Armada:

And Elizabeth, in the manner of the ancient Roman emperors, rode into London to give praise to God for her own and her subjects' glorious deliverance. In robes of state she was carried through London in a triumphal chariot from the Palace to the Cathedral of St. Paul.

We had a good place in the cathedral. We saw the ensigns and colours of the vanquished Spaniards displayed.

The citizens of London stood on one side of the street, proud in the liveries of their several companies. The street was hung with blue cloth, and with the banners made a stately and gallant prospect. We saw many we knew in the cathedral. I knelt beside Mary Sidney while the Queen said prayers at Paul's Cross. I think we both prayed for Philip. I do not cease to regret his early death, a loss to England beyond all enduring. Only two years ago people went to see his funeral ship, draped in black with black sails, come up the Thames. But people forget. Now was a day of thanksgiving.

The Queen herself exhorted the people to render the glory to God and extol God's name in thanksgiving. The people answered in a great litany of praise and gratitude.

Women waited on the cliffs of Hartland and watched the sea bring in the wrecked ships of Spain and the Spanish dead. When the toll of great ships was counted, of the one hundred and fifty sail which had left Coruña, fifty-four came back.

Richard Hakluyt sat in his chambers in the Temple and wrote in his great book:

Thus the magnificent, huge and mighty fleet of the Spaniards, which they termed at all places invincible, such as had sailed not upon the Ocean Sea for many hundred years before, in the year 1588 vanished into smoke.

Again to Ireland went Sir Richard, his aides with him. Sir Walter Raleigh went along and many of the cadets of great families.

The Queen was giving out her rewards, and Irish land cost her nothing.

Lady Grenville accompanied her husband. Thomasine went to London to be with Philippa. Spring planting time came again. Stowe remained closed.

In late summer Dame Philippa decided to establish herself for a time in Plymouth. There was an old house there that had belonged to the Tremaynes, her dead husband's people, over beyond the fortifications to the west.

Thomasine went with her. She was quieter now. She had learned to make her manners gracefully when she went out among Philippa's friends; to listen to gossip and not repeat. Thomasine never spoke of John Arundell or of Colin. Philippa let her go her own way in that matter. She could not make the girl out.

Thomasine, on the other hand, thought Philippa sorrowed

465

for Sir Philip Sidney. When Philippa suggested Plymouth, Thomasine thought she wanted to get away from London and all that reminded her of that noble gentleman. People spoke of him as a man cast in heroic mould; how, dying on the battle-field, he had passed his cup of cold water to a wounded soldier saying, "Thy need is greater than mine."

"Whom the gods love die young," Philippa had said one day as she sat reading in the garden. Thomasine was close by, sewing a long seam in a linen skirt.

They were both silent for a long time. Suddenly Thomasine said, "If I could only go to Merlin's cave, I would know . . ."

Philippa looked up from her folio. "Know what, my dear?"

"The old man would make his magic smoke. Then I would know what the future holds."

Philippa looked at her strangely. "Where is the sorcerer who makes pictures in smoke?"

"Uther is his name. He dwells at Tintagel in the great cave at the base of the cliffs below King Arthur's castle." She leaned forward, her eyes shining. "Some old wives say he is Merlin himself. . . . I don't know. I know only that he sees out beyond." She stopped, gave Philippa a quick glance. "Do you think me a silly?"

"No, Thomasine, no. Shall we start in the morning? I will order the horses. We will spend the night at Trerice, the Arundells' seat. Then you will see for yourself the house that may one day be yours and John's."

Thomasine flushed but made no comment.

In the early morning they rode out of the court-yard. Philippa's woman and her steward rode in her coach. The leather-covered boxes that held their habits were strapped on the boot. The coachman drove out the gates, a footman beside him; the lackey jumped to the seat on the rear.

They came to Tintagel the second evening at sunset. They left the tire-woman and the coach at the inn and rode directly to the cliffs across from King Arthur's castle. A deep declivity divided the land, ending in rocky shingle.

Thomasine rode first, calling a greeting to shepherd and herd-boy as she went. They came to a slate-covered cottage near the edge of the cliff. Farmer Wyatt and his wife Elsie ran out to greet her. The woman embraced Thomasine. "My child! My little child!" she cried, tears streaming from her eyes.

466

"Elsie is my nurse," Thomasine explained to Philippa.

The groom rode up and assisted Philippa to dismount, making a saddle with his hands. The sea-wind was blowing from the west. Salt touched her lips and stung her eyes.

The woman curtsied to Philippa and made her welcome. Wyatt showed the grooms where to stable the horses for the night.

They entered the cottage, and Elsie showed them to a neat room with a slate floor. Two small beds, each covered with a woven counterpane, two chairs and a carved chest made up the furnishing.

"Tea will be ready in a moment, mistress," she said to Thomasine.

Thomasine followed her when she left the room. "I want to go to the cave," she said, "directly after we have eaten."

They made their way down the stone steps cut in the cliff. The tide was high. The waves beat against the giant cliffs and broke into spray, running a mill-race between the great rocks that stood in the water like the Pillars of Hercules.

Thomasine walked ahead. She had taken off her habit and put on a blue skirt and bodice of white, such as farm girls wear. She was without shoes or hosen, and her dark hair hung loose to her waist. She had a lanthorn in her hand. They left Wyatt seated in a cranny in the rocks half-way down the steps.

Thomasine took Philippa's hand. She walked along a little ledge in the cliff that hung out over the water. The tide was rushing below, through the narrow cleft in the rock. They came to an opening so low they must stoop to enter. They were inside a great cavern, black as Erebus.

Philippa uttered a little cry.

"You will see in a few minutes," Thomasine whispered. "Do not fear. I know the place well. I could walk through with my eyes shut. See? Yonder is Uther's fire—the fire with which he makes the smoke."

Philippa saw at some distance a feeble glimmer of light.

Thomasine raised her voice: "Uther! Uther! It is I, Thomasine."

A hollow voice answered which at first Philippa thought was an echo. "Thomasine, I knew you were coming. I saw you riding. There is a woman with you whose hair is the color of ripe maize."

467

Philippa stood quite still. Terror flooded her veins and turned her cold.

"Come to my fire, if you must know the future." A man rose from a stone and stood beside the fire, a tall man, incredibly thin, with great eyes that burned in the firelight.

"Do not fear Uther. Fear only the future, lady. Sit." He motioned to a bench cut from the stone of the wall.

"Thank you," Philippa managed to say.

Thomasine was at ease, almost gay. "I am older now, Uther. I want my future. You promised me you would tell me when I was a woman."

"You are still too young to know your mind, Thomasine. It wavers like the tide between the rocks, rushing in and rushing out. A blond man and a man whose hair is dark. Why must you choose? Wait! Wait!"

Thomasine was silent. After a time she said, "Won't you tell me my future in the smoke?"

"No need, little miss. Your future is plain. You will waver, waver, and not know your mind. Come to me when you are a woman grown."

He turned his thin face with its burning eyes to Philippa. The fire seemed to glow and send out a radiance. There was no flame. "The lady wants to see ahead. . . . Sometimes it is not wise. Have you courage?"

"I have courage." Philippa's voice was firm.

He lifted a vial from a shelf in the rock and poured it on the flame.

The smoke poured out and filled the room. The man crouched at the fire. After a time he raised his voice. It was toneless, without vibration, a dead voice. "I will obtain an answer from the spirits I invoke."

The rock wall of the cave was at their backs. Thomasine drew close to Philippa and caught her arm. Philippa's eyes were fixed on the vial the man held. What was he saying? Was he exorcizing the Devil with his black art? A tremor of fear passed through her body. Her hands and feet were cold. Moisture came onto her forehead. She started to rise, but she could not move. She raised her eyes. There was a little light coming through the entrance of the cave. She heard the great roar of the ocean rushing between the rocks. Rhythm of the ocean beat in her temples. Her wrists pounded. Her vitals were clutched by terror. The girl beside her sat with eyes fixed on the flame.

The shape beside the fire had no outline, no substance. It was a wavering column of smoke, seeming to rise to the roof of the cave and spread, making a fog.

A voice came through the murk. "Emperor of the Legions of the Spirits of the West, Mighty Behemoth——"

Philippa struggled to move. She was as stone.

"Appear! Appear, attended by Ashtoreth, thy unvanquished consort! Appear! Appear, I adjure you by the secrets of the Styx, by the depths of darkness, by the wandering stars, by Hecate's deep silence, come! Appear, resplendent and lovely!"

There was a strong sighing, like the wind in a storm. The light flickered and burned low. The wild "seed of vapour" flashed. Philippa saw figures moving in it—a ship, a great cliff beyond . . . smoke from deck guns . . . a man lying on the deck, a wounded man.

Another knelt at his side.

Another flash closed them from her sight. When she looked again, two men lay on the deck. They were still . . . still as death.

She struggled and cried out. She was released from the spell. Thomasine caught her arm. "There was nothing—no future in the smoke. Oh, Philippa, I am sorry. Uther," she cried, "why was there no future?"

There was no answer, only an echo against the rocky walls of the cave.

CHAPTER 31
BATTLE OF THE REVENGE

English waters were clear of the ships of Spain, but on the Plate Route Spanish galleons still sailed, carrying the wealth of the New World.

This irked the Queen's ministers. Why should English sea-captains stop at home, farming land, building water flumes, lingering about the court, listening to plaudits for past ventures? Let them go out and seek the Spanish ships with their rich cargo of hides, gold and pearls. Let them cross the Equator, the "Burning Line" of the mariners, to trade with Brazil, open new trade routes, intercept the Spanish. It was well known that the silver and gold of Peru was brought overland to Porto Bello or Cartagena, then by the Plate Route to Spain. The first stop of the ships that sailed the route was at Havana, the next at the Azores. So let English ships hover about the Azores. When the galleons came in for sweet water, to repair damages or take sick men ashore, they would be off guard, an easy prey.

The Queen listened to her ministers. Avarice was strong in her. She called in her sea-captains, the men who had fought the Invincible Armada, the men who had sailed into all the seas of the world, and the men who had seated the colony in Virginia. They must now set sail again, hide in the shadow of the rocky cliffs of the Azores and wait to fall upon the richly laden flotas, before Philip of Spain could send armed ships to cover and defend them.

Richard Grenville was called home from Ireland by the Queen's order and made Vice-Admiral to Lord Thomas Howard. He was given a ship, the *Revenge,* the same ship Admiral Drake had sailed when he went out into the Channel to meet the Armada. She was fast and sailed well, but she had been a ship of bad luck from the day she was built. Only Drake's good fortune had outweighed the ill fortune of the *Revenge.* Now Grenville had her, but was he also fortune's child?

470

There was a great reunion at Stowe, when Sir Richard came back. He had been to London, where he and Lord Thomas Howard had called on the Queen and kissed hands on March 10, 1591. They had their instructions from Walsingham to sail for the tropics. Grenville would have been pleased to linger at Stowe for a little time, but the Queen was impatient. She needed gold, and it gave her pleasure to seize gold from Philip of Spain. Again Grenville would take with him, as his gentlemen-at-arms, John Arundell and Colin. Dick Prideaux he would leave behind, for he was soon coming of age; he moved his belongings from Stowe to New Place, the home of his people. Philip Blount was still in Ireland.

The last week of Grenville's stay at Stowe he yielded to John Arundell's pleas and made public the approaching marriage of John and Thomasine. They would be married on Sir Richard's return from the Azores.

Colin had slipped into his new position at Stowe with small difficulty. Even old Pooley the shepherd and Nurse Marjory called him Master Colin. He listened to the good wishes that were showered on John and Thomasine. He entered with zest into the gaieties that followed the announcement, the dancing and the merry-making. He laughed with the jolly company of young men and women who came to the betrothal ceremonies. But his heart was dead within him.

John went about in a dream. He could not keep his eyes from Thomasine's face. She was quiet and demure. Lady Grenville thought her conduct exactly suitable for a young lady. She was very pleased with Thomasine's improvement. But like Dame Philippa she knew nothing of what went on in the girl's mind.

Only Sir Richard guessed. He called Thomasine to his cabinet, one evening not long before he left, and questioned her. "I am your guardian, my dear. I stand in place of your father. I want to do for you what I would do for my own daughters. John is a good boy, trustworthy, honest. It is in every way a suitable marriage. You have an ample dower. John has many manors and much land. You are certain to be happy if you put your mind to it. I'm sure of John. . . ."

Grenville smiled as he looked at Thomasine's downcast eyes, her solemn face. "I'm not so sure of you, Thomasine. Is your new dignity of the surface only? Are you wild at heart?"

She glanced up swiftly to see if he were mocking her. His

smile was gentle and affectionate. "Oh, Sir Richard, I fear I am wild at heart. . . . Will I make John happy?"

"If you try, my dear—and if there is no other man in your heart."

She was silent for a moment. "There is no one else—not now."

Grenville watched the changing expression on her mobile face. It must be Colin, he thought, but that will not do. Colin belongs to the New World, she and John belong to the Old.

He laid his hand for a moment on her shoulder when she rose to leave. "My dear, you can make your own happiness, and the happiness of those about you, but in matters of marriage it has always been the custom to accept the decision of parents or guardians. There are other things to consider besides youthful emotion. You understand, don't you?"

Thomasine hesitated a moment. "I will try to understand," she said. "I wish Dame Philippa were here. She is so good, so understanding. I think she is the most wonderful woman in the world."

Grenville said, "I will tell her what you have told me. She will be pleased."

"Is she coming to Stowe?" Thomasine's voice was eager.

"No, I do not believe she will come to Stowe before I leave. I was thinking of Plymouth. Perhaps she will be in Plymouth." He turned and took up some papers from his table.

Thomasine went away. She was vaguely troubled by something in his voice. She met Colin at the bottom of the stair. He had doublet and hosen and a blue velvet cape over his arm. He paused when he saw her and stood aside to allow her to pass up the stairs.

She lingered, standing on the first step, her hand on the railing. "Do you want to go to sea again?" she asked.

"Not particularly. But I want to be with Sir Richard."

"Would you rather be sailing to Virginia?"

His eyes brightened. "Yes, yes. I will voyage to Virginia one of these days. Nothing can deter me from this desire—not the fact that the savages killed those brave fifteen men from Sir Richard's ship who volunteered to stay on Roanoke, nor the fact that we do not know to this day what became of the colony Master John White took out four years ago."

"It would pleasure me to go to Virginia."

"You? Virginia?" He glanced at her gown of fine blue taffeta, at the ruffles of Honiton on her sleeves and ruff. "You?" he repeated.

Her eyes blazed at him. "Yes. Why not? Do you think I am always like this—bowing, holding out my fine petticoats, sitting demurely sewing a seam? Don't you remember me riding my pony on the moors? Don't you remember the harvest? . . ." She paused, frightened by his look.

"I remember too much," he said sadly. "I remember that you are betrothed to my good and loving friend John Arundell. I hope you will be very happy, Thomasine. He loves you dearly." Colin turned away so she would not see his face, lest he betray himself.

Neither spoke of the stone house. Perhaps she was afraid. Colin was afraid lest the old passion rise. He must think only of John, of John his dear friend.

Thomasine watched his changing expression. For a moment she was on the verge of speech. Then she turned and ran upstairs without speaking. Her eyes were clouded with tears.

They danced at Stowe that night. All North Devon and Cornwall were there to say farewell to Richard Grenville and wish him good fortune.

Before dawn he and his gentlemen rode up the hill to Kilkhampton, a brave sight surely: a small but goodly company clad in bright armour, with banners waving in the morning breeze. The vale of Coombe had never looked so beautiful, Sir Richard thought. The fields were turned, the fresh earth was planted for the harvest. His eyes rested on Stowe, walled and towered and secure, within which were his family and his possessions. His sons were growing to swift manhood, his two fine stalwart sons. He must take them with him on some voyage, or perhaps after this it would be better if he remained home at Stowe. Mary would like that—dear Mary, so occupied with her children, her household and the management of her own estates.

He glanced at Black John. He was biting his lips. Colin showed nothing in his face. . . . Colin . . . He must make more effort to know what went on inside Colin's head. On this voyage he would try to learn. He wondered sometimes about the lad's feeling for Thomasine. . . . The sun came over the moor. The strong Norman tower stood out, black and grim against the red sky of morning.

473

They rode into Plymouth by the eastern gate late the third day. The sailing master had brought the *Revenge* down the Thames and anchored her in the Pool. Tomorrow at sunrise they would sail for the Azores.

Philippa received Grenville in the little parlour on the second floor. The Barbican and the Pool were plainly visible from the mullioned window. The old black and white house where she lived had been built in the early days of Henry the Eighth, but it remained sound and comfortable. They sat by the window at the small table where they had supped, and talked of the voyage.

She said, "We have had a sorry record. I saw Martin Frobisher when he came in from the Azores in October year before last. He had taken two ships, both of them rich. He told me that the Spanish *flota*, which they had failed to intercept, did not carry the great treasure. He was sure the Spaniards would wait until last spring to send it. John Hawkins told me the same. He was wild to be at sea early. He was irked because the Queen countermanded his sailing orders. You know how he barks. He said, 'I am out of hope of ever performing any royal thing.' He spoke with bitterness, for he thought the treasure would measure up to five million ducats and we would be too late to catch them. We were. It got through just a year ago. When Frobisher and Hawkins were out again—Frobisher in the *Revenge,* now your ship lying in the Pool yonder—there was nothing for them to catch. All through the summer and into the autumn they waited, only to hear at last that the *flota* had been turned back by foul weather. And now there's a two-years' treasure fleet to come. You've heard all this. Will we be too late again?"

Grenville smoked his long pipe in silence. He felt they had been slow to organise. "My Lord of Cumberland is not ready yet. Lord Thomas says he will not wait."

"What ships do you have?" Philippa asked.

"The *Defiance* is the admiral. Then there are the vice-admiral, the *Revenge,* and the *Bonaventure,* the *Nonpareil.* These are five-hundred-ton ships. The *Crane* is two hundred and fifty tons, the *Charles* and the *Moon* are about seventy tons each, and there's the barque *Raleigh,* the victualler. We may have two more, the *Golden Lyon* and the *Foresight.* They are already off Flores."

"Is my Lord of Cumberland to join forces?"

"No, he will cruise off the coast of Spain. It is meagre business, Philippa. I don't like it—lying like birds of prey, waiting. I tried to get ships in North Devon. There was none available at Barnstaple or Bideford. Their hundred-tonners are in the Newfoundland trade. Padstow offered a fishing boat of twenty tons, but I refused it."

Philippa got up and went to the window. She wore a soft gown of yellow silk, embroidered in pearls. Her slim waist was set off by a deep-pointed bodice. Her yellow hair was wound about her head, a black ribband plaited in the heavy braids. She looked very young and altogether desirable.

Richard watched her. They both avoided speaking of the night at Grenville House. He wondered if anything so filled with ecstasy could be repeated. He tried to keep his mind on what she was saying.

It was late March. A soft breeze floated in through the window.

"I must make out with what we have at hand," he said after a silence. "I have trusty gentlemen with me. Captain Langhorne is my captain of soldiers."

"Have you any Bideford men on the *Revenge?*"

Grenville laughed. "Do you think I would sail without Bideford boys to man my ship?" He walked to the window and stood beside her, looking at his ship. The *Revenge* filled the eye. She was trim but she was staunch. She could fight.

Philippa said, "Are you pleased with the *Revenge?* Martin Frobisher told me she's a swift sailer."

"Drake's ship." He smiled without rancour. "Second best. What do you think?"

"I think whatever ship Richard Grenville commands becomes first."

"Ah, Philippa, you make me my own man again. It is always so. You know my needs." He let his hand fall on her arm.

She turned to him. "I have said to myself that we must hold things as they are. I have been close to heaven with you, but I must not press too hard against the doors. We are firm people, you and I. We must not give way and hurt those about us."

He stroked her arm slowly. "I know. I have said the same thing more than once. But tonight, tonight, I have another feeling so strong it will not be stilled—a premonition, a

475

warning of my doom. When I entered my cabin to-day, I saw a white sea bird caught in the window. I released it gently. It circled about me once and flew away."

"I do not believe old tales. It is not true. It cannot mean——" Philippa hesitated to speak the word "death."

"The same thing happened once before, when we were sailing from Hispaniola to Virginia. That was a warning, Philippa. I shall perish in the sea as my father perished in the sea. I have always known that. Do not look so sad, my sweet."

She thought then of Philip Sidney. He too, had looked into the future and had seen his doom. Now he was dead. Another thought rose, more terrifying: Merlin's black cave, the cloud of smoke, the figure lying dead—was it on the deck of a ship?

She turned to him, burying her face against his breast. His arms tightened about her. "There is still time," he said. His voice held laughter and swift excitement. "I am still a man, and very much your lover, my sweet Philippa."

Five months the English ships cruised about the Azores without seeing the Spanish flota. They captured a small merchant ship or two; then a larger prize that yielded ten thousand pounds sterling; but no ships from the Plate Route. They waited, and the men grew impatient. Lord Burghley sent out more victaulling ships, but there was not enough green food. The men of the English flotilla came down with an epidemic. The *Revenge* was hit so hard that more than half the crew were unable to stand up on the deck.

Grenville determined to take them ashore on one of the Portuguese islands and stand by to protect them. The Portuguese would sell food. He gave orders to sail for Flores.

Young Master Colin was put in charge of reconditioning the sick men, a hundred and twenty-three in all. Like Sir Richard he was solicitous in his care of these good fellows of Devon, whom he had learned to love well. With rest and fresh island fare his efforts were so well rewarded that after a week thirty-three had been returned to duty, a welcome addition to the depleted crew.

In the morning of August thirty-first Lord Thomas Howard signalled, "Spanish ships of war are in sight. Let the *Revenge* make ready to sail."

476

Grenville made his reply. He would not sail until the last man of his sick whom he had put ashore was safe back on board. Those on the *Revenge*, seeing the admiral and the other ships set sail, showed their misgiving.

Grenville's face was stern as he watched the small boats bring his men from the island to the *Revenge*.

"Steady now, lads!" called Colin. "Gently there! Lay old Tom along the sailing thwart, abaft of Waters and Jameson. You, Watkins and Jones, in the stern-sheets with the others!"

The seamen handled the water and provisions briskly. They cared for their mates tenderly. The Spanish squadron might be upon them, but they moved surely and smartly about the loading of the four boats. The long hours of ship and gun drill showed in their every movement.

Colin shouted, "Boatswain, call the look-outs from the ridge! We are ready to put off. Master John's and the gunner's boats are ready too."

In the ships across the small harbour boats were being hoisted. To the westward off the beach of Villa Franca, the *Defiance*, Admiral Lord Thomas Howard's flag-ship, embarked. The *Golden Lyon* and the *Bonaventure*, already making sail, stood across the harbour mouth, headed to the north-eastward.

They would take station, according to plan, between the victuallers and the ships of Spain.

"How stand they now?" Colin queried of the look-out as he came scrambling down the rocky foreshore.

"A scant three leagues to the southward, sir, holding close along the coast, as though the fools thought to find us with no watch aloft at all! They are formed in two columns here on the eastern coast. A third column stands on to the westward of the island. Do they aim to circle Flores and catch us in a trap 'twixt their fellows and the shore?" He laughed. "They know not our good *Revenge*."

"Nor our good Sir Richard, I vow." The boatswain called to the look-out, "Lay you two to one he has those three great galleons for prizes ere sundown."

"Not so, my lad," said Colin. "We will show them our heels, standing first to the north-eastward as though to run for England. Then having given them the slip, we will circle to the west and southward and lie in wait for the plate fleet from Havana."

"More of gold and less of hides, I say," the old boatswain

grumbled. "I relished not the stench of that last cargo."

" 'Twere a shame to let them off so," said a topsail hand, harking back from dreams of the booty in the flotas to the business of the Spanish men-of-war, now close at hand.

"Their admiral there in the lead must be one of the new Apostles, sixty guns or more, they say, and fifteen hundred tons of burthen. We could use a ship or two like her."

"Not for mine, for sure!" The boatswain was emphatic as the oarsmen bent to their task. "Let them have their high-cargued sides, their fancy-figured cannon and their gilded sterns. I'll put my trust in plain fast ships of stout English oak, nimble in stays, with a full outfit of good English ordnance. Bideford black is my colour. No gilded cedar nor painted sails for mine."

"Aye to that!" growled a bronzed seaman from Padstow, his seaways learned these twenty years in the snug little vessels of the pilchard fishing fleet and in the hard ships of the Queen's Navy.

Colin laughed in his heart at the tough assurance of these stout men of Devon, yeomen and harriers though they had been short months ago. Now trained and polished by the sailing master and the master gunner, they held a full measure of the pride that filled the English fleet—pride in their ships and in the glorious victory over the Invincible Armada three years before. Some of these men had served in the *Revenge* under Drake and Frobisher and Hawkins. Their skill and daring were examples to the newer crews.

"Too many husbandmen in the Navy," the boatswain muttered as an oar caught and slipped in the lock.

"The steward at Stowe says the same when he needs more men to plant." Colin laughed, knowing well how the demands of the fleet had drained England of her men.

Aboard the *Revenge* Sir Richard Grenville paced the breadth of the deck. He watched the *Defiance,* with Lord Thomas Howard clearing the headland on the starboard tack. He wondered what the manoeuvre meant. He turned away to observe his own boats coming from shore. He was impatient to get his ninety sick carried aboard. His boats had been the last to put off from the narrow beaches of the high and rocky shore of the Isle of Flores. He began to chafe at the delay, to wonder whether the luck of the *Revenge* were running true to form.

He recalled how Sir Richard Hawkins had described her as

"ever the unfortunatest ship the Queen had." Grenville remembered her coming out of Ireland with Sir John Perrot, when she was like to be cast away on the Kentish coast. Under Sir John Hawkins she had grounded off Plymouth before going to sea in '86 and later as a result sprung a leak off the coast of Portugal. On her return to Plymouth she had beaten upon the Winter stone and run twice aground, lying for two and twenty hours on the shore, until forced off by the rising tide.

In the spring of that very year Sir Richard had heard that she was in evil fortune again. While at her moorings in the river, in light ballast, unrigged with only bare masts, she had managed to capsize, turning keel uppermost, to the great disgrace of the docking master.

But on the other hand she was a fast ship and the Queen was building five more of her type. He looked along the deck and at the rigging. She was a sweet ship. Under Drake's command she had met the extreme fury of a storm so severe that Lord Thomas Howard's ship was obliged to take shelter at Falmouth. But the *Revenge* rode out the gale and pursued the Armada up the Cornish coast.

Oh, well, perhaps her evil luck was dying. Let Don Alonso de Bazan send his great ships. England would match him.

The *Revenge* rode with her anchor hove to short stay, with all in readiness to make sail and be away. Her decks were cleared for action, her cannon were full loaded with round shot, and her battle ensigns streamed from the fore and main.

As the first boat came alongside, the order rang out to the forecastle, "Heave round the anchor! Heave right up!"

Before the last boat was hooked on, the topsails filled with the wind that blew straight from Spain and the *Revenge* gathered way, easing out of the bay on the starboard tack.

Being by far the ablest sailer of the six English men-of-war, she closed steadily on the *Defiance*, the *Bonaventure*, the *Crane*, the *Foresight* and the *Golden Lyon*, all sailing under fighting canvas, their mains furled, to give them greater ease of manoeuvre.

The *Defiance* had, with the *Lyon*, taken station behind and on the weather quarter to present the greatest force to the enemy, as was the custom in rear-guard action. All six stood fair for England.

The victuallers, by reason of their poorer sailing qualities, the moderate breeze and the need for the screening protection of the fighting ships, had fallen off to leeward of the battle line. They were drawing away to the east of northward, under full press of canvas, save only the *George Noble* of London, a nimble and weatherly two-hundred-tonner, whose bold master quite evidently was bent on bringing his small force of arms into the impending action and thereby somewhat lessen the grossly uneven threat presented by the fifty-three ships of Spain.

Fifty-three ships to fight with their little fleet! Grenville's spirits rose. What did they care how many came? They would fight them all, each in turn.

His boats secure, Colin had the sick laid out as comfortably as might be on the ballast stones deep below the waterline in the most protected place available. Then he ran to the poop deck to look to the readiness of the swivel guns. "Loaded with ball?" he queried of the gunner's mate.

"Aye, sir," came the reply, "with a hundred more and two hundred bags of grape near by."

The six small pieces here on the after cubbridge head, like their mates on the forecastle, would give a lively reception to boarders. They were a ready protection for the waist gunners, already sweating over their beloved thirty-two-pound cannon and twenty-four-pound demi-cannon amidships.

Colin turned to Black John Arundell. He was commanding the musketeers on the poop. His duty was to protect Grenville, his flag captain and his navigator. Colin saw the look of elation that spread over his companion's thin Gallic countenance as he witnessed the amber flame of the opening broadside of the *Defiance*. Hardly had the white smoke rolled across her deck when the *Lyon* followed suit.

"The action is joined!" John shouted in his excitement. "Fifty-three Spaniards and seven of us! Let Spain do her worst. My Lord Howard will give them a sample of English Midlands iron."

John ran to report his observation to the Admiral. When the cannons' roar reached their ears a great resounding huzza rose from the men of the *Revenge*. After the long wait battle fever was once more upon those men of Devon.

Cheer followed cheer as the English broadsides swept the galleons. With only their bow-chasers able to bear, they lumbered on, their rigging bitterly punished by Howard's fire.

Colin watched Sir Richard. He had expected to find some

show of satisfaction. The Admiral's patience had been worn thin waiting for his sick to be borne aboard, though God knew he would never have left them there on Flores to fall to the rack and thumb-screw of the Spanish Inquisition, no matter what Howard's orders were. Now he stood black and silent as the *Revenge* drove onward, the Spanish still well without his guns' range.

The ships of Seville in the nearest column, two furlongs beyond the reach, lay on his beam. The Biscayans of Bilbao were more distant to the eastward on his weather bow. The eight fly-boats, under Don Luís Cuitiño, were still farther to windward, farthest of all from the island, but were well back on the starboard quarter.

Sir Richard, perceiving that the Biscayans could not long withstand the punishment being dealt out by Howard, reckoned aright that they must soon haul their lumbering hulks closer to the easterly wind in order to bring their broadsides to bear. Then indeed the superior speed of the *Revenge* would begin to tell. Even as he watched, the topmast of the leading galleon shuddered and then slowly and with gathering momentum slid forward and came crashing down on the forecastle.

Grenville knew without seeing how her helmsman fought to haul his slowing ship out to larboard of the battle line, to save falling afoul of the next astern. That does it, Sir Richard growled to himself.

As if Don Alonso de Bazan had heard Sir Richard's words, the galleon rounded up to starboard, hauled parallel to the English line and sent her first salvo thundering into the *Golden Lyon*. As the *San Bernabé*, a mighty and puissant ship of the Biscayans, swung into column, her three and thirty great cannon spoke. The *Defiance* answered, some shot falling short but some sending splinters flying from the Spaniard's bulwarks. Again the *San Bernabé* spoke, this time to better effect.

In the waist below, the master gunner assayed his first ranging shot. "Short, a cable's length!" Sir Richard cried. He swung around to estimate the distance to the vast and ponderous ships of Seville, now fallen back upon his larboard quarter. Swinging his glass back to starboard, he suddenly saw that the hot little fly-boats were bearing off as if to run through the lee of the action, in swift pursuit of the heavy

481

English victuallers fleeing along the rocky coast of Corvo, the smaller island that lies north of Flores.

Up ahead the engagement of the *Defiance* and the *Lyon* developed a general action, first the *Bonaventure,* then the *Foresight,* joining up. The *Foresight* and the *Crane* found the range and began to hammer the whole length of the Biscayan column. Still the great ships of Seville in the leeward column remained unengaged.

Sir Richard said to John, "The sluggish curs will find that they must fall off and join the fly-boats chasing the helpless victuallers. This act adds nothing to the glory of Spanish arms."

The victuallers, he saw, would become trapped to the northward of Corvo between the fly-boats and the Sevilliards. The leeward squadron, now clear of Flores, hovered to the westward toward the declining sun.

The *San Bernabé* lay to windward on the starboard bow of the *Revenge.* Sir Richard hardly deigned to give her notice. He glanced across his fo'c'sle to his flag captain. He called "Ready?" He saw the master gunner's assent, heard the captain's reply, "Ready. Aye, ready."

Grenville gave the signal that launched the *Revenge* thundering into her mission of destruction.

The great *San Bernabé* shuddered to the first salvo. A wild cheer swept the length of the *Revenge.* The second broadside tore into the now stricken Apostle. From the waist of Richard's ship came the deep-throated Devon cheer, "Grenville! Grenville and England!"

Still no smile lighted the ice-blue eyes of Sir Richard. This was stuff for boys. Please God, let the *Revenge* find work fit for men.

To Colin close behind him Arundell said, "If we were to put about now, we could rend open her starboard side and give her double reason to respect the Queen's *Revenge.*"

Colin's voice rose in excitement. "Look now, John. See, the *Bernabé* is wounded in her side, but even so she has put some shot through our stores ship there."

"Aye, the *George Noble.* It's just as well, for it keeps the Spanish gunners from finding our range."

Seeing one of the great Apostle ships assault the bold but ill-armed *Noble,* Colin heard the long-silent Sir Richard give voice at a great shout, "Captain, make ready about!"

In a trice he ranged close down along the starboard side

of the hapless Apostle with salvo after salvo of round shot from his cannon and grape from the swivels, and did not pause as she drew off, for his stern-chasers took up the destruction after the broadside ceased to bear.

The larboard battery now roared into action. Taking the range from the bow-chasers, it commenced its work upon the preoccupied Biscayans to windward. The port battery was clear of the shattered *San Bernabé,* and Sir Richard, between the two Spanish lines, could open fire on the ships of Seville to leeward.

In a flash of protective rage he had succoured the *Noble* and supported Lord Thomas. He had given the Sevilliards cause to desist from playing hounds to the victuallers' hare. His pleasure rose at the huzzas of his men.

In the moment of triumph the blow was struck, not by the Spaniard, but by the English.

From the mizzen look-out came the frenzied cry, "On deck there! The admiral of our fleet has cut his main! All others follow. They disengage the action. To the northward now they stand."

For a moment Grenville and his men stood frozen. Never in all history had an English ship been so deserted. With a mighty curse on Howard he brought his fist down on the rail. "Traitors and dogs!" he shouted, his face black with rage. "Traitors and dogs! Run and be damned to you!"

Seamen came tumbling on deck from below. They watched the fleeing English fleet, mouths open, incredulous. Then violence of black rage assailed them. They shook their fists, screaming, "Cowards! Cowards!" Gunners shouted their wrath: "Cowards! Cowards! Cowards!"

John Arundell cursed with the men. "Howard's in league with Philip of Spain!" he cried. "May the wrath of God blast him down!"

Colin answered, "A Cornish curse on him: May he burn in hell!"

Fifty and three mountainous galleons of Spain closed in for a kill. In the gathering twilight the *Revenge* stood alone to fight a battle for England.

CHAPTER 32
DEATH OF THE REVENGE

It was characteristic of Richard Grenville that he gave no further thought to Howard. He was a stubborn man, strong, some said rash, in his undertakings, but he never turned back once he had set his hand to a task.

Darkness was falling. The *Revenge* was still his ship.

The Spanish were closing in. Before his eyes was the full power of the stately galleons, with their spreading coloured sails, ranged in two columns.

His heart leaped. Here was the dream of all sea-fighters. There was space to sail between the lines, with action on both hands, the chance to put the enemy into confusion and see the cross-fire of their guns do destruction upon themselves. Here he could profit by the superior sailing qualities of the *Revenge*.

He spoke to the flag captain. "Haul her close to the winds, Captain. I wish to pass between their columns."

"We will never make it, sir," the captain shouted his protest. "We cannot weather their leeward squadron."

"Damn their leeward squadron! Hold your course, sir! Steady as you go!" roared Sir Richard.

It was a close thing indeed, too close. The great *Ascención* of Seville lay dead ahead, head on, her masts all in a line, coming down upon the little *Revenge,* a vertible mountain of wood and canvas towering above her. But the nimble little ship clawed up to windward like a cat on a pole, and in the extremity the great galleon was forced to spring her luff, yield way to her tough little adversary.

The *Ascención* trembled as the *Revenge's* cannon roared and recoiled back in their breechings.

"Three salvos to their one!" cheered Colin.

The Spaniard's broadside could bear but momentarily as she bore away to port to avoid collision with the determined Grenville.

Meanwhile the larboard tiers roared defiance to the Biscayan line.

The second Sevilliard in turn was forced to yield to the weather gauge, her futile fire but briefly threatening the *Revenge*.

It was a bitter scramble. "How she eats her way to windward!" Colin cried as his smoking swivels ceased to range. "Look! We cross the avenue. We draw near to the Biscayan line."

"Too near!" shouted John. "The *San Felipe* will take our wind."

The sailing master, intent on gaining every inch to windward, had done too well. The *Revenge* had all but finished her fearful execution and got clear when she began to lose her way. She had come close under the lee of the high-cargued *San Felipe*, last ship in the column. They all saw what was happening, but it was too late. The little *Revenge* dragged slower and slower.

"She will not answer her helm!" the captain shouted, his voice rising in alarm. Aloft the canvas slatted against the rigging, and the topgallants by turns filled and fell slack. The lower sails lay totally aback, their air stolen by the towering galleon. The *San Felipe* rose above them like a ship of doom. Her countless soldiers fingered their muskets, holding their fire, as the range slowly closed.

In the *Revenge* Sir Richard, seizing the opportunity to take full advantage of the newly contrived bar-shot, ordered, "In the orlop there! Load the second tier with bar! We'll lower their walls a deck or two. Aim at the water-line! Aim well!"

The bar-connected spheres tore great gaping holes in the sides of the Apostle as she ranged alongside, her soldiers pouring into the waist of the trapped *Revenge*.

The *San Felipe* grappled and some nine or ten of her soldiers got aboard the *Revenge*. But the grappling ropes parted and the two ships drifted apart. From the cubbridge heads the grape from Colin's murdering pieces dealt swift death to the Spanish soldiery swarming in the waist below.

The *Revenge* drew clear, her sails filling as her wind came free of the lee of the *San Felipe*.

"Cut her main! Bear off to starboard! Go large! Set courses west by south!" The captain's orders rang out as he made to dash for the open-sea.

"Stay your orders, Captain! We fight. There has been enough of flight this day."

As the ship swung off, they sought but briefly to dissuade

485

Sir Richard. Then as the *Revenge* swept round, Grenville bore down upon the ships of Seville and once more charged on between the Spanish lines. Thundering death and damnation from culverin and cannon, he bore valiantly onward in the failing light, his trifling five hundred tons pitted against twelve of the finest ships of Spain.

Now perceiving that Grenville was bent on repeating his sweep up the lane between the Spanish column, Don Alonso de Bazan ordered the fifteen-hundred-ton *San Felipe* to close down again on the hapless Englishman.

As the *Revenge* slowed, General Marcos de Aramburu's Castilian galley came up from astern and threw boarders from the bow onto her poop, but those who remained of the soldiers of the *San Felipe* were now driven back from the forecastle into their own ship, and that great galleon, her sides torn with bar-shot, hastened to get clear of the devastating English broadsides.

This action threw the *Revenge* against the shattered *San Bernabé*, her first adversary, which, dead in the water, grappled the *Revenge* like a dying man. As the soldiers of General Martin de Bertendona struggled to board the *Revenge*, Colin's swivels swept their fire along the bulwarks and the Spanish dead fell back into the sea. The tide of combat surged across the deck to the starboard side, threatening to overcome the *Revenge*, but the stout Devon lads flung the boarders back, only to turn and meet a new threat as the *Ascensión* grappled to starboard, followed by another galleon across the bow and a fourth across the stern.

Those at the sides were so beaten by the heavy cannon of Grenville's lower tiers that they were obliged to withdraw from the action, giving place to two more.

All night long the battle raged about the *Revenge*, with never less than two great galleons at her sides. During the night the *Ascensión* sank, and another ship. Ship after ship came at them until, in all, fifteen Spanish men-of-war had been at her sides. And still the *Revenge* fought on.

The fire from the Spaniards was murderous for the heroes in the *Revenge*. She resisted with all her strength. The courage of men from Devon and from Cornwall filled her body from bow to taffrail. Her mainsail was gone. It trailed like a pall over her side, dropping into the water.

The enemy prepared to board again. All night long she

had fought them back. Heaps of Spaniards lay on her deck, drained of the last drop of their proud blood. With them lay her own dead and dying.

John Arundell and his little company formed a ring around Grenville, his captain and his sailing master. With pistol and sword they would make a living wall beyond which no Spaniard could advance. That was Black John's task; the captain and the sailing master could give no orders now. The *Revenge* could no longer move save with the rise and fall of the waves that lapped against her sides. All night Don Alonso de Bazan had signal lanthorns hung lighted on the *San Pablo* to draw his ships into the channel together.

The madness of high courage was in the hearts on the *Revenge*. They would fight to redeem the cowardice of Howard and his pack. They would show the Spaniards that Grenville's men and Grenville's ship would never turn tail and run.

Ill men crawled on hands and knees from the hold, carrying powder strapped on their backs, struggling to their feet to fight and die as brave men should, not like rats in the dark of the hold. They were county lads who knew the sky and the sun and the stars, the wild wind of the moors and the dash of the angry sea against rock walls.

John Arundell sank on the deck to rest for the moment while there was brief respite from the battle. Many followed his example. They had fought off the boarders. The boarders would come again, but the moment of rest meant much. One boy brought water, and another wine. The weary men drank thirstily

Colin and a gunner's mate, a handy lad from Bude, washed the wounded, bandaged arms and legs and bodies as well as they could, working in the dark with only a candle lanthorn to give light.

Grenville went among his men, laying a hand on brow or shoulder, speaking words of encouragement. By a dying man he knelt to pray. "The night is dark but with the light comes courage and hope."

Black John Arundell cleaned his sword and watched his leader. He thought of Sir Richard, with his high forehead and his soft blond curling locks, sitting in the low-mullioned window at Bideford, his cup of malmsey before him, a lute by his side—a steadfast man, conscious of his proud race, of his descent from the grandfather of the Conqueror, of cen-

487

turies of valiant deeds; a man harsh toward cowardice in others, at times tender as a woman, a man to follow to the death. Many an Arundell and many a Grenville had fought shoulder to shoulder in battle on land and sea. Arundells and Grenvilles had died side by side together.

Black John too encouraged the men. "We will fight," he said stubbornly, "no matter how many ships of Spain come pounding against our sides. Four we have already sunk, and we remain afloat. Will you ever forget our brave *Revenge* thundering down the lane between the fifty and three, our guns blazing, raking them fore and aft?"

The men, even the wounded, cheered at his words. "Her's a brave good ship," a Cornishman cried. "With six of her we could whip all Spain."

"Aye, aye, we could!" The cry came from the men who lay on the deck snatching the momentary rest.

John went back to his post. He tried to think of the lines of a Greek poet he had studied not so long ago and struggled to translate:

Who knoweth if to live is but to die,
And death life's gates, to those who have passed by? ...

He could remember no more. He sat down and leaned against a cabin door. His eyes closed. The sleep of the weary is merciful.

It was near midnight when Richard Grenville received his wound, a glancing blow from a musket ball, which creased his forehead. He fell to the deck. His men rushed to him.

The madness of courage was on him, even as he lay speechless on the upper deck. He would not be moved. Waving his hands and arms, he directed the fighting until speech came back to him.

Colin came to his commander during a lull in the fighting. Sir Richard was stretched on the deck, his back against the wall of his cabin. He was ghastly in the light of a candle lanthorn. "The *Revenge* is a wounded ship," he whispered to Colin, "sore wounded, but not yet dead. By God, we will fight them! What does it matter? We are ready for death or for life. Bring me my master gunner, Colin. I will give him orders when to sink the ship. Find John. Stand close together in the fight that will come in the morning."

The wind rose. It was blowing from the land, driving sea-birds before it. They flew wildly, flashing in and out of gun-fire flashes. Bewildered by storm, wind and fire, they drove into the billowing canvas and fell on the decks. One white gull fell at Richard Grenville's feet. It lay stunned, its curved beak against his foot. It's black, unblinking eyes seemed fixed on the wounded warrior. Grenville, unmoved, turned his eyes to Colin. There was no fear in their blue depths. A strange look—was it recognition?—resignation to his fate?

John Arundell woke to the clarions' alarm and the call of the lookout: "Boarding party forward! Boarding party aft! Boarding party to leeward! Boarding party starboard!"

The first streaks of dawn streamed across the sky. He jumped to his feet, unsheathed his sword and stood on guard. Grenville came out of his cabin. His face was set and hard as the cliffs of Hartland Point. He was in full armour, but his head was bare. The wound had been washed and bandaged. John thought he looked as the gods must look, strong, unyielding and valiant. He had never seen Sir Richard so magnificent, so commanding.

"They will do their worst now," Grenville said, "but let the Spaniards come with their fifty-three ships and their ten merchantmen. Let them come! We will show them how true men fight."

He turned to John. "Send a man to fetch Colin. I want him." His grim visage softened. "My two brave boys. I want you both. Together we will strike a blow for England."

John gave the order. A few minutes later Colin ran up the companionway. His face was white. "Sir," he said, "you called me?"

"Yes, Colin. I want you here beside me—you and John. Back to back we will fight them down as long as may be. After that we are in God's hands. His will is ours."

John ran into the cabin and fetched Sir Richard's helmet. Grenville pushed it away. "No. I will not cover my head or my face. I will meet Don Alonso de Bazan uncovered, eye to eye, to show him there are Englishmen who do not run."

Colin's heart swelled with pride. Here was the lion of England. He watched him step forward. A shrill whistle sounded from the nearest Spaniard. A few moments and the devils would make another attempt.

Grenville raised his voice: "You are valiant men and you

489

live or die to the glory of England and your Queen. Take your aim well. Waste no powder. Fight and die as West-Countrymen have always fought and died—with courage."

The huzzas that rose gave the Spaniards pause. What manner of men were these, who had fought the night through and were ready still to fight against such fearful odds? Were they devils or men?

Grenville clarions sounded. The men waited for the first hand or the first dark head to show over the side.

The enemy came with a rush, sea-soldiers from four great ships of the line. Armoured and armed, fresh from a night's rest, they scrambled up the side, only to be fought back savagely by the hacked swords and bent pikes of the *Revenge*. No Spanish soldier lived on her deck. Many fell into the sea screaming or landed on the deck of their own ships.

Men from one of the great Apostle ships rushed across the bridge and jumped to the deck. Soon the *Revenge* was covered with dead. Cries of the wounded, curses and prayers rose and filled the soft morning air.

Fifteen times Grenville's men repulsed the enemy. Fifteen times they broke away from grappling hooks and boarders. The Spaniards shifted ships. They brought on fresh men. But the wounded company of the *Revenge* fought savagely, desperately, with the courage of heroes who had the strength of the gods in them.

The high cliffs of Flores were black with islanders watching and waiting. People ran along the beaches dragging in the wounded and the drowned. As the sun went higher in the heaven, the human flotsam grew, hundreds of dead Spaniards.

The *Revenge's* guns still blazed, doing murderous damage to assaulting ships. As one ship sank, another came forward.

A gunner's mate ran to Colin. His face was grey with fatigue. Sweat poured from his forehead and ran rivulets in his powder-marked face. He had a wound in his forearm, around which was tied a rag stiff with blood. "Sir, the powder is almost to the last barrel and all our pikes are broken."

Colin said, "Give out what powder is left, equal share to each gun. Tell the men to hold fire for the last. After that we will fight with clubbed muskets, cutlasses and swords."

Suddenly a new ship came rising out of the smoke. She

sent fresh men to board the *Revenge*. A few got past, then more.

"Guard our Admiral!" sang out a man aloft. "They are swarming the poop. 'Ware, Sir Richard! 'Ware!"

John sprang forward, sword in hand, to engage the first man over, Colin was at his elbow. Three men circled Grenville closely, making a wreath of living flesh 'twixt him and the enemy. He pushed them aside. With his long sword he sought the foe.

Below them the fight raged, pike and staff, cutlass and axe. The West-Countrymen fought furiously, but where a Spaniard fell, two more rose to take his place, until the deck was strewn like a slaughter-house and the scuppers ran with blood.

Eight ships were sending boarders now.

Colin engaged a Spaniard, a tall man armed with a swift sword. As he fought, he heard John Arundell cry, "A rescue! A rescue! Grenville!" Colin thrust his sword through the neck of his foe. He drew out the blade. Blood spurted over his face and almost blinded him. Wiping his eyes with his sleeve as he ran, he found Arundell standing astride the mighty form of Grenville. Sir Richard was down, wounded in the head by a harquebus shot. Black John's sword was flashing, whipping around him like an arch of fire.

"A Grenville! A Grenville!" The clarions were blowing. On a Spanish galleon a drum rolled. . . . Men were yelling, swearing. . . .

Colin engaged, standing shoulder to shoulder with John. He saw a dark-faced man creep up the ladder, a knife in his teeth and a sword in one hand. He was a giant. His eyes were on the fallen Grenville. Colin cried out, " 'Ware the ladder!" John had seen the man. He leaped forward. The Spaniard towered over him, lunged for Grenville. John thrust his body forward and took the sword through his heart.

Colin caught the giant off guard while he was drawing his sword from John's body. They fought back and forward until Colin's strength began to fail. With a last tremendous effort he caught the man fairly through the neck. The Spaniard swayed against the rail. His body splashed into the narrow water between the ships.

Colin ran to John, The bright blood oozed from his lips. A great redness was over his leather tunic. Colin bent over and lifted his head. It fell back limply.

Grenville murmured slowly, "He is gone, the true brave lad."

Colin knelt beside Grenville, staunching the wound in his head. As he knelt, a shot from a Spanish ship struck the superstructure, splintering the wood. A Devon man fell, his arm over Sir Richard's body.

Colin heard a wild victorious shout, *"Felipe y España!"*

Grenville raised himself on his elbow. His voice was loud. "Master Gunner, split the ship and sink her! Never the *Revenge* into the hands of Spain!" He dropped back. He did not know that the master gunner lay dead on the deck and the ship was already Spain's.

A Spanish leader, Don Alonso de Bazan's captain of staff, came aboard the *Revenge*. He stood looking down on Grenville, now happily unconscious. Blood flowed down his white cheek and the corner of his mouth but he was still breathing.

Colin got to his feet, swaying from side to side. Two Spanish officers came up to him and took their places one on either side of him. He understood from their actions that he was their prisoner. They were very young and very serious. There was no triumph in their faces, only a sort of bewildered incredulity that so small a ship, so small a company of men, could cause such damage to the Spanish fleet.

Spanish seamen lifted Sir Richard gently and placed him on a litter. He opened his eyes. Colin sprang to his side and took his hand. He pressed Colin's fingers. He did not speak until the Spanish captain addressed him courteously and asked would he mind if they carried him to the *San Pablo*, where a surgeon waited to dress his wounds.

"I care not what they do with my body, for I esteem it not," Grenville whispered to Colin in a broken voice. He closed his eyes. Perhaps he swooned. Perhaps he did not want to look on his shattered ship.

Colin was thankful that Grenville had not seen the Spaniards lower John's canvas-wrapped body into the blue sea; that he had not beheld the ensign of England hauled down and the banner of Spain rise and spread out on the breeze.

The prize crew coming aboard the *Revenge* stood aside for the litter to pass. They glanced curiously, with solemn eyes, as the wounded commander was carried away from his ship. Beyond them Devon lads and lads from Cornwall stood under guard. Tears were streaming down the faces of the most hardened of them.

The officer in charge noted the emotion of the English prisoners at the plight of their great Admiral. He ordered the litter-bearers to halt. He motioned to the Englishmen that they might walk past to say farewell. Seamen, gunners and officers moved by, looking sadly on the wounded man. Grenville's eyes remained closed. His face was waxen. His fair hair and beard were matted with blood from the wound in his temple. They were disconsolate, knowing that they looked for the last time. The old seaman from Padstow knelt and kissed Grenville's hand. Others followed. Some sobbed. Colin blinked and fought to keep back the tears.

The captain of staff nodded to his men and they bore the litter across the boarding plank. They permitted Colin to go with Grenville. For that he was grateful.

On the second day Grenville opened his eyes and spoke. The surgeon nodded to Colin, who had sat all night in the cabin by Grenville's great bed. The Spaniard whispered, "He wishes to speak—but quietly, señor, quietly." He went out of the room.

Grenville watched him go. His face was calm, his blue eyes were untroubled. He spoke so low that Colin was obliged to bend over him to hear his words. "A paper, Colin, and a quill. Write what I say."

Colin took up paper from a table. The quills and ink were ready. He knelt by the bed, his paper spread on the counterpane, his ear almost touching Grenville's lips.

"Say to them at Stowe that I died . . ." He paused. After a moment his voice was clearer. "Write, Colin: 'Here die I, Richard Grenville, with a joyful and quiet mind . . . for I have ended my life as a true soldier ought to do . . .'" He stopped. His breathing was labored now. Colin fetched a cup of wine and held it to his lips. "'. . . a true soldier that has fought for his country, Queen, religion . . . and honour . . .'" He sank back against the pillow, very white, his eyes vividly blue, his blond hair falling over his moist forehead. Colin's hand trembled so he almost blotted the page. "'. . . whereby my soul most joyful departs out of this body . . . and shall leave behind it the everlasting fame of a valiant and true soldier. . . .'"

Colin heard a movement behind him. The Spanish officer and the surgeon had come into the room, but Grenville did not see them. His breathing became heavy and broken. Suddenly he spoke clearly.

" 'But others of my company have done as traitors and dogs, for which they shall be reproached all their lives . . .' " His voice sank again. Sweat stood on his forehead. The surgeon wiped it away with a cloth. " '. . . all their lives and leave a shameful name forever. . . .' "

His voice faltered at the last. His breathing was slower. There were long pauses, when Colin thought he had drawn his last breath.

The officer took the paper and quill and laid them aside. The surgeon's fingers sought the pulse in Grenville's throat. Sir Richard shivered once. His hand grew cold in Colin's clasp. He murmured something. Colin thought he spoke one word: "Stowe."

He did not move again or speak. Presently Colin felt a hand on his shoulder. The surgeon said softly, "A great man has passed, señor." He crossed himself devoutly. "God with him forever!"

All night the body of Richard Grenville lay in state. Dressed in court suit of white satin, his sword still at his side, he lay under the red velvet canopy on the great carved oak bed of a Spanish admiral. Clean-shaven, his blond hair and beard in order, he appeared asleep, serene and at peace.

Colin watched beside him, seated on his left hand. On his right a monk in brown robes knelt, murmuring prayers. Great candles in gilt sticks stood at the four corners of his bed. On the panelled wall hung a painting of Philip of Spain, his thin lips parted in a half-smile. A guard stood outside the door, their faces masklike and motionless.

All night officers and men from the Spanish ships passed by the door quietly, in an orderly way. Perhaps they held joy in their hearts that an enemy was slain. Perhaps some did honour to a true and valiant soldier. Colin stayed with him until the end. At daybreak they carried him to the ship's side, wrapped in canvas and the Grenville banner from his own ship. The courteous Spaniards had provided for this fitting ceremony and for the clarions to sound as Richard Grenville's lifeless body slipped overboard into the blue of a tropic sea.

The sea claimed him, and he claimed the sea that he loved.

Colin followed his captors to the boat. He was taken to a house on the cliff which lodged a Dutch merchant.

The sky was black and thunderous, the air heavy, without life. He had no life himself. He turned to walk to the white cell-like room they had assigned him, but his feet refused to move. He caught at the back of a chair. It was too far away. A weighted blackness rushed upon him, shutting out the light.

That night the storm burst. Never had there been such a storm in all the days of the island. The people closed wooden shutters, bolted heavy doors and took to praying. They knew that the great sea-captain had brought the storm. Perhaps he rode away in the storm to Heaven or Hell—no one knew whether he were man or devil.

The great "Campo Verde" did not go into the sea alone, for he was master of his ship, and the ship came to his calling.

The *Revenge* sank in the storm, carrying her wounded men and the Spanish crew who sailed her.

The islanders saw her, all sails spread, rushing on to her doom and the doom of her captors. She did not go alone. She called Spanish ships to follow, and she led them to their destruction, for they followed her on and on to the Island of Terceira, there to cast themselves against the great cliffs. The *Revenge* was avenged.

For days and weeks and months the islanders were dragging bodies of the sailors and soldiers of Spain from the beaches, until ten thousand men had been cast up by the sea. Out of the great fleet of fifty and three no more than twenty or twenty-five galleons ever returned to Spain. And out of the double flota from the Indies no more ships than that got through. Some say Spain lost more ships than she had lost in the Invincible Armada. The God of Storms had again fought on the side of the *Revenge*.

"Man or devil?" The islanders still ask the question. When the hurricanes blow and the violent seas pound against the headlands, sometimes the clarions of Grenville float out above the storm, calling ships to follow the *Revenge* to her death against the cliffs of Terceira.

CHAPTER 33
VOYAGER'S RETURN

A year and a day passed before the door of the prison in Cádiz opened and Colin was free. He did not know until months later that it was Dame Philippa who paid the ransom money. An officer met him at the gate of the prison and conducted him to the docks. Here he went aboard a vessel bound for Norway. A month later he sailed from Bergen to Great Yarmouth. He found there a boat carrying fish to the London market. Five days later he rode through the gates of Stowe.

Talking to Lady Grenville was not so difficult as he had thought it would be. More than a year had passed and she had gathered up the threads of her life bravely and with tranquillity. Colin wondered if there were not a certain peace now that had not existed in the days when her husband had gone to the New World or set sail elsewhere on the Queen's business.

She listened without speaking until he had finished the heroic story. "Thank you, Colin," she said quietly. "I am glad you were with him and with John Arundell. It makes it easier for me to know that someone who loved him and whom he loved and trusted was with him to the end. My brave Richard! He died as he lived—without fear, at peace with his God."

Colin said, "The Spanairds held him a hero and gave him a hero's tribute: flags lowered, the long roll of drums, the cannon salute and at last the sound of clarions as they lowered him into the sea."

She was pleased at this. "Even the enemy . . ."

"Yes, Lady Grenville. He was a very great admiral in their eyes, an enemy to be feared and respected."

Mary Grenville was silent for a time, clasping and unclasping her thin white fingers. "He would be pleased with Bernard," she said. "Bernard has applied himself diligently. He is now Knight of the Shire, as his father was. Our married daughters are content in their new homes. Dear, dear John

496

has his father's questing soul. The sea draws him. He is a true Grenville."

She hesitated a moment, watching his face. "Thomasine is sad, Colin. John's death hurt her deeply, but youth is strong, resilient. I would not wait too long."

Colin looked at Lady Grenville, startled by her words. "Did you know?" he asked.

"It was Dame Philippa who first called my attention. Then when I observed you and Thomasine I knew she was right. Sir Richard wanted her to marry John. It would be a suitable match, he told me."

Her smile was sweet as she looked at him. "Perhaps I am being very sentimental, dear Colin, but there is something so beautiful and tender in young love, and I was sure that Thomasine loved you and not John."

Her expression changed to one of sadness. "Dear John! We loved him devotedly. It comforts me greatly that they are together—a brave knight and his squire."

Lady Grenville was silent a moment. Then she rose and crossed the room. She took a key from her girdle and unlocked the escritoire where Sir Richard had always kept his papers. She selected a paper labelled "Colin." "Here is something my husband asked me to give you if he did not return. It is a deed to the manor near Stratton."

Colin opened the paper. His strong lean fingers trembled a little. A letter was attached to the document.

Colin, my dear friend:

I want you to own land, for land is the basis of all wealth; an acre or a hundred, it is the same. Perhaps you will decide to go to the New World. That would please me, for we must struggle until we have a firm colony in Virginia. But do not forget the Old World.

For that reason I bequeath to you the Manor of Highcliff near Stratton. This will keep you close to Stowe, if you decide to marry and live at home in England.

I watched you closely, Colin, during the months at Roanoke. I have been well pleased with your conduct in all circumstances. God with you!

Your friend,

Richard Grenville

Colin could not speak for emotion. Mary Grenville leaned

forward and laid her hand on his. "You have proved yourself, Colin. You have his blessing and mine."

He lifted her hand to his lips. "How can I thank you, dear Lady Grenville?"

She smiled gently. "By going to Thomasine and telling her what is in your heart."

He found Thomasine in the inner court, standing on the mounting block. A stable-boy, new at Stowe since his departure, was holding the bridle of a lively bay mare. Colin strode across the cobbled yard to assist her. Instead of holding his hand for her to mount, he lifted her by her narrow waist and swung her into the saddle.

"You are boasting of your strength." She laughed. "Come, ride down the vale with me." She called to the boy, "Bring a mount for Master Colin."

They rode down the vale toward the mill and climbed the rolling hill. There, in sight of the sea, they dismounted and walked along the ancient Roman wall. At the summit they seated themselves on the grass.

During the long lonely nights at Roanoke and those recent longer nights in prison he had thought of a hundred things to say to her. Now he was close to her, he could not speak. He could only look at her, wondering at the beauty of her dark eyes, the little pulsing hollow at the base of her throat.

She leaned toward him. She lifted his hand from the grass and turned it palm upward. "The brand has grown faint," she said softly. "I can scarcely see the outline. Oh, Colin, how many nights I have cried because I hurt you! You must have hated me, I was so cruel."

He raised her hand and held it against his cheek. "I have always loved you, Thomasine, from the first moment I saw you riding down the lane between the hawthorn hedges. Your stormy eyes, your rebellious mouth, your contemptuous glance told me I was a serf in your sight. Of a sudden I was enraged at your insolence. I determined at that moment to stand upright, eye to eye with any man. And from that moment I was your passionate slave. Before ever your brand was on my hand, I was marked your lover for always."

Tears came to her eyes. "Oh, my dear, my dear," she whispered, "hold me close and kiss me. The waiting has been so long."

After a long while she disengaged herself from his arms

498

and spoke of John. "If he had returned, we would have married. Sir Richard willed it for what he thought my good, and he had the right to dispose of me. I would have tried to make the best of it. I would have made a poor wife, I fear, though there was no one I respected or trusted more than John. We were friends, deep, affectionate friends. I have sorrowed for his noble death. But, oh, my darling, it is you that I loved."

They rode home slowly. The sun had dropped behind the horizon. The Vale of Coombe was deep in shadow. The last glory of the sun tipped the rounded hills and the young green of the fields. Over the woods of Stowe the rooks were circling. And as they rode they talked of Virginia.

On the Island of Roanoke the green vines of the grape and the wicked brambles twined riotously over the falling dwellings of the First Colony. Bushes grew thick and rank along the broken palisades.

Indians had come and gone away. Sea-chests had been dug up and their contents scattered. Pieces of armour lay rusting in the sand. A man's shoe hung on the limb of a tree. The wind had blown the sand high against the gates, and the crumbling walls made a picture of desolation. And all was ruin and decay.

At the water's edge where the *Tyger* had moored, white cranes and blue herons stood deep in the water, poised to strike for fish. Ducks sought haven, and a cormorant sat on a floating log. Overhead a flight of geese winged their eager way to the Great Lake.

But on the sea ships still sailed. In the Old World men talked to their sons of Sir Richard Grenville's colony of a hundred men who had sailed to Virginia, and their sons dreamed of a time when they too would venture to that fabulous land. And on the Ocean Sea gallant ships still sailed westward to a New World.

The One Hundred and Eight Men
who lived for one year on Roanoke Island in
Virginia, the First English Settlement in America.
1585-1586.

Master Philip Amadas	Roger Large
Master Hariot	Humfrey Garden
Master Acton	Francis Whitton
Master Edward Stafford	Rowland Griffyn
Thomas Luddington	William Millard
Master Marvyn	John Twit
Master Gardiner	Edward Nugent
Captain Vaughan	Edward Kelley
Master Kendall	John Gostigo
Master Prideaux	Erasmus Clefs
Robert Holecroft	Edward Ketcheman
Rise Courtenay	John Linsey
Master Hugh Rogers	Thomas Rottenbury
Master Thomas Harvie	Roger Deane
Master Snelling	John Harris
Master Anthony Rowse	Francis Norris
Master Allyne	Matthew Lyne
Master Michael Polison	Edward Kettell
John Cage	Thomas Wisse
Thomas Parre	Robert Biscombe
William Randes	William Backhouse
Geffrey Churchman	William White
William Farthow	Henry Potkin
John Taylor	Dennis Barnes
Philip Robyns	Joseph Gorges
Thomas Philips	Dougham Gannes
Valentine Beale	William Tenche
Thomas Foxe	Randall Latham
Darby Glande	Thomas Hulme
Master Ralph Lane	Walter Mill

Richard Gilbert
Steven Pomarie
John Brock
Bennet Harrie
James Stevenson
Charles Stevenson
Edward Seclemore
John Anwike
Christopher Marshall
David Williams
Nicholas Swabber
Edward Chipping
Christopher Lowde
Jeremie Mayne
James Mason
David Salter
Richard Ireland
Thomas Bookener
William Philips
Randall Mayne
James Skinner
George Eseven
John Chandeler
Philip Blount

Richard Poore
Robert Yonge
Marmaduke Constable
Thomas Hesket
William Wasse
John Fever
Daniel
Thomas Taylor
Richard Humfrey
John White
Gabriel North
Bennet Chappell
Richard Sayre
James Lacie
Smolkin
Thomas Smart
Robert
John Evans
Silvester Beching
Vincent Cheyne
Hance Walters
Edward Barecombe
Thomas Skeuelabs
William Walters

ABOUT THE AUTHOR

INGLIS FLETCHER's greatest fame rests on her books about early North Carolina, although her first two novels, *White Leopard* and *Red Jasmine,* were about Africa. Travel was long one of Mrs. Fletcher's chief enthusiasms. With her mining engineer husband, or often alone, she journeyed to remote mountain camps in Alaska and into the interior of Africa, where she went to study witchcraft and native customs.

Once back in the United States, she began, haphazardly at first, to hunt through records in California's Huntington Library for information about her early North Carolina ancestors. As she searched through the colonial documents, her interest grew until the names became live, vivid men and women and eventually the characters in such stories as *Raleigh's Eden, Men of Albemarle, Lusty Wind for Carolina, Toil of the Brave* and *ROANOKE HUNDRED.* The Fletchers lived in an old plantation house called Bandon, right on the scene of the historic events which come alive in Mrs. Fletcher's writing.